OUT OF BOUNDS

FORBIDDEN ROMANCE COLLECTION

LAINEY DAVIS

FORGING PASSION

A ONE-NIGHT-STAND PREQUEL

For Jenni Hermoso
#ContigoJenni

CONTENT NOTE

This book contains inappropriate and harassing behavior from a male character in a position of power. While his actions are not described in graphic detail, some readers may find the dynamics disturbing or uncomfortable. Please read with discretion.

The author in no way condones this type of conduct. The character's behavior represents an unfortunate reality for many women and people of marginalized genders. His characterization aims to bring awareness to systemic issues in sports culture and society as a whole.

While the depicted events are fictional, their impact is very real. If you find this content too upsetting, you may want to pass on this title. Please take care of yourself.

CHAPTER 1
WES

I flash my ID to the airport security and kick off my shower slides, sticking them alongside my phone in one of those gray tubs before I hoist my bag onto the belt. This isn't my first time traveling for soccer and I know better than to let my gear out of sight. No way in hell will I be breaking in emergency cleats from a box store near the airport.

I step through the metal detector, and no sooner do I grab my phone from the belt when I hear it buzzing and see the rapid, incoming messages.

> DAD:
>
> Where are you?
>
> DAD:
>
> Seriously, Wes. Enough. Where are you?
>
> DAD:
>
> Do you want to give your mother a seizure? Pick up the phone, son.

That last message is specifically designed to guilt me, but I'm not falling for it. Mom's epilepsy has been stable for years and Dad can fuck off.

I recognize that leaving school with only one year to go seems like a foolish choice, but if I want to get serious about playing pro soccer, about playing for the national team someday, then I need to focus on my game.

Sure, it's messed up that academics are the distraction in my student-athlete world, but it's the truth. I'm putting in at least 20 hours a week of practice, conditioning, weight training, and watching film. I'm studying the game so much I literally have nothing left in the tank when it's time to hit the books.

So yeah. I skipped out. At least, I can see how my dad views it that way. I let my college coach know about my plans to step down. I actually filed the papers to withdraw from school, too. I'm officially unaffiliated with the university. As of tomorrow, I'm a free agent, ready to show off my game to all the scouts at the elite open-invitation camp in California.

Technically, it's a camp for the U.S. national team coaches to look at potential players leading up to the Olympics, but I know I'm not ready for that milestone. I'm there to get picked up by a pro team hoping to round out their roster with fresh legs and healthy knees. Mid-season, long after the draft, these teams have ditched the guys who couldn't cut it or snapped their ligaments. Scouts swarm these camps with contracts at the ready.

Do I want to piss off my family? Do I want to ditch my cousin, who's been my roommate and teammate for years? Of course not. But Wyatt's on his own path, and I need to do what's right for me. At least he's not irate about it like my dad. Although, to be fair, Wyatt knows where I am right now, and my dad is apparently having a stroke because he thinks I'm missing.

Thatcher Stag can't stand not knowing where his family is every second of the day. I know he's overcome some abandonment trauma, but seriously, no parent needs to keep "find my phone" tracking on his 21-year-old son.

I grit my teeth and fire off a text to my mom, promising her that I'm just fine, that I know what I'm doing, and that I'll be in California for a few days. I'd have thought with two brothers as professional athletes, my dad would understand a lot more about seizing opportunities while my body is fresh, but he's too focused on me keeping non-soccer options open that he can't see it's costing me opportunities on the field.

I'm seizing the day, damn it.

I enrolled in this open camp, and committed to a year in the championship circuit playing semi-pro if things don't work out for me this weekend. Where will I land? I have absolutely no idea. It could be London, Chicago, Miami…that's the beautiful thing about the beautiful game. It's truly global and as long as I'm willing to live out of a suitcase—which I totally am—the opportunities are mine to pass up. And I'm done passing this particular ball. Wyatt and I have the lease on our apartment until the end of the month, so I have plenty of time to figure out where to stash my belongings.

But if I have anything to say about it, I'll know everything I need by the end of this weekend when the pro soccer coaches are fighting each other to pull me off their discovery lists.

I shove my phone back in my sweats and grab my duffel from the security belt, looking around for my slides. An irritated female voice hollers at me. "Hey, that's my bag, asshole."

I whip my head around to find a barefoot Latina woman glaring at me, toned arms crossed over her chest as her red-tipped toes dig into the tile floor. She looks murderously angry, dark hair in a braid over one shoulder, dark eyes glaring out from above tawny cheeks flushed with frustration. She is exactly the kind of woman I'd chase if I had the time and energy for such things.

But I don't, I remind myself quickly. She moves her hands to her hips, causing her t-shirt to stretch across her chest. It reads OU SOCCER. My breath rushes out of my body. The temptation is extreme—I love athletic women. I love joking around with them and I love the feel of their bodies against mine. And sexiest of all, this one is annoyed with me. "You have my bag."

I look down at my duffel and see that it is, in fact, not mine. There are no scuffs on it, for starters, and it's got the name MORENO embroidered on the side instead of STAG. "My bad," I say, slipping the bag off my shoulder and handing it to her. She snatches it with a huff and looks past me, I assume searching for her shoes.

Which seem to be caught up in a line at the machine, where the security agent is scowling at my actual soccer bag. The angry woman sniffs. "What did you do? Leave your tape scissors in there?"

"Shit." My stomach lurches because I definitely did leave my athletic tape scissors in the side pocket of my bag. I look around for someone to explain, but they're already beckoning me toward a podium. I can tell they'll be wagging a blue-gloved finger at me for my error.

I pad over there in my socks—my slides are still somewhere on the belt —and explain about the scissors. "I understand that you have to take them," I tell the guy, who rolls his eyes so hard I can almost hear it.

"This is serious, sir. You can't bring weapons onto a plane."

"Yes, I understand that. Like I said. I'm sorry."

He tosses the scissors into a bin next to the podium and gives my bag a final rummage, wrinkling his nose at the pungent odor from my shin guards. "Please make sure to take all your belongings from the belt," he says, shoving the bag in my direction. I nod and grab my stuff so I can hustle to my gate.

The flight is half boarded by the time I get there and as I make my way to my seat, I can't help the grin that splits my face. Moreno is sitting in the seat next to mine.

CHAPTER 2
CARA

I'M TRYING NOT TO STRESS. IT'S NOT GOING WELL. I WAS JUST A TOTAL BITCH TO a guy in the security line because he picked up my bag by accident. Gah. But I basically have everything riding on this weekend and I have no filter right now.

Which is why I have a whole string of apology messages to send to my roommates back at school for rushing out of our apartment in a huff to catch my flight. I could have had a ride from Shante if I was capable of accepting help from anyone. I could have gotten here much earlier, and not had to sprint from the shuttle bus only to get stuck in the security line behind a guy who is far too attractive for his own good.

"Nope," I say as I fill my water bottle from the fountain near my gate. "Not looking at men right now, attractive or otherwise."

I took a two-hour bus from my college in Ohio, followed by a city bus and an airport shuttle, and that's only today's part of my journey. I've been on this path to this training camp my entire life, from the first time I laced up a pair of cleats. No—from the moment I watched women like Brandy Chastain and Megan Rapinoe slay on the pitch and begged my parents to *buy* me a pair of cleats.

All the hours in the weight room these past four years, all the conditioning, all the physical therapy for sprained ligaments…it all comes down to this moment.

They announce boarding for my flight, and I make my way onto the plane, tossing my duffel bag into the overhead compartment before

LAINEY DAVIS

settling into my seat. Since I'm still allowed to use my phone, I decide it's time to eat some humble pie and I text my roommates.

MIDFIELD MAMIS

Made it to the plane!

SHANTE:

Oh, she's talking to us now.

TONI:

Probably forgot something she wants us to bring her real quick.

I'm so sorry I was a total bitch this morning. I'm so nervous, guys.

TONI:

We know, girl. You're going to be great. Don't even worry about it.

SHANTE:

Toni, you know she's worried.

I mean, I wasn't gonna say anything snippy. But yeah, I'm a wreck.

SHANTE:

And?

And I love you, and you're the best teammates and the best roommates and I'll tell you everything as soon as I get back.

ROSALIE:

We know you're going to kill it and we already planned a carbo load for Monday.

SHANTE:

Since when are we eating wheat?

ROASLIE:

I mean, maybe it's zoodles and meatballs.

TONI:

Zoodles are NOT pasta. I don't like pretending. And we don't have to follow a nutrition plan anymore. Except for Cara. <3

> Okay, well, I'll eat whatever I can with you, and I'll love it.

SHANTE:

Love you!

ROSLIE:

[heart emoji. Soccer ball emoji. Trophy emoji]

The flight attendant starts telling people to put our phones away, so I slide mine in my pants pocket just as the last passenger hustles on to the plane.

I look up and of course it's that white dude from security, whose giant duffel no longer fits in the overhead compartments because they're all full. I watch his muscles move inside his t-shirt as he hoists up the lids to nearby bins, then pulls them back down. His ass is right at my eye level and, not gonna lie, I stare. He's got a perfect bubble butt accentuated by his gray sweats and I suck in a breath, wondering if he will turn to face me and try the bins on my side of the aisle, because then I'll really get an eyeful.

Even if he didn't have a soccer bag with tape scissors, I would have spotted him as someone in training. That level of arm muscle doesn't just show up on a guy.

I do like to appreciate athletes. One thing that's true about all of us, we work our bodies to the limit, and we look damn good. I've had my share of adventures on tournament weekends. There's a pretty standard rule that my soccer teammates don't sleep around with the men's team, or even the men's teams for other sports at our school. Too much risk for distraction and drama, even if there's a smaller number of female collegiate athletes who are interested in men to begin with.

"Aha! Got it." The guy slams the bin shut with a grin and looks around, almost like he's expecting back pats. He brushes his shaggy brown hair back from his forehead with one hand and looks up and down the plane. I spy the one remaining empty seat on this plane: right next to me, and I groan as he sinks into his seat.

The flight attendants walk through the aisle for the safety demonstration, and I notice that both the male and female crew pause to smile at the sweatpants guy. A woman wearing the demonstration life vest stops in the aisle and beams at him, touching his arm. "Remember, anyone can blow the tube to inflate." She inserts the red plastic between her pursed crimson lips and winks before continuing down the aisle.

He smirks. "I notice she didn't offer you a personal safety demonstration." Is he talking to me?

I look over at him and he's got his brows raised, fingers tapping on his long legs, one of which spreads way into the aisle and the other is smashed against the seat in front of him. "How do you know I didn't get my one-on-one before you got onto the plane? You were awfully late…"

He grins. "I'd say I was right on time." At least that leg isn't pressing against mine.

"You going to follow her to the back of the plane for a snack?" I reach up and twist the air vent to full blast as the plane starts to taxi. He chuckles.

"I better stick close by in case you need rescuing. I have, after all, had some advanced coaching."

A puff of laughter escapes my lips before I can think of a retort. I like this sort of flirting because it keeps my mind off the pressure of this try-out camp.

He tips a chin in my direction. "Soccer, huh? OU? Me, too." I arch a brow at him. "I mean, not at OU obviously. You going to the camp in Cali?"

"I am. You, too?"

He nods. "I am."

I exhale. "So, your guts are twisted, too?" I wince. Maybe he's totally confident. Hell, for all I know he's already capped for the national team. I don't follow the men's game at all. But I'm relieved when his face softens, and he nods.

"Oh, I'm a total wreck." He twists to offer me his hand to shake. "Wes Stag, striker."

I grip his hand, feeling a flutter in my belly at the warm, firm contact. "Cara Moreno. Midfield."

"I hate midfield," he laughs. "It's exhausting."

"Hmm. Maybe try upping your fitness routine." We both laugh and then grip our respective arm rests as the plane jolts off the ground. Our forearms are pressed together on the arm rest between us, and I focus on that as we hit the sky. My phone flies from my pocket and skitters into the aisle and Wes reaches to pick it up.

He holds it out to me, and I slide it from his hand. His middle finger lingers, sliding down my palm and making me shiver. "We should get dinner or something when we land. My agenda doesn't start until morning."

I press my lips together, considering. I really need to network on this trip, and I'll have a roommate at the hotel anyway. But there's no harm in a meal before I check in, right? In the silence, Wes raises his brows, expectantly. He's gorgeous and funny, and he knows about soccer. High level soccer.

I can't shake the feeling it would be a mistake to turn him down.

But I also worry it's a mistake to say yes.

"We'll see," Cara says, toying with the end of her braid and then tugging on her tray table. I envy the way she has enough space to pull it all the way flat. My legs are way too long to even consider it. My knees get smashed every time the guy in front of me adjusts his weight. But squashed up close to a beautiful, sassy soccer player, I don't mind as much. Hopefully she can distract me from the spasms I'll probably get in my back from folding my body like a crouching insect.

"Well, Cara Moreno, you have to at least promise to sit next to me on the shuttle to the hotel. Wait. Does the women's team stay in the same hotel as the men's for this thing? Do they want to risk everyone … canoodling?"

I realize too late that I've revealed myself to be a first timer at this elite camp, but Cara seems unfazed. She turns her body slightly so she's almost facing me in the cramped space. I can smell her, fresh powder and floral soap. I want to bury my face in that braid and inhale. "Not sure how you don't already know this about women's soccer, Stag, but there's usually plenty of same-gender canoodling regardless." She laughs, and I realize I'm hanging on to some really outdated assumptions. Cara bites her lip and says, "I'm at the Summit."

I nod. "Same. So, about that shuttle ride…"

* * *

We flirt the entire flight, joking about the agenda, realizing the men's and women's teams share some staff members. I'm careful not to mention my relation to the coaching staff of my hometown teams. I'm not sure why

I don't tell Cara that fitness coach Lucy Moyer is my aunt, or that my uncle coaches the professional men's soccer team in Pittsburgh. Cara seems blissfully unaware of my family, and I realize it's a relief. I spend enough time worried that people think my relatives pulled strings to get me where I am.

Maybe they did back in high school and maybe they did to get me seen by the college scouts. But I'm pretty confident that I made my way here today on my own merit. My college coach sure didn't make any calls on my behalf after I quit the team.

Cara flops her head back against the seat and sighs. "I have so much riding on this weekend. You know?"

"Trust me. I get it."

She turns her head to stare at me, her dark eyes intense, like she can see right inside my head. "How can you stand it? The pressure? Sometimes I feel like, if I am this messed up about the possibility of making the national team, maybe I'm not cut out to wear that jersey anyway."

I shake my head and place my hand on hers on the arm rest. She doesn't pull her arm back or flinch, so I keep it there. "Don't think like that. Anyone would be a mess going into this camp. Even the veterans. It's not like their spot on the roster is etched in stone. It's a big deal to put yourself out there and risk being told you don't have what it takes."

She smiles. "It feels good to meet someone who gets that."

"Same, Cara. Same." I tap my other palm on my thigh, realizing my right leg is almost touching hers. How are these planes so small? The warmth of her body radiates into me, despite the blast of air she's got blowing from her vent. "I'll let you in on a secret." I can't believe I'm about to speak all this out loud, but what do I have to lose? She's on the same path. She doesn't know my history, but if she's trying out for the national team, she knows something about what my life has looked like on the pitch. "I don't even expect to get called to the Stars and Stripes. I'm here to get seen by the pro scouts."

Cara's smile lights up her entire face and she tucks a few tendrils of loose hair behind her ears. "Wes," she whispers. "Same!"

When we land, Cara and I grab our duffel bags—each of us with the proper bag this time—and she does agree to ride the shuttle with me to the hotel. But I can tell her head is already into her purpose for being here. Tonight isn't the night to let loose. Cara mutters to herself on the shuttle bus and I fight back the urge to squeeze her knee, to reassure her that she'll be great tomorrow. I have no idea how she'll play. How she'll respond to the pressure of being scrutinized. But something tells me she will rise to this occasion and shine above the other players.

As we pull up to the hotel there's a huge crowd of soccer players sprawled all through the lobby, with some chaos as people try to get checked into their rooms. I see a bunch of familiar faces and I hear a woman with a clipboard calling Cara's name from over near the vending machine.

She waves and holds up a finger, turning toward me. "So."

I slide my hands in my pockets. "So."

Cara rolls her eyes and pulls out her phone. "You should give me your number. You know, in case I have questions about life vests or something."

I grin. "You want instructions for how to blow a tube?"

Cara doesn't blush and she doesn't back away. She thrusts the phone toward me. "By Saturday night, I'll be ready for some turbulence."

I enter my number into her phone and then call myself, silencing the phone with one hand as I pass back hers. But I don't let go right away, stroking her hand with my thumb instead. I like that this has become a thing with us already. "I'll help you assume the brace position, Cara." I wink at her.

She smiles a tight-lipped half-grin and hoists her bag higher on her shoulder. I watch her walk away toward her competition, admiring the rear view as she leaves.

And then I turn to face the guys I've played against for years in college, the guys who are even bigger rivals this weekend than ever before. Time to get my head in the game.

CHAPTER 4
CARA

As a division one athlete, I've gotten used to some pretty swanky accommodations for soccer functions, and this training center is no different. The hotel is super clean and spacious, with all-white linens that I'm scared I'll get muddy later when I'm covered in grass and dirt from the field.

I'm rooming with a white woman named Jay, who played keeper for Seattle. I've played against her before, but never really got to know her. When we get to our room, we toss our bags on the ground and look at one another, hesitant.

She runs a tattooed hand through her short, straight hair and sighs. "I really don't like sleeping next to the vent thingy. Is that okay?"

I sigh right back in relief. "I really prefer sleeping further from the door! This is great."

We spend some time unpacking, swapping small talk to break the awkwardness. We both just graduated and have our sights set on the pros, with the national team as a "someday" goal.

"They're taking younger and younger players, though," Jay says, pursing her lips as she lays out her goalie kits on the dresser. "Maybe I've already missed my window. I don't know."

"Well, I worry about the same things, but I'm sure the competition is tighter for keeper since there's only one of you." She's got an array of pale blue, black, and lime green outfits. "Do you have to bring all of them with you all weekend in case we scrimmage?"

She shakes her head. "Nah. I just wanted to be ready."

. . .

We both like to fall asleep to white noise and we turn in pretty early to help combat the jet lag, but not until we chug water with electrolyte tablets stirred in. Jay cranks the volume on a sleep sounds app on her phone and we snap off the lights. And then my brain goes haywire, running through all the skills I know I need to perfect, all the flaws I can't unsee after the last round of film I watched with my college coach.

I can't do this all night and I silently chide myself for obsessing. But if I stop thinking about soccer, that only leaves thoughts of Wes. It's seriously unfair for someone to be that good looking. He's the total package: funny, tall, fit, and confident. I don't regret skipping dinner with him tonight since both of us really do need to concentrate. But I can't help fantasizing about what it will be like if we really do sneak away from the crowd after the last session ends on Saturday.

Will he really help me take the edge off? Unwind and forget the stress and pressure for a few minutes? Maybe it'll actually last longer than a few minutes with Wes. Or maybe we'll both be too exhausted to copulate after 16 hours of intense, high-level soccer.

Jay and I sit together on the shuttle bus to the training center. Apparently, the men and women are training in a different area of the facility, which makes sense since we need all the space in the locker rooms and offices.

"Wow." Jay and I stop in the tunnel to the field, looking out on the perfect grass in the California sunshine.

"Yeah," I tell her. "Wow." I know we've each experienced some pretty big stadiums, but this is beyond. This is the home of pro soccer for men and women, a stadium that regularly sells out with 20,000 tickets. "This is where it all happens."

"Damn right." Jay claps me on the back. "You got this, Moreno."

I punch her in the upper arm. "You got this, too."

Every woman in this locker room is the best of the best on their university team full of elite players. Or, I realize, the best of their professional club team. I try not to gawk at the group of women along one side of the locker room because I've definitely waited in line for each of their autographs in the past.

"Jay," I whisper. "We are in the same locker room with—"

"Don't be weird, Moreno." Her eyes widen and she shakes her head. "They're trying out this weekend, same as us. Right? All of us earned the right to be here."

"I wish I had your confidence about it," I mutter. I think back on the summer I spent living at school instead of going home. My parents were sad about it, but I wanted to graduate in August and focus on my game, rather than tack on one more semester. I clocked 30 hours a week on individual skill work with our positional coaches. I lifted weights until my thighs busted out of my jeans.

Jay's right. I can't afford to fuck this up by forgetting that I'm a bad ass.

I also can't forget the reward I've set up for myself at the end of the weekend…

CHAPTER 5
WES

THIS MORNING'S SESSIONS WERE BRUTAL, AND I LOVED EVERY SECOND. EVERY guy here is better than the best guys on my university team, and I've been keeping up just fine. I know I'm right where I belong, and when we get a break to hydrate, I wander over to the fence with my sports drink, leaning back and just taking in the scene.

The women are using the field inside the stadium this morning while the men train on one of the practice fields, and we're switching this afternoon. But from this angle I can see through the stadium gates onto the field and the women are scrimmaging.

I chug the rest of my drink and walk a bit closer, trying to see.

A streak of red catches my eye and I stare at the best midfielder I've ever seen. She's got MORENO on jersey back in white letters.

Cara's braid flies behind her as she attacks up the sideline, two defenders on her back and ready to pounce. I watch, mesmerized, as she plants a foot and weaves right, the ball following along like it's an extension of her cleats.

Her movements are graceful and devastating as she darts into gaps that shouldn't be wide enough. Cara makes it all seem effortless, pulling the ball back with one toe and changing direction to hug the sideline. As she approaches the goal, I can see she has the keeper beat. She's got a clear shot and it's going to smash into the back of the net.

Except she doesn't strike. She fakes right and sends a sweet pass to a teammate, who toes the ball into the center of the goal. "Fuck," I whisper.

Now that was a boss move. The coaches watching the session take notes and I see one of them whip out a phone, tapping frantically on the screen.

It shouldn't be this hot. She's not trying to be sexual right now. But I'm hard as a goal post watching her move. Honestly, I think I drool a little bit, but I pretend it's sweat and wipe my face with my jersey as I hear my name being called.

I indulge in one more glance as Cara's teammates swarm around her for hugs and high-fives. She's sort of shy about what just happened, her full, pouty lips tipped in a small smile.

"Stag! Let's move!"

I jog toward the sound of the coach's voice, ready for my own scrimmage and my own chance to show off my skills in a game scenario. As the striker coach pulls me and the other guys in to talk strategy, I marvel at just how specialized the training is at the next level of soccer. Even though I played D1 in college, we had all generalized coaches except for the goalies.

I'm spending this entire weekend not only showing these coaches what I can do, but also learning from them. I'm guessing the men's and women's staff have some of the same training plans because Coach Bev tells us the objective is to move the ball along the sideline and pass toward the center for the shots on goal.

It's easy to see why some guys would want to be glory hogs for a camp like this, to score and put points on the board. But I commit to showing Bev and the other staff that I can follow instructions and adapt to the gameplan.

On the pitch, I feel a little like Cara, moving the ball well, outwitting defenders. When I do see a shot on goal from the right corner, it's hard as hell not to take it, but as soon as I pass to another guy from my row, I can hear Coach Bev bellowing in delight.

Soon after, an air horn sounds, signaling our lunch break, and everyone makes their way to the locker rooms. I take my time on the walk over, feeling damn good about my morning, and Coach Bev shouts my name.

"Stag! Looking good out there. This your first open camp with us?"

I nod and she elbows a man standing next to her. I know Bev isn't on the national team staff, but I recognize her companion as the president of Soccer USA. "Lou, keep an eye on this one, hey? You'll be hearing his name in a few years."

Lou holds out a hand, smiling. "Lou Rubeo. And what name should I be looking for?"

"Wes Stag, sir." I shake his hand and he pats my upper arm.

"Stag. I'll keep that in mind." He raises his brows and walks in a different direction as Bev falls in step beside me.

"Don't mind him. Or do. But I've got you on my list, kid."

Now it's my turn to lift my brows. "What list might that be?"

She waves a hand. "It's a mental list for now. But I'm going to make sure you're in for the exhibition match tomorrow. I want you to be seen, okay?"

I nod rapidly. "Thank you. I want to do my best out there." She smiles and pats my upper arm, shooing me toward the locker room.

I strip out of my cleats and socks and into shower slides, feeling like a million bucks even as I make my way to the training room to get help stretching my lower back. Everything seems to be falling into place. I'm not usually superstitious. I don't keep the same socks all season or give up shaving during playoffs or anything like that. But I can't help but wonder if Cara Moreno is my lucky charm.

CHAPTER 6
CARA

"You saucy minx!" Jay claps me on the back after our morning scrimmage ends. "I thought you were going to score right between my legs, but you fired off that pass. So great."

I laugh, still high on the endorphin rush of perfecting the strategy the coaches asked for. "Thanks. I bet you would have blocked it if I took the shot. But we were working on that decoy move."

Jay shakes her head. "Well, it freaking worked. You grabbing lunch?"

"Yeah, I just have to change shoes quick."

"Cool. I'm grabbing a bag of ice for my shoulder. Meet you up there?"

I nod and she clacks off toward the training room, still wearing her cleats and today's bright orange goalie kit.

I'm still shaking with happiness at how I played this morning. I don't know if it's the sunshine or the atmosphere or if I just click with this group of players, but I can objectively say I'm kicking ass at this camp. I walk slowly toward the locker room, taking my time and basking in satisfaction, and I hear footsteps as someone approaches.

"Hello, there."

I turn and see a guy in a Soccer USA polo. He steps closer and I realize it's not just any guy, but the president of the whole organization. I recognize him from television when I've seen the national team play. "Oh. Hi."

He smiles and his eyes dip to my chest. "You looked pretty good out there. What's your name?"

"Uh, Cara. Cara Moreno."

"Nice to meet you, Cara. I'm Lou." He holds out his hand, and when I shake it, he doesn't let go as soon as I expect him to.

Cold dread snakes up my spine, like someone dumped a bucket of ice over my head. His smile creeps me out more than the handshake. Maybe because this guy is really important when it comes to the national team? I decide it must be my nerves and I pull my hand back, placing it on my duffel bag and holding it tight against my side.

"Well, I've got my eye on you, Cara. Hope to see a lot more of you."

I'm about to stutter out a thanks when Jay rounds the corner with the ice. She glares at Lou, who looks up at her and immediately backs up a few inches. Jay tips her chin. "We should get up to lunch, Cara."

I nod. "Yeah. I'm starved."

Lou smiles, but it's a false smile, even creepier than when he held my hand in his. "You ladies enjoy your meal."

I mutter another thanks and Jay says nothing at all as Lou walks away, whistling.

"You okay?" Jay is stern and serious, and I worry she thinks something bad happened.

"Oh, yes. Totally. I think I'm just exhausted." My hands are shaking a little as the adrenaline wears off from earlier.

She nods, her face still apprehensive. "Well, let's get some protein."

We make our way to the cafeteria and pile our plates with chicken breasts and sweet potatoes. By the time we've each had a few mouthfuls, we're laughing alongside the other people at our table as they verbally rehash the morning's cardio activities.

"Let's just skip as high as we can for a mile and a half," Jay jokes. "Really test out the strength of our sports bras before we scrimmage."

Everyone laughs until our sides ache and I'm back to feeling great. I'm sure I was overreacting to how Lou from Soccer USA made me feel and I chalk the experience up to hunger and adrenaline from the scrimmage. The afternoon session goes amazing just like the morning, even if I am utterly exhausted by the end. I decide to skip the shower at the stadium. I'll wait until I'm back at the hotel when I can take my time with a bottle of tea tree conditioner, so I check my messages while I wait for the shuttle bus.

My group chat with my roommates is full of good luck notes, videos of professional players scoring goals and celebrating, and then a picture of my entire college team after a workout. Every one of my teammates wishes me the best, even the ones I just graduated with who didn't make the cut for the open camp.

I'm still choked up and emotional when I get out of my shower, but Jay is fired up, bouncing around the room in a swimsuit. "There you are! Come on, everyone is doing hydration recovery." I furrow my brow in confusion, and she shakes her head. "We're invading the hotel pool. Grab your suit."

I laugh at myself. "For a minute I worried I forgot an active cool-down session or something."

Jay tosses me a towel from the bathroom. "No, we're just going rogue and enjoying some sunshine. Some of us live in Seattle, where we never see that yellow guy up there."

I quickly slip into my two-piece. It's not the sexiest bathing suit from my drawer—it's the functional one I use for ice baths, so the top has a lot of coverage, and the bottom is more boy shorts than bikini. "Okay, ready." I toss a long t-shirt over my head and shove my feet back in my shower slides.

The two of us head down to the hotel pool and find the entire space is crawling with soccer players. Jay whistles. "That is one fine display."

I nod, staring at the corner of the deck where a group of men are shedding shirts. "Mmm, yes." I look over to Jay and see she's got the same expression on her face as she stares at a group of women in two-piece suits similar to mine. We laugh at one another and drop our towels on the nearest lounge chair.

"Too bad we have to stay focused." Jay sighs.

"No harm in looking though, right?" I slide into the pool, the heated water a delicious surprise. "Oh my god, this feels amazing." I say it to Jay but when I lean my head back in the water and then right myself and open my eyes, I see that she's swum off toward the deep end and Wes Stag is looming over me from the pool deck.

"It looks amazing," he drawls as he drops to sit on the edge, dangling his legs into the water.

I smooth my hair back from my face and stretch my neck. Wes Stag without a shirt is entirely unfair when I'm trying to keep my head in the soccer game. But then again, if I let my brain rest and destress for a bit, maybe I'll be sharper tomorrow.

"Wait," Wes says. "Were you talking about yourself or the pool?"

Do I have the energy for this level of flirting after a hard day of soccer? "You should get in and research that question," I tell him. *Yes. Yes I do have the energy for this.*

Taking the invitation, Wes slides into the water and submerges fully, coming to stand and shaking the water off his golden muscles. I lean close, trying to make out the tattoo he has on his chest. "Oh," I smile. "A stag. I get it."

He traces the tattoo absentmindedly. "It's kind of a family thing. The laurel branches are for my grandma."

"So, everyone has the same tat? That's pretty cool."

He nods, running his hands along the surface of the water, not making any bones about checking me out. So I drink my fill and stare right back. I mutter, "if all the guys have the tattoo on your chest, where do the women get it done?"

He winks. "You'll have to become a Stag woman and find out, won't you?"

"Oh really? How does one become a Stag woman." I back away from him in the water and he follows, both of us squatting low so we're fully submerged up to the neck. "I'm a try-before-I-buy kind of gal…"

I like how I feel when I'm with him, confident, flirty, like I can say anything I want, and he wants to hear it. I can be up front in my interest in boning him and he clearly feels the same way. It's refreshing. It's thrilling.

He reaches out to touch my shoulder and I welcome the contact. My body leans back against his touch almost instinctively. It feels so different from when that Lou guy was near me in the hall earlier. I shudder, chasing thoughts of him away and focusing on Wes and his finger tracing my shoulder blade.

"It would look good on you here," he says, palm skating along my bare shoulder blade. "But it would also look hot on your upper arm." He moves his hand to the dip of my bicep.

This thing between us is electric. I know if I looked down, I'd find him at least half hard and I resist swimming to him, pressing against all that magnetic heat and muscle. The universe put him in my path at that airport, sat him right next to me, and now gifted me the chance to see Wes Stag all wet and warm in this pool.

I close my eyes. We still have a big day tomorrow and I cannot let myself slip away for a quickie with so much on the line.

I exhale through pursed lips and back away from him a few inches, leaning my back on the edge of the pool. He slides up beside me and I turn to face him. "Tell me about your family. Where are you from?"

"I'm a Pittsburgh boy, born and raised. My entire family is there." He looks up, pondering. "Well, some of my cousins are away at college. There are a lot of us all in school at once." He chuckles. "Our dads sometimes curse their choice to all having kids at about the same time."

I smile. "I have a big extended family, too. Mexican Catholics and all that."

"Extended family—not a lot of siblings?"

I let my toes float up out of the pool, noticing that the polish is chipped on one of my big toes. Probably where a striker stepped on me earlier today. It'll hurt later. "I'm an only child. My parents got divorced when I was young and neither of them had any more kids." I shrug. "They get along okay."

We talk about my upbringing in Ohio, how I suffered through over a decade of Catholic girls' schools. "My parents would have sent me to an all-girls' college, too, if I hadn't gotten a scholarship to OU."

"Thank god for Title IX, then, I guess." Wes taps his hand on the concrete pool deck.

"You know about Title IX?"

He scoffs. "Everyone knows about Title IX. Or…I guess everyone in my family. Do people usually not know?"

Wes seems taken aback as I explain how many people in Ohio have never heard of women's soccer, even in this day and age, and how many people are surprised I earned a free college degree playing soccer and expect to play professionally.

His eyes widen at that. "Man, my one aunt is an Olympian and some sort of high-powered court judge. She got involved in getting the US women's hockey team equal pay."

"Holy shit, really?" As he talks, I learn that passionate feminism is now my biggest turn-on in a guy. He keeps going.

"And another aunt coaches professional soccer—men and women. I guess in my family we just talk a lot more about those sorts of equity issues."

"That's amazing." I nudge closer to him. I want to tell him that I'd like to meet his family, to see this group of people who teach their sons about gender equity. But I'm not here looking for love. I intend to be a woman who is paid to play pro soccer, and I've spent decades convincing my parents that such a thing is possible.

This thing between us is totally happening—it'll be hot and fast. The gravy on the feast of this weekend. I chew the inside of my cheek and look at him, reminding myself that all bets are off the second tomorrow's afternoon session ends.

Jay shouts my name and waves a towel. "We're grabbing dinner. You in?"

I nod and turn to Wes. "That's my cue."

"Until tomorrow, Moreno."

I can't tell which is the more impressive feat: acing that plan on the field today, or walking away from a very wet, half-naked Wes Stag.

CHAPTER 7
WES

I watch Cara climb out of the pool, the sun glinting off the muscles on her back and shoulders. She walks away with her friend, drying herself off with the too-small hotel towel. There shouldn't really be anything sexy about a woman dabbing pool water off her neck, but I'm fully erect in the shallow end as she clacks away in her shower slides.

Under normal circumstances, I'd have her against the wall by now, our tongues tangling. But she's right—we've both got a lot riding on this weekend. I guess the anticipation adds to the intrigue, too. By tomorrow night we'll both be amped up and ready to unleash our inner beasts.

I splash water on my face and pat my own hungry stomach, wondering when the guys will head into the cafeteria for dinner.

Someone has to start that party train and climb out of the pool. I make my way over to the chair with my stuff and almost bump into a woman hustling into the fenced-in space. "Woah, there," she says, gripping my arm with a strong hand. And then she looks up to see my face. "Wesley Stag? I wondered when I'd see your mug."

"Aunt Lucy?"

My aunt swats at my arm with her clipboard. "Stay right there, mister. I need to give my card to a prospect and then you and I are having a chat."

I dry my hair and slip into my t-shirt as I watch her continue hustling with one of the women's players at the far end of the pool. Aunt Lucy pulls a card from her fanny pack and gestures excitedly as the player beams. I didn't think individual team fitness coaches would be at one of these camps recruiting, but I guess the Pittsburgh Hot Metal sent a deep bench to scout talent.

Lucy smiles at her prospect, shakes her hand, and then my aunt whips her entire body back to me, her face shifting to a stern scowl. She kicks a recliner toward me and sinks onto another one. "Sit." I do. "Wes. Your father is beside himself. Your uncles had to take him running and rough him up so he'd calm down. You want to tell me when the hell this family started keeping secrets and making huge decisions that leave other Stags in the dark?"

I sigh and lean forward, my elbows on my tired thighs. "Aunt Lucy, if I gave my parents advance notice I wasn't finishing school, they'd overstep. They'd go to the bursar and pre-pay tuition. You've met my dad. He's stubborn as hell."

"Oh, trust me, I'm familiar with the Stag man form of stubbornness." Aunt Lucy rolls her eyes. She's married to my Uncle Hawk, who only found out about his brothers as an adult when he was transferred to Pittsburgh's pro soccer team. I was about six years old when my family learned there was a fourth Stag brother…who happens to have a different last name from the rest of us. They've had a lot of years to make up for lost time, though. My extended family is insanely close.

Aunt Lucy leans forward and looks me in the eye, grabbing hold of my chin. "You could have at least talked to me and Hawk about your plans to go pro right away. You know we would have given you advice. Made introductions…"

Her voice drifts off as I shake my head out of her hand. "I don't want handouts because of my family. I want to sign with a team because I'm the fucking best player for the roster." She breathes in and out through her nose a few times, her hands tapping her clipboard. A thought occurs to me. "Uncle Hawk isn't here this weekend, is he?"

I can't help the flinch my face betrays at the idea of my uncle activating the family group chat from the bleachers. I'm sure he and Aunt Lucy are less than thrilled that I swore their son to secrecy regarding my plans. Honestly, I'm impressed Wyatt sat on this news and I definitely owe him big time.

"No, Wes, your uncle is home prepping the Forge for the playoffs while half his starters are here trying out for the national team."

I nod, because I assumed she'd be back doing the same thing with the women's team—half the reason I chose this particular camp to take my shot. I knew word would get back to everyone eventually. I just wanted to go into the inevitable hard conversations having made my mark. I'm assuming I will leave here tomorrow with offers. I've bet my whole future on it.

I scratch the back of my neck and make a face of contrition at my aunt. "So…why are *you* here, then?"

"Gah." She runs her hands down her khaki shorts and leans forward. "I got an urgent text about a keeper, a midfielder, and an unbelievable striker that our rivals in Louisville are planning to woo." She shimmies her shoulders. "I made myself available for the last-minute first-class direct flight out here."

I laugh, imagining her sprinting from the stadium in Pittsburgh to the airport in her polo shirt and fanny pack. She'd probably get there faster than if she drove, half because the traffic there sucks and half because my Aunt Lucy is fit as fuck from so many years training professional athletes and putting her workout money where her mouth is.

"Well, I hope you counter-woo your prospects successfully. Any player would be lucky to have you on their coaching team."

She grins. "Okay, okay, enough with the ass kissing. Wes, what's your plan here? Lay it out for me."

I throw my hands in the air. "You're looking at the plan. I declined my scholarship for this year and withdrew from the university. I worked my ass off over the summer to get fit for this weekend and I intend to leave here with offers."

She furrows her brow and looks at me skeptically. I show her my palms. "Yes, I have a fallback plan. If somehow, I leave here without any interest, I'll play for one of the academy clubs for a year and get my ass to the next open camp and the one after that until I get called up."

"Wesley."

I shake my head. "I know my parents' stance on education. I fully intend to finish my degree once I'm done with my professional career. Which is what your husband did, if I recall. And Uncle Ty. I don't need to tell you there's a limited window when my body can handle being a pro athlete."

She sighs. "No, Wes. You don't need to tell me that. But I still don't approve of your approach to this, doing it in a flame of subterfuge. Your dad was embarrassed to be kept in the dark, kiddo. Why would you do that to him?"

We stare at one another for a few beats. I have no good answers for her except that she isn't there when my parents unleash their anxieties on me. Education is so important to my mom that she can't see why I'd pursue anything until I have a degree under my belt. Her epilepsy prevented her from doing so many things physically and I don't know if she really gets that my body is the thing I'm focused on right now.

But my dad is a fucking artist. Yeah, he has a fine arts degree, but he knows what it means to slip into a trance and just let your body do its thing. It makes me nuts when he insists I put my studies ahead of literally everything else. Soccer *is* my everything.

"I have no good answers for you, Aunt Lucy. I'm 21 years old. I'm not relying on them for rent or cash or tuition. If I thought they'd support me in this, I would have come to them with it. I am sorry I kept you and the uncles in the dark—and Aunt Juniper. I don't know. I guess I never expected you'd stage a mass intervention to get my dad to cool his jets."

She rolls her eyes. "Please. All those men do is intervene with each other to cool their jets. You've dug a bit of a hole for yourself, Wes."

I lean back on the recliner. "I'll dig myself out of it after this weekend when I know more about what's in store."

She bites her lip and looks around. "Well, obviously I can't tell you anything in that regard, but you're a smart kid. You know I'm not the only coach who jumped on a plane this weekend."

I grin, but I know better than to push her for details. "There's a lot of top talent here, eh?"

She stands up and whacks me with her clipboard. "Get some food. Get some rest. Play your ass off tomorrow and plan a good grovel with the family ASAP."

I follow her into the hotel feeling pretty damn good about my choices leading up to this moment.

CHAPTER 8
CARA

"I want to see crisp passes out there, ladies. Lots of touches on the ball." Coach Akemi wanders up and down the lines of athletes, staring at our feet as we pass the ball and sprint between cones. We've spent the whole morning focusing on fundamentals, basic skills from my preschool days. "The team that has the best ball control is the team that takes home the gold," Akemi says, as if she can read my mind when I start to question the drill.

I think of my roommates, my fellow midfielders on my college team. We always pair up for these drills and we just know each other's style so well. I barely have to look when Shante, Toni, or Rosalie is across the cones from me. I just know they'll deliver the ball directly to my feet and, like a magnet is attached, I can send it right back where it needs to be.

It's hard for me to imagine building that familiarity from scratch, but I knew that would happen after graduation. There was never a second when I thought I'd stop playing soccer. My whole life has led to this moment, to the consideration for the pro women's soccer league, and someday to the national team. My midfield mamis aren't looking for the same experience. They all have graduate school on the horizon and Rosalie hasn't even looked into recreational soccer near where she's heading in Chicago. I need to create new bonds with new players.

So, I focus on my fundamentals here, with a partner I've never seen before, and remind myself that I'll settle into a team. I *will* get signed after this weekend and I will find a group of middies I click with. I punctuate this thought by stopping the ball with the inside of my foot and pushing it to the outside before chipping it across the lane to my partner, whose name I forget. She smiles and dribbles the ball.

"Looking good, Moreno. Nice work." Coach Akemi tips her chin toward the sideline where an army of assistant coaches furiously take notes on all of our performances. Just when I start to worry we will spend the entirety of the day on passing drills, Coach blows her whistle and tells us to huddle up.

"Coach Pat has been putting together some new rosters based on yesterday's scrimmage performance. They will read off your teams, and that's who you will be with for the rest of today's session."

I edge my way closer to Coach Pat, hoping they've put me on the same team as Jay, so I don't have to shoot at her in the goal today. Sure enough, Coach puts us both on the green team and Jay mimes an excited roar when she hears both our names.

There are 60 of us players, split into four teams, and we spend the rest of the morning cycling through more fundamental skills before the coaches send us off for lunch. Jay drapes an arm around my shoulder and hands me a cup of water as we make our way toward the cafeteria. "I've had enough first-touch practice to last me the rest of my life, I think," she jokes.

"Just wait until we practice shots on goal later." I elbow her in the side, glad to be forging a friendship outside my college network, with someone else focused on the same goals as me. I'm about to make another joke about the agenda when I hear a voice coming toward us.

"Oh good, the two of you are together. That makes things easier." A fit, white woman with shiny brown hair in a ponytail jogs up beside us and smiles, beckoning for us to step out of the sun into the shade of the tunnel toward lunch. "Can you chat for a minute?"

"Sure." Jay furrows her brow, confused.

"I'm Lucy Moyer, fitness coach for the Pittsburgh Hot Metal." Jay's brow stays furrowed. "I'm new to them this year—I was coaching the men's side before that."

I take a deep breath, attempting to calm my racing heart. A coach from a pro team has just pulled me aside to chat, with a pleasant look on her face. Lucy produces two business cards from a fanny pack and Jay and I each grab one. "The two of you really impressed our scouts yesterday. I flew out here to see for myself."

Jay's eyes fly wide, and she seems to bounce in her cleats.

"Wow," I stammer. "Thank you."

"Thank *you*," Lucy grins. "We really need more depth in the midfield, especially someone good with set pieces." I think back to the corner kick I took yesterday, that Jay swatted away like it was a slow pitch softball. My frustration must be evident on my face because Lucy says, "I was happy to see a fantastic kick with excellent form, and I was excited to see such solid defense on such a banger. Also, with excellent form." She looks at Jay thoughtfully. "I can tell you really work on your core strength and leg flexibility."

The two of us are beside ourselves. I know I haven't had any preparation for next steps since I wasn't in the draft this past spring. I was so focused on getting here, I didn't think about what to do and I'm unsure how to act when it came to the results. I'm guessing Jay hasn't, either. Lucy gestures at the cards we're each holding like they're made of delicate spider webbing. "My cell is on there. Reach out." With a smile she jogs off toward the striker for the blue team.

"So, that was amazing." Jay shakes her head and holds just the edges of the card, trying to keep from smudging it with sweat, I guess. I'm doing the same.

"Are you a hugger? I need a hug right now."

She nods and I throw my arms around her, both of us jumping up and down and squealing before composing ourselves. "Right. Let's fuel up and kick ass this afternoon."

"Check and check."

I nudge her with my elbow as we wait for our food. "You have to go up against the striker from the blue team today."

Jay grins. "She's got nothing on you, roomie. Me and my flexible hamstrings are ready for her."

Someone's gaze bores into me as I sit down with my food. I look over to see Wes gulping down ice water, his throat working spectacularly as he drinks. He and I feel inevitable, our plan to meet later an exclamation point on an amazing morning. I send him my best smile, which he returns with a wink before he heads back out to the field with the rest of the men.

THE FINAL CAMP WHISTLE BLOWS, AND I FEEL INCREDIBLE. FOR A FEW minutes…before the aches and pains set in and my body screams at me for torturing it for 48 hours. I join the parade of sweaty guys heading toward the training room and am pretty happy to see they've got a lot of help, so nobody has to wait very long.

I sign in and get on a table pretty quickly, telling the trainer that the worst pain is in my lower back. He frowns at the clipboard. "Did you participate in the cool-down stretches after the clinic?" I nod and wince when he sets a hand on my flank.

"I think I took an elbow during the scrimmage."

He hums and lifts up my shirt, nodding. He pokes around for a bit and says, "I'm going to hook you up with some stim for 20 minutes. I assume you've had this treatment before?"

"Ugh." I groan in response, wiggling out of my shirt and tugging my shorts down a few inches to expose my lower back for the sensors. I actually love getting hooked up to the TENS machine, feeling those gentle electric pulses in my muscles. It's the next best thing to a real massage. I moan in relief as the trainer gets me all hooked up. He sets the timer by my head and moves on to the next guy. I close my eyes and think through everything that happened.

I played my ass off this weekend. I took a huge gamble to be here, threw away my final year of college eligibility. After some of the conversations I had with the staff here, I'm feeling confident it all worked out. I haven't gotten any official calls yet, but I would expect those to filter in tomorrow morning after the scouts spend this evening unloading to their coaching teams across the country. Hell, maybe even across the world if the rumors are true that some scouts from the UK were watching today.

The stim machine gives me a jolt in a good spot, and I let out a moan before I can help myself. I open my eyes to see most of the guys have filtered out of the training room and the women's team is starting to file in as their session wraps up. My eyes connect with Cara's where she's seated on a table a few down from me while a trainer wraps bags of ice around her shins.

I give her a lazy smile. I am tempted to imagine her hands on my lower back, but I don't want to be sprouting wood here in the training room. That's for later, in private. Ideally with her, if she's still game.

She gives me a look that assures me she is still ready to celebrate and burn off some adrenaline. I smile wider as she licks her lips. I love that she's got the same priorities as me, the same expectations. We both emphasize our game right now, above our personal relationships. Neither of us is going into this expecting forever. Not at all.

She presses her teeth into her plump bottom lip, and I want to fly off the table and capture her tongue with mine. Her expression shifts like she can tell how turned on I am and her confidence is so damn sexy. I never realized before I saw Cara how hot it is when a woman knows what she wants and knows damn well how to get it.

I'm not talking about sex, although her openness about that is hot, too. Cara Moreno can play fucking soccer. She's like me, knowing in her tendons that she's one of the best in the world, capable of competing on the professional stage. There is nothing like that.

I'm glad I got to see her play from afar yesterday, got to see her skill on the field. She's a stunning, incomparable player and I cannot wait for her to direct all those physical strengths toward me.

The tension slips out of my muscles, both because of the treatment and because I'm imagining her straddling me on my bed, me lying back as she does the work to bring us both over the goal line.

The trainer pats Cara on the knee and moves on to the next athlete. Cara hops off the table and takes her time getting her bag. I've been in that place before: she'll wear the bags of ice on her legs until we reach the hotel and then she'll be all set. She bends over to fuss with the zippers, giving me an eye-level show that includes her entire, perfect ass just a few feet from my face. She is absolutely doing that on purpose.

The room is nearly empty now, just a few other athletes and one trainer remaining. Cara approaches my table and her hand trails along my leg, fingers tickling the hairs on my calf, the back of my knee, and fuck! She just keeps on going.

The timer beeps and I yelp, causing Cara to giggle. I struggle to sit up and shout over my shoulder, "Hey, is it ok if I disconnect myself?"

The trainer is stretching a woman's hamstring and glances over at me. "You think you can get all the stickers? Maybe your friend can help you out?"

Cara grins and nods, hands coming to my lower back. Her touch sends stronger shock waves through my body than the machine as she peels off the sticky circles. Her breath is hot against my ear as she says, "I know that stings. I'll kiss it later."

"Later? Fuck that. We're getting out of here immediately."

She giggles again and yanks off the final sticker, patting my back afterward to ease the sting. "I have to eat first. I'm starving."

I run a finger down the side of her neck, watching her shiver a bit as she continues to rub her palm on my back. "I've got something I can feed you, Moreno."

She smacks me and backs up, arching a brow and looking murderous. "I'm serious, Stag. I need protein. Do not make another joke."

I laugh and tug my t-shirt over my head. "I was going to tell you we can order room service. I don't know what you were thinking."

She bites her lip. "What about your roommate?"

I furrow my brow at her. "You have a roommate?"

"You don't have a roommate?" I shake my head and toss her a protein bar from my bag. "I can't believe the men don't have to share rooms. Fuck you."

I place a hand on her lower back, steering her out of the room and toward the last remaining shuttle bus. "Please do, Cara."

CHAPTER 10
CARA

WES AND I ARE AMONG THE LAST PEOPLE TO LEAVE THE STADIUM, SO WE HAVE the shuttle bus practically to ourselves. Practically, but not entirely. It's really unlike me to get physical with an audience, but I can't seem to help myself with Wes.

I'm relieved he doesn't have a roommate, that we can go back to his room and not mine. Not only because it would be awkward to navigate all that with Jay, but because I like that I can leave if I want to. I'm not here to get attached. I can't risk the mental distraction, especially if Coach Lucy comes through and I get an offer after this weekend. I can afford to distract myself for a few hours, but then I need to get serious about my future as a professional athlete.

And *then* I need to explain it all to my family, who still thinks I'm playing for fun on the side and doesn't seem to grasp that soccer is what paid for my college education.

But first, Wes Stag.

He guides me to the back seat of the bus and his hand is on my thigh before his butt hits the seat. He nudges the side of my neck with his nose as he whispers, "Is this okay?"

"God, yes." I choke out the words in a whisper, trying to keep my head facing forward. There are a handful of staff members in the front rows, conversing, and two other players seated not far behind the staff.

I turn my head to look at Wes and want to drown in the dark pools of his eyes. His pupils are totally blown and I know mine are the same. I want him. I want him for his body, I want him because I feel so fucking horny after the work of the weekend. I want him because I want to roar and feel so god damned good celebrating this milestone in my life. I have wanted this for so. Long.

And so has Wes. There is so much unspoken understanding between us, and I want that, too.

His fingers rub my thigh, feeling so good and warm on my screaming muscles. "Everyone else is probably in the pool right now," I whisper.

"Everyone else doesn't have a sexy woman in their arms."

I laugh, thinking of Jay. "My roommate might."

"Good for her." His voice is low, almost a growl. He looks hot as fuck all disheveled from playing, all relaxed from the stim on his lower back. We both smell like sweat and I know if I licked him now, I'd taste the salt of his exertion on his skin. The thought of it should gross me out, but it turns me on even more. I memorize the expression on his face right now, wanting to remember everything about tonight. How I feel as an athlete and how I feel as the woman Wes Stag desires.

The bus hisses to a stop outside the hotel and Wes grabs both our duffel bags in one hand, my hand in his other as he tugs me down the aisle and into the lobby. I rip the bags of ice off my legs and toss them in the trash as we walk through the hall. He summons the elevator with a knuckle and the second it arrives, I'm flat against the back wall, his arms around me. His chest is pressed against mine and I can feel every hard inch of the body he works so hard to perfect.

"Did you like watching me get an electronic back massage, Cara?"

I nod. His face is so close to mine. I could stick my tongue out and taste him, but the anticipation is almost as hot as I know kissing him will be. "I could watch you do anything." He pulls me even tighter against him and I feel a bulge in his shorts. I never anticipated this—electrifying attraction. The intensity of it. I wonder what he's thinking, but I don't have to guess for long because the elevator dings and Wes pushes off the wall, nodding his head toward the door as he backs out of the small space.

"Come watch me adore you, then."

I follow him down the hall, my cheeks hurting from smiling. Wes drops our bags outside his hotel door but has to root around for his key. I step up behind him and my palms go to his ass before I can think better of it. It's like he bent over right there to taunt me with his soccer glutes. "My god, you're firm," I mutter, giving him a squeeze as he grunts and straightens.

The door opens and he pulls me inside. I squeal as he pushes me against the wall.

He brushes the sweaty hair from my face with one gentle hand and then finally presses his mouth against mine. It's not just a kiss. It's a searing celebration.

His hands press into my sides as his lips move against mine and I sneak my tongue into his mouth with a sigh. It's good between us, hot and aggressive—we both grunt in satisfaction as our bodies fuse together.

Wes pulls back a bit, nibbles at my bottom lip. "What do you think about starting off in the shower?" He sniffs the air, a bit musty from our combined physical exertion.

"Mm," I nod and lick his neck, reveling in the purring sound he makes as I do. "I like that idea, Mr. Stag."

I wanted her the second she yelled at me at that airport, but now as my eyes dip to her lips, I might catch fire if I don't kiss her. She tastes like trouble, and for a minute I worry that sex with Cara will be too much. I have too much on the line to get attached, and Cara Moreno is the kind of woman I'd want to lock down.

I shake my head. I don't do those things. I don't enter into long-term relationships with women, and I don't incorporate emotions into my weekend flings. We kiss against the wall of my hotel room and all thoughts flee my mind as I open my eyes to see her looking satisfied and starving all at once. I like that I am bringing her what she needs and also leaving her hungry for more. She's horny as fuck for me, and I like how that feels. I like it very much.

When a whiff of my own armpit distracts me, I suggest we start our adventures with a shower. I should have thought of this sooner. My hands fist in her jersey, feeling the silky material under my rough hands. "Take it off," she says, reaching for the hem of my own shirt. I slide hers over her head and move to touch her bra but she shakes her head.

She steps back and her hands go to the elastic band at the bottom of the bra. "This will be wet and gross."

I slip my jersey off quickly so I can watch her wrestle out of her bra. I soak in the view as her tits spring out of the stretchy fabric—perky, golden globes with red-brown nipples standing stiff, calling to me.

"Fuck, Cara." My palms press against those beautiful nubs, rubbing and skittering as she sucks in jagged breath. "I could take you right here, against this wall. You're so fucking sexy, all firm and quivering for me right now." I thrust my hips against hers.

"Please, Wes," she begs, but she doesn't know what she's asking for. Not yet.

"Shower," I grunt, and pull myself back from her. I watch as her knees almost give out, and realizing this strong, powerful woman is literally weak for me is hotter than anything else.

I trip into the bathroom and crank on the shower, yanking down my shorts and briefs in one tug as Cara steps into the room. We both still have our socks on and we each hop around a bit trying to peel them off.

If I'm honest, I've never done this before, undressed from my kit in front of a woman. I've gotten a BJ after a game before, but that didn't involve the sort of intimacy I'm finding in watching Cara pull her sock off her toes. I moan as each red-tipped digit appears, and I know that after we shower, I'm going to kiss her feet. That's a first for me, too.

When did I last feel this way? So free? I've had a constant struggle over the years with the pressure of elite sports, and I've loved every second of it. But there's something about this woman that lets me relax, puts the stress of all that to the side. How did I just find Cara Moreno now, on a flight to my future?

I test the temperature of the water and gesture for Cara to climb in the shower, where I get my first look at her completely naked. I trace a hand down her side, murmuring to her that she's fucking incredible. Her fingertips trace my abs, running along the line of muscle on my thigh.

It's hot as a fever in the shower and I want to explode at the sight of her dripping wet, beads of water sliding down her gorgeous body. She presses me against the shower wall and grinds against me, slippery and warm, supple, and so fucking firm.

She reaches for the bar of soap and rubs it between her palms, setting it back in the soap dish before working her hands into a lather. And then she runs those foamy hands down my chest, down my stomach. I suck in a breath, hoping she's going to reach for my shaft, but she chuckles and starts soaping up my thighs instead.

"You're cruel," I growl, reaching for the soap. "Two can play at this game." I wash her upper arms as she scrubs my chest. She arches a brow at me, soaping up my back and my ass cheeks while I skip over her boobs and palm her butt.

Finally, with a wicked grin on her face, she slides a soapy palm around my cock, taking me in her hot hand and stroking me from base to tip. I watch her looking at my length in her hand, loving the "mm" sound she makes as she rubs against me.

I reward her by tracing a thumb from her naval down to the neatly trimmed triangle of hair that points toward her clit. It's like an arrow, guiding me toward the prize and she gasps when I reach the destination. "You like that?"

She responds by yanking my shoulders forward, slamming her mouth into mine. Her tongue mimics the motion of my thumb as I slowly stroke along her seam. She's wet and slippery. Warm and inviting me in.

Cara suddenly drops to her knees in the tub, her hands tracing through the hair on my thighs as her tongue snakes out and circles the tip of my cock. "Fuck, Cara, wait."

She pulls her head back, confused. I know if she puts those pouty lips around my dick I'll explode in her mouth in seconds, and I'm just getting started here. I hoist her to her feet again and shake my head, dropping to my knees in front of her instead.

"Fuck, Cara." That's exactly how I feel, what I want to do right now. I don't want to make love to him. I don't want to have sex. I want to *fuck* this man who just inexplicably stopped me from going down on him in the shower.

I was here, ready to put that delicious cock right into my mouth when he hauled me back to my feet and pressed my back against the tile.

When he sinks to his knees in front of me, I have to grip the soap dish to steady myself as I realize what he plans to do.

I've never had a man excited to go down on me, certainly not like this. Wes looks up with hunger in his eyes as he sticks out his tongue and licks along my core. The sound that comes out of me is obscene, but I don't have time to worry about it as he slides fingers through my wetness. There is nothing selfish about Wesley Stag, not in the bedroom department.

My soreness melts from my consciousness as he licks and strokes, his eyes boring into mine all the while. My head sinks back to the wall and one hand drops to his wet, dark hair as he teases, chuckling, driving me mad with want.

I breathe out, "Oh god, yes, Wes. Fuck. Fuck, that's good." He rubs a cheek against my thigh, his skin just a little bit scratchy with incoming stubble. When he finally touches my clit again with his tongue, the pleasure starts to circulate inside my belly, inside my spine. It radiates down my legs the more he touches and licks. As Wes strokes my pussy, everything goes fuzzy until I finally come in an explosion, screaming and writhing in the shower.

I'm still trembling and moaning as Wes stands up, holding me close and rubbing my back. "I've got you, baby. That was so beautiful. You're perfect when you come for me. God, you taste good."

I lean against him, unable to function in the aftermath of a destructive orgasm, and then I realize he's gently soaping my hair. His fingers massage my scalp as he mutters about how fucking good I taste, how delicious it was when I came on his tongue.

I tip my head up to look at him, blinking as the shampoo stings my eyes. Wes gently guides my head toward the shower spray, rinsing me as I come back into my body.

As I return to consciousness, I reach for him, rock hard beneath my hand. His erection stands almost upright against his stomach, pointing at my bellybutton. Going down on me turned him on, and that realization weakens my knees even more.

I go with the urge and sink to the shower floor, grinning up at him as he grips the wall and swallows. Fuck, his throat is sexy. I grab hold of his length and lick a bead of pre-cum from the tip, enjoying the low moan Wes releases when I do. I circle his tip with the tip of my tongue, then the flat of it, and then I make eye contact with him as I slide him inside my mouth.

He tastes salty, tangy, but clean since we've been in the shower for god knows how long by now. My tongue circles the head of his cock, and he releases an anguished cry. "Fuck, Cara, I want to watch you do that. You're so fucking beautiful with my cock in between those lips of yours, but I want to come inside you."

I shrug and kiss the tip of him, making my way back up to my feet and reaching behind me to shut off the water. "By the way…" I reach for the towel he grabs from the rack on the wall. "I get tested all the time for soccer. I'm healthy. I should have said that before…"

He grins, grabbing his own towel and briskly scrubbing himself dry. "I'm healthy, too."

And then he hauls me into his arms, bride-style, striding from the bathroom and flinging me onto the giant bed. He dives on top of me and stretches an arm to the night stand. "I took advantage of the 'health bin' in the training room yesterday."

I look into his drawer and laugh at the handful of colored condom wrappers and packets of lube. "I didn't know there was a health bin."

He nods, settling himself between my legs, which I gladly wrap around his waist. "We're hot athletes. They know we're going to fuck each other."

"Are you going to fuck me, though? Because I only had one orgasm so far and you're just talking and talking here…"

"Were you expecting two?" He arches a brow and my eyes fly wide before he bursts out laughing. "Because I'm giving you at least three, Cara. Mark my fucking words."

Wes grabs one of the packets of lube and bites open the end, drizzling it along my chest and giving me a look that's absolutely filthy. I realize it's a warming lube as an amazing heat spreads with the liquid. My boobs are shiny and slick, and he adjusts his body so his cock is lined up with my chest. "Push your tits together, Cara."

I comply, watching as his cock disappears between them. He puts one hand on the headboard and the other by my face as he begins to slide in and out of my slicked-up boobs. The tip of his cock appears and I tilt my head to lick it, which makes him gasp. I start to rub my nipples with my thumbs as he moves, the sight both lewd and incredibly sexy. I'm deeply turned on and my arousal starts to drip down my legs. "Wes," I gasp, and he pulls out of my chest, reaching for his pleasure stash and coming up with a foil packet.

"Is this still okay, Cara? Do you still want to do this?"

I nod, words escaping me as I stare at him.

"You have to say it, babe. I need an enthusiastic yes."

"Yes, damn it, Wes. Please fuck me right the hell now."

He grins and settles back between my legs, one hand guiding his hardness right where I need it most. He slides inside, praising me for being so wet, which sends another gush of moisture right to my core.

His chest sinks down to mine, and the lube heats up even more as our bodies slide together. "Wes." All I can do is moan and repeat his name as he fills me. The hand that was guiding his cock returns to my clit and gently rubs as he strokes in and out of my body.

The pressure is perfect and I dig my heels into his butt, thrusting up to meet him, savoring the stretch of him sinking inside me fully. "You feel so good, Wes." He kisses me and pulls out, leaving me empty, on the edge of an orgasm. "You fucking tease." I swat at him and he sinks back in, hard.

My breath leaves me in a grunt as he smiles. "There she is. That's it, Cara." He puts his thumb back on my clit, his palm holding my hips down against the bed as he pounds into me. I come again, harder than the first time, thrashing on the bed and loving the weight of him on top of me, the pressure of him holding my hips still while he continues to roll his own. I pulse around him, sensing every inch of his heat. "Two down, babe."

Wes pulls out abruptly and cups my cheek. "Can you be on top? I want to watch you ride me."

I nod and he flips onto his back, tugging me up and onto his body. I reach for his cock and slide on, bracing my palms against his chest while I adjust to the angle, the fullness.

"Christ, Cara, look at us." He stares down between my legs, watching his cock slide in and out of my body, studying my body stretched around his, swallowing him, welcoming him in. We both watch as I tilt my body and ride him, leaning forward until I know I found the friction I need to come a third time. My eyes widen as it builds. "That's it, baby. Let it happen. Good girl."

And with those words, I fall apart. I tighten my body and release all the pleasure I have and then a secret store of it I wasn't aware of. It floods out of me as I writhe and moan on top of Wes. I come with him deep inside me and he follows, grunting and shouting my name until I collapse onto his chest, panting.

That was the best sex of my life.

"I agree," he says, his voice low and his words slow. I hadn't realized I said that out loud, but I don't regret it.

"Come here," he says, sliding out of me, and tugging off the condom. He tosses it into the trash can by the bed and then pulls me into his arms. He looks at me like I discovered fire. And maybe I did—maybe this spark between us engulfed the entire world while we were in here. I have no idea and no desire to leave this bed to find out.

Wes wraps his arms around me and I'm so secure.

This doesn't make sense. I should be climbing off the bed, gathering my things, and sneaking out of his room. This is a one-night stand, but it feels like so much more. I knew what I wanted when I came up here, but this was … something else.

I know it's ridiculous, but what we just did has changed me.

I look up at him as he runs his fingers through my damp hair and then he kisses the top of my head. "Want me to order up some food?"

"God, yes, please."

CHAPTER 13
CARA

Wes orders practically the entire room service menu. We can relax our eating plans a bit now that we've finished the training camp, so we gorge on bread and pasta, making jokes about the meatballs.

"I've never eaten spaghetti naked before," I admit, sitting cross-legged on the bed where he just blew my mind.

"Same, honestly. But it's kind of fun." He winks as he slurps in a long noodle and I shove his shoulder.

"Of course you can wink." I take another bite of food.

"You can't wink?" He gestures at me with a breadstick, and I reach for it, laughing when he snatches it back. "You can't have my stick if you can't wink, Cara. It's a rule."

"I'd like to see this rule in the handbook, please." I snatch the stick from his hands and he laughs, reaching for a napkin.

We finish the food and Wes sets the room service tray on the table next to the bed. His room is pretty small, but the fact that he has it all to himself shows me how wide the chasm still is between men's and women's professional soccer. I don't want to think about that now, though.

I lean back on the bed on my forearms, admiring the look of him, naked and satisfied, his hair messed up from rolling around with it all wet. I wiggle my toes as Wes settles himself on the pillows and then reaches for one of my feet.

"What are you doing—oh, god." He starts to rub my foot, his thumbs pressing along my arch, knuckles pushing against the ball and heel. "Where the fuck did you learn how to do this? Holy shit, Wes." I lean

59

back, knowing I'm ruined for all other men for eternity now that I have had a naked foot massage from Wesley Stag. "Goooddddddd."

"If I had known you'd make those sounds and that expression on your face, I'd have led with this," he says, switching to my other foot.

I want to tell him that would have been gross because my feet would still have been sweaty from my cleats, but I lose all ability to form words when his tongue slides along the sole of my foot. He groans as he slides his lips to my toes, kissing the tips and then easing them into his mouth one at a time, sucking gently. It's very, very sexy and like nothing I've ever experienced before.

"Fuck, Wes. Please keep doing that."

He groans and complies, changing to my other foot before I open my eyes and see him practically unhinged with want. His cock is rock hard again, bobbing against the dark hair on his stomach as he strokes my foot. Wes tugs gently, pulling me closer until my feet are flat against his chest and my core is flush against his straining cock.

He keeps eye contact with me as one hand rubs my foot and the other dips between my legs, stroking. I purr as he slides a finger inside me, then another. Since when do I purr? "That's it, Cara. Does this feel good?" I nod as he switches to the other foot, his left hand now cupping my sex. His thumb presses against my clit, already an expert at the pressure and rhythm I need. I gasp and clench when his index finger traces along my body back to my ass and he grins as he lightly traces the puckered skin there.

"Another time, maybe," he says, turning his head to kiss the bottom of my foot. He keeps his thumb pressed against my clit and continues rubbing my foot until I'm gasping and coming apart for a fourth time, awash in new sensations.

When I can think again, I yank my foot from his hand and haul myself to my knees, crawling up the bed toward his cock like a jungle cat stalking a meal. He lets me take him into my mouth, sighing and settling back on the pillows as I give his rod the same treatment he just gave my feet and my pussy combined. Wes drops a reverent hand to my cheek as I slide him to the back of my throat. It's not long before he groans and stiffens. His abs contract and he gasps, as if startled by the intensity of his orgasm. Wes shudders and spurts into my mouth, and then he groans again as I swallow every drop.

• • •

He falls asleep soon after and I cuddle up against him, turning off the light and allowing myself to sink into the cocoon of his arms while my brain cranks into overdrive. I think about the weekend, about how I played. I'm confident I put my best self forward at this camp, on the pitch and in this bed. I blush, remembering Wesley's curious finger on my ass. The two of us could create something explosive together, but then I remember we came here with a specific mission.

Our game is important to us. I have no idea where I'll wind up after tomorrow, and he could go anywhere as well—rumor had it there were scouts from Europe here to see the men playing. My thoughts drift to the national team, knowing that's no longer a pipe dream but a real possibility for me in the years to come.

For one instant, I remember the uncomfortable way the Soccer USA president made me feel in the stadium before Jay called my name. Before I can dwell on that moment, Wes pulls his arm tighter around me. I drift off to sleep in his embrace.

My eyes fly open before dawn. The light shining behind the curtains is purple, like the sun hasn't quite made up its mind whether to rise. *What am I doing?*

The whole point of doing this in Wes's room was that I could leave, head back to my room and get a proper rest before my long flight home. I cannot get attached to orgasms and foot rubs. I have to focus, keep my eye on my goals.

I slip out of bed slowly, but Wes is out to the world. My body aches from the long weekend of too much exercise, and my crotch aches from the dick I rode last night. But I ignore the slight sting. As quietly as I can, I gather up my things and use the light of my phone to dig out a clean-ish change of clothes from my soccer bag, thankful I don't have to squeeze myself back into the disgusting post-workout clothes from yesterday.

I slip out of Wes Stag's room for a walk of shame. Except, I don't feel very shameful. I feel pretty incredible and I smile as I weave through the hall. I call the elevator and grin when I see Coach Lucy Moyer inside.

"Oh my god, it's you! I was just coming to slide a note under your hotel door."

"Seriously?"

She nods, thrusting a piece of paper into my hands. "I want you to have your agent call this number as soon as possible," she says, tapping a number highlighted in bright yellow. "You're going to get multiple offers today and I'd like Pittsburgh to be part of that conversation."

The elevator door shoves against Lucy's sneaker, and she gestures me inside the car. "I, uh, don't have an agent." I bite my lip and then grimace. There's so much I'm unprepared for. So much. A further reminder of why I can't lose my head in a man, no matter how many orgasms he hands out in one night. A boyfriend won't get me where I need to be professionally.

Lucy grins and unzips her fanny pack with a flourish. She fishes out a card and hands it to me. "I want you to call this number immediately, then." I look at the card. Lucy continues. "Don't worry about the time or day. This woman is fair and fierce. Call her." The elevator door slides open, and I see we've gone down to the lobby.

Lucy gives me a small push. "I have to go hunt down two more prospects, Cara, but call that number." She mimes punching numbers onto a phone as the elevator door slides shut.

I'm left standing in the lobby with all my dreams in my hand. It felt a little like fate brought me here this weekend to cross paths with Wes Stag, but that's not it at all. He was fun. We go together like smoke and fire. But this is my purpose. This is my future.

I'm alone. I'm aware of that reality before I'm fully awake in a room where I should have the gorgeous body of Cara Moreno draped over my chest.

I can't fight the disappointment that simmers, even though I know what last night was to both of us. It was a celebration. Releasing a pressure valve. We both have a lot riding on the camp from this weekend and riding each other was a celebration and a release.

Except, it didn't feel that way to me.

I did things with Cara that I've never done before, never wanted to do. We had a connection and a lump forms in my throat when I realize that was clearly a one-sided assumption. She didn't even leave a note. I reach for my phone to see if maybe she texted me, and it starts ringing in my hand.

Unknown number.

I have to answer it, in case it's an offer, but I'm not prepared for the volume that comes bellowing at me at … I glance at the alarm clock … 6:30.

"Wes! Baby!"

"Hello?"

"Don't you know my voice, kid? That's okay. Listen, your Uncle Hawk told me to give you a ring, said you're going to need me today."

I comb my memories, trying to place the too-chipper voice on the other end of the phone. "Brian?"

"The one and only." My uncle's sports agent starts praising my game, comparing me to the family legacy, whatever that means. I wake up more fully and start to process the meaning of his call.

"Wait. My uncle called you?"

"Damn right he did, and not a minute too soon. The sharks are swimming outside your door, baby."

I glance toward the hotel door and see a bunch of slips of paper on the carpet. Huh.

"Listen," Brian continues. "I'm not going to dance around. You know I was a good partner for your Uncle Hawky and made him a shit-ton of money over the years. I can guarantee you the same treatment the second you sign an agreement with me. I can text it to you, and I can be on the phone with those sharks in the lobby of your hotel within minutes. Where do you want to land, Wesley? Name your team."

I drag a hand through my hair. "Name my team? Seriously?"

He sighs. "Okay, not quite that awesome. But give me a ranked list. Word on the street is that your debut will be electric."

If my uncle called his agent, that means Aunt Lucy wasn't kidding when she hinted that my "subterfuge" worked in my favor. My stomach flutters and I stand up, pacing the floor. I catch a glimpse of myself in the mirror, with obvious sex-tousled hair, swollen lips, and scratch marks on my chest. Cara sticking around to celebrate would feel too good to be true. Last night she made me feel like I can do anything, achieve anything I want.

This morning, it's all happening … but she's not here. I sigh as Brian talks about numbers and sponsorship plans. It all sounds great, actually. So maybe it was better to have one perfect night than keep things going, grow frustrated with one another as we dive headfirst into intense schedules and camera shoots and too much travel. That's no way to kick off a relationship.

"Sounds amazing, Brian. Text me the thing to sign."

A pang of sadness stings me—my dad isn't here with me when I sign my first contract with an agent. I'll most likely be signing with a pro team in a few hours without my family celebrating. My Aunt Alice would have made a grain-free cake out of vegetables or some shit. My cousins would have gotten kazoos and done a damn parade around the Highland Park fountain if I'd looped them in.

Or they wouldn't have done anything, because my mom would have cried, and my dad would have glowered at me and I would have stayed in school another year and blown my ACL. I can't grieve what didn't happen any more than I can regret my choices.

Brian texts me an agreement and I sign it with my thumb on my cell phone, alone in a dark hotel room.

A few seconds later, Brian texts me instructions to head down to the lobby in twenty minutes, and he'll video chat with me while I have a conference with an offer. And there it is: my new life...the one I planned for. The one I set in motion.

I should want to call my cousins, or the guys from my college team, but the first person I think of is Cara. Did she get a similar offer this morning? Should I find her room and go another round with her to celebrate, real quick before we both fly out? Does she have an agent? Maybe I should send her Brian's contact info...

These thoughts swirl in my mind as I brush my teeth and slip into the only clean clothes I have left: sweats and an old Pittsburgh Forge t-shirt of my Uncle's.

I step out of the elevator on the ground floor and turn the corner, toward the conference rooms. Toward my new life.

I STAGGER OVER TO A COLUMN AROUND THE CORNER IN A QUIET HALLWAY, staring down at the card and the offer note from the Pittsburgh Hot Metal. Is this really my life? I have a fleeting thought again that I should run back up to Wes's room and tell him, but that's too much. He was pretty clear that he's not looking for long term.

But damn it, we shared something powerful. And I know he'd want to celebrate this moment with me. With my future squared away, maybe it is possible that I can think about something romantic, too. With the right guy it could work—and Wes Stag would definitely understand that soccer would be my top priority, that I'd be flying all over the country and spending long hours at the stadium studying the game.

Maybe we won't have time to be each other's everything, but maybe we can also be something. Somehow. If I can rise above my doubts and make a splash to the pro soccer coaches, surely I can maintain some sort of meaningful friendship … with benefits?

I take a moment to experience some of the joy bubbling inside me, squeaking and bouncing on my toes, letting my duffel bag fall to the ground and then freezing when it makes a loud sound in the echoey space. A man pokes his head around the corner from a conference room and I cringe a little inside when I see it's the Lou-guy who creeped me out in the tunnel the other day. "Hey there," he drawls, and I force a smile onto my face. He's wearing a Soccer USA polo again and I am fairly confident he's someone important with the national team staff.

"Hi," I mutter, folding my note from Lucy and stooping to get my bag.

When I stand up, I realize Lou is in my personal space again, one arm on the column and the other reaching for my bag. Stunned, I hand it over to him and he drops it to the floor again.

Every muscle in my body tenses as he smiles a weird, creepy grin. I can't quantify my feelings, but I know he's not interested in my soccer skills. *He's a predator.* The thought frightens me because I know he shouldn't be—he is a man in power in a world I'm trying to access. Every neuron in my brain is panicking but I also know that I can't just dart away because, well, I fucking came here to be seen by the national team. And that's this guy, apparently.

"Did I see you talking with Lucy Moyer yesterday?" I nod, trying to avoid eye contact. He leans in a little closer, his voice near my ear in a whisper. "I'm so glad. I've had my eye on you, Cara Moreno. I think we can expect big things."

My voice cracks as I frantically try to respond in a way that might satisfy this guy while somehow also communicating that I do not like this type of attention. "Thank you, Mr. Rubeo." Everything I have is clenched right now, my arms stiff and frozen in place, my feet cemented to the tile floor. My breath comes in rapid bursts. "I, um, really need to go meet with Coach Moyer…"

He nods but doesn't back out of my space, his mouth still twisted in a lewd smile that will haunt my dreams. "You do that, Ms. Moreno. We want to make sure you are all squared away on the right track." He traces one finger along my shoulder with his final word of that sentence, tapping the top of my arm before turning around and finally, blessedly, stepping back.

The air returns to my lungs in a whoosh as he takes another step further from me, saying, "Ah. Mr. Stag! Glad I caught you in time."

And then I see Wes in the hall, staring, face twisted in confusion. His eyes bore into mine as Rubeo drapes an arm around Wes's shoulder, guiding him toward the conference room. Wes turns his head back to face me one final time, his expression pained, before he closes his eyes, swallows, and faces Rubeo with stoicism.

As they step into the conference room and shut the door, I fear every possibility I might have had with Wesley Stag is gone.

FORGING GLORY

A SECOND CHANCE ROMANCE

I'M ALONE.

I'm aware of that reality before I'm fully awake in a room where I should have the gorgeous body of Cara Moreno draped over my chest.

I can't fight the disappointment that simmers, even though I know what last night was to both of us. It was a celebration. Releasing a pressure valve. We both have a lot riding on the camp from this weekend and riding each other was a celebration and a release.

Except, it didn't feel that way to me.

I did things with Cara that I've never done before, never wanted to do. I felt like we had a connection and a lump forms in my throat realizing that was clearly a one-sided assumption. She didn't even leave a note. I reach for my phone to see if maybe she texted me, and it starts ringing in my hand.

Unknown number.

I have to answer it, in case it's an offer, but I'm not prepared for the volume that comes bellowing at me at … I glance at the alarm clock … 6:30.

"Wes! Baby!"

"Hello?"

"Don't you know my voice, kid? That's okay. Listen, your Uncle Hawk told me to give you a ring, said you're going to need me today."

I comb my memories, trying to place the too-chipper voice on the other end of the phone. "Brian?"

"The one and only." My uncle's sports agent starts praising my game, comparing me to the family legacy, whatever that means. I wake up more fully and start to process the meaning of his call.

"Wait. My uncle called you?"

"Damn right he did, and not a minute too soon. The sharks are swimming outside your door, baby."

I glance toward the hotel door and see a bunch of slips of paper on the carpet. Huh.

"Listen," Brian continues. "I'm not going to dance around. You know I was a good partner for your Uncle Hawky and made him a shit-ton of money over the years. I can guarantee you the same treatment and the second you sign an agreement I can text you. I can be on the phone with those sharks in the lobby of your hotel. Where do you want to land, Wesley? Name your team."

I drag a hand through my hair. "Name my team? Seriously?"

He sighs. "Okay, not quite that awesome. But give me a ranked list. Word on the street is your debut will be electric."

If my uncle called his agent, that means Aunt Lucy wasn't kidding when she hinted that my "subterfuge" worked in my favor. I snuck out here to California against the advice of my parents and without their support. I gave up my college scholarship for this try-out and I almost can't believe the gamble paid off. My stomach flutters and I stand up, pacing the floor. I catch a glimpse of myself in the mirror, with obvious sex-tousled hair, swollen lips, and scratch marks on my chest.

Cara sticking around to celebrate would have been too good to be true.

Last night she made me feel like I can do anything, achieve anything I want.

This morning, it's all happening … but she's not here. And neither is my family.

I sigh as Brian talks about numbers and sponsorship plans. It all sounds great, actually. So maybe it was better to have one perfect night than keep things going and grow frustrated with one another. We both will be diving headfirst into intense schedules and camera shoots and too much travel. That's no way to kick off a relationship.

"Sounds perfect, Brian. Text me the thing to sign."

I feel a pang of sadness that my dad isn't here with me when I sign my first contract with an agent, that I'll most likely be signing with a pro team in a few hours without my family celebrating. My Aunt Alice would have made a grain-free cake out of vegetables or some shit. My cousins would have gotten kazoos and done a damn parade around the Highland Park fountain if I'd looped them in.

Or they wouldn't have done anything. My mom would have cried and my dad would have glowered at me, and I would have stayed in school another year. If I'd stayed in school, who even knows what would have happened. I probably would have blown my ACL. I can't grieve what didn't happen any more than I can regret my choices.

Brian texts me an agreement and I sign it with my finger on my cell phone, alone in a dark hotel room.

A few seconds later, Brian texts me instructions to head down to the lobby in twenty minutes, and he'll video chat in while I have a conference with an offer. And there it is: my new life … the one I worked hard for. The one I set in motion.

I should want to call my cousins, or the guys from my college team, but the first person I think of is Cara. Did she get a similar offer this morning? Should I find her room and go another round with her to celebrate, possibly real quick before we both fly out? Does she have an agent? Maybe I should send her Brian's contact info…

These thoughts swirl in my mind as I brush my teeth and slip into the only clean clothes I have left, sweats and an old Pittsburgh Forge t-shirt of my Uncle's.

I step out of the elevator on the ground floor and turn the corner, toward the conference rooms. I'm about to video call Brian when I see something that halts me in my tracks.

Lou Rubeo, president of Soccer USA, has a hand on Cara's shoulder, his lips a centimeter from her ear. I watch as his other hand moves to brush a hair back from her face, the same face I had my lips all over just hours before.

I feel nauseated, watching this man put his hands on the woman of my dreams. I guess if she can sneak out of my bed and into his arms an hour later, she's not the woman I thought she was.

I don't know why she is going for a high-powered soccer executive, and I don't have time to care. She's on her path and I'm on mine. I'm glad she's not looking toward me. I am glad she doesn't see my face as I stab the call button for my agent.

I turn on my heel and walk toward the conference room.

My roommate, Jay, slides down the hall of our apartment in her socks, singing some wake-up song she says she learned at camp as a kid. I throw a pillow at her from my bed. "I'm going to start sleeping with the door closed if you keep doing that."

She pokes her head into my room, a toothbrush dangling from her mouth. "You should probably sleep with the door closed anyway, Moreno. What's wrong with you?"

"Remember how I said my parents were deep into Catholic school dogma?" I shrug, sitting up in bed. "I wasn't ever allowed to close my bedroom door except when I was changing. I guess it's hard to break that habit."

In college I had three roommates from my soccer team. We called ourselves the Midfield Mamis, and we lived in a two-bedroom apartment near campus. I'm not sure if we closed our bedroom doors then because we all went to bed super early or if we passed out exhausted from training and studying. Jay continues brushing feverishly as I try to gather my hair off my face. I swear it got bigger as I slept or else it's just making itself at home in the Pittsburgh humidity. I'm told I'll get used to the weather here —balmy one minute, windy the next, but rarely sunny.

Jay rolls her eyes. "We can make our own house rules now, Cara. Ones that make sense!" She slides away, humming as she finishes her dental scrub. She and I are rookies on the Pittsburgh Hot Metal. We met at the tryout camp a month ago and I was excited when she asked if I wanted to find a place with her near the stadium in Pittsburgh.

I kick my door closed and change into workout gear. I can't stop smiling as I pull on the black socks, shorts, and t-shirt for my team. I want to pinch myself and make sure this is real, that I am actually a professional soccer player.

This has been my goal, my dream, for as long as I can remember. And now that it's here, I love that I still have goals, things to work toward. I want to start in a game and score for my team. I want to be chosen for the national team and play in the Olympics.

Everything I've ever wanted relates to soccer, to physical achievement and competition. I remind myself of this each time I think of that try-out weekend in California. When I secured my spot on this team. That weekend I also met someone I could very well have lost myself to.

It would have been easy to fall into Wesley Stag. I could bask under his intense gaze, writhe in pleasure as he strummed my body for hours. Everything was intensified with Wes, and the way he focused on my pleasure…it shook something inside me.

Growing up under such strict rules meant sex—even solo sex—was forbidden and had to be a stolen moment. It took me years to own my sexuality and that night with Wes was an epic, shattering explosion of pleasure.

I snort and slam my dresser drawer shut because those hours were short-lived. He made that very clear by refusing to answer my calls or respond to any of my texts.

Ghosted.

Ditched like the one-and-done I should have assumed I was to him. I brush my teeth and weave my curls into a long braid, definitely not thinking about the slide of Wes's fingers running through my hair, massaging my scalp.

"You ready to head out?" Jay jangles her car keys in the hall, pulling me from my heated reminiscing.

"Yep. Wait. I need protein."

I pull my door open and grin when I see my roommate holding one of the egg muffins we prepped on our day off. We filled cupcake tins with scrambled eggs, turkey sausage, feta cheese, and spinach, so we'd have a quick breakfast that met all our nutrition guidelines from Coach Lucy.

The fact that we both eat them cold while leaving the apartment at the last possible second solidifies our status as best roommates ever. Some women wake up early to perfect their makeup. Jay and I sleep in and bond over food. We operate in practiced efficiency as we approach the car, me holding both our bags and tossing them in the back seat while Jay navigates her keys, muffin, and coffee mug, still humming camp songs.

The September sun is just starting to rise as Jay's Honda pulls into the lot outside the stadium. The women's team has the field first today, and I love our cardio session by the river. We run laps and agility ladders as the freight trains roll past. We sprint in intervals as the tugboats blast their horns behind the coal barges chugging up the Monongahela River.

I feel part of the industry here, maybe because my team is named for the liquid iron still manufactured in the valleys nearby. When Coach tells us to start running the steps in the stadium, my legs threaten to liquefy from the exertion. But I remind myself that I am forged of strong will. I fought to get here. I'll fight to stay here.

The whistle blows, signifying the end of morning workout, and I sink into one of the benches near the grass. One of the trainers tosses me a drink, and I shield my eyes from the sun as I chug it down, watching as the men's team takes the field.

And of course I see him. My regrettable dalliance, Wesley Stag, plays striker for the men's team here. I can't let go of what happened in part because I see him every damn day at work, and the hot dummy doesn't even look at me.

I suck down the rest of my drink, glaring at him, until Lucy waves us all to join her in the tunnel. "I'm turning you over to Coach Ben, folks. I believe you have film next, then lunch and afternoon drills." She pats her clipboard and waves as we all pull off our sneakers.

———

I must carry a sour look on my face the rest of the day, because Jay asks me about it on the way home. "You're usually in a better mood after chicken teriyaki." She lowers the volume on the radio, inviting me to spill my guts as we navigate traffic on the Fort Pitt Bridge.

I can't help the sigh that rumbles out of me as I plunk my head against my window. "I saw Wes again today. He didn't look at me."

"That guy again? Come on, Cara. He's not worth all this space in your head."

"I know that, but it's easy to *say* I'll forget about him after he ghosted me, and it's another thing to literally see him every day and experience him not even making eye contact. I actually think I might be invisible to him."

"You're the furthest thing from invisible."

"Thanks, friend. If it helps, I do hate that I'm fixated like this."

Jay taps the steering wheel and chews on her lip for a few blocks. "Have you considered that, this…" She gestures toward my face. "Might be more about something else than it is about what's-his-name?"

"You know his name is Wesley."

"Only because you don't shut the hell up about him. But seriously, what about talking to Big Jim?"

I groan a little at her reference to our sports psychologist. He leads multiple sessions a week about mindset and trusting our teammates, and the content is always inspiring. It's just that Jim blinks. A lot.

"Do you think I could I talk to him over the phone?"

She shrugs. "It's not a bad idea. I mean, he's there. He's a resource. Maybe email him?"

I pop my lips a few times, considering. I haven't cemented a starting spot in the lineup yet. Maybe this hang-up on Wes is holding me back somehow. I clench my stomach, trying to ignore the voice in my gut wondering if Jay is on to something about my issues running deeper than Wes ignoring me.

Because I probably do know why he ghosted me, and I don't want to remember the slimy sensation freezing me in space as Lou Rubeo, the president of Soccer USA, invaded my personal space at the hotel and served me a huge helping of the creeps when he touched me. The last time I made eye contact with Wesley Stag was the moment Rubeo ran an uninvited finger down my face.

"I'm going to talk it out with my chicas. They'll probably tell me to call Big Jim, too."

"When are those chicas going to find me a lady-friend? There are not enough lesbians in Pittsburgh."

"Toni hooked you up with a cheering section when we traveled to Chicago last week."

Jay grins and waggles her eyebrows. "Exactly. Remind me where the rest of them live?"

Jay parks in the garage under our building and I rattle off the current locations of my friend group, texting them as I walk to let them know I need one of our chats.

By the time Shante replies from D.C., she's already spoken to Rose and Toni.

SHANTE

Emergency video pedis, 10am east coast
tomorrow.

TONI

That's 7 for you, Rosie-bug

ROSALIE

Excuse me, I am a very important PhD candidate
studying insects. I am not personally an insect.

"Jay, we're doing pedicures tomorrow. You in?"

"Hell no, I'm not in." She shouts from her room and then I hear the shower turn on.

I holler louder and I know she hears me tease, "Fine. Keep your rhino hide, but don't ask me how to meet more single ladies."

She pokes a head into the hall, clutching a towel around her tattooed chest. "You really think it's my feet?"

I laugh and shake my head. "I mean, nobody wants that rough sandpaper with them in bed."

"Ugh. Fine. I will exfoliate but I'm not doing polish." She slams the door as I confirm that I'm in for video pedicures.

We Midfield Mamis have been doing this for years—sitting for hours and massaging our feet while we unload everything weighing on our minds. We slough off bad vibes along with dry skin and finish the whole procedure with pampered toes and unburdened souls.

My college friends have retired from soccer, moved on to graduate school and corporate America. But they're still my safe place. I should open up to them about what's been going on, and I don't quite understand why I haven't.

I don't want to douse Jay with cold water by running a competing shower, so I wait for her to finish her scrub. We could shower at the stadium, but both of us prefer the luxury of our own bathrooms. It's the best part of this apartment, apart from the proximity to the water we can see from our balcony.

Each bedroom has an ensuite bathroom. It feels decadent.

I step onto my little piece of paradise, aka the balcony, while I wait for my turn with the hot water heater.

It's not much. All I have out here is a folding chair and a few plants that should be hung, but I haven't had a chance to buy stands or install hooks. And it's mine.

I'm here despite my parents' disapproval. I'm here regardless of their insistence that I'll never meet "a nice boy" to settle down and raise a family; that I am not putting my degree to use; that this career can't possibly bring lasting stability.

Those are their concerns, and their battles. I remind myself of this even as I hyper focus on the "nice boy" who did just as my parents said he would: turn his back on me.

"Yoga for athletes" is not how I predicted I'd spend my afternoon while my professional soccer team travels to Louisville for a match without me, but Coach…my uncle…suggested I work on my flexibility to really give myself a chance at a roster spot.

It's been a bit of a blow to my pride coming into the team as a permanent bench warmer. When I left my senior year of college to sign with a professional team, I definitely thought I'd roll into town a star player. Until I prove myself, I spend my days as "generic defender" during drills while the starters work on game strategy. These days, it feels like everyone views me as generically expendable, from my coach on down to the woman I met at the tryout camp.

My career has to be my focus right now. There's only so much time to claw my way onto a professional soccer lineup and I'll do anything necessary to be one of those starters.

So here I am, running late as I make my way to Pipe Fitters, a fitness studio in the east end of the city where I'm told the staff is discreet and the clientele won't post pictures of me on social media.

Class is in session when I hustle in the door, and I kick off my shoes near the studio as I grab the last mat from the bin. I try to shake it open somewhere in the back row, but the teacher smiles and waves me toward a spot near the front.

My knees lock when I see that, of course, the space is next to Cara Moreno. Great.

It's been bad enough trying to avoid her at the stadium for the past month while everyone raves about how great she is on the field. Now I have to pretend she didn't stomp all over my emotions as we sit side by side and open our chakras, or whatever we're doing in yoga class.

I could leave now, watch a yoga video on YouTube or something, but I want to play professional soccer more than I want to avoid this woman, so I grunt, adjust my shorts, and plop the mat into place as the teacher welcomes us all to take our place.

Cara doesn't see me yet because she's bent over, stretching with her perfect ass in the air. My brain immediately flashes to an image of me behind her in the shower, Cara bent over just like that as I soaped her spine and played with her clit.

Cara finally looks at me as I settle in. I try to keep my face neutral and look forward, but I see her in my periphery. She appears ... hurt. Confused? Screw that.

"This will be a restorative practice, meant to open your hips, relax your spine, and ease those knots in your busy shoulders." The teacher's voice is soothing as she paces the floor between the rows of mats. It occurs to me that maybe yoga is the secret sauce that keeps Cara in her starting spot, even as a rookie.

A quick glance around shows me a few pro football guys, a hockey player I recognize. I feel better, more at ease knowing I'm among like-minded professional athletes. Do I even get to call myself that since I haven't played one minute of pro soccer yet? If my uncle thinks this will get me where I need to be, I'll fold my foot in half and drag a knuckle down my arch like the teacher suggests.

As I work my toes apart, I keep seeing Cara from the corner of my eye. Her toes are painted burgundy now, and I wish I wasn't thinking about how beautifully that color contrasts with her tan skin.

"Give each of your toes a little tug and feel the blood moving into them." The teacher pats me on the shoulder gently, pulling my concentration back to the intense stretch in my feet. The last time I played with a foot, it was Cara's. And now I'm hard in yoga class thinking about her toes in my mouth.

I'm relieved when we switch to some hip opener poses, even more so when we rotate so I'm facing away from her. Until I realize this means she's staring at my ass as I widen my stance and hinge my hips forward.

It's fair to say my concentration is not where it needs to be if I'm going to draw the full benefit from this class, and I try my best to focus on my breath, to listen to the instructor. Until she says we are going to rely on a partner for the next series of hip poses.

I close my eyes, willing her to pair me with the linebacker on my right instead of the gorgeous woman messing with my feelings. "Cara, I'm going to ask you to team up with our newcomer today, if that's alright with you?"

I feel the teacher's hand on my arm as she turns me toward my one night stand. Cara pinches her lips together, looking everywhere but into my eyes. Whatever. I lie on my back with my knees bent and my feet on the floor, staring at the ceiling like I'm about to endure a medical procedure. When instructed, I pull one knee toward my chest and tip my foot toward the ceiling, wondering where the partner part comes into play.

"Okay, class. Let's have our standing yogi press a palm into our stretching partner's foot. Yes, just like that, Dustin. See how Jameel's hip is slowly stretching?"

I refuse to look as Cara's palm connects with the arch of my foot. I close my eyes, accepting this delicious stretch, but I can't focus on it too much because my junk is going to create a problem. By the time we switch to the other side, I'm fully erect and I open my eyes to see Cara kneeling between my legs. Her face hovers a foot above my crotch as she presses onto my foot.

My eyes connect with hers and I know she knows how my body is responding. If I had any say in the matter, I'd be flaccid, or better yet, I wouldn't be here at all.

A cramp burns in my lower back and I groan, rolling out of the stretch and rocking back and forth on the mat until the teacher arrives to talk me through a pose that releases the pain. Mercifully, she sticks by me for the remainder of the poses.

But at some point, I realize this leaves Cara to work with another partner, and I don't like it any better when I see a lanky dude pressing on *her* foot with his face hovering above her crotch. Why am I so messed up in the head over this woman? A bigger man would confront her, clear the air.

I'm not feeling very big as we pack up our mats, and I try to sneak out the way I came in, but I hear Cara's voice as I'm spritzing my mat with cleaner. "Can we talk?"

"I have nothing to say to you." I roll up the mat and start walking toward the bin near the exit.

"Five minutes, Wes, is all I'm asking. Then you can go back to ignoring me."

"Me, ignoring you?" I toss the mat into the bin with a muted thump. "That's rich, considering your attention span when it comes to men."

She shakes her head. "I knew you thought that. I knew you had misinterpreted what you saw. That's why you ghosted me when I could have really used a friend."

"Oh, you found a friend all right."

Once more, my memory is active, pulling up the cozy scene I walked in on as I went to sign my contract with the Forge. I saw his hand on her cheek as she stood there with no bra, probably still smelling like sex. With me.

Cara's face contorts as if I've slapped her. She clutches at her stomach and grips the wall with one hand. She swallows and shakes her head. "I can't believe I thought we could talk this out."

She pushes past me toward the exit. "Go on and leave then, Moreno. Again." I know I'm being a dick, but I can't seem to control myself.

Cara stops and looks over her shoulder at me, and I'm a little surprised to see her eyes welling with tears. She wipes her face and shoves the studio door open, leaving me alone in the hall.

Her tears give me pause. They seem out of character from what I know about her. Cara entered that tryout camp feisty and confident. She knew exactly what she wanted that entire weekend and made no bones about grabbing everything from multiple scouts' attention to my junk in a vice grip. And she left with a pro soccer contract, so something worked in her favor.

I don't know what to make of her outburst, but I don't have time to dwell on it anyway. My own career is on the brink of collapse. She did me a favor when she made sure our one night stayed that way.

CHAPTER 4
CARA

I slam the apartment door so hard that Jay springs up from the couch where she'd evidently been napping. "Cara?" Her face wrinkles and I close my eyes, taking a deep breath.

"Yes. Sorry. I just got a little carried away."

She frowns and rubs the back of her neck, then clicks off the television. "I thought yoga was supposed to be relaxing."

I sink into the couch next to her. We have a rare day off today and were each assigned different active rest. "I wish I'd gotten your stretchy band workout instead."

Jay snorts. "Yeah, right. Because it's so relaxing to squat a thousand times while Coach Lucy controls the resistance."

"I'm guessing you didn't have to defend your honor to a pigheaded striker at least."

Jay sighs audibly. "Is this about your reindeer?"

I swat her with the pillow. "His name is Stag, weirdo."

She shrugs. "It's funnier to call him a reindeer. Especially if he's being a douche."

I open my mouth to protest but my phone chirps with an incoming text. I glance at the screen and see that it's from Toni, whom I forgot I was supposed to call this morning.

"And now he made me stand up my friends. I can't with this guy."

"Let it out, Moreno. Get it over with."

I elbow her again and prop the phone up on the coffee table, clicking the icon to join the video chat in progress. All my chicas glare at me, pumice stones in hand and I wince.

"I forgot fancy-foot time. I'm so sorry."

Rosalie wags a finger at me. "I'm up at the crack of dawn! I don't do this for just anybody."

I grimace but Jay kicks my foot with her own. "We've got some rhino hide happening over here, folks."

Shante wags a finger at me. "That's what you get for leaving us in the lurch, chica. Did you even pre-soak and remove your polish from last time?"

I pry myself from the couch and scoot to my bathroom to grab my pedicure kit. When I get back to the living room, I'm touched to see that Jay got me a tub of warm water and a towel from the kitchen. "Go on," she whispers. "Shave your callouses like a block of parmesan cheese."

"You are disgusting, and I love it." Toni snickers from the tiny screen in the living room and I dunk my feet into the water. "One of these days we're gonna get you to join us," she shouts to Jay, who grunts and heads down the hall to her room.

She halts mid-stride and turns, poking her head back into the living room to shout, "Make sure she tells you about the reindeer. We have to get her to clear her head about that guy, no matter how great his antlers are."

I throw a pillow down the hall at her as she disappears into her room with another cackle.

When I look back at the screen, Rosalie is gesturing with her pumice stone. "Cara, babe, I can either tell you how my feet are starting to become real human feet now that I'm not running 30 miles a week in cleats, or I can remind you that you are working very hard to get selected for the national team leading up to the Olympics."

"Feet, please," I groan while my friends drown my voice in a chorus of "mm hmm."

"The fucking Olympics, Cara." Shante starts dabbing a cotton ball on her toes, scrubbing off last week's plum polish with gusto.

"Look." I cross an ankle over my lap and get to work with the callous shaver, noticing that my friends no longer even need to use this tool since, as they say, they've stopped playing soccer. They also don't get to spend their mornings watching the sun rise over the river. They no longer have world-class coaches helping them condition their bodies for maximum performance. But they know damn well how much these experiences mean to me.

"It's not like I was looking for him to be my boyfriend. I just really thought we connected and, well, it hurt my feelings when he ghosted me."

I bite my lip, feeling guilty that I'm not opening up to them about the added anguish of not knowing what to do about the creepy situation I found myself in with the president of Soccer USA. I don't even know how to explain it out loud, but I do know Wes Stag noticed something amiss. And instead of asking me my side of things, he jumped to the worst conclusion.

I get to work on my heels as I tell them about seeing Wes at yoga class. I leave out the details of how fine he looked in workout tights and a fitted t-shirt. "He's just … so done with me. And yet I have to see him every day."

Rosalie pulls a sympathetic face and leans close to her camera. "Cara, that sucks. What are the chances that your fresco hookup from camp would end up signed to the same city as you?"

Shante perks up. "Oh, I could tabulate the chances. How many pro women's teams are we up to now?"

"Thank you, stat doctor," Toni interrupts. "We don't need the actual numbers. What Rosalie is trying to say is that we know it stings to see him every day and think about that rejection. But we also know you will feel terrific once you do get past it. Like, are you seriously going to even think about him when Coach Akemi is handing you a red, white, and blue jersey?"

Rosalie nods. "Así es, chica."

Toni shakes a bottle of pink nail polish, rattling the little beads inside as she blends the colors. I reach for my matching shade as she asks, "You know what's better than a boyfriend, querida?"

Jay chooses that moment to re-enter the conversation, plunking next to me on the couch and shouting, "Literally everything." We all crack up laughing and I make room for her in front of the screen. Jay won't paint her nails, but she does reach for the lotion and starts to work on her feet.

"Seriously, though," Toni adds. "An Olympic gold medal will last a hell of a lot longer, look better around your neck, and open more doors for you than any boyfriend ever has."

As my friends erupt in a chorus of support and applause, I feel a lot better about the whole thing. After I end the video chat, Jay gives me a pointed look. "Do they still not know about how Lou Rubeo treated you?"

Her words feel like a slap. I shake my head and my mouth works up and down. "I haven't been able to find the words."

She frowns and places a hand on my shoulder. "The way he was getting in your space in the hall at lunch in California? That wasn't okay, Cara. I saw how he was looking at you, and that's not how professionals assess one another."

I blink rapidly in disbelief. I remember that Jay had come around the corner the very first time I encountered the soccer president. His actions that day had made me uncomfortable. Jay doesn't even mention how he escalated his creep factor, and the fact that she remembers even the one indiscretion makes me shaky.

My eyes start watering, and my chest feels tight. "Jay, he's ..." I think about how I felt both times I encountered him. How it should have been the very best experience of my life but I just felt...small...instead.

"He's a predator. I smelled it all over him. And he's messing with your head right when you need to be at the top of your game. Do you want me to go with you and tell someone? What do you want to do, Cara? I got you."

I lean forward and wrap her in a huge hug, and she pats my back.

"Well, now I got lotion on your shirt."

A laugh escapes from my throat, lightening the pressure a bit. I decide to ask Coach Lucy for advice, and Jay agrees to hold me accountable to do so.

———

The next morning, I feel both heavier and lighter as I drive us to work. I will happily admit that the yoga practice loosened up my hips a ton and I don't miss the big smiles from the coaching staff as they watch us work through our drills.

We scrimmage through a few different lineup combinations and Ben, our head coach, claps his hands as he blows a series of long blasts on his whistle. "Hot damn, gals. Who's ready to slay some Boston ballers?"

My team erupts in cheers, and he claps a few more times. "Go on and eat and get cleaned up and I'll see you in the theater for film in an hour."

He practically skips into the tunnel, and I notice the men's team filing out of their locker room, ready to take the field. I decide I want to get this over with before I see Wes again, so I hustle after the coaches to find Lucy.

I tap her on the arm, asking, "Can I talk to you for a second?"

She turns, smiling, but sees my face and her expression turns serious. "Of course, Cara. Come into my office."

I follow her and sit on the edge of the seat opposite her desk, not wanting to get sweat and grime on her nice chairs. Rather than walk around and sit in her own chair, Lucy perches on the edge of the desk, hands folded on her lap. "What's up?"

I look around her, to a picture of her family. There is a series of framed photographs on her desk of her with the men's coach, her with a little boy and a series of that same boy growing toward manhood. She's also got a wall of photos of a person who must be her daughter, looking fierce as she stares straight into the camera with dark hair and grey eyes. That woman looks like someone who would kick Lou Rubeo in the balls if he ever touched her face.

I take a deep breath. "Have you, um, ever felt … weird … around the staff from the national team?"

"Pah!" Lucy laughs. "Only every time I see them. Bev and Pat and Akemi are odd ducks, but I think that's what makes them so good at what they do."

I shake my head. "No. I mean, the management staff. The office guys."

Lucy frowns and grips the edge of her desk. "Did something happen, honey?"

I swallow and nod. Then I shake my head. "It might have been inadvertent? I just … felt … super uncomfortable when Mr. Rubeo was—"

My words leave me. It feels almost like I wet myself as a hot wave rolls over my body. Am I embarrassed, I wonder, or shamed? I don't know how to even describe what happened in a way that doesn't seem like I'm making a mountain from a mole hill.

Lucy's frown deepens. "Cara, he fails to set me at ease. I've just always had a yucky feeling about him. You can tell me if he crossed a line. I want you to know that anything you tell me, I believe you. You are an essential part of our organization and I'm on your side."

I nod my head a few times and tears leak down my cheeks, adding to the warmth that's still flooding my body. "It was more that he just kept getting into my personal space? And then right after I saw you in the elevator in California … he … touched my cheek?" Her eyes harden and her nostrils flare. Lucy leans forward and grasps my hand, nodding. "He backed me up against a pole and I worried he was going to kiss me." I close my eyes as I spit out that last part. I do not add that I think he only stopped because Wes came around the corner. I certainly do not add that I'd just left Wes's bed, naked, and he thought I was preparing to jump into someone else's right away.

Lucy makes a low, angry sound and squeezes my hand gently. "Honey, that is not okay. It's not okay that you didn't feel safe or that you had to worry about someone from your place of work—because you were most certainly there for a job interview, make no mistake. Gah! I'm just so angry."

I nod rapidly, exhaling deeply as a weight lifts from my shoulders. Lucy clucks her tongue and releases my hand. "What would you like to do, Cara? Do you want me to help you file a complaint?"

"Oh. Gosh, no. I can't do that." I think about the upcoming US friendly match against Germany, how selections are meant to begin in the next few weeks. "I feel better just talking about it with you."

Lucy takes a deep breath and looks over my shoulder at the photos of her family. "You know, Cara, I have experience with that sort of man. Personal experience." Her expression hardens. "Statistically, he's not going to stop at just making you feel uncomfortable."

I swallow thickly and lean against the back of the chair for support. Lucy exhales deeply a few more times. "I'd like to make sure you're not alone in any spaces he might be. In fact, I am going to have the whole team put the buddy system into play while we're in Boston. We've got the press hounding us anyway with playoffs coming up. Everyone on the team can probably use backup."

I swallow a few more times and bend down for my bag, fumbling to try to open my water bottle. Lucy stoops to help me and rubs my back as I drink deeply. "Thank you," I tell her, my voice wavering.

"Of course, Cara. Would you like a hug?"

I nod, sinking into her embrace, listening to my stomach gurgle with the first real hunger I've experienced in weeks.

THE YOGA MUST HAVE WORKED BECAUSE UNCLE HAWK SAYS I'VE HAD MY BEST week yet. I'm still not on the travel roster, but I'm feeling better about my chances of getting there. After Sunday morning training, I walk into my Aunt Alice and Uncle Tim's house right on time for family dinner. Which means I'm the last to arrive because this family shows up early any time there's food up for grabs. I can hear the ruckus from the front porch—the sound of four Stag brothers, their wives, and whichever of the eleven Stag kids are not currently away at school.

I can also smell the feast from the front porch, the aroma of garlic and herbs making me wish I could stay here forever, maybe roll around in that scent. Aunt Alice has been working around athlete meal plans ever since Uncle Hawk played pro soccer and now all my cousins' college coaches are jealous of the lean protein and whole grain smorgasbords. She regularly photographs them to post on the teams' social media pages.

I brace myself for a record scratch silence when I step into the kitchen, brimming with my tall, athletic relatives. I sidle up to the counter and snatch a piece of shrimp cocktail from a platter, managing to get it into my mouth before my aunts smother me in hugs. "Wesley!" Alice and Aunt Juniper squeeze me from each side and Aunt Lucy tips her chin at me from where she's deep in conversation with my mom.

It takes a minute for my mom to see me and when she does, her face shifts from calm into obvious concern. "Wes," she whispers. "Come here." She holds her arms out for a hug, and I step into her embrace, not realizing how badly I missed this until her red hair is tickling my nose while I lean over her. She starts smoothing my shoulders and checking me for damage before sliding the shrimp plate toward me on the counter. "Eat, babe. Your Uncle Hawk is whittling you down to bare bones." She turns to look for my uncle, who leans against the wall, holding a beer and listening to my Uncle Ty prattle on about the ice hockey tots he coaches. "Hawk!" Mom points a finger at him. "Why is my son so thin? He needs his strength for his back."

Uncle Hawk takes a swig of his beer, glancing around the room. I don't see my dad yet, so I guess he and Uncle Tim are outside manning the grill. "Emma, your son is at top form. He's lean, agile, and he's finally got loose hips."

Mom squeezes my side, which tickles, and I twitch under her grasp. "He's too thin."

I want her to stop worrying about old injuries. I also want to mutter something about not commenting on people's bodies, which she drilled into us for years. I have vivid memories of her shaking a finger at Ricky and me, her silver life alert bracelet clinking as she spoke. But I want my parents to be cool with me more than I want to be right, so I pat her hand. "I feel great, Mom. Squeeze my bicep." I flex for her and Aunt Juniper swats me with a towel.

Mom leans back and frowns. "Your back feels great, too?" *And here we go.* My cousins Odin and Gunnar cram literal handfuls of popcorn into their mouths, snickering when they see my expression. I scratch the side of my head with my middle finger as they pass the snack bowl to our cousins Stellen and Byron.

"My back is just fine, Mom. I told you—the physical therapists know what they're doing. I followed their instructions to the letter, and it barely bothers me anymore." It's not totally a lie. Just the part about it never hurting. I've actually felt great in the week since I took that yoga class. And besides, every professional athlete has aches and pains while they're in season. I keep waiting for my uncles to back me up on this, or maybe for one of my linebacker or hockey star cousins to pipe up that they, too, have recurring pain.

"Cut the crap, son. I wrote the book on fake stories." My dad must have come in the porch door while I was talking. He stands with his tattooed arms crossed over his chest, forearms flexing as he clenches and releases his fists. "Your mother and I were there in the room after you took that hit during college playoffs, in case you forgot. The team doctor mentioned surgery and possible paralysis."

I roll my eyes and cram another shrimp in my mouth. "He absolutely did not say I'm at risk for paralysis." Mom holds up a hand, but I shake my head. "He said the surgery to repair a herniated disc can sometimes damage the spine. And then he reminded you guys that all surgery has risks." I don't want to play this card, but it's been months of this sort of treatment from my parents and I've had enough. "Was it not risky for an epileptic person to get pregnant? Twice?"

Dad shoves off the wall and strides toward me. His nostrils flare as he jabs a finger into my sternum. "Watch your mouth."

"Hey, Thatch, I'm gonna take the kids to set the table while Alice finishes up in here." Ty grabs a huge stack of plates and gestures toward my cousins, who reluctantly put down the snack bowl and pick up baskets of silverware and napkins, following my uncles into the dining room.

In the meantime, Dad steps toward my mother, who rubs his back with her palm, tugging on her hair with her other hand. "Wesley, why would you choose that risk? A game isn't the same thing as the choice to grow a family."

I grab my own hair with both hands, the sting grounding me as I prepare to explain myself *again*. "Mom, I don't know how else to explain to you that there's nothing else that makes me happy. That soccer is my creative flow state. You write books because you said the stories scream at you to be set free, right?"

I turn to face my dad. "You blow glass because the images haunt you until you give them shape. You said that." I lean forward and grip the edge of the counter. "I feel that way about my sport. When I blow past a defender or send the perfect pass to a teammate, it's like all is right in the world for that second. The next second, I make some other sort of magic happen, together with another teammate."

I pound a fist on the counter, making Aunt Alice jump, and she backs out of the room with a plate of chicken, mouthing her apologies. Alone with my parents I let my head fall forward, closing my eyes. "I'm not going to tell you I don't worry about my back. I mean, it's my spine. I get it. But Mom, Dad…you have to let me pursue this opportunity. Do you know how few people are capable of playing professional sports?" Dad opens his mouth to talk but I straighten up and charge ahead. "Maybe I only get a year of this. Maybe I never get to start in a game. But I have to try. I have to give everything while I can and trust that you've given me the tools I need to figure out the next steps when we get there."

Dad swallows, his throat bobbing underneath his trimmed beard that's got streaks of white sprouting up throughout. Mom clutches his hand.

"Wesley, it's not easy for parents to forget the sight of their child crying in pain."

I nod. "I know that, Mom. I know. And just like you asked your parents, I'm asking you to trust me with my own body. I'm asking you not to put me in a glass cage." I look my father right in the eye. "You always told Mom she can do anything, that you'd be right by her side if she needed help. Well, now I need you cheering for me."

I don't give them a chance to respond. I'm not actually ready to discuss this further, so I walk past them into the dining room and grab a chair at the far end of the table, in between a few of my cousins. The massive crew has already decimated the platters of food my aunt prepared, and I have to fight through elbows to fill my plate. I eat quietly, looking around the table at my family, who mercifully ignores me while they talk about the non-soccer pro sports teams here in the city.

Uncle Ty's former hockey team, the Fury, haven't won a cup in years and my cousins all get heated as they talk about the pre-season exhibition games being played in Australia this year.

I'm glad for the comfort of the banter, the emphatic analysis, and the way my cousins tease each other about their predictions. And then I see my Aunt Lucy looking as miserable as I feel and wonder what else is going on. From everything I've seen and heard, the women's team has been crushing it on the field, so I have no idea why my aunt's face looks so tense as she talks to my uncle. He grips her leg under the table, nodding, before he leans back and scratches his chin.

Aunt Alice stands, then, and asks the kids to clear the table, even though the youngest kids here are twenty years old. This invites a mass eruption of dessert predictions from among her own offspring. My uncles, aunts, and parents all wander into the living room with their wine glasses.

I shouldn't drink alcohol during the season, especially when I'm working so hard to secure a starting spot on the team, but I snatch an empty glass from the table and walk up behind my Aunt Lucy, who has a bottle of white tucked under her arm. "Hey." I gesture for the bottle, and she frowns at me. "I'm having half a glass. Are you my aunt today or a member of the management team at work?"

She tips the bottle and pours me a few mouthfuls of wine, arching her brow before she brings the entire bottle to her lips and takes a deep swig.

"Woah. Can I ask what's got you so upset? You're not usually a big drinker, Aunt Luce."

She sighs and wipes her mouth with the back of her hand. "Cara

Moreno and Jay Whittaker got tapped for the national team after our match with Boston the other day."

My eyes fly wide, and it feels like my eyebrows will disappear into my hair. Why the hell was Cara upset at yoga if she made the national team? "Um, that's phenomenal. Isn't it?"

Lucy nods. "Yes. Absolutely." She flashes a forced smile and takes her wine to the back porch, where she gestures wildly at my Uncle Hawk. I swallow the tiny portion of wine in my glass. It tingles in my mouth. I haven't had anything outside my meal plan since ... I close my eyes against the memory of gorging on breadsticks and cheese pasta in bed with Cara at the tryout camp in California a few months back. We both decided to indulge in between rounds of the most explosive, intense sex of my life.

Lost in my memories, I don't hear my Uncle Tim talking to me until he snaps his fingers in front of my face. "Wes? Hello?"

I shake my head. "Sorry. What was that?"

He rattles a blue recycling bin at me. "I asked if you could go out back and dump that by the garage."

"Oh." I set my empty glass on the counter. "Sure. Sorry."

He grunts and grabs a sponge to scrub off the counters and I make my way down the basement steps and out the back door. I don't intend to eavesdrop on Hawk and Lucy, still arguing on the deck above me. But they're pretty loud.

"...what do they expect me to do, Hawk? The man made her uncomfortable enough that she said something to me. That speaks volumes." My aunt's voice cracks and I hear her gulping wine. I pause in place, resting the bin of recycling against the wall. If I dump it now, the rattling cans will alert them, and they'll stop talking...so I guess I'm actively rubbernecking on Lucy's drama at this point.

Uncle Hawk's voice is low, and I know he's trying to soothe her. "You have to be up front about it. Talk to the player rep, at least, or someone from Tim's legal team."

My aunt scoffs. "Like Tim ever handled anything quietly."

"Lucy, do you really want this kept quiet? Cara Moreno is more important to the organization than some guy in a suit with a desk job."

I'm so startled to hear Cara's name that I drop the bin and, as predicted, my aunt and uncle stop talking. Hawk leans over the deck rail to ask, "Everything okay down there? Oh. Hey, Wes."

I wave a hand. "Just dumping recycling for Uncle Tim."

Lucy frowns. "Better get inside for cookies before your cousins take them all. Alice used the monk fruit sweetener this time. Whatever that means."

I smile at her. I'd wrinkle my nose at whole grain cookies with odd-sounding ingredients if I didn't know from experience that those fuckers are going to be damn delicious, despite being packed with spirulina.

I head inside, back up to the kitchen, trying to make sense of why Aunt Lucy would be talking about Cara. Aunt Lucy mentioned a sticky situation with the national staff, and I remember Lou Rubeo all cozy with Cara in the hall in California. And then Cara cried as we argued after yoga.

A tingle of doubt skitters through my gut as I think of Aunt Lucy's concerned face, at the way she sounded so tortured when talking to my uncle. What did she mean, Cara was uncomfortable? I'm about to grab a cookie when something else about that trip sparks hesitation, a hiccup in my gut.

What if Rubeo was a predator instead of Cara seeking out that kind of attention? The president of Soccer USA making a pass at one of Lucy's players would definitely be the sort of thing that would set my aunt on edge.

I think back to the moment I lost Cara, to that vision of her in the hall with Rubeo. I walked around the corner to see him leaning in toward her, suggestively. I saw his finger tracing a line down her cheek. But what did her body language convey? I can't even remember. My memory only picks back up from the moment her eyes met mine and I almost let her see how much it stung to have been left.

I realize with staggering, horrifying clarity that I misjudged her. That she's been trying to tell me for weeks that something terrible happened and all I did was ghost her and leave her alone to deal with the effects of a slime ball making her feel unsafe. I've been swimming through a haze of hurt feelings that I wanted something more with a woman who walked out on me … only to realize I fucked everything up beyond recognition.

"I have to go." I blurt this declaration loud enough that Mom hears. She makes her way toward me through the throng of Stags, but I don't stop to hug her. I have to find Cara and apologize.

I dash out the front door as my father hollers for me to come back, but all I can think about is making amends.

"I just don't know what you want me to say, Cara." Mama sounds like I interrupted her with something frivolous when I called her and Papi to tell them I got chosen to represent our country in a friendly match against Germany. They've been divorced for years, but we always do a three-way call for these weekly chats. Apparently so they can present a united front that I'm still and forever doing it wrong.

"Mama, really? You can't say, 'Felicidades, Cara! I'm so proud of you?'"

She sniffs.

Papi makes a humming sound. "And they're paying you a salary to play football like the men?"

"Yes, Papi. God, I've been explaining this to you for months. And I'm not playing *like* the men. I play women's football. I'm a professional athlete."

"Watch your language, Cara." He snaps a reprimand like I'm still a child. And maybe it's childish to expect them to understand after all this time.

"We just want you to think about your future. What about starting a family? Having babies?"

"Yes." Papi chimes in with his machismo opinions. "These footballers earn millions. Messi is in Miami earning $50 million. Your cousin saw him at Costco."

I roll my eyes, glad they can't see me doing so to find another thing to chastise me about. "Messi is married with kids."

"And you're earning millions, yes?"

"Papi, you know I'm not."

"Mm hmm. Well, a man don't like a woman who earns more than him anyway."

"Luis, that's not true and you know it." I know better than to hope my mother is on my side with this interjection. She starts listing telenovela starlets with "ordinary" husbands and would continue for hours if I didn't cut her off.

"I'm not playing soccer to find a husband. I'm playing soccer because I love it and I love this freaking country and I thought you'd be proud that I will be representing it."

"Such language. Is that what they teach you at these schools with the men and women in class together? Is that how you talk to people in Pittsburgh? What does your priest say?"

I dig a knuckle into my temple with the hand not holding the phone, trying to decide what to say next. A knock at the door catches me off guard and I glance down the hall. Jay is out on a date with a woman who asked for her autograph after our last home game, so I worry that she forgot her key or something. "Mama, Papi, I need to go. Someone is at the door."

"Just think about what I said, Cara. You can still come back and find a job here in Findlay."

"Mami, I appreciate that. I will call you soon, okay." I hang up and throw the phone on the sofa, muttering to myself about my contract, feeling thankful that I have at least three years here in Pittsburgh where most people seem to understand that women have other goals in life than making babies.

Whoever's at the door knocks again, hesitantly, and I shuffle over to the peep hole. I gasp audibly when I see Wes Stag on the other side of the door.

"Cara, I came to apologize," he says as I press my back against the door, one hand to my chest as if I could still the racing heart inside my ribs. "Can I please come in and talk to you? I brought you something."

I should tell him to get lost. I should ignore him and hide in my room, ghost him like he did to me. He was so mean and dismissive when I tried to talk with him after yoga. For some reason I lean to the side and look through the peep hole again. Wes has one arm above his head, leaning on the door, face close to the little lens. His eyes seem sincere.

I sigh and open the door and melt a bit when his face shifts into a grin, like he's happy to see me. He holds out his hand, displaying a bright blue cube. "I brought you a power adapter." I arch a brow in confusion. His grin widens. "For when you're in France, with the national team. So you can charge your phone and stuff…"

I blink at him, unsteady on my feet. How does he know I got selected? How is it that this man who doesn't even like me understands the significance of my achievement so much that he bought me the perfect celebration gift? "Thank you," I whisper, accepting the cube and turning it over in my hand.

Wes points at the adapter. "There are different plug configurations depending on where you're going. See here? I guess the outlets are shaped different in Australia compared to Europe." He smiles at me, expectantly. Waiting. I look between him and the cube, unsure what to do. "So, can I come in and apologize now?"

I shake myself back to the present moment. "Yes. Sorry. Um, do you want something to drink?" I groan, embarrassed that I'm offering hospitality and my own apologies to someone who already said he came here to offer me those things. "We can sit on the couch."

Jay and I don't have a dining table. We eat at the counter, where we have four high stools, two of which are piled with clean laundry yet to be sorted and put away. The small table in the entryway is currently covered in mail and canned tuna—just a few of the side effects from a series of away matches.

Wes seems not to notice and walks to the couch, easing his long torso into the corner. He places his hands on his thighs and waits for me to join him. I pluck my phone from the other corner of the couch and set it on the end table, turning my body to face Wes.

"You seem frazzled," he starts. "Is this a bad time?"

I shake my head. "You know, just dealing with parents who don't understand why I'd want to play professional sports."

"Ah." He nods knowingly. "I know a few things about that." He swallows and rubs his palms along his jeans. I try not to think about the thighs I know hide beneath that dark denim. "So, I overheard my Aunt Lucy today at dinner."

I wrinkle my nose. "Should I know who that is?"

His brows shoot up and he stiffens. "Lucy Moyer? Your assistant coach?"

I tap my fingers and squint. "Coach Lucy is related to you?"

Wes barks out a laugh. "It's so refreshing when people don't know my whole family history." He shakes his head, smiling. "Hawk Moyer, the men's team coach, is my dad's brother. He's married to Lucy." My mouth forms an "oh" of surprise. "You can imagine the mind fuck it creates for me when I'm trying to prove myself and people think I just made this team because of my family."

"I … had no idea."

He waves a hand in the air. "So, my Uncle Ty played pro hockey, too. And my dad and Uncle Tim are lifelong runners. All us kids—there are 11 of us all together—all of us are athletic whether we like it or not. Many of us are playing D1 sports in college or putting ourselves out there for the pros. My cousin Odin is probably going to play in the NFL."

"Wow. Well, you know my family doesn't believe real women play sports."

Wes extends a hand like he wants to touch me but changes his mind and drapes it over the back of the couch. "Let me know their address and I'll have my Aunt Juniper send them a picture of her Olympic medal hanging in her judge's chambers at the courthouse downtown."

I chuckle, imagining my parents not knowing what to make of such a passive aggressive package. But then I don't know what else to say. "Um, you said you were going to apologize?"

He nods and licks his lips. "I don't know where to start so I'm just going to dive into it." I nod and swallow. Feeling exposed, I grab a throw pillow and clutch it to my chest. "I fucked up, Cara. I saw you and Mr. Rubeo standing together in the hall and I assumed the worst of you when I should have seen the worst in him."

I inhale a shaky breath through my nose and tears well up in my eyes as Wes brings up Lou Rubeo.

"My aunt didn't mention anything specific—she had no idea I was lurking nearby, anyway. But she said something at family dinner about there being issues with the staff on the national team. And, well, I couldn't help but remember how upset you were after yoga." He drags a hand through his hair and squeezes his eyes shut. "God, Cara, I'm just so damn sorry. I should have trusted you…I should have trusted what we shared together. Instead, I just made everything worse."

I close my eyes and a single tear rolls down my face. "I really felt a connection with you in California."

He slumps further into the couch, his proud shoulders sagging. "I felt it too, Cara. Like nothing I ever felt before. I'm embarrassed that I ruined that."

The air is thick with regret, and I want to tell him it's okay, that we can pick up where we left off…but he hurt me. His actions and his words… and lack of words…it hurt me. I'm already dealing with enough rejection from my parents plus navigating the delicate situation with the national team, when the flipping president of the organization makes me want to vomit. "I appreciate you coming here to apologize," I manage to tell him. I take a deep breath and release the pillow long enough to tuck my hair behind my ears.

He smiles and reaches out a hand to finger the end of my ponytail. I accept his touch, missing the contact I once savored with him. "I also came to congratulate you. I'm proud of you for making the cut." A beam of light expands inside my chest at his words, at his recognition of me achieving a lifelong dream. "When do you leave for training camp?"

I hug the pillow again, this time in excitement. "Not until later. National camp isn't supposed to conflict with league play, but we made the playoffs … as you know."

Wes's smile is even larger now and he leans one elbow on the arm of the couch, grinning. "Of course, I know. I'm vying for field time in our own playoff run myself."

I laugh, sinking happily into comfortable conversation with this man, who understands my work, my ambition. Even if he was a dick about it, he found a really thoughtful way to apologize. "I'd love to come to a game and see you play, Wes. If it works out."

His sneaker taps on the floor, and he shifts his posture, bringing his body just a bit closer to mine. "We could look at our travel schedules…see if that will work out anytime soon? I want to see you play, too." His smile would melt the ice off the sides of our freezer—and it's got quite a lot of buildup since Jay and I haven't been here to keep up with monitoring it.

"We can do that." I grab my phone and pull up my calendar, and he does the same.

CHAPTER 7
WES

MY NAME IS ON THE ROSTER AS A SUB FOR THE FORGE GAME AGAINST Charleston. Not a starter, yet, but this is the first time I'll be eligible to take the field as a professional athlete. I should feel an irresistible urge to call my family with this news, especially since I want to get to them before my uncle blabs. But when I see the roster posted by the showers, my first thought is to tell Cara.

It's only been a few days since I made amends, but we've been texting back and forth. She's going to be able to watch my game this weekend, since the Hot Metal plays Charleston's women's team the same day. The women play first, though, so I'll be warming up and unable to watch her play.

I hurry and change into my sweats and shoot her a text message.

> Call me after your practice? I've got news.

"Wes, got a second?" My uncle pokes his head out from his office and I nod, sliding the phone in my pocket as I walk toward him. "Shut the door, kid." I do, and then my uncle beams and claps his hands slowly. "I couldn't be any more proud of you if you were my own son, Wesley. You really stepped up your game the last week or so, bud."

He tousles my wet hair and I bat his arm away. "Ah, knock it off, Uncle Hawk. And thank you. I've been working hard."

He leans against the edge of his desk, arms crossed over his chest. "Have you talked to your parents any more since dinner at Tim's?"

I shake my head. "We'll work it out eventually. I do wish they could come see me play. I wonder if my coach knows whether I'll actually get any time on the field…"

"Do you want me to be your uncle right now or your coach?" He winks at me, then smooths a hand along his chin. "I don't really see Thatcher and Emma traveling for this one, though. I think it's parents' weekend at your brother's school."

I shrug. "All the more reason to keep working for a start in a home match, right?"

"That's the attitude." He claps me on the back and then pulls me in tight for a hug. "All right, I stink. Get out so I can shower."

I laugh and head toward the parking lot, checking my phone. I grin entirely too hard when I see a text from Cara, even if it is just a thumbs up emoji. I know she's feeling tender after how I treated her. This isn't like California where we were both immediately on the same page about being majorly into one another. If I ever want her to be mine again, I'm going to have to work as hard with her as I will on the field for that starring role.

I decide to hit up Costco and because I'm a good Stag who thinks of the herd, I text my cousins to see if anyone needs anything.

YOUNG STAG GROUP CHAT

Who needs ten pounds of Doritos?

WYATT:

You're not really going to eat that crap in season are you?

ODIN:

I will always eat Doritos. And a few pounds of beef jerky, please

PETEY:

I'm going to silence this thread for awhile since I doubt you're going to deliver to me in Ithaca.

STELLEN:

Always bragging about that Ivy League education…

Wes, I'll take cheese sticks.

Which kind?

STELLEN:

All the kinds. I don't care. Surprise me.

GUNNAR:

Better toss in a bucket of dairy pills if Stelly is
going to be pounding cheese in the apartment.

STELLEN:

Fuck you, Gun. I'm going to fart on your pillow
right now while you're at class.

They carry on this way while I drive to the store and fill a massive cart with snack food, most of it healthy. I'm about to check out when I wheel the cart past the pasta aisle and notice an end cap with bouquets of fresh flowers. Do I want to be a guy who buys a woman flowers, and maybe pays a custodian to slip them in her locker for me?

I check my watch and it's barely three. I still have plenty of time before rush hour traffic makes this plan ridiculous. The bouquets are only $9, so I toss one on top of the cart before I can change my mind. Only, when I get back to the stadium, I don't need to find someone to infiltrate the women's locker room for me because I spy Cara walking out the side gate with her roommate.

I throw my Jeep in park and leap out with the flowers. "Hey, Cara," I shout as I jog toward her, realizing I must look ridiculous or frantic or both.

She turns toward my voice and then sees the flowers. She tilts her head to the side, confused.

Her roommate looks at the flowers and then into my face and squints. "I'll see you at home, Cara. I gotta go."

"Wait," Cara shouts. "We rode in together."

"What?" Jay holds a hand over one ear. "I can't hear you over the train. Sorry, gotta go. Bye."

I make a silent note to buy Jay something nice for meddling on my behalf. I grin and put one hand in my pocket, holding the flowers out toward Cara with the other. She looks around as her teammates file out of the stadium, heads bent and talking to one another. I get the sense Cara doesn't want people at work to see her getting flowers from someone on the men's team, so I step behind a brick column and gesture for her to come closer. I choose not to believe she's feeling awkward about getting flowers from me specifically.

"What're these for, Wes?" She bites her lip and looks down at the bouquet again like it's some massive gesture and not a grocery store bunch of flowers.

"Well, I thought of you when I saw them. So I bought them."

She smiles, like she's trying not to but can't help it. The tiny pull at the corners of her mouth does something to my heart rate. I love knowing I made her smile. Half-smile. "Is that what you wanted to talk about? I was about to call you when you shouted my name!"

I shake my head and shake the flowers until she takes them from me, sniffing the bouquet. "Nah, these are separate. I wanted to tell you I made the sub roster. For Charleston."

"Wes! That's outstanding!" Her entire face lights up and I can tell that she means it, that she's truly happy for me.

"Would you want to celebrate with me?" I'm operating totally off book here, utterly astonishing myself as these ideas fly into my head and a little too invested in her response to me putting myself out there. "I'd love to buy you an herbal tea. Plus, you know, I hear you need a ride."

She laughs and I know she's aware there isn't much we can eat or drink at a restaurant leading up to a game, not with our nutrition plans. "That sounds nice, Wes. Thank you."

I gesture toward my car, stopped haphazardly. Cara laughs as she sees some women from the Hot Metal swerving around my Jeep on their way out of the stadium parking lot. "I think we'd better get a move on since you're causing a traffic jam."

She sniffs the orange and pink flowers and I keep my distance, even though I'd love to put an arm around her. Smell her hair, tell her that I think talking things out with her opened me up more than the yoga class did and really let me shine this week to earn this spot.

I unlock the car and lean past Cara to open her door, but she's already flung open the back door to toss her bag inside. Her nose wrinkles and she looks around at all the boxes in the car. "What's that smell?"

"Oh, god. Sorry about that." I lean past her and shove the boxes to make room for her bag. I do notice that Cara sets the flowers gingerly on top, out of harm's way. I smile and explain, "My cousins wanted seaweed snacks and beef jerky. I think we're getting some sort of chemical reaction from the paired odors."

Her head flies back as she laughs. "Have you tasted those seaweed things before? My one roommate used to love them."

I shake my head and accept that I'm not going to be able to open the door for her as Cara slides past me and into the passenger seat. "They taste like a fart. And they give you *horrible* breath."

"Note to self: do not eat seaweed snacks near Cara."

She buckles her seatbelt and leans an elbow on the window, turning her body toward mine while I drive. "Don't avoid them on my account. You need your iron to play for the Forge."

"Are we making metal jokes now? Hot metal jokes?"

"Okay, okay. Enough Steel City puns." She taps her fingers on her legs in time with the music over the radio. I head up Forbes Avenue toward the Oakland neighborhood where four of my cousins share a college apartment. There's a tea shop nearby.

"Is it okay if I stop quick and unload all this cheese and stuff? I have a key to my cousins' place, so it'll be quick."

"That's fine. Are we talking about cousins like *actual* cousins or like how every Latino family friend is my auntie and their kids are my cousins?"

"Oh, these are my actual cousins. My dad is one of four, and each brother has … a lot of kids." I put on my turn signal to head down Atwood Street toward the university-owned apartment building where a lot of athletes live, including my extended family. I parallel park in a loading zone by the fire station across the street and hop out, filling my arms with an awkward stack of boxes. I'm about to tell Cara that I'll be right back for the rest of it when I notice her standing beside me, arms laden with jerky and chips.

"Lead the way," she grins, and I marvel at how in sync we are, even now when our friendship still has an undercurrent of hesitation. I shake away the thought and hurry toward my cousins' apartment. But then I realize I don't have a spare hand to get the key from my pants pocket. I'm in the middle of an awkward maneuver to rest the boxes against the wall and pull my hand free, when Cara says, "Here. I got it." Before I can say a word, she slides her hand into my sweats and plucks out the keychain.

I grow immediately, achingly hard at the heat of her touch, at the memory and familiarity of her body near mine. I draw in a shaky breath, worried I might actually come in my pants like a teenager. "Which one is it?" Cara shakes the keys, questioning, and I shake myself back to reality.

"The one with the purple ring," I manage to choke out. Cara unlocks the door and holds it open for me. I drop the boxes just past the threshold and gesture for her to do the same with her armload.

"Shouldn't we put the cheese in the fridge? I don't want it to go bad." I'm well aware that any lingering here could lead to a cousin returning from class, or waking up from a nap, and I'm not ready to subject Cara to the Stag family brand of inquisition. She already knows my aunt and uncle and I tell myself I don't want to impact any professional boundaries she's established at work.

She's on her way back from the kitchen before I can tell her the cheese is fine for a few hours. Beaming, she walks past me into the hall, and I lock the door behind us as I follow her. "That's so nice of you to take them supplies, Wes. I never had a big family like that."

"You're an only child, right?"

"Mm hmm. I have relative-cousins in Florida, and like I said, I have 'cousins' near home … but they wouldn't exactly drive to my college apartment with care packages."

I swallow, remembering the tension with her parents and their outdated views on women in sports. "It helps that we all live close by, I'm sure."

"Well, anyway, I think it's nice." Cara once again gets herself inside my Jeep before I can open the door for her, and I'm left on the curb looking weird as I watch her buckle her seatbelt.

The tea shop ends up not having seating, which leads to me driving Cara home and sitting on her balcony in a camp chair. She's got a sweet view of the Allegheny River, and we sip our drinks as we watch people rowing crew and kayaking. She smiles at the water. "Is it weird that I love watching the water sports? It just looks so peaceful, somehow."

I slurp my tea. "Not weird at all. I think I told you my Aunt Juniper rowed crew in the Olympics. All of us took rowing lessons from her."

"That's so cool."

I shake my head. "It looks cool, maybe, but those people are masochists. Nothing has ever burned my lungs more than Aunt June barking me through a power 20."

Cara laughs and leans forward on the rail, the breeze blowing her curls around. "What about the kayaks, then? Are those harder than they look?"

I swallow the urge to make a joke about things looking hard, but I can tell Cara catches her slip because she lifts her eyebrows as she slurps the rest of her iced tea. There's a weighted pause where we just look at one another. I want so many things … to kiss her and hold her, to shout over the balcony that I got called up to the roster.

I'm about to tell her I need to quit while I'm ahead, make an excuse and head home, but her roommate starts shouting from the living room.

"Cara! We got our workout schedules from Akemi. You're gonna want to go to bed immediately and rest up." Cara smiles knowingly, and I can imagine exactly what she's thinking. She's got that dread of how hard it will be on top of her Hot Metal workouts, plus the simmering burn to demolish the benchmarks. I remind myself that work has to come first for her, and it should be that way for me, too. We both have too much to prove to get lost in flirtation.

"I get it," I tell her, my voice softer than I intended. "I'll let you get your rest. Sounds like you need it."

"See you at work, Stag." She grins and crunches an ice cube from her glass, and I actually experience a pang of jealousy from a frozen shard of water.

"See you at work."

I'M NOT SURE HOW WESLEY STAG AND I TRANSITION FROM AN HERBAL TEA hangout to making each other lunch on alternating days, but all week, I've been prepping turkey wraps and slicing carrots into intricate shapes, constantly trying to up my lunch game before I meet him outside the stadium in between drills and film and his physical therapy. We eat by the river unless it's raining, watching the barges chug past and waving at the occasional morning booze cruise.

Yesterday, he handed me a joke lunch full of that seaweed stuff, so today I disguised a turkey meatloaf to look like a cupcake, topped with riced cauliflower frosting and chive sprinkles. I hand him the container and bat my eyes, awaiting his response. Despite my hesitation around him and my anxiety that he'll ditch me again at the first sign of trouble, I'm growing addicted to the way I feel when I'm around Wes.

"Dessert for lunch? You're pretty confident in yourself now that you're on the national team roster, Moreno." He winks and sniffs the food. His brow furrows. "What is this?"

"I promise it meets our dietary parameters." I shift my posture so I'm leaning forward with my elbows on my knees, my own meatloaf container still sealed since I didn't decorate mine any special way.

"Did you call my Aunt Alice or something?"

"You know I have no idea who your relatives are, Stag. Try it!"

Wes wrinkles his nose, shrugs, and takes a bite of the cupcake. I watch his face shift as he tastes the savory food when he was expecting sweet. I laugh as he moves through shock and into acceptance and actual enjoyment. My meatloaf is damn tasty, thank you very much. "Id dis meatloaf?" Wes covers his mouth with his free hand as he chews.

I nod and take a bite of my own dish, feeling nostalgia when the taste of oregano with a touch of cumin hits my tongue. I swallow my bite and explain, "I used black beans to bind it all since I know you're off rice right now."

"I love it. I'm not going to be able to beat this. What did you use for the sprinkles?"

I shrug and nudge him with my shoulder. "Are you admitting defeat? Is the great Wesley Stag giving up and naming me lunch-making champion?"

"Nah. Not really. Besides, I have a few days to figure it out since we travel tomorrow, right?"

I nod and enjoy the shiver rolling through my body. I'm excited for this away game. "Coach Akemi will be in Charleston watching."

He smiles wistfully. "I wish I could watch your game, too."

"I know you do. But I'm also excited to see yours. Jay and some of the Hot Metal are going to stick around for at least the first half."

"How generous."

"Hey, come on. How many of your teammates can name a player on my team?"

"Fair point." Wes finishes his cupcake and takes a deep pull from his water bottle. He fidgets with the cap and stares out at the water for a bit. "Are you doing anything tonight?" I hesitate just long enough that Wes quickly adds, "I was planning to watch a game and wondered if you wanted to join me."

A flurry of emotion whirls inside me at the prospect of alone time with Wes. Will we touch? Will I be able to recover if we don't? This man and I have an electric connection when he's not snapping to conclusions. I'm not sure how to navigate that, and I'm not sure how much I can let it distract me from my career right now. "What game? Whose house?"

He taps his lips and I can tell he knows his answer will determine a lot. "How about your house if Jay doesn't mind my presence? And … maybe the last World Cup final?"

"I'll see you around six." I stand and brush the crumbs from my lap, gathering up my stuff so I can head back inside for my strategy session. Wes follows and I notice a slight wince as he stoops to grab his bag.

He knocks on my apartment door at 5:59 and I point finger guns at Jay, who insisted he was one of those guys who viewed time as a social construct. "Whatever, Cara. He better have food with him."

She opens the front door to reveal a long pair of legs in grey sweats, topped with a stack of takeout boxes that hide the chest and face of our visitor. "Did someone request food?" Wes bends his head to the side of the stack and grins. I force myself to look away from the sweatpants. Jay grabs the top few boxes so Wes can see where he's going, and they spread stuff out on the counter while I run around grabbing plates and silverware from the dishwasher.

"Wow, I didn't know you were bringing an entire feast."

He shrugs. "Three professional athletes can put away a lot of calories, right?" He points to the boxes. "These are actually from my Aunt Alice—the chef I was telling you about. She knew I'd be missing family dinner on Sunday, so she dropped off a huge care package."

"Wes, you didn't have to bring us your special family food." I try to imagine a circumstance where I'd share ropa vieja if my aunt sent me some from Miami.

"Shut up, Cara. I want the chef food." Jay is already digging into a container of grilled chicken and zucchini.

Wes slides a box toward me and my mouth waters at the smell of mustard and garlic. "It's really fine. You have to remember, my entire family lives within a few miles. If Aunt Alice knew Jay was craving this sort of thing, she'd probably start delivering weekly."

"I'm not gonna say no to dat." Jay squeezes her eyes shut in bliss as she devours the savory food.

"Are you watching the Lionesses game with us, Jay?" I arch a brow at her because she told me she wasn't sticking around.

"Lionesses?" Wes squints around a mouth of broccoli.

"England? World Cup final?" I wash down an incredible mouthful with a swig of water.

Wes puffs out a laugh. "I thought we were watching France versus Argentina."

Jay grins and claps us each on the back. "As much as I'd enjoy watching you two figure out that you have to specify which World Cup you meant since there's one for each gender...I'm going to watch the Seattle versus Louisville game with the other keepers." She strides toward the door and glances back over her shoulder. "In case you weren't sure, we will be watching women play soccer." Jay's cackle echoes down the hall as she leaves, and I frown at Wes.

"Do we really have to watch men's soccer?"

"Are men so gross?" He winks at me and takes a final bite of food, wiping at his mouth with a napkin.

I ball up my napkin and throw it at him. "Sometimes, yeah. But I want to watch the women's final from last year and assess the competition."

Wes's eyes dart to the couch, where the remote lies on one of the cushions. Before I can react, he dives over the back of the couch, one long arm extended toward his goal.

"Oh, definitely not, Stag." I spring over the side of the couch. He jumped first, but I'm closer and my fingers wrap around the end with enough time to spare for me to smash the power button. "Ha."

Wes hauls both legs over the couch and under his body, using his leverage to wrestle the remote from my hands. He smashes the voice control button and shouts "show me Messi versus Mbappé."

"Don't you dare," I yell at the television in vain as the Argentinian and French flags appear on the screen. I elbow Wes in the side and lean over his lap, digging a nail into the microphone icon on the remote. "I want Spain versus England."

The screen flickers and … a random international men's game appears. Wes and I both deflate, and he groans. "I get it, Moreno. I'm sorry. Even the robots think men's soccer is the default."

I want to say something in response. I want to curse the patriarchy. But my chest is heaving, and my face is a few inches from the bulge in the center of Wes's sweatpants and all thought seeps out of my skull. Gingerly, I sit up and nestle into the corner of the couch, relinquishing the remote as Wes pulls up the women's final match.

"God, this is a good game," he whispers a few minutes in as we both adjust ourselves to the far ends of the couch. He pauses a few times to point at the screen, and I smile, appreciating his commentary. By half-time, we're an inch apart from one another on the couch, staring at the screen and barely blinking, even though we both know the outcome of the game. England gets a yellow card soon after and Wes nearly punches a hole in my coffee table as he shouts at the referee on the screen.

"Easy there, big guy." I rub a palm on his back, realizing as I do that it's probably a bad idea, but not caring enough to pull back my hand. Wes turns his head to smile at me—a warm, full-faced expression with teeth and twinkling eyes—and my heart stops a little bit. More than half of me wants to dive into him and finish what we started in California. My skin tingles just thinking about it, with my hand resting on his ribcage. Breathless, I lean back against the couch as the game continues on the television.

Wes relaxes his posture as well and soon I feel the warmth of his arm around the back of the cushions. By the time the game ends, I've got my head on his shoulder as his fingers draw gentle circles on my shoulder.

CHAPTER 9
CARA

THE WOMEN'S TEAM FLIES SEPARATELY FROM THE MEN'S TEAM FOR OUR Charleston match. Jay grumbles about our connection in Baltimore since, based on the flight board at the airport, it seems like the men flew direct. "It's all the little shit like this that just fills me with a boiling rage sometimes, you know?" She kicks a trash can in the security line.

"Trust me, I get it. I grew up in a family where the men actually sit at the dinner table waiting to be served plates of food." Even though we do all get security pre-check as a job perk, there are so many of us that our line moves just as slowly as the regular security line. "How close are we to booking a full flight, just us? If we paired up with the men, I bet we'd be close."

Jay leans in for a retina scan and sniffs. "With the athletic trainers, I bet you're right. Just makes me hate the national office suits even more, if they think stuff like this is equitable."

Her mention of the national staff has me reflexively tightening my stomach. I'm grateful for the distraction of the x-ray machine. Once our team is through the checkpoint, we pile into the shuttle to the terminal. I see Coach Lucy talking heatedly to Coach Ben and a pang of discomfort washes over me. Is it my anxiety that leads me to suspect their disagreement is related to Lou Rubeo? They could just as easily be arguing about our starting lineup.

Once we're near our gate, Lucy peels off from the group to make a phone call. I don't mean to eavesdrop, but her voice rises as I approach. "Hey, babe. Yeah, he's going to be there … I haven't decided yet … Yeah, I know your brother can support me, but I'd like to avoid bringing a lawyer to a press conference if I can help it."

I slow my pace as much as I can without seeming obvious, and I spend both legs of our flight trying to calm my stomach, worrying that opening up to Coach Lucy created problems for the entire Pittsburgh soccer franchise.

Jay and I split up at the hotel in Charleston—each of us is rooming with someone else who plays our position—and while I like my fellow mid-fielder just fine, I don't know her well enough to open up about my off-field worries. As a result, I take the field Saturday morning with a whole suitcase of unprocessed emotional baggage.

I can't quite chase away the blockage. It's like a fog at the periphery of my vision throughout the game and I keep getting elbowed by defenders. My footwork is sloppy, and I bobble the ball a few times.

At one point I move to receive a clearing kick from Jay, but instead of cradling the ball gently to the ground so I can run with it, I lock my ankle and it bounces wildly from my foot straight to the feet of Charleston's best striker.

Worse, I freeze in shock over my mistake instead of tearing down the field after her. She weaves through our defensive line, plants her foot, and kicks the ball into the top corner of the net, past Jay's fingers. Ben subs me out with 20 minutes left in the match and I don't even question it. I slump into the sideline shelter, staring at the field and hoping my replacement has her shit together enough to turn the tide. She doesn't, and the ref whistles for the end of the game.

Coach Ben sighs and heads over to shake hands with the opposing coach. He turns back to face us. "Tough one, folks." Ben gestures his head toward the tunnel and everyone shuffles toward the locker room for our post-match meeting. I start to follow and I feel a hand on my shoulder.

"Hey, Cara, you okay?" Coach Lucy offers me a cup of hydration drink, which I accept with a shrug. She offers a watery smile. "You seemed distracted on the field. Want to talk about it?"

I shake my head, still staring ahead. I hear her inhale, hesitate, exhale. "I want to follow up with you about our conversation in my office. I want you to know that I took it very seriously, but as you know it's a very complicated situation."

"Ha." The sound puffs out of me, and I turn my head to face her, finally. She smiles as we lean against the wall in the tunnel.

"I'm sure you know the national team staff is here tonight. I meant what I said in the locker room about sticking with a buddy. One thing we know about these types of men is they behave differently with an audience."

I drain the rest of the liquid in the cup, crumple it, and toss it toward the wastebasket. I mutter my thanks to Coach Lucy, and walk toward the rest of the team in the locker room.

———

It's hard to drum up enthusiasm from my teammates to watch the men's game after our loss on the pitch. "I'm going no matter what," I say, toweling my hair after my shower. I know I'm just a rookie who came on board late season, so I'm not surprised when Jay is the only Hot Metal player to join me in the bleachers as the men take the field.

"Think anyone would notice if I ate an entire funnel cake?" She sniffs toward the concession stands longingly.

"Don't do it! You'll hate yourself in the morning. Besides, it was my fault that striker got the ball to begin with."

Jay flicks me in the shoulder. "We have four perfectly good defenders on our team who could have stopped her. Plus, you know, me."

"What's your point?" I spy Wes in the group of gold jerseys and my heart flutters a little, the first semi-joyful emotion I've felt in a few days.

"My point is that we should all be jointly eating funnel cake as a coping mechanism because we are all to blame for that loss. Not just you taking on the responsibility. Is that the reindeer?"

I squint to make sure, because a lot of the guys look the same from this distance. "Wow. He's starting. I thought he was a sub."

"Good for him." Jay claps and puts two fingers in her mouth, whistling. Ordinarily I'd call my Midfield Mamis to decompress, or at least vent-text them while I watch, but if Wes is starting, I want to pay attention.

I smile as the ref blows the whistle and the Forge center kicks the ball to Wes. I can't make out his facial expression from here, but I suspect he flashes a cocky grin to the Charleston player as Wes pulls the ball back and spins away, streaking up the right sideline with his teammates in fast support. Wes drives all the way to the top corner before sending the ball right in front of the goal and another Forge player heads it into the net.

"Boom!" Jay stands to applaud, shaking her head and whistling again. The stadium erupts with boos from the locals while the small Pittsburgh fan section bursts into song.

I keep my eye on Wes, whose teammates crash around him for high fives after that assist. Is it my eyesight or does he wince when their center slaps him on the back? I've been noticing a lot of wincing from him lately…

The Forge dominate the play for most of the first half, spending the whole time up near the Charleston net, but they don't find another goal. Charleston kicks the ball out of bounds and for some reason, Wes moves to take the throw in. Jay notices this as well and asks, "Why the hell would they have a striker take the throw?"

Wes looks down the line to where his teammates are moving fast, sprinting to get open. He draws the ball back to throw it and it arcs over his head right to the foot of the charging Forge striker, who slams it into the back of the net, dead center. But I'm not looking at the celebration on the field. I'm staring at Wes, crumpled on the grass in pain.

CHAPTER 10
WES

WHEN I MANAGE TO OPEN MY EYES, I SEE MY UNCLE'S FACE A FEW INCHES from mine on the sideline. "Is it your back, son?"

I groan in response, nodding a few times. The training staff makes their way over to me, patting me up and down like they're searching for blood. "Back," I grunt as another spasm rolls over me. Am I seriously hunched on my side in the grass a half hour into my first professional soccer game?

"Can you sit up, Wes?" The trainer, Randy, asks, offering a firm hand and tries to get me upright. I'm blowing air like a woman in labor as white-hot pain burns down the left side of my body. This is just like before when I was out for months with a bulging disc.

The same fucking injury, despite all my training, despite the care I've taken with my muscles. Hell, I even went to a flipping yoga class, and I'm still slumped against my trainer on the grass while an entire stadium whispers to themselves about whether I'm paralyzed.

Randy and Uncle Hawk get me to my feet, and I squeeze my eyes shut, dizzy with the pain. I hear the applause as I hobble to the bench, and I can just make out the announcer calling for a substitution. I've just fucked up the entire strategy Uncle Hawk had going into this match, but I guess I should find some comfort knowing we are at least up 2-0.

I realize they aren't steering me toward the bench at all but taking me down the hall to the training room. "Guys, at least dump me on the bench with the team. Come on."

"Come nothing," Hawk says. "You're worth more to me healthy and you're going to see the doctor."

I growl in response, eventually assuring him I can manage the walk with Randy in support. I know he has to get back out to the pitch. Before we can argue about it, Aunt Lucy appears at my side to help me the rest of the way to the table in the training room.

I collapse onto the table, eyes squeezed shut as the doctor pokes and prods, rubs me with Icy Hot, and hooks me up to electric stimulation for my aching muscles. The trainer quickly sticks a bunch of electrodes to my back and turns on the machine, sending waves of tingling sensation through my body. They drape a heating pad over my back and then, from the sound of things, someone else has blown their knee, so I'm left unattended to wallow in my misery.

"What happened?" I pry an eye open to find Cara Moreno staring into my face, her own etched with concern.

"Back. Probably a disc." I grunt in between pulses from the stim, feeling drowsy after the adrenaline disco my body just experienced. I feel her hand on my forearm, soothing me. I should probably respond in some way but can't get it together and I must start dreaming, because I think I hear my Aunt Lucy talking to Cara.

"Did you walk in here alone?"

"More like ran." Cara whispers, clearly upset. "I was worried about Wes."

"We had a plan in place, Cara. I told you he was going to be here. He's probably on his way into the training room right now for fuck's sake."

Cara's grip on my arm tightens. This must all actually be happening. I hear her mutter an apology, asking if she can please stay with me until the MRI.

"MRI?" I lift my head at that, dislodging the heating pad on my back. Aunt Lucy shifts it back into place.

"Yeah, kid. Healthcare moves faster in the pros." She winks. "You're a hot commodity now. Did you know they're counting the throw-in as an assist?"

That draws a smile and a smaller, happier moan from me. I hear a flurry of voices in the room and Aunt Lucy says, "Well, I have to go. Cara, please stick with Wes, okay? And protest if they ask you to leave unless I come back for you."

The worried masses flock around the other guy with the knee pain and I hear a scrape as Cara drags a folding chair close to the table where I'm beached. "How long until they wheel me into the MRI? Did they say?"

"Dunno. It still blows my mind that Charleston has on-site imaging. You'd be on an ambulance right now if we were back home."

"Maybe I'll add an MRI machine to my contract demands when I renew."

I expect Cara to laugh at my joke. It feels so obvious to me that I'm probably going to be cut from the team once the scan reveals irreparable spinal damage. My parents' words echo through my head as the electrodes pulse into my damaged spine.

I open my eyes when I realize she's not laughing. She's just sitting with me, tracing her fingers up and down my arm like she doesn't know what else to do. Which is fine, because this feels nice. "You're so pretty," I blurt, turning my head to the side and pressing my cheek against the blue vinyl covering the table.

"Well, you're not half bad looking, Stag." Cara grins. I remember that I made huge assumptions and fucked up the opportunity we had to be together. It's entirely my fault she doesn't think I'm 100% good looking. But she's here. That has to mean something.

We're just on the cusp of being friends again … I don't even know if she wants more than that. It's probably just as well, since I doubt she wants to be seen with an unemployed former athlete with no college degree. Maybe I could join her fan club and keep making her lunch.

"Hey." I open my eyes again and her face is so close. If I could manage to lift my head up off the table, I could kiss her. I try it anyway, and my nose collides with her forehead as a ripple of sparks fires down my sciatic nerve.

"Fuck!" I slap the table in pain, more alert now that I've made an ass of myself and further irritated my back.

When I open my eyes again, Cara swallows. I watch the lovely line of her throat moving above the black polo shirt. The letters Hot Metal shimmer across her chest in red foil, a tiny Pittsburgh Women's Soccer embroidered in gold above one boob. "Would you like me to kiss you, Wes? Is that what you were trying to do?"

I snort. "Trying. Failing. Story of my life lately, I guess. Thought I could at least manage to kiss a woman, but nope." I pop the P, lulled into a drunken stupor again by the tens machine and the fumes of the menthol ointment on my back.

"How about this," she rests her hand on my cheek and smiles. Then she leans in and places the world's most chaste kiss to my forehead.

Before I can ask for more, the medical staff announces that it's time to stick me in the MRI tube.

THE PAIN MEDS MAKE ME DROWSY, SO I DON'T REGISTER THAT MY FAMILY HAS filed into my apartment until I hear my mom wail. Her eyes brim with tears … unless that's the light playing tricks on me.

I'm sprawled on my stomach just aware enough to realize I drooled on my pillow. I'm pretty sure I'm naked. I know Uncle Hawk got me a first-class seat for the flight back so I could fully recline with heating pads, but that was peak muscle relaxer effectiveness, and I was super out of it. I guess my uncle got me into my apartment and dumped me into my bed too, but I doubt he'd take off my underwear.

Have I even showered since the game?

"Oh, Wesley." Mom runs a finger through my hair and climbs into the bed with me. "What happened?"

"Uh?" It feels like too much effort to turn my head, so I'm staring at the door when Dad leans through it before crossing his arms and frowning.

"Your aunt made you containers of food and your cousins are out in your kitchen making a chart for who is going to sit here with you, just until you're off the pain meds."

Mom tisks at him and pats my hand. "Thatcher, that's not necessary. I can be here the whole time."

"Emma, you cannot be here around the clock taking care of Wes *and* taking care of you. Remember your book launch?"

I notice Dad doesn't reference Mom's epilepsy, but I'm glad he's making her let my cousins pick up some of the work taking care of me.

Wait.

"I don't need people to take care of me." I find the will to roll onto my back, my arms following along on a few second delay from when my brain tells them to move.

"Is that so?" Dad walks over to my bed and squats on the floor next to it. I focus on the tattoos swirling around his forearms. I should get more tattoos. "When did you last take your meds? When are you due for another dose? When's your follow-up appointment with sports medicine here in Pittsburgh?"

"Thatcher, enough." Mom scolds him while rubbing my shoulder. I hope someone scrubbed me off so she's not getting sweat slime all over her hand, but I smell the menthol ointment on my pillow and know that I'm pretty scuzzy. "Wes, your cousins and I *want* to be here with you. Nobody will get in the way of your routines. We'll just hang out on your couch and use your Wi-Fi and make sure you take your pills."

Dad grunts. "And wipe your ass."

"I don't want anyone to wipe my ass. I definitely do not want my mother to wipe my ass."

Through narrowed eyes, I see my father squinting and rubbing his beard. "Do you think you can wipe your own ass right now?" He sniffs. "When's the last time you tried?"

"Thatch, you're being a lot right now." Uncle Hawk's voice of reason clears the fog in my brain, leaving room for frustration that my parents are bearing down on me like I'm still in preschool. "The team can send home health aides over twice a day until he's got more range of motion. I told the kids to set up a schedule to drive him to P.T., which will be the most important thing for his recovery."

"Health aides? Some untrained doofus earning minimum wage? I don't think so, baby brother. We've got this sorted." My dad's nostrils flare as he shakes his head.

My uncle starts arguing that the Forge pays good money for qualified professionals, and I tune them out as they bicker. I roll toward Mom, who has settled into the bed with her shoulders against my headboard. "Was Dad like this when you had seizures?"

She chuckles. "He used to bring me ham sandwiches. Oh, one time he sent a massage therapist to the house!"

I adjust my posture and wince in pain. "I'd take some of that right now. Better than him threatening to have Odin follow me into the bathroom."

"What if I just stayed over here for tonight? Would that be okay? You're still my baby, Wesley."

"I'm not going to kick you out of my guest room. But that's mostly because I can't stand up right now."

She plants a kiss on top of my head as the Stag family narrates their progress putting a care plan together. "Mom?"

"Yeah, kiddo?"

"Did Uncle Hawk say what the diagnosis was? From the MRI?"

She smiles a wobbly smile. "Herniated disc. Same as last time. Your father and I would like you to consider surgery."

I'm not in the mood to discuss this with my parents. I'm not going under the knife if I can continue to treat my spine with steroids and physical therapy. I know my parents don't want to hear me say I plan to get back on the field as soon as I'm able, so I just let the brain fog settle back in as I close my eyes amidst the din.

That's when I hear a female voice and realize I must be dreaming. Cara laughs nervously and I hear her say, "I should have realized he'd have family here to support him. I'll come back another time."

Except maybe I'm not dreaming, because the mattress shifts as my mother climbs out of the bed. "Goodness, no, dear. How thoughtful of you to come see Wesley and … did you bring him a cheeseburger?"

"Can he eat cheeseburgers?" Dad sniffs audibly, so I do, too. I smell Cara's meatloaf and pry my eyes open again.

"You're actually here?"

She nods and stands in the hall, shifting her weight from foot to foot. She's still dressed in her team polo and team sweats. She must have gone right home from the airport and made me a snack without even stopping to change first. My stomach swoops at the thought of her rushing to help me. I'm pretty sure my face splits into a dopey grin.

For once, the Stag family is silent as they stare at Cara, waiting for her to speak. I hope my entire family isn't out in the living room. It'd be better if just, say, six or seven of my cousins were looming over her at my door rather than the baker's dozen tall, lanky guys in peak concern mode.

Cara swallows and I try to sit up a bit. "I did bring a burger, but it's not actually a burger … well, the patty is but the bun is mostly cheese and egg …" She holds up the clear container and I grin, and for a minute I can't even feel my back hurting. "It's an illusion," Cara continues as my family just blinks at her until Dad clears his throat.

"Emma, why don't we all go down the street for a coffee and finalize the ride schedule like Hawk suggested. Wes can visit with his friend."

It feels strange to hear my father refer to Cara as a friend. The word seems totally inadequate, and yet more than I should be hoping for after how I treated her. We have such a tenuous companionship since I apologized, and I remember how she sat with me in the training room after my injury. It's got to mean something that she drove here with a special treat. Right?

I croak out the word "friend" groggily as Mom leaves my room. I hear murmuring and the sounds of footsteps in the hall, finally the thunk of my heavy door closing, and I sigh audibly. "It feels different when it's just us here," I tell her.

Cara sets the gift on my nightstand and bites her lip. "Nobody told me your prognosis. I've got your phone, though. Here." She sets something on the night stand next to the fake burger. "I gave your bag to Coach Lu—to your aunt."

"Herniated disc," I mumble. "My family will want surgery. I will opt for steroid injections and heavy P.T. If I'm not fired."

"Come on, Wes. They're not going to fire you over this. You had two assists in your professional debut."

"They've let good players go before."

"Your uncle isn't dumb. How long are you out?"

I stare at the ceiling. "Probably six weeks. So … you know … the rest of the season."

"Well, then you'll have the entire off season to really dig in. You'll be a beast by training camp."

I turn to look at her and her smile lights up her whole face. My brain tells my hand to reach out and stroke her hair or cup her cheek, but my arm doesn't listen to me and it just sort of flops around on the bed. Cara frowns at my chest and sniffs. "Have you showered?"

I shake my head. At least I think I do.

"Hm." I wonder if she's thinking of the last time we showered together. I definitely am, and the mental image would have me hard as hell if these pain killers weren't slowing all my reflexes. Or maybe I am hard? Cara leans closer. "I could help you. I think I could."

I love the idea of that, of her naked against me again, soaping up my body while I watch the water bead off her nipples. God, I want that. But I know this isn't the time to make that leap. I want to do things right with Cara. I want to earn her trust back properly. I swallow. "My uncle said home health aides would come for that stuff."

"Oh." She seems disappointed, like I've rejected her. I can't trust anything I say right now.

"I want to watch you shower," I say, and she laughs. Maybe I'm doing okay here? "When I'm not on drugs I want you to help me shower. No.

That's the wrong thing. Someday I want to shower you again, Cara. With your toes."

Cara laughs and I hear the door open again. My family must be back already. Cara rests a hand on my forearm and leans close. "I fly out to Germany in a few days with the national team. I came to tell you I'll be gone for two weeks ..."

"I'll miss having lunch with you."

She laughs and nudges the fake burger so it's within arm's reach. "I expect you to watch the U.S. friendly matches on TV and discuss them with me when I get back."

"If the TV can find them, I'll only watch your butt." I hope I just told her I plan to watch every minute of her matches, even if she's on the bench. I might not have a career much longer. But I do have a woman I find fascinating. "Charge your phone?"

"I already packed my adapter." Cara winks. For a moment I think she's going to lean in and kiss me on the mouth, but my mom appears behind Cara.

"It is just so nice of you to think of Wesley. And to bring him a gift. I'm Emma Stag, his mother. I think I forgot to say that before."

"Cara Moreno." Her face blurs into my mother's red nest of curls in my drug-altered vision. "Wes, I'll see you when I get back, okay?"

I nod. At least this wasn't goodbye. I hope she doesn't realize I'm a limping has-been athlete already and ditch me for someone who can complete a throw-in without breaking his back. I fall asleep to the sound of my parents walking Cara out of my apartment.

CHAPTER 12
CARA

I've probably stared at his text a thousand times since I woke up. It's funny. I was so convinced that a relationship would take my focus away from my game, get in the way of progress. The reality is that I'm somehow sharper knowing Wes is back home rooting for me.

It doesn't make sense. I've always had people rooting for me. Shante and Rosalie and Toni all plan to fly to Paris for the Olympics and have each convinced their local pubs to air today's friendly against Germany.

Not that it was a heavy lift. We play at 4pm, so that means Wes and Shante are watching me at ten in the morning their time. I find it hard to imagine Toni or Rosie will be awake and at a bar for soccer in their time zones.

I wonder if Wes will leave the house to watch the game or sit alone in his apartment, brooding. His injury rattled his family, and I can't help but wonder if that's what has him feeling so hopeless about the whole thing. I've seen athletes overcome much worse, and I know he can get back out there.

I'm lost in these thoughts in the hotel dining room, stirring muesli into my yogurt, when I hear shouting from the coaches' meeting in the conference room. Coach Akemi never loses her cool, but she's shrieking at someone with enough ire to freeze my arm in place.

"… change my coaching roster in the middle of an international tour?"

The response is muffled, and Coach growls. "What happened to total autonomy to select my own staff? This is bullshit."

Coach bursts from the room and down the hall as my team stares after her. All of us had been pretty subdued pre-coffee, but Jay raises her brows at me from across the room. I shrug and then stiffen when I see Lou Rubeo exit the conference room. He looks around the dining room with a fake grin on his face and I slouch to hide myself behind the menu holder on the table.

By the time I straighten my spine, the rest of the Soccer USA staff is filing toward the elevator, silently, looking like we lost our match. I don't like feeling as if the opponent is the president of our organization, rather than the opposing team on the field.

I choke down a few bites of breakfast and decide to retreat to my room before our film session. I guess that's why I come across Coach Lucy in the hall, her tear-stained face red and splotchy as she stabs at the elevator button. "Oh, Cara." She sighs and smiles. "Good luck today. You don't need it, but I know you'll kick ass out there."

I frown. "You won't be there to see it?"

She shakes her head. "Unfortunately, no. But I don't want you to worry about that today, okay?" The elevator arrives and Lucy drops her bag in the door to hold it open. She pulls me in for a hug. "Stick with your team-mates and play like you trained. I will be watching no matter where I am."

She backs into the elevator, picking up her bag, and the door slides shut, leaving me feeling confused and unsettled. I slip into my room and drink a glass of water. I check my phone again, stare at the message from Wes and realize he sent it in the middle of the night. I wonder if he was lying in bed when he did so.

That sends an entirely different set of sensations rioting through my belly, but it shakes me from my funk enough to head back downstairs. The team is gathered in the conference room ready for film, but Coach Akemi hasn't reappeared yet. I slide into a chair near the other midfielders. Sabrina, who plays opposite me, gestures for me to lean in. "They fired Lucy," she says, shaking her head.

"What?? When?"

Sabrina shrugs. "What I heard is Lucy filed some sort of complaint against someone on the office staff, and they responded by sending her home."

"In the middle of our tour? That's insane."

She's about to say something further when Coach Akemi walks into the room and sinks noisily into her seat at the head of the table. "You've all heard by now. We are without a fitness coach until the organization deems fit to provide us with a new one. My choice for this team was dismissed, but she left notes to get you all warmed up and then cooled down after today's match." She looks at a piece of paper in front of her on the table. "Prep swimsuits for after the game. Apparently, we're doing hydrotherapy."

She doesn't field questions, just reaches for the remote and turns on the video of yesterday's scrimmage, stopping every few seconds to zoom in on someone's positioning or compliment our passing. "We feeling good, folks? Ready to kick some German booty today?"

We all cheer a yes, but it lacks the energy we normally build when we're yelling en masse.

Our ride to the stadium is subdued. I can't tell if our warmup is as well or if this is just what it feels like to focus before a national team match. Jay finds me in the locker room and elbows me until I smile for a selfie with us in our jerseys. "This is for the mantle, Moreno. No, we should blow it up huge with a flag and a bald eagle canvas."

"You want me to take a pic of you guys?" Sabrina tugs at her navy shorts and Jay nods. We squeeze one another as we smile for Sabrina and, despite the situation with our coaching staff, the reality sets in. I'm wearing a USA national team jersey. I'm about to take the field for my country in a match against Germany. As long as I don't screw up out there, I will be back here in Europe for the Olympics in less than a year.

My smile is genuine and Jay air drops the picture to me. I send it to Wes, and he responds almost immediately.

WES

Red, white, and blue looks good on you two.

ME

That's my new favorite poem.

WES

Put the phone down and get out there already.

I do as he suggests. I think of him watching as I stand for the national anthem. I think of my friends back home and briefly wonder if my parents are tuned in. I quickly file those thoughts away with my questions about Coach Lucy as *too big for before the game*. And then I'm jumping in place, waiting for the ref to blow the whistle.

"Are you up, Wes? Oh, there you are."

"Shh." I wave a hand at my mom and raise the volume on the television. I don't need the announcer to tell me the German striker is pressuring Cara hard along the sideline, and I forget my mother is in the room when Cara manages to toe the ball back and fire a pass to her teammate. "Hell yeah! Get 'em." I try to rise and cheer, but then I remember that my back is still tender and the reason I'm home watching soccer on a Saturday morning is that I'm not with my own team in Phoenix *playing* soccer this weekend.

"What's this? USA?" Mom sits next to me on the couch and hands me a glass of juice. I see that she's got some pain meds in her other hand, and I frown, keeping my eyes on the television.

"Shh. Soon halftime."

Mom shakes her hand with the meds until I swallow them, and we both stare at the screen. I whoop when a German defender kicks the ball over the back line. "Yes! Corner."

I lean forward, ignoring the sting in my spine as the camera zooms in on Cara. I smile like a fool, watching her spin the ball as she waits for the ref. "Oh. Is that your friend? It is! The girl with the fake cheeseburger."

I ignore my mother as I watch Cara set up her kick. "Come on, come on." She nods her head and takes her shot. It soars up in front of the net and her teammate heads it in like it's nothing. "GOAL!" I stand, fists clenched, cheering, and I look over at my mom, whose face is stretched in a huge grin. The ref blows the whistle for half-time and I mutter a curse that the camera switches away from the on-field celebration. I was hoping to see Cara again, to stare at her beautiful face as she smiled after her assist.

"Anything you want to tell me, son?" Mom gestures at the television and hits mute on the remote as the commercials come fast and furious.

I sink back into the couch, heart racing. I loved watching my girl kick ass out there. And then I freeze, because I just thought of her as *mine* when she's anything but. Cara has so much going for her, so much to lose. She's said a bunch of times that she had to fight her entire family and centuries of the patriarchy just to slip that jersey over her head.

What have I got to offer her? Cases of beef jerky I'm not even supposed to lift for a few more weeks. I swallow. "She's my friend, Mom. We met at the camp in California."

"And now you both play here in Pittsburgh?"

I nod. She hums. "What?" I shouldn't snap at my mother, but I don't want to pull my eyes away from the screen.

"You know our family rules about safe sex, right, Wesley?" She rests a hand on my arm, and I whip my face toward hers quickly, which sends sparks of pain up and down my spine.

"Oh my god, Mom, yes. I know the rules. She comes first. She comes twice. Wrap it up. I know. Ow." I hear a rattling sound as Mom hands me a few pain pills, which I take from her without looking so I can watch Cara adjust her shorts before she takes a free kick. I followed all the rules with her, and I still blew my shot. But I'm working on it.

Mom taps at her chin and frowns. "Have you heard from your uncle today? I wasn't sure if Lucy called him since he's got to keep his head in his own game …"

"I'm on injured reserve and Uncle Hawk is Coach Hawk right now."

"Mm. Well, you should know that Lucy got dismissed from the national team today. In fact, she's on a flight home right now." I turn my head to face my mother, slowly this time, eyes wide. She nods. "Your Uncle Tim is in stiff lawyer mode. It's quite impressive, as always."

I grab the remote from Mom as the game comes back on the screen for the second half. I don't want to blink for fear I'll miss a camera pan on Cara. This time, I focus on her face, trying to assess whether she's reeling from whatever went down with my Aunt Lucy. I wonder how the team will explain the optics of dismissing someone from their coaching staff mid-tour, when they still have two more friendlies to play before they head back to the states.

All I see is a woman focused on her game until Cara is subbed out at the 60-minute mark. I reach for my phone, sending her a quick message I know she won't see for hours.

> Terrific assist. Textbook corner.

And then I worry she will think I'm trying to mansplain her efforts, so I send a series of explanatory follow-up messages.

> Obviously I know you know that.

> I just mean it was great to watch. And I'm happy for you. You looked great out there.

"Wes, enough." I remember my mother is still here in my apartment, eyeing me as I send rapid-fire texts to Cara. Mom grins. "You don't want to overwhelm her, bud."

I swallow and set the phone on the arm of the couch. I blow out a sigh. "You escorting me to PT later? Is that why you're over here today?"

She rubs my leg. "I'm over here because I love you, silly. But yes, it's my turn. I promise I won't try to stay and watch. I have to work on some edits anyway."

"Appreciate that, Mom." I glance at the screen. The US is still up 1-0 with a few minutes to go. I decide I wouldn't mind at all if Cara came with me to PT and watched me bear crawling across the gym and stretching out across the foam rollers. But she's got much bigger and more important things to do than sit around and stare at my recovery process.

I ask Mom about her book, hoping to shift the energy and distract me from my sorry state.

"I'm glad this one's about done." Mom frowns. "I might like to write another one about this situation with your Aunt Lucy. I don't like all the inequities I'm still seeing between the national teams. The men play at a much better time slot for an American audience, don't you think?"

I fudge my way through a conversation, not sure I want my investigative journalist mother delving into misogyny of American soccer when I'm just trying to claw my way back onto the payroll. But then I glance at the screen as the game ends, and I see Cara's face. She should be elated right now. She just claimed the assist for our nation's only goal in her first international match. But her smile is pinched, and her eyes seem hard.

"That sounds like an important book project, Mom."

She smiles and ruffles my hair. "I'm glad you think so, sweetie. You ready to start walking to the car?"

Slowly, with a lot of grumbling and questioning my life choices, I follow my mother to her Volvo.

MY FIRST INTERNATIONAL TOUR WITH THE NATIONAL TEAM ISN'T WHAT I expected at all. I thought I'd feel a surge of pride exploding in my chest as I stood on the field while the national anthem played. I thought I'd wave at the camera and think of all the little girls watching, realizing they can do this someday.

Instead, it's been confusing and fraught. We won our games, but not like we should have done. The ghost of Coach Lucy's dismissal hovered around the bench, the locker room, the field itself. Nobody said as much, but I have to believe this was related to Lou Rubeo and what I confessed to Lucy about how he creeps me out.

I also think about Jay's comment that I am probably not the only woman he treats that way...if he felt bold enough to act like that where anyone could see, he probably worked up to that perceived invincibility gradually.

The long flight home is uncomfortable emotionally and physically, and when we land Jay mumbles that she's going to hire a rideshare back to our apartment rather than take the bus. I'm debating joining her as we head down the escalator to the baggage claim, but then I see a familiar face holding a sign.

Wes Stag stands leaning against a column, wearing a suit and a chauffeur's cap, holding a piece of cardboard with MORENO scribbled in black marker. The sight of him is so totally unexpected, and so welcome after all the travel, that I almost cry. Instead, a laugh bursts from my mouth. I jog down the final stairs to hug him and find myself surrounded by his familiar soapy scent as strongly as I'm circled by his arms. "What are you doing here? I thought you can't drive on your pain meds?"

He hooks a thumb over his shoulder toward a similar-looking man slouched on a bench, playing with his phone. "My cousin Wyatt is actually the driver." Wes shakes the sign. "Thought I'd make myself useful. Via my cousin."

I feel lighter than I did since Germany, when Lucy got sent away and Coach Akemi started shouting. Another laugh floats out of my parched throat and I hug him again, gently so I don't jostle his back. "This is such a nice surprise. Thank you." I glance at Jay, who has descended the escalator with a wide-eyed stare. "Do you have room in the car for one more?"

"I've got room for five more." Wes laughs. "We took our uncle's minivan since I didn't know how much stuff you had."

"More like you didn't trust me to drive your Jeep and I don't have a car."

"Anyway ..." Wes waves at Jay. "We've got room for your goalkeeper. Jay, you want a ride home?"

She nods and jostles her way toward the clump of passengers waiting for bags.

"I'm Wyatt, by the way." Wes's cousin extends his hand. "I heard about you rolling by with fake burgers, but I was at a tournament in San Diego."

"Cara Moreno. And playing in Cali is marvelous in autumn. Good for you!" A red light begins flashing above the baggage carousel and Wes moves like he's going to grab my luggage for me.

Wyatt claps a hand on his shoulder. "Not this time, cuz. Nothing heavier than a milk jug, remember?"

He sighs and shakes his head. "This fucking sucks."

I rub his arm. "I'm really sorry. You'll have to catch me up on what the PT said since I talked to you last. Was that when I was in Spain?"

"Look at you, playing so much international soccer you can't even remember where you've been." I suspect he's trying to avoid the subject, but I know I can get him to talk later. I'm surprised by how good it feels to anticipate talking to him alone.

Wes makes Wyatt pull Jay's and my bags as we wheel our way to an ancient minivan in short-term parking. "Shotgun," Jay shouts, and climbs up front, where she wedges her travel pillow against the window and falls immediately to sleep.

I smile at Wes in the captain's chair across the small aisle from me. "It's a little like that flight to Cali," he says, referring to the day we met, when the flight attendant was hitting on him during her safety spiel.

"Mmm." I yawn. "Except nobody in this vehicle is going to offer to blow your tube."

"That's going to be enough of that," Wyatt scolds from the front seat. He blasts heavy metal from the stereo and merges onto the highway, scowling. I know if I fall asleep now it will mess up my chances to get back on eastern time, so I force myself to stay awake on the ride home.

It helps that Jay knees the power button on the stereo and shuts off the music. She and Wyatt bicker about appropriate decibel levels until Wes suggests he turn this car around.

Jay flips both of them off. "Cara, don't get me wrong. I'm happy to save fifty bucks on this ride home. But your reindeer are driving me nuts."

"Reindeer?" Wyatt arches a brow and catches my eye in the rear-view mirror.

"That's what Jay calls the Stag family when she's feeling feisty."

"So, always, then," Wes deadpans, extracting bottles of water and granola bars from a pouch behind the driver's seat.

"Whose car is this again? These are delicious." Jay tears into her bar and I just nod in approval.

Wyatt explains, "My Uncle Ty retired from hockey to be a full-time dad." He shrugs. "All four of his kids are in college now, but he still stocks his dad wagon like he's hauling our entire crew to the playground."

The Bluetooth in the van picks up an incoming call on Wyatt's phone and we all listen to the robotic voice chant, "Incoming call from Unknown Number," before Wyatt growls and stabs the button to decline the call, which puts the heavy metal music back on until Jay growls and turns the music off entirely.

Jay guzzles her water and tosses all her trash into a tiny wastebasket in between the front seats. "I'm going back to sleep. Do not put that screaming music back on." She punches her pillow and closes her eyes again.

"So." Wes turns to face me, winces, and sets his spine in line again, facing forward while awkwardly trying to talk to me beside him. "You guys had a clean sweep."

I nod. "Yeah, Coach is pleased. We won't get a chance to train together for a few more weeks. And then we have a tournament in March ..."

"And then Paris." Wes grins.

"So freaking cool, Cara." Wyatt drums his hands on the steering wheel as he waits to merge into the Fort Pitt Tunnel. I haven't lived here long enough for this view to get old, the way the city reveals itself in golden sparkles as we drive through the tunnel.

I press my face to the window as we drive over three rivers in quick succession before the view fades into the highway embankments and over-passes. "Sorry. What was that?"

Wes is smiling again and shakes his head. "I was just saying you shouldn't let it go to your head, but I see you're still a Pittsburgh girl at heart."

"Our building is just up there." I point for Wyatt as he enters our apartment complex, and then I poke Jay in the shoulder to wake her up. "Thank you both so much for the ride home. Talk to you soon?"

I raise my brows at Wes, who furrows his and shakes his head. "I'll walk you up, if that's okay."

"Of course. It won't bother your back?"

"Nah. You've got an elevator, right?" Jay and I hoist our bags from the back of the van, and I notice Wes leaning through the window of the mini-van. Wyatt waves and drives off. Wes slides his hands in his pockets. He's ditched the cap and jacket, loosened the tie, and has his shirt sleeves rolled up. The transformation has my heart racing. "Wyatt had an errand to run. He'll come back for me in a bit." He holds a hand up. "If I'm in the way I'll just wait for him outside. No pressure to host me."

"Don't be silly. Come on." I feel a strange second wind setting in and I think about the melatonin I bought in case I wanted help with the jet lag.

Jay slumps against the wall in the elevator, moving around with her eyes closed when we approach our floor. "I'm beat. I don't even have the energy to make jokes about you, Stag."

I pat her on the arm, still feeling alert myself. Probably because Wes is here… "Night, Jay." She waves and slams the door to her room, leaving her bag propped against the wall in the hall.

I chuckle and rest my own bag beside hers. We have a washer and dryer in the apartment and I'm sure our gear will be standing on its own by morning, but even if I'm too wired to sleep, I don't feel like doing laundry. "You want some water? I don't know if we have anything else."

"Water is great." Wes slowly lowers himself into the couch and I make my way over to him with two plastic Hot Metal souvenir cups of tap water. He holds his up to toast. "To Team USA."

"Salud." I smile as I drink. I feel at ease with him, like a piece of myself is missing when we're apart and I can be a whole person. Which is strange because I haven't known him long. I decide it's probably because we've already been intimate. Then I flush, remembering how he put my toes in his mouth …

He clears his throat. "So, my family is in kind of an uproar. My aunt wasn't supposed to come home."

I set my cup on the table and let my head flop back on the couch. Wes angles his body toward mine, gingerly. "Wes, I just know it's about Lou Rubeo. I told her, you know … how he made me uncomfortable and invaded my personal space."

"Cara, he touched you without permission. Not just a handshake type thing. That's harassment."

I close my eyes. "I know. And Lucy knows, and I'm sure she said something to someone … and look where that got her."

"You know my uncle's law firm represents the interests of the Forge and the Hot Metal. Lucy won't take this lying down. She has an army of angry lawyers making a battle plan."

"Lawyers?" The word makes me shiver. Lawyers were always synonymous with austerity in my family. My parents got along just well enough to be civil to one another after they divorced, but not without footing extensive legal bills. I remember having to go to court, talking to judges about my living arrangements. It was terrible as a child. It feels even more daunting now, when all I want to do is play soccer.

"Yeah, Cara. Lawyers. Harassment is illegal. You have a right to feel safe at work." I swallow, unable to verbalize how those words impact me. I don't know if I feel unsafe per se. But I sure am distracted from my game whenever I know that man is anywhere nearby.

"I was just hoping Lucy would find some sort of solution where …"

"Where what? Someone would scold him, and he'd admit wrongdoing and knock it off?" Wes's eyes are wide with disbelief.

I sit up. "Yes. That is what I hoped would happen."

He scoffs. "Fat chance of that. If a guy like that has to be told not to treat colleagues that way, I don't think he's going to receive the message. Not really."

My body starts shivering. I'm not sure if it's the jet lag finally catching up to me or the weight of Wes's words. I reach for the water again, and my hand shakes so much the water sloshes onto my lap. "Here." Wes steadies my hand, guides it to my mouth so I can take a sip. "Are you okay? What can I do?"

I breathe in the scent of him. He smells faintly of menthol ointment. I've never seen him in dress clothes before and I take a moment to settle myself, staring at his forearm where it rests on my leg. I love the look of his dark arm hair over his pale skin, the green veins just visible beneath his powerful muscles. I lower my hand onto his. "I could really use a distraction right now, Wes…"

I lean toward him, ready for a kiss. I can see his chest rise and fall a few times before I close my eyes and then … nothing. He doesn't close the distance between us.

I open my eyes to see his boring into me, dark and sincere. He tips my chin up so our faces are level. I feel his breath whisper against my skin as he says, "You could never just be a distraction to me, Cara."

"Wes." My voice is a whisper. I don't know what to make of this, of my attraction to him paired with his rejection of my physical advances.

He runs a finger through my hair and my body leans toward his touch. "You're exhausted and overwhelmed right now. When you kiss me again, I want it to be because you can't stand not kissing me." He swallows and I watch his throat work, remembering how it felt to lick along those cords of tendon. "We both have a lot going on right now. Huge, uphill battles to fight. I don't want to rush into anything physical and skip past the emotional stuff."

I breathe a few times, half in his arms, half arched away in rejection. I don't know what to say, how to tell him I feel a throbbing ache only he can calm … but also, he's probably right that I'm just looking to distract myself rather than really enjoy Wes Stag for all that he is.

"How about a hug?" His face is hopeful, and he twists slowly, gently to face me, opening his arms awkwardly.

I nod and sink against him, feeling him pull me tight, like I'm precious to him, like I'm the only thing that matters. Like I'm not some evil person who invites unwanted attention from Rubeo-type-men. Wes holds me and rubs my back and runs his fingers through my hair until I must fall asleep. When I wake up in the dark, I'm alone on the couch, but someone has tucked me under the comforter from my bed, a full glass of water beside me on the coffee table, my phone plugged in to charge beside my head.

I SWEAR, PHYSICAL THERAPY AT THE SPORTS MEDICINE CENTER IS JUST AS HARD as training at the stadium. My therapist, Savage Sofiya, is a homicidal maniac, insisting I can lift more, stretch farther, and move faster than my body tells me. I show up every day, sometimes twice, and work until my muscles burn. I work until I barely think about Cara asking me to distract her and my dumb ass saying no. I know offering her a hug was the right thing to do, but that doesn't make me want her less.

Days out from holding her until she fell asleep, I'm drenched in sweat, chugging water, and fighting to concentrate as Sofiya growls at me to give her five more kilometers on the rowing machine, this time with resistance. "Are you serious? Haven't I been here for two hours already?"

"Is two hours too much for you? Should I call your coach?" Sofiya taps at her watch, and I growl, moping back to the sweaty machine with a sigh. By the time I'm done, I feel like an overcooked noodle, but I'm not allowed to stretch out and stick to the floor. Sofiya orders me over to the mats to stretch and cool down.

I comply, too tired to argue, until Sofiya blows a whistle and starts applauding. "Everyone! Wes just touched his toes! Look at that spine flexion!" The room bursts into applause and I realize I am indeed bent all the way over, fingertips on my sneakers.

"Huh." I hold the position a bit longer until I hear a familiar voice cheering louder than the others.

"You got this, Stag!" I look between my legs to see an upside-down Cara pumping her fist and cheering for me like I just scored a goal for the

Forge. She puts two fingers in her mouth and whistles, and I didn't know she could do that. I straighten up, worried the sight of her will turn me on so fast I'll tent my shorts.

Sofiya pats my shoulder. "See you tomorrow, dude. Lots of water tonight."

"Yeah, yeah. Thank you," I add, backing toward the door and Cara, who grins and gives me two thumbs up. "You're here? I mean … I wasn't expecting you." I rake a hand through my sweaty hair. "I'm glad to see you."

"Glad to see me awake, you mean?" Cara laughs. "Wyatt reached out because I guess Jay left her headphones in the minivan. Yada, yada, I told him I'd bring you home today."

I grin, feeling my energy return at this news. Is it ridiculous that I'm excited she came to give me a ride home from physical therapy? I should be embarrassed by how excited everyone here is that I touched my freaking toes. But considering a few days ago it hurt to twist side-wise in a conversation, I guess I should let myself feel proud of this milestone.

"You ready?" Cara twirls her keys around one finger. "Although, if you're rowing and touching toes now, does this mean you can drive again?"

I shrug and refill my water bottle at the fountain, reaching for my phone and house keys from the little cubby where I stash my stuff during PT. "I stopped taking the narcotic pain relievers days ago, so probably. I see the doc again tomorrow afternoon." Cara falls in step beside me on the walk through the massive building. There are full-size athletic fields inside and most of the professional sports teams in Pittsburgh use the facility for medical support.

I'm overcome with an urge to wrap my arm around Cara, pull her close against my side as we walk. I resist it, though, because I don't want to send her mixed messages after I turned her down for a kiss in her apart-ment the other night. But I also don't want to just climb in her car and have her drop me off right away. I squint into the bright sky as we push open the doors to the parking lot. The facility is located along the river, and a bike path meanders by. I scratch the back of my neck and ask, "do you want to go for a walk or something? Are you free?"

She smiles and nods. "Sounds nice."

I gesture toward the trail as a cyclist breezes past. "You know, this goes all the way to D.C."

Her brows lift. "Seriously? How far is that?"

I shrug. "Dunno. Maybe a few hundred miles? I think my Uncle Ty and Aunt Juniper rode their bikes on it once, though. Took a few days."

"I bet that's gorgeous this time of year."

All around us, the trees are bright yellow, dropping oblong leaves that crunch under our sneakers. It is beautiful, but not like her. "You're gorgeous," I blurt, regretting my lack of filter. "I mean—"

She touches my arm. "Thank you, Wes. You're not bad looking. Especially all bent over to touch your hairy toes."

I nudge her with my shoulder, enjoying the fact that it doesn't hurt for me to do so. "Hey, about the other night … I just wanted to tell you, I'm not *opposed* to kissing you. You know that, right?"

Her cheeks flush, and I like that look even more than the sight of her here among the yellow leaves. "I guess I know that." She runs her hands through her ponytail and looks at me sideways. "It'd be easier if we just banged it out and ignored all the other stuff, though."

"Ha. Maybe." I rub my back. "Hey, can we sit? I don't want to overdo it."

"Of course!" Cara rushes to the side of the trail and brushes dried leaves and twigs from a bench overlooking the rusty old steel mills. "You all right?"

I nod. "Yeah. Just got tired all of a sudden." I stretch an arm along the back of the bench, and she leans into it. We watch a barge chug up the river. "Do you want to talk about any of the stuff with the national team? Have you seen Aunt Lucy since you got back?"

Cara sighs and slouches against the bench. "I really don't like talking about it. But I will if you want to." She presses her lips together. "Practice with the Hot Metal has been fine the past few days. But I haven't talked to Lucy alone, no. Maybe I'm avoiding her?"

I let the hand stretched along the bench rest on her shoulder and give her a squeeze. "It's all just so gross. I hate when people make other people feel small. Or powerless. I feel really powerless right now with this stupid injury and that's not anything near the same scale as what you're dealing with."

"What do you mean? You can't even play right now."

"Yeah, but I'm not ever—for any amount of time—worried someone sees me as anything other than an athlete." My eyes bore into her, and I think again of Lou Rubeo touching her, thinking he has the right to her body. If he walked by in this moment, I worry I'd strangle him. To me, Cara is power and grit personified, and I got the biggest rush of my life when she invited me to touch her, when she chose to be intimate with me.

Knowing some man is out there trying to take that choice from her fills me with blinding rage. I stuff that back down, though, because she doesn't need my ranting and raving.

We sit in silence for a few minutes and then head back to her car. She cranks up some pop music and drums on the steering wheel as she heads west. "Oh, hey." She glances over at me, and my breath catches again at the sight of her golden skin in the sunlight, brown eyes smiling brightly. "Are you up for yoga again this weekend? We have a bye …"

"I'd love that. Man, what have I become? A guy who likes yoga."

"It's good for us."

"Yeah, yeah. But yes—maybe I can even drive us."

CHAPTER 16
WES

It turns out I am indeed cleared to drive, and I celebrate this independence by hauling my carcass to PT for early sessions so I can still watch film and sit in on strategy talks with the Forge.

My uncle acknowledges my presence in the room with a tip of his chin and continues explaining a new formation he wants to try in our playoff match against Detroit. Unless this turns out to be a miracle strategy, this will probably be the last game of the season. I'm actually glad I made plans to go to yoga with Cara during it, because I need the distraction from all the emotions it brings up knowing my first pro season was such a glorious disaster.

"We'll miss you out there, buddy." One of the other strikers, Alejo, holds a hand out for a shake.

I give him a small smile in return. "Wish I could be with you guys. Man, it was brutal watching that game against Richmond. You were a beast."

Alejo pretends to brush dirt off his shoulder and we both laugh. "I'll see you around."

I spend the rest of my night wondering if it's too pushy for me to call Cara. I'm utterly distracted, wishing I could be with her for all my meals, wanting to text her during all the long pauses where I don't have any other human interaction. Maybe it was a mistake to live alone … especially when I'm so used to my family surrounding me at all hours.

Or maybe I'm totally smitten by Cara Moreno and letting it get in the way of my mental recovery work.

Whichever it is, I'm super early to pick her up in the morning and my mood immediately lightens when she climbs in my car smelling like clean cotton, wearing bright blue leggings and a fitted workout tank that hugs her taut abdomen.

I spend the entire drive to the studio wondering why exactly I turned her down for hot sex, especially knowing how explosive we are together.

"This might be the last time we get to hang out for a bit." Cara talks around a hair tie between her teeth as she works all her dark waves into a ponytail.

"I'll bite. Why's that?" The Hot Metal are also in playoffs, but I don't get the sense anyone expects them to advance much into October. The Forge are about to wrap up. I sort of thought we'd both have even more time on our hands.

"I overheard Lucy and your coach talking about you."

"You were eavesdropping?" I tease her, but I love that she was nosing around, interested in me. I love that I'm in her thoughts like she invaded mine all last night.

Cara pats her hair and smiles. "I think the medical team might clear you for off-season training."

"Ah, but that assumes the off-season starts tomorrow. Are you saying you don't have faith in the Forge today?"

"Without you? Not a chance."

I spend the entire rest of the drive glowing from her praise, but trying to be cool so Cara doesn't see how much her words affect me.

We bend and stretch our way through the class side by side, and my back doesn't bother me once. It's stunning how a few weeks of powerful muscle relaxants and intense physical therapy have me almost back to fighting shape.

It's even more incredible that we're in a room with what appears to be half the professional hockey team, and Cara hasn't even sent a lingering glance toward any of the beefy men surrounding her in Yoga for Athletes. I know because I've spent all my calming breaths watching her. She is, of course, focused on her breathing, and keeps her eyes on her own toes.

Cara has short-term goals she needs to achieve, an arc she has to complete this year with the national team. I remind myself that I'm a diversion for her. She said as much the other night. I blow out a breath, glad I said we should take things slow. Both of us have a lot on the line.

At the end of class, Cara seems totally blissed out in corpse pose and I feel like I have ants in my shorts, so I duck out of the room early to get a drink and wait for her where I won't disturb anyone. I check my phone and sure enough, I have a voicemail from the Forge team doctor.

"Wesley, Dr. Dansey, Forge Football Association. I reviewed your case with your physical therapist, read your files, and looked over your most recent images. I'm happy to clear you to return to off-season workouts with the team starting in two weeks, barring any spectacular on-field episodes today. Any questions, you know how to reach me."

I like how he ends the call without a sign-off. I aspire for that level of efficiency someday, like my Uncle Tim. Just brusquely offering the most important bits of information and saving any other niceties for his family.

And Cara. I'd be nice to her regardless of anything else happening in my life. The thought warms me, and I finally see her emerge from the studio, smiling and walking slowly, like she's drunk on endorphins.

"Hey." She drags out the vowel sound, gliding toward me in her bare feet as I fish both of our sandals from the cubby we shared when we arrived.

"You were right about your gossip." I show her the phone screen with the automated transcript of the voicemail. "I'm back to work."

I can't rein in the grin that splits my face, but I almost fall over when Cara squeals and places her hands on my shoulders, stretching up to kiss my cheek. I feel the warm echo of her lips on my skin as she dances and claps. "Wes! That's fantastic. I'm so happy for you."

I rest a palm to the place where she kissed me, smiling so hard I wonder if my face will crack. "Can I take you out? To celebrate?"

Cara turns her head, brow arched mischievously. "You mean like a date? Because I have to tell you, Wesley Stag, I'm going to expect a good-night kiss at the end of a date."

I lean against the wall with one arm raised, my best grin flashing all my teeth at her. "Oh, it's absolutely a date, Cara."

"Jay, how are her feet looking? Don't lie to us." Shante shouts from the video chat in my bathroom as I get ready for my date. By which I mean styling my hair and trying to locate some makeup that isn't crusty or expired.

Jay pokes her head in the door. "She's wearing socks, chicas. But I'm guessing they're pretty rough."

"He's not going to see my feet." I shout this around a mouth full of hair pins as I try to tame my mop into an up do. I give up and decide to comb it instead, since I never wear it down and it's looking nice and shiny today.

"We just want you to be ready, querida." Rosalie waggles her eyebrows. "It's been a minute for you, right?"

I glare into the camera and my friends laugh. "Do I criticize your grooming choices from afar? No. I do not. Shante, were your feet supple and smooth when you went out with that person from the finance department?"

Toni cackles.

Shante wags a finger at me. "My feet were perfect, as always." She rocks back in her chair and wiggles her toes at the camera. "I'm telling you, since I stopped playing footy, I can play footsie instead. My finance sweetie approves."

I frown at her as I yank a comb through my hair one final time. "They saw your toes on your first date?"

Toni clears her throat. "This isn't exactly your first date with Wes, though."

Jay, who apparently stayed in the bathroom for the conversation, grunts. "Those two hang out all the time. And I like it because it involves free food for me, and sometimes rides from the airport." I stare at her. She shrugs. "He seems really into you, Cara."

Toni, Rosalie, and Shante collectively sigh so hard I think heart emojis might shoot out of my phone.

I bite my lip. "I don't know if I'm ready for *really into me*, though. I'm dealing with…" I flip my hands around in the air in what I hope is an all-encompassing gesture. "And, you know, I'm training for the Olympics."

"Yeah you are, chica!" Toni blows me a kiss and I smile.

"Look, I don't want anyone to suck on my toes today. But I wouldn't mind a little tonsil hockey."

"Gross." Jay throws a clementine peel at me. "Please don't call it that."

There's a knock at the door and my friends unleash a series of giggles and whoops. "I'm hanging up. I still have to finish in here." I end the call before they can protest, hurrying to swipe gray shadow on my eyelids. "Can you let him in and tell him I'll be out in a minute?"

Jay rolls her eyes and heads toward the front door. I hear her whistle, followed by muffled voices as I dab mascara on my lashes, and I finally locate a tube of lip gloss that seems like it's in good shape. Some of my teammates wear a full face of makeup if they know a match is going to be televised. Me? I have to beg and borrow supplies when my name gets called for a press conference. But I want to feel special tonight, so I take some extra time emphasizing my features. I step back from the mirror and smooth my hands down my dark jeans.

I found a loose-fitting hunter green sweater that hangs off one shoulder and I managed to cram my bulging pro-soccer calves into a pair of brown leather boots that stop just below the knee. I have no idea where Wes is taking me on short notice, but I figure this outfit will work unless it's someplace really fancy. I hope it's not someplace swanky.

I step into the hall and Wes stops his conversation with Jay at the sound of my shoes on the floor. I smile, watching his eyes widen at the sight of me. He looks pretty damn good himself in a ribbed turtleneck and black jeans. "Hey." He grins but his eyes dart over to Jay and he hesitates. "You ready to head out?"

"Be safe, you two." Jay laughs at her own joke as she grabs her keys and a puffy vest. "I'm going to a movie with the strikers. I'll be late on purpose." She winks and leaves as I shift my weight.

Wes walks toward me, and he smells delicious. I sense a subtle cologne or maybe aftershave. "Cara, you're gorgeous." He reaches out a hand to touch me, like he can't help himself, and I lean my head into his palm.

"Thank you. You look nice, too."

He tips his head toward the door. "Come on. I have a surprise for you."

"Shouldn't I be surprising you?" I lock up and follow him down the hall toward the stairs. "You're the one with the big news this week."

Wes drapes an arm around my shoulder as we walk toward his car. "Just let me show you the surprise."

We drive a few blocks, over a bridge, and head up toward Wes's neighborhood. The Allegheny river is beautiful in the dark, with all the city lights reflecting off the water. Wes parks outside a brick building that looks like it once housed a factory of some kind.

He rushes out of the car to open my door and extends a hand toward me as I climb out of the car. "Okay, so, this place isn't open yet."

"Then why are we here?" I frown, looking at a few windows where light shines from inside.

Wes shakes his head. "I mean it's not open to the public. My aunt—the chef—hooked me up with the owner when I said I needed to find a place I could take you that would fit with your meal plan for the national team."

"Wes, that sounds like a lot of hassle. I thought we'd be—"

He holds up a hand as we approach the door. "Turns out the owner of this place is a huge football fan. Moved here from Spain. She couldn't wait to bring us in to test things out with her staff and her menu and whatnot."

Wes tugs the door open to reveal a space under construction. I can see exposed brick walls and shining floors, but he guides me toward a set of stairs. We make our way up a few flights, and he pushes open a door to the rooftop. I gasp at the beautiful, intimate space.

Cushioned benches are arranged to look over the river, with a low table set with candles. There's room up here for a few tables, but it seems tonight it's just us up here. Strings of fairy lights ring the balcony, and a fire crackles in a low grate.

Wes lifts my hand and kisses my knuckles, his lips warm against my cool skin. "Do you like it?"

"I love it." My voice is a whisper and I let him guide me toward the bench, where he snuggles up close to me. The fire warms us from behind and I look around, enjoying the muffled sounds of the cars on the roads below. It all feels so far away while Wes is so close, like the two of us are nestled in a secret perch.

I hear the door open and turn my head to see a server dressed in black, carrying a tray. "Good evening, Ms. Moreno, Mr. Stag. Chef sends some water infused with rosemary and ginger for you to enjoy while you look over tonight's menu."

He hands me a dainty glass with a sprig of herbs garnishing the cool liquid. The menu is hand written on card stock and I gasp again when I see the list of courses. Everything from the almond crusted zucchini appetizer to the tarragon chicken to the yuzu tart dessert fits easily into my food parameters. But unlike the bland chicken and veggies Jay and I subsist on most of the time, this meal promises to burst with flavor and texture.

"Wes. This is incredible." I take a big gulp of my water, overcome with excitement for a restaurant meal I'm actually able to enjoy.

"You're pretty incredible, Cara. I'm not just saying that."

My cheeks heat and not from the fire.

The server returns with the appetizer and asks if we're interested in anything else to drink. I bite my lip. "I'd love a glass of red wine with the main course if you could recommend something?"

He smiles and nods. "Yes, indeed. I recommend the tempranillo with tonight's flavor profile. For you, sir?"

"I'll have the same, please. And maybe a pitcher of this water in the meantime?"

Wes offers me the plate of nutty zucchini discs, and I pinch one with my fingers, seeing no silverware yet. "Oh god, this is amazing." We both chew and moan about the delicious veggies until the plate is clear.

At some point, our server comes to clear the appetizer and delivers soup and salad so quietly I barely notice. Wes adjusts his posture, I assume to accommodate his sore back, and I miss the closeness of his body even if it's easier to eat as we're seated more upright.

"I wanted to really go big this first date since I'm not going to see much of you for a bit." Wes winks as he spears asparagus wrapped in cured meat.

"Well, I'd say you hit the back of the net. Mmm." I snag the final roasted pepper from our salad plate and take a quick bite. "But not gonna lie, I'm really excited for Palo Alto. If we beat Jamaica we'll be in amazing shape for the group stage."

He listens while I rattle on about each country's prospects at the Olympics, and at some point, he starts rubbing my hand with his thumb as I talk. It feels so natural, this physical connection but also spending time with him in this romantic setting. I don't have a flutter of nerves, perhaps because we've already seen each other naked.

But I did expect at least a little unease. Instead, I just bask in the glow of him, his warm smile, this entire thoughtful experience.

He clears his throat and rests his hand flat on top of mine, asking, "Who did Coach Akemi name to replace Aunt Lucy?"

And there's the ball of lead hitting me in the stomach. "Not sure who it is. Some guy from Texas, I think? He emails all the workout plans and such. We'll meet him at the camp."

"Surprises me that she picked a dude. Isn't everyone else on the staff female?"

I smile. "Yeah, Coach Akemi is big on women leading women. Well…" I think about Coach Bev, from the men's team. "I guess she's just big on women in leadership positions."

Wes grunts. "Would be great if she had more sway in the national team office."

I groan. "I wonder if we win a gold medal if that will give her more pull? Akemi was so, so angry when they fired Lucy without her input."

Wes sits back in his chair and looks at me intently, considering. "Have you told anyone about what happened? Other than my aunt?"

I shake my head. "I keep hoping that was the end of things, that he knows she knows and will maybe watch his step or something." I adjust my posture and drink some water. "We have a new rule that Coach Akemi kept up even after Lucy left—we always travel with a buddy in the stadium. It's been good for a lot of reasons, actually. The press sometimes sneaks in and tries to catch players off-guard with questions we're not supposed to answer."

"They do that sometimes with us, too." Wes's eyes shift toward the door, and I smell the savory warmth of our main course.

Our server sets down our chicken and a glass of wine for each of us. "Buen provecho," he says with a bow.

"Gracias por todo," I respond and the server winks at me before backing down the stairs, leaving us alone with our drinks and our meal.

"It's pretty hot that you speak another language." Wes nods his head in approval. "Americans really suck at that kind of thing."

"I am American." I nudge him with my boot, and he concedes my point with a wince.

"Sorry. I just did that thing where I forget that we don't have a national language or universal heritage."

"Mmm hmm." I grin at him. "Te salva que eres bello."

He lifts my hand and kisses my knuckles again. "What does that mean?"

I wink. "I basically said it's a good thing you're hot."

"I'll take it."

WES RAISES HIS GLASS AND I CLINK MINE AGAINST HIM, SAVORING THE TASTE OF the wine. One glass should be fine with my meal plan, especially considering everything else here is on the list of "knock yourself out" foods.

I don't want this date to end. Between the food and the spicy wine and the ambiance, it feels like some sort of fairytale. Plus, Wes has been staring at me intently for hours now and I could melt under the heat of his gaze.

"I want to do better with you, Cara. I want to be a better friend and listen more, and I want to be here cheering for you as you crush it with the national team."

The smile splitting my face might strain my face muscles if I'm not careful. "You are a good friend, Wes. Thank you." I rub at his leg with my foot, gently this time, and his promise of a goodnight kiss starts to feel really inadequate for what I'd like to do with him right now.

Wes scoots back around the bench so he's sitting right next to me again, our cleaned plates off to the side. I remember that we haven't yet had dessert, and just as Wes slides an arm around my shoulder, our server reappears with a tart and two spoons. "Here you are, sir, madam. And you can take all the time that you need." He ducks away before I can thank him, and I turn my head back to Wes to see him aiming a spoonful of yellow custard at my mouth.

He tilts a head in question, and I open my lips. Wes slides the quivering spoon of tangy citrus into my mouth, and I nearly die of bliss right there on the rooftop. "I've heard you make those sounds before," he whispers.

I'm sure my pupils have dilated fully by now. "Doesn't even compare.

You have to try this." He opens his mouth like a baby bird, and I swat at his chest, but I don't want to deprive him of this delicacy, so I spoon some custard up for Wes and feed it to him, gently.

"Oh shit." His face brightens as he works through the seven stages of ecstasy involved in this dessert. I balance the plate on his long thigh and the two of us press close together, sharing an orgasmic flavor experience that's heightened by my desire for him. Based on the size of his pupils and the ragged breaths he draws whenever I press on his leg for leverage as I scoop up yuzu, Wes feels the same level of barely contained lust.

"Take me home." I place the spoon back on the empty plate with a clang. Wes nods and springs to his feet, tugging my hand and guiding me down the door.

The white-clad woman at the foot of the stairs must be his aunt's friend, the chef who created our feast. She speaks with a heavy accent as she asks us how we enjoyed our meal. I beam at her. "Muchas gracias. La cena estuvo deliciosa."

Wes, standing behind me, pinches my butt and I jump. "What she said. Gracias. Truly."

Chef winks at me and I yelp as Wes hauls me out to the car.

His hand splays across my thigh as he drives back to my apartment, and I feel the heat radiating from his body as we finally climb the steps to my door. When Wes finally presses my back against the door and leans his body against mine, my knees threaten to buckle. "Cara, I can't get you out of my head." His voice is ragged, almost pained.

"I don't want you to," I whisper. And it's true. Above all the stress and the intensity of work, I have Wes Stag as a comforting, sexy blanket. He makes me laugh. He takes me for fancy food. And he'd better kiss me, or I will actually burst.

His face hovers an inch from mine until he grabs my face with both hands, pulling my mouth against his.

I moan, sliding my tongue into his mouth, the taste of him familiar and fascinating. Deep sounds of pleasure rumble from Wesley's chest and his hands move to my back, my butt. I rock my hips against his as he nibbles my lower lip, feeling the thick bulge inside his pants and loving that I put it there.

I let my head tilt back against the door as Wes sucks on my neck and licks his way from my throat back up to my mouth. "I want you." My voice is so assertive when I meant for it to sound sexy. And maybe it does, because he growls and pulls his head back so he can meet my eye.

"Are you desperate for me, Cara?" I nod and he thrusts his hips against mine, pushing me back against the door with delicious pressure. He grazes a knuckle down my chest, not quite touching my nipple through the layers of sweater and my bra. I whimper at the tease. "I could make you come on my hand right here in the hall. Would you like that?"

Another nod and I lunge my mouth toward his, our teeth knocking together with the force of my kiss. I groan as Wes's long fingers crawl along the hem of my sweater, finding their way inside and into the waist of my jeans. "Yes," I breathe, letting my own hands trail along his chest. His body is firm and his heart thunders beneath my palms. I tilt my hips as his finger makes its way inside my panties.

"Oh, fuck, Cara, you do want this, don't you?" I whimper as he traces the needy bundle of nerves, not yet applying the pressure he knows I need.

"Let's go inside." I reach behind me for the door, fumbling for the knob, forgetting that I have the keys in my clutch that I seem to have dropped on the floor.

Wes rests his forehead against mine and presses harder against my clit. I forget what I was just asking him, what I needed. Nothing exists apart from that exploring digit and the heat of him holding me up. "Let me see, Cara. Come for me. Show me."

My mouth falls open, but no sound emerges. We stare into each other's eyes and my hands freeze with his shirt bunched in my fists. Wes circles and presses, his long fingers sliding along my seam as his thumb presses firmly against my clit. "So wet," he whispers. "So slippery for me."

I nod my head and feel a burst of energy erupt behind my belly button. The ball of pleasure rolls toward my center, throbbing and pulsing until it ripples through my entire body. Gasping and rocking, moaning and shivering, I come on Wes Stag's hand just like he asked.

He cups my sex until the waves subside and then slides his hand from my jeans as my breathing slows. I stare at him through half-closed eyes as Wes lifts the finger that had just been inside me, to his kiss-swollen lips. He sucks his finger, and my hands drop to my sides as he growls. "Delicious."

"Wes."

"I love hearing you say my name. Have I told you that before?" I shake my head. "Well, I love it." He bends toward me, kissing me gently. I see and feel his bulge inside his jeans, and I extend a hand to reach for his length. Wes steps back.

"Wes?"

He kisses my forehead. "I still want to go slow. Is that okay?"

"That was slow for you?" My eyes fly open finally as I start to take in that we are not going to have penetrative sex.

"No, Cara. That was slow for *you*." He kisses me gently and swallows, smiling. His hands are on the door on either side of my head, and I can smell my arousal still clinging to his fingers.

"What about you?" I glance down at his crotch, seeing his junk twitch beneath his jeans.

"I will dream of the sight and sound and taste of you coming for me, Cara, the whole time you're gone."

A thought occurs to me, and I bark out a laugh. "Are you saving the milk until I buy the cow? Is that how the saying goes?"

Wes cocks his head to the side, a crooked grin lighting up his face. "I just want to give you something to look forward to when you get back." I swat at him again. He grabs my hand and kisses it, palm-side up this time, with a naughty lick. "But seriously, Cara, we both have so much on the line. I don't want either of us to be distracted from our work right now."

"You're not a distraction, though. You're ..."

"You told me you need a distraction."

I shake my head. "I thought you'd get in my head and strain my focus, but it's the opposite, Wes. You keep my mind off the bullshit."

"Cara, you need to sit with the bullshit. You need to work through it until it doesn't have any power over you. I don't want to be a distraction from the bad stuff. I want to be..." Wes drags a hand through his hair and shakes his head. "I want to be the man who makes you feel seen and understood and celebrated."

His words hit me like a kick to the shins, knocking my breath away with their impact. A hot tear rolls down my cheek and Wes brushes it aside with his thumb. He stoops to pick up the bag I dropped and reaches in it to hand me my key ring. With the echo of his words still ringing in the air, he presses one final kiss to my lips and smiles, not as brightly as before. Wes waves and walks down the hall.

It's been a week since Cara left for California and I swear I can still taste her, still smell her hair. Memories of our date keep me up at night, in a good way, and the anticipation of a repeat keeps me focused during off-season training sessions.

Uncle Hawk keeps saying he's only looking for 80% effort during our scrimmages and drills, but I feel like I'm pouring out 110% just to keep up with the guys at their relaxed pace. I'll get there, though.

As I drive to the stadium, my bluetooth tells me I have an incoming message from Cara. "Shall I read it aloud?" I get a kick out of the British accent I set for the robot voice in the car, and I talk back to her like she's a real person.

"Please do, darling."

She responds in her slow, monotone. "Cara Moreno says game tonight against Jamaica wish you were here they moved me to false nine."

"Oh shit!" Cara had been hinting that her coach was playing around with some different formations. Cara usually plays deep midfield, like Uncle Hawk did, which is pretty grueling since she's involved on defense and offense. False nine puts her up closer to the opponent's goal.

"Darling, please respond to Cara Moreno."

"Sure, Wesley. I can do that. What would you like to say?"

"Holy shit exclamation point that's incredible period I can't wait to watch period."

My British robot repeats the message to me, and I tell her to send it, noting that it's pretty early in the morning on the West Coast. I'll have to check the game schedule and make sure I get the time difference right. We just have a short cardio workout this morning, so it shouldn't be a problem.

I stroll into the locker room, nodding at the guys. Most of the team are wearing headphones and scrubbing the sleep from their eyes. Our nutrition guidelines are a lot looser in the off-season and I'm pretty sure I can smell the alcohol wafting off our starting goalie. I haven't made much of an effort to hang with the team. It felt weird since I was injured and unable to play for the end of the season. I've just been chilling with my cousins in their apartment, playing video games like we've always done.

"Wes!" My uncle sticks his head out of his office and beckons me over. I yank my practice jersey over my head and click over to him in my cleats.

"Yep?"

"Can I get a ride with you to family dinner? Lucy drove this morning and she's … not feeling sociable today."

"Sure." I had forgotten about family dinner, which is dumb because it's been going on every Sunday since before I was born. I guess what I really did was forget today is Sunday. "I might have to leave early, though."

"Hot date?" Uncle Hawk waggles his eyebrows.

I sniff. "No. I'm watching the US versus Jamaica game." I hesitate before adding, "Cara's starting."

He purses his lips, and his brows lift in a "well, well, well" sort of expression. "Gotcha. Well, that match is the reason for my wife's foul mood today. I'll watch with you, if that's okay? Avoid the bear and all that."

I want to ask him more about Lucy's response to her dismissal from the national team, but I also want to get my mind ready for training this morning. I tell my uncle he's welcome to a ride and I head out to the field to warm up.

I think about Cara trying a new position as we run agility ladders. I imagine how her brain must be in overdrive, learning new places she has to be on the field, new patterns of running. I decide to shake things up myself, leading with my left foot when I'd normally use my right, and so on. It works great and I find I'm faster than I expected at this stage of my recovery.

I test out a longer stride on some sprint drills, too, and it feels weird but puts me over the line ahead of the other strikers. I was so worried that starting any sort of meaningful relationship with a woman would take me out of my game. I feel giddy as I realize that just thinking about Cara inspires me to go deeper into my training.

My face hurts from smiling in the last set of wind sprints and when my uncle blows the final whistle, he calls everyone in to a huddle. "Men. Can we all give a 'hell yeah' to Wes for that performance today?" The guys pat me on the back. "Inspirational recovery, kid. Hell yeah on three."

―――――

By the time I finish showering and changing into clean sweats, Uncle Hawk is waiting for me on a bench in the locker room. He holds up his phone. "Good news. Your Uncle Ty is going to put the game on his giant television, and we'll all watch together."

I open my mouth to protest that I won't be able to focus with a thousand Stags gabbing and cracking jokes, but Uncle Hawk holds up a hand. "Everyone knows we're there to support Cara and the rest of the national team. Your mom is still gunning for you to bring her around to meet the family properly some time, by the way."

I grunt, remembering my mother not-so-subtly bringing up my sex life the last time we hung out. "Mom is a sucker for anyone who makes care packages."

We drive to my aunt and uncle's house and I can tell we're among the last to arrive. The entire block is lined with SUVs, which are probably an impractical choice for city living, but most other cars are too small to accommodate the long-legged Stag men.

Chaos erupts from within as we open the front door, and I smell onions and tomatoes simmering in the kitchen. "We're going to eat chili while we watch." Uncle Ty bellows from behind a stack of bowls he starts lining up on the kitchen island, which is tricked out with every topping anyone ever thought might go with a vat of chili. But because this is Pittsburgh, there's also a bucket of French fries.

I notice that my family has saved me a coveted spot on the couch to watch the game. My cousins are all sprawled out on the floor and my aunts are chatting with Mom at a high table with stools that's angled to face the screen. I give a wave to my dad, standing in the corner with a huge bowl of food.

Once everyone is seated, Mom stands up on top of her stool, which elicits a growl from my dad. "Emma, be careful."

"Relax, Thatchy. I'm taking a picture for Wes to send to Cara." She taps at her phone a few times and I hear the camera sound. "She should know she's got a cheering squad."

"USA! USA!" Odin and Wyatt start chanting as the national team appears on the screen, arms linked on the sideline as the national anthem starts. Warmth spreads through me when I see Cara, who has her eyes closed as she sings along. She seems calm, which is great because I know she'll be amazing out there. She's worked really hard for this.

"Wesley, are you going to send her the photo?" Mom leans over the table behind me.

"Not during the game, Mom. She doesn't have her phone on her right now anyway."

"Which one is she?" Gunnar squints at the screen when the camera pans to the full field after the Jamaican anthem.

"False nine." Uncle Hawk surprises me with his awareness of Cara's new position. He shrugs when I glance over to him. "Lucy's been getting updates from Akemi."

"This whole thing must be so difficult for Lucy." Aunt Alice rests her head on my Uncle Tim's shoulder. He grunts in response but doesn't say anything. "Tim, I know you're not allowed to talk about it, but can you at least—"

"Ssshhh!" Wyatt waves a hand as the match kicks off. I'm relieved that my family, with so many serious athletes among us, knows when to hush up if it matters.

My bowl of chili sits forgotten in my lap as I stare at Cara. The new position puts her in the center of the field, and it seems like every other pass comes right to her. She moves the ball so accurately, sending perfectly timed passes to the forwards. The US dominates the field from the first whistle, and it feels like only seconds pass before Cara has a breakaway. She feints right and moves left and then, swish. I imagine I can hear the net ripping from the force of her goal.

"What a cannon!" Wyatt springs to his feet, pumping his fist. My other cousins all start chanting "USA, USA" and I'm not going to lie. It feels amazing knowing my family is this excited about the success of someone I care about.

A few minutes later, Cara intercepts a pass and lets loose a long ball that shouldn't go into the net, but the Jamaican keeper misjudges the angle and the ball sails right in past her glove. Mom leans forward again to say, "Oh, Wesley, she's wonderful." Mom ruffles my hair and I lean back into her hand, catching sight of Dad out of the corner of my eye. He's smiling.

The rest of the game goes by in a blur of refilled bowls, cheering, and zero goals from Jamaica. We're down to injury time when I see an unmistakable streak of dark hair in the center of the screen. Cara sprints, seemingly out of nowhere, to intercept a pass and nobody can catch her as she charges right for the goal. Her new position puts her in exactly the right place to make these sorts of moves.

She shifts her weight, fools a defender, and spins past another. Stopping to plant her foot, Cara swings and snaps the ball into the corner of the net. I'm on my feet screaming, barely registering my mom yelling, "I can't see! I want to see the replay."

"Emma, stop standing on the damn stool. You'll break your neck." Dad strides over to her and must intervene because Mom's red mop of curls starts bouncing in my line of vision. I don't need to see the replay. The series of moves is burned into my brain. My girl is incredible.

My girl.

"A tremendous display of talent from the young Pittsburgher," the announcer is yelling above the crowd in the stadium. My family eventually calms down. People start washing dishes the second the ref blows the final whistle, but I stay where I am because I want to see as much of Cara as they'll show on the television. Thankfully, my family knows to wait a bit before they start teasing me about her.

The camera pans along the players as they shake hands, and the US captain preps for an on-field interview as she swaps jerseys with the Jamaican captain.

I lean forward to look for Cara, milling around in the background with the rest of the team, exchanging hugs, bouncing, clapping hands. Everyone seems impatient to congratulate her and she accepts all the praise graciously, smiling brightly and turning to face each well-wisher.

Then I see a guy I know she won't be happy to greet. Lou Rubeo walks onto the field, shaking hands with all the US players. I grit my teeth, understanding that this is part of his job as president of the organization. But...I must be hallucinating because I swear, I see him approach Cara and spin her around to face him.

And then I swear I see him grab her face with both his hands and kiss her on the mouth.

My Cara.

This man has his lips on her on international television. Her body stiffens. I see her arms go rigid. He's gone as swiftly as he arrived, shaking hands with staff from the Jamaican team. Like he didn't just assault my girl.

I can't breathe. I imagined that, right? As the camera pans away from

Cara, I just about convince myself that the whole thing was a messed up illusion, until Wyatt snaps off the television and shouts above the chaos. "What the actual fuck was that?"

I look around and my entire family is silent, mouths open in shock and disbelief. It was real. That actually happened.

I yank at my hair and then I have to get out of there. I sprint from the room and out the front door before I can register who is yelling my name.

I BARELY MAKE IT TO THE TRASHCAN IN TIME BEFORE I PUKE UP WATER AND bile. My body violently heaves, screaming at me from the inside. The burn in my esophagus grounds me as reality sinks in: Lou Rubeo just grabbed me and kissed me on the mouth, in front of 20,000 fans and an internationally televised audience.

"Cara!" Jay's voice breaks through the fog as I grip the edges of the trash barrel in the tunnel leading to the locker room. I turn my head toward her voice and see her face etched with concern.

She places a hand on my back as one final retch takes over my body. "Come on, friend. Let's get you in the locker room."

The press starts rushing to the tunnel, heels clacking on the polished concrete. I don't know how many of them saw what happened or if they're just excited about the outcome of the match. It's hard to tell what's real. Rubeo just moved on from what happened like it hadn't happened at all, and nobody pulled him aside or dragged him away.

As soon as Jay guides me into the locker room I sink onto a bench and rest my head against the wall. Coach Akemi bursts through the door and skids over to me on her knees. "I just heard what happened. Cara! My god. Where is your agent?"

"My agent?" My eyes feel swollen and it's hard to see individual faces from the crowd now hovering around me. I haven't talked to my agent in a few weeks. I'm still too new for endorsement deals. I'm not sure how she would respond to her client being grabbed and kissed against her will. Is that even something the rest of the world cares about?

Coach Akemi places a reassuring hand on my shoulder. "They're going to want a statement from you, honey."

"Who? Who is they?"

Coach waves a hand around. "Everyone? Soccer USA. The Olympic committee. The World Association Football Union. The press …"

"What is there to say?" Jay hands me a bottle of water and I start chugging. She pulls the bottle back.

"Easy there, bud. Go slow so you don't puke it up again."

A male voice slips through the crack in the swinging doors to the locker room. "Everyone decent in there? We've got a hungry press corps out here, gals."

I don't recognize the voice, but it doesn't seem to matter. Coach bellows back, "We're all naked. Tell them to wait." She returns her gaze to me, eyes serious. "Cara, I want you to go into the coaching offices and call your agent. She'll answer, I promise." Coach stands up and looks around the room. "Hogan, get Moreno's phone from her locker and throw it over here, please."

My teammates have all been standing around staring, silently, as this interaction unfolds. Hogan shakes herself and heads for the shelf in my locker, extracting my phone. "You're blowing up, Cara."

I nod and take the phone from her, seeing countless notifications. My hands shake as I bring myself to my feet and I notice my thumb scrolls over a message from Wes.

Holy shit! That's incredible. I can't wait to watch.

My stomach drops further, if that's even possible. Wes was watching. He saw another man kiss me. My legs tremble as I walk to Coach's office, worried he'll once again think I sought out that behavior from Rubeo.

Worried he'll think I liked it.

Worried Wes will see it as a rejection of him. Tears roll down my cheeks as I remember our night together before I left for training camp.

I sip water slowly, preparing to look for Alex Steele's number, but my phone rings and it's her calling me anyway. "Hello?" My voice sounds like, well it sounds like I just vomited stomach acid.

"Soccer USA just called me, babe. They want a statement."

Alex doesn't have time for small talk. She told me that when Coach Lucy first gave me her number, and I haven't minded before, but now I really need some context. "I don't know what that means."

Alex sighs. "It means they're going to want you to say *boys will be boys*."

I freeze and try to ignore the spiders I sense crawling on my skin. "That's not what happened."

"Anyone with a brain can tell that. Hell, social media even seems to agree you looked terrified, and the internet doesn't agree on anything."

"It's online already?"

"Oh, lady. Do me a favor and turn off all your notifications. No. Have your roommate do it. Are you alone right now?"

I tell her Coach sent me into her office, presumably so she could deal with the media. I do hear quite a ruckus out in the locker room.

"Soccer USA plans to say Rubeo was 'caught up in the moment' of your decisive victory and couldn't contain his joy about your tremendous talent blah blah bullshit blah."

I forgot that I scored a hat trick, my first since high school. For a second, a bit of calm settles over me and I almost smile. And then Alex keeps speaking. "They're going to want you to confirm that you, too, were overjoyed and happy to share in that proud moment."

"That's not what happened."

Another sigh. "I know, and I'm going to tell them that. But I don't need to tell you what it's like for a woman to work in the sports industry." I purse my lips. "Total fucking sausage factory, Cara. You should assume everything you're assuming is accurate."

"Well, it sucks. I'm just…trying to make America look good on the soccer field."

"I know. Do you want to sleep on it? Which I recognize is a bullshit phrase because I doubt you'll sleep tonight."

She agrees to tell the organization that I need time to draft a response. I hide in Coach's office for a long time, staring at a gray metal cabinet until Jay comes in to tell me the media has left.

She waits for me while I shower and change. By the time we get on the team bus, the mood is joyful. People are celebrating our victory and someone hands me a paper cup of champagne.

Hogan smashes a button on a bluetooth speaker and Queen's "We Are the Champions" blasts throughout the bus. It's easy to shove down my agony about what happened after the match, especially as everyone around me seems so focused on what happened in the 90 minutes we spent working together on that field.

I let my body dance down the aisle and toss back the champagne, accepting high fives as the team chants "golden boot! Golden boot!"

We pull into the hotel parking lot a few minutes later and the team heads straight to the hotel bar, everyone piling duffel bags in the lobby, forgotten like the weight of what happened to me.

Coach Akemi waves for me to come over to her. She holds out her phone, brow furrowed. "Is this what your agent agreed to?"

I see a social media post from Soccer USA, predictably stating that Rubeo was caught up in the moment...but I also see a quote presumably from me, where I supposedly said, "we were all overcome with excitement. These things happen."

CHAPTER 21
WES

Cara isn't taking my calls. I know she and Jay are back in Pittsburgh because I asked my Aunt Lucy. I've sent what I hope are compassionate messages to Cara. I even sent flowers to her apartment with a note about how I'm thinking of her and on her side no matter what.

I know in my bones that she never said "these things happen" about that monster assaulting her. I've seen how upset she was for months after he just touched her face. There's no way she's not suffering from being grabbed like that in what should have been an overwhelmingly joyful celebration of her talent.

I decide to linger at the stadium after the Forge training this morning, since I know Hot Metal is doing off-season workouts in the afternoon. But

I must miss Cara's arrival because eventually I hear the sounds of the team taking the field.

Determined to make contact with Cara, I go grab some lunch and hurry back to the stadium to meet her after the workouts. Armed with chicken salad, grapes, and a pumpkin tart, I position myself right outside the locker room. And then I wait.

At first I scroll social media, but I opt against that as I see more head-lines from fuckers making it sound like Cara is making a big deal out of nothing.

The locker room door creaks open and I straighten, expectantly. No Cara. Jay sees me, though, and walks over. "Hey, Stag."

"Jay. Is she in there?"

She shakes her head. "Dude, I'm concerned. She went back to the weight room after we finished sprints. She's going to burn herself out in more ways than one if she keeps this up."

My shoulders sink at this news. "Does my aunt know she's doing extra workouts? Isn't that frowned upon?"

Jay shrugs. "Lucy knows. She's in there with her."

"Oh hell, my uncle is going to flip out."

Jay nods. "Already happening, Stag."

I hold out my container of chicken salad toward Jay, whose eyes light up. "Here, you take this. I'll go see if I can do anything."

She shouts after me as I walk toward the weight room. "You're welcome to try."

I can hear my uncle bellowing in frustration.

"Lucy, you're 45 years old. Do you really want to blow out your ACL over this?"

I hear feet pounding and the treadmill whirring. When I open the door, I see my aunt in a full-out sprint, barely sweating, staring straight ahead as she runs. Cara matches her stride for stride, also ignoring my uncle, who paces the room while tugging at his gray-streaked hair. "If I didn't think you two would trip and fall, I'd unplug those machines. God damn it, where is Tim?"

As if summoned by the universe, my uncle appears behind me, straightening his tie, several underlings in line behind him. "Lucy, Cara." Tim tilts his head, his expression demanding attention be paid. My aunt flicks a button on her treadmill and hops to the side rail as it slows to a stop. Cara follows suit. Neither of them are even breathing heavy as they straighten out their shirts and stare at my uncle. Nobody seems to have noticed me yet, so I lean against the back wall.

"Yes. Well. Here's how things stand." My uncle waves a hand toward a colleague, who hands him a piece of paper. "Soccer USA is holding firm to their 'boys will be boys' statement. Alex Steele has been quite clear that Cara never approved the statement they attributed to her." Uncle Tim hands the paper back to his colleague and folds his hands in front of his waist, looking down from his impressive height at Cara and Lucy while my Uncle Hawk grinds his teeth. "Right now, our choices are to go along with these statements—"

"Absolutely not. No fucking way." Uncle Hawk throws his arms in the air. "Lucy was fired from the national team for bringing up this guy's bad behavior and then he escalates to televised assault? No."

"Thank you, Hawk, for summarizing the problem." Uncle Tim keeps his gaze trained on Cara as he scolds his brother for interrupting. "Cara, my firm and I cannot represent you in this matter because it's a conflict of interest. We are employed by the Hot Metal, who are a franchise member of Soccer USA."

Cara looks like she is going to hyperventilate, but Aunt Lucy squeezes her hand reassuringly. Tim gestures toward a woman near the back of the room and I see my Aunt Lucy sag in relief and recognition. "Cara, this is my friend Tawnya Kimani, partner at Jones, Lynch, and Kimani. *She* has enthusiastically offered to take your case."

"My case?" Cara looks confused and I want so badly to cross the room and offer her a reassuring hug.

Aunt Lucy wraps her arms around Tawnya and I remember that they're old friends. Wyatt grew up hanging out with Tawnya's twin sons. "Hey," I pipe in from the back of the room. Everyone turns to look at me like they're just now realizing I'm here. "Doesn't Tawnya's husband own the Forge? Isn't that a conflict of interest, too?"

Tim shakes his head. "At this stage we don't believe so. Tawnya will draft a letter seeking disciplinary action against Rubeo, as well as an accurate statement from Cara about what happened."

"About what happened to Lucy, too, right?"

Everyone stares at me for a few moments before turning their heads toward Aunt Lucy. She stands up straighter and adjusts her shirt collar. "I'd like to focus on what happened to Cara but am prepared to join into the calls for disciplinary action if needed."

That statement seems to set the legal people into action, and they don't really seem to need input from anyone else at the moment, which doesn't stop my Uncle Hawk from following them into the hallway, shouting about the nonprofit organization he started to help fund legal support for women who have been abused.

Abused. The word hangs in the air until Cara and I are the only ones left in the weight room. She stares at me, and I can tell that the next words from my mouth will either drive her to collapse or give her the strength to walk out of here in one piece.

I swallow and pull up the bag from the deli. I clear my throat. "I brought you lunch. I'd offer to eat with you, but I gave mine to Jay and it's long gone."

I watch Cara's face melt into relieved contentment. "Thank you," she whispers, taking the bag from me and sinking onto a weight bench. I perch on the end, not sure if she wants me close enough to touch her, but hoping she might. I miss the feel of her in my arms, the solid, strong weight of her.

"This is really good, Wes. Do you want to share it with me?"

I wave a hand at her. "I'll get something at home. You need your strength." I don't say that she needs it for the brewing lawsuit and media circus. I also don't say that she needs it as she keeps preparing her body to compete in the Olympics.

She wolfs down a few bites before slowing to stir the chicken salad, glancing over at me. I edge a bit closer to her and she seems to relax even more. "Wes, I'm so tired."

"I bet you are. Jet lag and all." I nudge her with my shoulder and smile. Thankfully she returns the expression a bit.

"I could really use a distraction from all this." She waves her hand toward the hall, where the lawyers are still conferring. By which I mean shouting.

I look back to Cara, fighting the urge to touch her, to run my fingers through her hair. "Have you thought any more about talking to someone about what happened?"

She growls and I know I've said the wrong thing. "All I do is talk and talk about what happened. Nobody even asks about my hat trick. They just want to know when I got so close to Rubeo. Close!"

I clench my abs and my legs to avoid exploding at the thought of him being close to her in any capacity. "I just want to make sure you have the help you need, that's all."

"What I need, Wesley, is someone to help me feel good for a few minutes so I can refill my tank. God, you're acting just like you always say your parents act when you're injured. Like it's the only thing you're allowed to talk or think about. Ever." She shoves the bag of food at me and stands. "I wasn't asking you to fuck me. I was just hoping we could hang out."

She stomps toward the door in a frenzy of dark curls. "Cara, wait, I'm sorry. You're right, okay?"

She slows but doesn't turn around. She mutters something and I lean closer, trying to hear. "Can you say that again?"

When she turns, the fire has dimmed in her eyes and she looks vulnerable, biting her lip and looking up at me. "Where do we stand?"

"What do you mean?" My heart rate picks up and I place a hand on the wall for support.

She swallows and I love staring at her body carrying out those basic functions. Every part of her is amazing. I should tell her that. But she says, "Asking you to kiss me before … it drove a wedge between us. And I want to be closer to you again, Wes."

I can't help the smile that tugs on my lips at her words. "I want to be close to you, too." It's the biggest understatement of my life, like saying Pittsburgh has a few bridges. "I'd love to hang out with you and, I don't know. Eat seaweed snacks."

She shakes her head. "Those taste like a fart."

I smile, feeling a sliver of hope. "I'll think of something we can do that smells nice."

Her face shifts into something not smiling exactly, but no longer miserable or angry. With a curt nod, she strides out of the weight room and over to her new legal counsel.

CHAPTER 22
CARA

SOCCER SWEETHEART CALLS FOUL OVER POST-MATCH SMOOCH
  By Ken Benton, Celeb Spectator

Romance or Rude? Sources Reveal Months-long Flirtation Between Soccer Star and Organization President
  By Nick Alders, A-List Almanac

Did Soccer Prez Cross a Line?
  By Tom Edwards, Bros, Balls and Banter

I haven't slept in a week. Between the jet lag, the media, and the stress of having to relive months of discomfort, I just can't get my brain to turn off. I know I look like shit. I know I'm playing like shit.

I keep hoping this next thing will be the one that lets me unclench and just ... pass out.

"Cara, mi niña, you need to take some time off and get some rest." Rosalie's accent thickens when she worries, so the sound of her voice really tells me I look worse than I thought. "This fucking guy accusing you of lying is bananas. I've seen the video."

"I don't want to talk about the video. Please." I massage my temples as

179

I lie on the couch with my phone propped on my lap, my friends' faces tiny squares of encouragement in a world increasingly full of people wanting to analyze my life.

"Okay," Shante pipes in. "Well, I read the new statement you put out. I mean, who hasn't?"

Toni shakes a finger in the air. "It's all over socials."

I bang my head against the arm rest a few times. "All of it is all over socials. That's the problem. I can't think. I can't even brush my hair without someone analyzing my intentions."

The newest layer of this scandal is Rubeo claiming the kiss was mutual. Nobody seems to remember that he was going with "caught up in the moment" as his non-apology. Now it's all a huge discussion about how I flirted my way into a starting position on the national team.

Rosalie frowns. "I'm going to start posting more screen shots of your goals in that match. Like…you scored *three* sick-ass goals. How is anyone curious about how you got picked to start?"

Shante sniffs. "God forbid someone just punish a man for doing something wrong."

I sigh. "Hey, chicas, I love you. But I can't talk about this anymore today."

Toni squints at her screen. "It's only 10."

"Exactly."

"Okay, Cara. We'll let you go so you can rest."

Seriously? My best friends can't talk to me about something other than my international scandal? They're hanging up? I wave in frustration and end the call as Jay shuffles down the hall from her room.

"I take it you're not coming in today?" She talks around a bite of breakfast muffin, and I realize I haven't taken my turn cooking. Or cleaning. I glance around the apartment and see the piles of junk mail and dirty laundry on every surface.

I groan and, instead of getting up, sink further into the couch.

"I'm glad you're taking some time, Cara. Don't worry about the apartment. We'll get to it." Her pep talk is interrupted by a knock at the door, and I lift my head to see Wes giving Jay a high five as they pass one another on the threshold.

He wrinkles his nose and sniffs. "And you accused my snacks of smelling like fart?"

I throw a pillow at him. "Shut up. It does not smell like farts in here. It's just …"

He grins. "I'm kidding. But I did think of something we could do that will smell nice."

"I'm not really in the mood to go out in public right now." I gesture at my disheveled state.

Wes walks around to the couch and lifts my feet, sliding his body under my heels and lowering my feet back to his lap. He starts rubbing my feet through my socks and I groan out loud, both from the friendly, familiar contact and because it feels sinfully good. "What if I told you it wasn't public? I set up something private. Just you and me and the person working there."

"Working where?" I close my eyes as Wes switches feet, pressing his knuckles into my arch. His fingers are strong and the pressure is perfect. I briefly wonder if he'll go into massage therapy when he stops playing pro, but I don't want to think about Wes's future. I want to bask in the delicious contact right now.

"Working at the surprise, fragrant date place I set up for us today."

"It's a date?" My eyes fly open.

He scrunches his face in adorable confusion. "I mean … isn't it a date any time we hang out? I thought … we were … dating …"

He sounds so uncertain, so concerned. A wave of discomfort pulses up the back of my scalp. "I hadn't thought about naming it. Everything is so confusing for me right now. God, everything I do is under a microscope."

"Hey!" He drops my foot and rubs a palm up my leg. "I'm sorry. You're right. We don't have to name anything, okay? But I did set up a special … appointment for us and I'd love to take you if you're up for it."

I bite my lip. "I really should clean up the apartment before Jay gets home."

Wes rubs a palm along his cheek and looks around. "It's not so bad. I'll help."

"What? No way. I can't ask you to do that."

He shrugs and pops to his feet. "I offered. Come on." He extends a hand toward me and, frowning, I take it and he hauls me to my feet.

"Don't lift me! Your back."

"How about you let me worry about my back and you sort through the mail while I get the dishwasher going?"

He doesn't wait for me to argue, but walks over to the sink and starts rinsing things, loading up our dishwasher like he has a masters degree in plate arrangement. My mother would be both impressed by his technique and confused about why a man would be touching a dirty dish.

I watch him work as I quickly shuffle through the mail, recycling most of it and setting aside two small piles of important stuff for Jay and me. Wes is still scraping oatmeal bowls when I finish, so I gather up the laundry and get the washer going. By the time I pull my head out of the front loader, he's got a broom in his hand and hums as he dances around my kitchen, sweeping.

"Are you singing 'Dancing Queen' while you sweep my floor?"

He hums louder, passing the broomstick from one hand to another. "In my head it's 'soccer scene.' I'm digging the soccer scene, get it?"

I can't help the laugh that escapes my mouth. "You're ridiculous."

"Hear the shout of the refereeeeeeee, oh yeahhhh. You can kick. You can slide. Kicking the goal of your liiiiiife."

Wes drops the broom and grabs my hand, twirling me around the kitchen as he croons made up lyrics. I laugh at him, each word from his mouth more ridiculous than the last, until he runs out of ideas. "You ready for our appointment?"

I sigh. "I guess I am. Thank you."

He leans in and kisses me on the cheek. "You're welcome."

Wes heads toward his neighborhood in his giant car, which I now realize he needs so his head isn't banging the ceiling. Every part of him is long and lean, and my cheeks heat as I remember a particularly long part of him I haven't seen in a long time.

He parks along the curb on Butler Street and I glance up, not familiar with this block of the bustling neighborhood. There are a bunch of bars and little restaurants with every type of cuisine, it seems, apart from Spanish … or Cuban, of course. Longing for my mother's cooking burbles up in me, palpable. I nearly sob but I reach for the door just as Wes opens it, his hand extended to help me out of the car.

I realize I'm in a trendy neighborhood in old sweats, with no makeup and uncombed hair. I stiffen, until Wes leans in and says, "You look perfect. We're wearing practically the same outfit." He grins and runs his hands down his hoodie. I hadn't noticed that his black and gold sweatshirt reads Hot Metal instead of Pittsburgh Forge.

"You're wearing women's soccer gear?"

He pats his chest. "I'm a huge fan. Have you seen their midfield?" He fans himself and I give him a shove.

He guides me toward a building with a very busy font on the sign so I can't make out the name. Something mix … and we walk inside to a wave of fragrance.

"Wes! Welcome. And this must be Cara." A sales clerk, whose name tag reads Alanna, approaches with a wave. "I'm so excited to do a custom pour with you both today."

"A what now?" I glance around the shelves and realize Wes brought me to a make-your-own candle shop. The walls are lined with hundreds of jars and scents, and it all combines to a lovely, fresh aroma. Alanna lowers the window shades, giving us privacy, and I glance around. "This is so nice."

Alanna nods. "Why don't you two have a seat and we can get an idea of what sort of candle you'd like to create."

Wes hops up on a stool and immediately says, "I'm making one for a very special woman who hates the smell of seaweed but always makes me think about water."

"Water?" Alanna and I speak at the same time, but he keeps his gaze on her and nods.

"Yeah. She gets into this flow state when she's working, and she's powerful and she sparkles. And she can be very dark and stormy."

Alanna smiles. "She sounds very special. Why don't you try some of these scents and see if any jump out at you." Alanna puts a tray of tiny bottles on the table in front of Wes, with labels like solar lily and bergamot.

She turns her gaze on me. "Are you looking for any specific mood? What scent profile are you thinking about?"

I try to name some of the things I'm feeling about Wes right now, but all that comes to mind is "gratitude. I am just feeling really grateful for my candle recipient."

Alanna smiles. "We can work with that, most definitely." She sets a wooden tray in front of me, and I start sniffing tiny vials, distracted by Wes enthusiastically inhaling and following each sniff with a loud "aaah. Nice."

Eventually, I pull out sandalwood, cedar, and something called labdanum. Alanna seems delighted by my choices and turns toward Wes. "Are you thinking of using them all?"

He shrugs. "It all smells really good."

"That would be a very complex scent indeed."

Wes grins. "Well, that's perfect, Alanna, because this person is very complex." Alanna nods and gestures toward a selection of jars, telling us to select a home for our candle creation while she gets the essential oils ready to mix into the hot wax.

I consider Wes for a few moments and then choose a smooth black jar. He spins around with a white jar in his hand, grinning. I notice a leaping deer painted on the jar—probably a reindeer for Christmas, but I let him have his moment of joy because it's adorable.

We return to the table and Alanna set us up with wax and wicks and tiny spoons to add our scents. As we work on the candles, I focus on the feel of Wes's leg pressed against mine, the joy on his face as he continues to inhale the tiny bottles of fragrance. I asked him to take me somewhere and take my mind off my troubles, and I would have never imagined pouring candles would tick that box.

"I'm calling mine Big Wick Energy," Wes says, sliding his complete candle to the edge of the table. "It's to remind my recipient of me."

I swat his arm. "You're bad."

He leans in to whisper in my ear, "No, Cara, I'm very, very good for you." And then he kisses my neck, and the pleasure of it sets my hands shaking. I dump a bit more sandalwood than I intended into the candle, and I decide to quit while it's still salvageable.

"Mine's called Don't Blow It." I smile at Alanna, who nods. Wes and I have the option to create professional-looking labels for our candles and we spend some time choosing ridiculous fonts. I can tell Alanna thinks we are goofballs, but honestly, it's such a relief to do something frivolous that I don't care what she thinks.

We get our labels stuck on our candles at last and Alanna explains that they need to set for at least two hours. "You can come back for them this afternoon, or any time this week if that works better."

"Thank you so much for your help," Wes says, fishing some cash from his wallet.

I pat my sweats, looking for my own money, but Alanna shakes her head. "Mr. Stag pre-paid for your session. But thank you, so much, for the generous gratuity." She nods her head toward Wes, who gives her a wink.

"You ready to get out of here, Moreno? We've got time to fill!"

———

Wes suggests we hang out at his place since it's only a few blocks away, and we move his car to his building so he can stop feeding the meter outside the candle place.

Except, when we get in his car, the radio comes on and it's a news report. "... today as the president of Soccer USA faces temporary suspension. A spokesperson from the organization declined further comment, mentioning an ongoing investigation into a personnel issue."

Wes lifts his hand to shut it off, but I grab his wrist. "No, wait, I want to hear this."

"…from within the soccer community claim Rubeo assaulted national team player Cara Moreno, allegedly grabbing her, and kissing her on the mouth without consent after a US victory over Jamaica. Tawnya Kimani, legal representation for Moreno, says more details will continue to unfold, and that her firm is prepared to pursue legal action."

Wes frowns and pulls into the garage at his building. "Legal action can mean all sorts of things."

"Shh."

"—meanwhile, sources close to Rubeo continue to assert that Moreno had been flirting with the soccer executive for months. They released a video of the soccer starlet celebrating after the match with her team, drinking champagne and allegedly unaffected by any form of alleged assault. To see the video and learn more about this story, visit our website at WBNA dot—"

Wes yanks his keys from the ignition, cutting off the radio. "A fucking video of you happy? Like you can't be happy about winning and still furious at …what he did?"

I swallow and step out of the car, walking slowly toward the elevator. "I really need to sit down."

"Of course. Sorry. Here I come." He clicks his key fob to lock the car and waves a different fob to summon the elevator. He stands opposite me in the lift, concern etched into his features. I stare at his neck, seeing tendons flex as he swallows and grinds his teeth together. His anger grounds me in reality, lets me believe I really am seeing and hearing all this nonsense about someone from my place of work behaving criminally and then denying it.

The elevator reaches Wes's floor and he steps out, unlocking the sliding door to his loft. "Can I get you some water?"

I should prop myself on a stool at his counter or sink into the couch in his living room, but I don't. I follow him over to the sink. "Wes, I need you."

"I'm here, Cara."

He turns to face me, but I shove him back against the counter. "No, I need you to fuck me."

"What? Cara—"

I shake my head and place my palms on his chest. "I need to be in control. I need to choose. I need to feel so god-damned good because I want to, despite what anyone else says. I need to know if I still can. Do you want me?"

He swallows again, eyes wide. "I wanted you from the moment you first yelled at me at that airport. But—"

I place a finger over his lips. "No buts. I need you. Right now."

CHAPTER 23
WES

I'M SO CONFLICTED. THE HOTTEST WOMAN IN THE WORLD IS SHOVING ME against my own sink and telling me to fuck her. But this woman has also been through a lot and just got out of the car listening to radio announcers discuss her like a social studies topic. That has to be messing with her head.

The last thing I want to do is give her something else to regret. "Cara." I swallow, trying to hold back the fear that what I feel for her is too big, too strong. "I...can't go all in like this and then lose you again."

I know it's not fair to bring up my own worries while hers are so big and so present. But I also can't give her what she needs without letting go of the control over my emotions—the last thing I have keeping me safe.

"I need *you*, Wes. Please. I'm not going anywhere."

Cara grabs my palm and presses it to her chest. I feel her nipples pebble through all the layers of her sweatshirt. She's been pretty clear for a few weeks that she wants this—it's been me putting on the breaks, insisting that she should want me for me, not as a distraction from what's hard in her life.

But she didn't ask me to take her mind off things just now. She asked me to give her control and choice. *"I need to feel good,"* she'd said. She grabs my other hand and presses it to her crotch. I feel the damp heat of her body and a groan escapes my throat. I growl and pull her against me. "You want to be in control, baby?"

She nods her head rapidly. "Yes."

"Tell me what you want." I lick my lips, waiting.

She smiles, a slow, spreading expression that slides over her face like a mask of happiness. Soon enough, I'll help her find that joy more permanently. For now, if she wants this, I'm going to give it to her. "Go lie on your bed." She tilts her head toward my room. "Take your clothes off as you walk."

I do as she says, and I risk a glance over my shoulder to see her following suit. We shed our sweats in a heap of fuzzy black and gold. I wonder if I should pause to pull off my socks, but Cara comes up behind me and I feel her nipples against the middle of my back.

I turn at the doorway and walk backward towards the bed and tip onto the mattress just in time to catch her above me. She straddles my waist, her heat against my thighs as her palms slide down my chest.

She seems to consider her next move, and I make my hands busy while she ponders. "Can I touch you?"

"Everywhere," she nods, pinching my nipples.

I gasp. "Fuck, Cara." My dick twitches in response to her rough touch and she reaches for it, thankfully with a more forgiving grip. She fists my cock as I tease her thighs, touching her lower belly, everywhere except the ball of nerves I know she's hoping for.

She moans in frustration. "I want to …"

"What, baby? Anything."

Her eyes flare, wide and dark. "I want to sit on your face."

"Oh, fuck, please. Yes. God." My head sinks into the pillow and I rest my hands on her golden hips as she makes her way up my body. I smell her, more potent and wonderful than anything in that candle shop, and as Cara grips my headboard, I inhale long and deep before she lowers herself on my eager tongue.

"Please, Wes." I lick her gladly, my hands digging into her rounded backside. The familiarity of her body, of her taste, tugs at my memory like warm sunshine. I play with her clit using my nose and my mouth together while my hands gently rest on her butt and she rocks back and forth, groaning.

"Oooh, yes. Just like that. Harder, now. Faster." Cara barks out commands and I follow like an eager soldier. I'm incredibly turned on at the sight of her dark hair spilling over her shoulders, her brown nipples bobbing as she jerks and shudders above my face.

I'm greedy for her orgasm, realizing I need to give it to her as much as she needs to claim it. "Come for me, Cara." I nudge her with my nose as I encourage her. "Be a good girl and come on my face."

I readjust my grip so I can slide my thumbs along her seam while I hold her over me. She sinks into place in my palms and both my thumbs slide inside her body just as she tumbles over the edge, an orgasm ripping through her as she pulses around my hands and tongue.

She grunts and thrashes, finally tipping to the side, panting. I roll to face her, grinning. We could stop right here, and I'd die a happy man, knowing I gave that to her. But Cara Moreno has no intention of stopping.

She shoves me onto my back again and climbs back aboard, this time tracing a fingertip along my ribs. She teases the sensitive skin from my belly to the root of my cock. "I haven't been with anyone since you, in California." She brushes her hair back, revealing a serious expression. We both know we're tested frequently at work, but I like that she's telling me this.

I shake my head. "Haven't either. No one but you." My breath comes in bursts as she starts playing with my dick, her grip the perfect pressure as she slides up and down my length.

"I'm on birth control. Monophasic hormone levels are supposed to help prevent ligament damage and—"

"I get it. You want to ride me bare." My mouth hooks in a crooked grin. The thought of sliding inside her, nothing between us, nearly has me spurting in her hand. "Yes. I'm so good with that. So, so—oh shit."

Cara lowers herself onto my shaft and we groan in unison at the sensation. I've never felt anything like this in my life. She is wet velvet inside, so slippery. More than that, I can feel the trust between us right now. There is nothing separating us with me inside her and that knowledge grips at my heart so tightly I whimper. I stare down at our joined bodies as she starts to rock herself above me. "Cara." Her name is a whisper, a prayer of gratitude.

But I remember that this is about her and what she needs. She grabs for my hands again, pulling them to her chest and I gladly play with her tits while she uses her hands to find the leverage she needs. Cara is on the brink of coming a second time without any assist from me.

I'm doing as I was silently told, stroking her nipples and pulling, pinching those hard little berries while she gets herself off on the friction of our pelvises rubbing together. "So ... fucking ... good," she hisses, and then I about blow my load when I see her reach between her own legs, finding the exact pressure she needs to cross the finish line.

"Oh, shit, Cara, I'm going to come." I give her about a second of warning before I blast off inside her, watching in awe as she melts above me. Her face is such a perfect picture of bliss, of joy and pleasure. I spurt again as I realize I helped her get there.

After I grab us some warm washcloths from the bathroom, I haul Cara into my arms and play with her hair until her breathing slows and I realize she's fallen asleep. Remembering the dark circles under her eyes when I first got to her apartment, I decide to hold her and keep her safe as long as she needs to rest.

CHAPTER 24
CARA

HE TEXTS ME THESE THINGS EVERY FEW HOURS AND IT NEVER FAILS TO PUT A smile on my face, even with everything going on at work. I need to continually remind myself that soccer is my job, that this is my professional work and 99 percent of the people at my workplace treat me as I would expect to be treated at work.

I light the candle he made me every afternoon when I get home, and I've made a habit of sitting and sort of staring at the flame, organizing my thoughts after my shower. It's like meditation, I guess. I never tried it before.

Most evenings I have stressful calls with my agent about the latest spin from the national soccer association. I didn't necessarily want Rubeo fired in the beginning. I'm not sure what I wanted … just for him to go away and leave me alone.

But I've come to realize that as long as he stays in the position of president, I'll continue to see him at every training camp, every international fixture. There's no way I could go to the Olympic Games and be expected to sit near him at a press conference about our team unity and pride for our nation.

Alex Steele is enraged that the board for Soccer USA won't fire Rubeo, so now in addition to getting him fired, she's urging me to make a plea to replace the patriarchal board of directors, too. "Nothing is going to change if we don't get rid of the people making excuses for abusers." Alex's anger and firm words make me feel like my own anger is okay. So, I take her advice at every turn.

Which is why I'm already geared up for a fight when my phone rings, but it's not my agent this time. Or my lawyer. It's my mother.

"Cara, I have Papi on speaker. We're outside the church."

"I didn't think you guys went to church anymore." I suppose we've skipped over the part where we pretend to greet each other with love and affection.

"Don't be profane. Of course we go to church." My father scolds me like he hasn't spent the past two decades of Sundays watching any professional soccer match fielding a player of Cuban descent.

I inhale and stare at my candle flame, thinking of Wes.

"Cara, what's all this in the news about you luring this man?"

"Mama, I hope you know I'm not luring anyone. I hope you think more highly of me than that." I clench my fists and concentrate on the candle, which sputters a bit with my breath. I sit back so I don't accidentally blow out the flame.

My father roars. "How dare he touch you? On television! How dare that man lay hands on a woman like that."

"We didn't have these problems with you at the girls' schools. This is why we were so worried about you at that college, going around with all these men. These men don't know how to behave themselves." I can hear my mother crossing herself, probably sitting on a bench near my father, perhaps ignoring the fact that they're sitting outside a church that doesn't allow divorce at all, let alone an amicable one like they had.

"I'm glad you can see that the man is the one with the problem here, Mama. I was just trying to do my job ... and honor my country." I add this last bit with a false hope that my father will chime in with one of his usual declarations about the impact of Cuban Americans on our economy.

Instead, he sighs. "We think you need to come home. You still have a room at your mother's apartment, and one at mine. You aren't safe there with those men."

I stare at the candle, thinking of Wes, thinking of how my experience here has led to me being named a starting player on the U.S. Olympic soccer team. My heart breaks that my parents don't seem to care about either of these accomplishments. They see only what the reporters suggest: that I somehow brought on Rubeo's attention by being a woman.

I take a stuttering breath. "I have to go now, Mama, Papi. I will keep you updated on my travel schedule. I hope you can still plan to come see the friendly match in Chicago."

I hang up before my father can reiterate that it's a long drive as the weather gets colder. A tear slides down my face and I flick it away, hearing a small hiss as the drop hits my Big Wick Energy flame.

————

"Knock, knock." Jay pokes her head in my room. I still haven't gotten into the habit of closing my door. I spend a lot of time thinking about how many years it's been drilled into me that it's always, always my responsibility to ward off the uncontrolled sexual urges of men. And any sexual urges I might have myself.

I remember how I felt on top of Wes the other day, how powerful and happy and strong. I remember the look of sheer delight on Wesley's face as he brought me to climax, and I can't believe I ever let anyone tell me it's not okay to want that experience.

I brush my hair off my face and smile at my roommate. "Hey. What's up?"

She purses her lips. "I know you turned off all your notifications and took all the social media apps off your phone."

I nod. I was getting inundated with direct messages from angry people. *It's just a kiss. We can't even kiss women now?* And those were the things from the nicer people. Jay volunteered to scan social media on my behalf and give me a summary if there was anything my agent or lawyer needed to know.

I should buy her a candle or something for that labor because I sure as hell can't handle that work.

"Well, I wanted you to see some of the stuff. Just some of it. Hogan and I copy-pasted some highlights."

"Hogan?"

Jay smiles and nods. "A lot of the Hot Metal keep asking how they can help, what they can do, all that sort of thing. Well, here." She hands me a piece of computer paper with a bunch of tiny screen shots pasted to it.

He's always been creepy to me, too. Used to stare at my boobs at press conferences. #WeStandWithCara

Rubeo is a criminal abuser. Touched my ass once—uninvited. #WeStand-WithCara

Nobody should have to deal with that abuse at work. And soccer is work. #WeStandWithCara

Current and former members of the national team all seem to be posting similar sentiments about Lou Rubeo. It seems like none of them ever thought it was bad enough to say something, but so, so many women felt uncomfortable around him, avoided being alone with him, or worse.

"Jay, this is … I don't know what to say."

She sits next to me on my bed and pulls me in for a hug. "You don't have to say anything because you already said the thing. And we believe you, Cara. Everyone who matters believes you."

Jay smacks a kiss on my cheek, and I burrow into her shoulder, feeling lucky to have been assigned her as my roommate all those months ago. I never thought I'd feel a connection with someone as intense and powerful as I had with my friends from college, but I'm starting to see that the women's soccer community is full of like-minded people.

"Anyway," Jay loosens her vice grip. "Does that candle say Big Wick Energy?"

I nod. She rolls her eyes. "Straight people are weird."

Jay heads out with Hogan and the defense, leaving me alone in the apartment with my feelings. So of course, my mind wanders to Wes.

We still haven't circled back to a conversation about our status. Are we dating? Does what we have defy labels? Either way, I'm eager to show him the print-out from Jay and tell him about my new hashtag.

When I check my phone, I see a note from him that he decided to take advantage of open hours in the weight room at the stadium.

I can drive down there and surprise him, and maybe he will invite me back to his loft for a remix of our adventures from the other day.

I deliberately avoid the radio as I drive to the stadium, letting the messages Jay showed me replay in my head instead to give me encouragement while I drive. We stand with Cara. Every woman on that curated list said the same thing: they stand with me.

I'm practically floating through the door, the green light from my badge flashing brightly in the dimly lit hall. I can hear the clang of weights and I'm sort of glad Wes is still here working out. He told me he's been killing it in scrimmages. I guess outrage gives him an edge. Or maybe it's the fumes of that candle I made him.

He catches my eye in the mirror as I round the corner into the weight room and his gaze darkens immediately. He's shirtless, glistening with sweat, bursting through a set of thrusters with a heavy barbell and plates.

His body is chiseled perfection. Every tiny muscle in between all his larger ones is flexed as he works the weight up and over his head. Wes grunts with the effort of the movement even as he maintains eye contact through the mirror. I lean against the back wall of the room, incredibly aroused at the sight of him.

He bends over to drop the bar, his bubble butt popped back in my direction, draped in mesh shorts that end midway up his tight thighs. Wes growls as he picks the bar up again and heaves it into the air, straightening to his full height and looking like da Vinci's Vitruvian Man sketch. My eyes drop to his crotch and sure enough, his bulge moves, seems to swell.

And then I yelp as Wes drops the weight to the ground. He turns and stalks toward me, his intention clear. He's a Stag ready to rut and I am ready for his horns. I giggle at my ridiculous analogy until he gets near me. I can practically smell the lust on him. It turns me on a lot.

Wes boxes me in against the wall, one forearm on either side of my face. "When did you get here?"

"Just now." I reach out and rest a hand on his sweaty chest, liking the feel of his heart racing beneath his skin.

"Did you find what you were looking for?" Wes tilts his head to the side, breathing heavily from his workout. Or maybe he, like me, is dizzy with desire right now.

"Not quite." I reach for his mouth with my thumb, intending to rub his lower lip, but he snaps his jaws and sucks my thumb into his mouth.

Wes releases my thumb with a pop and studies me, considering. Wordlessly, he presses off the wall and starts toward the door, extending a hand for me, which I take.

He tugs me into the men's locker room, gives a quick look around, and nods as he strides toward the shower. "I'm filthy, Cara. You have to know that."

I swallow and nod. "I can see that."

He grins. "And you like that, don't you? You like it when I fuck you dirty." I nod, watching as he drops the shorts to the ground and kicks off his sneakers. "Get naked, now, or I'm going to throw you in there with your clothes on."

I hurry to comply, excited by his rough words. We haven't had this kind of sex since California—this inevitable, horny sort of coupling that's rough and kinky and delicious. A breath after I peel off my last sock, Wes has me backed against the tile in one of the locker room stalls. There's no curtain, but I also know there's nobody else around and I release a moan as he dives in to begin sucking my nipples in the hot spray of the water.

Steam from the water forms a cloud in the shower stall, softening the sting of the harsh fluorescent overhead light. I peer through the mist at the dark head and gray eyes of Wesley Stag, who sinks to his knees and wedges my thighs apart. He grunts as he squeezes my thigh and hooks it over one of his shoulders before he dives in and starts licking my center like it's the last phase of his cardio workout.

I sink into the tile, my hands resting on his messy, damp hair as I let the pleasure overtake me. This is what I need. I need the way he understands me, knows what I want and likes what makes me feel good.

And there is no question he likes this. Wes moans with pleasure and reaches between his own legs to fist his cock while he pulls me closer and closer to the cliff with his tongue.

"Oh god. Damn, that feels good. I need you." My words come in short bursts with long moans in between and then I'm coming on his mouth while I feel his dick bopping me in the ankle as he works it furiously with his fist.

I thrash around in the shower stall as he brings himself to his feet, still rubbing at his erection. I move to reciprocate, not caring that he hasn't washed himself off yet, but Wes shakes his head. "I won't last, Cara. And I want to come inside you."

I swallow, my stomach turning flips and my legs still shaking in the aftershocks of the orgasm he just delivered. All I can do is nod before I'm hoisted from the ground. Wes rests my butt on the small shelf meant for toiletries, and before I can protest that my weight will break it off the wall, he nudges in between my legs and thrusts inside me. He holds my thighs with his strong hands, the shelf just taking a bit of my weight as he begins to fuck me hard.

My spine digs into the tile and I hear the combined sounds of our grunts, our skin slapping, and then a low, keening wail I realize is coming from my throat as Wes releases one of my legs to reach for my clit.

"Wes! Wes! Yes, please keep doing that." I grip his shoulders, slippery and swaying, as he pulls a second orgasm from me.

I feel his hairy thighs against the back of mine as he lifts my legs higher, hooking my ankles over his shoulders. He's so deep inside me now, the tip of his cock bumping my cervix and causing me to bear down on him.

"Oh, fuck, you're so tight, baby. You like when I'm fucking you this deep?" I nod my head and he grins wickedly, moving his hand from my clit and massaging lower, further back.

He finds the tight pucker of my ass and I remember how he started to play with it when we were together in California. I'm running out of energy now, sure he's fucked the breath out of my body, but a jolt of molten steel warms my entire body as Wes pokes the tip of his little finger inside my most private place.

I come apart in his arms, and I hear him growling that he's coming, too. I feel the pulsing surges of it, the warmth inside me, and I hear him purring into my ear. "You're so beautiful, Cara. So fucking hot and perfect right now. Christ, look at you. Look at you." I glance down and I can see myself spread around him. His wrist is angled beneath one thigh, and I can feel his finger still inside my channel, which grips him tight like my heart.

"Take me home, Wes."

He nods and kisses my temple. I rest against the wall of the shower while he soaps up his hands and gently washes my body, then his own. We dress quickly and head towards his place.

We hold hands walking back to his room, like teenagers on a date, and I love the freedom and silliness of that. I wake up in his bed, tucked tight against his side, feeling safer than ever before.

KISS-GATE AT WOMEN'S SOCCER FRIENDLY
  By Ken Benton, Celeb Spectator

Outcry Over Post-Match Celebration
  By Amanda Peters, Fame Frenzy Online

Cancel Culture Comes for Celebrating: Can we even show excitement anymore?
  By Nick Alders, A-List Almanac

My uncle, in coach-mode, texted the entire team to let us know there's increased security at the stadium for the time being. Even though it's the off-season, and the pro teams don't have mandatory workouts yet, there have been a ton of paparazzi hanging out trying to take pictures of Cara.

I received a special, bonus series of texts from my entire family warning me to keep my cool and let the lawyers handle everything, no matter what these guys say.

It's not easy.

If you had told me I'd spend the tail end of my first pro season injured and then removing social media from my phone because I can't handle the trolls coming after my girlfriend, I'd have laughed in your face.

Girlfriend.

Cara hasn't used that word, and I haven't pushed her again for a label. I want to trust my gut on us, that we are in a good place together. She spends almost every night in my bed, curled up in my arms. And that's better than any sort of label.

———

Cara and Jay had a special strategy video call with their coach from the national team, so she stayed at her place last night. Instead of waking up to have lazy sex, I drag myself out of bed to head in for cardio and weight training.

I see the light flashing off what looks like a thousand camera lenses as I approach the gate to the parking lot. During business hours, the stadium parking lot is used by commuters who mostly work downtown, so there's no real way to keep the media out of the lot as long as they pay their parking fee.

Something tells me they're happy to drop $20 per van so they can swarm the gates, begging anyone who walks by to talk to them just for a minute. I keep my head down and my hood up as I shuffle past them, eager to connect with the security guard nodding me toward the player entrance.

"Thanks, man," I say, offering a hand to the guard to jostles me through the reporters all asking my name, if I know Cara Moreno, if I ever got "carried away" after a soccer game.

"You got it, Wes." The guard shakes my hand and I feel guilty that he knows my name and I have no idea who he is. But then I remember I'm a pro athlete in a city that worships its sports teams.

"Hey, man, let me know if you ever want an autograph or anything." I realize it sounds a bit desperate as I say it. I'm a rookie nobody who only played in one match, after all, but the guy's face brightens.

"That would be great! Me and my old man are tracking your whole family. We got a Ty Stag rookie jersey, signed, from when he started with the Fury."

"That's awesome. I'll make sure and grab something for you, okay?"

He gives me a salute and I make my way into the locker room, reminding myself that there are still good people out there in sports fandom. Not everyone is chomping at the bit, eager to tear down the players.

"We can't fucking do anything anymore." I hear the voices of my teammates in the locker room, shouting about something.

I make my way to the bench by my stuff and start wedging my bag in the narrow, vertical space. "Tell me about it." The guy on my left, Harrison I think, kicks at a roll of tape on the ground. "One of those fuckers shoved a camera lens right in my face. Almost chipped my tooth."

I grunt. That's aggressive and unnecessary. "They shouldn't behave that way."

Harrison nods. "All because some chick can't handle a kiss." He throws a shoe into his cubby, but I freeze where I stand.

"What did you say?" My words come out sounding harsh, but I mean for them to cut glass.

Harrison looks at me. "I said some fucking chick can't handle a little celebration kiss and now we all live in a police state."

I wait a beat, sure some other guys on the team will speak up. Will say something in Cara's defense. Will decry the slime ball who grabbed her against her will. But nobody does.

And all the frustration, all the rage I've felt for months ever since I realized this guy was making her uncomfortable to start with? It all flies out of me through my fists as I shove Harrison up against the wall, screaming and bashing his shoulders off the divider between our two storage shelves.

"What the fuck, man?" Harrison tries to get a punch in to my ribs but I grab him by the shirt and spin him so we're standing on opposite sides of the bench. I duck my shoulder and move to dump tackle him like my football-playing cousins taught me.

All the years of growing up with a brother and eight male cousins come to a head as I transfer decades of horseplay into an outlet for my fury. I dig a knuckle into Harrison's sternum, a knee into his thigh as I swing.

He gets a punch in on my jaw but I barely feel it, pummeling him with both hands as I straddle his body on the sticky floor of the locker room. I'm screaming, shrieking with rage when I feel a pair of hands lift me off Harrison and I finally realize my uncle is in my face yelling my name.

I snap my mouth shut and drop my hands to my sides. Uncle Hawk is breathing heavy and gives me a shake. "In my office, Wesley. Now! Harrison, come back in an hour. Bring your agent. We're going to talk about your morality clause."

My uncle keeps a hand on my shoulder, steering me toward his door while he mutters about asshole men who don't get it.

"Did you hear what he said?" I sink into a chair and press the heel of my hand into my eye. It's throbbing. Harrison must have popped me in the face more than once.

"Yeah, of course I fucking heard him and half the team saying things that, frankly, upset me a great deal. I was in the middle of arranging a training about intimate partner violence prevention when you went ballistic and took it into your own hands." He swipes a hand along his desk, scattering pencils and post-it notes. "Which I expressly told you not to do, Wesley."

I wince. Between the pain in my face and the sting of his words, I'm starting to feel like a real heap of garbage. "So, what happens now?"

He leans on the edge of his desk with his arms crossed and brings one hand up to massage his graying temples. Uncle Hawk takes a deep breath. "Now you go and see a psychologist, Wes."

"What?" I recoil. "You're sending me to a shrink?"

He glares at me. "Shrink? Seriously?" He shakes his head. "Look, I know you know this, but your aunt was going through some crap when we first met. She and Wyatt went to counseling for a long time, and it wasn't until I finally did, too, that I was able to let go of some of my own anger about the whole situation."

I rub my face, mirroring his action, but wincing in pain. "I didn't know that you were in therapy."

"Hell, kid, everyone needs therapy. Which is why we have a psychologist on call, ready to work with all the athletes in this program. I would hope people would take advantage of that gift voluntarily, but now I'm going to mandate you attend as a condition of you returning to my active roster."

"You can't do that."

"The hell I can't!" He kicks the leg of my chair. "Don't mess with me on this, Wes. Get your ass up to Doctor Georgia and get your head on straight." He stalks toward the door and pulls it open before stopping and turning toward me. "Cara needs you at your best. This is going to get uglier before it gets better."

He strides out of the room, yelling orders at the guys as he heads to the field, where I guess I won't be joining him today.

CHAPTER 26
CARA

Jay growls as I enter the kitchen. I can't get ahold of Wes and was up half the night worried something happened to him. I considered messaging his cousin Wyatt, but I chickened out.

"What's up, roomie?"

"Fucking Rubeo. I know I'm curating the news for you, but his *mother* is on a *hunger strike* and is hospitalized. She's refusing to eat until his name is cleared."

"What?"

Jay nods. "I'm dead serious. She won't stop until the world stops besmirching her son's good name."

203

I swallow a knot of bile, wondering if it's possible to puke from disgust. I've already vomited from exertion and, after the last USA match, from trauma and fear. What's a little revulsion retching? "His mother thinks I'm lying?"

Jay growls and punches the couch cushions. "Bae, a lot of people say you're lying."

I grip the edge of the counter, frozen in the middle of the room. "But the hashtag…"

Jay sighs. "Come on, let's sit and come up with a plan here. Because yes. There is a hashtag. There are people supporting the shit out of you, but there are also a fuck-ton of people making it all worse."

Jay and I already decided to arrange our training in another location since there's been so many paparazzi at the stadium. The studio where Wes and I took yoga for athletes has a bunch of workout space that Jay and I have been using to follow Coach Akemi's workouts for the national team.

Jay microwaves a pair of egg muffins and I choke one down as she drives us to Pipe Fitters. I like the atmosphere, with brightly colored walls painted with positive affirmations, and I come close to enjoying myself during the workout. But each time my stomach pings with a well-earned hunger, I think of Lou Rubeo's mother, refusing to nourish herself until I … what? Say the kiss was consensual?

Indicate that it's normal and fine for someone to grab me at work and kiss me without permission? I'm back into a rage before the final set of kettlebell moves. "I can't handle this, Jay. I can't handle any of this."

She heaves a weighted ball into the air, aiming for a spot high on the wall. "You can and you are. It just sucks, Cara." She grunts and throws the ball again, and I decide to join her even though this isn't on my workout plan. It's cathartic, hurling a heavy ball into the air and sinking into a squat as I catch it.

When we finally head home, I'm ravenous and almost okay about that, mentally. I whip up a giant bowl of tuna salad and prop my feet on the coffee table, connecting my phone to the television screen so I can call my chicas and see them on a bigger canvas.

"Cara, querida. I'm taking Twitter off my phone." Shante snaps her fingers in rage as she frowns.

"Twitter isn't even a thing anymore anyway." Rosalie waves at me but then frowns as well. "But I know what you mean. All this bullshit. When do you have to go back? Will he be there?"

"What do you mean?" Toni is eating actual popcorn as she settles in for our call. She's still wearing her lab coat, and I smile, thinking of her as a lead investigator on her own research study already.

Shante rolls her eyes. "Cara is gonna have to go back to California with the national team. You know—to get ready for the Olympics? And that monster is in charge of the whole sport sooooo, you know. He'll be there, right?"

The hand holding a forkload of tuna stops midway to my mouth. I drop it into the dish. I had not stopped to think that if Lou Rubeo isn't fired and the board won't suspend him, then of course he'll be present at camp. He'll be carrying on his work like it's any old day of the week.

Shante squints at me. "Cara? You okay, chica?"

I shake my head. "I … didn't stop to think that he'd be at camp."

Jay comes into the room fresh from her shower. She waves at the camera and my friends blow her kisses. "You didn't think who would be at camp?"

Rosie snorts. "This fuckwad with the mama on a hunger strike, that's who."

Jay's eyes widen. "Oh, shit. You're right."

I grip the arms of the couch. "We leave in a week."

"What's your lawyer say? Hang on. Someone's at the door." She walks over to the intercom and squints at the image, then pushes the button. "It's your reindeer." She sits on the arm of the couch. "Has your lawyer said anything? Or Alex Steele?" Jay turns to the screen and addresses my friends. "Did you know she's my agent, too?"

"Good for you, girl." Rosalie smiles briefly, then her face slips back into rage mode. "Cara, what *did* Alex Steele say about this?"

My mouth opens and closes a few times but then Wes bursts through the door to my apartment and I see from the corner of my eye that he has a massive shiner. "Wes?"

The tuna bowl clatters to the floor as I spring out of the couch. "What happened?"

He waves a hand and saunters over to the couch. "It's nothing. I just … can I come sit with you for a little?"

Shante, Toni, and Rosalie are literally leaning into the camera as if they can get closer to Wes and examine his face as I'm doing. I gently trace the outline of his bruising. "This isn't nothing. What happened?"

"You want some ice?" Jay talks around a mouth crammed with tuna salad. She must have picked my bowl up from the floor and helped herself.

Wes shakes his head. "I took an elbow to the face during a scrimmage, that's all."

Jay arches a brow at him and swallows her food. "Must have been one hell of a corner kick if elbows were flying that hard. Your keeper okay?"

Wes waves a hand and then turns to face my friends. "You must be the beloved Midfield Mamis."

"Oh, we are." Shante nods. "I've heard about you, Wes Stag. I know where you live, and I know who your family is."

He snorts. "Most people know who my family is."

Shante makes a sound like "mm hmm," and shrugs. "Well, I don't have time to tell you that if you hurt this woman, I'm going to wax your pubic hair and feed it to you."

"My god." Wes claps his thighs together and I slide closer to him on the couch, making room for Jay, who still has my tuna.

I'm grateful for the chaotic distraction until Rosalie shakes her head and groans. "Wesley Stag, you did not get that in a scrimmage. You were in a brawl."

"What?" Jay, Toni, Shante, and I yell in unison as we all turn to face Wes, who closes his eyes.

"Some of the guys were upset about the added security at the stadium. You know, for the paparazzi."

"So? I'm upset about it, too." Jay tosses the empty food bowl on the coffee table and crosses her arms over her chest.

Wes takes a deep breath. "Well, one of the guys said something I'd rather not repeat about the Rubeo incident. And I lost my temper."

My friends all start shouting that they're glad he stood up for me like that, how they hope he taught that guy a lesson. All I can hear is that my worst moment has infiltrated the locker room of the men's team here in Pittsburgh and that someone very important to me feels the need to violently defend my right to exist without being grabbed.

"I can't do this." I say the words quietly and repeat them more decisively.

"Can't do what, sweetie?" Rosalie mimics petting my hair like she used to do in person if something upsetting happened.

"I can't go to the camp. I have to boycott. If they won't fire Lou Rubeo, I won't play."

The room is silent for a few beats and Wes grabs my hand, squeezing. Jay drapes an arm around my shoulder and hands me my phone. "You better call Alex. She'll want a heads up, or maybe she will be the one to call Akemi."

Wes nods and keeps on squeezing my hand. "Maybe call Tawnya, too? You'll probably need a lawyer since this is a contract issue."

I take a deep breath, preparing myself to make these calls, feeling calmer than I have for weeks. I'm not going to just casually give up my dreams, obviously, but I feel a sudden certainty that this is the way forward, that boycotting and refusing to play, refusing to score goals for the United States, is the way to get them to listen when I say I won't be treated like that.

Jay springs to her feet. "If you call Tawnya, ask her for a referral for me, too."

"You, why?" Wes chuckles. "You gonna beat someone up?"

"No, asshat. I'm boycotting the national team, too." She rests a hand on my shoulder. "If you're not going to camp, I'm not going. We have to get rid of this guy. Together."

CHAPTER 27
WES

I don't know what to wear to therapy. On television, whenever someone's in therapy they seem like they stop on their lunch break from an office job. My office is a soccer field, and I'm not allowed on it until I deal with this, so I go with a polo shirt and black jogging pants.

I knock on Dr. Georgia's door and pull at my collar as I wait uncomfortably in the hall. The door opens, revealing a short woman with dark skin and a wide smile. "Wesley Stag! Good to meet you. Come on in." She opens the door and gestures into her office, which is painted yellow and manages to capture the gray Pittsburgh light and make it seem sunny.

"Call me Wes, please."

She nods and sinks into an armchair. She has a small desk in one corner, but the rest of the room is filled with different types of furniture. There's a massage table along one wall, a couch, and a wingback chair opposite hers. "Sit anywhere you like."

I nod and perch at the edge of the wingback.

She smiles and clicks her pen. "Your coach asked me to talk with you about the altercation in the locker room. But I'd like to start by just checking on how you're doing overall."

I scratch my head. "What do you mean?"

She shrugs. "How have the last few months been for you? Your medical records indicate you've had quite a comeback from an injury."

I shrug. "Parts have been great. I'm playing pro soccer, right?"

She nods. "You are indeed." And then she waits.

And I wait, and I realize I'm supposed to keep talking. "So, yeah, I had the injury and that sucked. But my girlfriend was really supportive while I was in physical therapy."

"It's wonderful to find someone who supports us when we're ill or injured." Dr. Georgia smiles. I try to decide if it's cheating if I don't go back and say the word girlfriend is presumptuous of me. Dr. Georgia continues. "Getting injured must have been disappointing, especially so early in your career."

I nod. "Disappointing. Yeah."

She taps her lip. "Is that what led to the fight in the locker room?"

A swell of anger pulses behind my ribs. "I think you probably know that the fight was about my girlfriend, who was assaulted on television, and Harrison said some fucked up things about it."

Dr. Georgia squints and does that slow nod thing. I hated it when my parents used to do it, and I'm not thrilled to see now. "My notes from the coaching staff indicate that you and Ms. Moreno are, perhaps, quietly dating, and also that Mr. Harrison made rude remarks, prompting the coaches to arrange for some intimate partner violence prevention education, and that you took issue with the remarks and physically attacked your teammate. Does that sound right?"

"Yes!" I growl the answer, because it is accurate but also so inadequate, I'm not sure what else to even say about it.

I stand and start pacing the office as Dr. Georgia keeps nodding. "You clearly care very deeply for this woman."

"Cara."

"Okay. Cara. My understanding is that she experienced harassment and you…" she gestures like I'm supposed to keep going. I don't know what to say. Dr. Georgia sighs. "You haven't been able to directly intervene. What's that like for you?"

I yank on my hair. "It's utterly infuriating, that's what it's like."

"Tell me more about that, Wes."

I roll my eyes and sink back into the chair. "She's worked so hard and she's so fucking amazing. Like, top of the world amazing. Unparalleled. And then she's dealing with this nonsense, and I can't do a thing about it. I can't protect her. I can't even get my own teammates to see why it's wrong for men to treat people that way. Like, how dare this small-ass guy make her feel powerless."

"Mmm. Yes. I see." Dr. Georgia nods.

"Sure, you see. The people who see, see. But I have no clue how to make this type of thing stop. Not a damn clue. I'm so angry."

"I can see that." Dr. Georgia starts taking notes on her pad of paper.

Who even knows what she's writing down. I realize I've been shouting, and half the stadium probably heard me bellowing. I take a deep breath.

"You know, Wes, it's admirable that you want to defend Cara." She smiles. "But you also must know you can't control others' actions. What you can control is being there for her, supporting her in constructive ways. Managing your own reactions."

I have my mouth open to tell her I am supporting Cara. I'm distracting her, I'm giving her what she needs. But I'm not managing my own reactions to anything. Not really. I snap my mouth closed.

Dr. Georgia clicks her pen again. "Many people who experience harassment feel powerless to stop it. And the people who love those experiencing harassment feel those same overwhelming emotions."

"I spend a lot of time imagining what it would be like to fly out there and throttle this guy."

Dr. Georgia says, "hm," and writes something else down in her notebook. "The desire to take action is understandable. Are you maybe making an assumption about what Cara needs, though?"

I grind my teeth together. "Cara needs to boycott the national team. She told me that yesterday and then asked me to go home so she could sleep alone."

"And that didn't feel good."

"Of course it didn't. She's my fucking girlfriend." Except that's not all of it. If I'm brutally honest, I feel a little guilty because I used to be some guy like Harrison, who saw Rubeo with Cara and didn't recognize how harmful his actions were.

Now, after what we've shared, I feel like Cara is mine, body and soul. And I think that might be the crux of my rage right now. This Rubeo fucker messed with something that's mine.

Dr. Georgia raises her brows and gestures for me to go on. "Do you feel like boycotting isn't enough? That you should do something in addition to her choice?"

I stare out the window. Dr. Georgia's office has an excellent view of the freight trains going opposite directions along the banks of the Mon River. "I guess I feel ineffective."

"Hmm. Sort of like when you hurt your back?"

I stare at her. I breathe for a few minutes and nod. "Yeah. Like that."

She clasps her hands in her lap. "It sounds like you have a bit of a tendency to downplay your feelings, whether physical or emotional. Does that seem fair?"

I shrug. "I have no idea. You're the expert."

"Well," she starts. "What happened with your injury? How did you process those big feelings about something so important?"

I snort. "First I had to get my parents to stop wailing that I'll wind up paralyzed."

"Your parents?"

I wave a hand. "Yeah. I hurt my back before, in high school, and my dad laid into me that I'm going to wind up in a wheelchair unable to take care of myself."

"That must have been extremely frustrating to hear on top of your disappointment at getting injured."

"Yeah. Okay. I'm sensing a theme."

She smiles. "And that is?"

I tap my fingers on the arm of the chair. "I hate feeling like I can't do enough, and then I hate it more when other people tell me not to do more, and it all just simmers."

"And then what happens?" She arches one brow expertly, and I briefly wonder if that skill is a prerequisite for becoming a therapist.

I sigh. "I snap." I think about my snap judgment when I first saw Cara with Rubeo in California, how I immediately assumed something awful. I think about screaming at my parents and eventually just not even telling them I was going to the elite camp to be seen by scouts. I think about tackling Harrison to the floor, and I decide he deserved that beating and I'm not going to waste more energy dwelling on that one.

Dr. Georgia sets her notebook on the floor next to her chair and leans forward. "We are out of time for today. But you made some insightful connections here about how you respond when you feel powerless or ineffective. I'd like to work with you to build some healthier strategies to process your emotions if you're up to that."

I nod. "I guess. What happens now?"

She smiles. "Now you go home, and we meet again next week, same time."

CHAPTER 28
CARA

WOMEN'S NATIONAL TEAM GETS EMOTIONAL IN THE FACE OF MORENO Accusations
    By Ed Realm, News and Views

Since When Is a Kiss Such a Problem: Can women stand up to competition on the field if they can't handle the celebration afterward?
    By Logan Henderson, A-List Almanac

Within minutes of Jay texting the rest of the players named to the national team, they all decide to boycott the camp in solidarity. A few of them even message me privately that they, too, had had uncomfortable interactions with Lou Rubeo. None of the players will agree to play until the organization fires him.

I have absolutely no idea what to do with that collective support and break down crying on the floor of the apartment until Jay calls Coach Lucy, who drives over to sit with me. She runs her fingers through my sweaty hair and doesn't say anything, just lets me cry out loud until my throat hurts.

"It's hard to process a big wave of love when you're used to a fight," she soothes. And then she starts to tell me about her ex, a man who manipulated her and made her feel small and eventually started stalking her. "The hardest thing for me at that time was accepting help from my soccer team … and from Hawk." She smiles as she says her husband's name, a far-off look in her eye.

Lucy takes a deep breath. "I would be remiss as your coach if I didn't encourage you to speak with a mental health professional about all of this." I stiffen. I know instinctively that therapy is good for everyone, and I've done a lot of work with the team and the sports psychologist, blinky eyes and all. But I didn't grow up in a family that encouraged me to talk about my feelings, and I certainly never had anyone in a position of power tell me that someone else is to blame for anything that happened to me.

Lucy continues, her hands still soothing me. "I can see why you might not want to speak with someone associated with the team, Cara. But I met some terrific professionals at the women's center, and I'd be happy to make a recommendation."

I sniff. So far, Lucy's recommendations have a 100% record of being amazing. My agent, who Lucy found for me, is actually flying in later today to talk more about the national women's team boycott. I draw in a breath and manage to sit up. Lucy hands me some water, which I sip gratefully. "I'd like that. If you could suggest someone to talk to." I bite my lip. "But I don't know where to start …"

Jay lets out a relieved sound and I remember that she's still here, draped over the back of the couch, concerned. "I've been to tons of therapy," she tells us. "It's great for my game, not that I'm playing right now. But anyway, just let the doc guide the conversation if you're stuck. Want me to drive you to a session?"

———

A few hours and a long shower later, I'm nestled into a comfy couch in a brightly lit therapist's office not far from Jay's and my apartment. Apparently professional athletes can get in to see professionals on the fly … that or Lucy called in big favors. The therapist is a Middle Eastern woman who told me to call her Amira. She smiles from an overstuffed chair across from me, her silver bob haircut glinting in the sunlight. "I read the notes your coach sent over, as well as the information from your intake form. Cara, that must be very difficult. How are you doing today?"

I shrug. "Not great? I don't know what to say."

Amira nods. "You must have worked very hard for a very long time to be selected for the national soccer team. Can you tell me about your soccer career?"

My eyebrows shoot up into my hairline. "My career might be over just as it's getting started." Amira waits patiently for me to elaborate. "I just feel like I'm always that little girl, begging the grownups to just be allowed to play. And they're always telling me I'm just a little girl who shouldn't want to."

Amira sits forward in her chair, elbows on her knees. "Can you tell me more about that? Who are the other grownups invalidating your talent?"

I roll my eyes. "My whole life. Everyone. My parents ... they wanted me to be a timid little princess in skirts, on the hunt for a husband. Now this fucking guy thinks all I'm good for is his sexual pleasure. Or something." A wave of nausea forces its way up my throat, and I cough into my fist to avoid vomiting at the thought of Rubeo's mouth against mine. I reach for a water glass on the table by the couch.

"Take your time." Amira nods and just waits. She really is a good listener. I take a few breaths to gather my thoughts.

"I just want to play soccer. I don't want to be a femme fatale out to get men fired. I don't want to be an icon. I just want to go to work, train hard, and play with my team. I've earned that."

Amira nods. "You certainly have. You are a tremendous athlete. Your coaches are unanimous in that assessment."

I grunt. Amira leans back in her chair. "Unfortunately, what you are experiencing is common for women in all career paths, and you're certainly in the limelight in a high visibility career like athletics." She leans forward again. "But this harassment and abuse does not erase your talent. You have accomplished so much, despite these obstacles."

I don't know what to say in response to that, so I just stare at her. She smiles and a few beats pass. I can't tell if she's waiting for me to say something else, so I just sip the water and stare at her.

"I worry I brought this all on myself."

Amira frowns. "Can you tell me more about that? I want to understand what you mean."

I tap at the arm of the couch, thinking about my parents, the shitty referees I used to have in high school who viewed officiating a women's game as a punishment. "It's like no matter how good I am, there are always all these people trying to undermine me. All the women's players. Like we're a joke or something."

Amira nods. "Not a funny joke, is it?"

I shrug. "Eventually it just feels like maybe I don't deserve to be here. Or maybe I do deserve ... whatever Rubeo is doing. Like that's the cost of playing."

Amira nods empathetically. She seems to nod a lot. "You did nothing to deserve being harassed and mistreated. The blame lies entirely with the perpetrator and those who allow him to remain in his position. Not you."

I stare at her.

"Let me repeat that, Cara. Because it's very common for people who have had these experiences to blame themselves. But this is not your fault. You did nothing wrong."

I blink a few times and turn away from her gaze. "I feel stupid for hoping I could just play soccer. Like … my boyfriend just plays soccer. He gets up and goes to work and gets a bigger paycheck than me and nobody thinks he's being cute. I guess it was naive to think I could have that, too."

Amira nods a few times more and taps the arms of her own chair, studying me. "It's not naive to expect fair and equal treatment. You deserve to feel safe and respected. This is in no way your fault."

The more she says that the stiffer I feel. Like a big ball of fire is crawling up my spine and squeezing my throat. It's very hard to believe her, to believe I've earned the right to my place among the soccer greats when so many others see me as an object. Jay has tried to keep me from the headlines and the comments online, but I've seen what people are saying. I've heard the names they're calling me.

Amira continues. "My office is a safe space for you to process unfair treatment. Whatever you feel is the right thing, and the only way through all this is to honor those feelings and try to understand them."

I swallow through the sludge of overwhelm. Amira smiles at me. "I'm so proud to have met you. You are a resilient, talented person."

The tears come again, and I let them. Amira sits quietly, patiently, while I cry. Afterward, I feel both empty and full.

I feel drained after therapy and all I want to do is take a nap, preferably with Cara in my arms. I figure she must be pretty overwhelmed, too, so I stop and grab us some food and head toward her apartment to see if I can convince her to take a siesta with me.

I raise my hand to ring the buzzer, but Jay flies out the building door and I grab hold of it. "Hey." I hold it open for her as she squeezes out.

"Oh. Stag. Hey. She's up there." Jay smiles. "She'll be glad you're here, I think."

And then she bustles off, shouting for her phone to send a message for her and growling when the robot voice seems to misunderstand her commands. I saw some of the headlines. I know the women's team decided to boycott their camp this coming weekend unless the national office fires her abuser.

I clench my fists against the flame of rage licking my throat at the thought of this guy. I try to remember that Dr. Georgia said this is normal. It's normal for me to feel angry like this. I just have to learn what to fucking do about it other than smash someone's face.

I take the stairs up to Cara's apartment two at a time and tap on her door. She pads over to it, and it sounds like she's wearing slippers or something. I'm staring down at the floor when she opens the door, so I see the leopard print fuzzy footwear before I glance up and see her face. "Cara." Her eyes are puffy and it's obvious she's been crying. I open my arms and she steps right in and I squeeze her tight.

Her scent wafts around me, like a fog of calm. I just feel right when I'm with her. I don't know that anyone else has ever understood me the way she has, and I don't know that I've ever known anyone else like I do her. She doesn't have to tell me she's feeling overwhelmed by her teammates stepping to bat for her. It's no light lift to get a group of women to put their professional sports careers on the line like this.

"I saw the news," I whisper, and she nods against my chest. "Want to take a nap?"

She pulls her head back a few inches to look at my face. "Is that a euphemism or do you really want to sleep?"

I smile. "I want whatever you want…" She frowns. "Okay, I want to actually sleep. But I'm game for whatever in a few hours if you let me hold you."

A sigh slips out and she seems to melt into me even more. I'm feeling pretty good, pain wise, and I stoop to grab her legs with one hand, hooking her up in my arms with a smile on my face. "Feels good to haul you around."

She reaches around and pats my back. "It doesn't hurt anything?"

I shake my head. "I'll tell you if it does."

A few short strides later and I'm placing her gently on the mattress. Cara has said before that she's got some weird hang-ups about doors being open, so I reach for it and catch her eye. She nods and I push it shut with a snick. Then I kick off my shower slides and crawl into bed with her, plucking the slippers from her feet and tucking her against my side.

"What did I miss?"

"Hmm." I love drawing sighs from her. I love making her feel good. She is such a fierce lioness. I have no doubt she could eviscerate anyone, mentally or physically, if she set her mind to it. And I get to hold her in my arms. "I saw a therapist …"

"Me, too," I whisper, kissing her ear.

"That shit is hard work."

I nod and squeeze the fingers she has laced through mine around her belly. I feel her drifting off, the slowing of her breath as she sinks into the mattress. The warm lure of sleep sneaks up on me … until my phone rings.

And it's the special, obnoxious ring I set up for my agent at his insistence. Cara groans and I roll away from her, reaching for the phone to quickly answer so the noise stops. "Hello?" I whisper in a way I hope conveys my irritation. Because what the fuck, man. It's the off season and he knows I just went to my mandated therapy session.

"Wes, baby." Brian has a way of talking to me like I'm simultaneously five years old and the most important person in his life. "I've got news."

"News you couldn't text me?" I wedge the phone under my shoulder and turn sideways, needing to touch Cara to ground myself. I rest a hand on the swell of her hip and wait.

"So, I know you're aware that the Olympics are coming up."

"Yeah. No shit."

"Don't talk to me like that, baby. I'm your daddy here."

"Brian, do not ever call yourself that again or I swear to god I will fire you."

"Fine, fine." He chuckles. "Did you see Lewis blew out his knee at camp this week?"

"What?" The starting left wing for the national team has been to three World Cups. I have a signed photo of him and my Uncle Hawk on the field together before Hawk retired.

Brian grunts. "Bad tackle at practice. Shitty timing for him and the team and all that."

I pull my hand from Cara's butt and drag my fingers through my hair. "That really sucks, man. Thank you for telling me personally, I guess."

"Wes. Baby. Beautiful, obtuse baby. Lewis is out and they need to replace him. They're calling up players to the training camp this weekend before the friendly match versus Colombia."

"I thought the women play Colombia."

Brian snorts. "The nation has a men's team, too, you know. Anyway, you're up, Wesley. I already emailed you the info. Best get yourself to the airport."

Brian hangs up and I stare at my phone in disbelief. Did I really just get called up to play for my country? I swallow, a thick knot of ... something ... sticking in my throat.

Cara rolls over and squints at me through sleepy eyes. "What was that about?" She rubs at her face.

"Shh. Don't get up."

She sits up. "I want to know what the call was about. You can tell me shit, too, Wes. I'm not totally fixated on my own problems."

"Hey, that wasn't what I was doing. I know you've got room for more than one thought at a time." I grin at her and kiss her cheek. She arches a brow and gestures for me to go on. I take a deep breath. "I got invited to the national team camp."

Her eyes fly wide. "Wes. That's amazing!" She takes a breath. Her face falls. "Oh."

"Yeah. Oh." I lean against her headboard, elbows on my knees and face in my hands.

Neither of us says anything, waiting for the other to speak. My mouth is dry and it's like someone poured sand on my tongue.

"What do you want me to say here?"

"I don't know. This has been my whole life. My only dream."

"I know that. And I know you know it's my dream, too."

I nod. "This is how we met in the first place—both of us chasing this goal. And now it's here at my fingertips."

She nods. She clenches her teeth. I think about how this chance might not come again. She just stares at me. I sputter. "You saw how an injury took me out this year. You saw that."

"What are you saying?" I tug on my hair, considering my words, but she spits out, "It should be an automatic no. No discussion."

"What the fuck?" Is she seriously dictating the terms of my career to me here? "Are you my dad now? Telling me what's best? This isn't just some snap decision I can push away without considering options."

Cara closes her eyes. Her chest expands as she takes a deep breath and then lets it out slowly. "I think you should go."

"I didn't say that."

"No, I mean I think you should leave my apartment. Right now, please."

"Cara, wait. We have to talk through this."

She shakes her head and points to the door. My phone rings again, Brian's piercing ringtone, insistent. "I have to take this."

"I said get out." Her tone leaves no room for discussion, so I grab my shoes and leave, the pinging shrieks from my phone chasing me down the hall like the horns of Jericho.

CHAPTER 30
CARA

I HEAR VOICES COMING FROM MY LIVING ROOM. I MUST HAVE FALLEN ASLEEP after I kicked Wes out of my room, because the light has shifted and it's nearly dark outside. I figure Jay must have invited people over, and I am about to pull a pillow over my head to ignore them when one of the voices floats close to my door. It's familiar.

"Cara, chica, get your cute behind out here." A series of knocks shake my door as the sleep fog dissipates.

"Rosalie?" I climb out of bed and shuffle to the door, opening it to see not only Rose, but Shante and Toni as well. My mouth drops open. Jay stands behind them, grinning.

My Midfield Mamis swarm into me, tackling me into the wall and squeezing me, muttering praise in Cuban and Puerto Rican slang as we all jump up and down.

"How are you here?" I pull my head out of the bramble of curls and hugging hands.

Shante pats my face. "We were going to come to your game against Colombia anyway." She shrugs. "Jay helped us switch our travel plans."

I clutch at my heart. "Is it possible to die of happiness? I'm so glad you guys are all here."

Toni shakes a finger at me. "You are not allowed to die, querida. Not with those feet."

Within ten minutes, I'm hustled to the sofa with my feet in a pan of warm water, the familiar sounds and smells of my former roommates surrounding me as I watch them initiate my current roommate into the healing wonders of a soothing pedicure.

"You owe me for this, Moreno," Jay says, but I can tell she's enjoying the feel of the warm water on her tired feet.

Shante has a laptop open, curating headlines and telling me there's something she wants me to see. "There's a hashtag. Did you know about the hashtag?"

I nod. "Yeah. I like it. We stand with Cara." I can't hold back my smile at the thought of that, even if it is only a few people among a loud chorus of assholes using different hashtags about the situation.

"No." Shante shakes her head. "No, I mean it's a trending hashtag, Cara. Look." She spins the screen so I can see. "There are over ten million posts from women supporting you, around the world."

My eyes adjust to the screen, and I see the posts, more each second. Stories of harassment at work and feeling inspired to speak up. Girls in high school posting about talking to the school board about equal equipment and field access. And dozens and dozens of former national team players who have experienced unwanted touches from Lou Rubeo.

"Oh my god." I point at the screen. "This is…"

"A tidal wave." Toni pulls my foot out of the water and up onto her lap and starts hacking at my heels with a pumice stone. "You threw a pebble into the ocean, and the ripples made a fucking tsunami."

With a triumphant huff, Shante pulls up a video. It's a compilation from the current national team. Everyone apparently sent in videos from their own homes, explaining the boycott and how they're not going to stand for this treatment from our national office.

"This is more than I ever thought I wanted," I whisper.

My friends squeeze me in support. "All eyes are on you," Rosalie chirps. "We see you. The world sees you. You have everything now."

A sob roars from my chest. "But I don't have Wes. He didn't stay."

Jay growls as I explain what happened before they turned up at the apartment. "Get me a hunting permit, Rosalie. I'm going to shoot a Stag."

"Fuck this guy. He had his chance." Shante slams the laptop shut. "We've got other shit to worry about." She holds out a selection of nail polish for me. "I'm thinking red. For the blood of your enemies."

"Where are my enemies? I mean, currently."

"We're doing a press conference, roomie." Jay smiles and pulls a piece of paper from her pocket. "In a few hours we're meeting at the stadium with Alex Steele, Lucy, all those folks. You get to read our statement out loud."

"Our statement?"

Jay grins and explains that our series of emails and text messages with the national team is now assembled as a manifesto, a set of demands for the international sporting body to clean house in the national office or risk the US women not participating in the Paris Olympics. The team manager even put together a list of financial hits the program will take without our national team out there driving ticket sales, merchandise sales, and premium television viewers.

"We're going to rain on them like molten, hot metal until they slice that misogynist cancer from the office." Toni nods definitively. "Now let's get you dressed."

CHAPTER 31
WES

I DON'T EVEN LOOK AT WHAT I'M PACKING IN MY BAG BACK AT MY APARTMENT. I don't remember the drive over here, either. I keep seeing Cara's face, so hurt and angry, and then I remember my own face when my uncle took me and my cousins to watch the national team play for the first time.

I was five years old with my face pressed against the bleacher railing, staring at the guys on the field, desperate to be among them someday. And even though I fought like hell through my injuries, I don't know if I truly believed I'd be here, invited to put on the Stars and Stripes to represent my country on the soccer field.

Like, who turns down this kind of opportunity?

Cara does. For good reason.

I don't know how to silence the voice in my head telling me I'm making the wrong choice. This has been my only choice for as long as I remember. I grab my cleats and shove them in my duffle bag. My flight leaves in three hours. I don't have time for second thoughts.

But my guts are roiling and I search for my phone. I can take a few minutes to call Uncle Hawk and ask him what to do. He's no stranger to this opportunity and he knows the stakes. I press the icon for his contact, waiting for the call to connect.

And I realize he's probably at home with Aunt Lucy, comforting her because *she* isn't with the national team right now, either. A wave of shame rolls over me, thinking about her getting fired and all the power of my family backing her up didn't change a goddamned thing.

I hang up the phone before Uncle Hawk can answer.

I stare out my window, even though it's dark and I can't see outside. I know what's out there: an entire world divided into people who are sick of the shit Cara and all women have to endure…and scumbags who let it continue by turning the other way.

"Fuck!" I scream and bury my hands in my hair, hoping I can somehow tug it all out in one symbolic yank.

I call Cara and she sends my call right to voicemail, but I deserve that. I wait for the robotic voice to finish and I blurt, "Cara. I'm passing up my chance. I'm taking a stand with you." And then, because it's true and overwhelming and necessary, I add, "I love you. I'm coming to find you and tell you in person."

CHAPTER 32
CARA

Coach Lucy, Jay and I take our seats at the table in the press room, which is currently empty because the stadium staff is giving us a minute to get our bearings before unleashing the hounds. And I know they're hungry as actual feral dogs for the scoop on this situation, especially as the men's team gathers in California for their international friendly match.

The thought of the men's team turns my stomach sour and I worry I might puke until Jay squeezes my hand on the table. I nod and Coach Lucy waves a hand at the guard at the door. He opens the swinging metal panel and a herd of cameras, microphones, and hairspray shuffles past him.

The seats in the room fill immediately and interns rush to bring microphones to the table, flashbulbs popping as photographers adjust their settings for the lighting in the room. I tune it all out and think about the statement I'm about to read.

Coach Lucy taps on the microphone a few times and the din settles down. "Thank you for being here tonight," she says. "I'm Lucy Moyer, former assistant coach for the women's national soccer team."

The press erupts into angry shouts and Lucy holds up a hand. "I say former because, as I'm sure you know by now, I was dismissed from my position after expressing my concern that one of my players was being harassed by the president of our national organization." Lucy purses her lips and I clench my butt, knowing it's almost my turn to talk to the cameras. "Rather than examine the issue, the national office sent me home hours before the team played an international match. And I think you all know what happened after that."

Another roar from the press. Hands wave in the air and everyone speaks on top of one another. The sound throbs through the room, the bright lights pulsing. I can't see or think. My phone starts ringing in my pocket and I smash the button to send the call to voicemail.

Lucy holds up her hand again and stands, pulling the microphone up with her. "At this time, Cara Moreno will read a statement from the collective players from the national team, about their choice to boycott this weekend's camp and match. Cara?"

Mercifully, the crowd of reporters remains quiet as I clear my throat and adjust the paper. "Thanks. Um, thank you all for being here." I glance up at them and they all stare. "I'm not used to the spotlight like this. I never wanted to be up here making statements." I clear my throat again, more aggressively, and Jay slides me a cup of water, which I clutch in one hand. "I just want to play soccer. All of us on the national team … we just want to play soccer. We aren't out here to be pretty. We aren't looking for relationships. We just want to play the game."

I pause to sip the water and hope the press will hold off their flood of questions until I read the whole statement. "Those of us playing professionally, we do so with lower salaries than our male counterparts, even if we score more goals and win more games. But we aren't here talking about that injustice." I stare at the crowd again. They wait, but I do see red lights flashing from the cameras, so I know this is being broadcast live … everywhere. "We are here, back at our homes and not in California, because our governing body is being led by a predator. A man who grabs women against our consent and kisses us without permission, who corners us in hallways to talk about our bodies…this is not a man who views us as professional colleagues. This is predatory behavior that has no home in any workplace. Because that's what professional soccer is for us: our work. This is our career. We train and we study, and we fight for this nation, for this sport, as professionals, and we demand to be treated as such."

I take a giant breath and see Jay nodding out of the corner of my eye. "That is why none of the women named to the national team squad will agree to play for this country until Lou Rubeo is removed from his position, and until the board that refused to discipline him is removed from their seats." I look over at Coach Lucy, who pumps her fist at me quietly. I nod. "We will now take your questions."

Another thunderstorm of noise erupts from the crowd, and I've never navigated one of these situations before, so I sit back in my chair and wait for someone to tell me what to do. Lucy is more adept at this atmosphere, and she points at a woman in the front row. "Pam. Go ahead."

The woman stands up. I gasp when I see she's wearing a shirt that says #WeStandWithCara. She smiles at me. "Pam O'Reilly. Fem Forward Press. Cara, what does it feel like to speak up after this abuse, and inspire so many other women to do the same?"

"Pardon?"

Pam smiles wider. "Our last count showed over 15,000 testimonials online of women and people of other marginalized genders who have spoken out against harassment or abuse in the workplace since hearing your story. Can you comment on how it feels to lead that movement?"

I blink at her a few times. "I didn't want to lead a movement. I just want to play soccer. I want everyone to be able to do what they want to do without worrying about anyone crossing a line."

Pam scribbles on her notepad, smiles, and sits. Lucy points to someone else in the crowd, who directs their question right back at her, so I take a few moments to catch my breath. I glance at my phone and see there's a voicemail from Wes. I start sweating because he's supposed to be on a flight into enemy territory right now. But I'll have to deal with that later. In my periphery, I see movement at the side of the table and notice some murmurs, but I keep my eye on the crowd, surprised to find more faces that seem supportive than the angry macho crowd I feared.

Lucy points to a guy near the back of the room, who stands and introduces himself as Peter Winters from Sports Daily News. "Yes, Cara, can you comment on why nobody from the men's national team seems to have a problem with Lou Rubeo or his leadership? Seems like if he was such a bad president, there would be unrest from that camp as well?"

I open my mouth to tell Peter that the men aren't experiencing sexism from Rubeo, when someone interrupts me. "One small correction there for you, Pete."

I turn my head to see Wes standing by the table, wearing a US jersey from a few decades ago. I furrow my brow and Wes smiles at me hopefully. Peter gives Wes a "go on" gesture to see what sort of correction Wes might have for him.

Wes reaches for the microphone, which I hand him. "There *is* unrest with the men's national team. I, Wesley Stag, was recently named left wing for the squad and am joining the women's team in their boycott. Anyone who grabs a woman and kisses her without consent has no business leading an organization. The game and this nation mean too much to me to agree to play under conditions like that." Wes peels off his jersey and throws it on the table. "I stand with Cara and the national team, demanding that Rubeo be fired, and the board replaced." Wes crosses his arms over his chest and indeed remains standing.

A tear slides down my cheek and relief washes over me. A ragged sob escapes my mouth and I press my hand over my lips to avoid it getting picked up by the microphones.

Lucy and Jay handle questions for I don't know how long and eventually the security guard ushers the press from the room. Finally, the only people left are Lucy, Jay, and Wes standing around me.

Lucy dips in to squeeze me in a hug. "Cara, you were fantastic. Total class act." I see her look up at Wes and smile. She rests a hand on his shoulder. "Good to see you, nephew."

"Thanks. I'm just glad I made it in time." They grin at each other until Jay groans and stands up.

"All right, all right." She claps her hands. "Who is taking me for pasta? I haven't had wheat in like five months, and I think this warrants a good emotional eat."

Coach Lucy smiles. "I'll take you up on that. Mind if we call my husband on the way?"

"I'm here, babe." Hawk Moyer pokes his head in the door, grinning. "Proud of you all." He blows his wife a kiss and Lucy and Jay make their way over to him, leaving me alone in the room with Wes and his balled up national team jersey.

Wes slides his hands into the pockets of his sweatpants and looks down at me. "My agent is pretty pissed I didn't tell him I was skipping my flight."

"Oh yeah?"

He nods. "He'll get over it." I tap at the table and Wes slides into the folding chair at my side. "I couldn't go through with it, Cara. I'm sorry I wasn't strong enough to say no right away. You deserve someone who stands by your side no matter what."

I press my lips together and try not to cry.

Wes reaches for my chin, and I tilt my head into his palm. His voice is a whisper as he says, "I want you to know how much I admire your strength. How much my entire family supports you as a player. God, Cara, you are like fire on that field and all I want in the world is to see you back out there."

"All you want? Really?"

He grins. "I mean, I'd take another date with you as an add-on. But yeah, babe. I want you to do what you were born to do." He fishes in his pocket and pulls out his phone. "Here," he says. "Look." Wes slides the phone across the table to me so I can see a photo of him standing with his arms raise, the dark hairs of his lower belly visible beneath the hem of his T-shirt as he screams in unadulterated joy. I can see a room packed with people in similar poses. "That's when you scored your third goal against Jamaica. That's my entire family watching you, so proud of what you can do."

I clutch the phone to my chest, swelling with emotions I don't know how to name. I've never had an extended family watch my game, let alone cheer for me in unison. Wes reaches for my face with his other hand, and I drop the phone, moving my hands to rest on his thighs as he stares into my eyes. "Cara, you make me a better player, but more important, you make me want to be a better man. You are the piece I've been missing my whole life." He draws a shaky inhale. "I need you, Cara. I love you."

I open my mouth to say I love him, too, that I need him and his big, noisy family that will hopefully continue to butt in when either of us loses our way momentarily. But Tim Stag bursts into the room with my lawyer, Tawnya, at his heels. "We have news, kids."

We whip our heads over to stare at the intruders. Tim smiles. "Rubeo. Is. Out."

CHAPTER 33
CARA

WES ASKS IF HE CAN DRIVE ME HOME AFTER OUR LATE DINNER AT THE restaurant. Considering I drove down here crammed in the back seat of Jay's sedan with Shante and Rosalie, with Toni up front admiring all the Pittsburgh lights on the water, I was more than happy to accept a more spacious ride.

Once we're in the car, alone, Wes turns to face me before putting his key in the ignition. "Cara, I know I have a lot of atoning to do. A long way to go to prove that I'm solid, but—"

I place a finger over his lips and lean across the console to kiss him. I tug on his shirt, pulling him closer, savoring the taste of him. It's been days since we've been physically intimate. Weeks maybe? I've lost track of time with everything that's been happening in my life. "I need you," I whisper against his lips, and the responding moan from his chest tells me all I need to know about his state of mind.

He swallows, and turns the engine over, and I settle into my seat facing him as best I can. "I thought you'd be shirtless when you pulled that jersey off." I reach across the gear shift for his leg, tracing along the muscle with my index finger.

"You wish." I can see his grin in the light from the street lamps along the bridge as he heads toward my place. "That would have been an entirely different sort of statement if I hadn't had an undershirt on..."

I hum contentedly along with the music, enjoying the look of him as we make our way to my apartment. "I have four women camping in my apartment right now," I mutter, realizing this is the first time I've seen my friends in person in months.

"I don't mind. They're important to you." Wes shrugs. "You're important to me."

A smile tugs at my lips and I remember something I wanted to tell him earlier, before things got heated. "I called you my boyfriend. A couple times. Is that okay?"

Wes turns to look at me, slaps the turn signal, and pulls to the side of the road. "Cara." He punches the button for his four-way flashers. "You can call me whatever the hell you want. I've been yours from the moment I laid eyes on you. I fucking love you, remember?"

Something warm spreads through me and I do remember. I remember that I was about to say it back to him before his uncle burst in the room with legal updates about our case. Both the men's and women's national team camps have been rescheduled, and Wes and I fly to California together in a few days, along with Jay and Lucy. Both the Forge and Hot Metal have plans for an airport sendoff for us that, frankly, sounds more exciting than any team-sponsored celebration we've had yet in the Steel City.

"I remember something like that." I squeeze his leg. "I'm bad at this kind of thing."

"What? Being a rock star?" Wes tucks my hair behind my ear, his elbows bumping against all the different knobs and gadgets in a car that's too small for his long limbs.

I grin into his hand as he strokes a thumb across my lip. "I'm bad at verbalizing my feelings. I'm used to expressing myself physically."

Wes's teeth shine white as he grins at me under the streetlamp. "I'm happy to have that sort of conversation with you, Cara Moreno."

"Good. Take me home, Stag."

We arrive at my apartment to a flurry of activity. I see Jay in the middle of a circle of my friends, who are applying hair pomade and glitter with gusto. "Jay …" I clutch at the door frame for support. "Are you wearing makeup?"

She bats her lashes at me and flexes, looking cute as hell in a shirt, tie and fitted pants. My chicas are in heels and skirts with gold hoops and popping curls. Toni smacks her hands together and turns to face me. "Jay's taking us to a gay bar. You aren't invited, pana."

"You're not taking me out with you?"

Rosalie points at me. "You seem tired … or at least like you want to be in bed." She smooths her down her shirt. "This pansexual princess is looking to dance," she says, twirling.

Shante and Toni bust out laughing and Jay pulls her phone from her pants pocket. "Ladies, our ride is outside." She winks at me. "We'll be gone for hours."

And just like that, they're off in a cloud of expensive perfume and laughter. Wes wastes no time closing the door behind them and locking it, then backing me up against the kitchen island. "Do you want to dance, Cara? I'm very good with feet."

I swat at his chest. "I don't think you meant that how it sounds."

He arches a brow at me. "How did it sound?"

Biting a lip, I rock back and drink him in. I can see the lines of his abs through the undershirt, the bulge in his pants that pulses along with his breath. "It sounded like you're going to suck on my toes again."

Wes growls and hauls me over his shoulder, his steps eating the distance between the kitchen and my bedroom. He kicks the door shut behind him and tosses me on the mattress. I clear my hair from my face and gaze up at him, the adrenaline from this evening settling in my stomach. Or is that arousal?

It all comes out to the same thing as I gaze up at the look on his face. Wesley Stag has sex seeping from his pores, from the dark stubble on his chin to the blown pupils in his gray eyes, to the hot cock pressing against my belly as he holds himself above my body, staring. "I love you, Cara."

My face melts into a smile and I adjust myself, taking more of his weight onto my groin, where the friction feels perfect. "I love you, too, Wes. And I want you. Real bad."

His mouth hooks to the side in a crooked smile. "Anything you want." Pivoting to the side and freeing up his arms, Wes reaches behind his neck to pull off his undershirt with one arm. I wriggle out of my top and pull down my pants, reaching for my bra to remove it until he stops me with a gentle hand.

"Can I?" I nod and he pulls the straps down from my shoulders. I usually wear sports bras. I'm not even sure if Wes has ever seen me in a regular bra and panties, but he seems super interested in the sight at the moment. He rocks back to sit on his heels, staring at me as he traces his hands along my side, fingers grazing the cotton at my hips, the cups of my bra.

"My god, Cara, you're everything I've ever wanted. Look at you." I glance down, seeing myself through his eyes. And I smile at the sight of his lips on my skin. I love the contrast between our skin tones. I love the feel of his big hands across my belly. And I love the sounds he makes as he pinches my nipples before licking each of them thoroughly.

Somehow, we both wind up naked and curled together, kissing and sucking each other's skin until I'm worried we'll both be covered in hickies. Wes seems less concerned, asking for more when I latch on to his neck right where it meets his shoulder. I suck harder and he groans, pressing his hips into mine so powerfully I nearly come from the contact.

My gasp brings him back into the moment and he draws back, adjusting his position again so he can fit a hand between my legs. "I want you to come first, because I'm not going to last."

I shake my head. "I want you inside me. Please, Wes? Oh, god, that feels so good."

He bites his lip, pressing his thumb against my clit and meeting my eye, seeking permission to keep going on his quest to get me off. "Fine. Okay. Oh, yes. Like that. Wow." I sit up on my forearms, watching as Wes moves his hand in my wetness. I watch as his fingers disappear inside my body, surrounded by sensation as his touch seems to spread through my entire nervous system.

"You're so damn beautiful when you come for me. I love making you feel good." He rocks his hips against my thigh, like he can't bear to not be moving, and I reach for him greedily, clenching my fist around his length. We taste each other's moans as I kiss him while he rubs until I soar over the edge, coming in his arms, knowing this is the man who would give up everything he's ever dreamed of for the chance to support me, to do what's right.

I'm still coming when Wes slips inside me, and I open my eyes to find his face an inch from mine. I am filled with him, stretched magnificently around his hot, smooth cock, and I feel closer to him than ever before. "I love you," I whimper as I start to move beneath him. "I love you so much."

"Cara. Fuck, baby. I have to come. You feel so good, and I love you so damn much." Wes thrusts a few more times and I feel the muscles of his butt work as he moves. And then he stiffens, and I feel his release, over and over, warm and pulsing. But more than that I feel the tears on his cheeks as he rests his face against mine, telling me over and over how much he needs me, how he will never, ever let me go.

CHAPTER 34
WES

"Yo, Cara, Jay, you guys ready to go?" Wyatt, impatient as always, hollers down the hall to my girl and her roommate. We have hours until the three of us fly with Aunt Lucy to play rescheduled matches with the national teams, but Wyatt insists we go early. He doesn't want to stick around the airport for the press circus, mumbling something about keeping a low profile.

Me? I can't wait for the attention as the four of us head out to meet the new Soccer USA president Eloise Lisange, who immediately reinstated Aunt Lucy to the women's team coaching staff and gave her and Akemi a giant pay raise.

"Coming!" Cara staggers out of her bedroom under the weight of two duffel bags. She will be out in Cali for a bit after the match because her agent landed her some pretty slick endorsement deals and she'll be shooting commercials. Both of us made arrangements to keep up our therapy sessions remotely while we're traveling with the national team, and I've been surprised by how much I'm learning in those conversations.

I rush forward to take one of the bags from Cara, but she shakes her head. "I got it, babe. Save your back for the match against Colombia."

I wink at her. "I'll save my back for you, baby, and lie on it gladly."

"Gross. I'm going to turn on the car." Wyatt huffs out of the apartment with Cara on his heels, the clips on her bag squeaking as she walks.

I hear her phone chirp, and she pauses to check it, mouthing that it's her mom on the line. "Mama? Papi? Yes, I'm on my way to the airport right now." She smiles. Things have improved ever so slightly with her parents since Cara gave that press conference on television and Telemundo did a feature piece on her as America's "it" sports star. Cara's voice fades as she makes her way down the stairs with Wyatt, but she sounds happy telling her parents about the game schedule.

My stuff is already loaded in Uncle Ty's minivan, so I poke my head in Jay's room to see if she needs any help.

I catch a glimpse of her rainbow stack of keeper jerseys as she zips her bag shut with a flourish. "Had to get the lucky socks squeezed in the corners, but I fit everything in one bag."

"Nicely done." I glance around to see if she actually only has the one bag. "Need a hand with anything?"

She clips a belt bag around her waist and slaps me on the shoulder. "I'm good, Stagly. Looking forward to a few nights without you sleeping down the hall."

She steps through the door, and I follow her so she can lock up. I lean on the wall and tell her, "I've been trying to get Cara to stay at my place to give you privacy."

"Oh, sure, it's *me* who needs privacy." Jay rolls her eyes and heads for the stairwell. I can hear the bass thumping in the minivan from the lobby of the building and I have to laugh at the tricked-out sound system in a Honda Odyssey with 200,000 miles on it.

Wyatt barely waits for the sliding doors to close before he stomps on the gas. Jay turns around from the front seat and shakes her head at me when she sees that I've reached across the aisle between the captains chairs to hold Cara's hand. "What?"

"I'm going to miss you, Moreno."

Cara furrows her brow. "What do you mean?" I squeeze her hand tighter while we wait for Jay to elaborate.

Wyatt grunts. "She means you're going to have to start staying at Wesley's solo pad, so you don't keep her up at night with your sexcapades."

Cara's cheeks flush but I refuse to feel embarrassed about the sounds I can draw from my girlfriend when I'm doling out multiple o's. And I'm overjoyed at the idea of her spending more time at my place, just the two of us. I pull her hand closer to me and lean over so I can kiss her knuckles.

We pull in front of the domestic terminal at the airport, and I see Wyatt clench his jaw. He hates the press and I know he wants to get out of here before anyone notices us as part of the celebratory send-off. I hop out and pull our bags from the back of the van and barely get my head out of the way as he closes the door via a button by the steering wheel. "Play hard, guys. Go USA!" He zooms away before we can respond.

Cara and Jay are grinning as they head toward the sliding doors to the bag drop. Both our teams fill the landside terminal, along with fans of the Iron Army … and all their drums, cowbells, and giant black-and-yellow flags. Cara starts dancing to the beat of the drum line as we walk in with our bags and the Hot Metal women notice our arrival.

"They're here," someone shouts into a megaphone. And all hell breaks loose as forty pro soccer players, our coaches, and our most rabid fans start chanting "I believe that we will win." Jay drops her bag and starts clapping along with the beat and Cara follows suit. I have no choice but to drop my own bag and twirl my best girl, dipping her for a kiss to the roar of the crowd.

Someone shows up with a tuba and only then does airport security intervene and try to shuffle us to the security line. But Cara, Jay and I all have pre-check, so we make our way to Aunt Lucy, who has a microphone and speaker that one of the fans must have set up for her. "Thank you, Pittsburgh, for this incredible send off."

The crowd roars. People pause on their way to their flights, taking pictures and cheering "USA, USA" before they head into the security line. This right here is how I always knew it would feel to reach this level of competition.

But I never dared to imagine I'd be here alongside a woman playing at this same level, that I could focus as much on her as I do my career—more intently, actually—and instead of turning my dreams to dust my relationship would fill me with more joy than a game-winning goal.

"Cara, Jay and I cannot wait to show you what a united national team can do under great leadership." I hear Aunt Lucy's voice and I pull myself together by pulling Cara tight against my side. She rests her head on my shoulder and hugs my arm. Lucy points at me and I wave at the crowd. "And my nephew, Wesley Stag, is excited to kick in a new era of men's soccer on a team committed to building equity at all levels of the game. Right Wes?"

"Absolutely." My words are drowned by another roar of the crowd. We wave and sign a few autographs before Jay starts tapping at her watch and the four of us make our way through the security line. I recognize the security agent who held me up for a pat-down the first time I flew to California for one of these camps. I give him a salute as he glances over my shoulder at the crowd, still pressing right up against the barricade to cheer us off.

I smile at Cara as I reach for our bags. She yanks hers from my hand

and wags a finger at me and tips her head toward the shuttle to our gate. I press into the train car, snuggling up against her as if the car is overflowing when really, it's mostly empty. Cara laughs and leans in to my embrace. "I love you, Wes. I can't imagine being here without you."

I run a hand through her hair and kiss the top of her head. "I love you, too, Cara. And you're never going to be without me again."

THE US MEN'S TEAM GOT KNOCKED OUT IN THE FIRST ROUND, BUT THAT'S pretty much what everyone expected. I didn't mind because it freed up all my time to watch Cara play, watch Cara take press interviews, and watch her sponsors shower her with gifts and good-luck flowers.

My girl is starting to get comfortable in the spotlight, but she still flushes the most beautiful shade of rose when people say something particularly complimentary about her athletic prowess.

Today was the semifinal match against Sweden and I was right there in the front row with Cara's college roommates when she scored the game winning goal. Honestly, I think I strained my back a little bit cheering as my lady whipped off her jersey and took a victory lap, abs flexing like a bad-ass. Cara's parents even texted me that they were impressed, and I promised to pass their felicidades along to her.

But first, my girlfriend needs post-match recovery, and I have big plans to take care of her. I've been extremely patient, helping little kids in line for her autograph and taking pictures, texting the Stag family back home with all the important updates like yes, Cara received Aunt Alice's care package and yes, she's definitely still moving in with me once we get back to Pittsburgh.

I made arrangements with Aunt Lucy for Cara to take her ice bath separate from the rest of the team. After she signs the final autograph and waves at the fans, Cara says, "Sorry, guys. I have to do my cool down so I'm ready for Australia in the final in a few days."

I put two fingers in my mouth and whistle, kicking off a new wave of

"USA, USA" chants as Cara makes her way to the locker room. I know what she will find there: instructions for her post-game recovery session in a different location than she's expecting. I'm waiting in the hydro therapy room with fluffy towels and massage oil when Cara sticks her face in the door.

"Wes?" Her brow is furrowed in confusion. "Where's the rest of the team?"

I shrug. "I didn't check their recovery schedule, baby. Only yours."

She crosses her arms over her chest, and I can see her wiggling her toes, painted bright red this time, apparently for the blood of her on-field rivals … according to Rosalie. "Does Coach Lucy know you're in here with me?"

"Babe." I set the towels on the bench next to the small pool of icy water. "Someone has to time you and make sure you don't stay in there too long. I don't want you to get hypothermia."

Cara laughs and kicks off her sandals, sliding her shorts down to reveal the hottest little pair of booty shorts. I hope she plans to take them off for her ice bath, but I'm out of luck in that regard as she starts to slither into the water in her sports bra and those perfect underwear.

I lick my lips as she hisses, sinking up to her armpits and resting her head on the side of the pool. "I should tug you in here with me."

"Nah." I squat down beside her. "I didn't play today. And my body heat would warm up the water too much."

Cara's teeth start chattering and I see huge goose bumps on her lovely, coppery skin. I glance at my watch. "Nine minutes left." She growls. "I know it sucks. But you're going to sleep so well tonight."

She splashes me and damn. That water is frigid. But I fully intend to warm her up after she's done in there, so I don't worry too much about my damp shirt. We have this room to ourselves and there's a perfectly lovely cushioned bench along the back wall.

"Take my mind off of this. Tell me what you thought of the game."

"Damn, baby. It was outstanding." We piece the match together verbally and I love the expression on her face as she describes sending that final kick right past that Swedish keeper's fingertips. "I didn't think anyone would get past her this tournament. Didn't she have a perfect save record before now?"

Cara smiles contentedly, her arms stiff against the sides of the cold pool. My watch alarm beeps, and she springs from the water like she was launched out by a rocket. I barely get to my feet in time to open the towel and grab her. "Why do we do this to ourselves?"

I shake my head as I rub her through the towel, trying to warm her arms. "They say it helps our central nervous systems. Or the lactic acid. Or something."

"Something." She rests her wet head on my shoulder, and I guide us both toward the bench, easing her until she's lying down, big brown eyes fixed on mine. "What are you going to do now?"

I grin. "Now I'm going to warm you up." I pull the bottle of massage oil from my pocket and wave it at her, enjoying the sleepy, contented expression on her face as I squirt some of the oil into my hand. "Why don't you take off those wet clothes?"

"Too tired." She curls the towel more tightly around herself and I reach for a foot, massaging the arch the way I know she loves, drawing beautiful groans from her mouth, that melt into moans when I chase my touch with kisses.

"Do you want me to help you take them off?" She nods her head. "Let's just start with the bottoms and see how that feels, okay?" I love acting like this is some sort of clinical examination instead of me preparing to fuck her senseless and then carry her up to her room to tuck her into bed by curfew. Cara lifts her hips and I slide the wet undies off. I shove them into my pocket, despite being soaking wet, because I plan to use them later when I'm alone in my own room.

I slick up my hands with more of the oil and work my palms along her legs, massaging her calves and firm thighs as she spreads her legs wider, resting her feet on the floor on either side of the bench. "That's it, Cara. Perfect."

I lean in a nose her mound as she opens wider before I slide a slicked-up finger into her folds, parting her for me as Cara's chest rises and falls more rapidly. "That feels so good."

"Mm, it's all for you, baby. Is that enough pressure?" I study her face for a beat and add another finger inside her, resulting in a huge buck of her hips and her hands slapping down on my shoulders. "All right. Maybe just one more finger, then?" When I slide the third finger into her heat, Cara keens, raising up onto her elbows with her mouth in a tight oh. She breathes through her nose, and I can tell she's trying to keep things quiet. "Don't worry. I locked the door."

Cara nods and lies back on the bench as I fuck her slowly with my hand. Once I feel the pulsing flutters inside her, I know she's close. I lean forward and lick her, tasting salt and musk and perfection as she whimpers my name. I love the sound of my name on her lips. *My* name. And I'm so turned on by her pleasure that I almost come in my track pants.

"Wes, please." She eases up onto her forearms again, staring at me.

"Please what, Cara?" I slide my hand out of her body one finger at a time. I know what she wants, but I want to hear her say it.

"Please fuck me. I need your cock."

I promised her I'd never leave her wanting, ever again. So, I quickly shove my pants down below my butt and pull out my dick, which is so hard it bobs against my stomach as I position myself between Cara's legs. My eyes latch onto hers as I slide home and I feel her body relax, like this was exactly what she needed to totally let go.

Cara reaches for my waist as I bring my hands to either side of her head. My body is bent at an awkward angle, but I don't care about anything except this connection we share. "I love you, Cara. Always." I grunt, driving into her as she starts to come. She moves to hold a hand over her mouth to muffle her cries, but I kiss her instead, swallowing her moans and feeding her mine in exchange.

I feel her orgasm rip through her and mine is close behind, starting at the base of my spine and tearing through my body as I mutter into her ear over and over. "I love you. I need you. You are incredible."

After I get Cara bundled up in cozy sweats, I user her outside to where I booked a car service. She doesn't have another match for a few days, and her coaches said there are no team meetings this evening. She's all mine at the Olympic Village … until curfew, of course.

Cara leans a sleepy head on my shoulder, humming contentedly along with the radio, and we hold hands as we walk to her room. I'm prepared for anything, whatever she needs, but I'm really hoping she wants me here with her. When Cara opens the door to her room, I'm glad to see housekeeping has delivered the care package of food from Aunt Alice. Both our stomachs growl audibly when we're hit with the aroma of freshly-cooked food.

Cara darts into the room and opens the box, moaning out an "mmm" that goes straight to my groin. I'm about to slip out the door and let her eat, when she calls for me. "Will you eat with me?"

"Of course. Not even a question." I close the door and walk toward the table and chairs. Cara sits and rests her chin on one hand, reaching for me with the other. "Will you stay until I fall asleep?"

A wave of warmth floods over me and I scoot my chair closer to hers, so her body touches mine while we eat until we're stuffed. Cara gets ready for bed while I clean up, and then we climb into bed together.

I rub her arm as she drifts off and I fight hard to stay awake. My thoughts wander to the future, to a lifetime of us supporting each other on the field and strengthening our connection off of it.

Once her breathing slows and I know she's asleep, I press a kiss to her temple and slide out of her room. I rest my head against the door, hating the national team rules that keep us separated right now but honoring her commitment to following them.

My phone buzzes as I head to my own room and I see a text from Wyatt. I click it open, expecting some sort of celebration after the women's game today. Instead, it's a series of angry emojis followed by a chilling line of text.

> I don't know what to do, cuz. My bio dad showed up today.

———

Want one more glimpse of Wes and Cara's happily ever after? My newsletter subscribers get a spicy bonus scene. Visit laineydavis.com to sign up for a post-workout workout story.

FORGING LEGACY

A FORBIDDEN ROMANCE

CONTENT NOTE

This novel contains mentions and descriptions of parental abuse and neglect, which may be triggering for some readers. While not gratuitous in detail, the story does explore the long-lasting emotional and psychological impact of this trauma on the main character, Wyatt.

Please be advised that the following topics are discussed or alluded to within the narrative:

Physical and emotional abuse; Child endangerment and neglect; Manipulation and gaslighting; Anxiety, panic attacks, and PTSD; Unhealthy family dynamics and strained parent-child relationships

My intent is to handle these sensitive topics with care and respect while realistically portraying the challenges of overcoming past trauma. Please take care of yourself when reading.

CHAPTER 1
WYATT

I HAVE ZERO DESIRE TO DRIVE MY COUSINS TO A CROWDED BAR JUST TO BE THEIR designated driver when they close the place down.

I have even less desire to deal with their nagging and whining, so I guess I'm showering and putting on some sort of decent clothing to leave the apartment. A rotating cast of my cousins has lived in this three-bedroom apartment for years as we worked our way through Pittsburgh University— where most of us are varsity athletes.

Which means when we get a night off from our nutrition plan, we make up for lost time. Or … they do, anyway. I don't like losing control like that. I don't want to do something I'll regret. Something I can't undo.

"Yo, Wyatt! You curling your hair or what? We're missing happy hour." My cousin Odin pounds a fist on my bedroom door. I can hear Stellen and Gunnar grumbling behind him in the living room. I glance in the mirror and smooth a hand back through my dark hair. I cram a baseball cap down low, hoping it's enough to keep people from recognizing me. I really hate crowds.

With a sigh, I flick off the lights and pull the door open in a carefully timed maneuver that sets Odin off balance. I don't move to catch him as he stumbles into my room; we all laugh as he curses me from the floor. "You guys ready to go or what?" I ask, grabbing the keys to my Range Rover and striding toward the door.

Stellen argues his way into the front seat and turns on both his seat warmer and mine. It's New Year's Eve and cold as balls outside. Most of the students are still away for break, but half the sports teams have matches. We're going out with guys from the football and ice hockey teams. Which tends to mean there will be tons of girls looking to get lucky, rattling off our stats, and asking for damn autographs on bar napkins.

Did I mention I hate all this?

"Are you wearing perfume?" Odin leans front and sniffs my neck.

I swat him away. "Knock it off, man. It's called soap. I showered."

"Gunny, doesn't Wyatt smell like he's wearing a little something?" Soon all three of my cousins are sniffing me, sniffing themselves.

I try to ignore all of it and look for a parking spot near the bar. Something must be going right between me and karma because someone pulls out of a space a few doors down. All four of us cheer as I put on my blinker, hoping the scent analysis is finished.

Odin pulls out his shirt collar. He is, of course, not wearing a coat. He's like his dad, my Uncle Ty—a furnace.

Odin bucked all sorts of Stag family traditions and started playing football.

My mom and dad are deep into the world of pro soccer; Uncle Ty was a legendary pro hockey player. Stellen's dad, my Uncle Tim, always preferred to boss everyone around—he's a sports lawyer who manages all their contracts.

Odin rubs his palms together and waits for the traffic to pass so he can open his door. "All right, men. Let the good times roll. I've got exactly twelve more hours to exercise my liver before I start training for the combine."

I chuckle. At least my coach gives us New Year's Day off, but then I'm a senior and I've got a different path to going pro in my sport. I'm more focused on working with my agent to get signed somewhere far from Pittsburgh. I need to get the hell away from the specter of my biological father.

My cousins walk ahead of me and into the bar, where a loud chorus of cheers erupts from the crowd of fellow athletes and sports fans. If I time things just right, I can slide in at the tail end of the ruckus and find a seat at the bar.

This is exactly what I do, tugging my hat down a bit lower and pulling my Aunt Emma's latest book from my jacket pocket to read. A bartender asks me what I'm having, and I grunt out a request for a soda. Aunt Emma wrote a significant nonfiction bestseller about sexism and the patriarchy in the world of professional soccer. My cousin's girlfriend, Cara, is part of the book because she got grabbed and kissed on international television by some jerk in the Soccer USA office.

I'm racing my way through a chapter about his eventual jail time when liquid splashes down on my pages. I snap my gaze up, looking to see who spilled a drink on my book. I find my face an inch away from the most fantastic set of breasts I've seen in ages.

The soft, rounded globes nearly press against my nose as their owner leans past me to hand drinks to customers who, I realize, are pressing against me from behind. I glance around and the line at the bar is at least three deep. The bartender doesn't seem frazzled, though. She and her rack move methodically, stretching and leaning to pour drinks, handing them to the waiting customers. Her fingers fly over the buttons on the register without her needing to look and she stuffs cash tips into the pitcher behind the bar as she mixes up soda with cheap liquor.

I decide not to say anything about a little ginger ale splashing on my book. I sip at the soda and stare at her, mesmerized. She's got curves for days—round hips in tight jeans, a gently rounded stomach beneath the previously-noticed incredible chest, which is highlighted by a tight black tank. I recognize her, but she looks different today somehow.

I don't go out much, but when I do, my family drags me to this place, and there isn't much turnover with the staff. All the athletes tip really well in exchange for adjusted drink strength as needed: strong when we're winning. Light on the liquor pours when we're losing. The staff here takes good care of all of us and, more than once, has distracted annoying fans who get a little too personal. I should remember her.

She catches me staring and winks at me as she pulls on two taps at once, perfectly pouring a pair of beers she then serves to another wave of patrons. I could watch her all night, but I realize that's creepy.

I try to focus on my book … but I already know the ending of that story. Cara is doing amazing. The US office got all new management, and every soccer team in the country, from the pro level down to the tiniest kid league, received new training and funds to support players of all genders.

What I don't know is this bartender's name, her story, or whether she'd ever consider letting me get a closer look at her incredible body.

Eventually, the crowd at the bar starts to thin a bit, and I manage to read an entire page of my book since she's out of sight. But then I feel her presence across the wood from me, and she leans forward, her hair blocking the light so I can't read. I look up to meet her gaze.

"Can I ask you something?"

I blink at her, unable to think of anything smart to say in return. You know, like "sure" or "of course..." *Words, Wyatt. Come on, man...*

Eventually, she puts me out of my misery, refilling my soda with barely a glance. "Why are you sitting alone at a bar, reading a book, on New Year's Eve?"

CHAPTER 2
FERN

"He's here again. Hot and bookish." My best friend, Thora, pinches my butt as I tie my apron snugly around my waist. I yelp and swat at her as she grins, tying her apron in place.

The two of us have been working together for years. Thora's mom gets us a lot of gigs working the bars at the various professional sports stadiums around Pittsburgh, but tonight is the Holy Grail of lucrative shift work: New Year's Eve at Fuel Up, a popular bar near campus. It's also my final shift, since I'm starting a new job this semester and can't commit to a regular bar schedule.

I pull my cheat sheet from my pocket one more time, looking over the cocktail specials. A lot of them are standard drinks with Pittsburgh-themed names: Molten Iron for a rum and Coke, Neville Island Iced Tea instead of Long Island…that sort of thing. "I'm ready," I tell her, flexing my fingers.

"You better be ready for a fat tip." Thora makes suggestive gestures and elbows me as I try to ignore the subject of my infatuation. He comes in every few weeks and sits alone at the bar with a soda and a book, looking dark, sexy, and silently responsible.

I stomp on her foot with my Converse sneaker, and she yelps. "Will you knock it off with the tip talk? I already agreed it is going to happen. Don't make it weird."

Thora is one of the few people who knows that all my hard work academically and financially has meant there's a certain gap in my life experience. Namely, I've never had p-in-the-v sex. Like a lot of teen girls, I initially wanted it to be with someone special, and I spent all of high school working my ass off for a college scholarship, which meant that someone special never fit into my schedule.

Then, it just all felt weird and awkward, and starting last year, I told Thora I'd settle for someone half as talented as my vibrator. But – I recognize a pattern here: – I wasn't willing to slow down my studies and fellowship applications to go out in search of anyone's tip.

So here I am, on New Year's Eve, in my senior year of college. All my paperwork has been submitted for all the things, and I have an incredible work-study position for the spring term. I told Thora I wanted to leave workaholic, sexless Fern behind and usher in the new year as a woman who enjoys herself every now and again.

It was Thora's idea to go for Mr. Designated Driver's big D. She guessed correctly that he'd be here tonight, ready to safely usher his friends home. Unless… I can convince him to take me home instead. Thora raises a brow at me as she serves a pitcher of beer to a crowd of muscular student-athletes.

My target is oblivious to it all, periodically flicking a long finger to turn the page of tonight's book. I lean forward on the bar, clasping my hands in front of my chest as I stretch to see if I can read the book title. Something about a Beautiful Game. I lick my lips and straighten my ponytail. "Can I ask you something?" He looks up at me, and his mouth opens and closes a few times. I probably startled him, so I just plow ahead. "Why are you sitting alone at a bar, reading a book, on New Year's Eve?"

His brow shoots up under the brim of his hat. "I hate crowds. I like reading." He shrugs.

I laugh. "Why not snuggle up on your couch with that book, then?"

And then he shoots me a real smile, a cocky grin that tips to one side before he licks his lips and closes the book. "Maybe I like having someone refill my drink while I read."

I pull out the nozzle and press the button to fire some more ginger ale into his glass. He laughs and watches me as I reach for a cherry to plop in. It's symbolic, although he doesn't know that.

I point to the book. "So, you're a soccer fan, then?"

He laughs again. "You could say that." He slides the book into his lap. "What about you? More of a hockey fan?"

I shrug. "I mostly think about juggling flaming bottles while mixing drinks. You know, really wow the crowds." A customer waves his hand, and I hold up a finger to the bookworm while I pour the guy a pair of cheap beers.

I catch my stranger's eye again and make my way back to him. He leans forward. "You're ambitious. I like it. But seriously, what are you into?"

I bite my lip and lean toward him. We're almost touching, and I can smell the ginger ale on his breath. I have to shout over the roar of the bar. "Honestly? I'm just trying to finish my degree and get out of here."

He nods, his eyes serious. "I can respect that. I'm right there with you."

I stare into his dark eyes, and I think my panties really do melt a little. "I'm Fern," I tell him, extending a hand.

"Wyatt." He gives me a shake, his hand warm despite the ice in the glass he's been clutching. "Wyatt Moyer."

The bar is three-deep with rowdy bodies, the jukebox is blaring, and I'm sort of just dumping various liquids into glasses and hoping for the best. I really can't ignore my work to talk to this guy, but now I know his name is Wyatt, and his palm is callused.

A customer waves a hand in front of my eyes to get my attention and Wyatt frowns, but I hold up an index finger again and wait on the newcomer. He leaves a soggy five on the bar, and I shove it into the tightly packed tip jar. My mouth waters, thinking about what I can do with that money. A new laptop, for starters, capable of running Python and saving my work. But if I get accepted into my dream fellowship in the U.K., I'll also need a ton of professional clothes, a student visa, the works.

I pour a few Molten Irons, envisioning the day I can actually afford my plane ticket across the pond. When I glance back at Wyatt, he's reading again. I keep one eye on him as I serve a round of beers mixed with a few pitchers of the spiked iced tea. I give a heavy pour on the rum, observing Wyatt's fingers turning the page gently, like he's worried he'll rip the paper. I watch as he uses his left index finger to smooth down the center of the book, pressing the spine open in a way that only seems lewd to me because I'm sex-starved. Surely.

There's a brief lull in the demand for drinks, and Thora catches me staring. She waggles her eyebrows, and I shrug. He's got a hint of dark stubble on his sharp jaw and full lips that tip up and down, moving between a frown and a small smile as he reads. His hand absently spins the soda glass, and I look my fill at his long fingers, the tendons in his hands practically dancing as he moves the cup.

It's now or never. There's only about two hours before midnight. Technically, I can leave whenever I want. I know Thora will keep my tips safe if I split before we close. I take a deep breath and grip the edge of the bar, standing in front of Wyatt. He puts the book down and looks up at me, smiling.

Emboldened by his warm facial expression, I charge ahead. "Any interest in me pouring drinks at your place? While you read ... or whatever?"

Wyatt rubs a hand on his chin, considering. I'm not great at this, but I sense a look of combined surprise and desire on his face. He's quiet for a long time, long enough that I worry I blew it and ruined everything. Oh, god, what if he's gay? Or taken? As if he can read the panic on my face, he blows out a breath. "You're gorgeous, Fern. But are you sure? There's a lot of guys here who can maybe ..." He looks around like he's trying to decide what a guy should be able to do for me.

I place a hand on his and meet his eye, drawing on confidence I had no idea lurked inside me. Desperate times, I guess. "Wyatt, I don't want a guy who can do anything other than get me off. I don't have time for more than that."

He takes a sip of his drink, chewing one of the ice cubes in his glass. I reach past his fingers and pluck the cherry back from his soda, biting it from the stem and hoping I don't look like an idiot. He leans back in his bar chair and I'm pretty sure he adjusts himself before he crosses his arms and squints at me. "Did my cousin put you up to this?"

"What? No. I don't know you. How would I know your cousin?"

Wyatt bites his lip and looks behind him, evidently spotting the cousin in question among the crowd of rowdy, laughing athlete guys. Wyatt pulls off his hat and rubs at his hair, which is a little long on top but shaved on the sides and back. Suddenly, all I want to do is run my hands through it, learn the shape of his haircut, and feel those sweaty strands between my fingers. He's hot. I look pretty good. This has to happen, right?

Wyatt nods, like he's finished having a similar internal monologue. "Your place or mine?"

I rip the apron off my waist and make eye contact with Thora, who claps a hand over her mouth and jumps up and down and makes the okay sign with her other hand. "Yours. I have to leave here through the back door. Meet me in the alley?"

On one hand, this alley is pretty private, and I feel a sense of calm knowing nobody is going to run up to me to ask about my season, my prospects, or my parents.

On the other, it's dark as hell and I hate that Fern was going to head out here alone in the middle of the night. I lean against the warm brick wall, waiting anxiously for her to emerge, questioning my decisions. What am I even doing, bringing a woman home for a one-night stand?

I've had teammates do this and wake up to find pictures of their ass plastered across social media. Something in my gut tells me Fern isn't going to do that. I get the feeling she's all business, all the time. And for some reason, she decided tonight her business is me.

The door opens with a burst of light and loud noise, and Fern slips into the alley, shivering a bit in her coat. I catch a brief look of hesitation on her face, but then she smiles and approaches me. "So, where do you live?"

I extend an arm for her to walk ahead of me down the alley and toward Forbes Avenue and my stellar parking spot. "I'm just a few blocks away, but my cousins made me drive." I glance at her and unlock the Rover. "Heated seats!"

Her eyes widen, seeing the car. I sort of like that she doesn't seem to know who I am. She clearly wasn't expecting a nice car like this. "Wow." She climbs inside and runs her hands along the leather arm rest. I close her door and walk around to my side, climbing in and turning on the engine as Fern massages my interior. Our hands brush when I reach for the gear shift, and I feel a jolt of electricity running through my body that has nothing to do with the V-8.

I clear my throat and flick on the button to warm Fern's seat. She smiles and settles in. "Wow. That heated up so fast. Okay, I'm never leaving this car."

I turn around to check behind me as I back out of the parking spot, catching her staring at me when I pull onto the busy three-lane street. "So, you'll be serving me sodas from the passenger seat?"

I sort of like cracking jokes with her. I relax into the idea of getting naked with this woman, getting up close and personal with her incredible curves. But when I glance her way, she seems tense, so I reach for her hand, running a thumb across her knuckles. "Just 'til graduation," she clarifies. "After that, I'll move out."

"Upgrade to an RV?" I turn through Schenley Park so I can loop back around to Atwood Street. Out of habit I give a wave to the dinosaur statue, feeling a bit dumb. My parents often took me and my sister to the history museum and joked about the dinosaurs playing soccer with their eggs.

Fern sighs. "Hopefully, I'll upgrade to a lorry. Or whatever counts as a luxury vehicle in England."

I nod. "I'm trying to move abroad myself. Do you have a job lined up?"

She shakes her head and closes her eyes, continuing to rub her palms along the now-warm seat. "I applied for a few fellowships. If it all goes to plan, I'll live in a van by the river Thames and get a PhD."

There are no spots near our apartment, of course, and I grit my teeth as I prepare to circle the block and look for parking. "You might be better off with an apartment you can walk to and from."

Fern sits up straighter. "Didn't you say you were your cousins' ride? How will they get home?"

I growl in frustration, turning onto a street two blocks from my door. "They'll have less of a walk than us now that all the parking is gone. I should have made them hoof it, to begin with."

Fern points to a spot on the left side of the street. "There's one!"

I nod and parallel-park while she stares at me again. Maybe I back up an extra time, just to be sure. I grin and unbuckle, turning to face her. "If you can stand the walk, I have the heat on in my apartment. No leather, but the couch isn't too bad."

Fern opens her door, catching me off guard. I run around the side of the car in time to at least close it for her. She smiles. There's heat in her gaze, and I take her hand, making our way down the street. She looks up at me, blowing her dark hair from her eyes. "You never said why you're leaving the country. Grad school?"

I shake my head, incredulous. She has no idea. This is amazing. "I've got some job prospects in Mexico." A half-truth, a small omission. I can be anybody I want tonight. I can be Wyatt Moyer for real, with a woman who hasn't memorized my stats or searched the internet for my parents, or bookmarked news stories from when my bio dad was arrested for leaving me in a hot car while he went into a bar.

"This is me," I say, fishing in my pocket for my keys and unlocking the outer door to the building.

"I thought these apartments were all for athletes…" Fern looks around, then her eyes widen, and she claps a hand over her mouth. "Oh, duh. You came in with all the athlete guys." She squeezes my arm like she's checking for muscles. I'm happy to have her find them. "What sport are you? Swimmer?"

I laugh. "Hardly. No, I play soccer." I tilt my head toward my apartment door and move to unlock it.

Fern follows me, babbling. "I should have known. Your book had a soccer ball on the cover. Sometimes, I'm so deep in my own business that I just don't notice other people's details. Which is probably a sign I wasn't meant to be a bartender long-term."

I set the book in question on the counter, along with my keys, while Fern looks around—I'm assuming for someplace to hang her coat. I'm not even sure what the most gentlemanly protocol is here. I'd grab her and kiss her right now, but that seems kind of overkill. I swallow but decide to just tell her, "You can put your stuff in my room if you want."

I gesture down the hall to the open door where my cousins gave me crap a few hours earlier. She nods and heads in there. I follow, snapping on the light to reveal a space I'm pretty glad I keep neat. She takes in my king-sized bed with a black duvet, a dresser full of athletic clothes, and a small desk with a lamp and laptop. She notices the bookshelf and touches the books, smiling at the rows of cracked spines. I've always been a reader—lots of time on buses to and from away games.

Fern sets her coat on my desk with a clunk, and I figure she has all her stuff in her pockets since she doesn't have a purse. My sister always has a huge purse that could double as a duffel bag.

I clear my throat. "I, uh, don't do this very often."

Fern bites her lip and nods. "Me neither."

"We don't have to do anything." I scratch the back of my neck and pull off my hat, tossing it on the desk on top of her coat. "I'm happy to keep reading my book while you bring me San Pellegrino."

Fern tosses her head back and guffaws. "God, even your soda is fancy." She takes a step toward me and runs a finger from my shoulder to my elbow. I twitch under her touch, feeling ticklish and electrified. "I didn't come here to pour drinks."

"Good." I lean forward and press my lips against hers.

CHAPTER 4
FERN

Man, this feels good. Wyatt wraps his arms around me, hands splayed across my back and butt as he kisses me. His lips are just as soft as they looked, and I love the feel of them pressed against mine. I can feel the warmth of his body, the delicious strength of him, and a moan escapes my throat as we kiss.

Kissing, just seeking pleasure for the sake of it, is so foreign to me. I'm so used to working hard toward specific goals. It's delicious, just standing here with my arms around him, exploring his mouth.

He seems to enjoy the sounds I'm making and releases his own deep moan. I pull back with a gasp, not expecting the vibrations that buzz through his chest at his sounds. Wyatt smiles at me wolfishly and then leans back in, biting my lower lip as he backs me up to the edge of his bed.

I sink onto the mattress, and he stands between my legs, running his hands through my hair, gazing down at me like I'm made of some precious material he doesn't want to hurt. "Just checking in with you, Fern. Are you comfortable with this?"

I nod. He nods back, finger tracing my cheek. "Good, beautiful, because I'm ready to give you a happy new year."

I start to laugh because it's an adorably dorky thing to say, but then he sinks to his knees and presses a hand to my sternum. I'm flat on my back on the bed as he lifts the hem of my shirt. "God, your body is incredible," he murmurs, planting kisses along the stomach I usually try to hide behind flowy or ruched tops. I don't even have time to feel self-conscious about it because Wyatt licks and nips his way along my ribcage.

I move to take off my tank and while he watches, literally licking his lips. "Fern, I've been hard for you since the moment you pressed your chest in my face at the bar." Wyatt seems surprised by the confession but also seems to recover quickly at the sight of my too-big boobs spilling out of last year's bra. "Holy shit, look at you."

I glance down to see what he sees, but my view is blocked by his head as Wyatt yanks off the bra and presses his mouth to my nipple. The wet heat of his tongue has me gasping, prickles of pleasure zooming through my body as he kneads and squeezes and licks, moaning and whispering praise the entire time. Why have I not made time for this sooner?

I place one hand on his shoulder, loving the subtle movements beneath his shirt. The more Wyatt suckles at me, pinching and teasing, the more I squirm beneath the weight of his torso. I realize he's working his way to the floor between my legs, and I crave pressure and friction against my center, but I can't quite get it in this position. I grunt in frustration and Wyatt looks up from his work.

He draws one finger down the center of my body, teasing at my crotch. The denim of my jeans is too thick, and I need more. "God," I curse, but I don't know what to say next. Do I just ... demand that he touch me?

"You need it bad, don't you Fern?"

"Yes. Thank you. Please." I don't even know what I'm saying, but he laughs, and I feel his long fingers unbuttoning my pants. Before I can form any sort of response, my legs are in the air, my jeans and panties are ripped off, and my thighs are smooshed against Wyatt's ears while his hands press the soft, sensitive skin of my upper legs closer to his head, like he's trying to drown himself in my body.

And then he spreads me open and studies me, like I'm a page in one of his books–intently, like there's nothing else in the room.

"Oh, I wasn't expecting ... oh, wow." I raise myself up on my forearms just in time to see Wyatt Moyer stare at my vulva like it's the most incredible thing he ever laid eyes on. And then, with a sigh, he leans forward and licks me there. "Wyatt!" He freezes and looks up, eyes questioning. "I'm all ... sweaty. I was just working for hours."

"And?"

I bite my lip. "And, doesn't it smell?"

He sniffs, and my cheeks heat. But he's not turning away in disgust. He looks like he is about to have a stroke from pleasure, somehow. "It smells like a pussy, Fern."

"Okay, but ... you like that?"

He dips a finger inside me gently, and I suck in a breath. I bear down on him involuntarily, arching my back to see if I can get any friction where I need it on my clit. "I like it a lot, yeah. It smells like you're turned on, and I really like that."

Well, I can't argue with him. If I hadn't been turned on before, the sight of him staring at my body with hooded eyes, blown pupils, and reverence would have me dripping all over his sheets. Who am I to deny him something he apparently likes, right? Right? Maybe if I had more experience, I wouldn't feel so vulnerable. Before I can protest again, Wyatt licks me again, slowly, his tongue flat and wide, and deliciously warm. "Oh, wow. Okay. Yes. Ohhhhhh wow."

Wyatt licks and thrusts his finger in and out. His hands are somehow everywhere on my body, all at once. I feel his fingers on my thighs, my nipples, my folds. I feel his tongue lapping and pressing until I'm a coiled spring of need. I realize my legs are pressed hard against his head, smothering him perhaps, but I am powerless to do anything but fist the sheets. I moan as he licks and glides and sucks until I'm tipping over the edge. Electric shudders roll through my body, lifting me up and out of my consciousness. I think I'm shouting his name. I think I'm squeezing my legs together in time with my waves of pleasure.

I drop a hand lazily to my stomach, and my eyes drift close. I stop moaning, switching over to a gentle hum as I enjoy the small aftershocks rumbling through my body. When I open my eyes, Wyatt is standing in front of me shirtless, dropping his jeans, palming the bulge in his boxer briefs with one hand as he wipes his mouth with the back of his other. I blurt, "Jesus. You look filthy. Like sexy-filthy. Sorry." I move to sit up, but Wyatt shakes his head, crawling over me like some sort of jungle cat predator.

"I am filthy, Fern." I scoot up the bed 'til I'm near the pillow, and he bows down, giving me his weight and kissing me, and wow. I definitely taste myself on his lips. My eyes widen in shock. One corer of his mouth hooks up in a grin. "What?" When I can't say anything, he smiles. "Hasn't anyone ever done that for you before? Made you come with their mouth?"

I shake my head, and his smile widens. "They've been missing out. You taste incredible."

Before I can ask him if he really means that, he juts his hips against mine, and I feel the thick rod of his erection. Is he hard like that for me? From getting me off? My blood fizzes at the thought that he enjoyed smashing his face in my sweaty snatch, especially as he starts groaning again, pressing his big hands into my boobs. "These feel so incredible. So soft. Your body is like a dream, Fern."

Wyatt rocks his hips against mine while he praises me, and I wrap my ankles around his knees, knowing I'm so wet that I'm getting his underwear damp. "Take these off," I tell him, like I know what I'm doing, and I start sliding the cotton over the swell of his ass and holy shit.

He wriggles out of his boxer briefs, and I look over his shoulder to see the most amazing backside. It has dips in the sides where the taut muscles of his legs meet those solid glutes. I press my palms into the dips, my fingers digging into his cheeks, and wow, I can feel the whole rigid length of him rubbing against my heat.

I tuck my chin and adjust myself on the bed because I want to see it between us, want to know what an erect cock looks like in person, and it's better than I imagined. Wyatt's shaft is long and darker than the skin of his butt. The uncut tip glistens with a bead of moisture, and I can't tell whether it came from me or him. I reach for it, amazed at how warm and smooth it feels in my hand, yet also impossibly hard. I rub the liquid on the tip with my thumb, spreading the fluid around the shiny head as he nibbles my ear and squeezes my boobs. Everything feels so good, so much, so amazing.

Wyatt rolls to one side, and I see him fumbling around the drawer of his nightstand . He pinches a foil packet between his fingers and moves to tear it open. I sit up. "Can I do it?" I am overcome with a burning desire to be the one to roll the condom onto him, to feel it snugly in place before he slides inside me. I'm not worried about pain, somehow. I've used toys in the past … a lot, of late. And I know my body is soft after he made me come that hard.

I'm throbbing with anticipation, with the need to have this part of him inside of me.

Wyatt stares in silent wonder as I take my time lining up the condom, rolling it down him slowly. When I glance up to meet his eye, we smile at one another like we just achieved something together. I have a moment of concern that I don't know what he likes, but then he asks, "You ready, Fern?" Wyatt runs a finger along my jaw again. I realize he already has things he does that turn me on. And he seems to like my enjoyment.

"Yes, please." I lie back down, settling onto the pillow and tipping my thighs open as he crawls back between them. Wyatt keeps his gaze locked on mine and uses his hand to line himself up, and then … it's happening. I feel him sliding inside, a burst of fullness followed by a pinch and then exquisite satisfaction.

CHAPTER 5
WYATT

I FREEZE WHEN I'M INSIDE FERN, OVERWHELMED BY THE SENSATION AND intensity of our connection. I stare down at her with my weight on my hands. She winces briefly but then seems to love what she's experiencing because I can feel her pulsing around me, drawing me in deeper. "Oh, yes, Wyatt. Please. Yes."

Fuck, this woman is so damn hot. She's like a creamy, delicious dessert, all curves and softness, wrapped entirely around me with her arms, legs, and velvety pussy. I could drown here, happily, enveloped in the tangy sweat of her. My sheets are going to smell like this for days, and I'm going to fall asleep achingly hard at the memory of how this feels right now.

I let her have a little more of my weight, and I think she likes that because she pulls me tighter against her torso. And then Fern starts moving beneath me, rolling her hips, muttering my name, spewing profanity. "Do you need to come again, beautiful? Is that what's wrong?"

I grin at her as her eyes fly wide, and she nods. "Yes. Please?"

"You don't need to beg me, Fern. Fuck, you feel good." I adjust my weight so I can touch her, reaching between us to press a thumb into her clit. She's so damn responsive. I can tell immediately when she likes something, which gives me so many clues about when she doesn't. It doesn't take me long to find the pressure and rhythm she needs to go wild. "You're making me lose my damn mind, Fern."

She seems beyond speech, thrashing beneath me. At one point, she sinks her teeth into my shoulder, and I can feel her coming, pulsing and squeezing around me. I can't hold back anymore. I put all my weight on my forearms and start rolling my hips with full intensity, driving her into the mattress, grunting like an animal until I feel the ball of white-hot pleasure building at the base of my spine.

Fern reaches between my legs and squeezes my balls, her expression pure sex. The feel of her, and the look of her, and the sound of my name on her lips sends me over the edge. I'm coming into the condom, pulsing inside her as I press my forehead into hers until I'm totally spent.

———

My chest heaves as I try to calm down. Fern traces a lazy hand through the hair on the leg I have bent up over her hip. I press a kiss to her forehead and her eyes fly open, almost like she forgot I was here. I smile down at her, wanting to stroke her hair and hold her tight. Which is insane because I never want to do those things. We just had a one-night stand. I should be itching to get her out of here so I can shower. "Hey," I say.

"Um, hey." She bites her lip and looks around. "I … should probably go."

"I'm still inside you," I point out, although I slide out when she shifts to sit up. I reach for her hand. "If you give me twenty minutes, we can do an encore."

Fern huffs out a laugh. "Twenty minutes, huh? That's the recovery period?"

I shrug and kiss her cheek. "Don't go anywhere."

I dash into the en suite bathroom to deal with the condom. I realize I don't have a washcloth , so I take a hand towel and run it under the hot water. When I get back to the bedroom, Fern has already put on her bra and her tank top, and she's looking around the room like she's searching for the bottom half of her clothes. "Hey," I tell her. "Lie back and let me take care of you a minute at least."

Her eyes widen and I gesture with the towel. She settles back onto the bed, looking down as I gently rub the towel between her legs, kissing her inner thighs. As I get closer to her pussy, she tenses. "Sore?"

She nods. "Just a little. It was totally worth it, though. I didn't mean—"

I grin. "It's okay." I dab at her gently with the wash cloth. "We don't have to do another round, but you definitely aren't walking home in the middle of the night."

"Oh, I wasn't going to walk. I live in Brookline…"

I scoff. "Isn't that at least two buses away? On New Year's Eve?"

She shrugs, and I toss the towel into the bathroom. At least it lands on the tile floor. I climb into the bed and try to tuck Fern against my side, running my hands through her hair until I feel her body ease up a bit. "It's one bus and one train." Her words are slow, sleepy.

"I'll drive you in the morning. Stay."

Fern sighs and wriggles against me, her bottom half is still naked. I wrap an arm around her, naked myself, and rest my palm on her butt. This is perfection.

————

When I wake up a few hours later, in the gray light of early dawn on a new year, I'm alone in my bed. No note, no Fern, no way to contact her for a repeat.

I sigh and drape an arm across my face as I hear Odin getting ready for the combine. It's probably just as well. I wasn't lying when I told her I couldn't commit to anything more than casual. If everything goes to plan, I'll be moving in a few months.

THORA

You ready to slay the day? [vampire emoji]

ME

Is that really the right image for that text?

THORA

I couldn't find a wooden stake emoji

ME

What, no Buffy GIF?

THORA

So, I take it you're not nervous. Now that you've
propositioned a hottie, you're ready for anything!

———

I HADN'T TAKEN THE TIME TO CONSIDER MY NIGHT WITH WYATT LAST WEEK AS
any sort of bravery benchmark. I guess my friend is right, though. I sort of
proved to myself that it's okay to ask for what I want and trust myself in
new situations. New Year's Eve worked out pretty damn well, after all.

But on the other hand, I'm not nervous about teaching because it's
basic algebra, and I am pretty confident I'm good at explaining those
concepts to other people.

I put on my "teaching outfit" that Thora helped me pick out: brand-new-used designer jeans from the thrift store south of the city, a bright yellow blazer from the same store, and a cute striped shirt I already had. Thora and I have been trying to build capsule wardrobes to mix and match professional pieces for when we start graduate school, and need to look less like bartenders.

I don't want my students to think of me as "that chick who always wears the yellow blazer." But some things are too good to pass by, even when funds are tight. Veronica Beard new with tags for seven dollars ? That's just good sense.

I take an early train downtown and smile as I blend in with the other commuters, transferring to a bus heading toward campus. Undergrads don't usually get the chance to be teaching assistants for recitations, but there are way more first-year math students than usual and fewer grad students to cover the classes this spring.

My mentor, Professor Yoon, suggested I submit an application. I'm pretty sure they just needed that as a formality, but I'm grateful for the experience ... and the money. I thought there would maybe be some more training or that I could meet some of the grad students who are also leading recitation, but they are basically throwing me in with the wolves.

They lecture twice a week in a huge auditorium, and then the third class of the week is broken up into twenty-student groups where we TAs answer students' questions and reinforce the material. Dr. Yoon sent out the syllabus to all of us, their admin let us know where there were cubicles we could use for office hours, and someone from the math department made sure I had a copy of the textbook. And that was it. No fanfare, but I guess they wouldn't have picked me for this gig if they didn't know I'm responsible.

I'm really looking forward to this, rather than feeling nervous. I like explaining things to other people. I like it when they ask me questions because seeing what others are confused by is a really interesting way for me to rethink the concepts. And I'm not in charge of the curriculum—just making sure the students grasp the material Dr. Yoon lays out.

Recitation is graded pass/fail based entirely on attendance, so I don't even have to worry about anyone getting mad at me over grades. I have my roster printed in a folder full of notes and a ton of extra copies of the syllabus. I did look over the names and there are a handful of older students. I'm assuming they couldn't fit the required math class into their schedule until now. Or maybe they forgot they had to take it to graduate. Or maybe they're just bad at math. For now!

I have daydreams of convincing them all that the language of the universe can be applied everywhere. I know they won't all leave here in love with algebra, but I know I can help them understand how to approach these concepts and how to succeed in this class.

I arrive at the towering building, with students streaming in and out of the revolving doors. I hold my head high as I type 23 on the elevator call box, and soon, I'm zooming up to one of the newer classrooms, full of projectors, whiteboards, and everything I need to write out complex equations larger than life.

I write my name on the board with ALGEBRA 1 RECITATION.

I spread my things on the podium at the front of the room but then decide I'd rather we all sit in a circle, so I pick a desk for my stuff and arrange the other chairs in a ring so we're all facing each other—or we will be once the students start showing up.

I slide into my seat and run my finger along my printed roster. I come across a student named Wyatt DeLuca. My cheeks heat, remembering my night with a different Wyatt.

Thora was right. Sex is a huge stress reliever. I couldn't walk properly for a day and a half after my night with Wyatt Moyer, but I took a hot bath, touched myself thinking of how I got that sore and went into this first week of class of my final semester of college feeling more relaxed than ever.

I shake these thoughts away as the first groups of students trickle in. I smile at them. "Hey, I'm Fern. Sit anywhere you like!" They do, mostly ignoring me and one another as they check their phones or work on the crossword from the student paper. I check my watch, and it's exactly ten, so I get up and walk toward the door to close it just as the last straggling students slip in.

I stumble when I see Wyatt—my Wyatt—duck into the room with a muttered apology. I back up toward my desk, hitting it and knocking my folder to the ground in a flutter of papers. He crouches to pick up the pile of syllabi, and his eyes meet mine as he hands them to me. I freeze in horror as I realize he's a student in this class. Why the hell would he lie about his name?

CHAPTER 7
WYATT

"MOM, I HAVE TO GO. I'M LATE FOR CLASS." SHE ALWAYS CALLS AT THE WORST times. I lean against the wall and close my eyes, knowing my mother means well but also wishing she'd butt out just a little. Most parents aren't intimately familiar with the process of getting signed to a professional sports team. Lucky me, both my mom and my stepdad coach professional sports teams.

I am lucky. I have amazing parents. I mutter this to myself as Mom keeps on offering pointers.

"You really should touch base with Brian. I can have Dad talk to him if you want. We'd love you to stay here in Pittsburgh. Imagine if you could play for your dad? Wouldn't that be so fun?" My stepdad, Hawk Moyer, is the only real father I've ever known. He embodies that role so completely it's hard for me to remember that I have a biological father…and I never use that word in reference to Nick.

I pinch the bridge of my nose. "Like I told you, Brian is talking to teams in Mexico. I'm really focused on finishing my degree right now, Mom. And I'm going to be late for the math class I should have taken four years ago."

She hums. "Okay, honey. I just love you so much, and I'm so proud of you." Her voice catches. "You've overcome so much."

"I love you, too, Mom." I see the last group of students walk into the classroom I'm supposed to join. The teacher, presumably, comes to the door to close it. "Gotta go, bye."

I hang up on my mom and jog to the door just as it's closing, and in my haste, I bump into the teacher's desk, sending a pile of papers fluttering to the ground. I worry I hurt her or something because she stiffens and doesn't move to pick anything up. I tug my hat lower on my head and crouch. I really wanted to get here early to remind the professor they're not supposed to say my name during roll call.

For one thing, I hate when other students in class identify me as "that soccer player." They don't know anything about me except that I'm good at sports. I wish there were a way to just ... be a professional athlete and not talk to fans. All the press conferences and fan fests just remind me of being in custody court. My parents are always talking to reporters. I should be used to the recognition, but it all makes my skin crawl.

I gather the last of the papers and look up to hand them to the professor. Except it's not a professor. It's Fern. From the other night.

Her eyes are wide, and she stands frozen in the middle of the classroom. I look around and see ALGEBRA 1 RECITATION written on the board ... along with Fern's name. Shit.

"Are you my professor?"

The question seems to snap her out of her shock, and she snatches the pile of papers from my hand. She strides over to her seat and clears her throat. I take this as my cue to pour myself into a desk. I was hoping to hide in the back, but she has all the chairs arranged in a circle so everyone can see everyone else. Great.

"I'm Fern and I'm the TA for this recitation," she says in a thin voice so unlike her confident bartender voice or even the voice she used in my bedroom. I cannot let myself think about her in the bedroom, especially if she really is my teacher. I tug on my hat again. I need to face the fact that she is in charge of my grade for this course.

I fucked my professor.

Fern takes a deep breath and holds up a piece of paper. "I passed the syllabus around, so you should each take one of those and look it over. I know it's weird that the semester started on a Thursday, and you're having recitation before you even meet Dr. Yoon. They will lecture on Mondays and Wednesdays. And of course, we meet on Fridays." She laughs a little nervously, and some of the other students join in, but most don't, and Fern's cheeks turn a little pink.

I've heard her make better jokes. "Anyway, today we're just going to review the schedule, and if there's time, I can preview the topics for next week's lectures."

She summarizes the syllabus, and students around me highlight the dates for the exams, which Fern will help administer but not be grading. "Oh, speaking of grades," she pulls out a folder. "Recitation is one credit, and that's entirely based on attendance. Everyone gets two absences, no questions asked, but after that ..." She points to the syllabus, where I can see that there's a basic rubric for how many points off we get for being late or absent. "So, I guess I should take roll." Fern starts reading out names, and the students around me grunt or wave in response.

My heart starts racing. Students look around, eyeing each other up and looking for recognition as the names are read. It's only a matter of minutes until they recognize me from billboards and last year's college soccer video game. I need to head this shit off at the pass. I blurt, "I'm Wyatt. I'm here."

I can tell by Fern's face that they have me on the roster under my legal name toward the beginning of the alphabet. "Wyatt," I repeat as everyone stares. "I'm probably the only one on the roster." I gesture at Fern's list, and she nods, moving her pencil. She continues on through the roster as people murmur.

It's already too late. People recognize me. I hear someone ask their friend if they heard I got a shoe deal. I wish. Except, not really, because that would be a lot of fucking publicity. I just need to buy myself some time to get signed. I can focus on endorsements and all that superstar crap later. I just need to seal my first deal and get myself established, hopefully far away from American soil, where nobody knows anything about me from before I got good at soccer.

By the time my heart slows, and I can concentrate, the students around me are packing up and filing out. I kill time reading a book until the room clears out, and it's just me and Fern.

"Wyatt, may I speak to you?" Fern's voice is oddly formal, and I nod, staying in my seat until everyone leaves. I'm definitely not having any sort of conversation in front of other undergrads. Fern seems to expect our convo to start immediately, and she sighs and shifts over to a seat next to me.

She smells great, floral and fresh. Her outfit is damn fine, too. I liked her in jeans and a tight tank top, but this look suits her a lot. She looks professional and confident. Or I assume she looked confident until she saw me and realized *she* fucked one of her students. I grin at that. Damn right, she did.

"Wyatt." Her tone is angry now. "Why did you lie to me?"

CHAPTER 8
FERN

WYATT BLOWS OUT A LONG BREATH, TAKES OFF HIS BASEBALL HAT, AND THEN shoves it back on his head, covering his eyes. "I didn't lie." I point at the roster, about to yell at him for gaslighting me, but he holds up a hand. "Not exactly. I just didn't tell you everything. It's not like we traded life stories."

I bite my lip. He's right that we didn't give each other a ton of information. But we did share something pretty intense. Or maybe it was just intense for me because I never did that before? Maybe that's always how sex is…an overwhelming connection and feeling that this other person can see directly into my soul and fill me with unreal pleasure…

"Look." Wyatt grips the edge of the desk attached to his chair so hard his knuckles are white. "The last name on your roster isn't supposed to be public information." I furrow my brow, and he explains that he has an alias. "I can't stand any association with the man who sired me, but that's what was on my birth certificate. So, I don't use it unless I have to." He takes off his hat and fiddles with his hair, a nervous habit apparently. "I go by Wyatt Moyer wherever I can. My mom calls it a stage name, but that makes it feel even more like I'm not really part of the family." He fidgets in his seat, and I stare, not knowing what to say about all of this. "Look," he pleads, eyes huge and doing things to my insides. "I did try to go into the system and change it to Moyer. I also tried to change it at the damn social security office, but that's a whole freaking production involving court and lawyers and shit."

Something about this revelation tugs at my heart. Maybe it's the look in his partially hidden eyes…the obvious pain and frustration there. "You're trying to change your name?"

He nods. "It doesn't feel like mine. It's my birth father's name, and he's a piece of shit. I go by my family's name, Moyer, and I swear I didn't try to mislead you or something to get in your pants."

My cheeks heat, and I grimace. "Well, I guess it was me pushing the pants situation."

He leans forward and grins. "You didn't have to push too hard, Fern."

It's my turn to take a deep breath. I stare down at the roster on my desk. "Okay. Well. I'm assuming you're not able to switch to another recitation section?"

He shakes his head rapidly. "My schedule is nuts between conditioning and weight room, and I'm not even in season right now."

"Mm. Well, I also have an intense schedule trying to finish with a double major in math and computer science, so that leaves us stuck together in a teacher-student situation." I fidget with the pen on my desk, not meeting his eye. "We need to keep things professional. No more flirting and definitely no repeats of New Year's Eve."

When I finally look at him, he's giving me a filthy look, like he's remembering every second of our night together before I slinked away from his bed like a thief. "Wyatt, I'm serious. I absolutely need this experience on my CV and—"

"Yeah, yeah. I get it." He flinches, like he's also trying to convince himself. "You're my teacher. I will be on my best student behavior. You'll barely notice me."

He grabs his backpack and heads for the door, leaving me to doubt my ability to ever concentrate in his presence. Staring at his ass in his gray sweats doesn't help me with this mission. Not one bit.

———

I'm supposed to meet Thora in the library to debrief. Neither of us has any other classes on Fridays, but since we both live so far off campus, we usually hang out and study together until lunch. She spots me approaching and makes exaggerated winky faces, fanning herself. "Fern, you look smoking hot. If I were your student, I'd have trouble paying attention."

I sink into the seat opposite her at the table. "You have no idea." She furrows her brow and I slump forward, head on my hands. "The guy from the bar is one of my students." Thora is silent long enough that I pop my head up to make sure she hasn't left. Her mouth hangs open a bit, and she blinks a few times. "Did you hear what I said?"

She grins. "Oh, I heard. And I've read this book before."

"What do you mean?"

Thora rubs her palms together. "Forbidden love. Hot as fuck student. Sexy-as-hell professor. I probably have ten of those in my e-reader right now." She rummages in her bag like she's going to show me her romance novel collection.

"I'm not going to read one of your steamy books right now, Thora. This is serious."

She waves a hand. "I know. But … is it serious? It's recitation, right? Graded based on if he shows up to class?"

I clench my whole body. "Yeah but coming to class could feel unsafe for him. Or uncomfortable. I might be making him uncomfortable."

Thora nods. "Yes, I can see how your overt sexual energy would be unsettling for a young student-athlete about to sign a pro soccer contract."

I frown at her. "He's going pro?"

Thora rolls her eyes at me. "Are you telling me you didn't even look him up online after he was inside your body? Hell, I looked him up the minute things calmed down at the bar. Oh! I have your tips." Thora reaches into her cavernous bag, rummaging around until she pulls out a bright pink envelope stuffed to the ripping point. "It's mostly ones, I think. Mine was."

I slide the money into a zippered pocket of my bag, pinching it between my thighs in case someone wandering past gets any ideas. Not that I really believe everyone is out to rob me. I just really need that money to end up in my savings account ASAP.

Thora runs her fingers through her hair and looks at me. "Fern, I get it. You know I get it. And honestly, you're both seniors. You're both clearly dedicated to your own thing. I think you're mature enough to ignore him for an hour a week while you plan your climb up the academic ladder."

I nod. She's probably right. The shock of seeing him today will wear off.

We try to get things done for a bit before I give up, too distracted by Wyatt and what could happen now that he's my student. "I need to go deposit those tips." I sigh. "And my mom will probably want to touch base about teaching anyway."

"You gonna tell her about Wyatt?"

I squint, considering. "It's not like I pour out my soul about guys and stuff like that … how would I even bring it up?"

Thora shrugs. "Mama Montgomery is very reasonable. And she'll sniff you out in a heartbeat if you don't tell her something. Why not just say one of your students is a guy you were interested in last semester."

I nod, tapping my fingers on my bag full of precious, dangerous cargo. "It's not technically a lie…"

I stand up, checking the time on my phone. "All right. I'll talk to you later. You working this weekend?"

Thora nods. I wave to her and run outside in time to catch the bus downtown.

———

I have an entire hour on public transit to figure out what to tell my mom, so by the time I get to the bank where she works, I'm feeling much calmer about the whole situation.

Mom looks up from her teller window , smiling when she sees me. I slide the pink envelope across the counter. "I'd like to make a deposit, please!"

She glances at the envelope, still taped shut. "You didn't even use any of it to buy yourself something nice?"

I make a face. "Mom. What am I gonna get that's nice?"

She sighs. "We can do a treat every now and then, Fern Montgomery. It isn't sustainable to keep living like monks while you save and save for the next thing."

I grab a deposit slip and start filling it out. "I know, Mom. And I am easing up a little. I told you I went out with friends on New Year's Eve after my shift. And I'm not even working this weekend." I don't add that my only friend *is* working, so I'm still not doing anything social. "We should have a movie marathon."

Mom's face brightens. "We can get takeout. You can tell me all the latest news about your fellowship."

I slide her the completed deposit slip. Mom doesn't ask for my ID, but I show it to her anyway. I don't want anyone to be checking a video or something and get her in trouble. "There's nothing to tell right now until they make their decisions. You know that, Mom."

And she does know it. She was once a bright student like me, applying for scholarships and looking at colleges. She got pregnant with me and moved in with my dad, and they both made a real go at juggling school and parenthood … until it got really hard, and Dad took off. He didn't go far physically, but he also never really seemed to mature much, and he's certainly never offered either of us any support, financially or emotionally.

Mom hands me a receipt for my deposit, and we both smile a bit at the balance number on my account. Slowly and steadily, I'm getting closer to my benchmarks. Assuming I get accepted into one of the programs … I can't let myself worry about what might happen if I don't. I say, "I'll make dinner tonight and queue up that new Reese Witherspoon movie for when you get home." I grin and squeeze Mom's hand. She squeezes back and waves me off.

CHAPTER 9
WYATT

"You're Wyatt Moyer, right? From the soccer team?" A woman with bleached blond hair sits in the seat next to mine as I try to slip into the back of the recitation section the next week. I glance over at her. Any other year, I'd be into her glossy pink lips and the view of her lacy bra from the cut-off collar of the baggy sweatshirt she wears. Today, I just want to get through class without angering Fern.

I'm not in the best mood for superfans. My legs are aching from lifting weights with the team this morning. My fingers are cramped from texting my parents repeatedly that I haven't signed any contracts yet.

"Yeah," I grunt, keeping my eyes on my notebook and hoping my body language communicates that this isn't going to be a lead-up to a hookup.

She slides her chair closer to mine. "My roommates and I *love* soccer. We were there for your hat trick this fall. Against Maryland?"

I nod. "Yeah. Thanks for coming out." I hate this. If I'm going to play pro, I know I need to at least be nice to fans. But honestly, it's all I can manage right now trying to figure out my professional life, stay in shape, and not pop a boner over the TA for this math recitation.

As I draw nonsense notes in my notebook, I see a hand with manicured nails slide a piece of paper onto my desk. I look up again and my fan is smiling at me. "That's my number. If you ever need to catch up on notes or whatever." She lifts her brows at me seductively. My mind reels, trying to figure out what I can say to politely let her know I won't be reaching out to her for homework help or anything else.

She's probably memorized every factoid about me online, and that always weirds me out.

I'm saved by Fern clapping her hands and shouting, "Okay, everyone, let's get down to reducing equations." She smiles and shakes her head. "That's sort of funny if you understand math concepts." She's adorable, making nerd jokes. Nobody laughs, of course, because it's ass-early on a Friday, and we're all here because we suck at math.

I try to sink low in my seat and stare at her, which is expected of students and teachers. Except I'm not looking at the right things. I'm not watching the numbers and letters she writes on the board—I'm staring at that lush ass and remembering how it felt to dig my fingers into her soft skin. When she lifts her arm to write on the board, I'm staring at her silhouette, wanting to palm her tits again, maybe while she whispers into my ear about finding square roots.

Fern was the absolute perfect distraction for me from all the pressures in my life, and now … I'm distracted by my distraction.

I'm so fucked. I wonder if I'd still be this into her if she wasn't my teacher. Would I go for a brainiac gal? I've never really sought anyone out for more than casual fun. I'm not entirely sure what I'm hoping for with Fern. Just a fantasy? A fucking amazing memory to use when I jerk off in the morning? A repeat, so I can carry around the knowledge that I boned my teacher?

She tosses the dry-erase marker on the shelf with a clatter and smiles at the board. "Does anyone else have a question about the substitution method?"

She looks around expectantly. Nobody moves or talks. I glance at my watch and see we're only about halfway through the session. I don't want her to have to stand up there while a room full of assholes makes her squirm. But I wasn't paying enough attention to what she was saying to come through and ask a question of my own.

Apparently, I don't need to worry about Fern, though, because she raises one eyebrow and crosses her arms, popping one hip out in a move I'm sure is unconscious but definitely communicates that she knows absolutely everything there is to know about whatever method she just mentioned. "Not one of you wants to know about using the distributive property? Hint: this will definitely be on the exam…"

Still, nobody talks. Fern circles the room once, and I can tell she's playing with us. She knows none of us have any idea what's going on, but everyone is paying attention now, leaning in as she talks. "Could it be that none of you remember what the distributive property actually is?" Fern laughs and returns to the board. "Let's break it down."

———

A half-hour later, everyone files out of the room. I can still feel the buzz in the air that comes when a bunch of people are all figuring something out together. Fern really is good at teaching this shit. I shove my notebook in my bag and try to slip out the back. I know if I look at her, I will betray something with my facial expression.

So, I'm not really paying attention when I leave the building, heading toward my apartment to grab some food before my afternoon classes. I pull out my phone to order takeout and see a series of texts from *him*.

> Can't avoid me forever, son.

I can picture my biological father, Nick, in my mind, glassy eyes looking dead inside. His muscles bulge like he's still hitting the gym for hours a day despite getting himself declared physically disabled and incapable of working — or paying a single cent of child support to my mother.

I hate that I reached out to him, that I brought this on. My hands shake as I scroll through the messages. The first time I reached out was to let him know I was changing my name. I had to file a notice in the newspaper. He was going to see it anyway. I figured we'd clear the air and move on, maybe get a beer sometime.

He immediately began demanding I send him money to make up for years of him being denied the right to be my father or something. I realized pretty quickly that I hadn't been catastrophizing any of those memories. This guy is a real piece of shit.

> Saw your name on a potential roster for the
> Olympics, kid. Be a shame if someone leaked dirt
> on your mother. Did I hear that she was accused
> of sexual misconduct?

I school my face to remain expressionless. The thought of my mother assaulting anyone is ludicrous, especially when she's been so active in trying to change soccer governance and fight for pay equity in the sport.

I lean against a wall for stability, trying to calm down amidst the crowd of students as they are leaving classes, parting around me like I'm a rock in a riverbed.

> You better start taking my calls, kid. Or I'll start
> making calls to other people.

A ball of hot nausea bounces through my stomach. I'm surprised to feel wetness on my cheeks when I press my knuckles against my face. For a minute, I worry it's blood from my father ripping open old wounds. But apparently, I'm just crying.

I wipe my face on my sleeve, attempting to block out the world, when I hear a soft voice call my name.

"Wyatt? Are you okay?"

I open my eyes to see Fern standing before me, her brow furrowed with concern. I try to force a smile, but it feels more like a grimace. "Yeah, I'm fine. Just needed some air."

She takes a step closer, her hand hesitantly reaching out to touch my arm. "You don't look fine. What happened?"

I shake my head, not wanting to burden her with my problems. "It's nothing. Just some family stuff."

Fern's gaze is steady, her voice gentle but firm. She bites her plump lip, and I shudder. "Wyatt, I can see that you're upset. You can talk to me."

"Can I?" I take a deep breath, weighing the options. Something about Fern's presence, the warmth in her eyes, makes me want to trust her.

"I heard from my father," I say, my voice tight. "He's not ... he's not a good man. He said some things and made some threats. It just brought up a lot of bad memories."

Fern's hand tightens on my arm, her touch grounding me. "I'm so sorry, Wyatt. Do you want me to call anybody for you?"

I shake my head, swallowing past the lump in my throat. "I'm fine. Seriously. He's just a blowhard. I'm going to head home." She looks skeptical. "My roommates are there."

Fern's voice is still soft, so it is different from her tone in class. "I know we don't know each other that well, but I'm here for you. If you ever need to talk or just need someone to listen."

Her words wrap around me, soothing the raw edges of my pain. I manage a small smile. "Thank you, Fern. That means a lot."

She returns the smile, her hand sliding down to gently squeeze mine. "Anytime."

We stand there for a moment, the silence between us comfortable and understanding. "I really messed up a few months ago and reached out to him."

She winces. "I went through a phase like that. Expecting my dad to be a real adult. Like TV dads."

I nod. "I figured ... I hadn't talked to him in over ten years. Maybe I was misremembering all the things that happened before Mom left him. It was dumb of me to think we'd just reconnect like friends or something. All I did was remind him that Mom has money now."

Her eyes are warm and understanding. "I'm sorry, Wyatt. That must have really hurt. And now he's ... being cruel?"

I nod and don't say anything else because what is there to say? Finally, I take a deep breath and straighten my shoulders. "So, yeah, I'm going home now. Thanks, teach." I add that last part as a reminder to myself that she's offering this support as part of some duty from the university. I'm pretty sure they all have to look out for students' well-being. But she looks a little stricken when I say it.

Fern nods, regardless. "Okay. My offer stands. Whenever you need it."

"I'll remember," I promise. "And Fern ... thanks again. For being here."

She smiles, warm and genuine. She gives a wave and crosses the street toward a crowded bus stop. I look away and wander home, trying to forget.

CHAPTER 10
FERN

It takes me ages to calm down after teaching my recitation section every Friday. I know the material pretty well, and I think I'm doing a good job of keeping the students engaged and learning the material. But it's just *so much work* to keep my cool in front of them and project a confident aura.

Especially when I've got Wyatt sitting there, hot and vulnerable. I found myself wanting to wrap him in my arms the other day, even though I knew I couldn't. I need to remember to look up resources for students like him who are having issues with their families. I'm sure the other teaching assistants are probably better equipped to handle those things. All I had to offer him was a stupid hand squeeze and listening ear.

I have so much riding on this class going well…so much. The stress of that alone would make my back sweat but add in Wyatt sitting in the circle of students each week, staring me down with his dark eyes. He always looks like he did when we were naked together—intense, dirty, vulnerable, and dominant all mixed together.

My phone buzzes in my bag, shaking me out of my thoughts. It's a text from Thora about meeting up for lunch. I smile and send her a thumbs-up. I have just enough time to sit in my cubicle across from Professor Yoon's office and chip away at my own coursework.

Saving my easier classes for my final semester was a pretty slick move. Sure, I had to work like a maniac last semester on all the advanced math classes, but I needed those completed before my grad school application anyway. I'm staring down a few months of a more relaxed pace.

I've been really enjoying my art class, which surprises me because I

291

pretty much never thought about art once before this. This week, I've been thrilled to read about how fractals are present in the work of famous artists like Jackson Pollock and Katsushika Hokusai.

I happily spend an hour on my paper for art history before my timer goes off to meet Thora in the cafeteria. She's already sprawled out at a table with a bowl of soup when I arrive. I don't want to interrupt her since she hasn't yet heard about her law school acceptance, and I know she's a bit of a mess. By the time I wait in line for my sandwich, and make my way over to her, she's got ink on her nose and has propped one of her pre-law textbooks on her empty soup bowl.

"Hey," I whisper, sliding into the seat across from her. "You gonna make it?"

She looks up at me and blows her hair out of her eyes. "To be determined. Ugh, is it past noon already?" She glances around at the crowded cafeteria.

I nod, mouth full of sandwich. I swallow and tell her, "I don't mind a working lunch if you need to get caught up. I'm reading about fractals as a tool to identify forgery in fine art."

Thora rolls her eyes. "I have no idea what any of that means. None of it."

I laugh. "That's okay." I wave a hand at her spread of books. "What are you frazzled about?"

"Ugh, I'm in this stupid argument class that's half full of jocks who give zero shits and half full of pre-law students who really need the credits. And, of course, the professor stuck me with another pre-law student for this project."

I frown. "Why is that bad?"

"Because now I have to actually collaborate and talk through the problems." She slams a book shut and picks up her soup bowl. I laugh as she licks at the rim. "God, this is good. So salty. Anyway, if I had a jock partner, I could just do the whole thing my way, be in charge, make sure it's all perfect. You know?"

I do know. We get along because we both have that desperate need for perfection and control. If we mess up, we both know the stakes and how even one lousy grade can set off a staircase of unintended consequences. I pat her hand. "I'm sure you and the other pre-law asshole will make a fine argument about …" I glance at the books she's been packing in her bag. "…the effectiveness of standardized tests. Thora that sounds boring as hell."

She nods. "It is. Did I mention we couldn't come to an agreement about our topic, and the professor had to *assign* one to us?" Shaking her head, Thora fixes her ponytail and then leans forward on her elbows, chin in her hands. "How was recitation today?"

I flush. She notices. "And what was he wearing this time? Maybe those mesh shirts they put on when they break into teams? With nothing underneath?"

"Thora Jansson, stop it right now!" The damage is done, of course. I'm thinking about Wyatt in athletic shorts and a mesh tank top, staring at me like he does in class.

She stands up and gestures for me to follow her. "You're the one who said you need to figure out how to let loose this semester. You haven't even gone to a party yet, have you?"

I shake my head, following her out of the cafeteria. "I think I already had my fun. And like I said, this art class is pretty cool."

"Jesus, Fern. One night of nooky and a class that's not impossible is not a formula for a fun final semester."

"Oh, like you're out there doing keg stands and snorting coke."

She laughs at me. "Is that how you think of fun? Drugs and being upside down?"

I shrug. "What do I know about relaxing?"

She links her arm with mine. "Come on. I don't have class 'til three. Let's go into the hotel across the street and steal desserts from the conference room."

I swat at her. "We can't do that. People paid for those."

"Yeah, and we're usually the ones being paid to serve them and clean them up. You know how many are usually leftover." Thora tugs my hand across Fifth Avenue into the fancy university building where—I don't even know what sorts of business people gather at these events. She's right that we're usually working with the catering staff. Hesitantly, I follow her into one of the ballrooms. She smiles and waves at the men and women in suits, making a beeline for the dessert buffet. Before I can blink, we're back outside, each holding a tiny plastic cup of mousse with a tiny wooden spoon.

Thora dots chocolate on my nose with her spoon. "See? Wasn't that fun? And nobody was eating them anyway."

Eventually, I relax enough to swallow the dessert. We sit side by side on a black metal bench, watching students rush past en route to class, eating decadent sweets. And I really do feel more relaxed.

Thora wanders off for her afternoon class, and I head home, wishing I'd saved some of the mousse to share with my mom. Inspired, I look up a recipe for mousse on my phone and stop at the store to grab the ingredients.

Another movie night with Mom and fancy dessert sounds like just the thing to kick off … well, a weekend full of coursework and not entirely relaxing. I'm fidgety because I'm used to working at the bar, but when I couldn't take weeknight shifts anymore, they filled my position with another bartender. It'll be okay. Soon enough.

My cousin Wes uses the term "competency boner" when discussing his girlfriend. Cara is one of the best soccer players in the world, and Wes was a goner for her the second he saw her in action. Well, not only is Fern Montgomery a fantastic bartender … she's also a really fucking good teacher. Sitting in class listening to her explain how to solve equations like nothing has me more than half-hard.

It's been at least three weeks, and I try not to make eye contact with her, recite the quadratic equation, and think about my steps for taking penalty kicks, but it's hopeless. I'm hot for this teacher.

I stare at my lap until she says, "Okay, that's it for this week. Let me know if you have any questions about the exam."

Shit. The exam. I've been so busy fretting about what damage my father might cause that I've really been struggling when it comes to my studies. I'm not a terrible student, but math has never been my best subject. My family is always saying sports use a lot of math skills, and I guess they're right, but I don't see how that translates to absolute value or whatever it's called.

I hustle out of the classroom, wondering what social activity my cousins are going to rope me into this weekend. I've been a lot less grumpy about driving their asses to bars since I got the vague hope that Fern might be working as a bartender, but I think she stopped doing that now that she's got this teaching gig.

I emerge from the elevator to find Odin and Stellan sprawled on the wooden benches in the lobby of the classroom tower. "Wyatt!" Odin looks up from his phone as Stellan yells my name. "We're doing a Costco run. You're driving."

I roll my eyes at them. "Why do I always have to drive? This isn't even a drinking event."

Odin shrugs. "Your car has the most cargo space. We need like 35 gallons of cereal, plus toilet paper."

I sink onto the bench next to him. "We are four guys living in an apartment. How much toilet paper do we possibly need?"

Stellen starts counting on his fingers. "It's been months since we restocked, man."

"Yeah, and I'll be graduating in a few months. The last thing I want to do is pack toilet paper when I go to Mexico."

Odin shakes his head and stands, offering me a hand to tug me to my feet. "You act like my brothers aren't lined up to take over the lease when you graduate this spring, dude. There will be Stags in that spot for years."

I walk beside them in the cold for the few blocks back to our apartment, where we dump our backpacks and fight over who will drive to the store. A series of texts comes through from my mom, asking if I'll have dinner with her tonight instead of Sunday. I show the phone to my roommates. "I will drive, but only because you fuckers are going to unload on the curb, and I'll go on from there to hang out with my mom."

Odin rubs his palms together. "That means you guys won't be at family dinner on Sunday, which means more of Aunt Alice's chicken for me."

I punch his shoulder. "I might show up Sunday, too. Just because my parents are out scouting or whatever doesn't mean I can't come."

———

An hour later, my car has been stuffed to the ceiling with packaged snacks and then unloaded in a snow squall; I'm finally on my way to the soccer stadium to grab my mom. I wave at the parking attendant, who has known me since Mom got this job when I was four years old, and I pull into a spot right by the stadium offices.

I could text Mom that I'm outside, but I enjoy going into her office. As a kid, I used to run up and down these halls, sneaking into the locker room where my dad and the other guys on the team would let me score on them. Now, Dad's retired from playing and is coaching the men's team, and the city has added a women's pro team to share the facility.

I start sweating when another message comes in from Nick—another number I haven't blocked yet.

You know it's slander for you to talk about me in the papers. I see these articles coming up. Big shot kid looking for a big contract, and the reporters gotta mention some bullshit from 20 years ago? Fuck you. I'm going to sue you.

A lump forms in my throat. I don't know what slander means, really, but asking my lawyer-uncle about it would lead to more questions than I know how to answer.

How the hell could I be on the hook for some reporter looking up public information that half the world already knows? I haven't let that man's name cross my lips to a reporter. Ever. I need to figure some shit out before I can deal with any of this, so I block the number and go looking for my mom.

She steps through the door of her office just as I'm shaking away this current wave of dread. "Wyatt! Come here, you look freezing." Mom wraps her arms around me and looks surprised that I'm taller than her, as if I haven't been taller than her for ten years now. "Well, I thought I could warm you up, but I guess we'll just blast the heat in your car. Where do you want to eat?"

I shrug, and Mom suggests we try the robot sushi place, where all the food goes by on a conveyor belt. "Yeah, that sounds fun."

I drive, and Mom talks about her roster leading up to the Olympics. She always played midfield, like my dad and me, and I like hearing her assess the women's national team. We get to the restaurant, and Mom keeps talking.

I think this is going to be a pretty easy meal with her until Mom grabs two plates of California rolls and holds them out of my reach. "I talked to Brian." I groan and she slides me one of the plates. "Why are you postponing a contract offer? And he said you turned down an endorsement opportunity?"

I take a bite of the sushi, but it all tastes like sand in my mouth. I can't tell her I'm waiting to sign a contract until I figure out if Nick can really sue me. Suppose signing something so publicly will set him off bringing up lies about her and Dad. "I've got some complications at the moment. But I'm handling it."

"That's what Brian said you said. I just don't know why you'd sit on something like that, honey. It's not like our family lacks lawyers who can help. Whatever it is. Uncle Tim is a huge donor to your school. I'm sure whatever is going on, he could—"

I snap at my mom. "I said I'm handling it." Her head jerks back, her expression pained. I sigh. "I also need to figure out what I want and what my career is going to look like. I want to begin my professional career as I plan to continue. Brian is always talking about building a brand. Maybe I'm not a cereal flake ambassador. Maybe I'm more of a deodorant icon."

Mom grins and shakes her head. My Dad and his brother Ty did a spot for Old Spice a few years ago, talking about Stag Swagger. "As long as you have a plan, Wyatt. But please know Dad and I are here for you. You can tell us anything." A silence hangs between us, and I wonder if she's thinking what I'm thinking—that I spent a ton of time in therapy telling first the psychologist and then Mom and Dad all the things that happened to me when Nick had visitation.

I've always walked around feeling like a stain on this family. The Stag family is full of massive success—professional athletes, incredible artists, and writers ... I know they don't mean to make me feel like the dark-haired stepchild, but that's precisely what I am.

———

I drive Mom home after dinner, endure extra-long hugs from her in the driveway, and head to my place to get caught up on my schoolwork while the apartment is empty. Except it's no use. I can't concentrate on my history paper, and no matter what I try, I can't figure out how to solve the practice problems Fern gave us to prepare for the exam on Monday.

I slam my notebook closed, and a piece of paper flutters out—the syllabus. I look at it as I go to shove it back in the folder and see an online forum for the recitation class. Chances are pretty slim that Fern or anyone would be on there at eight on a Friday night, but I log in mainly to satisfy my curiosity.

Sure enough, I'm the only student in the room; everyone else's name is grayed out ... except a bright green dot next to Instructor.

Fern.

Hey. I type in the chat window quickly, realizing I should elaborate. *I'm stuck on the problem about filling the bags of sugar.*

I stare at the screen for a few breaths. I'm about to slam my laptop shut and watch reality television instead when I see some floating dots appear in the chat window. Oh shit, Fern is typing back. I try not to imagine her in comfortable clothes at home, maybe not wearing a bra, perhaps those fantastic tits shaking a bit as she types furiously to help me.

Where are you stuck?

My lips part, thinking about her naked even as she's trying to help me with math. Why is this hot for me? I'm seriously fucked in the head. She's trying to help me with my math homework; it is her job. Fern seems perfectly capable of forgetting our night together, treating me just like any other student. Which is what I am. A student who is stuck on a math problem about weighing bags of sugar: *I got the heaviest possible bag, but I don't know how the equation can find the lightest possible bag of sugar.*

Fern asks me a few questions, which initially frustrates me because wouldn't it be easier if she just told me what I'm missing... but finally, I see what to do on my own. I actually feel the tension leave my shoulders as I type a formula into the chat box, and then when Fern types, *perfect! You got it!* I feel like I just scored a fucking goal in the last instant of a game.

Thanks so much, Fern.

I bite my lip. *I mean Ms. Montgomery. Thank you for helping me on a Friday night.*

My pleasure. Does she really mean that? Oh, god, I can't think about pleasuring Fern.

I stare at the screen, unsure if I'm expected to respond if she's still sitting there. My heart thunders in my chest, but I type, *You're really good at explaining this stuff. I mean it.*

Thanks, Wyatt. I appreciate that. Good luck on Monday's exam. Have a good weekend.

Again, I should close the computer. I should walk away. But her instructor dot stays green. She's still sitting there on her end. It's not like I can type anything I'm really thinking, especially not on an official university server. But damn, do I want to know what she's wearing, what she's doing after this, why she'd be monitoring the online support forum on a Friday.

By the time her green dot turns gray, I'm fully hard, aching in my jeans, remembering how she looked spread open on my bed, how she tasted when she was so nervous about being sweaty. I close my computer and move to my bed, wishing I could still smell and feel her there as I unzip my jeans, take myself in my hand, and relieve myself to the memory of Fern Montgomery's O-face.

MOM COMES UP BEHIND ME AT THE TABLE, LEANING OVER MY SHOULDER TO KISS the top of my head and peek at my computer monitor. "You're doing work on a Friday night?"

I shrug. "I'm usually *working working* on Friday nights."

Mom pulls up the other chair at our small table for two. "I'm glad you have a bit more room in your schedule this semester. I thought you'd go do fun teenager stuff, though."

I try not to roll my eyes. "Mom, I'm 22 years old."

She winces. "Okay, okay. But still. Where's Thora?"

I suck on my teeth. "I think she's working the hockey game tonight. She got one of the bar stands that has a tip cup, so she was excited for that." Neither Mom nor I need to mention that I don't have other friends. Everyone from high school is either involved in their adult lives by now, with kids or full-time jobs, or else far away at their colleges, working weekend gigs to supplement their scholarships.

Mom tilts her chin toward the computer. "Well, what are you working on? I saw you smiling at the computer when I came for a drink of water."

I flush. "I was working on a paper, but then one of my math students was in the forum asking for help."

Mom tilts her head, looking at me strangely. "One of your students, hmm? What's that about?"

I wave a hand and close the computer. "He's someone I knew from before … one of the regulars at Fuel Up. It's been … weird having him in the class."

Mom frowns. "Fern, I don't need to tell you what can happen if you lose yourself to a man."

I press my fingers into the scratched surface of the table. We've had it as long as I can remember, and I'm pretty sure it came to us nicked and scuffed. "You don't need to tell me again, no. And like you said, Mom, I live like a monk. So, there's nothing to worry about."

Mom crosses her arms. "It's not that I don't want you to go out and experience dating and love and adventure." She sighs. "It's just all so … fragile. You know? Like there's only a tiny icicle between having a good time and making a choice you can't unmake."

I nod. We've had this conversation a lot. Too many times. This conversation is why I work so hard at my studies, but it's also why I went wild on New Year's Eve, and now I'm having to pretend like I'm not a hot mess every time I see or even think about Wyatt Moyer.

I sigh. "I'm going to go to bed. I love you."

I reach for her hand, and she squeezes mine. "Love you, too."

In the morning, I feel restless in our apartment. Mom is at work, and Thora is most likely still asleep. I take the train downtown and grab a bus to campus, head into my usual spot in the library, and freeze in my tracks when I see the very cause of my unsettled state.

Wyatt sprawls in a chair by the wall of windows overlooking Forbes Avenue. His long legs, clad as usual in gray sweats, seem to take up the entire floor. He wears a university t-shirt despite the January chill, and his baseball hat is tugged low over his eyes. His dark hair peeks out a bit from the edges of the hat. I wonder if he's due for a cut or just likes it shaggy that way. And I can't be wondering such things about one of my students.

I pause and look around, trying to find another place to sit and get some work done, but something causes Wyatt to look up, and his eyes catch mine. I have one of those moments where the rest of the room fades away, it's like I'm peering down a tube. All I can see is Wyatt, framed by bright daylight, smiling at me.

"Fern! Hey."

I nod and look over my shoulder again. Now that he's seen me, is it rude if I don't sit near him? Instructors sit in libraries with their students. I've done it myself lots of times. I sigh and walk toward the seat next to him, opposite a low table with just enough space for both our notebooks. "Hi yourself. I don't usually see you here …"

He shakes his head. "Well, technically, I'm supposed to be at cardio this morning, but I have a meeting with my agent later, and … you probably don't care about any of that. Sorry. Hi."

I swallow and tuck my hair back behind my ears even though none of it had come loose from my ponytail. I wish I had tried a little harder with my appearance today, but I'm in old jeans, an old bar t-shirt, and a huge sweater that probably has holes. "I don't mind. Will you get in trouble for missing cardio? With the team?"

Wyatt sets his book down on the table. I see that it's the same one he was reading a few weeks ago, when I met him. But now he's nearly done with it. "I won't get in trouble, no. I would have entered the MLS draft and been gone from here, but I have some shit I need to finish up." He shakes his head. "That's not what you want to hear about, either."

I fuss around with my bag, pulling out my pencil sharpener and scrap paper I rescued from the recycling bin in my classroom. "You mentioned a hard time changing your name. What's the problem with that?"

"You really want to know?" Wyatt leans forward toward me like he really wants to tell me about this, like he needs someone to listen.

"Sure. I'm a pretty good problem solver."

He laughs. "Yeah, that's true. Well. Like I said, my bio dad is a piece of shit. My step-dad has always wanted to adopt me, but dirtbag wouldn't relinquish his parental rights. It was a whole fucking thing my parents dealt with for years." His face shifts, like the memories make him uncomfortable. "I couldn't get a passport. You need both parents to sign for that to leave the country. So, my whole family couldn't travel unless they left me at home. Which, to their credit, they never once complained about where I could hear them." He puffs out a breath. "But my parents are both heavily involved with the national soccer teams, and Dad competed in the Olympics a few times…Mom coaches all over Europe. They always had to leave me and my sister home with family."

"You have a sister?" I'm not sure why this is what I latch onto in that whole heartbreaking story, but the rest of it is so foreign to me. A family that competes internationally in sports? Forget about it. My dad can't even hold down a job.

Wyatt nods. "Birdie. Yeah. She's an elite soccer player, too. Anyway, the second I turned 18 we got the passport sorted out. But I wanted to change my name, to be like the rest of my family." He bites his lip, scooting his chair closer, like someone might be listening to him. "I went to try and do it myself, and they make you run an ad in the newspaper that you're changing your name and offer a number if someone objects."

"What? That's nuts." I never heard of anything like that. "My mom didn't have to do that when she married my dad...not that that lasted longer than a few seconds."

Wyatt waves a hand. "If you're married or divorced, it's easy. But otherwise, they think you're trying to avoid credit card debt, so you have to go through hoops. I didn't hoop properly, and I wound up poking the bear."

I frown. "Your bio-father, you mean?"

He nods. "Yeah." He groans. "It's so dumb. I called him thinking–I don't know. That we'd be buddies or something? I wanted to tip him off that I was changing my name."

I shrug. "That doesn't sound dumb. I always hoped my dad would be my buddy, but I gave up trusting that he'd ever show up when he said he was going to."

Wyatt drags a hand through his hair. "Yeah, well, once Nick caught wind of what was happening, he started threatening me."

A chill runs through me, and I hug my arms to my chest. There's something about the look in Wyatt's eye: this big, muscular athlete with a wealthy family and resources being scared of someone. "What did he say?"

Wyatt shakes his head. "I'm not getting into all that. I just can't have him stirring up shit for my parents. That's what he'd do, mostly. Create bad press. Tell lies. Drag my mom's name through the mud again." He sighs like the weight of the entire library is crashing down on his strong shoulders. "She worked too hard to get away from him and make something of herself, to get me away from him."

I bite my lip and tap my finger on my lap. "But you're kind of a big deal athlete, from what I hear."

He grins at this. "You've been hearing stuff about me, Fern?"

I roll my eyes. "Knock it off. That's my point. People talk about you."

He nods. "Yeah, and every time they do, it's only a matter of time before they run a search, and news articles come up about poor Wyatt, the kid who had to be rescued by the police." Wyatt looks over my shoulder and out the window at the bustling city. Students pour out of the 7/11 and the Dunkin' Donuts. Tourists stop at a sidewalk cart to buy university t-shirts. Here, we're just two people under a lot of pressure, in different ways, trying to keep our noses down and get through it all.

A fist of anguish punches my heart, thinking of a little boy going through that again and again his whole life as that scary incident comes up in every news article about him playing soccer. "That sounds awful. The police thing."

He nods. "I was thinking maybe I blew it out of proportion in my mind, you know? But once I actually reached out to him … he showed me that I had it right all along."

I should hug this man. Student or not … he's hurting. Unsure what to do, I reach out and squeeze his knee. "You couldn't have known that he'd threaten your family. It's been years. I get why you thought he'd work on himself."

Wyatt puffs out a laugh. I grin. "I have fantasies about my dad going on meds or something. Getting a therapist. Getting a job… buying me a birthday card." I shake my head. "What will you do after you graduate? You said you have an agent?"

Wyatt swallows, and when he meets my eyes, he looks more vulnerable than I felt the night he took me home. "I'm trying to play internationally. But I need to sort out my name to sign my contract as Wyatt Moyer. It's important to me."

We stare at one another for a long time. "Can't your agent help with that?"

Wyatt groans and sinks lower into his chair, dragging a palm down his face. "He's my dad's agent, too. And my cousin's. Like I said, I can't have any of this impacting my family. It's something I really want to do on my own. Like … a lot of stuff has been handed to me over the years. It feels like the least I can do is sort out my legal problems."

I'm not sure what to say in response to that. I know family law is a horrifying ordeal. My dad hasn't even been unpleasant or vindictive, and it was still a nightmare for my mom for a long time. So much was out of her control, always. And she always felt like she was being scrutinized by the court. I can't imagine how much more stressful that would have been if my father had been abusive.

Neglectful, sure, but never abusive. I want to reach out to Wyatt, to gather him in my arms and tell him I understand. But that feels like crossing a line, so I just press my lips together and nod. "Thank you," I stammer. "For telling me all that. I won't betray your trust."

He nods, takes a deep breath, and stares up at the ceiling while he blows it out. Then he points at his notebook. "Feel like talking me through *those* problems again? I'm not feeling good about the exam."

A warm current flows through me at the thought of helping Wyatt, of working closely with him on the language of the universe. "Sure. Tell me where you're the most stuck."

We spend the next few hours talking through the various word problems and I figure out that Wyatt's been forgetting how to count negative numbers. I draw a few number line sketches on his scratch paper, and it's like flipping a switch for him. He solves the rest of the problems quickly and finally jumps to his feet, pumping his fist. "Hell yeah!" He holds his hand out, I think, for a high five, and I slap his palm tentatively. And then my stomach gurgles louder than his celebration whoop. "Oh, crap. What time is it?" Wyatt looks at his expensive smartwatch. "Want to go grab lunch? The least I can do is buy you a sandwich for helping me on a weekend."

I wave a hand. "I packed. And you don't need to thank me. It's my job to help."

Wyatt puts a hand on his hip, scowling down at me. "It is definitely not your job to help on a Friday night or a Saturday. Come on." He beckons with his hand and reaches for my bag. "We can have a very public sandwich. You can tell me about your ..." He glances down at the notebook I never even cracked open. "... trigonometric identities. What does that mean, anyway?"

I open my mouth to explain, and he holds up a finger. "Tell me at lunch. Come on, Fern. Please?"

Then he flashes puppy eyes at me, and I throw all my reservations on the ground and stomp on them in my sensible, well-worn sneakers as I stand up to accept lunch with my student.

Fern seems just as uncomfortable being seen or recognized as I am, so I suggest a diner a few blocks from the main drag. I tip my chin at the host, who is bussing tables, and Fern and I settle into one of the tall booths near the back.

Just as I watch Fern shrug out of her coat, a flustered server drops off a pair of laminated menus, still damp from a wipe-down, and plunks red plastic water cups in front of us. "Be back in a few," they say, hurrying off to another table. Fine with me.

I don't need to study the menu. I always get a grilled chicken breast with broccoli and a side of wild rice if I'm in the off-season, which I am right now. I pretend to study the menu, but really, I'm staring at Fern. She's so damn pretty, in addition to being insanely capable. Her dark hair and eyes stand out against her fair skin—Fern's complexion is almost like porcelain, but I know there's nothing fragile about her.

And god, she's curvy and soft. But never delicate. She has a wide smile she doesn't use very often. I sigh. She's been pretty clear about the stakes if she gets in trouble with her teaching gig. I shouldn't be trying to get her to smile at me.

The server comes back while Fern is frowning at the menu. I kick her gently under the table. "Remember, this is my treat to thank you for the help with the absolute value stuff."

She rolls her eyes, and the server looks back and forth between us. "You guys ready to order?" They tap a pen on an old-school restaurant notebook. That's why I like this place. No digital anything. I don't even think they take credit cards. It's dimly lit, always full, and the food is pretty good.

I glance at the server and give them my order, trying to adjust my pants in response to Fern licking her lip as she settles on what to eat. "I think I want the Reuben," she says like she's not sure. Man, how long has it been since I ate one of those? I make a mental note to treat myself in celebration once I secure a contract.

The server takes our menus, and they rush off to hand the slip to the kitchen staff. Fern folds her hands on the table and looks at me with those huge eyes of hers. "So, you're eating healthy stuff, but you're not in season, but you're skipping workouts and trying to get a professional contract? Is that about it?"

I laugh. "I know it all sounds insane. It's just what I'm used to. It's actually been pretty easy to eat clean in my family since all four of us are in elite athletics. And my Aunt Alice is a chef, so she spoils us all."

"Oh man, a chef in the family would be my undoing." Fern reaches for her water, and I can't help but stare at those full lips wrapped around the paper straw. She frowns and pulls it from her glass. "I can't handle how these feel in my mouth once they get wet." She picks up the cup and takes a sip, and it's much less evocative, which I guess is good for my still-tight pants.

"What about you," I ask her. "You said something about a fellowship?"

Fern nods. "I applied for a bunch of them. It's not like I can go to grad school without full funding. But I really want to study in London."

I lean forward, fascinated. "Why London?"

She beams and absolutely glows in the low light of this deli. "Imperial College in London is one of the best places in the world to study algebraic geometry."

I snort. "I don't even know what that is!"

Fern waves a hand. "Advanced math stuff. But the connections would be incredible. Cutting-edge research in cryptography and cybersecurity. Financial engineering. Gah!" She shimmies her shoulders, looking adorably excited. "A whole world of opportunities."

I nod. "And you didn't have a ton of opportunities before."

"Yeah." She shrugs. "You know how it can be. It sounds like you started out with a single mom…" I nod. Fern continues, saying, "Mom always wanted to study finance. She's incredible with numbers. She and my dad met in high school, got pregnant, got married, and tried to make it work with community college. Still, they didn't have a ton of support, and…" Fern drifts off and looks up at a restaurant employee who slides our plates on the table and practically takes off at a run to gather more from the counter at the kitchen window.

I slide her plate closer to her and grab my own, adding, "And your dad couldn't handle when shit got hard, so your mom made do."

Fern nods. I lift my water glass and hold it out toward her. "To strong women." I wink as she clinks her cup against mine. We have a lot in common, even though it doesn't seem like it from the outside. Sure, I had a lot going my way for the majority of my life. But the baggage of the early years is still weighing me down in a big way that I can see Fern understands. She doesn't seem grouchy and moody about her struggles, though. She just digs in and works around the clock toward her goal.

Fern picks up her sandwich, the gooey sauerkraut and sauce dripping out on the side of her hand, and takes a bite. And she releases a sound I heard a few weeks ago when I had my head between her thighs. "Shit, Fern, it's no wonder I like spending time with you."

Fern chews, blushing, and frantically reaches for napkins. "This is a mess," she whispers, and I think she means more than the sandwich. I'm about to say something else I shouldn't, something flirty and inappropriate, but a pair of students walks down the aisle toward the bathroom, and they recognize me.

"Hey! You're Wyatt from the Viper soccer team, right?" I close my eyes, take a deep breath, and nod. "Man, you had a phenomenal season! Hey, can I get an autograph?" The one guy reaches forward and snatches Fern's spare napkin, sliding it my way.

She stares at him and his companion, wide-eyed, unused to having her meals interrupted by fans. They look over at her and quickly glance back at me. I don't like that they don't say hello to her. Sure, she's not famous, but she's clearly someone important to me if I'm sitting here with her at a restaurant. Instead, the shorter of the two guys looks at Fern and asks, "You got a pen we can borrow?"

Fern's mouth works up and down, and I can tell she's about to reach for her bag to dig for a pen, but I hold up a hand. "Hey, guys, we can do a quick selfie, but please don't inconvenience my friend or take her things." I slide the napkin back toward Fern as the taller guy nods and hands me his phone.

I extend an arm to get the three of us in the photo. No way am I asking Fern to take it. I smile, tight-lipped, and hand the guy his phone back, barely acknowledging them as they walk off.

"Wow," Fern says, chewing on another bite of sandwich. I scowl. "You really don't like getting approached by fans, do you?"

"Was it obvious?"

She laughs.

I shake my head and spear a bite of chicken. I chew, swallow, and reach for my water. As I do, my hand brushes Fern's as she reaches for her water at the same time. I stare down at the place where our skin touches, feeling searing jolts of electricity run through me. It's like a pinched nerve but in a really good way.

In a moment of impulse, I lose all sense of … well, sense, and I lean forward, reaching for Fern, like I'm going to pull her face close to me and kiss her right here in the restaurant. For the briefest moment, I think she's going to reciprocate, but she pulls back and starts shaking her head. She stiffens.

"Wyatt," she whispers. "We can't do that. You can't do that. I'm your TA, and we need to have boundaries."

I nod. "I'm sorry," I tell her, and I'm about to say a whole lot more when my phone rings. It's the loud, brassy ring I assigned to Brian, my agent. I sigh. "I'm sorry," I repeat, gesturing at the phone in my hand.

She nods and takes another bite of the her sandwich. I stare at her eating as I accept the call. Brian doesn't even wait to be greeted; he just launches into news of a potential contract offer from a team in Mexico. I know Fern can hear him. I know everyone in the deli can hear him.

Fern takes one more bite of the sandwich and shrugs her arms back into her coat. I hold a hand over the phone. "You don't have to go," I say quietly.

She shakes her head and places a palm on my shoulder. I feel the warmth again, the sizzle, but I know her intention is not to encourage that type of energy. "You should talk to your agent. Thank you so much for the food, Wyatt. I'll see you in class."

She makes her way out of the crowded restaurant as Brian rattles on and on about the money we're going to earn together, about the suntan I'll get in Guadalajara. I can't manage to rustle up excitement for this opportunity, especially knowing I'm no closer than I was before to sorting out my legal name. I barely pay attention as Brian talks through his plan to woo the team. Despite the heavy odor of fried food and grilled meat, I still imagine I can smell Fern and her snow-dusted hair.

My mind reels from the disappointment of not kissing her, from the opportunity I might have to let slip away, from all of it. Eventually, I toss a bunch of money on the table and walk out, making my way home where at least my cousins can distract me with their carefree nonsense.

CHAPTER 14
FERN

MY HEART RACES AS I RUSH FROM THE RESTAURANT IN SEARCH OF THORA. I make a beeline for Fuel Up and sure enough, she's behind the bar washing glasses, getting ready for happy hour. She glances up when the bell rings above the door as I enter, and I must look frightened because she dashes over to me and wraps me in a hug.

"What the hell happened?" She brushes my hair back from my face and studies me like she's looking for bruises. I don't need to tell her they're all internal.

I take a deep breath and blurt, "I went to lunch with Wyatt, and he tried to kiss me, and I panicked."

She laughs and shakes her head, clutching at her chest. "Fern. I thought something actually bad happened to you. Jesus." Thora walks back to the bar, slapping a towel over one shoulder and continuing to shake her head.

I follow and slide my butt into a stool, my mind racing. The thought of Wyatt's lips on mine sends surges of heat through my veins, but the fear of the consequences of kissing a student is like a bucket of cold water, shocking me back to reality. "I'm serious, Thora. This could be really bad."

She squints at me, considering. "But you like him?"

I groan. "I really do. He makes me feel …" I try to verbalize the connection I feel to him, but I just shrug. "He's just great."

Thora winks. "Doesn't hurt that he's fly as hell and probably has an ass you could bounce darts off of."

I press my palms to the bar and purse my lips. "I can't stop thinking about him. Not just the physical stuff. All of it."

311

Thora sighs. "I get it. He's hot, and you two have chemistry, and it sounds like he's a sexy, moody orgasm vending machine."

I wince. "That's all true and accurate. But …"

Thora's eyes soften. "I know it's not just about the physical stuff, Fern, and that you're focused on what's at stake here. Your career, your dreams. But you also deserve to have fun and feel good."

I sniff. "I hoped you'd tell me to be careful and that I've worked too hard to risk it all for a guy."

Thora grabs a clean glass and starts polishing it with the towel, winking. "Not my style." The familiar clink of glasses and hum of conversation fill the air as more patrons trickle in. The bell above the door tinkles again and a group of students makes their way toward the televisions along the back wall, showing pro hockey and basketball games. Thora raises her brows. "That's my cue to get pouring. You going to be okay?"

I flap a hand at her. "Yeah. I just needed to vent about it."

"What kind of bartender would I be if I wasn't here for you when you needed to vent?" Thora grins and sets a pitcher under the tap.

I say goodbye and leave the bar to bury myself in classwork. As I head home, I try desperately not to think about my moodiest student. I take a deep breath, pushing thoughts of Wyatt from my mind and shaking away the echoes of his intense gaze and the warmth of his touch.

Monday morning arrives, gray and frigid, matching my mood as I make my way to campus and the algebra lecture hall. "Is Dr. Yoon here yet?" A student is waiting outside the lecture hall when I arrive early to set things up for the exam. Their eyes dart from their watch to me and back, cheeks flushed.

My arms are full of test papers, so I try to communicate with my eyes that I need help opening the door. They do not get the hint. I sigh. "No, they will be arriving in a bit. Could you grab the door for me?"

"Oh. Sorry." The student opens the door and follows me down the aisle toward the lectern, asking what will be on the test and whether they can look over the paper before we begin.

I set the stack on the podium, letting my forearm cover the papers. "I'm really sorry, but it's a timed test. I can't let you look before the exam begins."

Their demeanor shifts—jaw set, body stiff. I can tell they're frustrated. I see a spark in their eye, and my heart rate increases. Are they going to hulk out over this? I try to think of how I'd respond at work to a customer who gives me the willies. Tending bar, I usually have a bouncer I make eye contact with, and I don't have to explain a damn thing.

Here, I'm apparently on my own with a kid who seems on the verge of a mental health crisis. They're about to begin a tirade of injustice when I see a dark figure looming behind them. Wyatt is early, striding down the aisle like he can sense my discomfort from the back of the room.

"Can I borrow a pencil?" He asks me this, even though I can see at least three mechanical pencils sticking out of his shirt pocket.

I swallow, relieved, as the frustrated student huffs their way to a seat in the front row. I nod and reach into my bag for a pencil. Wyatt's fingers linger on mine as I hand over the yellow wood. I make eye contact—a huge mistake—and a flush creeps up my neck. I remember the charged moment at lunch, the near kiss, and I think about how artfully he handled the situation just now…appearing to rudely interrupt while actually rescuing me from a frustrated, panicked undergrad.

I like the idea of having someone swoop in, someone looking out for me, even with little stuff like this. But this is a very dangerous thing to yearn for, and I have two decades of experience with the realities of trying to count on someone else and eventually giving up on him. My mom and I are solid, but I still see the impact of how my dad messed her up—messed us both up.

Dr. Yoon enters the auditorium to a flutter of the student's questions, and Wyatt releases my hand. With a nod, he shuffles to the back of the room and sinks low in his chair, tugging that hat low over his eyes. I can't tell if he's nervous about the test. He shouldn't be. By the time we left the library, he had a great grasp of the material.

I try to listen as Dr. Yoon firmly sends the anxious student to their seat. I need to learn to set boundaries like this if I'm going to enter academia someday. At the very least, I'll be navigating students like this in graduate school. But I can't concentrate, and Dr. Yoon actually snaps their fingers to get my attention when it's time to distribute the papers.

My hands tremble slightly as I pass out the tests, especially when I get to Wyatt's row and see his dark eyes following on my every move. I take a deep breath and remind myself to stay focused as I hand out the last of the papers.

Dr. Yoon taps on the microphone at the front of the large room. "You may begin." There's a brief roar of papers being flipped over, a flurry of pencil scratches, and then all I have to do is pace the aisles, making sure nobody is visibly cheating.

I try to keep a watchful eye on the students, but I find myself glancing at Wyatt more than I ought to. I notice things like how sexy he looks with his brow furrowed in concentration. How he taps his pencil when he's thinking. How he flexes his fingers along his thigh with the hand not holding the pencil.

The hour crawls by in a tumult of my racing heart. I'm sweating when Dr. Yoon finally announces there are five minutes left. I take my place beside the podium, and the students who have finished early file up to submit their tests. "Make sure you put your name on the front page," I say repeatedly, and a number of students retract their paper to label it after the fact.

The class period ends, and the final students make their way up front. Wyatt lingers behind, approaching me with his paper. "Thanks for all your help," he says, his voice a low rumble that vibrates every tendon in my body. I nod and look down to see he's holding out my pencil. When I close my hand around the tip to take it back, he squeezes the eraser end and grins.

A warmth spreads through my chest before I can stop it, before I can remind myself that I'm trying to leave the damn country, and the last thing I need is to feel any sort of anything for a guy, especially one who is off limits.

Wyatt leaves the lecture hall, and I get to work stacking the test papers. I turn to hand them to Dr. Yoon, who is packing up their messenger bag. "Here you go."

They glance at me. "I usually have the TA's grade the exams and only come to me with questions."

"Oh." I bite my lip. "I'm not sure I know how to distribute these to the group?"

Dr. Yoon frowns, pausing as they pack up their things to leave, and I realize just how little preparation I've had for this TA gig. Dr. Yoon shifts their weight from foot to foot, clearly in a hurry to leave, and seems frustrated to have to explain the basics to me. "Aren't you all on a group chat? An email thread?"

A lump forms in my throat. I hate feeling unprepared. "I'm not on one of those, no. How can I get the list of names of the others?"

They sigh. "I'm sorry. I have a committee presentation. I'm sure you'll figure something out, Fern. You're very bright."

They rush from the room, leaving me with the stack of tests. I close my eyes and take three deep breaths. I will go to the math department office and ask one of the admins for advice. Admins always know everything. This will be fine. They're right—I'm resourceful.

Wyatt is slumped on a bench, staring at his phone, when I open the door. I huff out a laugh. Of course, he's here. I sink onto the bench next to him, and he smiles at his phone as he continues typing. "Can't get enough of me, Montgomery?"

"Yep. That's me. Obsessed." I shuffle my bag around so I can put the stack of papers inside. "How do you feel after the test?"

"You should grade mine right now and tell me how I did." He slides his phone into the pocket with his pencils, looking at me expectantly.

"Ha. How about no. I am absolutely not getting involved in grading yours." I feel a flutter of anticipation, wondering if he'll touch me. Wanting him to touch me. Knowing he shouldn't.

As if he can sense my distress, he eases away from me on the bench. "Sorry. I'm being pushy. I just really think you're awesome."

His cheeks get small spots of pink, causing me to flush as well. I laugh. "We're both worked up over this test, I think."

He smiles. "I'll let you get to grading. See you Friday?"

I nod and watch him walk away. I gather my things and head toward the math department office, where the admin pulls a list of the other student teaching assistants for Dr. Yoon's class. When I lean on the wall outside the office to email the group about divvying up the tests, I see an unread message from Imperial College in London.

I gasp as I click to read it.

Dear Ms. Montgomery: I am delighted to inform you that you've been selected...

I stop reading and close my eyes. My heart races. Is this really happening? I hum a little bit and open my eyes, returning to the message.

...for our graduate fellowship in algebraic geometry, including tuition remission, a monthly stipend, accommodation in our private graduate student housing, as well as a meal plan for our residential dining halls. Assuming completion of your degree and receipt of final transcripts...

I stop reading again, eyes watering. This is it. This is what I've been working for. My dreams are so close I can feel them with my fingertips. I stamp out thoughts of Wyatt and his exam and his soccer career. I need to focus on finishing this semester.

I pull up a group chat with Thora and my mom, typing three words in all caps:

Their responses come almost immediately, and I smile, knowing I'll be celebrating with them.

CHAPTER 15
FERN

Thora and Mom flank me as we walk up Forbes Avenue in the fading daylight. I was excited that the timing worked so they could both be in the neighborhood to celebrate with me as soon as I got the note from Imperial College. Thora points at the bougie new chain restaurant with a bright sign. "This calls for milkshakes," she says, tugging us inside.

I try not to look at the price tag for three shakes—they don't even have alcohol stirred in, so why on *earth* do they cost this much—and we find a high table to sit. Mom's eyes water as she holds up her plastic cup brimming with whipped cream and cherries. "To my hardworking girl, who never takes her eye off the prize."

"Cheers to that!" Thora plucks a cookie from the top of her treat and bites into it.

I click my cup against each of theirs and savor the sweet drink. "It all feels surreal," I say after swallowing. "Like … this has been the goal for so long. What's the goal now?"

Thora rolls her eyes. "Getting the damn degree, Montgomery. That's the goal. Do you have your student visa yet?"

I shake my head. "No, I needed the acceptance letter first."

"Oh, right." She taps her fingers on the table. "Not gonna lie, I'm anxious about my own acceptance letter now."

Mom squeezes both our forearms. "I just know you'll both be heading off to London together. Thora, what makes you want to do a law degree over there, though?"

Thora's eyes widen, and she waggles her brows. "International business, baby. I want to go everywhere. I want clients in Tokyo. I want to facilitate deals in Delhi. London is a starting place."

I set down my milkshake and squeeze Mom's hand. "Don't worry. I plan to come back stateside after my degree. I'm just looking for a very specific program expertise."

Thora laughs. "Only about 30 people in the world understand what you do with your math, babe. And that's fine because you're a beautiful algebra wizard."

Mom's eyes watery as she sips her shake. "Fern, you've always seen numbers differently from other people. I don't know where that comes from, but it's very special, and I know you've worked so hard." She dabs at her eye with a napkin.

I draw in a shuddering breath. "Mom, you've been supportive. Always. We did this together. I wish you could come with me!"

She waves a hand. "Maybe someday. For a visit." We share a grin until I feel my phone buzz in my pocket. Frowning, wondering who it could be, I glance down. It's Wyatt. I forgot I had given him my number at lunch. I press my lips together and send the call to voicemail as Thora and Mom talk about how nice it would be if Mom flew first class to see us both in London. Thora snorts. "It's not like anyone from my family will be coming over."

I slurp the last of my shake. There's no way I'll be hungry for dinner after this. "Never say never, Thor."

She squints and points at the ceiling. "The only way my parents are coming to London is if they're on the run from the law." Thora's purse begins to beep. "Ah, shit. I gotta get to the arena. I'm working the hockey game tonight."

Mom glances at her watch. "I should ride with you. I don't like to take the train too late." She looks up at me. "How long are you staying on campus, sweetheart? You said you have TA work to do this evening?"

I nod. "I want to get a head start on grading these exams alongside the other folks, get a sense of the routine and all that."

Mom frowns. "But you won't stay too late? Or splurge for a car if you do?"

There's no way I'm splurging on a ride share after we just had expensive milkshakes, but I nod my head to appease her. Public transportation is perfectly safe if you know how to use your elbows, which I do.

Mom and Thora wave and head to catch a bus toward downtown. They sandwich me in a hug on their way out of the shop, and once they're gone, I fiddle with my cup, deciding it can't hurt to listen to Wyatt's voicemail. His voice comes through the phone in a broken, muffled torrent about threats from his father and demands for money.

It's hard to ignore the undercurrent of panic in Wyatt's voice as I listen to his message, and I head instinctively toward his apartment a few blocks away, worried.

———

I knock on the door, hoping it's the correct one, and am greeted by a giant who shouts something about food delivery. "Sorry," I mutter. "I must have the wrong apartment…"

But then I see Wyatt over the man's shoulder. He sits on his couch, staring at me wide-eyed, face pale. He looks so vulnerable; I want to rush over and wrap my arms around him. The guy who answered the door looks at me, turns over his shoulder, and says, "There's a chick here for one of you." He snaps his gaze back to me. "What's your name?"

"She's here for me." Wyatt appears in the doorway, shoving the man out of the way and reaching for my hand.

He tugs me wordlessly through the apartment and straight into his bedroom. I worry there will be a chorus of teasing, but the entire production is met by awed silence by his roommates, who all seem too tall and too muscular for any of the furniture. I begin to understand why the athletes get their own apartment buildings—everything is bigger in here. They probably have reinforced box springs under their mattresses.

"Fern." Wyatt's voice is gravelly, pained. "You came." He sinks onto the edge of his bed and props his elbows on his knees, cradling his forehead in his palms.

I stand in front of him and rest a hand on his shoulder. "You sounded so upset. Want to tell me what happened?"

He shakes his head and I begin to stroke his shoulder, tracing a fingertip from his ear, down his neck, along the firm swell of muscle. He seems to lean into my touch, so I continue, and eventually, he says, "I feel like I'm putting my entire family at risk, like I'm just some outsider exposing them to trash and scandal."

I sink next to him on the bed and pull him into my arms, resting his head on my shoulder. His body shakes. My mouth is right by his ear as I whisper, "I know they don't feel that way about you. I can tell they'd want to fight this guy alongside you, Wyatt."

His voice is muffled by my shirt. "You haven't even met all of them. The Stag family is intense."

I rub my palms along his back and his arms, just holding him close to me. "From everything you've said, I think they'd get intensely protective of you."

He shakes his head. "That's the problem. They'd drop everything and go wild. And they probably *would* lose endorsements. I can't be the reason any of them lose an opportunity." He draws back to look at me, and his eyes are red and watery. "I'd never forgive myself if my parents got pulled from coaching the national team."

I swallow, looking around for water and not seeing any. I soldier on, voice thick. "What makes you think the team wouldn't rally around them?"

He sighs and pulls back further, reaching for his aunt's book on his nightstand . "This is all about corruption in the national office. My cousin Wes? His girlfriend was the woman who got grabbed and kissed on television. Did you read about that?"

I frown. "It sounds familiar … didn't she start a whole movement? And a clean sweep in the management with a vow to do better by their players?"

Wyatt seems to collapse, like he can't let himself trust that anyone would possibly be on his side in all of this. "Hey," I tell him, kicking off my shoes and curling up in the bed beside him. I let my hand rest on his face, and he turns toward my palm like a plant angling for sunlight. "I know it's hard to trust people when you're used to going alone. I get it. I was raised by a single mom."

He nods, cuddling closer to me. I've never felt this before, another person relying on me for comfort like this. Let alone a man I find attractive. A man who made me come harder than my expensive (and totally worth the cost) vibrator. I cannot think of Wyatt's bedroom skills right now. He's upset. I knock his baseball hat off his head and bury my fingers in his dark hair instead, gently stroking his head. It's intimate and soothing for both of us. His breath begins to slow, and I can feel him calming down.

"Okay," I tell him. "If this feels like too much, I'll shut up. But you know my friend Thora?"

He nods. "You've mentioned her."

I continue to stroke his hair and tell him about Thora's pre-law adventures and some of the case studies she's described to me. "There's a clinic on campus for legal aid. You see a law student, but it might be more confidential than talking to an official person who might know your family."

Wyatt draws back, frowning up at me. "What good would a student clinic do? I have an agent…"

I nod, bracing myself for him to not want to hear any suggestions. "I just remember Thora talking about petitions for confidential name changes. So, you wouldn't have to advertise it. I'm thinking a student could at least help with that."

Wyatt is quiet for a long time. Just as I worry he's fallen asleep, he curls a little tighter against me and says, "That could be something."

"It could," I whisper. "I'll get the clinic info from Thora. I can go with you if you want or not—whatever you need."

He looks up at me again, brow furrowed. "Why would you help me like that?"

I shrug. "I like you. We're friends. I think?"

His lips tip up in a small smile. "Yeah, something like that."

He burrows back into my shoulder, and I stroke his hair some more. "What were you going to do tonight? Before you came here, I mean?"

I smile against the top of his head. "I was drinking a milkshake, and then I'd probably read."

His voice is muffled against my shoulder. "What flavor milkshake?"

I laugh and swat at him. "It was hazelnut with little chunks of pretzel. And cherries, of course."

"You're into cherries."

I shrug against him. "I guess so. Sometimes."

I like this cuddly side of him, even as I begin to remember that he is off-limits in this regard. But my urge to help him overpowers my doubts, so I ask, "Want me to read to you since I'm here?"

He pulls back, meeting my eye. "That would be amazing."

"Yeah?" He's unexpectedly enthusiastic, so I disentangle myself from him and crawl toward his bookshelf, studying the spines. "Is that Megan Rapinoe's memoir?"

He stretches out on his back, grinning. "Yeah. I love that one. I know she has a version for adults, but that one's signed."

My jaw drops. "Seriously?" I glance inside the cover, where I see the book is indeed signed and personalized. "Well, we have to read this one, I guess." He nods, and I crawl back to him, sliding under his head so it's on my lap as I open the book. I begin to read, brushing his hair off his forehead with one hand while I recount young Megan's struggles with teachers who didn't like her, with anger she wasn't sure how to contain until she got a soccer ball at her feet.

Each time I glance down, Wyatt's eyes are closed, and I worry he's asleep until he grunts in laughter at the Rapinoe tradition of cleaning out the fridge. "Leftovers don't exist in this apartment, either," he tells me. He waves a hand toward the door. "Those monsters eat everything. Everything."

I close the book and set it aside. "My mom and I eat a pot of soup for like an entire week. It's just us."

He smiles. "Some pros and cons to both those refrigerators, I guess."

I feel warm, happy, and relaxed. I know a crisis for him brought me here, but even if it's forbidden, I'm glad to be right where I am.

"Where were you tonight? Other than milkshakes?"

I glance down at him, and I can't contain the smile that tugs at my mouth. "I was celebrating." He raises his brows, questioning. "I got into my grad program … with funding."

Wyatt draws back, grinning. "That's incredible, Fern. You rock."

A flush builds from my core to the tips of my ears. "It feels pretty damn good."

His gaze heats, and he sits up. "Did you feel all celebrated out? Cuz I can think of some pretty good additions to your milkshake experience."

He licks his lips and snakes a palm onto my hip, tugging me tight against him. I inhale sharply, feeling him fully erect, hard and hot.

I glance down at his sweats, noting the outline bulging between us. "A celebration, hm?"

He nods, splaying his long fingers wider against my butt, digging in and squeezing. "Are you interested in that?"

I close my eyes. "Nobody will know?"

He looks over his shoulder toward his bedroom door. There isn't a sound from outside the door, not even the video game. I have no idea what time it is or how long we've been in here. "They're not going to tell anyone, trust me," Wyatt says with a small smile. "We know better than to blab about who goes in and out of the bedrooms here."

I lick my lips and, rather than prolong the conversation, lean forward to kiss him.

He's familiar and exceptional, warm lips pressing against mine while a tiny moan escapes his throat. I love the feel of it, the sound of his wanting. I rock my hips against him as his hand stays on my ass like all he wants in the world is to feel me pressed into his crotch.

"Fern," he whispers and sucks on my tongue, sending spirals of sparks along my spine. I nibble on his lower lip and explore his mouth with my own tongue, wriggling until my nipples feel the friction against his chest.

I move a hand from his head to his waistband, fingers finding the smooth, taut skin of his abdomen. I trace along the top of his sweats, where his stomach is hairless and firm and so, so warm. In a flurry of elbows and muscular forearms, he whips his shirt over his head and throws it across the room, leaving me with the magnificent sight of his torso. When he rolls onto his back, I can't help but straddle him, pulling off my own shirt and then returning my palms to his chest as he settles me onto his erection.

Even through my jeans, the friction feels perfect. I can tell I'm wet, all the way through my underwear, and Wyatt confirms this when he reaches between my thighs and grins, finding the evidence of my arousal. "Oh, Fern, you gorgeous thing."

I bite my lip and reach behind my back, unclasping my bra. The straps fall from my shoulders, and Wyatt reaches up to slide my hands away. He cups my breasts greedily, squeezing and kneading. "Your body is so fucking incredible," he rasps as I continue wriggling on top of him. In an athletic move I can't comprehend, he sits up without using his hands, and his mouth is back on mine as he continues to touch my boobs, eventually moving to pinch both nipples between his thumbs and forefingers. "Beautiful," he murmurs, never taking his eyes off me.

"That feels so good," I manage to moan, and then I gasp when he dips his head to lick first one nipple and then the other. He leans back, admiring the wet nubs in the dim light from his nightstand. I think about a book Thora gave me once and I stiffen, wondering if Wyatt would be interested in recreating one of the spicy scenes.

He licks and rubs, seeming to enjoy himself immensely as I sit with my hands on his shoulders. Eventually, he looks up, rubbing his cheek against one breast like it's a satin pillow. "What's on your mind, Montgomery?" He arches one eyebrow as I bite my lip. Sensing my hesitation, he straightens. "What's up?"

I take a deep breath and close my eyes, then drop a hand between our bodies, causing him to hiss when my palm rests on his cock. "I was wondering if you'd want to try something …"

I bring my other brow up to match the first at Fern's hesitation. "Beautiful, I'm 100% sure I'm interested in trying whatever's on your mind." The fact that this woman is curious about something in bed has me harder than ever, and I was pretty fucking hard from the moment she put her arms around me, despite being upset and panicking about my family.

Fern has a way of making it feel like things will actually be okay, like there might be a solution out there that doesn't involve me giving up soccer or something like that. She leans in close, lips against my ear. I can feel her breath hot on my cheek as she says, "Would you want to put your cock between my boobs?"

I stiffen, genuinely afraid I'm going to come in my pants at the very thought of burying my dick between Fern's creamy tits. "Holy shit, Fern."

She stiffens. "We don't have to. It was just an idea."

I flip her onto her back in an instant, causing her to yelp. I'm fumbling with my nightstand drawer with one hand, frantically searching for the lube as I yank down my sweatpants and boxers with my other hand. "Fern. There is nothing in this world I would enjoy more than that. Wow. Found it."

I hold up the bottle of lube, and she frowns. "What's that for?"

"Oh." I shake my head. "Oh, gorgeous, I'm going to slick you up and rub my hands all over you until you're shiny and smooth, and then you're going to hold those awesome boobs together as I grip the headboard and glide in and out."

Her mouth drops open in a sexy oh as I flip open the lid on the bottle of lube. I grin when her hands land on my butt, and I grin even wider as she gasps as the drops of liquid land between her breasts. "Fuuck, Fern," I whisper, watching the rivulets of lube drip along her sternum. When I'm sure there's enough, I get to work spreading it around.

She lies back on my bed, hair all messed up, plush body all soft and warm on my sheets, shining as I lube her up. I set the bottle on the night-stand so I can concentrate, making sure her nipples get some of the action. "Oh, that feels so good, Wyatt," she purrs. Her hands are on my thighs now, everywhere but my erection, which is good because the second she touches me, I know I'll explode. "This is so hot."

I nod. "So, fucking hot. You ready?"

She nods and grips the sides of her boobs. "Oh my god. Fuck, Fern. Jesus." I grip the headboard and slide in, groaning each time I see the head of my cock appear at the top of her cleavage. My breath bursts out of me like I've just played 89 minutes, but I can't lose sight of the goal. I have never felt this turned on in my life … until Fern gets the idea to stick out her tongue and lick the tip of me the next time I thrust.

She meets my eyes and does it again, and before I can warn her and I can distract myself, I come right there on her chest, splashing my release all over her with a grunt. "Oooh, Wyatt, yes," Fern moans, dabbing a finger in the mess I made. "My god, that was hot." Rather than horrified, Fern seems hornier than ever by my early explosion.

The second I regain consciousness, I yank off her jeans and underwear. I dive down the bed between her thighs as she adjusts her posture, sitting up a bit so she can see what's going on. Fern keeps one finger in the sticky splatter on her boobs and the other hand in my hair as I spread her thighs and lick her. With a few thrusts of my tongue, her head falls back against the headboard. I love watching her come apart like this. She's always so put together, in charge, and confident. It's like I'm the only one who gets to see her this way, disheveled after getting exactly what she asked for.

I move a thumb to her clit, remembering how she liked firm pressure there last time. She tastes like she's desperate for this, and I get hard again, remembering how she was so wet, she seeped through her jeans when we were making out. I tongue her seam, and slide a finger inside feeling her pulsing around me. "That's it, beautiful. You got this." I trace the sensitive skin of her inner thighs, giving her pussy a break until she clamps her knees against my ears. Laughing, I dive back in until I feel the waves and ripples rolling through Fern's body. She drops a forearm over her mouth, stifling her moans as she comes, grunting my name. I hold a finger inside her while she rides it out, and then I kiss my way back up her body, pausing when I get to her chest.

"You are so hot when you come," I tell her.

Lazily, she rolls her face toward mine. "You're just saying that because you're the only one who's seen it."

I frown. "What do you mean?"

She shrugs. "Nobody else has ever been able to do that, Wyatt."

A swell of pride mixes with frustration that she hasn't always gotten what she deserves in bed, which is constant pleasure and satisfaction. I kiss the tip of her nose. "It is my pleasure and my fantasy to see you this way, Fern Montgomery. Fucking look at you."

I glance down at her body, and she does, too, squirming a bit. "I'm a mess."

I nod. "Let's clean you up in the shower."

I do, and then I carry her back to my bed, and she falls asleep beside me, fingers in my hair as I keep a palm on her amazing ass. I know this is a risk for her, that she's got more to lose here than me, and that makes it that much better to know that she's here for me right now. It feels so right like this is exactly where each of us needs to be.

I WAKE UP TO THE SOUND OF WYATT'S ALARM, PAIRED WITH A FIST POUNDING on his door. "Yo, cuz, we're heading to the weight room. You in?"

Wyatt grunts an affirmative-sounding syllable and rolls to face me. I feel the bed shift, my senses slowly turning on. He plants a kiss on my forehead.

"What time is it?" I don't even want to open my eyes. This can't be when he gets up every day.

"Probably five," he croaks. "But you don't have to rush out of here. Sleep as long as you want and let yourself out." He kisses me on the forehead. It's nice, like how I imagine a boyfriend might wake me up if we lived together. But Wyatt cannot be my boyfriend because he is my student and also because I'm leaving the country in a few months for grad school.

I roll on my back with a groan. "I should go home and shower before class."

I open my eyes to see Wyatt changing into workout gear. His smooth, muscled skin seems to glow in the low light he turned on in the bathroom. By the time I shake the sleep from my eyes, he's brushing his teeth with one hand and pulling on a sock with the other. "Seriously, stay. Nobody will be here. All four of us are going to work out."

Wyatt disappears into the bathroom, and I hear the water running. He appears back by the bed, smelling minty, and kisses my forehead another time. And then he smiles, and he looks so sweet and vulnerable I can't help but swoon right back onto his pillow. "Okay, I'll just close my eyes for a minute."

Wyatt laughs and waves, backing out his door to the grunts of his cousins. I hear low voices and a door close, and then … I'm alone in Wyatt Moyer's apartment. It feels strange to think of him by the other name, the one he's trying so hard to shed, the one he believes is keeping him from the career he longs for, and the family harmony it sounds like they've fought really hard to build.

I think about how very anxious he is about the whole thing, wondering how long it's been since he talked to a therapist about his past trauma. He mentioned counseling from when he was a child, but it sure sounds like he needs help sorting out his feelings now.

I'm drifting back off to sleep, thinking about how good my body feels after offering him a distraction last night. It was a distraction for me as well and a damn good way to celebrate my acceptance into grad school. Hopefully, Wyatt is right, and nobody in his family will mention me at all, even in passing, to anyone on campus.

Just as I'm convincing myself his cousins don't even know my name and that my secret is safe, I hear a door open. And then I hear Wyatt's bedroom door open. Totally bewildered, I clutch the sheet to my chest as a woman stomps into the room, flicking on the light. Noticing me in the bed, she drops a suitcase on the ground and groans. "Well, shit. This fucking figures."

My cheeks heat in embarrassment and confusion. She exits the room and I hear a lot of commotion out in the living room and kitchen area. Cupboards slam, and music begins to play. I hurry out of bed and get dressed in yesterday's clothes, knowing my hair looks bad as I slept with it wet after rolling around with Wyatt. My cheeks flush remembering how he gently washed me in the shower, how we came together in his bed afterward so tenderly, so slowly. I didn't think I'd have anything left in me after he used his tongue on me earlier, but Wyatt surprised me by coaxing another massive orgasm from my body with his hand while he stroked in and out of my body.

I shake my head and grab my backpack, stepping into the hall.

The woman is sprawled on the sofa with a hand over her eyes. "You don't have to leave. I was just looking for a place to crash in peace. My brother doesn't usually have overnights."

"Brother?" The word is out of my mouth before I can process all the parts of her sentence. Wyatt doesn't bring girls home, or if he does, he doesn't tell his sister about it. Did he mention a sister? Everything is so fuzzy right now.

The woman curls into the sofa, pulling a hooded sweatshirt over her face. Her voice is muffled by the back of the couch. "Look, I'm sure you're delightful, but I am going to pass out until one of them gets back from cardio or whatever."

I stand in the middle of the room, not sure what to do. I'm fully awake now, and I decide I might as well head to campus. I can keep plugging away at the stack of exam papers while I try not to panic that this apparently-exhausted sister of Wyatt's might report our relationship to the university. Which would trigger a cascade of disasters including removing me from the position, taking away the paycheck that comes with it, and probably causing Imperial College to reconsider my fellowship offer.

Nope, I cannot let myself have a staircase of terror thoughts.

I send a message to Wyatt as I wait for the bus to the campus library.

> Met your sister this morning ... I guess she
> needed a place to crash?

And then, because I know I won't be able to concentrate without asking, I add

> Do I need to worry about her mentioning our
> sleepover to anyone?

she's sort of forbidden or if she's just fuck-hot, but there's no way I'm concentrating on class this morning with those sorts of memories so fresh in my mind.

When my phone pings with an email, I see it's from Fern and immediately open it. The student law clinic is every Tuesday and Thursday morning, so basically, right the hell now. I change into a nice shirt and slacks—a big change for me since I'm usually wearing athletic stuff—and step into the living room to whistles and jeers from my cousins and my sister, who is now fully awake and playing video games with Odin. "Where the hell are you going?" She sniffs, like I'm wearing ripped clothes and a grease-stained shirt instead of business casual.

"I have a thing," is all I give them. I grab a pea coat from the closet and slip it on, immediately realizing it must belong to Odin because it's fucking huge, but I don't pause to change. I head directly to the clinic, and mercifully, there are only a few people in line ahead of me. One of the clinic workers seems to be the bartender friend Fern mentioned. I frown—I don't know if undergrads are equipped to handle the kind of shit I am here to discuss. But it seems like Thora is mostly handling registration, so I relax a bit.

"Oh," she says, making eyes at me. "It's you! Name, please?"

I hesitate. "Um, that's sort of why I'm here…"

She squints. "I need a name to put on the case file. What's your current legal name?"

I look over my shoulder. "Can I just write it down?" I don't think there is anyone here who might recognize me. I don't have my signature hat pulled over my face, but we're also not really in an area full of undergrads. Everyone mulling about the clinic seems to have shit they're distracted by.

Thora shrugs and slides me her electronic tablet. "We're in the age of modernity. You can type it."

———

I'm sitting outside staring at my official petition for a confidential name change. The law student had access to all the old court records, and it was super uncomfortable rereading those documents. I had sort of suppressed the court appearances from when I would have to go to his house for visitation, and he would refuse to feed me if I cried or made noise, and Mom kept trying to change the custody order.

I'm a little twitchy remembering all the incidents my mom never found out about because the police never got involved. But the supervising lawyer at the clinic today said we didn't even need to get into all that because there was enough paperwork from custody court paired with the threatening texts.

I was embarrassed to tell them that I initiated contact, but I think the law school folks understand what it's like to hope your parents will raise you.

I gave them a check that was less than a tank of gas in my Range Rover, and they're going to file all this stuff for me with the magistrate.

All I want to do is call Fern and thank her, properly. But she's spooked about my sister. Fern and I never seem to get enough time alone. I realize I have just the way to overcome that obstacle, in a place where Fern won't worry about us being seen or anyone reporting our relationship to her boss.

I look at my watch. I have no idea what her schedule is like on Tuesdays, but I do know she has a mailbox in the math department. I form a plan and scrawl a note to her on the back of the law clinic flyer Thora handed me outlining their services and fees.

As I make my way to the math building, I hope I run into Fern in person, but I don't hold out much hope of that. I slip the folded flyer into the pigeonhole above her name and head home to prepare while I wait for her response.

CHAPTER 19
FERN

"Ms. Montgomery, can I speak to you for a moment?" Professor Yoon summons me from the cubicle where I'm grading papers near their office.

"Sure. What's up?" I sink into the seat opposite their desk, cringing a little at how informally I just answered them. They always seem so serious and busy. I can't get a read on them.

They set down a stack of papers and glance at me over the top of their glasses. "I heard about your acceptance to Imperial College. Congratulations." They don't smile when they say this so I'm not sure how to respond.

"Thank you?" My voice tilts up at the end of my sentence. "It's a huge honor."

Professor Yoon takes off their glasses and folds their fingers together. "It's an honor for us as well, to have prepared a student for such a prestigious program. I will be following your career with interest." I can't quite tell, but it almost seems like they smile, so I relax a bit and let out a huge breath. They pick up one of the papers from their desk. "I'm told you are avoiding grading the word problems on the exam?"

My cheeks flush. Have the other teaching assistants been talking about me? My heart races a bit. "Um, well, some of the students' answers have seemed partially correct and I wasn't sure how to give credit for those."

Professor Yoon chews on one of the stems of their glasses. "I do not typically award partial credit. Math is a very precise endeavor, as you know." I nod. They sigh. "It occurs to me that you have not had the benefit of an orientation. The other teaching assistants get a bit of guidance when

337

they arrive for graduate school. Have there been other gaps preventing you from completing your work?"

My eyebrows shoot up. There have been so many gaps I don't even know where to begin, but it won't do me any favors to ask them to start at the beginning. Especially since we're a month into the semester at this point. I clear my throat. "Um, not that I can think of? But I might not know what I don't know… my recitation grades are still just pass-fail based on attendance, right?" They nod. I think of Wyatt, of how I should have mentioned a prior relationship with him a long, long time ago, but now that ship has sailed halfway to London. "I'm good," I stammer. "I'm enjoying learning the ropes."

Now Professor Yoon actually smiles. "You won't need ropes for long. You won't even have the burden of teaching your first year in England."

I am surprised to learn they think of teaching as a burden. I think about how much I enjoy breaking down the concepts with my recitation students and how it helps my own thinking for my work when I have to explain basic concepts. I shrug. "It's a great scholarship."

They nod. "Well, back to it." They slide me the pile of exams, and I head back to the cubicle to re-do them. Right or wrong. No gray area for Professor Yoon. I need to keep that in mind.

I pass the row of mailboxes on my way and see that there is something in mine. I grab the slip of paper and see that it's a flyer from the student law clinic.

Wyatt.

I look over my shoulder, which is ridiculous because I would surely hear if there were someone else in the hall. Seeing no one, I unfold the paper and see a handwritten note from him on the back of the form.

Sorry again about my sister. Thanks again for the law clinic advice. I have so much to tell you. Let me take you somewhere we can talk? Say yes. Call me.

I sink back into my seat in the cubicle, staring at the mountain of exam papers, thinking about my own coursework as well as lesson plans for Friday's recitation. What does he even mean, take me somewhere?

I grade papers for another hour, trying to get as many done as I can, which is a little easier now that I'm not giving anyone room for doubt if they got the answer wrong but the approach correct … it's not a policy I would choose, but it's not my call.

What is my call, is the hushed conversation I have with Wyatt from the 23rd floor, where nobody is around because I checked. Twice.

"Hey," he answered. "You got my note?"

"I did," I whisper, which I realize might make me seem even more suspicious if someone shows up. I remind myself that nobody would have any idea who I'm talking to as long as I don't use his name. "What did you mean?"

I can practically hear him smiling, which is unusual for him. "My family has a house in the mountains, right on the ski resort in Hidden Valley. Let me take you there?"

I puff out a laugh. "I don't ski. Is there even snow?" Our winters have been incredibly mild lately.

He scoffs. "We wouldn't be going there to ski, Fern. Although I can teach you if you want." I frown. He continues. "I'd cook for you. And there's a hot tub."

A vision of Wyatt shirtless in bubbly water is impossible to tamp down in my mind. Fuck, that sounds amazing. "When would we even do something like that?"

"Any time. Nobody uses that place during the week. Do I remember that you only have one class on Thursday? We could go Wednesday afternoon, skip your class, get back in time for you to be my teacher Friday ... "

I am positive my entire face and neck are bright red at this point. Two entire nights in a mountain cabin with Wyatt Moyer sounds like something from a romance novel. One of the books where I got my idea for that thing we did the other night. "I can hear you breathing hard, Fern." Wyatt's voice teases me. "I'm sure you've never skipped a class before in your life, and you probably know all the material."

I bite my lip. My Thursday class this semester is the art history class I saved for this year because it's pure enjoyment. It doesn't even count toward my degree, although I'm using it as an elective. The professor is one of those people who gets me to see the world differently and think about art not just as a bonus but as an important part of being human. "I don't know if I *want* to miss my Thursday class," I admit.

"Hm. Well, think about it. I can make it worth your while. Over and over again ... in the hot tub. On the counter. On the rug by the fire..."

"Okay, okay. Wow."

"Are you blushing, Fern? I wish I could see. Snap a picture."

I hear someone come up the stairwell and turn to see a red-faced student huffing and puffing a bit. Hopefully, they see me in a similar state and assume I also took the stairs up here. "You have to stop talking that way."

"Meet me at my apartment tomorrow?"

I bite my lip. "What do I even bring?"

Wyatt laughs. "Strip of condoms and a bottle of lube?"

"Wyatt!" I swear I'm going to pass out if he keeps talking this way.

He laughs again. "Just comfortable clothes. There are sheets and towels at the house. I'll take care of all the food and everything. Including you ..."

———

We hang up, and I immediately call Thora, who texts me that she picked up a bartending shift and can't talk. I feel this counts as an emergency, so I make my way to the bar on Forbes Avenue, where I first met Wyatt Moyer on New Year's Eve.

Thora is slinging bowls of soup and pints of dark beer to the lunch crowd, and I make my way up to the bar, grabbing a stool at the far end, hopefully out of earshot of ... well, everyone.

Thora's brow furrows when she sees me, and she slides a menu my way along the bar. "What are you doing here? You never spend money."

I lean forward. "I have to tell you something."

She bites her lip. "Bowl of soup?"

I glance at the prices on the menu. "Cup of soup."

She nods and disappears, serves a bunch of food and drink to some other patrons, and makes her way back to me, where she starts rinsing glasses. "What happened?"

I tell her about my chat with Professor Yoon and Wyatt's indecent proposal. She grins. "I did see him at the clinic. He left there pretty happy. He had some weird thing about his name?"

I wave a hand. "That's not our business. The point is he wants to ..." I don't even know how to describe what he seems to be offering.

She leans across the bar and takes a bite of my soup. "He wants to sex you up in a fancy-ass ski chalet where nobody is going to interrupt you."

"I'm sure it's not a chalet."

Thora arches a brow. "You really haven't looked up his family at all? They're, like, super famous Pittsburgh royalty."

I frown at her. "I had no idea."

She nods. "I've been doing a little stalking action on his cousin Odin, arguably the hottest Stag."

I recoil. "Odin? He's …" obnoxious … loud … not Wyatt … I'm not sure how to finish that sentence.

Thora pats the bar. "He's in my argument class. I'm supposed to work with him on the next paper."

I laugh. "Well, you'll like that. He's an athlete so you can probably–"

"Boss him around? Take over the project entirely." She beams. "You know me so well." A bell rings from the kitchen, and Thora rushes off to grab another order, shouting over her shoulder. "It's okay if you're smitten with Wyatt. There are way more sexy dudes in his family, though, for the rest of us. And you should definitely go to the *Winter Palace*. Do it for the rest of us, toiling away behind the bar." She leans back and presses the back of her hand to her face like a fainting Victorian woman.

I roll my eyes at her and finish my soup.

I jump when my mom rests her hand on my back. And then I groan. "What time is it?"

Mom pulls up the seat next to mine. "It's almost six. I just got home. Have you been here all day?"

My back aches, and I stand, trying to stretch as I simultaneously blink to wet my dried-out eyeballs. "I have all this grading to get done for Professor Yoon."

"Mm." Mom frowns at the stack. "I thought you had a whole week for those?"

I bite my lip. I've already decided to go with Wyatt. I hate missing my class, but I also rarely do anything spontaneous. I never do anything decadent. "I'm, um, going out of town for a few days this week. With a friend."

Mom arches a brow. "A friend who is *not* Thora?"

I laugh because Mom knows as well as I do that Thora and I are never going to ditch class and work mid-week to go adventuring. At least not while we're undergrads. Who knows what will happen when she's a Rhodes Scholar and I'm in "fancy math school," as she calls it. "A friend who is not Thora." I shrug, not wanting to upset my mother or give her all the sordid details. "I'm trying to live a little. Be young. What are you always telling me?"

"Hm. Mid-week? What about class?"

I sit back down next to Mom. I glance at my stack of papers—only a few left. "I've never missed a single art history class, and everyone gets one freebie with no penalty. And I'll be back before my math recitation on

Friday. And as you can see—" I point at the stack. "—I'm well ahead of the curve with my work for that gig." I lean my head on Mom's shoulder. "Think of it like the spring break I never took."

Mom sighs and kisses the top of my head. "You're right. I trust you. You're always responsible, and you're older than I was when I had you."

I frown at her. "You don't sound so certain."

"Well, you're not giving me many details." We both laugh and Mom gets up, opens the fridge, and we set to cooking dinner together, my stack of papers forgotten for the time being. As I stir and chop, I think about how many people seem capable of no-string flings. This trip with Wyatt doesn't have to mean anything. I can let him ravish me away from the prying eyes of soccer fans on campus and anyone who might put my TA position in jeopardy.

This can be a delicious cherry on top of my undergraduate career before I head off to … well, frankly, more of the same hard work in graduate school. Just on a different continent with different things to see on weekends. From what I've read, Imperial College takes graduate students on weekend excursions to the moors and day trips to Stonehenge. I feel a little giddy thinking about a theoretical advanced math discussion about Stonehenge with a bunch of like-minded students.

And I'll be a train ride away from Paris! The idea of seeing the Eiffel Tower when I've never even seen the Statue of Liberty is a bit surreal. Mom heads to her room after dinner, and I finish grading, typing in the last of the grades, and packing up the papers to drop off with Professor Yoon first thing in the morning. Before I try to sleep, I pack my ratty old swimsuit, which will have to do, along with my best sensible underwear, dark jeans, and a few tops like the one I had on New Year's Eve when Wyatt apparently fell hard for my rack.

———

In the end, I don't get much sleep at all, anticipating my big sordid adventure. But when Wyatt picks me up outside the math department, I forget all about being tired. I climb into his black SUV, sink into the leather seats, and smile as he points the car east and heads toward the mountains.

"Tell me about this place," I insist as he merges onto the highway and calmly enters tunnel traffic.

Wyatt grins, a wide smile I'm not used to seeing on his face. "My dad and his brothers all went in on it when Uncle Tim turned 40. It's nice having a place big enough for all of us."

I lean one elbow on the window and rest my head on my hand. "When you say all of us … how many is that, exactly?"

My whole family is me and Mom, so I'm fully unprepared when Wyatt spits out the number 19. My jaw drops as he ticks off aunts, uncles, and cousins. "Oh," Wyatt adds. "There's also Grand and Lolly. Dad's mom, Lolly, married my mom's friend Patty—my Grand." He shrugs. "So, 21 if they come to stay when we're there." He scratches his chin. "Wes is feeling pretty permanent about his girl, but we haven't all been together since he's been with Cara. I bet it'll be 22 of us for Christmas."

I try not to imagine making it 23, try not to think about being in this fantasy castle bursting with family … with Wyatt.

He tells me the place has an indoor soccer field, a theater room, a pool *and* a hot tub, and enough bunk beds for an entire soccer team. "The best part is the big table, though," Wyatt adds. "It's really, really nice when we all sit together eating amazing food Aunt Alice makes. She's the chef. I think I told you about her."

I smile at him. "You sound really happy when you talk about your family."

He frowns at this. "Yeah." He sighs. "I've been caught up in this shit with my bio dad. Ever since he started contacting me … making weird threats. It's been heavy. I guess I get nostalgic for big Stag getaway weekends."

As Wyatt exits the turnpike, the big buildings of the city give way to rolling hills and frosty trees. "I guess it really is colder up here in the mountains."

He nods. "Yeah. I told you, it's an escape to a different world." We drive along, and I wonder if I should ask him about his progress with the name petition, but I decide it's too soon for anything to have happened, even if he was able to pay to fast-track things.

Before I can fret about it too long, Wyatt turns into Hidden Valley Ski Resort and points up the hill. "We're headed up there, right on the slope."

My eyes widen. "Won't people *see* the house if it's on the slope?"

He shrugs. "Sometimes people on the lift can see you if you're in the hot tub during the day. But we'll be very secluded tonight, Fern. I promise."

His last word carries so much heat that I shiver, so far gone my lust overtakes all my worries about being seen by … exactly who do I think is looking at me from the ski slopes? Certainly, not anyone who is in the position to tattle on me to the math department about making out with a student in a foggy hot tub on a rich family's deck.

"Here we are," he says, pulling into the driveway to a massive house with a sloped roof and multi-story windows overlooking the forest.

"Wow," is all I can muster, and when I look to my side, Wyatt is staring at me.

"Yeah," he says, not looking away from my face. "Wow."

I carry the cooler and grocery bags inside while Fern drops her bag and stares around the great room. Not gonna lie, the first view of this place is always spectacular. By the time I make a second trip in from the car, she's figured out the remote for the fireplace and turned on the recessed lights above the massive wooden table.

I decide right there in the doorway that I'm going to spread her out on that table and make her come. My own private feast. I drop the last grocery bag on the counter and walk up behind her, looping my arms around her waist as she stares out the window. I kiss the side of her neck, feeling her melt into me. "Want a tour?"

She shakes her head. "I just want to stand here for a bit, if that's okay."

"Whatever you want." I nuzzle at her, letting my hands trace across her soft belly, growing hard as she sighs and stares at the beauty of the Laurel Highlands. She rests her head back against my shoulder, and I startle, realizing how fucking good it feels to just hold her this way. I have no worries here, no responsibilities.

I don't even have cell reception to worry if my agent is going to call, or my new lawyer. Until I connect to the household Wi-Fi, I'm in my own little world with Fern Montgomery. I reach for her hand. "Come on." I give it a tug. "Let me show you our room."

———

I walk Fern down the hall, past the bunk room, up the stairs, and into my parents' bedroom. My dad and each of his brothers have a room with a king-sized bed, and there's a queen suite in the basement for Grand and Lolly. But there's no way I can achieve what I need to with Fern in a bunk bed, so I take her into the first room at the top of the stairs.

She's in my arms in a flash, mouth sealed against mine as I flick on the light and then hoist her into my arms. She wraps those thighs around me as I walk toward the bed, and when I finally sink on top of her, it's like the world exhales.

"Wyatt." Fern's voice is in my ear, her breath hot on my skin. I feel the heat between her legs as she keeps them wrapped around my waist.

"You look so good here with me," I tell her, admiring the flush in her cheeks before I tug her shirt up and over her head. "God, your body is so luscious." She smiles as I kneel above her, palming her boobs.

Fern tugs at my shirt, struggling to sit up, so I help her out and pull it off with one hand behind my neck. And then we are skin to skin, moaning into each other's mouths. I slide down her body to lick at her nipples, and she drags her fingernails down my chest.

"I thought this was going to happen in the hot tub," she whispers, biting my trap muscle and then sucking the spot where her teeth pinched me.

"Mmm," I lick each nipple and then thumb the wet peaks. "We can do that after. To recover."

Fern opens her jeans and slides them down her hips. I do the same with my pants until we're both fully naked on top of the covers. "Shit," I freeze. "I left the condoms downstairs in my bag."

Fern pouts. "You better hurry and get them. You can't leave me like this, Wyatt." She spreads out on the blanket and drops a hand between her legs.

"Fuuck, Fern. Do not move." I sprint down to the doorway and grab my entire bag, taking the steps three at a time as I rush back to find her … not in the same position at all. No. Fern has rolled onto her stomach, the glory of her naked ass on display for me as her dark hair spills over one shoulder and she presses up into some sort of yoga cobra pose that pushes her tits together.

I almost choke on my tongue. "My god, Fern. Look at you." I throw the bag onto the bed and dive on top of her, feeling the swell of her ass against my dick, which is harder than I ever thought possible.

Her voice is husky when she says, "Mm, you're so warm." She turns her head to the side, and I kiss her as I fuss with the bag with one hand.

Finding the condom, I yank it on as quickly as I can and then nudge her thighs open, settling between them.

"I want to take you like this," I whisper into her ear. "All spread out for me, that incredible ass where I can see it. Oh, my, you *are* wet." My fingers spread her open, finding her pulsing and hot and so soft.

"Wyatt!" Her cry is a gasp as I pull my hand out from her body. "Oh god, I need…"

"Mm, I know what you need." I kiss her shoulder and line myself up behind her, one palm on her ass and one on the base of my cock as I notch up and start to push inside. The sight of her like this, spread around me, soft and perfect, almost has me losing myself before I even finish a stroke.

"That's it," I tell her as she buries her face in her hands, disappearing behind a curtain of hair. "Look how easily you take me, gorgeous."

And she does. Fern swallows me inside, pulsing and hot around me. "Wyatt, it feels so good like this." She presses her forearms into the bed and shifts her hips back, moving to meet me as I start to thrust inside her. I let her take all of my weight, leaning over her and sucking on her shoulder as my hands search for her breasts. "Oh," she moans. "Oh, do that some more." I pinch her nipples as I grind into her, and she tilts her hips.

"Fuck, Fern, can you get up on your knees? I need to touch you, beautiful." She lifts herself up, giving me access to her clit as I snake an arm around her hip. I band the other across her chest and, feeling inspired, pull her upright so we're both on our knees. Fern grips the headboard with both hands, pinned against me as I flick her nipples and knead her clit, all the while thrusting inside her and trying not to come until I hear her shrieking and feel her pulse around me.

And then we're both coming, shaking, collapsing in a fit of giggles and released tension, curled together on the bed in a sweaty, sated knot.

When I finally tuck Fern into a fluffy towel and tug her out back to the hot tub, a bottle of white wine and two glasses between the fingers of my left hand, she's already sex-drunk and utterly relaxed.

And then she sees the sky full of stars, away from the lights of the city, sparkling above the treeline as the steam from the hot tub swirls upward. "Climb on in," I tell her, gesturing for her towel, which I hang on a peg by the hot tub along with my own. I've never been naked in my family's hot tub before, never brought a woman here to curl against my chest with a drink under the stars. "This is amazing," I whisper.

Fern turns her head, incredulous. "Wyatt. I know. But surely you're used to it by now?"

I shake my head. "How could I ever get used to this? Look at you." I squeeze her waist before turning to open the wine and pour us each a glass. I set the bottle on the shelf behind the headrest in the corner of the hot tub, where the jets are cranking.

"Well," she blows her hair away from her face and accepts a glass of wine. "Look at you. And look around."

I nod. "We are both incredible, and the scenery is pretty okay." Fern throws her head back, laughing, and takes a sip of her drink.

She rests her head sleepily against my shoulder. "I don't think I'm going to be able to do much else tonight after all that."

"You don't want to do *all that* again?" Just the thought of it has my dick twitching against her back, but I guess she doesn't notice it with the water jets because Fern sighs into her wine glass.

"I really don't think I can handle that again."

"I'm up for the challenge if you are." I grin and squeeze her hand, and we both sip and stare at the stars.

Fern turns to me, arms around my neck, facing me in the dark water. "I should tell you something."

I nod. "I've told you plenty of things."

Fern smiles and runs her fingers through my hair in that way I love so much. "You're the only person I've been with. Like that I mean."

I frown. "Like what?"

She shrugs. "Like, put their penis inside my vagina." Another smile, and she presses a kiss on my forehead. "It was something I really *really* wanted to do on New Year's, and I'm glad it was you because it was incredible."

I'm not sure what to say in response to that, so I just stare at her a few beats. I set my wine glass on the shelf and pull her tighter against me. "Thank you," I whisper. "For trusting me with that. I'm ... touched? I don't know what word to use."

"Don't let it go to your head," she says with a laugh, reaching past me to get my wine glass and handing it to me again. "I just didn't want you to be the only one confessing things about your identity."

"I appreciate that." I settle back against the headrest, appreciating how intimate it is here with her, curled up like this, but also so natural and really fucking nice.

The jets shut off after twenty minutes, reminding me that I need to keep Fern hydrated and probably fed if I want to make good on my promise to ply her with orgasms. I hop out of the tub and quickly wrap my towel around my waist, opening hers up for her to step in as she gingerly climbs down the steps.

"It's a lot nicer getting in than getting out." Her teeth chatter as I grab the wine, flip the lid back on the hot tub, and run inside, where I grab a container from the cooler and slide it into the oven.

By the time I've heated up our meal, I've thoroughly warmed Fern up by the fireplace. After we eat, I warm her up again in bed and we fall asleep in each other's arms, as if we can stay this way.

As if we're both not on the brink of leaving the country, facing potential scandal, or technically forbidden from being together. None of that seems to matter as I pull her tighter against my chest, one palm on her butt and her palm above my heart.

I WAKE UP TO THE SMELL OF COFFEE. I OPEN MY EYES TO FIND WYATT KNEELING by the bed, holding a steaming white mug. He's smiling, looking so content and relaxed.

A lazy smile tugs at my own lips as I work to sit up in bed. I realize I'm still naked and a little bit sore. But it's wonderful. He's shirtless, too, and climbs back in bed beside me, a mug of his own in his hand. "Morning, beautiful."

He clinks his mug against mine and cuddles against my side. And this might be the best way I've ever woken up in my entire life. I'm delightfully warm and comfortable. I sip at the coffee, which has the perfect amount of milk and nothing else.

He kisses my neck in between sips and feeling content; I do the same. Until we're tangled together, mugs forgotten, making out like morning breath doesn't matter. Despite the ache between my legs, I'm desperate for friction yet again, and I move to straddle Wyatt in the bed. Until he grips my wrist. "There's something I really want to do with you."

I furrow my brow and look at him, brushing my hair back from my eyes. "Something we didn't already do last night?"

Wyatt grins wickedly and scoops me into the air. Both of us naked, he sprints down the stairs as if I weigh nothing at all, and I yelp as he begins to lower me onto the wooden table by the massive windows overlooking the ski slopes.

I glance to my side, seeing the chair lift in operation on the mountain.

"Wyatt!" I drop a hand to cover my breast even as he spreads my legs open, positioning me at the end of the table. "What are you doing?"

He sinks to the floor, his long legs kneeling on the wood, torso aligned with my thighs. "They can't see in, Fern. Tinted windows."

I feel his palms on my legs and bite my lip, studying the glass. "It doesn't look tinted—oh!"

He starts licking me, long, slow strokes of his warm tongue. He gently places one thigh and then the other over his shoulders so I'm surrounding his head as he burrows between my legs. There's nothing for me to do but run my fingers through his messy hair and relax into the sensation.

Wyatt licks me like I'm a dessert. Here, in this mansion on the mountain, he makes me feel like I'm the most precious, necessary thing he ever dreamed of. It goes on for what feels like ages until I'm moaning his name and arching my back, waves of pleasure crashing around me. Every time I open my eyes, I see Wyatt's face, his eyes dark with lust and his lips glistening with my own moisture. It's filthy and wonderful, and I come, shouting his name until it echoes off the pristine walls.

After, he carries me back up to bed, where our coffee is waiting. And it's almost like it never happened, except I'm fully sated, and he's hard as stone, one hand lazily stroking himself while he drinks his coffee and stares at me.

I set my mug back on the nightstand and turn to face him. "That was pretty special, you know."

He grins. "I've been dreaming of doing that." I stare down at his crotch, loving the way his hand looks fondling his length.

I run a hand along his chest. "What exactly do you do when you dream of that?"

He arches a brow, setting his empty mug on his nightstand. "I think you know what I do, Fern."

I climb over him, one leg on either side of his, but settle myself midway down his thighs, not touching him where he's glistening and leaking. I like the feel of his hairy legs against my smooth ones. "I want you to tell me. And show me." I bite my lip, placing my hands on his shoulders. He sucks in a breath and moves his hand more rapidly along his cock.

"I touch myself until I come," he whispers, eyes closed. And then his eyes fly wide, staring at my body, my face.

"I want to see," I tell him, and I really, really do want that. I want to see his head thrown back in ecstasy, hot ropes of release splattering his rock-hard abs. "Show me, Wyatt. Show me what you do when you think about eating me out on your dining table. Show me how it turns you on to make me come so hard."

"Fuck, Fern." His hand flies along his dick, his other flailing through my hair, finding purchase, tugging. It stings, electrifying. We lock eyes, and I watch his face contort as he gets closer to the edge. I can see why it turns him on so much to go down on me. Inspired, feeling brave, I scoot backward and out of his grasp. I stick out my tongue and taste the tip of him, a salty burst of moisture on my tongue. "Oh, gorgeous, you don't have to. I wanted to make today about you …"

Wyatt is panting like he's just finished a match. I place a hand on his thigh, the other on top of his own hand, grasping his erection. "This is about me," I whisper.

And it's true. As I slide my mouth onto him, I can feel the power I have in this moment. I can feel his surrender, the awe and appreciation he's experiencing alongside the evident pleasure. I'm delighted to learn I can draw groans and grunts from Wyatt's mouth as I lick and suck, tease and kiss. His hand drops away, cupping my chin. When I glance up at him, with several inches of him in my mouth, his eyes fly wide, and his head drops back. Wyatt emits a bellow and comes forcefully into my mouth. I pull off, licking at the drops of his pleasure but watching greedily as more white ropes spray up onto his abs. It's filthy and just what I wanted to see.

When I reach out to dab a finger in the mess and then taste that, too, Wyatt seems to actually pass out.

———

Hours later, or maybe it's days or months … we're finally dressed, cuddling in the kitchen while he heats up some sort of breakfast casserole he brought in the giant cooler of delights. I can't stop kissing him and giggling, touching him as we wait to eat. It's like any millimeter of space between us is far too much after what we just shared.

And then I hear a car door slam, the sound of women laughing. I stiffen. Wyatt hasn't heard yet. He's nibbling at my chin when the front door of the house opens to reveal a woman with a salt-and-pepper ponytail flanked by an older woman with a short bob and … my art history professor.

The three of them stop laughing and stare at us, the older two women tittering with laughter and the younger one dropping her hands to her hips. "Wyatt Henry De Luca! What the hell are you doing here?"

CHAPTER 24
WYATT

"Fern, wait!" She ducked out of my arms and sprinted up the stairs when my fucking mother barged into the house. I'm torn between wanting to run after Fern and tell her everything will be okay, and facing the apparent repercussions of bringing her here without checking in with my family that they weren't using the place.

Mom stands in my way, hands on her hips, while Grand and Lolly laugh hysterically behind her. "Wyatt Henry De Luca," she repeats. And that does it.

"Do not use that name, Mom. I've asked you so many times."

She shakes her head, appalled. "That's your response right now? An irritation about semantics?"

"It's not a fucking irritation. God, you know how much I hate any connection to that name. It makes me sick." I try to shove past her after Fern, but she places a hand on my shoulder.

Mom's face softens. "Wyatt, baby. We need to talk. Your friend is okay. Nobody is going to chase her down." I grit my teeth, wondering if Fern is spooked enough to jump out the window upstairs and ski to freedom. I decide she's not that foolish and I follow Mom over to the sofa, thankful she didn't head for the wooden table I still need to clean off.

"I think I know her," Grand says, glancing up the stairs where Fern disappeared. "Is she a student? She is. She's one of *my* students." Grand laughs, joining us on the couch. "Imagine that!"

"Glad you find this so amusing," Mom snorts. "Wyatt, what are you doing here? You know there's a schedule for the ski house."

This is the first I've heard of a schedule, but it shouldn't surprise me, knowing my family. I wonder how many times this happens—someone bringing a romantic partner out here only to be thwarted by another Stag looking to relax in peace and quiet. I glare at my mom. "I thought you were in Texas with the national team."

She sneers. "That was days ago. This is my relaxing wind-down after our loss. Which you'd know if you checked the AirTable your uncle set up."

Lolly holds up her phone. "It's an app, dear. See? Your dad is coming out tomorrow, and we think maybe Birdie can join us on Saturday!"

I drag a hand down my chin, and then the oven timer scares the shit out of all of us. "That's the casserole," I mutter. I jump up to pull it out of the oven before it burns when a thought occurs to me. "Why didn't Aunt Alice say anything if she knew you guys were coming? She made me all this food … "

Mom arches a brow. "You told your aunt you were having a …" Mom bites her lip. "Romantic getaway? Here?"

"Well." I stare at the French toast mixture. "Not exactly. But I asked her what food would be good for a few days away with someone I'm trying to impress and —" I end my sentence abruptly when Fern appears at the stairs with her bag, eyes red like she's been crying. "Hey," I shout, rushing over to her. "You don't need to leave. I told you I'd take care of you."

Fern tries to hide her face, and I put together what Grand just said. She's one of Grand's students. I'm one of Fern's students. Fuck.

Grand stands and reaches for a plate, helping herself to some of the casserole. "I think we should all sit down and eat and have a conversation." She starts walking toward the table.

"No!" Fern and I shout together before my grandma can sit at the head of the table.

Grand arches a brow and pivots toward the island, lowering herself into one of the bar chairs. She pats one next to her and looks at Fern. "Have a seat, Ms. Montgomery."

I stand frozen as Fern sinks into the chair next to Grand. Lolly mutters something about running to town for coffee, and Mom stares at all of them like she can't tell what's going on.

Finally, Mom says, "Well, Wyatt, introduce us." She crosses her arms over her chest, adopting a stance I've seen her take while bossing around professional athletes on the soccer field.

I lick my lips. "Mom, I mean Lucy Moyer … this is Fern Montgomery.

Fern, this is my mom, and I guess you know my Grand … what are the odds of that?"

Fern looks pale and Grand slides her a glass of orange juice she procured from my cooler. Smiling, Grand reaches for the champagne I had chilling in there alongside it. "You were doing it up right, Wyatt. Mimosas are a great idea, I think. Lucy?" Mom shakes her head.

Still looking pale, Fern sips at her drink. "Cheers," Grand says, holding up her flute. She smacks her lips and pats Fern on the arm. "Fern—can I call you Fern when we're not in class?" Fern nods. Grand smiles. "Fern, I think it's great that you and Wyatt are having a good time together. My wife Holly will be the first to tell you I'd forget about that scheduling app for the house, too. There's plenty of room for all of us here if you two want to stay."

I groan and Mom huffs. She mutters something under her breath about disinfectant and I flush, knowing there are a few surfaces here I planned to scrub before we left. Grand squeezes Fern's hand. "And isn't it interesting that you're here during our class time, and I'm here, too? I guess we both played hooky today." Grand smiles, fussing with one of her earrings. She looks over at my mom and asks, "Am I remembering that you were trying to keep things quiet when you started dating Hawk? That was right after that terrible incident with the hot car." Grand winces and looks over at me.

I remember when I met her—when she used a brick to smash the window in my father's car to get me out of the heat, saving me from suffocating. The weight of the memory washes over me in nauseating waves and I sink into the chair on the other side of Grand. Mom swallows and reaches for a champagne flute. "Hopefully that was a very different circumstance," Mom says, sparing a small smile for Fern. "I'm sorry we didn't get to meet each other properly. Fern, is it?" Now Mom's smile is genuine. "I've never gotten to meet one of Wyatt's girlfriends before."

Fern's eyes widen. "Oh, it's not…I'm moving…"

I clear my throat. "We're just hanging out for now, Mom." Realizing I can change the subject to much easier material, I add, "Fern got accepted into a PhD program in London."

Grand claps her on the back. "That's wonderful. Is it related to math? You've been so interested in that fractal article."

Fern nods and starts talking about algebraic geometry, which keeps them all from asking about my contract, my father, my mess and my forbidden entanglement with my TA. By the time Lolly gets back from the store, the four of us have finished all but one slice of the breakfast casserole and I've managed to spray the table clean while scrubbing up the island from our meal.

I get the sense Fern doesn't want to actually finish out our second night here—not with my mother and grandmothers—so I hurry upstairs to change the bed linens. I come down to find Fern white-faced while my grandmother promises not to mention her to Professor Yoon, the big shot math guy in charge of Fern's job. Grand waves a finger in the air. "I know Jae-won from the LGBTQ faculty summit. We go way back. But they don't need to know we were both skipping class today." Grand meets my eye and I know I'm going to have a lot to discuss with her once I get Fern back home.

CHAPTER 25
FERN

I can't find words to talk to Wyatt in the car as he drives me back to Pittsburgh. I pick at my cuticles while he navigates the twisting roads until I guess he can't take the silence anymore and yells, "I can't believe my fucking mom and grandmas walked into my sexy vacation."

I turn and stare, biting back a laugh. "Sexy vacation?"

He grins. "Was it not sexy?" Wyatt waggles his eyebrows, and I relax a bit.

I sigh. "It was very sexy. But very dangerous, apparently. Your grandma is my professor."

Wyatt scratches his chin. He hasn't shaved, and the dark stubble coming in looks really good on him. It makes him look like a pirate. "My Grand isn't going to tell anyone about us, you know. That's not how she rolls."

I burrow deeper into the passenger seat. "It's not a conscious thing always, though. It's a comment at a staff meeting or a knowing glance my way when Professor Yoon can see … there are a million reasons this was a terrible idea, and I probably should have just told my advisor about you back in January, and now it's way too late for that. I'm really worried that everything I've worked for is going to sink into a pit of farts."

Wyatt waits for a beat after my explosion of anxiety, finally saying, "Does it feel better to get all that out? That was a lot … "

I don't look at him. "It was a lot, and no. It doesn't feel better." Except it kind of does. Verbalizing all of that makes it sound a little less … daunting. What if I went to Professor Yoon and told them about Wyatt? Would they write a letter to Imperial College? Would they withhold my transcript? Unlikely. But the possibility is still there.

Wyatt drives through the Squirrel Hill Tunnel, and we are nearly back in my neighborhood. If he was an ordinary boyfriend, I'd have him walk up and say hello to my mother. But he's not my boyfriend, and we're coming back early from an illicit mid-week tryst. My mother is at work. "Wyatt." I look at him as he pulls up along the curb outside my apartment building. "We can't do this again."

He nods. "Trust me, I'm figuring out the calendar app as soon as I drop you off."

I shake my head. "No, I mean, we can't do this." I gesture back and forth between us. "We need to maintain a professional relationship, and that's it."

He frowns. "We are way past all of that, Fern. You know I'm not going to say a damn thing, and I'm not going to any faculty meetings. I don't even talk to Professor Yoon."

I take a deep breath and close my eyes. "I can't jeopardize my future, Wyatt. I don't have a safety net like you do."

When I open my eyes, he's frowning at me, expression turning angry. "That's not fair, Fern. You know about how my family is at risk right now."

I extend my palms his way. "Exactly. I know you're facing a lot and working through a lot of challenges. You have a lot on the line as well. We both need to keep our distance from one another."

Wyatt opens his mouth to say something, but I grab my duffel bag from his back seat. "I'll see you in class tomorrow morning."

Except I don't see him in class. I mark him absent and dismiss the group early. Everyone is anxious about mid-terms, and I set up two study sessions as requested by Professor Yoon. Later that day, I meet with them to review the plan for the rest of the semester. I don't mention Wyatt and my prior relationship with him. Professor Yoon doesn't ask me anything about the recitation.

For two weeks, I spend most of my waking hours in my cubicle outside their office, grading quizzes, not thinking about Wyatt, skipping over his test paper and redistributing it to another TA's stack.

During the final study session before spring break, I'm just about to relax into my role at the front of the room when Wyatt slips into the back.

His hat is pulled low, but I can see the dark circles under his eyes like he hasn't been sleeping.

Well, none of us sleep at this point in the semester. I'm sure elite athletes are supposed to be better at it than the rest of us, but I'm feeling the pinch as well, trying to get everything lined up so I can spend next week dealing with my visa and passport applications while my fellow students are all out on a beach somewhere getting wasted.

I briefly wonder if Wyatt will go to a beach for spring break, if he'll seek distraction or comfort from some bikini-clad girl at a tiki bar. I glance at him and decide that, no, that's not his style. The man who avoids crowds and brings books to a bar will probably spend the week working out and reading some new book about knee injuries in pro athletes.

"All right, folks," I say, dusting off my hands after writing an equation on the chalkboard. We're in a larger room than my typical recitation space, so I have to speak louder to more students. "Who can explain what we do next in this equation?"

A few students in the front row forget that parenthesis come before addition in the order of operations, and I see Wyatt's cheeks flush when I gently correct them. Is he, too, struggling to solve for X? I decide to circle the room, glancing at everyone's paper and pointing out where people need to redo their work. My heart races as I approach Wyatt's desk. I pause in front of his chair. "Can I see?"

He meets my eye, his gaze hot and intense, and moves his hand away. His neat writing reveals that he did the addition and subtraction before multiplying, and I shake my head. "Stay after, and we can talk this through, okay?"

He nods silently, and my breath seems caught in my throat. I take final questions and dismiss the class. A few students linger, checking in with me about the homework problems and the exam review guide. Wyatt remains in his chair at the back of the room, reading a paperback with a soccer ball on the cover, until the last student slips out and closes the door behind them.

We're alone in a lecture hall, both of us silently breathing, looking at one another. Can he feel this tension, too? I realize I miss him, the feel of his hands, the pressure of his lips against mine. "Did you forget Please Excuse My Dear Aunt Sally," I whisper.

He shakes his head. "I never knew it to start with."

I laugh and sit next to him, gesturing for his paper. I write PEMDAS at the top. "Pemdas," I say. "The order of operations. There's a set way you have to approach a problem..."

He looks at me for a long time. I can hear his breath, and I think maybe I can hear his heartbeat, too. "I usually go about things in the wrong order, don't I?"

He stares down at his hand, and I wonder if he's trying not to touch me, trying to restrain himself from placing his palm on my thigh the way I'm struggling not to wrap my arms around his neck. "Well, we're doing things in the right order now, yes? We have to."

Wyatt shakes his head. "I'm not going to be able to do that, Fern." He leans in and before I can blink, his mouth is on mine. His kiss is fierce, the pressure intense, and so, so good. I've missed the smell of him in my nostrils, the feel of his hair sliding around my fingers.

"Wyatt." I breathe his name into his mouth, and he pulls back, his eyes shining and wet as he stares into mine. "We can't."

He nods, and the moment is broken. He draws back, shoves his paper in the pocket of his sweatshirt, and stalks out of the room without another word.

CHAPTER 26
WYATT

I CAN'T BELIEVE I KISSED HER. I'VE BEEN WITHERING INSIDE, TRYING TO KEEP away from Fern for weeks, and then I kissed her. I had to go to the damn study session because I missed class, and she's been very clear that the pass/fail grade for this course is entirely based on attendance. So, then I had to sit and stare at her gorgeous face and brilliant brain as she explained all these concepts to 100 students.

I don't even want one student to look at me, and she stood up there covered adorably in chalk dust while 100 pairs of eyes looked at her.

An unknown number rings my phone as I'm hurrying home from the study session, and I send it to voicemail.

I reach the apartment, stop in the kitchen for a protein bar, and make the mistake of pulling out my phone. I hear Nick's sick voice in the message, telling me he's going to send old videos of him and my mother to the press.

It's all too much: his sneering voice, his threats, the rejection from Fern when she's the one person who has made me feel at ease this entire year. My heart races, and a buzzing sound takes over my awareness. I'm choking on the protein bar, sweating, sinking to the floor in the kitchen, pressing my palms over my ears.

I don't realize I've been shouting until I see Odin's face in front of mine, his hands on my shoulders. I can't hear him, but I see his mouth moving. He's saying my name.

Eventually, he wraps his arms around me. Eventually, I hear his words. "I got you, man. I got you. You're okay, dude."

———

I don't know how much time passes or how I get to the sofa, but once I can hear and see again, my cousins are all pressed against me, concerned. Odin, Stellen, and Gunnar each have a hand on my body, grounding me. Odin, who should be asleep getting ready for the Black and Gold football game this weekend, pulls me in for a hug and plants a kiss on top of my head. "Cuz, you gotta tell us what's going on. This is scaring us, man."

Stellen holds out my phone. "Can you start by telling us what the fuck this is about?"

I blink at him a few times and then sink back into the couch. I close my eyes. Odin says, "Don't make me call Wes to come over here. He says you've been a moody bastard this entire year, and he's not wrong. He's been checking up on you, man. So, let's have it. We stick together, right?"

I nod and pull up the message transcript. I can't handle hearing his voice again. They all read it, cursing. "He's been at this shit all year. He wants money, I think. Or just wants to win? It all started when I tried to change my name." My cousins all sit rapt, silent, waiting for me to continue. They know how much I hate it when the media brings up my past, but they don't know anything about what's currently happening. I tell them how I've been trying to get my name changed, how initially I had to report it in a newspaper, and that's when he really started harassing me. I tell them how I don't want to sign a pro contract with anything linking me to that piece of scum, how I want to be a full and legal part of the Moyer-Stag clan.

"It doesn't matter to me that my dad has me in his will or whatever. It's not about money to me. It's about belonging."

Odin coughs. "Do you think you don't belong with us? Is that what this is?"

I blink at him. "Not entirely. But sort of. I mean, I'm literally the ugly step-child in this situation."

Stellen groans. "Not one of us cares about who your bio dad is, fucker. Do you think we treat Cara like she's not part of the family? She's stuck with us, dude. And you've heard the stories about how all our dads came through for your dad when your mom got the restraining order on Nick all those years ago."

Stellen stands up. "Actually, I'm calling my dad. And yours. This isn't okay, man."

"Please don't, Stell. Odin, come on. I've been handling this on my own."

Odin stands up with Stellen, and Gunnar joins them. Odin glowers at me. "I found you on the floor in the kitchen having a panic attack, Wyatt. You are not okay. That's just facts."

Stellen steps away, and I hear him murmuring into the phone. When I try to get up and stop him, Odin and Gunnar press me back onto the couch. Odin places a hand on top of my head. "I'll sit on you if I have to, but you're going to stay here and endure a Stag family meeting right the hell now."

———

Ten minutes later, my dad and uncles Tim, Ty and Thatcher are crammed in our living room, all gray beards and crossed arms and confusion. Uncle Tim passes out a cardboard box full of fancy bubble water. "This situation seemed to call for San Pellegrino," he says.

My dad frowns at him. "Since when do we drink this shit? I thought you were bringing whiskey."

Uncle Ty shakes his head. "The boys are in season, Hawk. You know they have nutrition plans."

Dad rolls his eyes and pops open his drink, wedging his body onto the sofa by mine. "Want to tell us what this is about, son?"

I shake my head. My cousin Wes appears in the doorway, looking disheveled. Dad frowns at him. "You're in season too. You have a fucking game tomorrow. I'm going to bench your ass."

Wes shrugs. "Some things are more important than soccer." He tells the room how I've been withdrawn since at least August and how I confided in him that I heard from Nick months ago.

Dad curses and crumples his empty can. "Does your mother know about this?"

I shake my head. "No, and this is exactly why I didn't want to get any of you involved. Mom has been through enough." Not only did she have to deal with my abusive father for years, but she also dealt with a sexual harassment crisis in professional soccer. She's been stressed up to her ears, and I even ruined her escape to refresh at the ski chalet. I feel sad and defeated as I tell him, "I'm not going to be the one to upset her. Not again."

Dad looks at me strangely and then, quick as a cat, snatches my phone from my hand. He scowls, and I know he's scrolling through my messages. I worry for a moment that he's reading my conversations with Fern, but then I realize he doesn't give a fuck who I'm sleeping with. He's reading the unknown number messages and transcripts from the calls I never deleted out of fear I'd need them for the police. Because I always knew Nick would come for me. I know he's not safe, and he's not mentally healthy.

A wave of shame crests and splashes over me as my Dad reads the messages and sees my inability to get rid of this guy and the potential to bring down this incredible family who never asked for this kind of drama.

Odin catches my eye as I'm twitching on the couch and moves so he's squatting in front of me, his massive body shielding out the noise in the room as people continue yelling. "Wyatt." Odin squeezes my shoulders. "Do you honestly believe this family won't shred anyone who tries to fuck with one of us?"

I shake my head rapidly. "No, that's not it. I–" A sob catches in my throat, and I just keep shaking my head.

Wes and Gunnar circle around me like we're in a huddle waiting for a medic on the field. Odin rests his forehead against mine. "You're not just a regular cousin. You're my brother, man. And I already have enough fucking brothers."

Gunnar flicks him on the cheek, and Odin barely flinches. Wes rests a hand on my heart, the gesture is warm and surprisingly soothing. Wes says, "Did you honestly think we'd kick you out or something? I'll tattoo my name on your chest right now if that's what it takes, bro. We Stags stick together. No matter what."

Gunnar nods. "No matter what."

The four of them manage to hug me tightly and slowly, the adrenaline works its way out of my system. We start breathing in unison, probably because Odin is loudly conducting a breath symphony with his nose, but the impact is huge.

As my dad shouts for Uncle Tim to read things, I expect to feel another panic attack brewing. But … I don't. I feel a sense of calm. Like, I'm finally, actually, in good hands. Thatcher walks around picking up empties for recycling. Uncle Ty shoos Odin and Gunnar to bed. They protest but listen to him. Wes agrees to leave when Uncle Tim announces that he's going to handle this immediately.

"What does that mean," Dad asks. "Handle it?"

Uncle Tim scoffs. He's a sports attorney and usually handles contract issues, but I know he has a long history of getting involved when his pro-athlete clients get tangled up with the law. "We will have a restraining order on file by morning," Tim says. "Nicole Kennedy Brady will oversee a media statement in collaboration with your agent." He looks at me.

"Where is Brian in all this? Did you at least loop in your agent?" I shake my head. Tim rolls his eyes so hard I'm worried he'll fall over. "We will control this narrative so tightly, Wyatt. What on earth led you to believe you didn't have the full support of the entire Stag family when this first happened?"

Dad places a hand on Uncle Tim's shoulder, calming him before he launches into a Tim-Tirade. "Thank you, brother, for handling the legal and PR details."

Tim's head recoils in shock. "Of course, I'll handle this. Wyatt, you're my nephew. Nothing is more important than family."

I close my eyes and hear the soft voices of my uncles, and then I hear my apartment door open and close. When I open my eyes, I'm alone in the living room with my dad. And I can't handle the look on his face. "Son," he whispers. I break down in tears.

A sob rips from my throat, the stress of months of these threats and not knowing what to do. Dad is next to me on the couch again, his arm around my shoulders. "Son, your mother and I should have noticed that you were struggling. We should have had your therapists from before on speed dial … or at least kept their cards."

My jaw drops. "Dad, no. You and Mom have been incredible. My whole life, you've been—" A sob catches me off guard as I think about how I loved my dad from the day I met him when I was four. I worshiped him, not just because he was a pro athlete, but because I could tell immediately that he really enjoyed spending time with me. I didn't have words for this stuff as a young kid, but I do now. I see how this family Mom and I found is the real deal, and I'm part of it. For good.

He wraps me in a hug and kisses the top of my head. It's easier for me to talk to him when I'm not looking at his face, so I tell his shirt, "I wanted your name. I wanted it so damn bad. To officially and legally be a full part of this family."

"Wyatt, you've always been my family. You know that."

I nod. "At first, I sort of wanted to surprise you. To sign with a team as Wyatt Moyer, to see my name in ink with a pro team, as the son of the great Hawk Moyer." We both inhale a shaky breath.

He kisses my head again. "You said you made progress on that front?" I nod and explain to him about the student law clinic and how I have a petition for an emergency name change. Dad chuckles, his voice calm and deep, his chest rumbling against mine in this hug. "I'm sure your uncle will get that fast-tracked along with the restraining order."

Dad grins, matching mine. Then his smile fades. "I hate that you know the official terms for these legal situations." We separate but remain next to one another on the couch. Dad lets out a long breath. "I want you to know that you are always more important than anything in my career, son. We're financially secure forever at this point. You know that, right?"

"Ugh. Yeah, Dad. I know."

"Well, then, you have to make me a promise that you won't face anything like this on your own ever again. We move as a herd. Or something like that."

I laugh and stare at the ceiling. "I promise I'll tell you all my troublesome shit from now on."

Dad hums and crosses his arms. I can feel him waiting to say something, practically feel him trying to form the words until he finally asks, "Want to tell me about the woman Birdie and your mother caught you canoodling?" He nudges me with his shoulder. "Or is that a secret, too?"

I cough and wrinkle my nose. "Dad. Come on. Canoodling?"

He shrugs. "Lolly says she's smoking hot."

I drop my head against the back of the couch. "She is. She's really smart, too."

I sit with my father late into the night, telling him about Fern, how I'm not supposed to be with her, how she's moving to England, and I'm hoping to move to Mexico anyway. He listens, squeezes my thigh, and tells me I'll know the right thing to do when the choice arrives.

"Nothing has to be forever, son. Unless you want it to be." He fiddles with his wedding ring, smiling like a sap freshly in love. It should be gross, but I've always appreciated how into each other my parents are. I wish this message had been the one that sunk in rather than the poison Nick always spewed. I wish I had realized sooner who my real family is.

Dad drapes an arm around my shoulder and rests his head against mine. "Do you know how weird it was finding this family as an adult? I spent my entire life with a father-sized hole in my identity, only to learn I had three brothers."

I smile, trying to imagine what it looked like when Hawk Moyer showed up at a Stag family dinner for the first time. "That must have been a shock to your system."

"Ha! Your Uncle Ty made me go running with them. After a full day of training."

I smile at the thought, even as my thighs ache in sympathy. The four of them still go running together at least once a week, making laps around Highland Park, squabbling. I swallow another lump of nerves and ask, "When did you ... accept that you were part of it? Like, really part of it?"

Dad hums and smiles. "They had to force me." He squeezes me. "But I think it was when they all showed up together in court for you and your mom. That was when I realized they were here with me for my dark times as well as my happy sports star moments. You know?"

I don't know how I grew up around all of this unwavering support and love and still managed to cling to the idea that I'm an outsider in their midst. Exhaustion muddles my thinking, and I fall asleep next to my dad on the couch, trusting–for now–that I have his support and that of my entire extended family.

I knew all along that they'd drop everything if I asked them to, but I never wanted to be the cause of any stress for them. But my dad is right—with all of them swinging their collective resources together, there is no need to think any of us will go down for this. I should have realized that they'd *want* to help me, just like I want to help them, whether I'm hauling their asses to Costco or helping Wes chase down the love of his life after a misunderstanding.

When I wake up, the afterglow of support is still with me. I feel hopeful that I can finally move forward with my life on my own terms and that I have the potential for the sort of future I always dreamed of.

Except, the dream of making a name for myself in Guadalajara doesn't feel as bright as it once did. I think instead of Fern's face after I kissed her. She's balancing on a thin wire, and she doesn't have all of this family support that I do. Who and what will pull her back if her involvement with me threatens her goals?

Maybe my dad is wrong about that part of it. I can see the woman I want to be with, and I have no fucking idea how to make that happen without destroying either of our paths.

CHAPTER 27
FERN

I FIND MYSELF DOWNTOWN WITH NOTHING MUCH TO DO BY TEN IN THE morning on the first day of spring break. Turns out, it really doesn't take that long to deal with passport paperwork when you show up with all the forms you obsessively studied online.

I could go back home and binge old seasons of *Call the Midwife* and have myself an ugly cry, or I could hole up in the campus library and get ahead on my work for my remaining classes. There's not much point to getting ahead other than trying to keep my mind off Wyatt and the haunted expression on his face the last time I saw him.

I bury myself in work at the library, finishing papers that aren't due for another month, finalizing calculations on math equations the professors intended to take all semester to solve. Each time a memory of Wyatt's body touching mine bubbles up to my consciousness, I growl, sharpen my pencil, and dig into my scratch paper hard enough to mar the wood surface of the desk.

Eventually, there's nothing left for me to do or grade or write. And my mind is still a hot mess of anxiety over London and heartbreak over the impossibility of meeting Wyatt when I can't ever have anything meaningful with him. I decide to find Thora, who said she is working concessions for the Forge and Hot Metal pro soccer teams. Of course, it's the pro soccer teams.

I check the time—the games start at 4 p.m. but it's just past noon. Hopefully, I can catch her on the phone, at least before she has to report to work.

"Fern! Where are you?" I hear a lot of noise in the background. She's either on a bus full of drunk people en route to the game, or she's making her way through a tailgate outside the stadium.

I sigh. "The library."

Thora scoffs. "I knew you would be. Hey, someone didn't show up for their shift. Want to come pick it up and at least earn a little money while you're moping?"

Usually, I'd say yes to something like this in a heartbeat, but I'm not feeling up to crowds or feeling able to concentrate on food orders, for that matter. "Thanks, but I'll just go home and mope in peace and quiet."

"Is this still about Mr. Orgasmic?" I hear a slam, and then the background noise fades. Thora has moved somewhere she's able to talk.

"Can you not call him that?" I groan. "But yes. I can't stop thinking about him."

"Look, I get that he's very sad, and that hot possum pout is very attractive. There are many, many examples of this in television canon. But you have shit going on, Fern. What if you find someone else to bang who is actually casual? Just go get your rocks off. Like a man would!"

I rest my head on my hands on the desk in the basically empty library. "I don't think I'm cut out for that sort of sexual freedom, Thor. It's not just that he's sad and it's not just that I want him because I can't have him. I think I like him and his dumb car and the way he looks at me when I talk about math…"

"Ugh, you sound like you haven't heard anything I've told you about the horror stories I see at the legal clinic."

I bite my lip. I know Thora knows a bit about Wyatt's legal challenges. She's right that she's told me all sorts of scary stories about men with legal troubles. Stalking. Tax evasion. Credit fraud. They all manage to find women and dupe them out of their life savings. "The good news here is that I don't have any assets to be duped out of," I tell her.

She sighs. "Trust me. He's not looking to take anything from you. I just mean … I shouldn't say anything." There is another clatter in the background, and I wonder how much longer she'll be able to talk.

"What shouldn't you say? You always say what you shouldn't."

"Ha. Fair." She takes a deep breath. "I just mean … sometimes things escalate. In addition to getting in trouble for boning a student, you might be in danger. Hypothetically. If you hitch your wagon to this guy."

I hadn't considered that if Wyatt might be in danger from his bio father, anyone he cares about would be, too. I have to assume that's what Thora is referring to, based on what Wyatt has told me about how desperately he wants to change his name and be rid of that association as best he can. But how would I be impacted? I groan and start packing up my things. Better to head home and induce a cry via television. "I know you're right that I should just let it all fade into a beautiful memory."

"A beautiful, orgasmic memory you can call up while you're living the high life in fucking London as a superstar genius fellow in super math school."

She's right. I have a lot on the line, and Wyatt is complicated. Being with him would be complicated and dangerous for many reasons. We hang up when someone starts shouting for Thora to hook up kegs of IC Lite.

I head home, wondering what Thora knows specifically about Wyatt's situation, about what his father might have done to escalate things enough that the student law clinic is aware. My phone starts pinging rapidly when the train exits the tunnel, heading south to my neighborhood.

Mom is checking in, of course, but so is Wyatt.

I stare at the phone, reading his messages over and over again.

WYATT

Are you okay? I wanted to check in.

WYATT

Some big stuff happened to me this week. Can I call you?

WYATT

You're probably somewhere studying like a good student, aren't you?

WYATT

Seriously, though. Can we talk?

I squeeze my legs together, not understanding my reaction to seeing him refer to me as a 'good student.' I nearly miss my stop thinking through all the reasons I shouldn't connect with him outside of class.

But none of those reasons account for the raw vulnerability he showed me telling me secrets about his past. Things he didn't even tell his family for fear of costing them opportunities. I don't *owe* him a conversation, but I want to have one with him. I want to hear what happened.

We can talk. When's good for you?

WYATT DRIVES TO MY NEIGHBORHOOD THE NEXT MORNING TO MEET ME FOR coffee. It's strange to see him here, where I grew up. My neighborhood is much more focused on football and baseball, as a rule, so he doesn't seem to be at risk for being recognized here as he would on campus with all the rabid college fans.

But when I peek in the window from the sidewalk and see him waiting at one of the tables, he actually looks a lot more relaxed than I've seen him anywhere outside of his family's ski house.

"Hey," I say, pulling up the chair opposite him and sinking into it.

He smiles, wide and bright-eyed, sliding a plate of pastries across the table toward me. "Hey. You hungry?" I shrug, reaching for one, and if possible, his smile widens. "I like that about you, Fern. The way you enjoy your food."

I flush and dab at my mouth with a napkin. "You said some stuff happened? Also, what are you wearing?"

He's got tight-ish black workout pants and a black jersey I haven't seen before under a plain black zip-up athletic jacket. Usually, he wears university team gear.

He grins. "This is for the soccer combine later today." He bites his lip, expression turning hopeful. "You want to come watch? It's basically a bunch of pro hopefuls in the region doing skills and drills for some scouts from international clubs."

My eyebrows shoot up. "International? Like the Mexican team you were looking at?"

Wyatt nods, pulling off his hat—plain black—and runs a finger through his hair. He doesn't place the hat back on his head, and I hold back the urge to tuck his loose, dark hair away from his forehead. He seems youthful and content. "Did something change for you, Wyatt?" I take another bite of the pastry, and he leans forward, clasping his hands on the table.

"I talked to my dad. And my uncles. About everything." He waves a finger in the air, and I take that to mean his entire situation with his name and the threatening texts and all of it. Wyatt grins. "Uncle Tim pulled a lot of levers. And my Aunt Juniper is a magisterial judge who happened to have night court last weekend." He reaches into his pocket and procures a creased photocopy, which he slides across the table.

"What's this?" I squint to read the fine print, but it's all legalese I'd usually call Thora to interpret.

"My name change. It's official." He pulls the paper back, expression a blend of awe and disbelief. "As soon as I deal with the social security office, DMV, and passport people."

"I just did my passport yesterday! I can help you with the forms." I clap a hand over my mouth, not at all sure why I'd offer that when he's apparently got a whole team of experienced lawyers and lawmakers shepherding him through this process.

But Wyatt reaches for my hand and squeezes it appreciatively. "I'd love that, Fern. Seriously."

I want to bask in the warmth of his skin against mine, but despite his trying to keep a low profile, I can't risk being seen intimately with Wyatt. I tug my hand free and reach for the pastry plate again. "So, you're officially Wyatt Moyer?"

He puffs out a laugh. "Wyatt Stag Moyer. I ditched the middle name for a better one."

"I'm glad for you, truly. Good luck getting your transcripts updated in time for graduation, though." I laugh derisively, and then I realize he probably doesn't care too much about his college transcripts if he's headed off to be a professional soccer player.

"Come to the combine today," he says, his voice low. "I'd love to have you there cheering me on. Yelling Moyer and having it be me you're calling that …"

I frown. "Won't you have your family there? And your agent and all that?"

He shrugs. "Yeah." He leans forward, closer to me. I can smell his soapy scent, his deodorant and laundry detergent, and his tangy Wyatt aroma. "But they're not you." I take another bite of the pastry, and Wyatt pulls out his phone. "I'm going to text you the info and your name will be at will-call. You don't have to talk to my mom or Grand or Lolly." He winks. "I hope you can make it."

––––––––

Wyatt leaves the coffee shop, and I sit with the tray of buttery deliciousness, worrying about what to do. I'd love to see Wyatt in his element, wearing little shorts. I'm so happy for him that he seems to have dealt with the albatross, although I can't help but wonder if his next steps ought to include some mental health support for the trauma that got him into that state to begin with.

I stare at the details in my phone about the soccer event. It won't be crowded with fans—most likely just family members and press folks. Since I already finished absolutely everything school-related, my only alternative would be another day glued to my couch watching sad television.

I dash home for a hat and sunglasses and make my way to the stadium along the Mon River. By the time I arrive, the athletes have begun their activities. The stands have pockets of families, many holding up signs, but there are a few scattered individuals in the bleachers. I make my way toward the seats behind one of the goals, avoiding eye contact with Wyatt's mother and grandmothers, who I can clearly see up in one of the fancy boxes along with a man who must be Wyatt's father. I can hear them shouting, and I glance to the field in time to see Wyatt receive a complicated pass from a coach.

Wyatt flicks a foot, seemingly effortlessly, and the ball sails into the net right in front of me. I can't help but whoop. And then he cycles through the drill several more times, scoring with each opportunity—sometimes off his left foot, sometimes his right, and sometimes using his forehead to nudge the ball into the net.

He's magnificent out there, totally in control of his body on the field. Other players sometimes crash into him, but he doesn't lose the ball. At times, he moves his foot on top of it, pulling it around the grass like it's attached to his shoe. I see people on the sidelines taking note of Wyatt's work, making phone calls, whispering to one another, and pointing at him. A ball of pride swells in my chest as if I had something to do with his success out there.

One of the coaches blows a whistle and the players break into teams wearing black shirts and white shirts. They start a game, and I wish I had paid attention during any of the times I worked with Thora at these events. I have no idea what's going on with the game, but I can see Wyatt's family pumping their fists and hollering whenever the ball is near him. Wyatt doesn't break his gaze from the field, though. He's focused, determined, dodging around other players with ease.

After a few minutes, he breaks free of a crowd of players, shakes off an elbow, leans back on one foot, and kicks the ball into the corner of the net past the diving hands of the goalkeeper. The stadium erupts into cheers, and I'm caught up in the moment, jumping to my feet to wave my hat around. And then he sees me, and I freeze. The whole stadium seems to melt away as he smiles at me and gives me a little wave. My cheeks heat as he wiggles his fingers in my direction.

Someone calls him off the field, and he disappears into a tunnel. I sit back down and try to pay attention to the action on the field, wondering if I should stay or go now that Wyatt is apparently done with his performance. I've made up my mind to head home and call him later, but someone puts a hand on my arm, stopping me as I go to leave.

It's a man with a camera, which seems to be recording. "Pardon me, miss," he says, his voice indicating a long history with a lot of cigarettes. "You're here with Wyatt De Luca?"

I frown. "I don't know anyone with that name." I try to shove past him, but he chuckles and stands in my way.

"Right, right. Goes by Moyer, doesn't he? I'm doing a little story on his family. Thought it would be good to include some quotes from the girl-friend. What's your name, honey?"

I stare at the man, not knowing how to respond. I know Wyatt is guarded with the press and I can't imagine he'd want to reveal anything about a romantic relationship in the news. He can't really avoid his parents coming up since they're part of the sport. But I feel pretty confident he'd support me telling this guy to fuck off. Except I don't say that because I'm too overwhelmed. I shove past the man and hurry toward the exit gate.

CHAPTER 29
WYATT

I FEEL FUCKING FANTASTIC. I HAD AN INCREDIBLE MORNING AND BRIAN PULLED me aside the second I stepped off the grass to let me know today is going to be an offer day.

For the first time, the idea doesn't fill me with dread. I've got my mom and dad in the stands, my legal shit sorted out, and a signed document from the courts ordering my biological scum rag to stay the fuck away from me and my entire family.

Plus, my girl is in the stands watching. I know I can't really call her my girl … Fern is my professor–instructor if we're being technical. And I'm moving to Mexico, and she's moving to London. But she's here. She came over to watch me because I asked her to, and that means the world to me.

I'm practically floating when I step outside the locker room to catch my breath and calm down while I wait for Brian to call me up to the conference room to sign paperwork. I lean against the brick of the stadium exterior, smiling at the train going past, and the barges on the river. This stadium has been my home base for almost my entire life. I spent hours here after school, running around while my parents finished work. Once Dad retired from playing and started coaching, I spent even more time here, running drills alongside the team like some bratty kid. Except, I could always keep up.

I hear a shout and glance toward the sound. I see a woman hurrying toward the light rail station and a crusty man with a camera in hot pursuit.

It's … Fern. What the fuck? "Hey!" I push off the brick and start following them, my cleats loud on the sidewalk. I shouldn't run and risk stumbling in my awkward footwear, but I will if I need to. Fern hears my voice and whips around. Her eyes are wide with concern until she sees me, and I watch as she immediately seems to relax. "Fern, is this guy bothering you?"

"Fern, is it?" The guy pulls out a notepad and starts writing shit down.

"Who the hell are you? Don't say her name."

He smiles and shrugs. "I'm just doing my job, kid."

"Moyer, I've been looking everywhere for you." My agent's voice appears over my shoulder, and I see him approaching from the corner of my eye. He stops beside me, hands on his hips, glowering at the cameraman. "Fuck you, Pella. You trying to get another libel suit? I will sue you before you get to your car."

The man—Pella, apparently—grins and shakes his head. "I just do what I'm told. Take it up with BuzzTalk."

He stalks toward the parking lot, chuckling, and I glare at Brian. "Who is that guy? He was following Fern." I gesture at her.

Brian scowls. "Do I know Fern?"

She opens her mouth, and I place a hand on her shoulder. "She's my fucking friend, and I don't want that guy bothering her. He wrote her name down and took her picture."

Brian nods. "I'll take care of it. This is what you pay me for. I thought we went over that when your dad called me about the name stuff." Brian shakes his head, fingers flying across the screen of his phone. My Uncle Tim appears on the sidewalk with us like he could smell another opportunity to dismantle someone legally. Fern looks like she's going to pass out.

"Hey, can we get her inside? Fern, come on, let me get you some water." I put an arm around her shoulder, but she shakes it off, eyes glittering like she's on the verge of tears. I nod and gesture for her to walk ahead of me and through the door into the stadium offices. We bypass the locker room and head for the elevator, Brian and Uncle Tim whispering about the gossip website, takedown notices, and defamation lawsuits.

They both seem totally casual about this situation, but I can tell that Fern is freaking out that someone is going to write about her and put her photo on the hottest celebrity gossip site around. I walk her toward the conference room, thankful there aren't yet any team reps in here and grab a bottle of water from the bowl on the table. "Tell me what happened," I ask, sitting in one of the chairs and bending to unlace my cleats. I'm done for the day, regardless of what the teams might still be looking for. There's no way I could play right now, all worked up about Fern and the press.

She swallows. "I was cheering for you. He took your picture on the field and then mine and … asked me things." She takes a big swig of water. "I tried to leave and he followed me. I thought he was going to get right onto the train with me."

I reach for her arm and she yanks it back. I close my eyes, remembering again that while I might have solved all my shit and gotten my ducks in a row, Fern still has everything to lose if people find out she and I are involved. "My family won't let them print anything, Fern. Okay? Do you trust that?"

She rolls her eyes. "The internet is forever, Wyatt. There's probably already a story on TikTok."

"There are always fucking stories about me on TikTok. Why do you think I worked so hard to change my name?"

She stiffens and I lean forward before I remember that she isn't comfortable being touched right now. I hold up my palms. "I'm sorry. I'm just trying to understand what happened."

Brian pokes his head in the door and says abruptly, "Pella filed some gossip piece already, but there's nothing there." He shrugs. "Just says you're the kid of soccer legends Hawk and Lucy, you've got a girlfriend from school, lists her name and the university." Brian squints at his phone. "Okay, it was just updated that … aw! You guys met in math class?"

Fern turns white.

I stand up and yank Brian's phone from him. "They have to take that down, Brian. There's a situation."

He frowns. "You're supposed to tell me about situations, kid. This is how it works. You tell me about the situations, and I handle them ahead of time."

I drag a hand through my hair. "It's only a situation for Fern."

Her face hardens, and she stands up. "Well, I'm so glad you see it that way. God, I can't believe I came here." She moves toward the door.

Brian holds up a hand, urging her to stop. "Hey, kiddo, a situation for you is still under my purview. What's going on?"

I open my mouth to tell him that our tryst on New Year's Eve became a huge liability for Fern's future career, but the rest of my family appears in the doorway. Mom, Dad, Odin, Stellen, and even Birdie shove into the room, shouting that the team from Guadalajara is on their way up to the conference room with a contract for me.

Fern shoves through all of them, and I follow her into the hall, feeling ridiculous in my socks and soccer gear while my life is both falling apart and coming together. "Fern, can you just wait?"

She whips around to face me. "For what? The press to publish more about me while you're signing? I have to figure out what I'm going to do, Wyatt. This is serious."

"Brian is going to take care of it. This is going to be fine."

She throws her hands up in the air. "You're so naive if you really believe that they can help me now." She snaps her lips together, closes her eyes, and takes a deep breath. When she opens her eyes, they're cold and distant. "Please don't reach out to me or contact me apart from class. I'm so happy for you and the contract you're about to sign. Thank you for helping me unwind. I hope you can understand why I regret ever trying to do that."

She turns on her heel toward the stairs. I want to follow her, but I'm literally pulled back by sets of arms. My family shouts congratulations that feel hollow and empty as Fern marches away from me.

———

I stare at the pen in my hand that I just used to check off a major life goal. I signed Wyatt Stag Moyer on a professional soccer contract, in black ink, with a boring ass ballpoint pen covered in teeth marks. Who even knows whose mouth was gnawing this Bic.

I should feel … better. I asked my family to give me a minute alone. We're all going out to celebrate later, but I need to calm down. I don't need to look up when I hear a knock on the door–I know it's my dad. I keep staring at the pen as he makes his way to the black leather seat next to me and squeezes my leg. "Hey, kid. Will you sign my jersey?"

I look over to see him holding a Guadalajara jersey. It looks way too big for him. "Where did you get that?"

He laughs. "Brian has a few things in the trunk of his Bugatti."

I sneer at my dad. "Since when does a Bugatti have a trunk?"

Dad ruffles my hair. "Okay, smart ass. The back seat then." Dad pulls a Sharpie from his track pants pocket. "You gonna sign it or what?"

The silky material feels smooth and cool in my hand, a tangible reminder of the dream I just achieved. I don't hold back the grin as I scrawl my name on the back of the jersey, which Dad slips over his Forge polo, a huge smile blooming across his entire face. "I'm really proud of you, you know." And then he sighs. "And I can see that you're upset about the reporter."

I nod and briefly close my eyes, picturing Fern's face. The hurt in her eyes when she left the stadium, the fear of losing everything she's worked for. It tears me apart, knowing that I'm the cause of her pain. "Fern has so much to lose. She … I hate that her knowing me exposes her like that."

Dad nods and taps on the table. He leans forward, his elbows resting on his knees, his eyes searching mine. I can see the worry etched in the lines of his face, but there's also a fierce determination, an unspoken promise there. "I had a similar conflict when I first got with your mother." His mouth tips in a small grin, like the memory is mostly pleasant now. "I don't need to remind you it's important to protect the people you love. Or that you have my full support and any help I can offer to do that."

I swallow a lump and twirl the pen in my hands. "I don't want Fern to suffer because of me, Dad. She's worked so hard for her future, and I can't be the reason she loses everything."

Dad pulls me in for a hug like I'm a kid instead of a grown-ass man who keeps acting like a child. Dad says, "Son, you've got a good heart. We'll figure this out together. Fern's part of the family now, and we take care of our own."

I shake my head against his shoulder. "She asked me to give her space. I want to respect that."

He hums, low and long. "That's a good instinct. But are you sure that's what she's really asking for?"

I nod and sniff through my nose, grounding myself, finally setting down the chewed-up pen. "Yeah. And I think I know how to offer her that distance and still make sure she's okay."

Dad arches a brow and rubs a hand across his stubble. "How's that, son? Want to run your plan past me? Or Uncle Tim?"

I shake my head and stand, clapping him on the shoulder. "I know what I need to do. I'm ready to go find everyone now."

Dad stares down at my feet and I remember that I'm standing around in my socks, and that I came up here right from the field. We both laugh, and he walks me to the locker room to get changed. I know what I need to do, and it's going to piss off my parents, but I know it's the right thing to do–for Fern. For her future. I'll sacrifice whatever I can to make things right for her.

I don't expect anyone to be around during spring break, but after I spent the night crying in my room, obsessively refreshing websites and my email, I can't handle being alone anymore. I travel to the math department, hoping Professor Yoon has decided to work from their office while things are quiet, and the students are away.

They don't seem like the kind of person who goes on a big bender for spring break, and I'm grateful when I see the light shining under their office door. I tap lightly on the wood, knowing I have to face this. Have to come clean about emotional baggage to a mentor who has always been dreadfully matter-of-fact and pragmatic. "Yes?" Their voice sounds muffled and sure enough, I open the door to see them behind a trio of giant monitors. They must be running a complex series of programs.

I step into the room and close the door behind me. "I was hoping I could speak with you." I sink into the chair opposite their desk.

Professor Yoon peeks over the lowest monitor, adjusting their glasses. "Ah, yes. Ms. Montgomery." They stand and walk around to the other side of the desk, leaning against it, hands at their sides, fingers tapping the surface. "I received a strange email yesterday afternoon with a link to an online article that no longer exists."

I nod. I hadn't realized the story had been taken down already. Maybe that means it's okay? That the story lacked veracity?

Professor Yoon seems to be waiting for me to speak next, so I add, "I went to the stadium to support Wyatt. He's one of my students in the recitation."

Professor Yoon nods. "Yes, I took note of that, as well as some official registration updates. Strange. It all showed up in my email at once. You know how I feel about email."

"You hate it?"

They laugh. "I hate most disruptions. This week is for long periods of uninterrupted analysis! Can you just *feel* the data forming patterns?" They clap their hands.

I tuck my hair behind my ears. "I'm not sure how the reporter was able to get information about me...or even if what they wrote was true ..."

Professor Yoon nods. "Yes, there did seem to be a FERPA violation."

"FERPA?" I frown, unfamiliar with that term.

Professor Yoon holds up their hands in a "mea culpa" gesture. "I have been so remiss in your training for this assistantship. The graduate students will have learned that it's a federal offense to release student registration information. But I'm also making a hypothesis that it was not you who told the reporter about Wyatt's enrollment in your class and subsequent withdrawal from school?"

"No, it was definitely not me, but—wait. Withdrawal?"

They frown at me. "Is that not why you're here today? To update your roster? Wyatt *Moyer* and his legal team wrote to update his transcripts with his legal name and then withdrew from the university. Something about professional obligations abroad?" They shrug. "Usually, in these cases, the students simply take an incomplete and finish their degree later. I have no idea why he would totally withdraw from the entire school over a gossip article ... Ms. Montgomery, are you all right?"

I dab at my face, where tears have started to fall down my cheeks. If Wyatt withdrew from school, that means he was trying to keep his word. He made it so he isn't my student, hoping to help me keep my funding. Nobody but my mom has ever made that kind of sacrifice for me. I'm not sure how to handle this. I close my eyes and say, "He did it for me, Professor. Because the truth is that he wasn't just my student. I've been ... involved."

I open my eyes to see Professor Yoon unmoved, blinking, waiting for me to continue. "I met him before the semester began ... and he had that whole name change situation, so I didn't realize it was him on the roster and —"

"And you didn't mention it or switch sections when you had the opportunity?" I shake my head. They tap their fingers on the desk again. "Well, this is a bit of a pickle ... but truthfully, I don't have time to map out all the prongs of this fork." They shrug. "The student has withdrawn and is, in fact, leaving the country. They were in a pass-fail recitation where the grade is based solely on attendance ... I assume you took accurate and unbiased attendance records?" I nod. They nod. "It would be very hard indeed to botch attendance records." They emit a deep sigh and peek over one of the monitors at the program running on the screen. I can see pink lines intersecting with green ones on the monitor as a graph forms, fractal patterns blooming across the three monitors.

"I ... don't want special treatment. I broke the rules."

"Did you, though?" Professor Yoon gives their chin another scratch. "The handbook specifies rules for interpersonal relationships between graduate students and undergraduate students, but you are both under-graduates. And like I said, he has left the university. Nobody has filed a complaint. Nobody has reported misconduct."

We are both silent for a few beats. Or maybe a few hours. It all feels agonizingly slow as I sweat in the plastic chair, curling and uncurling my toes inside my shoes while I wait to see what's going to happen with my assistantship. I finally dare to ask, "So, what happens now?"

Professor Yoon takes a deep breath through their nose and holds up their hands again. "Now, you continue your excellent work leading up to the final exam. You seemed to enjoy preparing the students for mid- terms. Would you be interested in leading another large study session the week before finals?"

I blink. "I meant what happens with ..." I gesture my hand in a circle.

Professor Yoon glances at their computer again. "Ms. Montgomery, do you think you can figure out how to update the class roster inside the university grading portal? If yes, I would say, please do so and carry on. I'd be most appreciative if you could leave me alone with my prediction model for the rest of the week."

As if that settled the matter, they walk back around to their side of the desk, sitting down with a creak of the chair springs and leaning forward to gawk at the monitors once more. Stunned, and confused, I leave their office and sink into a seat in one of the cubicles. There are no graduate students around. No undergrads looking for test grades. Just me and my tattered laptop I pull from my bag. I wait for it to groan into life and log into the grading software. My screen shows a flashing alert that one of my students has had a status change. In a few clicks, I update Wyatt's name in the system and remove him from my grade roster.

It really happened, then. He's leaving school and moving to Mexico. And I'm carrying on like none of it ever happened.

Except it did happen. I was with him, and it changed me, opening me up to an adoration I never expected and care and comfort I never imagined. And it's all gone again, a reminder that I can either have turmoil and affection or hard work and professional success.

With a sigh, I shut down my computer and make my way to the library. There is still work I can do to prepare for my studies at Imperial College.

CHAPTER 31

WYATT

ALL I DO IS PLAY SOCCER AND USE THE TRANSLATE APP ON MY PHONE. I've been down here for three weeks and already got kicked out of my Spanish class because I kept getting lost and showing up late. I get that I can't be disrupting the other students. I've only got myself to blame.

There's one or two guys on the team who speak enough English to give me shit on the field and joke around a bit, but I miss my cousins. I miss Pittsburgh and being near water. This is the farthest I've ever been from a river for any real length of time. I had no idea how much it impacted my sense of place.

But the soccer is good. Really fucking good. And nothing compares to that feeling of hearing the announcer say my name—Wyatt Moyer—to a sold-out stadium full of rabid fans.

That's what I talk about when my parents call. I send them selfies of myself with kids who asked for my autograph. The first time it happened, I had this vivid memory of meeting my dad for the first time. Mom had gotten tickets to the Forge game, and he had just been signed. I wore that tiny, autographed jersey until I grew enough that the seams started to stretch.

By then, we lived together, and I could have had a thousand jerseys. But that first one felt so special. Someone famous took the time to talk to me. I try to keep that in mind, even if I can't understand half the words these kids say to me.

I'll get used to it.

I'm walking to my rental from the stadium after practice when my phone rings, and I see it's my Grand, so, of course, I pick it up. "I miss you so much," I blurt by way of greeting.

"Hey, guy, I miss you, too. Tell me, what trees you see?" Grand has a thing for hugging trees everywhere she goes, and she goes bonkers for species we don't see a lot in Pittsburgh.

I walk toward a leafy little guy and squint at it. "I don't know what half of these are called," I admit. "This one looks like … floppy?"

"Could it be a corn plant?" Grand sounds so curious, I can almost see her looking up the flora of my new city while we talk.

"I guess? I don't really know Grand."

"Well, you'll send me a picture later, I bet."

I chuckle. "Sure. I'm walking home from practice now."

"I took a guess you would be." I hear a tap turn on. "I had a nice meeting today with the LGBTQ faculty group. Lots of folks there from other departments."

"Oh yeah?" It's unusual for Grand to call me with these sorts of work specifics, even though I was a student at the school where she teaches.

"Mm hm. Professor Yoon was there."

I stop walking. "Is this about Fern?"

She hums. "Sort of. I did mention that they had had you as a student and that you're my grandson. They seemed surprised that you withdrew rather than take an incomplete to wrap up your degree after you get settled."

I adjust my bag to the other shoulder and switch the phone to my other ear. "Grand, I don't really care about the specifics of all that. I'll get it sorted eventually."

"I was wondering the same things as Jae-won, actually. I know we didn't get a chance to talk about school in all the hustle to get you to your new team."

I reach the hotel where I have a long-term rental set up while I'm supposed to be looking for apartments. I take the stairs up to my suite while Grand lists all the reasons a college education is important for everyone, especially when I'm just a few credits shy.

"Look," I tell her, clicking the door shut and flipping the deadbolt. "It was the easiest way for me to get on the road quickly," I lie. The truth is withdrawing from school was worlds easier for Fern. If I made it so I was no longer her student, there was no chance for repercussions from the BuzzTalk article.

Although, Brian tells me the writer and editor are getting slammed *and* someone from the university is in trouble for releasing information about me. Who knew I had federal rights to privacy about my enrollment?

"Well," Grand continues, "Jae-won and I also have a student in common. Fern."

"I forgot you had Fern in class this semester." I sink onto the edge of the bed, trying not to put my grandmother on speaker so I can look at photos of Fern on my phone.

"Yeah. She's doing some really cool interdisciplinary work with advanced pattern modeling and art forgery identification. I'm writing her a letter of introduction for someone at her graduate program in London."

My heart swells at that, the idea of Fern getting a leg up. I like that it's based on something she did with her own incredible brain and work ethic. Nothing to do with me pulling strings or swinging my family name around. Fern probably likes that, too. "I'm sure she's going to be a rockstar over there," I mutter.

Grand hums again. "Well, I'll let you go. I'm supposed to remind you that the Stag herd is flying down for your match against Cruz Azul, and your Uncle Tim wants to have a board game night afterward."

I scoff. "Sure. Let's sling colored tiles around while the fam is on vacation."

Grand laughs. "Azul is a fun game. But I think you're right that the beach would be a better choice."

"Are you and Lolly coming down with them?" I can't figure out if I hope she is or isn't … I want to grill her for more information about Fern but also avoid all discussion of her until she's settled into her fellowship and safely funded where she needs to be.

"Nah. Gotta get ready for finals. Love you, Wyatt."

"Love you, too."

———

The next few days are a blur of training, film, and trying to understand what Coach is asking of me. The team here has a very specific style of play, really aggressive offensively, and I'm up to the challenge. I just … am slow to process the strategy through the language barrier.

So, I'm mentally exhausted when I walk back to the hotel the night before the match and totally unprepared to find my family sprawled out in my suite.

"The hell?" I barely get the curse out before I'm bombarded by hugs and hair ruffles. Even my sister wedges herself in for a hug. "Shouldn't you be in Palo Alto? I thought you have camp?"

Birdie shakes her head. "You got your weeks messed up, dude. I had this next week off to be home for your senior night stuff ..." She shrugs, and Mom gives her a side hug.

"We're all excited to spend time with you here and see you play, babe." Mom stretches up to kiss my cheek, and I bend over to let her.

My cousin Wes and his girlfriend, Cara, are sprawled on my sofa, watching a British Premier League match on the television on mute. "We've both got a bye week," he says without looking away from the screen.

I grin, happy to see my space full of family, even if it's a little shady that someone from the staff let them in here. I guess my parents have sway with fans of La Liga. Dad pushes off the wall, waiting until everyone peels off me to give me one of his crushing hugs, lifting me in the air with a grunt. "Wow. I keep forgetting you're big now."

I grin, wrapping my arms around his waist and lifting him easily. We both laugh as I set him down, and he says, "All right, all right. Show off."

I show them the view from my window—boring apart from the trees Grand cooed over. I show them my gear, feeling a swell of pride just seeing the name MOYER in glossy white vinyl on the back of my practice jersey. My game kit will be hanging in my locker when I get to the stadium, and I like that they'll see that, too.

But Mom looks wistful, and Wes barely glances away from the game. Which, to be fair, is tied with just a few minutes of injury time remaining. Birdie tells me she ordered room service since she and my cousins are on a meal plan. I am supposed to be, too, but I've been slipping a little now that I have access to incredible street tacos.

We cram around the table, and my family is oddly quiet and polite. "You guys are acting weird," I tell them around a mouth full of corn.

Dad and Mom exchange a glance and she sighs, reaching for my hand. "We talked to Grand, you know. We hadn't realized you withdrew from school."

I point at Wes, who never even finished his senior year. "We already went through all this with him last year. My body only has so many years to do this kind of work. Dad, you didn't finish school, either!"

He nods. "You're right. But I also never dropped out to protect someone from a publicity scandal incited by a criminal in violation of his no-contact order."

"Wait, what? Nick was behind this?" I throw my napkin across the table, feeling nauseated at the thought of that man somehow determining my life path in any way.

Mom closes her eyes and takes a deep breath. "He tipped off the reporter. He was able to speak with the admissions office, too, since he had your personal information." She points a finger at the ceiling. "But your Aunt Juniper and your dad's foundation are mandating training for any public-facing university employees, reminding them about the rules and who is allowed to access student data."

I rock back on my chair, tugging on my hair. I thought I was past all this mess. The stress of it creeps up and over me, not quite to the level where I had that panic attack back in Pittsburgh…but not far from it.

Dad squeezes my arm. "I want to say a few things, okay? First of all, you know I started my career in the UK. The competition is excellent, the coaching is world-class, and there's no language barrier for you."

I bristle at his mention of the UK. I stare at him and Mom, wondering how much they know about Fern and if it's weird to feel excited about this suggestion.

Dad folds his hands on the table and continues. "The shared language would be really useful when you're working on your mental game." He points to his head. "Your mother and I feel sick that we didn't check in with you about your past, what you've been through."

I growl. "I'm over all that. You did your part. I had therapy for years." I'm not really over it … I'm just distracted by thoughts of moving closer to Fern without any risks to her career. But she hasn't reached out, and she told me she wanted space. She might not appreciate me showing up in town with my caravan of issues.

Wes snorts. "Dude, I'm in therapy now. I don't know how anyone would deal with the pressure of pro-sports without therapy, and that's without someone trying to sabotage my life."

Cara smiles sadly and nods. "Also, in therapy. And, you know, someone did try to sabotage my life. So, I'm here if you ever want to talk about that."

"I definitely don't want to talk about it. I came here to forget about all of that. Look, I appreciate that you're all concerned about school, and I definitely appreciate that you're behind me with legal resources. I can't wait to play tomorrow with you here. Family is everything to me. You all know that."

Dad crosses his arms, and Mom leans her head on his shoulder. "You can't run away from those challenges, Wyatt. They're faster than you, and they have more endurance. The only way to slay those dragons is to sit down with them and talk through it. With professional support."

"Thanks for the pep talk, Coach." I leave the table and head into my bedroom, slamming the door.

———

Eventually, I hear my family head out of my room, leaving me alone with the clawing, sickening realization that they're right. About all of it. I fucking know I need to get my head straight about all this stuff with Nick, and I have no idea why I'm reeling at the thought of starting up therapy again.

That's a lie. I know it's hard work and exhausting, and they're right that I'm using all my extensive energy on my game and navigating a new space where I can't even read the menus at restaurants. If I'm honest, I'm not trying too hard to assimilate here. At least half of my sour mood stems from missing the competent, kind, and sexy-as-hell math genius whose life I almost blew up. I pull out my phone and stare at a picture I snapped of us at the ski house. My heart lurches in my chest, missing her. Is it even possible for me to transfer to the same city as Fern without pissing her off?

I search her name online and smile, reading the profile her university put up about her interests in … advanced math words I don't know how to pronounce. London is a big place, and I'll be traveling fifty percent of the time. If she tells me to fuck off, I can disappear from her life just as easily there as I can here. But what if she's happy to see me? What if things could be better once both of us have a stronger foundation?

I wait a few hours to see if any of this starts to feel ridiculous, but the opposite happens. I start to get excited about the potential of a transfer. Of a change in plans that might bring me near the best woman I've ever met.

I text Brian to see if there's space in my contract to put me on loan.

CHAPTER 32
FERN

I CAN'T BELIEVE I LET THORA TALK ME INTO WORKING CONCESSIONS AT THE Black and Gold game. The stadium is packed with rowdy students and alumni, all here to cheer on our football team one last time before graduation. The air is electric with school spirit, but I'm just not feeling it.

"Come on, Fern,". Thora nudges me as we fill up cups with ice. "This is our last hurrah! We've got to make the most of it."

I force a smile, but my heart's not in it. "What does it say about us that our hurrah is working while other students party?"

She laughs. "Totally on brand for us."

I should be over the moon right now - I've secured my fellowship in London, I'm on track to ace all my classes, and I'm about to graduate with honors. But all I can think about is Wyatt.

Thora must sense my mood because she gives me a knowing look. "You're thinking about him again, aren't you?"

I bite my lip, feeling the heat rise in my cheeks. "I can't help it, Thor. What we had ... it was intense. I've never felt that way before." This is the first I've felt up to discussing it out loud. I've spent the weeks since spring break in a sort of waking coma despite Thora's efforts to drag me out of my own funk.

She sighs, handing a customer their change. "I get it, babe. But you said it yourself - it's for the best. You're both heading in different directions."

"I know, I know. It's just ... he gave up so much for me. He left school, Thora. To protect me." My throat tightens at the memory. I don't know what to make of his gesture and subsequent disappearance. I did tell him not to contact me. I squirm, wondering if I should reach out to him.

Thora's eyes soften. "That just shows how much he cares about you, Fern. But you can't let that hold you back. You've worked too damn hard to get where you are."

She's right; I know she is. But that doesn't stop my mind from wandering to stolen moments with Wyatt - the way his hands felt on my skin, the intensity in his eyes when he looked at me, the depth of the connection between us. Was that love? Do I love him? I don't even know how to recognize that emotion.

Thora must read my thoughts because she bumps my hip with hers. "Hey, no more moping. There will be plenty of hot, smart, non-student men in England. Trust me."

I can't help but laugh. "Speaking of England, did you sort out your paperwork for the Rhodes fellowship?" Thora was accepted into the program because she's a badass but hit some hiccups with her visa and passport.

Her face splits into a huge grin. "Nothing will keep me from Oxford, baby!" She takes a breath. "But I'm still working on the identity verification. Turns out when your parents are drunk when you're born, they spell shit wrong on the paperwork."

"Thora!" I throw my arms around her. "That's a nightmare. I hate that for you."

We ignore the line of customers for a moment. She grips my hands. "I'm on it. I'm not above asking everyone I know for help. We're going to tear up London together," she vows, eyes sparkling. "Different schools, not too far apart. We've got this."

I feel a rush of affection for my best friend. She's been my rock through all the drama with Wyatt, never judging, always supporting. Knowing she'll be with me in London makes the whole thing seem less daunting. "Please let me know if I can help."

"Well, well, well. If it isn't our favorite bartenders." A familiar voice breaks through our conversation. I look up to see Wyatt's cousins grinning at us from the other side of the counter. I pinch my lips together and wave nervously.

"What can we get for you boys?" Thora asks all business. I don't think she recognizes them.

As they place their order, I can't help but study their faces, looking for traces of Wyatt. The family resemblance is strong, but none of them have his particular brand of intensity. Which makes sense, since he's not biologically related. But they all definitely have a similar swagger.

"Are you here to see Odin play?" I ask, trying to keep my tone casual. Thora turns at that, brow furrowed.

Stellen nods. "Yeah, it's his last home game. He's hoping to make a big impression before the draft."

Thora groans audibly. "Odin fucking Stag. I should have put it together." She smacks her forehead. Stellen, Gunnar, and I stare at her. "He's in my arguments class. He's the one driving me crazy, refusing to do anything on the final project."

I glance at her. "I thought you *wanted* to take over and do everything?"

She waves a hand. "I'm going to handle it. What do you other Stag assholes want to eat?"

They laugh and order a bunch of food, which I start to prepare as Thora takes their money.

Just then, a collective gasp rises from the crowd. I whip around to the TV screen just in time to see Odin crumple to the field, clutching his leg. The announcer's voice blares over the speakers. "Odin Stag is down. It looks like a serious injury, folks."

The Stags go pale, abandoning their food and rushing off to find their family. I turn to Thora, expecting to see relief that she won't have to deal with their antics anymore. But her face is stricken.

"Oh god, Fern. What if I cursed him? What if this is my fault for complaining about him?" Her voice shakes.

I pull her into a tight hug. "Hey, no. This is not on you. Injuries happen in sports all the time. It's a risk they all take."

She nods against my shoulder, but I can tell she's not convinced. The weight of the moment hits me - in the blink of an eye, everything can change. All those dreams, all that potential, can disappear in an instant. My heart aches for Odin and his family. But I can also see how the weight of Thora's and my own dreams has impacted us. We both have a hair trigger when it comes to catastrophe. What's that line from *Dirty Dancing* about balancing on shit?

Odin will come out of this just fine, but Thora and I don't really have people to pull us out if we start sinking. "Come on," I tell her. "Let's focus on this shift, and then we'll take a look at your paperwork drama."

We both finish our shift robotically, and I don't even think twice about splurging for a ride share home rather than fighting the crowds on the train from the stadium. Mom is waiting for me with grilled cheese sandwiches, but her face falls when she sees me walking in the door.

I sink onto the couch with a groan and Mom walks over, handing me a plate. She perches next to me on the couch, waiting for me to spill my guts.

The scent of melted cheese and buttered bread wafts toward me, and my stomach grumbles in response. I take a bite, savoring the perfect blend of crispy, golden-brown bread and gooey, comforting cheese. I swallow, then tell her someone I know got hurt in the game today. Mom frowns. "That's awful, dear. But you seem more upset than I'd expect for … something like that."

I take another bite. She always gets the bread toasted perfectly. Crispy and brown, crackling with flavor. I swallow again. "It's Wyatt."

Mom raises her brow. "The person who took you on your getaway?" She nudges me with her shoulder, and I nod.

"He's not just *a* person, though, Mom. I think he's *my* person. And he left." I don't add *because I told him to leave.* She tilts her head to the side, listening. I set the plate down on my lap. "He left school, and I think he left the whole country. He was trying to get a job in Mexico … I haven't looked." I blow a raspberry with my lips. "I know it's crazy, but I miss him, and I can't imagine my life without him now."

Mom puts an arm around my shoulders. "I didn't realize you felt so intensely about someone. Why didn't you tell me?"

I shrug. As I sit on the couch, the weight of Wyatt's absence settles heavily on my chest. It's like a piece of me is missing, and I can't shake the feeling that I've lost something precious. "It's all very new. Or … it was. It's all over now. And I guess I'm sad about it."

Mom's brow furrows with worry as she listens to me, her hand gently rubbing my back in soothing circles. I can see the love and concern in her eyes, and it's a comfort to know that she's always here for me, no matter what. She's my constant. But I still ache. Mom rests her head on my shoulder. "Oh, honey. Love is never easy, is it?" I shake my head, and she squeezes a bit tighter. "I think you just need to give it time. If you two are meant to be, you'll find a way to make it work."

As I lean into my mother's embrace, her words echo in my mind. Maybe she's right. Maybe Wyatt and I just need time to figure things out. But the pinch in my heart reminds me that waiting is easier said than done and that I'm not in a position to go where he is. Not for the next five years.

———

The next morning, I wake up feeling a bit more settled, but the weight of

Wyatt's absence still lingers. I know I need to keep moving forward, so I text Thora and suggest we visit the Stags to check on Odin.

At least it will give me something to focus on besides my own heartache. Thora and I head for the Stags' apartment, a tin of cookies in hand. "I just want to check on him," Thora says, shifting nervously. "And apologize for any bad juju I might have sent his way."

I rub her back soothingly. "It's going to be okay, Thor. He'll appreciate the gesture."

"I'm still not doing his portion of the project," she mutters.

I nod, knocking on the door. "That's fine, babe." I knock again.

When the door swings open, it's not Stellen or Gunnar standing there. It's Wyatt.

I feel the air leave my lungs in a rush. He looks just as shocked to see me, his eyes widening. But then a slow, warm smile spreads across his face, and my knees go weak.

"Fern. Hi." His voice is soft, almost reverent.

"Hi," I manage, my heart pounding.

Thora groans beside me. "You two are so obvious." She grabs the cookies from my hand. "Is Odin here? We brought snacks."

Stellen appears behind Wyatt. "Snacks?"

Thora peers past him. "Yeah. For *Odin*. Is he here?"

Stellen winces and looks at Wyatt, who starts scratching at the back of his neck. Wyatt says, "He tore his Achilles."

I frown. "That doesn't sound good."

Stellen shudders. "He had surgery last night. Gonna be months of rehab. He's still in the hospital for observation. Are those cookies?"

Thora clutches them tighter, and my stomach twists at the thought of Odin's injury. He's always so playful, but I know he must be serious about his sport to play at this level.

"I'm heading to the hospital to see him," Stellen says. "Want to come?"

Thora nods, casting me a significant look as she follows him out the door, Gunnar trailing behind. And then it's just me and Wyatt, alone in the apartment.

"I missed you," he says without preamble. "So much. But I was trying to respect your boundaries, give you space ..."

"I missed you, too," I admit, my voice catching. "I can't stop thinking about you, about us."

His eyes search mine, full of longing and hope. "Come sit?"

I nod, letting him lead me to the couch. The apartment is a mess, with half-packed boxes scattered everywhere. "Is someone moving out?"

He sighs, running a hand through his hair. "Yeah. I didn't take much with me to Mexico, so I need to get the rest of my stuff." He looks at me. "Did you know I went to Mexico?"

I shake my head, then I nod. My mouth is dry, and when I try to talk, no words come out.

Wyatt gestures around the room. "I signed with Guadalajara after the combine. The same day as all that press drama. Hey, Fern, I'm so sorry for any stress I caused you. You shouldn't have to feel unsafe just knowing me, coming to a sporting event."

My heart races. I can feel the pulse of it thumping in my ears, which are hot and sweaty all of a sudden. "I …" What am I going to tell him? That I didn't feel unsafe? That's not true. But I felt more unsettled when he disappeared, even though I flipping told him to leave me alone.

Wyatt fills the silence. "I, um, have some shit to sort out." He taps his head. "I'm a little fucked up from what happened with my … with Nick." My face softens at his admission, and I reach for his hand, squeezing it, relishing the feel of him.

Wyatt swallows. "I actually have a trade in motion. I was going to have my stuff sent to me from the apartment … but I flew home last night when I heard about Odin." He trails off, the weight of his cousin's shattered dreams hanging in the air.

"I'm so sorry," I whisper, squeezing his hand again.

He grips my fingers, drawing strength. "It's the risk we all take, you know? Every moment on that field is a gift. We never know when it might be our last."

His words hit me like a punch to the gut. Life is so fragile, so precious. And I know that so why don't I ever translate that to things that bring me joy? Why are we wasting time apart when we could be together?

As if reading my mind, Wyatt takes a deep breath. "Fern, I need to tell you something. I'm transferring to West Ham United. For at least a year."

"In London? But I thought …" My head spins, trying to process this new information.

"The language barrier was too much in Mexico on top of everything else I'm dealing with, and West Ham has an amazing psychology team I'll be able to work with." He smiles and turns so he's facing me directly. "But also, I want to be close to you," he says, his eyes boring into mine. "While you chase your dreams, I want to be there to support you in whatever way you'll let me. Because I lo-"

I cut him off with a fierce kiss, pouring all my pent-up emotion into it. He responds instantly, his arms coming around me, holding me tight. In that moment, everything falls into place. This is where I'm meant to be. He's not a roadblock. This relationship feels necessary, a vital part of me moving forward.

None of the challenges that happened this year have been his fault or my fault alone. We made these choices together, and every step of the way, we've overcome obstacles. This reality sinks in as I press my lips to his, clinging to his shirt, and moaning into his mouth. With Wyatt by my side, I feel like I can conquer anything.

When we finally break apart, I'm breathless and giddy. "I love you, too," I whisper against his lips. "I think I always have."

His answering smile is blinding. Wyatt is my home, my heart, my forever. As he lowers me back onto the couch, our bodies tangling together, I know that whatever the future holds, we'll face it together.

As I lower Fern onto the couch, our bodies intertwined, I can hardly believe this is real. After all the heartache and uncertainty, she's here in my arms, telling me she loves me. I've been so consumed by my own nightmare that I never stopped to believe or even hope I could have something like this.

My hands roam her body, reacquainting myself with every curve and contour. Her skin is just as soft as I remember, her scent just as intoxicating. I trail kisses down her neck, savoring the little gasps and moans that escape her lips.

"Wyatt," she breathes, her fingers tangling in my hair. "I need you."

Those three words set me on fire. "Yeah, you do, gorgeous." I sit up just long enough to tug my shirt over my head before diving back in, capturing her lips in a searing kiss. Her hands explore my chest and my abs, leaving trails of heat in their wake.

I remember how she has trusted me for this kind of intimacy, how I'm the one who made her feel safe enough to let her guard down when all she's ever done is build a fortress to protect her on a path to a different sort of life. I slow down, savoring the feel of her, physically and emotionally.

We undress each other slowly, reverently, as if we're unwrapping the most precious gifts. When we're finally skin to skin, I have to take a moment just to look at her, to memorize every detail of this perfect woman beneath me.

My eyes drink in the sight of her luscious curves, the soft swell of her breasts, the dip of her waist, the tantalizing flare of her hips. I run my hands along her sides, marveling at how her body yields to my touch, supple and pliant, but I know she has a core of steel inside.

This gorgeous body covers an unshakable strength and resilience. Fern has become my favorite story, one I want to read over and over again, even as it's still being written. She's faced so many challenges and overcome so much, and she's never lost her warmth, compassion, and incredible capacity for love. Or is that just for me?

As I lower my mouth to her breast, taking a nipple between my lips, she arches beneath me, a breathless moan falling from her lips. Her nipples harden so fast. I pinch them, loving the way they respond to my touch. Her eagerness lights me on fire and sets off a primal need to pleasure her, to worship every inch of her. Fern has become as vital to me as my family, familiar and comforting ... but meeting very, very different needs.

I swing my attention on her breasts, licking, suckling, teasing, until she's writhing beneath me, her nails digging into my shoulders. The contrast of her soft flesh against my hard muscles is intoxicating, a heady reminder of how perfectly we fit together in every way.

"You're so beautiful," I whisper, trailing kisses down her stomach, memorizing the way her muscles quiver under my touch. "I love you so much, Fern."

Her eyes, dark with desire, shine with unshed tears. "I love you, too. More than anything."

I pour all my emotion into the next kiss, letting my actions speak louder than words ever could. As I settle between her thighs, the heat of her drawing me in, I'm once again struck by the incredible gift of her love, her trust, her surrender.

"I'm on the pill," she whispers, breath hot on my ear. "And there's never been anyone but you ..."

I draw back. "What are you saying?"

She shrugs. "I want to feel you inside me with nothing between us, Wyatt. Nothing but us."

I swallow, trying not to explode. "I get checked all the time. I'm healthy, Fern. And there hasn't been anyone since you." I blink away moisture and smile at her. "You're it for me, baby."

She smiles and licks her lips, reaching for me. I hiss when she wraps a palm around my length and moan as she guides me between her thighs. I lock eyes with her and sink inside, the sensation so overwhelming I collapse on top of her, giving her my full weight.

"I like how heavy you feel on top of me," she says, wrapping her legs around me. I kiss her throat and settle onto my forearms so I can see her, wanting to see her face while we do this.

We move together like a symphony, our bodies perfectly in sync. Each touch, each caress, each thrust is a declaration of love, a promise of forever. The way she embraces me, her soft curves molding to my hardness…it feels like an unbreakable connection.

When we finally come apart in each other's arms, spent and sated, I hold her close, marveling at the way she fits so perfectly against me. Her body, so soft and yielding, is like a safe haven in a world that's been so harsh and merciless.

This is where I belong. She is home.

———

I pace the arrivals gate at Heathrow, my heart racing with anticipation. I tried bringing a book, but there's no way I can concentrate on reading it, so I shove it in my back pocket and stare at the arrivals board again. Fern's plane landed twenty minutes ago, and I know it's only a matter of time before she clears customs and makes her way to me.

The past month has been a whirlwind. Between settling into my new team, finding a flat, and starting sessions with the psychologist, I've barely had a moment to catch my breath. I've literally been counting down the days until Fern gets here. She sent me 30 images from the art class she took with Grand and told me to put one up on the wall every day until we could be together. Sort of sappy, but I like having someone to be that way with.

I call her every day, even if the time zones are hard with my training schedule. Fern doesn't seem to sleep anymore, so it worked out. She's been wrapping up her finals and packing up her life in Pittsburgh while I've been scoping out all the places I want to show her in London. I offered to fly her mom out here with her, but Ms. Montgomery doesn't have a passport yet. She and Fern are making plans and soaking in their time together, and I hope they'll let me help out when they're ready. What else am I going to do with this sort of paycheck?

Finally, I see her emerge from the sliding doors, her face lighting up when our eyes meet. I rush forward, sweeping her into my arms and spinning her around, for once not caring about people staring. "You're here," I murmur against her hair, breathing in the scent of her. "You're really here."

I'm vaguely aware of a few people snapping photos of us. One of the first things I talked about in therapy was my aversion to the press, and how important it is for me to make a good impression with fans. I have all sorts of mental exercises I work through to remind myself that it's okay for the world to see me successful and happy and that my father can't take that from me.

So now, I let it happen. Thankfully, nobody tries to interrupt us. Until my phone emits a quacking sound. "What the hell?" I glance down to see a group text from my cousins.

> **YOUNG STAG GROUP CHAT**
> ODIN
>
> Did you know I can manipulate your notifications from afar? You're still on the family plan!
>
> STELLEN
>
> Epic.
>
> GUNNAR
>
> We're going to video call you during family dinner this weekend. Tell Fern she has to tune in.
>
> ODIN
>
> Can you put her on the family plan so I can fuck with her phone notifications, too?

Reading over the exchange, Fern laughs, a joyful sound that sends my blood buzzing. "I'm here. And I'm not going anywhere."

I cup her face in my hands. "Welcome to London, love. Ready for the adventure of a lifetime?"

Her smile is brighter than the sun. "With you? Always."

Hand in hand, we make our way out of the airport, ready to take on the world together. It's not going to be easy. She's in an intense academic program. She's gonna be a hot doctor. And my life is intense. But I know we can handle anything as long as we have each other.

Fern is my rock, my guiding light, my forever home. And as we step out into the bustling streets of London, I feel a sense of peace wash over me. This is exactly where we're meant to be, side by side, chasing our dreams and building a life together.

She and I are forging a new legacy, one that's entirely our own—one that recognizes the power of love, resilience, and the unbreakable bonds we share. It's a legacy I'm proud to call mine...ours.

EPILOGUE: WYATT

5 MONTHS LATER

"I can't believe you splurged for first class." Fern curls to face me on the comfortable bed in the plane. We've shifted things around a bit to be next to one another and the little pod is surprisingly cozy and private.

I tuck back a strand of hair that has sprung loose from the sleep mask she hasn't yet pulled over her eyes. "What's the point of earning all this pro soccer money if I can't take care of you?" She rolls her eyes and tugs the mask over her face, wriggling a bit under the downy blanket. Her body slowly starts to relax against mine, and I kiss the top of her head before tugging my own mask in place.

I only get a few days off between matches this Christmas, so if I'm going to visit my family with Fern, I want to be as comfortable as possible. Flying first class from London to Pittsburgh is the first big splurge I've made, and I don't think I can ever go back now that I've had the incredible food and lay-flat seats .

I don't sleep much on the flight, but I enjoy the long stretch of time with Fern in my arms. She technically lives in the student housing on her campus but spends what nights she can at my flat between my travel commitments. This cuddle fest above the Atlantic is a real luxury.

When we land in Pittsburgh, I try to play it cool, so I don't tip Fern off to the next round of surprises. We get to exit the plane first, which means we sail through customs to find my cousin Wes waiting to give us a ride, along with …

"Oh my god! Mom!" Fern runs to hug her mother, dropping bags on the floor. Wes grins and hugs me around my own bags before stooping to pick up Fern's. She and her mom are dancing around, crying, and squeezing each other. I try to gently usher them to the side, so we don't block people coming through the security doors.

"I missed you so much," Fern and Heather Montgomery sob in unison. Grand and Lolly finally helped Fern's mom get her passport, so she's going to fly back with Fern in January to tour around London a bit before the spring semester, or Hilary Term, as Fern tells me they call it. I'm sending them both first class, obviously.

The final surprise for Fern is our destination. Rather than exit the highway for Pittsburgh, Wes keeps heading east toward our ski house. Fern and her mom are so busy talking in the back seat that they don't notice until we hit the snowy side roads in the mountains. Fern presses her face to the window and coos. "Wyatt Stag Moyer, I thought we were staying with your parents?"

I grin at her from the front seat. "We are. We're staying with my parents in their ski house. Along with Wes's parents, Odin's parents, Petey's parents … Grand and Lolly …"

"Okay, okay. Wow." Fern clasps her mom's hand. "Are you ready for 21 people in a huge house? Because I don't know if I am."

Heather laughs. "I went to a Sunday dinner with all of them last week to help plan Christmas." She pats Fern's hand. "It'll be fun."

Wes navigates his Jeep carefully up the icy roads, and it doesn't take long before we see light glowing from the massive windows of the Stag Chalet. Fern and Heather both sigh. I can already feel the familiar, comfortable warmth. And then Wes opens the front door, and chaos slams into us. But I smile because that's familiar, too.

Aunt Alice shoves a drink into Heather's hand and ushers her off to sit by the fire with Aunt Emma and Lolly. Stellen and Gunnar grab all our bags and complain about having to stay in the bunk room while Fern and I get our own space in a new room we all agreed would be better served as a sleeping space than a room just for foosball.

I'm about to feel compassion for Gunnar, but he slings me over his shoulder and drops me in the hot tub, fully dressed as the rest of my family watches and laughs. I spit a mouthful of hot water in his face, grinning, and he strips to his boxers and climbs in with me. It's good to be home, with family.

The past few months have been simultaneously incredible and incredibly difficult. I've got a lot of mental stuff to work through, but I'm learning that therapy is a lot like any other sort of training. I put it on the schedule, I show up, I do the work, and I feel the results. I've been playing the best soccer of my life with West Ham, and they just bought out my contract for four years, which means Fern and I don't have to search for our next home base together until she's done with her PhD.

She emerges from the house with a huge smile on her face and fluffy towels draped over one arm. "Are you okay in there?"

"I'd be better if you were in here with me instead of this guy." I hook a thumb at my cousin, who tries to dunk me, gives up, and sprawls against the back edge of the tub.

Fern shivers a bit and looks at Gunnar. "No Odin this year?"

He shakes his head. "Not this time."

Fern opens her mouth to add something, but a door opens above us, and my mom pokes her head out into the dark. "Dinner is in five minutes. Whoever is out here, come in and wash your hands."

Fern laughs. "I love that washing hands is the important to-do item before dinner when you're fully clothed in the hot tub."

I hop out of the water and accept one of the towels from my ladylove. I consider taking them both and leaving Gunny to freeze, but I opt for kindness. By the time I'm changed into dry sweats and have clean hands, the entire family is seated at the huge wooden table.

Wes has his arm around Cara, Birdie steals sips from Dad's wine ... even Uncle Tim seems relaxed with his whole family under one roof. A crackling fire and a massive pine tree decorated in silver-glitter popsicle sticks from our youth give the entire room a cozy vibe. Fern squeezes my leg, and I'm glad to see she doesn't look nervous at all. She and her mom are used to quiet holidays with just a few people, but everyone here has accepted them as part of the growing family.

I've got enough therapy under my belt to see it was always this way. I've always been welcome here, part of the fabric.

Uncle Ty approaches the table with a huge platter of meat, Aunt Alice right behind him with a massive pot of ... something I'm sure I'm allowed to eat because she's amazing that way. Uncle Ty holds up the knife like a microphone and says, "Before we dig in, someone needs to hand me their phone so we can send a picture to Odin."

Alice sets her food on the table and reaches into her back pocket. "I've got you covered. But you've got longer arms."

He grins, turns, and extends the phone as far out as he can, squints at the screen, and then leans back to make more room. "I think we can get everyone in. Heather, Fern, squeeze in a bit more. More than that. Perfect."

He snaps a few shots, and I know half of us will have crossed eyes or pursed lips, but the result will be perfect: flawed and overflowing, with plenty of room for everyone.

———

Can't get enough of Wyatt and Fern? My newsletter subscribers get a bonus scene! Visit LaineyDavis.com to sign up.

FORGING CHAOS

CHAPTER 1
ODIN

I WAKE UP IN A HAZE, MY VISION BLURRY AND UNFOCUSED. NOT SURE WHY, BUT there are some harsh fluorescent lights above me. Something smells like chemicals—antiseptic.

Panic rises in my chest as I try to piece together what happened. I attempt to sit up, but a sharp, searing pain shoots through my ankle, forcing me back down with a groan.

Last thing I knew, I was flying down the football field, defense bouncing off me like hailstones—until one of them didn't, and I went down like I'd been struck by lightning.

The memory hits me like a freight train - the game, the tackle, the sickening pop as I went down.

I was hoping it was a dream.

Instead, it is a nightmare.

I know where I am.

Reality crashes down like thunder: I'm in a hospital bed.

Did I at least score the touchdown?

The thought flits past, and I almost laugh at how ridiculous it seems now. Here I am, laid up in a hospital bed, and I'm worried about whether I got the ball over the line in a stupid spring scrimmage that doesn't mean anything. But that's who I am - or who I was. Odin Stag, star running back. The guy whose entire future hinged on his ability to dodge tackles and sprint down a field.

I just yeeted my Achilles, and I know what that means.

So, what am I now? A patient. A statistic. Another athlete whose dreams just fizzled out like a passing storm.

I'm pulled from my spiral of self-pity by the sound of the door opening. My mom walks in, her eyes red-rimmed. Dad's right behind her, his usual happy expression cracking around the edges. I can see the worry etched into the lines of his face, the fear he's trying so hard to hide.

"Hey, kiddo," Dad says, his voice gruff with emotion. "How're you feeling?"

I paste on my best grin, determined not to let them see how scared I really am. "Like I just went ten rounds with a freight train," I quip. "But you should see the other guy."

Usually, this sort of thing has Dad roaring, coming back with bad puns. Today, he just nods. Mom lets out a watery chuckle, perching on the edge of my bed. She married a hockey player. Ty Stag—Pittsburgh legend. None of this should be new to her, but I guess it's different when it's your kid laid up like this.

Her hand finds mine, squeezing gently. "Oh, sweetie," she murmurs. "We were so worried."

Before I can respond, the door swings open again, and a doctor strides in, all business. He knows my dad, because of course he does, and they shoot the shit until the doc seems to remember I'm here. He launches into an explanation of my injury, throwing around terms like "complete rupture" and "surgical intervention." I try to follow along, but my mind keeps catching on to phrases like "extended recovery time" and "physical therapy."

What does this mean for my future? For the draft next year? For everything I've worked so hard to achieve?

My parents pepper the doctor with questions I can't bring myself to ask. How long until I can walk? Run? Play again? Each answer feels like another nail in the coffin of my dreams. As the doctor leaves, an uncomfortable silence settles over the room. Things must really be bad if Dad isn't making a dumb joke about deodorant or trying to grab Mom's butt.

"Well," Dad says finally, forcing a smile, "at least this gives you some time to focus on class, right? Might even boost that GPA of yours."

I know he's trying to help, to find some positive in all this, but it just makes me feel worse. Their presence feels suffocating right now. I'm torn between wanting their comfort and needing space to process this on my own.

I'm surprised my entire extended family isn't here right now. The Stag family bench is deep, with three uncles, three aunts, and seven cousins usually up in my business. But I remember that they *were* all here before the surgery, and Dad sent them home when I went under the knife. I don't want to see the entire extended crew right now. I don't want to see anyone.

First, I need to figure out who I am now.

My drug-addled mind repeats a bunch of thoughts. I'm not going to be a professional athlete. I might not even be able to be an Uber driver. And I know damn well my family will want me to look on some bright side or keep my spirits high or whatever rainbow bullshit.

Right now, I need to focus on the realities of what's going on with my body: agony, yes, but also…deterioration. A torn Achilles is very much an Achilles heel. A career-ending injury. That's just math.

I've spent my entire life planning a professional sports career. I was raised by an Olympic rowing mother and a professional hockey player father, and all my brothers are gearing up to follow in Dad's footsteps. Where does that leave me? Even after I physically recover from this nightmare, I won't be the same person I was before.

I was my Norse god namesake … wielding lightning or some shit. Now, I'm a has-been in an entire family of superstars.

"Odin?" Mom places her hand on my arm, and I meet her eye.

I clear my throat and ask her to take me to the bathroom to have something to do. Mom presses her lips into a line. "Honey, you're not supposed to get out of bed yet…"

I squint and look over my left shoulder at a catheter bag full of piss. I laugh. I can't even control my bladder right now. I am totally, utterly at the mercy of these machines. Yet, the reality of it is that I haven't been controlling anything for years. I eat what Coach tells me to. I lift what another coach tells me to lift. I follow the rigid path toward the pros because that's my legacy.

That's the plan.

But not anymore.

I sigh and reach for the clicker the nurse told me about with my morphine drip. I click until the monitors start to beep, and I fall asleep listening to my parents in manic planning mode with a zillion different specialists huddled around my bed.

Rationally, I know I didn't curse anyone. It's just plain lousy timing that Odin Stag happened to get hurt moments after I complained about having to work with him on my final project for a class I absolutely need to ace.

People complain about group projects all the time. Just small talk. How was I supposed to know he'd go down like a dump truck full of gravel the second I finished my rant about him being a shitty research partner.

It's not that I think he's not smart. I don't trust anyone but my best friend Fern.

Anyway, just in case the universe is testing me, I'm making Odin cookies. At home in my parents' kitchen with the window open and a fan blowing to keep the plume of my father's cigarette smoke away from the baked goods.

I really don't bake. But how hard can it be to follow the instructions on a bag of chocolate chips? I'm pretty pleased when the first pan I pull from the oven looks exactly like the photo on the bag, like actual, regular cookies. I smile, scraping them from the pan onto a towel I set on the table. We don't have any foil, and we certainly don't have the cooling racks the instructions recommended. Hell, we only have one cookie sheet, and it looks like it's been in the house for five decades.

My dad must have caught a whiff of the cookie's success because he hollers, "Bring me a few of those, will you?"

I grind my teeth. Nothing is preventing him from getting up from the couch himself. It's one thing when he asks me to bring him a drink on my way past. I'm not working today. I'm not waiting on people. Plus, these are spoken for.

I ignore him and get to work scooping balls of dough onto the pan for the second batch, thinking about Fern's offer to accompany me to Odin's apartment to deliver the cookies. She's dating his cousin, who also lives there. I encouraged her to make a move on Wyatt, and that seems to have worked out great. Fern assures me nobody has mentioned a single thing about me having cursed Odin into a significant injury.

It's self-centered of me to even imagine I caused this. I'm well aware. I lick a wayward hunk of dough from the outside of my hand before I slide the pan into the oven. I'm well on my way toward a peace offering I plan to combine with a reasonable insistence that I take care of the entire project for our shared class. If Odin is hurt, he'll have much to deal with recovering. That's just facts.

"You hear me?" Dad's voice startles me. He stands at the entrance to the kitchen, leaning against the wall with his arms crossed. "I asked you to bring me one of those."

I swallow back the urge to point out he *demanded* several of the cookies. Instead, I smile and explain, "These are a gift for a friend, Dad. He's sick."

He steps toward the stove. "You can make a few extra for your own family. If he's sick, he can't eat all that."

I place my body between my father and the cookies. "They're not for you." My voice is sharp, harsher than I ever speak to my parents, even though they provide absolutely nothing for me at this point in my life. My scholarship covers rent for me to live here, more than my fair share of the groceries. I've helped pay my way in the world since I was tall enough to work under the table at all the shitty restaurants my parents bounced between. I'm leaving here in a few months, just as long as I maintain my perfect grade point average and meet the expectations of my graduate school fellowship.

Dad's lip curls up angrily. "Think you're better than us now? Cookies for your fancy school friends? Is that it?"

I shake my head. "That's not it at all. These cookies are a gift. For someone in pain."

My father looks at me like I'm the enemy and turns on his heel, heading back to the living room, muttering about how his own kid won't cut him a break.

I realize there's no way the entire batch of cookies will fit in the empty nut container I brought home from the bar. After I clean up the kitchen, I glance at the overflow, about eight beautiful cookies. I fight an impulse to cram them in my mouth or shove them in the garbage. Instead, I pile them on a plate, leave them on the table, and walk out the back door with my get-well gift for Odin.

By morning, I'm exhausted from nurses entering my room every five minutes overnight. They're gradually pulling tubes out of my body, which is great, but I would pay any amount of money right now for an hour of uninterrupted sleep.

I pay casual attention as the morning nurse reviews plans with me. Something about benchmarks to put weight on my foot and later to drive. I'm getting a knee roller and fancy physical therapy courtesy of the university football team, but I'm entirely dependent on others to get me to and from the facility. Great.

They pulled the tube out of my junk so at least I could pee on my own…under supervision and with several orderlies holding me upright. What a hero I am. If only the jersey chasers could see me now.

The nurse tells me to prepare for discharge around lunchtime and leaves me in peace, but the door to my room bursts open again immediately.

This time, it's a girl I vaguely recognize from one of my classes. She's with my roommate Stellan, who looms behind her, tugging at his shirt collar.

What the hell?

Thora, I think her name is. She's tiny and loud in class, and I think I'm supposed to work with her on a project. She's clutching a metal container to her chest, looking flustered and out of breath.

"Odin!" she exclaims and rushes to my bedside like we've known each other for years. "I brought you cookies."

Stellan leans on the wall, clearly out of breath from trying to keep up with this pint-sized, treat-yielding woman. I'm about to ask what the hell she's doing here when she barrels on, "I feel responsible for this." She waves a hand around at my leg, which is engulfed in my brand-new plastic boot. "I was bitching about working with you, and there you were on the television. And then all this happened. Not that I think I control evil demons or something. I'm not the real Thora."

I stare at her. "Am I high? Are you here right now?"

Stellan waves. "She showed up at the apartment. I offered to bring her in. She has cookies." He points at the tin, and she nods.

"I am sorry to interrupt while you're sick. Are you sick? Injured. It's just that I wanted to let you know…about our class project. It's due soon, and with you being…well, here, I wasn't sure how we were going to finish it, and I need this grade to maintain my scholarship, and-"

I cut her off, overwhelmed. "Seriously? I'm lying here in a robotic cast with my career in shambles, and you're worried about a class project?"

Thora's face falls, and I see the moment she realizes how she's come across. "I- I'm sorry," she stammers. "I didn't mean…Of course, your health is the most important thing. I just… I cannot get a bad grade on this assignment. I have a fellowship lined up for grad school, and I can't lose it. I was wondering if you wanted me to go ahead and do the whole project. And I made you cookies."

Something in her voice, in the desperate look in her eyes, makes me pause. She waves the metal tin at me, and I reach for it. For the first time, I look at Thora—not just as the bossy, intense girl from class but as a person with dreams and fears. Plus, I know something about losing a shot at a big dream.

"Grad school, huh?" I say, my tone softer now. "What are you going to study?"

I fumble with the cookie tin lid as Stellan scratches his neck.

Thora reaches for the container and opens it for me, handing me a cookie. I feel a little zing as our fingers touch, but it's probably because I'm high on painkillers. Or something.

She tells me she won an award and is going to study international policy in England. I can't keep up. The meds are kicking in big time, and I'm groggy and struggling to chew the cookie. When I open my eyes again, I see Thora holding the foam cup of water near my face, tapping my cheek with the straw.

Is she taking charge of this situation? I don't hate it.

I sip and meet her eye, not sure what I see there, which tracks, because I'm not sure of anything right now.

I swallow the water and say, "Thank you." She nods and sets the cup back on the table. I try to move the container of cookies, but my arms aren't paying attention to my brain right now.

I arch a brow. Or maybe I squint. I'm not sure, but Thora shifts her weight uncomfortably. Stellan sighs and walks over to the bed, placing his palm on my head like he's some sort of priest offering a blessing. "Hey, man," he grunts. "Sucks about your foot."

I nod. At least, I think I do. He shakes his head and reaches for a cookie, but I have just enough concentration left to swat his arm out of the way. "Those are mine," I growl.

Thora presses her lips together. "Okay, well, I wrote my cell on the cookie container. I don't need it back, by the way. I just wanted you to be able to contact me. About class."

Stellan sets a hand on her shoulder, and something unpleasant flicks through my chest. What's his deal with Thora? He says, "I'll take you back to the apartment."

She shakes her head. "No, thanks. Fern and Wyatt are going to be making up for lost time." She checks her watch. "I have a shift soon. I can walk."

Stellan frowns at her and glances at me. I try to frown at him. Something is off about this. I wish my head were working. He groans and says, "I'll drop you at the bar, okay? And I won't touch any more of his cookies." My cousin tosses a grin at me and then walks out of the room, squeezing my good leg on his way out the door. Thora follows, looking uneasy. I can't get a read on her.

But then, I can't get a read on anything right now. Except I'm pretty sure she plowed in here to tell me she's going to do our whole project without me, and that stings more than my incision. I am literally not in control of any part of my life, from my digestion to my rehab schedule.

Maybe I can handle a group project.

"Don't count on doing the paper alone," I bark.

She turns to face me from the hall, brow furrowed. "Sorry, what?"

"It's a team grade," I tell her, tapping my fingers on the metal container that looks like it used to contain multiple pounds of shelled and salted peanuts. "We're a team. We'll do it together."

Stellan blinks at me, and Thora taps her foot on the floor. "Maybe just call me when you're home," she says. I can tell she thinks I'll forget this conversation. She and Stellan leave, and I stare at the ceiling, waiting for discharge. I give up and fall asleep, thinking about Thora's pouty lips as she offered me water.

I SLIP INTO FUEL UP, THE TRENDY BAR WHERE I WORK TOO MANY HOURS, MY mind a whirlwind. The familiar scent of stale beer and greasy bar food hits me, but it does nothing to calm my nerves after seeing Odin so messed up. My hands shake as I tie my apron, and I nearly drop a glass while setting up the bar.

"Real smooth, Thora," I mutter to myself. "First, you act like a weird robot in front of the injured hottie, and now you can't even handle basic bartending tasks. A stellar day all around."

As I start serving the early crowd, my mind keeps replaying the scene at the hospital. Odin's shocked face when I burst in, babbling about our project like some kind of sociopathic academic drone. God, there I was, this crazy-eyed loudmouth, more concerned about a class assignment than Odin's injury.

A customer snaps his fingers at me, jarring me back to reality. "Hey, sweetheart, you gonna stand there all day, or can I get another beer?"

I plaster on my best fake smile. "Coming right up, sir. And hey, maybe we could work on using our words instead of treating me like a dog? Just a thought."

As I pour his beer—extra foam because fuck him—I can't help but draw parallels between this interaction and my behavior at the hospital. Was I any better than this entitled jerk demanding Odin's attention when he was clearly in pain? Some Rhodes Scholar I am. I can't even manage basic human empathy. Although … I didn't infantilize Odin with a chauvinistic pet name, so at least there's that.

The bar door swings open, and in walks Fern, practically floating in a post-sex haze. I'm happy she had a reunion with her hottie. Odin's cousin, I remember. Family.

Fern's hair is mussed, and a small blue bruise is peeking out from under her collar. I raise an eyebrow as she approaches.

"You and Wyatt made nice, I take it?"

Fern grins, unabashed. "Oh, hush. You were the one who turned me into this person. What is it you always say? Stick a peen in it and forget for a while?"

Her words sting more than they should. "Yeah, well, some of us have more pressing concerns than getting our rocks off."

Fern's smile falters. "Okay, spill. What happened at the hospital? And don't say 'nothing.' I know your 'I fucked up' face, and you're wearing it hard right now."

I sigh, glancing around to make sure no customers need me before leaning in. "I may have royally screwed up with Odin today."

"How? Didn't you give him the cookies? Men love cookies."

I groan, recounting my disastrous hospital visit. With each word, Fern's eyes grow wider. When I finish, she lets out a low whistle.

"Wow. That's...something."

"I know. Who does that? Who bursts into a hospital room and immediately starts talking about a class project? I'm a monster, Fern. A grade-obsessed, compassionless monster."

Fern reaches across the bar, grabbing my hand. "Hey, stop that. You're not a monster. You're just...intensely focused. And under a shit-ton of pressure."

I snort. "Yeah, because that makes it so much better. God, what if they revoke my fellowship? 'Sorry, Ms. Janssen, we've decided you lack the basic human decency required to represent our institution.'"

"Thora, breathe. They're not going to revoke your fellowship over one awkward interaction. And let's be real, you've got so much riding on this project. It's not unreasonable to be worried about it."

I nod, knowing she has a point. But the guilt still gnaws at me. "I just...I should have been better, you know? He's lying there with his life in shambles, and all I could think about was my stupid GPA. A rational person would have just sent the cookies with his cousin. And a note."

The bar starts to fill up, and I throw myself into work, grateful for the distraction. But even as I mix drinks and fake laugh at terrible jokes, my mind keeps drifting back to Odin. To the way his blue eyes had widened in surprise when I burst in, to the hurt that had flashed across his face at my callousness.

During a lull, I can't help but check my phone. No messages. Not that I expected any, but still. My finger hovers over Odin's contact info that Stellan gave me when we left the hospital. He was weird about it, too, like I'm interested in Odin for sexy times and not just a means to a four-point-oh.

Should I text Odin? Apologize? But what would I even say? 'Sorry I acted like a robot with no feelings. Hope your catastrophic injury isn't too inconvenient for my academic goals.'

Fuck that. I did offer to do the whole project so it could be one less thing he worries about. Is academic integrity important to him? I don't know which way is up at the moment.

So, instead, I respond to a text from my mom, firmly telling her that no, I will not stop for cigarettes for Dad on my way home. I wish this happened rarely enough that I was shocked about the request, but I am not.

As the night winds down, Fern finishes chatting with the staff and prepares to leave. She fixes me with a stern look. "Promise me you'll be kind to yourself, okay? You're allowed to have conflicting feelings. You're allowed to worry about your future and still care about others."

I roll my eyes, but I can feel a small smile tugging at my lips. "Yes, Mom. I promise to practice positive self-talk and all that jazz."

She grins, pulling me into a quick hug. "That's it. Now go home and get some rest. And maybe think about texting that current obsession of yours."

"He's not my anything," I call after her, but she's already out the door, leaving me alone with my thoughts again.

As I walk toward the bus home, the cool night air clearing my head a bit, I allow myself to really think about Odin—not just as a project partner or an inconvenience to my plans, but as a person. What must he be going through right now? His whole future, everything he's worked for, is suddenly up in the air. And yet, when I saw him, he still managed to be kind, even in the face of my spectacular social ineptitude.

He must have been on some intense pain meds, based on how his pupils looked in the hospital. Not that I was looking at his pupils at all.

I think about his family, too. The way they rally around him, their love and concern palpable even to an outsider like me. It makes me ache a little for reasons I don't want to examine too closely. Fern's always talking about that family, how tight they are, and how they support each other. It helps when you always have your basic needs met and don't have to panic about money constantly.

And I'm going to become a person who works to change that! We can become a country where everyone has that sort of chance, dang it. I just need to finish this last month of college and step into my true purpose: Thora Janssen—International Policy Researcher. Rhodes Fellow. All around policy changemaker.

And then, unbidden, my mind drifts to less...academic thoughts. Like how Odin looked unfairly attractive even in a hospital gown. Or how his hand felt when our fingers brushed as I offered him a cookie. I shake my head, trying to dislodge these unhelpful thoughts. This is ridiculous. I do not have time for a crush.

As I reach my parents' house, I make a decision. I'll find a way to make this right. To balance my coursework with human decency. To be worthy of a Rhodes Scholarship and, more importantly, deserving of Odin's forgiveness.

But as I crank up my air purifier and climb into bed, my last thoughts before sleep claims me are of piercing blue eyes and a smile that makes my heart do somersaults.

I am so, so screwed.

I SIT IN THE FRONT OF MOM'S CAR AFTER GETTING WHEELED OUT TO THE CURB, cramming cookies in my mouth and staring out the window as she drives me home. When we get to my apartment, we realize it's not an accessible building. There are stairs everywhere.

I stand outside the door, one leg resting on the knee roller, one hand on the handlebars, the other clutching that damn tin of cookies.

Mom stares at the steps into the building and the stairwell up two floors to the apartment I share with my brother and cousins. "Odin, I'm so sorry." Mom gestures at the stairs like she is the architect or something. "This isn't accessible at all, is it? Not even a ramp…"

I sniff. This building is for student-athletes, so it makes sense that there's a minimum expectation of walking ability. Mom sighs. "I'll run up and grab your brother, okay? We'll get you inside."

I have no idea what the plan is to get me upstairs. I'm not crawling up the steps. I guess I'd let Gunnar give me a piggyback ride. Lord knows I've carried his drunk ass up to our apartment that way before.

Gun and Stellan make their way outside, along with Mom, who looks like she wants to cry. Gunny claps a hand on my shoulder. "This sucks, bro," he offers. I grunt at him.

Mom fiddles with her car keys. She's double-parked outside the building, and people are starting to stare at us as traffic backs up behind her black SUV. "I'm just going to move the car, and I'll come in with your things, okay?"

I wave a hand at her because what do I care where she parks?

Stellan walks around my knee roller, checking out the foam pad where I'm supposed to rest my cast. I can put weight on my knee, but not under any circumstances, my foot or lower leg.

Gunnar points a thick finger at me and says, "I assume you don't want me to throw you over my shoulder?"

"Fuck you." I flip my brother the bird because this is how we communicate our love when our parents aren't around.

Stellan scratches his chin, squinting at the apartment entrance. "I think we can hop this together," he says.

Gunnar nods. "Odin, you put your left hand on the banister, right arm around me, and we'll hop you up. Stelly can carry this contraption."

"Why do you get to help him hop?" Stellan is now put out over not being chosen to help his invalid cousin up the stairs. I groan and finagle my roller toward the banister, testing my weight on the creaky railing.

"I'm his brother, asshole. When your brother gets hurt, you can help him hop."

Stellan flicks Gunnar in the ear. "Don't say that about getting hurt, man. You're going to jinx us."

I kick the knee roller away with a growl. "You guys going to fight all day or help me inside?"

"Sorry, bro." Gunnar slides up against my side. "I won't even pinch you this time. Or tickle you. Maybe." He wedges his shoulder under mine and locks an arm around my waist. We're about the same height, so it works okay. After a few days lying in a hospital bed, I'm weaker than I want to admit, so I give him my weight and hop up the few stairs to the apartment door.

I use the roller to get down the hall and then rely on Gunny again to get up two flights of stairs to our apartment, which I realize I'll have to leave every morning for PT. "How is this shit going to work," I ask the room at large.

There's an uncomfortable silence as my brother and cousin shift their weight and stare at their backpacks. They need to get to class. Mom walks in the door carrying the football uniform I forgot I was wearing when they rushed me to the hospital. Someone stuffed it in a clear plastic trash bag, which is probably where it will stay. I'm not sure what happened to my pads or helmet. I guess I have to return the jersey to the athletic department. That's a problem for another day.

"What do you need to get comfortable, Odin?" Mom sets the bag on the ground and looks around the apartment. There are a lot of cardboard boxes stacked all over since Wyatt is moving out, but the place is otherwise not too messy—for once. Typically, Mom is full of jokes and comments about our filthy kitchen and toilets, but today, she wrings her hands together and stares at me, her eyes shiny, like she's trying not to cry.

You and me both, Mom.

"I'm just going to bed," I say, testing out the knee roller on the apartment carpet. I glide my ass to my room and am glad to see I fit through the door pretty easily. From there, I quickly hobble into my bed; once settled, I realize I didn't set myself up with water, snacks, or anything. "Can you bring me my cookies, Mom?"

I'm 22 years old, asking my mother to bring me a box of cookies. But she does it, smiling. She sets the tin on my nightstand along with a glass of water and a clementine. I know we don't keep fresh fruit in the apartment, so this is clearly pity fruit. "Isn't this for your snack later?" I reach for the cookies but point at the orange.

She smiles. "Your father can bring me another one. He likes visiting my chambers."

"Gross, Mom." My parents are always making weird sex jokes about her judge's office.

She ruffles my hair and kisses the top of my head. She reaches into her pocket and sets a few pill bottles on the nightstand. "I'll call around four if I don't hear from you that you took these, okay?"

I nod and adjust the covers. I hear her talking softly to Gunnar, and then I hear the apartment door close. I'm alone. I cuddle the tin of cookies to my chest like it's a throw pillow. Did Thora really come to the hospital to give me shit about a group project? I guess she at least brought me some cookies. I stare at the phone number on the lid of the tin. Should I thank her? Or give her shit for being a jerk about schoolwork?

I decide to send her a text.

ME

Hey

THORA FROM CLASS

Sorry. Wrong number.

ME

It's Odin [deer emoji]

THORA FROM CLASS

Oh shit. Sorry! How are you? I'm so sorry I was such a jerk yesterday. There you were in the hospital after surgery, and I was bugging you about class. Don't even worry about it. I'll write the paper and put both our names on it.

I stare at her message. It's not like I ever care much about my classwork. Under ordinary circumstances, I'd happily take credit for her work and be done with it. But nothing is ordinary anymore. Before I can think too hard about it, I write back:

No way. I can't have you putting my name on something I haven't even read. What if you do a terrible job?

THORA FROM CLASS

Okayyyy well…are you going to be able to work on it? From the hospital?

ME

I'm home now, actually. And I no longer have football practice eating into my spare time, so…

THORA FROM CLASS

So?

ME

So why don't you come over? We can work on it this afternoon when my pain meds wear off, and I can think clearly.

THORA FROM CLASS

Today? Are you sure? We have a few weeks.

ME

I literally have nothing else to do.

This is partly a lie. I'm supposed to schedule meetings with my academic advisors, coach, the financial aid people, and my athletic trainers. I have a whole team of people who care about their investment in my attendance at this school as a football player. But here I am, for a change, doing something as a student.

ME

Bring more cookies.

I toss the phone on my nightstand without waiting for her reply, and I roll over and finally grab a few hours of sleep.

CHAPTER 6
THORA

"I'M SUPPOSED TO GO TO HIS APARTMENT." I BLURT THIS INTO MY PHONE WITH no preamble, but Fern is used to this style of communication from me.

"Well, it's not like he can get to you very easily," Fern replies, her voice far off like she has me on speaker while she's doing other things. Which I'm sure she is. We graduate in less than a month, and Fern leaves immediately to go to grad school in London. I will be in Pittsburgh without her for the entire summer before my fellowship starts at Oxford. Fern continues, explaining, "Wyatt told me Odin is on a ton of pain meds. Or he's supposed to be, but he's being stubborn about taking them, so he mostly lies around moaning and growling."

I immediately picture him moaning, not in pain but in pleasure. The man is smoking hot, but he knows that. He's a Division One athlete. Of course, he knows his body is a wonderland. I clear my throat and check the time. I have a few minutes before my history class. "So, do I just go over there and sit on his bed with him?"

"They have chairs," Fern says. She's basically married to Odin's cousin Wyatt, who lived in the same apartment until he left to play professional soccer abroad. She's probably had sex on the chairs over there. I shove that thought away and croak out an affirmative sound.

———

Sitting in class, I pay half attention to my professor as I stress about going to Odin Stag's and trying to work on our class project. It was easy to

437

picture him naked and move on when we were just regular classmates. He doesn't even sit near me. But, our professor assigns random pairings for each project and it was my turn to get paired up with the athlete in class. I really thought he'd be glad to have me do the whole thing. I know he wasn't serious when he said it might not be good. I mean, I don't want to sound cocky, but I'm a Rhodes scholar. I don't do bad work.

Odin's apartment is near the bar where I work so it's nothing for me to go over there in between class and my shift. I'll have to figure something out for dinner. These mundane thoughts distract me from all the bigger stressors weighing down on me lately. I've spent my whole damn life trying to change my circumstances, and I'm right on the cusp of succeeding. I can smell it above the exhaust fumes and alley pee in Odin's neighborhood.

I don't know how I ended up driven to excel academically in a house full of long-time service workers and people with an addiction. My dad's been on house arrest for months now, and Mom has a record, too, making it hard for her to get any sort of job that offers a decent wage.

My grad fellowship is meant to be me studying international policies around parole and incarceration. Everyone from my neighborhood seems to cycle through generational patterns of poverty, petty crime, and disproportionate consequences.

But just winning this fellowship isn't enough. I know enough about the world to know the deck is stacked against me. I don't have a passport yet. I'm saving up my tips to deal with that and get myself a laptop and a new wardrobe. Oh, and a flight. I have to really save up to afford a flight overseas.

Ugh, it's all swimming to the surface again and making me twitchy, so I bite my lip and walk faster. If I can make headway on this class project with Odin, I won't feel strangled by all this other stuff.

Someone holds the door open for me at Odin's building, and I walk up and knock on their apartment door. I hear a grunting sound from inside that might be an invitation to enter. I hope it wasn't a sex noise. I tentatively open the door and see Odin sprawled on the couch, his booted foot elevated on the arm, long, hairy legs sticking out from a pair of athletic shorts that cling to all the lumps and bumps around his crotch.

Nope, not gonna stare at his crotch. I move my eyes to his face and smile. "Ready to get to work?"

He frowns at me, almost like he forgot I was coming over, but he shrugs, and I make my way over to the armchair next to his head. "We need a right-sized topic that we can write about for five pages. I was thinking we should argue for increased government funding for colleges and universities."

He shakes his head. "You're not going to just boss me around and bull-doze the whole report, Thora." I…like how my name sounds coming out of his mouth. I like it too much. "That topic sucks."

I scoff at him. "Maybe because you never had to worry about paying for school, Mr. Scholarship."

He arches a brow at me. "Pretty sure Fern told me you're on scholar-ship, too, Ms. Bossy."

"I'm not bossy." He stares at me. "I'm assertive. I have to be. People think they can run over me otherwise."

He snorts. "Because you're pint-sized."

"We can't all be six-foot-eighteen." I wish I had a pillow to swat him with. I actually glance around his living room, looking for one, but they're all either under his head or the heel of his boot. I take a deep breath. "This isn't productive. What topics would *you* like to pursue for our paper, Stag?"

He stares at the ceiling and laces his fingers together behind his head, which makes his t-shirt ride up and shows me a tan, smooth expanse of belly skin looking taut above the waist of his shorts. "We should still do something related to low-resource students and school funding." His sentence surprises a huff out of me and he squints. "You don't think I know a million guys on the football team who are only here because of sports? Trust me, nobody is telling these guys they're smart like you."

"I…never considered the people on athletic scholarships."

Another sniff from Odin. "You and a lot of other people. I'd love to have time to take harder classes. We spend almost 40 hours a week on football stuff and still have to take 12 credits."

The fridge hums to life in the uncomfortable silence as we both realize I've been sanctimonious. Again. "Okay, so what's the topic, then? Path-ways to college for kids with low-income families…"

"Ethics of athletic scholarships."

"Ethics of tuition at all?"

"Oh!" He sits up. "My mom loves talking about how community college should be free. I guess that's different than universities?"

"I'm not really sure, but I'll write that down. Community college should be free. We can look at what other countries do and charge?"

Odin grins. "We can work with this." We each dive into internet research, making a list of sources and potential argument topics until an alarm goes off somewhere in Odin's apartment.

He sits up and claps his hands, swinging his casted foot around to rest on the coffee table. Then he winces when I guess that puts pressure on his heel. He blows out a breath and grabs a bottle of pills from the table, swallowing some with another grimace.

I chew on the end of my pen. "You all right?"

"Don't," he says, his voice sharp. He must see me flinch because he runs a hand through his hair and fiddles with one of his earrings. I never realized he had his ears pierced before this. I wonder what else I never knew about Odin Stag. "I'm pretty beat," he says. "I'll look some stuff up and text you, and we can get started with an outline." I stare at him. "What? You didn't think I knew how to outline?"

"Are you kicking me out of your house?"

He furrows his brow. "No, but I am going to go to sleep. So, unless you want to sit here alone while I'm snoring…"

I sniff and shove my notebook back in my bag. "We really can probably do most of this over email."

"Huh-uh," he barks. "I hate that shit. Back and forth, ten thousand messages when a three-minute conversation would solve it all. We should meet in person."

"How's that going to work? We both have insane schedules." From talking with Fern, I know that Odin and all the athletes are up before dawn for weight training and have team commitments until late at night.

Odin gestures at his leg. "I don't know if anyone told you, but I'm not exactly running sprints with the starters right now."

I bite my lip, and my cheeks heat. Of course, his schedule must be a little more open now. He said as much. I try to cover. "How was I supposed to know your schedule for follow-up treatment? Anyway, *my* schedule is still insane."

"You're here now," Odin declares with another shrug. "Just come back at this time on Monday."

I snort and shake my head. "That's too far out. I will *call* you tomorrow when I get a chance."

"Fine," he says, and closes.

"Fine!" I mutter as I slam the apartment door and walk away, grinning despite myself.

CHAPTER 7
ODIN

I haven't been to class since my injury. How long has it been? A week? A year? I only left the apartment once to follow up with my surgeon, and it was such a debacle getting up and down the stairs that I haven't bothered since.

So, I don't know why I'm up and dressed and slithering down the stairs on my ass to wheel myself to this arguments class. I pretty much decided to withdraw from the semester and finish later. I have nothing else to do in the fall. Except if I withdraw now, that leaves Thora without a partner.

We've hung out together daily, working on this project when she has time between her classes and her grueling schedule at the bar. She wants to take over and do this whole project herself, on her timeline, and…I don't want to let her do that for some reason. The girl gets under my skin. So maybe I'm dragging myself up Forbes Avenue to prove something to her.

I growl in frustration when a car is parked too close to the corner, blocking the curb cut, and I can't get my knee roller up without a hassle. Some jagoff honks at me when the light turns, and I question every one of my life choices to date.

Despite all of this, I'm always on time for class and events. People think I'm really laid back, but I guess growing up in a house with world-class athlete parents rubbed off on me. I'm disciplined about my schedule when I care, which I did until I got hurt.

I park my roller in the back corner of the class and wedge myself into the too-small desk, sprawling my cast into the aisle but unable to do anything about it. Thora walks in, and I watch her eyes widen at the sight of me. She hurries to a desk in front of me and sinks into the seat, her dark hair flouncing over her tiny shoulders. She really is a small person.

"What are you doing here?" She hiss-whispers like it's some secret or like I'm an intruder.

I shrug. "Attending class? With my project partner?"

Her eyes roll hard enough to make me dizzy. "Aren't you supposed to be in bed with your foot elevated or something?"

I waggle my eyebrows at her. "You like thinking of me in bed, Janssen?" An adorable flush blooms across her cheeks as the professor makes his way into the room and dumps his stuff on the lectern he never uses. Professor Ferda likes to sit on the edge of a table, facing us but still looming above us. Except I'm pretty much at eye level with him, sitting. Not that I've made a habit of making eye contact.

"All right, scholars," he says, clapping his hands. "We've got what? A week left together? By now, you've got all the basic concepts for forming effective arguments, persuading an audience, and utilizing a call to action, right? Right?" He waits for us all to murmur at him, and he smiles. "So, I'm going to give you all a chance to workshop your final presentations. If you're not already, please move to sit with your partner. You'll have five minutes to organize your outlines, and then I will have you swap with another group."

Professor Ferda hands out a worksheet with things we are supposed to look for in each other's outlines. I'm one thousand percent certain Thora, and I have all this shit in place already. The last draft of the outline she sent me was so detailed I spent a half hour just crossing things out and whittling it all down.

Which she points out when she flings our printed outline onto her desk and glares at me. "What's with all this? Those were good ideas."

"We would have gone over the time limit," I insist. "It's more refined this way—three main arguments. We can't get into the weeds talking about socialized healthcare and paid parental leave when we only have ten minutes. We need to stick to education."

Thora frowns. I could already tell she was one of those people who spews out the entire context of every possible angle before she can get to the meat of an argument. Except when she's sparring with me, it seems. And I kind of like that she gives me shit on a regular basis. Who shows up in someone's hospital room to yell at them about group work? This girl.

"The free healthcare is important, though. It shows the Scandinavian values."

"Are we talking about the merits of socialism, or are we talking about free college?" I raise a brow and cross my arms.

She huffs. "They're the same thing." She crosses her arms.

I'm about to tell her she's absolutely incorrect when Professor Ferda stops by my desk. "Hey, Odin." His voice is saccharine, like I'm seven and scraped my knee. "I was sorry to hear about your injury. I wasn't expecting you back in class after your advisor reached out."

I shrug. "I haven't talked to him this week. I would never leave Thora high and dry." I wink at her, and that seems to piss her off, so I file that away to do it again sometime.

Professor Ferda nods and purses his lips before saying, "Okay, great. Well, why don't you two switch papers with Jean and Malcolm?"

———

I let Thora scribble all over the other group's notes, watching as she mutters to herself the whole time. Class ends, and we get our paper back with only a few smiley faces in the margins. I can tell this bothers Thora, so I thank Jean and slide the paper into my sweatpants pocket. "Where to now?" I ask Thora, and she rears her head in confusion.

"Um, I work."

I frown. I hadn't considered that she had shit to do and wouldn't just come back to my place for more arguments. If I'm really honest, I want her near my bed in case I convince her to join me in it. I scratch my chin. "At the bar?" She nods. "But it's slow during the day if you want to finish our sources in between customers?"

I shrug. "I guess I'll be a barfly then. I've never been to a bar during daylight hours…"

"I can't believe this is how you're going to spend your afternoon." She tugs on her backpack straps.

I realize I haven't exactly told her that this paper is officially the only thing I have going on until I start physical therapy. I get myself situated on the knee roller.

She winces. "Are you going to sit there and bug me?"

"Ah, so I bug you? Sounds interesting." Veins start pulsing in her neck, and I laugh. "I'll sit on a bar stool, and eat some soup or something, and work on our bibliography."

Thora bites her lip, which is probably the only plump thing on her body, and I stare as she works her teeth along the rosy, sensitive skin. "I guess that's okay."

I start rolling back down Forbes, and she walks beside me. "Don't you usually work evenings?"

She sighs. "I work whenever I can get in there. You know I'm moving to the UK this fall, right?" I shake my head. She hums. "Fern and I both are. She's there long term but I'm just there for a year. And I need so much stuff I can't afford yet." She pauses while I navigate a curb cut, successfully this time. "You probably don't care about my airfare or professional wardrobe."

"I care. I'm not an asshole."

"Oh, no, you're renowned for your benevolence." Thora laughs. "What do they say about you? That you rack people up by the horns or something?"

"Well, nobody's going to say that ever again, are they?"

Thora stares at me with her mouth hanging open. "Oh my god, Odin. I'm so sorry. I keep doing that to you. How can you stand me?"

"I'm not really sure I can," I joke. We get to the bar, and she holds the door open. I'm happy to see this place has a ramp from the curb. I guess the owners want everyone to be able to access their cheap beer and fried food. I make my way to the stool at the end of the bar, and Thora walks behind it, tossing her bag somewhere and tugging on a black apron.

"What'll it be, Stag?"

I consider this. She's right about the meds not mixing with liquor. But this place serves all kinds of fried food I'm never allowed to eat while training. And I'll never have anyone telling me what to eat again. I slap the sticky wood surface of the bar. "Bring me the app platter."

She frowns. "That's meant to serve four people."

"App. Platter." I enunciate each syllable and pop all the p's until Thora laughs and shakes her head. I watch as she types in my order and then hurries to serve some preppy kid who thinks he's cool because winks at the bartender.

She walks off to pour his beer, and I glare at him when he sets a crumpled dollar in a ring of condensation on the bar. He walks off with his beer as Thora heads to the kitchen, presumably for my food, and I reach in my wallet for a five, placing that guy's shitty tip along with my addition on a drink napkin, nice and smooth and dry.

When Thora sets the food in front of me, she sees the tip, and a smile spreads wide across her face. She folds the bills neatly and adds them to the jar by the register.

I eat all the fried food, knowing it will make my gut churn. It takes me five minutes to type up our sources for our essay, so I take my time and watch her work. I confer with her between customers and add some stuff that we can use for our presentation to a list on my phone.

I was going to pester her into returning to my apartment after her shift, but I'm exhausted between leaving the house and eating all the heavy food. I text my cousins to come get me and leave a twenty folded neatly by my plate.

I force myself to walk away because if she sees me, she will refuse the tip, and I want her to have it.

———

When I get back to the apartment, there's an envelope sitting on my pillow. I frown at it because the edge is ripped like one of these buffoons opened my mail. I sit on the edge of my bed and chill my irritation when I see the letter is only addressed to "Mr. Stag," which could really be anyone here.

My guts churn when I see that it's a check from the college football video game that made me into a character. I knew this was coming, but it still feels like shit to see it sitting here. What the fuck am I supposed to do with this money? What kid wants me in their damn video game anymore?

I consider ripping up the damn thing, but that feels disrespectful to Thora, who is still working behind the bar and will be for hours. I shove the check and the envelope in my desk drawer and pop a pain pill, hoping for sleep.

CHAPTER 8

THORA

"THORA! GET THE DOOR!" MY DAD BELLOWS FROM THE LIVING ROOM, WHERE I'm sure he's sprawled on the couch from the night before. Chances are pretty high that he was drinking, but chances are also pretty high that his probation officer won't stop by today to check.

I brace myself to dash through the cloud of cigarette smoke before it occurs to me that people don't usually knock on the door at eight in the morning. I poke my head out of my bedroom. "Are you sure it's not the P.O.?"

Dad snarls, and I sigh, grabbing my backpack. I try to spend as little time as possible at my parents' house and even less time away from the air purifier and dryer sheet haven I rigged up in my bedroom. I know I can't do anything about having grown up poor, but I sure can try to keep the cigarette smoke smell away from my clothes, hair, and school supplies.

I shoulder the heavy bag and peek through the smeared glass pane on the door, shocked to see Odin Stag waving up at me from the sidewalk. Yanking open the door and stepping outside, I hiss, "What are you doing here? How did you know where I live?"

Odin waves at a black vehicle idling in the street, and the driver peels off with a deliberate screech of the tires. Odin shakes his head. "A, I got a ride from my brother so I could go over our bibliography before it's due today, and B, you shared your dot with me the other day."

I furrow my brow. "I shared my dot?"

He shrugs, adjusting his giant frame on his knee roller device. "On your phone. The tracking thing."

I lean against the stoop, still wondering how he managed to knock on the door without climbing the four concrete steps. Maybe his brother knocked for him? "I never shared my location with you."

Odin grins, one of his earrings twinkling in the morning sun. "It's possible. I asked Fern where you live."

"Why would you do that? She would have told me." I didn't realize Fern chats with the Stag family, especially since Wyatt moved out of the country.

Odin rolls closer to me. "Like I said, I wanted to talk about the project before class, but you weren't answering your phone."

I slide the device in question from my coat pocket, and sure enough, I missed a zillion texts from Odin and Fern, as well as a few calls. "Oh, sorry. I set it to do not disturb when I was at the bar, and I guess I forgot to turn it back on."

"Seems unlike you, Janssen." He winces, and I realize he must be uncomfortable. I bite my lip. "I, um, can't really invite you up." I gesture vaguely at my parents' row home. "But we're just a few blocks from Constellation Coffee if you want to go sit and talk?"

He checks a very fancy watch and shakes his head. "Nah, we better start moving to campus. Don't tell me you walk the whole way from here?"

I scoff at him. "I take the bus. Do you not know about the bus?"

He shrugs. "Never had to worry about it before this." He waves a hand at his foot. I think about how close his apartment is to campus and remember again that I've had an unconventional education. That's why I usually only hang out with Fern. She gets it. She lived at home all four years, too, and we were queens of finding library space to camp out on long stretches between classes. We know where all the free food is around campus and the best places to nap without worrying that anyone will snatch our bags.

"Come on, big guy." I start walking up the hill toward Penn Ave. "I'll show you the splendors of the 93 bus." He rolls alongside me quietly, grunting a bit at the rough spots in the sidewalk. I slow my stride and absolutely do not stare at his ass in his gray sweatpants. I also don't admire his shoulder muscles, obvious and visible even in his hoodie. "You've got to be six feet tall," I mutter, and he laughs.

"That's what you're thinking about right now?" Odin growls as his roller catches on a tree root. He hoists the device up and over the uneven surface and says, "I'm six-four. And before you ask, so is my dad, and all my brothers are right around that range. We grow 'em big in the Stag family." I'm treated to a wink that sets my pants on fire, and I know this guy knows exactly how good he looks, but I am swooning like a jersey-chasing fan regardless. If I were the sort of person who went to sporting events, I'd be screaming over the railing right now at half-time, begging Odin to fire a t-shirt cannon my way.

I try to cover my ogling by explaining, "I was just thinking about how we will get you inside the bus. Some of them have a ramp that flips out, but some just…" I try to demonstrate how the buses sort of squat to let old ladies step aboard.

"Don't worry about me," he says. I nod and point at the bench inside the bus shelter. He shakes his head. "We can stand. I'm serious. I have enough people worrying about me and treating me like an invalid. Talk to me about our sources for class."

I'm about to tell him about conference proceedings I downloaded from some university in Portugal when I spot a bright red bus chugging up Penn Ave from the Strip District. I wave at the driver, who stops and stares at Odin. Does the driver recognize him? I guess so in this sports-obsessed town. The bus beeps and squats down, and I don't know if I should get in first and help him or…actually, I have no idea what to do because there's no way I could lift him or anything. He gestures for me to get on, and I do.

He heaves his knee roller in the door, and I grab it with one hand as he muscles the rest of himself into the bus. He's not even breathing heavily. The driver and I both look at him, impressed. I shake myself out of my stupor and tap my student ID on the fare box. Odin arches a brow and fishes in his pocket for his wallet, clearly unused to having his ID at the ready to gain access to buses and, probably, dining halls.

Everyone on board watches as he rolls down the aisle to the accessible seating. I stand in front of him, and he scowls, clearly grappling with some sense of chivalry and the dueling reality of his temporary impairment. I cross my arms over my chest and frown at him until he sinks into the seat, tucking the roller in between his enormously long legs. I consider sitting on his lap, on his good leg, obviously. Would he even notice my weight? I shake my head as the bus chugs forward. I steady myself on the pole by Odin's head, and he glances up at the strap hanging from the bar far above my reach. "Neither of us is well-suited for this," he says with a shake of his head.

I shrug. "Beats walking, I guess."

———

Once on campus, the sidewalks are better maintained, and the buildings have ramps and elevators. We get to class a little bit early and settle into seats in the back of the room. I pull out my ancient laptop and open my mouth to tell Odin about the new source.

"What the hell is that thing?" Odin points at my laptop, which whirs noisily. I glare at him. "Is that a telegraph machine? Why is it so big?"

I punch him in the arm, which stings because his body is pure muscle. He shakes his head and removes a shiny, lightweight laptop from his bag. "You said something about Portugal?"

I can smell him seated this close together. His laundry detergent smells expensive, and there's a whiff of either hair gel or deodorant or maybe cologne with an alpine scent. I like it…too much. I guess it's fine that I'm attracted to him. What straight girl in Pittsburgh wouldn't be? I can give him a huff and work on this project and still achieve what I need to get out of here in a few months.

"Did you just sniff me?" He leans close to my ear to ask this, and his breath melts over my cheek and neck like honey. Shit, this is bad.

"Yes." I turn to face him, meeting his blue eyes with my dark gaze. "You stink."

A laugh rumbles out of him as the professor walks into the room. "You lie, Thora."

My tiny little research partner is into me, which is great because she's hot. I don't see an issue, apart from the fact that my life is ruined and my foot is in a giant cast. And, also, I can't move very well. I pay minimal attention to the teacher through the rest of class, demand that Thora come to my house whenever she's done with her shit today, and I wheel myself toward home.

Only I don't get very far because my athletic advisor appears out of nowhere, jogging toward me on Forbes Avenue. "Odin! Hold up, please."

I squint at him, backlit by the sun. Behind him, construction cranes work on new classroom buildings, likely partly funded by revenue from television contracts for my football team. Meech looks pissed, which is fair. I've been blowing him off for a few weeks. "Hey, Meech."

Demetrius Thomas is in charge of keeping the entire football team in line—academically, behaviorally, you name it. Most of the time, he's worried about our academic eligibility to play ball, but I suspect his vigorous chase down the city streets today is more related to scholarship shit. He wheezes a bit, holding his hand on his chest as he catches his breath. "Been trailing you since the Cathedral of Learning, kid. Your brother tell you I came by your house?"

"He might have said that. A lot of people have been stopping by." This is always true—girls with flowers. Football fans wanting to know what my injury means for their fantasy draft. My coaches.

Meech leans against the window of the Seven-11. "You're supposed to be withdrawn from school, Stag. Medical withdrawal. What are you doing going to class?"

I sniff. This guy is still acting like I will play football in the fall for my final year of eligibility. Meanwhile, I'm months away from even walking again. Exactly one running back has ever come back from a ruptured Achilles tendon, and he was already on a pro team when he got injured. I stare at Meech and lean on my knee roller. "I have something I need to do next week, then I'll sign the forms."

Meech arches a dark brow above an angry set of eyes. "You need to address this before finals. You haven't been going to class, Odin. Failing out is different from a legitimate withdrawal for an injury."

There's no way I'm pulling from this final presentation now. Thora would be smug about doing it all herself, and she'd fuck it all up, trying to argue the entire internet. I'm not sure why I care so much about this stupid assignment, but I also know she's got a lot riding on her perfect grade point average. "I don't know what to tell you, man. I have a presentation I have to do next week. I will roll directly from there to the registrar's office. Or yours, if you can handle that stuff."

"What day next week?" He crosses his arms over his chest, standing over me. Meech played ball back in college, too. Didn't go pro. Now spends his days wrangling assholes like me. I'm actually pretty good. I don't get my girlfriends pregnant. I don't blow my rent money on tattoos. My big annoying flaw is staying enrolled in school when I ought to bow out.

"Tuesday," I tell him. "I'll be done by ten." I turn around and roll toward my house before he can shout after me. I don't think he follows me, but I don't check.

———

It's obvious my parents were at the apartment. By the time I get myself back up the stairs, the fridge has been stocked with soup and grilled chicken. There's a bowl on the coffee table full of little baggies of roasted almonds, and approximately 700 bananas teeter on a rack on the counter. I cram almonds into my mouth and play video games until a tap on the door announces the arrival of Thora Janssen. I look at my watch. I've been ignoring the world for hours. I guess my brothers and my cousin Stellan all went straight from class to workouts.

"Come in," I shout, hoping I left the door unlocked.

She slips in and sinks onto the couch beside me. "God, what a day. I was at the law clinic this afternoon. You wouldn't believe the things human beings do to one another, Odin. It's horrifying."

"I forgot you work at the law clinic." I adjust my posture so I'm facing her as best I can.

Thora nods. "I mean, it's volunteering. But yes."

I nod, too. "Yeah. You helped Wyatt get his shit together. Turned his whole life around."

Thora purses her lips. "Honestly, I just check people in for the most part. It's people like your mom who are actually doing the work. They're the ones who change lives."

"Okay, but you're there helping. Someone has to check people in. Right?"

She makes a face at me, like she wants to stick out her tongue or leave rather than accept appreciation. I grunt. She must think I'm a gorilla. Maybe I'm just hungry. I hear a sound and stare at her. "Was that your stomach?"

Thora looks sheepish. "Yeah. I'm going to grab dinner after we finish our draft."

I frown and shake my head. "We should eat. My parents brought soup."

"Soup?" She looks like she never heard of it before. Or maybe she's not used to parents who make food. Her family sounded bitchy when I knocked on her door this morning.

"Yeah. I'll share if you heat it up for us."

Her face lights up. "Deal. You've got clean bowls and stuff, right?"

I flip her the bird, and she cackles, yammering at me about mean landlords and terrible employers while she heats soup on the stove.

She carries two steaming bowls to the couch, a pair of spoons tucked into her back jeans pocket. I stare at them. Am I supposed to reach in and pluck them out, thus touching her ass? Does she want me to touch her ass? She was ogling mine earlier…

"Hello? McFly?" Thora waves a hand in my face. She sets the bowls on the coffee table beside my boot cast and must have been asking me something.

"Say again? Sorry."

"I was asking where you keep the napkins." She glances around and, spotting a roll of paper towels, strides toward them to rip off a few. The question about the spoons is answered when she pulls them out with one hand, tucks a paper towel into my hoodie pocket, and hands me a bowl of soup, all in one smooth motion. Seeing my impressed face, Thora smiles.

"Bartender skills." She grabs her soup and sits beside me, close enough that I can smell floral perfume above the garlicky aroma of my dad's minestrone. "Oh shit, this is good. Your parents made this?"

I nod, slurping some of the broth. A surge of emotion hits me along with the flavors on my tongue. Dad started cooking when he retired from pro hockey to raise me and my brothers. Not sure why I feel like sharing, but I blurt, "My dad stayed home to support my mom's judicial career." Thora's eyes go wide. I take another bite of soup, and she matches my movements, silently waiting for me to tell her more. "Mom's on the Commonwealth Court now, but she did family court for a long time. She's Juniper—"

Thora gasps, cutting me off. "Juniper Jones, is your *mom*? Holy shit. She's a hero. I met her at the student law clinic a bunch of times. She's *amazing*. She remembered that I was going for the Rhodes scholarship. She's your mom? Of course, she is…"

I eat more soup, but I'm not sure how to respond to all of that. I'm more used to people freaking out about my dad. I guess there are more sports fans in my social circle than…are court fans even a thing? Law fans? "You want to be a lawyer?"

Thora nods and sets her empty soup bowl on the coffee table with a clang. "I'm definitely going to be a lawyer. I told you why I'm going to England, right? To study international approaches to child welfare and recidivism for nonviolent crimes? Your mom is the star of a bunch of case studies I've read for class. Didn't she start in sports law? That always seemed out of character to me…"

I finish my soup and stretch forward, batting Thora's hand away when she tries to help me reach the coffee table. I might not be able to do much, but I can set my own fucking bowl down when I'm done eating. I pop my evening pain meds into my mouth, swallow, and explain, "Mom had to switch jobs sort of abruptly, and my Uncle Tim had an opening." I turn to face Thora, adjusting my cast to sit sideways on the couch. "Can we be done talking about my family now?"

"Hm. Sure." Thora reaches for her backpack and pulls out the laptop, which is really more of a barely portable desktop machine on its last legs. "Let's crank out a draft."

———

She has, of course, written most of it already and included way too many footnotes and parenthetical asides, which I delete until she acknowledges that my version is much more streamlined and effective. We get most of a draft down while she gets us more soup. By the time she leans back with her hand on her belly, I'm exhausted but still hungry. This would be the perfect time for me to make a joke about eating my next course…between her legs. But it wouldn't be a joke. Not for me, anyway. I scratch my neck. "I have to do something else. My head is spinning." I make my way to my feet, and Thora looks concerned. When I frown at her, she schools her features. "I'm not fragile, you know."

"Ha! I can see that. I just…want to be helpful. That's all."

I rest my knee on the couch, so I'm not putting weight on my bad foot; like a good patient, I scratch my neck. I haven't shaved in a while. Maybe I'll grow a beard now that I don't have to wear a helmet over it. She continues to stare at me like I'm fragile until I stretch and sit back down on the couch. "All right," she says, looking at her phone. "Let's map out a plan to finalize this and practice our oral presentation." She clacks away, sending notifications to me, which I ignore as the meds kick in and begin to dull the throbbing in my lower leg.

I must be dozing off because Thora startles me by resting a hand on my shoulder. "Hey," she says, and I don't like the soothing tone in her voice. I like it better when she's mean to me. "I'm going to head out."

I try to respond, but all that comes out is a grunt. She stands up and then bends to grab her backpack, and my lizard brain overtakes my rational mind, and I rest my palm on her backside. I don't squeeze or rub. I…hold it like a firm little watermelon, all for me

Thora glances back over her shoulder, a laugh in her eyes. "Can I help you?"

"I don't know, can you?"

She chuckles and lifts my hand from her ass, placing it on my chest and patting it in place. "Some other time, Stag, when you're less stoned."

"I'm going to hold you to that," I yell after her when she closes the apartment door. At least, I think that's what I say. I fall asleep before I can check.

By Friday, I'm barely taking any more of the pain meds, and Thora and I have hit a groove. I leave the apartment only to go to the arguments class, and she comes over between class and work. She doesn't bring up the ass incident, but she also looks away less often when I catch her staring at my junk. I'd say we're about even.

At one point, she throws her pencil across the room with a roar, and I stare at her, not used to seeing her react that strongly. "Was it something I said?"

She shakes her head. "No. I'm just being a brat. Sorry. I really wanted to work tonight, but my manager shifted me to Sunday."

I scratch my stomach, and maybe I let my shirt ride up without fixing it. "Won't you get a lot of tips during the football game on Sunday? That's a good thing, right?"

She sighs. "You're probably right. I hate being so close to finishing all this, like I can taste it, but I'm still so far off." She stares at my stomach, giving herself a long look. "You don't want to hear about this stuff."

"I don't mind. You might have noticed I don't have much going on right now."

"That's not the same as listening to your unfortunate classmate whine about growing up poor and getting shafted at work."

I grin and gesture at my crotch. "You want to talk about getting shafted, Thora? I'm very open to that." She throws a pillow at me, but I deflect and grab the one behind my head, throwing it back. She giggles. "Seriously, though. I'm very interested in that discussion if you are."

Her cheeks flush, and it's really satisfying to achieve that. She bites her lip and says, "It's not a good idea, Odin. I'm counting on this grade."

"You think I'm going to piss you off before we present next week?"

She humphs. "You already piss me off."

"Well then, what's stopping us, gorgeous?"

Thora rolls her eyes, grabs another pencil from her bag, and returns to scratching away in her notebook. I prop my laptop on a couch cushion and scroll through articles about public universities in Germany until she throws another pencil. I eye her cautiously like she's a bomb about to explode. "What now?"

"I can't concentrate."

I rub a hand across my chest, teasing, and say, "Because of my rugged good looks? It's the cast, isn't it?"

"I just really need to be done working today." Okay, so she's not in the mood to joke around. Noted.

I close the laptop, figuring I've learned all there is to know about tuition-free higher ed in Europe. Thora starts gathering her things like she's going to leave me here alone on a Friday night, and I sort of panic. "Want to play a game or something?" The question comes from nowhere, but as soon as I ask it, I realize I'm desperate for her to say yes. I can't be alone in this apartment; it's too hard to leave, and we have a really fun game shelf thanks to decades of Stag family competitiveness.

She picks up both the pencils she threw and taps one against her cheek, considering. Finally, she shrugs, and I exhale. "Sure. Like checkers or something?"

"Checkers? Are you ninety years old?" I grab my knee roller and scoot over to the shelf by the never-used dining room table. I peruse the options and grab a small box of cards from the top. "How about Taco, Cat, Goat, Cheese, Pizza?"

"What?" Thora laughs. "I don't think any of those words go together."

"Oh, they definitely do." I tip my chin at the table. "Get your ass over here and prepare to go down."

She humphs again and walks toward me, sliding past my scooter and into a chair. "You should know that I don't lose, Stag. And I never go down first."

I kick the knee roller aside and open the box, shuffling the cards as I stare into her eyes from across the table. "Care to make things interesting?"

She shakes her head. "You know I've got no money."

I shrug. "Bet something else then."

"No way." She leans toward me, trying to see the cards. "You'll just pick something dumb like making me write the whole paper for you."

"You wish. Tell me what you want if you win."

She taps her chin and stares at me, her dark hair coming loose from her ponytail, almost like her whole body is drawn toward my hands while I'm shuffling. "If I win, I get to borrow your car tomorrow so I can run errands."

I scoff. "I would have lent you the car regardless. But if that's what you really want." I start dealing the illustrated cards, face down.

"Well, what are you playing for?" She looks up at me, equal parts innocent and irritated, fierce and caring.

I deal us each a twelfth card, pressing my index finger into the top of the draw pile in the middle of the table. I stare at her as she bites her teeth into her plump lip, thinking about sinking my teeth into it. I think about how she's so bossy, so regimented, and streamlined and how much I'd love to see her frazzled. I want to see her fall apart, close her eyes, and moan. I really shouldn't ask for what I actually want if I win, but what the fuck do I have to lose? I lean back and cross my arms. "If I win, I get to watch you get off."

CHAPTER 11
THORA

I LICK MY LIPS AND STARE INTO THE BEAUTIFUL, CHISELED FACE OF ODIN STAG. Did he really just say he wants to watch me touch myself? I've never done that in front of anyone before. We've been joking about getting frisky, and it's pretty clear we're both into each other. I'm half tempted to counter-offer a full-on sex-fest if he wins, but his offer intrigues me.

"You want to watch me get off? That's it? How is that a treat for you?"

Odin's eyes fly wide, and his head draws back like I just told him the Earth is flat or something. "Are you serious? You don't understand what would be awesome about watching a woman give herself an O?"

I hitch up one shoulder and tap my fingers on the table. "Fine. If that's what you want. Easy. Tell me how to play since you won't win anyway."

Odin grins, one half of his broad mouth hooking up to the side as he explains that we are going to take turns reciting the phrases "taco," "cat," "goat," "cheese," and "pizza." Each of us will flip a card while we speak. If the card matches what we say out loud, the first person to slap the pile wins.

"And there are special cards," he explains, holding up one featuring an illustrated beaver.

"You're serious with this? I thought you'd have some sort of...sophisticated game. Are we really doing beaver faces?"

"Thora," he says, shaking his head. "This is clearly a groundhog." He knocks on the table, shows me a gorilla card, and pounds on his chest. "I don't know what gave you the idea that anyone in this apartment is sophisticated."

461

That draws a laugh from me, and I watch as he shuffles again. We begin. We trade wins for a few hands, each of us gently slapping the table when I say pizza and flip a pizza card, and he says goat and reveals a cute little horned critter.

But then, we stop being gentle. I see his stack of cards growing taller, and I'm a little more vigorous bringing my hand down on the top of the heap. "Yes," I hiss, ignoring the feel of my nails digging into his palm. He winces and frowns, his face going serious. With a nod, he picks up the pace.

"Goat," he says, flipping up a narwhal, and I immediately clap my hands together over my head as if they were a horn. The whole thing is absolutely absurd, and I'm having more fun than I've had in months.

We're about even when the door to the apartment opens, and his room-mates limp in, groaning about practice. Stellan looks over at us, and his face brightens. "Will you deal me in?"

"No," Odin and I both yell simultaneously. He quickly flips a card, saying, "cat," and I follow rapidly with an emphatic "goat."

Odin's eyes don't leave mine as he flips cards. He must be staring at the deck with his peripheral vision, a skill he thinks he has over me as an athlete. But a bartender uses every part of her eyeballs, too. I can spot a hand waving for a drink from a crowded corner and a wedge of illustrated Swiss just as easily. "Cheese!" I wail, slamming my hand down…on top of a hunk of muscle and tendons.

"Gotta be faster if you want that sweet SUV, Jansson." Odin cackles as he straightens his cards. The other Stag guys take a seat at the table, watching us as they cram tuna in their mouths straight from the can. I don't know if I've ever been that hungry in my whole life, but I have never played Division One sports.

Odin's brother Gunnar peeks at Odin's card stack and whistles through his teeth. "Getting close to a W, bro." Gunnar looks at me. "Think you can beat him if you draw a gorilla?"

Odin and I ignore the banter and the stench of tuna, flipping cards and slapping at a pace that has my heart racing. Soon, the pile in the center of the table has at least 20 cards on it, and tension thrums thick in the air of the apartment.

Gunnar and Stellan lean forward, fascinated, but I will myself into the zone. I don't even really care about borrowing Odin's car, and I'd probably get myself off in front of him for free, if I'm honest. It's been too long since I used my pocket rocket, and I really should take care of that tonight, now that I'm all keyed up from this stupid card game.

But I want to beat him. I want to watch Odin's eyes flash in frustration when I win, and I want to see how he responds and hear what he'll say when I rub his defeat in his smug, sexy face. Is this why people play sports? God, this is invigorating. "PIZZA," I bellow, turning up a card that features a grinning kitty.

Odin purrs, although I don't think it's on purpose. His brothers elbow each other in anticipation. Whoever wins this hand will undoubtedly win the deck. I only have one card left. Odin tosses out a grinning slice of pepperoni as his deep voice shouts, "TACO," and time stops before I flip my final card.

I say the word cat but don't glance down soon enough. Odin notices the gorilla and leaps to his foot, pounding his chest before bringing his giant palm down onto the heap of cards. It's over. He's won. And he's not being coy about it. "Yessss," he roars, pumping his fists in the air.

And then, before I can register what's happening, he grabs his knee roller with one hand and hauls me over his shoulder with the other. We're gliding toward his bedroom like luggage on a baggage belt, and he dumps me onto his bed with a bounce, standing over me, chest heaving, looking sexy as fuck in the glow of his desk lamp.

I tuck my hair behind my ears and try to catch my breath as he stares at me. Odin drags a palm down his chin, chest rising and falling dramatically. "Fuck, Thora, I'm sorry. You okay?"

I laugh. "Yeah, I'm great. That was…something." Odin sits in his desk chair and kicks his knee roller away, propping his booted foot on the end of his mattress. His room is one long tube with a giant bed at the far wall and a dresser opposite the desk. There's a second door I assumed was a closet, but Odin hooks a thumb toward it and explains, "There's a bathroom if you need to get yourself ready."

"Get myself ready?" I arch a brow and lean back against his headboard. He has an actual headboard! I have a shitty twin mattress on a futon frame. I'm sure my parents dumpster dove for it when I was in elementary school.

A slow smile spreads across Odin's entire face, like a cat about to go after the leftovers from Gunnar's tuna feast. "I'm claiming my prize, Thora. So, let's see it."

I look around the room and bite my lip. "Oh. Okay, so here's the thing…"

CHAPTER 12
ODIN

I HAVEN'T BEEN HARD SINCE MY SURGERY. I REALIZE THIS WITH STUNNING clarity as my dick swells to life at the thought of Thora touching herself in my bed. I don't know if it's the pain meds or the brain fog, or the crushing reality of my future being destroyed, but my cock has been as limp as my prospects since my tendon exploded.

"So, here's the thing," she starts, but she doesn't look like she wants to call things off.

"Tell me, beautiful." I lean forward, hands on the arms of my desk chair, ready to jump into action.

Thora squishes her face, wrinkling her adorable nose and pursing her plump lips. "I need battery backup if this is going to work, and I didn't exactly pack for a sex party when I left for class this morning."

I nod. "Okay. Anything else?"

She looks surprised by my calm, and her eyes dart around my room like she's looking for a vibrating dildo. "Well, I usually use a book. And…"

"And?" I bring my good foot to the floor and lean forward, hands on my thighs.

She waves a hand at my bedroom door. "I actually have the book…in my bag. I was going to read it on the bus home later."

I puff out a laugh. "You read your sex book on the bus?"

She frowns. "It has a good story, too. It just…also has good sex in it…"

"Right," I grunt and hop up to my feet, lunging for the knee roller.

"Wait. Where are you going?" Thora jumps off the bed and follows me as I make my way to the kitchen. I stretch my arm up on top of the fridge and grab the basket we keep up there as Thora scurries over to her backpack and picks it up.

Stellan, Gunnar, and my twin brothers stare at us as I wink at them and roll back to the bedroom with Thora hot on my wheels. Thankfully, they don't say anything rude that might spook her. I need this, damn it.

Thora closes the door behind her and perches on the edge of my bed, pulling a tattered paperback from her bag and dropping the bag to the floor. "Why do you have an Easter basket?" She tilts her head at the bundle on my lap, and I grin.

I crack my knuckles and explain, "My mom and aunts stock a 'safe and satisfied' kit for the apartment." I pull a strip of condoms from the top of the basket, followed by a carton of Plan B. Thora crawls up on her hands and knees to get a better look, and I let myself imagine her doing that naked. I bet I can fit her entire boob in my mouth—like a tiny apple. I decide I'll ask her to touch her nipples while she's giving me my prize in a few minutes.

I keep digging in the basket, searching for what she needs. She squints. "Is that a pamphlet for PreP?"

"Yeah." I shrug. "Why?"

She shakes her head. "Why would you guys need that? Unless…"

I clear my throat. "My brother is bi, actually, but the basket isn't just for us." I chuckle. "We're supposed to share with all our friends. Aha!" I find what I've been looking for and hold up the box.

Thora's eyes fly wide as saucers. "A cock ring?"

I nod. "A vibrating cock ring." I toss her the box. "And now it's yours, even though you don't have a cock for it."

She stares at the picture of the blue silicone ring with a vibrating nub meant for his pleasure *and* his partner's. Thora's eyes go from mine to the box and back before a crazed laugh escapes her throat. "Wow. This is unexpected, Odin."

I prop my boot back on the bed and cross my good leg over it. I lace my fingers together behind my head and lean back in my chair. "We good? 'Cause I'm ready when you are."

Thora's whole demeanor shifts. Her eyes drop to my crotch, and I let her look at the growing bulge I've got stretching out my shorts. Eventually, I'll drop a hand down there and give it a squeeze, but for now, I'm just looking forward to the show. What will it even look like when this feisty woman goes after her clit with the toy?

Thora licks her lips again and reaches for her book. It falls open to a page she appreciates, and I nod, encouraging her. "Read out loud," I demand, and she actually blushes. Again. "Oh, honey. Is that too much for you?"

Thora gives me a look and tugs down the zipper on her jeans. I grab my phone and put on a playlist at max volume. Even still, I hear the hum as she activates the toy, which thankfully came charged in the box because I was probably going to cry if we had to wait an hour for it to juice up. She adjusts her posture and leans back against the headboard, which lifts her tits a little more and gives me a nicer view of her hand moving up and down slowly inside her pants. I see that she's inside her underwear with the toy and I wonder if she's shaved bare or if she has dark pubic hair. I think about asking her, but she starts to read from the book.

"Linus knew he shouldn't be looking through the ferns by the creek, but he couldn't help himself as Sally hiked up her skirts, revealing creamy white ankles and trim calves that seemed sculpted from marble."

"That's what turns you on?" I lean forward, adjusting my legs so I can sit up.

Thora glares. "It gets hotter. It's kind of what we're doing, actually."

"Yeah? Sally's gonna get herself off in the creek?"

Thora blushes some more and then lets out a little gasp because she's still got the toy on her clit. The book falls out of her hand, and I stretch until I can just reach it. "Let me see." I take the book and watch as Thora settles herself back on the bed. As if she can read into my fantasies, she drops one hand to her nipple, which I can see pebbled beneath her t-shirt. "Fuck," I whisper, thumbing to the dog-eared page.

"As Linus crouched, he nearly gasped aloud when Sally's hand continued reaching higher and higher beneath her shift until she surely reached her quim. He steeled himself so he didn't fall into the water as he continued to watch the woman he had no business wanting as she touched herself in broad daylight in the creek beside her traitorous father's cabin. Shit, Thora. What is this?" I look over the book and see her mouth half open, eyes hooded. Fuck me, I can smell her arousal, rich and spicy, behind the sweet smell of her detergent and whatever perfume she wears. "You really do get off on this, don't you, gorgeous?"

"Keep reading," she moans, the hand down her pants moving more intentionally as her nipple hand rubs faster.

"There is no fucking way I can concentrate on this book while you're making those sounds, Thora."

She opens her eyes, seemingly surprised that she has, in fact, been making noises. But oh, has she. Tiny inhalations, shuddering gasps. I memorize every single one, planning to use them all later as I brutalize my cock in the shower. "Look at you," I whisper. "You're fucking close, aren't you?"

She nods her head, and I hear a zing as she must crank up the speed on the cock ring. I long to jump onto the bed beside her, to watch or even join in, but our bet was that she would get herself off, and the prize is so much sweeter than I ever expected. Thora Janssen has lost all her composure, all semblance of haughtiness. I might as well not even be here as she tweaks her nipple and rolls her hips, and presses that toy into her clit.

"Your pussy needs to come, doesn't she," I say, eyes fixed on the body part in question.

"Oh, god," she whines, and her hips fly up off the bed.

"Yeah, Thora, work that clit with my cock ring. Let me see, gorgeous. Fuck, that's perfect." I drop the book and press a hand to my dick as Thora comes, thrashing around on my bed with her eyes closed and her lips pressed tightly together.

I'm overcome with the need to do this again, to see if I can get her to scream. To insist that she yell my name before I let her come. I'm desperate, I realize, to touch her.

"Can I kiss you?" I'm out of the chair and perched next to her on the mattress before she can respond, needing to be closer to her body after... all of that.

Her mouth drops open, and then she presses her lips together. "I don't know, Odin..."

"Right. Right." I sit on the mattress but let my hand fall to her leg, and she seems to like that, so I rub some small circles on her jeans. Her breathing slows to regular as we sit and stare at each other.

Her hand drops to her side as she tries to calm down. I watch her chest rise and fall, slower and slower, until her breathing appears normal, and she zips up her pants. She must have clicked off the cock ring because she stares at it, silent and still and bright blue in her palm. "Where, um, should I put this?"

I close her fingers around the toy and squeeze her hand, relishing that contact with her. Shit, I'm wild for her. "It's yours, Thora. Nobody else is gonna use it."

"Not even you?" She gives me a look that makes me wish I had two good legs so I could slam her up against the door and fuck her senseless.

Eventually, she sets the toy on my pillow before gathering her hair and attempting to put it in a ponytail. "So, I need to get home."

I shake my head. "No way. It's late. I'm not letting you go out there alone, and I can't handle the stairs right now."

"Well, Mr. Bossy, I still have to run those errands tomorrow, and I want to get an early start since the buses run less often on Saturday."

I dig around in the dish on my desk until I find my keys, and I toss them to her. I'm happy to see her catch them with one hand. She's competent at this shit, and it's fucking hot. "Take the car. I can't drive it anyway."

She shakes her head. "That wasn't part of the deal. I lost the game."

I scratch my chin and stare at her, thinking. I sigh. "Okay, what if you drive me to PT, and then it's a favor for me, and you can use the car to get Sally a new shift or whatever the hell you have to do." I point to the book on my desk.

Thora's cheeks turn pink again. "Sally's shift is just fine." She stares at the wall, seeming to consider her options, and she shakes the keys in her hand. "What time do you need to be picked up? I guess I could take you. You're sure I can use the car?"

"Thora. Do I look like the kind of person who says shit I don't mean?" I cross my arms over my chest as she laughs and nods, reaching for her bag.

"Okay, okay. What time?"

I tell her to grab me at nine, and then she's gone, shoving my keys in her pocket like they belong there. I realize too late that she's forgotten the book, so I pick up where I left off, glancing through the chapter to read about Linus watching Sally whack off in the ferns. And then he can't help himself and has to touch his own turgid member, which reminds me again of the first boner I've sprung in two weeks.

I look at my bed, where the blue cock ring sits on my pillow like a kinky hotel treat. I adjust my body to my usual side of the bed, which now smells like Thora, and move the ring to my nightstand. I finish reading the chapter growing harder than before.

I slide my hand down my shorts and give my cock a squeeze, remembering how Thora looked in my bed, touching herself, pinching that tiny nipple. Fuck, she just let herself go all the way to oh-town while I watched. I give myself one more hard tug, remembering the shape of her mouth as she came, and I'm erupting all over my shirt.

I shiver with the force of my release, warm cum spurting everywhere like it's been pressurized for a month, and someone opened the faucet. That would be Thora, I guess. I yank off my shirt and use it to half-assedly clean myself up, dabbing at the white gunk on my stomach, and I realize I got jizz all over Thora's book. "Shit," I mutter, trying to mop it up with the shirt, but the ink smears, and the pages are already starting to wrinkle. "Fuck it," I mutter, reaching to turn off my light. Before I fall asleep, I vow to grab her a new copy of the book while she's out running errands in the morning.

DAD GRUNTS AT ME FROM THE COUCH AS I WALK IN THE FRONT DOOR ON shaky legs. I'm a tiny bit nervous Odin's car will get sideswiped while parked on my street overnight, but he parks it on the street at his place, so he's probably got fancy collision insurance.

I was *not* expecting tonight to happen. I had the most intense orgasm I've ever had with another person…by myself. I'm not exactly sure what happened, to be honest. But it was hot as fuck. I give my father a tip of my chin on my way through the living room. I need to get into my room where I can breathe and call Fern.

But Dad grabs my arm on the way past. "Grab your old man a cold one while you're up?"

I press my lips together. I hate enabling him. His ankle monitor certainly doesn't impede him from walking to the kitchen, and I seriously doubt he left the couch today to move his body, look for work, or do anything at all helpful to our family. Mom has been working doubles at Ritter's since Dad got arrested, plus picking up serving shifts with Fern and me at the sports stadiums on weekends.

I sigh. I'll be out of here soon, and once I finish my fellowship, I'm not moving back into this house, no matter what. I'll have better financial prospects by then. "Sure, Dad," I mutter, hurrying to the fridge and grabbing a can of Milwaukee's Best Lite from the door, where it's crammed in among the expired mayonnaise and barbecue sauce.

I toss it to my father as I walk to the stairs, and he hollers. "You're gonna shake it up, Thora. What the hell are you doing that for?" I shake my head and hear the fizz as he opens the can regardless. I don't look back as he slurps at the foaming beer. I'm already dialing my best friend's number as I dart into my room, where I immediately spray myself with air freshener. I spend way too much on this stuff, but it's worth it to me not to have to walk around campus smelling like an ashtray. At least, I hope I can mask the stench.

Fern picks up, voice groggy. "'Lo? Thora?"

"Oh my god, you won't believe what happened," I blurt, recapping my evening with Odin.

"Wait," she interrupts. "I thought you were just going over there to work on your project?"

"Oh, we worked on it." I sink onto my bed and kick off my shoes. "And then…we did the other thing."

I hear her suck in a slow breath and whistle. "So, he didn't join in? He just watched?"

"He fucking told me what to do and sat there watching. Then I left, and I'll pick him up for PT in the morning. I have his car."

"Huh." Fern yawns, then says, "I had no idea Odin had all that in him. He usually just jokes around and plays video games when I'm over at Wyatt's."

I unhook my bra and get ready for bed. "I think maybe his injury has fucked with his head. He's different in class, too. I don't know how to explain it."

Fern tells me the whole Stag family has been worried about Odin, how he is ignoring calls from the university, and his father is worried about his mental health. It feels like a violation to hear this third hand from Odin's cousin's girlfriend. "I guess it's none of my business."

"Sorry. So, it was good? You don't usually…finish with guys."

I smile. She's right. I enjoy sex. I have a lot of it when I want to. Sometimes, I can boss a guy around and convince him to work my vibrator into the action, but more often, they get all huffy about the suggestion and leave me on the precipice to finish up later, on my own. "He seemed really into it. But what does it mean?"

"Does it have to mean anything?" Fern asks this as if she's some sort of expert rather than an intellectual currently enjoying her first-ever relationship.

"I have no actual idea," I tell her. While I'm not really one for repeats with guys, I also don't sleep with dudes I'm going to see again unless they happen to stroll back into the bar, in which case I just sort of ignore them until they go away. I sigh. "I need to try to sleep before I spend the day tomorrow with the guy."

Fern giggles. "Update me when you're back. Oh, are you getting your visa and stuff tomorrow?"

I shake my head, even though she can't see that. "Tomorrow is professional attire at the thrift shop. Maybe multiple shops since I have free transportation." We hang up the phone with me promising to share outfit photos and her promising to come with me to the post office to get my passport as soon as I have the money.

———

In the morning, I drive Odin's beast of a car back to retrieve him, enjoying the heated seats even if the SUV is too big to comfortably make tight turns in Pittsburgh's narrow streets. I shouldn't have tried to wend my way through Bloomfield back to his place, but it's too late now as I sing along to the radio while gingerly navigating the Belgian Block side roads.

Even with the fancy shocks in Odin's bougie car, I feel the rumble of the tires along the uneven granite bricks until my bones rattle. If I drove any faster, I might not need to use a vibe to get myself off. But I'm not going to think about sex in Odin's car. I'm taking him to a medical appointment.

I'm surprised to see him waiting outside when I arrive. I suspect he got his roommates to help him down all the stairs before they left for practice or whatever because Odin looks like he's been leaning on the signpost for a long time. "You're late," he says by way of greeting.

I look at the clock on his dash and furrow my brow at him. "How do you figure?"

He tosses his knee roller in the back door and hops on one foot into the passenger seat. "Because I was waiting for you." And then he flashes me a grin, so I know he's just giving me shit, but also still thinking about last night. I can just tell.

I swallow and fiddle with the rearview mirror. "Where am I taking you?"

Odin directs me south of the city to the facility where the professional football team practices. "You get to go here, too?"

He laughs. "We share field space with those guys. And medical staff, too. You can park in the close spots." Odin pulls an accessible parking tag from his hoodie pocket and clips it on the rearview mirror.

"Am I...supposed to wait for you? I don't know how long these things take."

He shrugs and fumbles as he tries to hop around and open the door to get his roller. I unbuckle and race around the car to help him, which seems to frustrate him. "I got it," he snaps. And then his face sags. "Sorry. This is my first appointment. It'll be like two hours. You don't have to wait, but it would be great if you could be back around eleven."

I shrug and hold the scooter in place while Odin adjusts his weight on the knee cushion. "The store I need doesn't open 'til ten anyway, and I wouldn't make it back in time once I got going."

We start to roll through the building and Odin doesn't even stop to look at signs. He must be pretty familiar with this sort of injury treatment. I wonder what else he's hurt through his years of playing elite football. We stop outside a wall of windows, looking in on a huge gym full of machines and padded tables and shirtless men grunting. Muscles flex as they lift themselves and lunge and pedal furiously on exercise bikes. "Wow," I say, totally distracted by the peak physical forms on display in front of us.

"Relax, Janssen," Odin grunts with the effort of opening the door for himself and wheeling through it. I can't believe they don't have one of those buttons to open the door, considering the people coming through it are presumably all injured. Again, I try to help him, and again, he growls and looks pissed off by the gesture.

There doesn't seem to be a waiting room, so I just follow him until we're greeted by a friendly woman in a polo shirt and shorts. "Hey, you must be Odin." She extends a hand, the other holding a clipboard. "I'm Prachi, and I'll be torturing you today." Odin laughs and shakes her hand while my eyes fly wide. I guess black humor is the norm here. Prachi glances at me. "Did you want to hang out in the lounge while Odin works?"

I glance at Odin for guidance, but he just slumps on his scooter, looking forlorn as the pro team's quarterback hops past us on one leg, then the other. I should probably be starstruck, considering sports are a religion here in Pittsburgh. Maybe it's the orgasm hangover, but I feel pretty chill. The only athlete I'm thinking about is the one pouting beside me. He doesn't suggest I stay and watch, though, so I guess I'm heading to the lounge. "Sure. Where is it again?"

Prachi directs me down a hall to the cushiest room I'll ever hang out inside. There are luxurious armchairs, trays of fresh fruit, and a fancy coffeemaker, plus little signs with the Wi-Fi password and bottles of sparkling water in a clear-front fridge. Athletes and their drivers apparently lead different sorts of lives than me, and I try to imagine Fern enjoying this sort of thing with Wyatt once they're settled in the UK. He just signed with a professional soccer team in London, so I'm sure this will be old hat for her soon enough. I text her a selfie from one of the chairs, a bunch of grapes in my hand and a bottle of San Pellegrino tucked under my elbow.

I wish I'd thought to bring my backpack. I don't even have a book with me, which reminds me that I left my copy of *The Redcoat* in Odin's room last night after… after. I'll have to make do with my phone to entertain myself, and I discover that the library has an eBook copy of the sequel to my beloved historical romance by Chloe Petals. I know she lives in Pittsburgh, but I've never had a chance to meet her.

I munch on the grapes and read nearly half the book on the library app before my phone starts ringing in my hand, startling me. It's Odin calling and then texting, telling me to get my ass outside to his car so we can leave.

I grab an apple for him since he's clearly hangry, and smile when I see him leaning against the car, a little sweaty and a lot irritated. "Session go that well?" I tease, unlocking the doors.

He grunts and tosses his scooter in the back. When we're both situated with the radio playing, I start to back out of the parking spot. "Am I taking you home?"

"Where's your errand?"

"Oh," I explain, "You don't want to come along on that one. I'm going clothes shopping."

His brows go up. "You gonna try shit on?"

I flush and nod. Why am I always blushing around this guy? I don't know if I've ever blushed in my life, but something about him makes me feel…vulnerable. Odin grins and rubs his hands along his thighs. "I'm coming with you." I shrug, not sure what to make of this development or even if this sexy, enormous football player would fit inside the dressing room at the thrift shop. I get the car turned toward the Birmingham Bridge so we can cross the Monongahela River. "That reminds me," he says, "I have to tell you something."

"What?" I ask, rolling my eyes. "You want a rematch?"

"No, smart-ass," he retorts, "I just—"

But I don't get to hear what he just did because right at that moment, there's a huge bang, and the car starts swerving like crazy on the bridge with six lanes of traffic.

CHAPTER 14
ODIN

"Oh my god, oh my god, oh my god," Thora chants as she grips the wheel and slams on the brakes. I hear a chorus of horns wailing around us as cars pass while my G Wagon swerves through traffic.

I clench my jaw, helpless, until she brings us to a stop in the bike lane, the bridge shaking and vibrating under the rush of cars and semis continuing to zoom along its span. "Fuck," I mutter, dragging a hand through my hair.

And then I look over at her, hands over her face, shoulders shaking. "Hey," I squeeze her arm. "You did perfect. We're safe." A car honks, and Thora shrieks, stabbing at the button for the flashers. "Perfect," I repeat, catching my breath. What the hell happened here?

Thora's breathing rapidly in little short puffs and won't make eye contact. She just keeps saying, "I'm so sorry. I'm so fucking sorry. I will make it up to you."

"Hey," I tilt my head to try and find her gaze. "Hey, Thora, I'm not mad." She snaps her eyes to mine, and she looks terrified. I concentrate on keeping my voice level. "This isn't your fault."

She shakes her head. "I will have to pay you back for the damage. I can pick up a few shifts and get you the money after finals and—"

"Hey," I try to rub a thumb along her hand where she's still white-knuckling the steering wheel. Someone put a huge dose of terror into this woman, and I want to strangle whoever made her react this way to what's probably just a flat tire. "Thora, I wouldn't expect you to pay to fix my car, okay? Let's go see what happened?"

She blinks, like she's trying to hold back tears, and I see her throat working as she swallows. "You're not mad?"

"I am not mad. Not even a little bit." And it's true. I'm enjoying myself with her a hell of a lot more than I enjoyed that session of PT, where I learned just how little I'm able to do with my right leg and how the fuck long it will be until I can wear a shoe, let alone walk…let alone run.

Thora whispers, "You're not mad," like it's her new mantra, and I watch her puff out a long, relieved breath before she claps her hands and transforms into a different person—the Thora I'm more familiar with. "Okay, so where's your jack and tire iron?"

She hops out of the car and walks around back before I can maneuver myself out, clinging to the door for balance as I work to keep my bad foot off the pavement. The front passenger tire seems to have exploded, which reminds me that I was supposed to get new tires this spring but kept putting it off because of football practice, and then, well, I thought the car wouldn't be going anywhere. "Shit, Thora, this is my fault. I was supposed to get these babies changed months ago."

Thora squats on the ground near the back seat, grunting as she lifts part of the floor, which I didn't realize was removable. She pulls out the tire iron, dropping it to the ground with a clang. I scratch my chin and reach for my knee roller in the back seat right before Thora flips it up and extracts a jack from beneath it. "How do you know where all this shit is in my car?"

She shrugs. "My uncle works on cars." She starts walking around to the back and flipping open the cover to the spare tire. "Well," she adds. "He probably runs a chop shop."

I flinch. "So, you know how to change a tire, but you were freaking out about doing it?" Cars whiz past us on the bridge, and Thora seems not to notice. She starts lining things up by the passenger side of the car.

"Um," she mutters, "Poor people don't usually drive reliable cars. I know my way around a donut." I notice she doesn't say anything about the freaking out part.

I stare as she works. "At my house, my dad always deals with spare tires." I'm not even sure if we've ever had a flat before, come to think of it, but Thora's mention of not having a lot of money makes sense since I'm pretty certain my parents have always kept up with car maintenance until my dumb ass came along.

"Yes, well, some of us have dads in and out of jail rather than keeping up with inspections." Thora frowns. "I'm not going to be strong enough to loosen the nuts, even if I jump on the tire iron."

"You're not jumping on the tire iron on the Birmingham bridge, Thora." I frown at the situation. Not only can I not play the sport I've spent my entire life dominating, but I also can't even change a fucking tire with my—what is Thora exactly? Anyway, with a woman in the car.

"Don't tell me what to do, Stag." She starts to stomp on the wrench, but it doesn't move. She can't weigh much more than a hundred pounds, and I know she's strong because she hauled the tire over here, but she's not "D1 football player strong." And neither am I—not anymore.

I stare down at my useless foot, resting on a wheeled assistive device. I'm about to pull out my phone and call my parents when Thora says, "I think what we need to do is balance your knee on my leg since I won't roll away, and then you stomp the lever with your good foot."

I blink at her. The idea is fucking weird, and the physics of it sounds wild, but I'd rather give it a try than have to call my mom to come get me when I'm out with a woman I want to see naked. "Hmm," I grumble.

Thora kneels on the ground like she's about to propose and pats her thigh. "Put the boot-knee here. You can hold onto the roof since you're a thousand feet tall." She's right about all of it, and when I finally get myself lined up and take an experimental stomp on the tire iron, we both hoot in celebration as the nut loosens with a screech. "I can't believe that worked." She grins, bending to move the tools to the next nut on the tire.

We work our way around, me grunting with effort and nearly falling, her stoically bearing the pressure of my awkward body, and then I stand by like an asshole while she jacks up my car and changes the rest of the tire. I snap a picture of her with my phone since she looks hot as fuck, with her face streaked with dirt as she tightens a lug nut on a six-figure car.

Which she shouldn't have to do when she's out with me. I realize she wouldn't even be here with me right now if I weren't broken, and I slide my phone back in my shorts pocket without looking at the pic.

A slamming sound shakes me out of my drama, and Thora walks back toward me, wiping her hands on her jeans. "I think I got it on there. Do you want to check the tire before I put the tools back?"

I grimace. "Why would I want to check?"

Her face tightens, and I can tell that she is not only used to people yelling at her, but she also somehow doesn't have confidence that her work is suitable, which means someone probably spent a lot of years screaming at her that she's not good enough.

What's my mom always saying about emotional regulation? Thora clearly didn't grow up with a lot of it around. "Right," she says, tipping her head toward the driver's side. "Well, let's get back in, I guess."

It takes just a few snaps and thumps for Thora to get the car put back together while I climb inside, fishing around the console for hand sanitizer and napkins. I present these to her, and she smiles like I just got her roses, so I decide I should definitely do that later to thank her for putting my car back in working order. "That was incredible," I tell her, turning in my seat and draping an arm behind hers. "You were amazing, you know that?"

She shakes her head. "I was a mess." I swallow a retort because now doesn't seem like the time to dive into her trauma.

"Hey, will you let me buy your outfit or whatever? I owe you big time for changing the tire."

She puffs out a laugh. "You owe me? I probably drove over a piece of glass or something stupid."

"Don't talk that way." I let my voice get stern and realize that's probably not the best way to talk to someone who is obviously upset. "I told you," I say with much more intentional calm. "I was supposed to get new tires, but I kept putting them off, and then I got hurt. This is on me. And no offense, but you'd have to have driven over a long stretch of razor wire to blow performance tires, baby."

"Hey." She snaps her eyes to me as she turns over the engine. "Do not call me baby. I know I'm small, but I am not diminutive."

No, you're fucking not, I think, but what I say is, "Don't pout like one, and I won't call it as I see it, Janssen." She seems to be sliding back into her usual self.

She snorts and turns off the four-ways, easing back onto the bridge toward Oakland. "Oh," she looks at me. "Where should we go? I guess we have to find a tire place?"

"The Mercedes place is on Baum. Weren't you going to some store on Liberty Ave? We can just do your errand first and drop the car after. I assume you won't go over—what's the speed limit for the spare tire?"

Thora pats my leg. "Now, who's a baby? We'll drive the speed limit and be just fine. But are you sure you don't want to go right to the dealer? I don't want you—"

"We are running your errand, and that's final," I bark. She nods and heads toward the Bloomfield Bridge. If I squint, I can probably find her house from up here, and I consider rolling up there with my brothers and cousins to scream in her father's face and see how he likes it. Between her mentioning prison and her obvious fear that I was going to berate her for a normal flat tire, he seems like he's probably a real piece of shit.

But my time is better spent building Thora up than worrying about someone who is not worth that kind of effort, especially since I can't physically intimidate anyone at the moment.

"I'm buying you an outfit," I say again, impressed as Thora parallel parks along Liberty near a row of shops. I point to a fancy clothing store I've heard my mom mention. "Let's go find you something in there."

She huffs at me, and I ignore her, rolling up to the boutique...where I discover I can't even get in the fucking store because it's got stairs outside.

"Hey," Thora places a warm hand on my arm. "You don't have to buy me anything, Odin. And I'm pretty sure the thrift store has an accessible ramp."

I flip the bird at the bullshit shop and scowl when a store worker sees me, eyes wide through the window. Whatever.

"I better fit inside the dressing room with you," I mutter to Thora, who laughs and shakes her head. We walk a block to the thrift store that does indeed have a ramp to enter.

"You wish, Stag." But her cheeks flush as she pushes open the door to the crowded shop, waiting for me to wheel inside with her.

ODIN DOES NOT, IN FACT, FIT INTO THE DRESSING ROOM OF THE THRIFT STORE. It's more of a shower stall, honestly, but Odin barely fits in the store at all. He's just such a huge human being, made bigger with his cast and scooter.

I walk up and down the aisles, searching for "professional research fellow vibe" pieces, and Odin creaks behind me, grumbling that there's no room for him. A dress catches my eye, and I lean past my companion. Spotting the original price tag on the shiny material, I gasp, startling Odin, who furrows his brow. "What?"

"It's new with tags. Oh! And it's my size. I have to try it on immediately." I shoulder past him toward the dressing room, and I hear him following. I wouldn't even know what it meant to find an Alice + Olivia dress in a Pittsburgh second-hand store except for Fern, and I have been daydreaming over an issue of *Vogue* someone left at the bar.

The polo sweater dress has white trim and fancy houndstooth buttons with a really fun spread collar. I'm not even sure what the black fabric is, but the whole thing slides on like it was made with me in mind. I am almost totally flat-chested with no hips to speak of, but as I tug the dress over my head and smooth it along my body, I want to cry because I look amazing. Somehow, this form-fitting dress makes my form look more feminine. I purr as I run my hands along my hips, staring into the tiny mirror in the dim light.

The sound must trigger Odin's impatience because he snaps the curtain open and then freezes when he sees me in the dress. I watch him taking me in, enjoying the obvious lust in his eyes as he stares at me in the $500 dress I'm about to buy for $6.99. His throat works as he swallows before saying, "You're getting that, right?" I nod, smiling. I start to imagine wearing it for him, which is stupid because he's my research partner, whom I fooled around with briefly. There will be no wearing things *for* or with him. Odin grunts. "I have to get out of here. I'll meet you outside in what? Half an hour?"

"Do you need me to go? I can take the car to the dealership as soon as I pay for this—"

He shakes his head. "I told you I'm buying you that outfit. I just need to…" He rubs at the back of his neck and gestures with the fingers gripping his scooter handle. "I don't fit in here." Odin reaches into his pocket, pulls out a wallet, and presses a twenty into my hand. "Half an hour?"

I nod as I watch him go and then work quickly to find a few more new-to-me outfits for my new life abroad. When I'm wearing these things, I don't look like someone whose father orders her to get him a shitty beer.

These are the clothes of a person with regulated emotions and enough of a cushion to approach an emergency with calm. I can't afford these clothes brand new, but I can sneak into them second-hand. I can reuse someone's discard, giving it a second life. I should have given Odin the money back, but something tells me he'd be weird about it, so I splurge a little on a pair of flats that go perfectly with the dress *and* slacks and a boat-neck top I imagine I'll wear while I walk along the Isis river in Oxford.

CHAPTER 16
ODIN

I WAS SECONDS AWAY FROM COMING IN MY PANTS AFTER SEEING THORA IN THAT dress. It's not even a slutty dress. In fact, it's super professional, which is what she said she wanted. But it clung to her body in ways that set off deeply unprofessional thoughts in my caveman brain.

If she weren't excited about how fancy it is, I would probably take her somewhere and rip it off her. Except I can't do the things I want to do to her because I only have one functional foot. That awareness calms my dick right down, and I wheel down the block toward the bookstore, remembering that I never did get to confess that I ruined Thora's book.

Thankfully, the bookstore has an accessible entrance *and* wide aisles, so I wheel myself inside in search of the romance section. This is where I find my mother...laughing and fiddling with boxes of books along with my Aunt Emma and one of her friends.

I stand there with my mouth hanging open, irrationally wondering if my mom somehow knew what I did to ruin the book I came here to replace.

I eventually realize that's ridiculous and wheel my way over toward her. And she clutches at her chest like she's about to faint. "Odin! You're out and about!" Mom clamps a hand on Aunt Emma's shoulder, and my aunt pats it supportively.

"I do leave the house, Mom. Come on."

She shakes her head. "Of course you do, sweetheart. It's just all those stairs. And you've been so grouchy when Dad and I have tried to call or stop by. Did you find the soup Dad left you?"

"Yeah. Thank you." I stare at the floor for a beat. "I know I've been in a mood. But I've also been leaving the house more."

"Well, what brings you in here? Did you come to help set up for the event?" Mom points at a sign, which informs me that Aunt Emma will be in conversation with Chloe Petals here at the bookstore, talking about the crossover between nonfiction sports books and the historical romance Chloe will soon release about Pittsburgh rowers in the 1800s. Mom, an Olympic gold medalist in rowing, is apparently the host of the event.

"I had no idea any of this was happening," I admit, fidgeting with my scooter, wondering how our entire family is going to fit in this tiny bookstore, let alone members of the public.

Aunt Emma grins. "We've sort of kept this one tight. I know the Stag herd is supportive, but this is more for our rabid fans. Well. Mostly Chloe's rabid fans."

And then the name clicks. Chloe Petals wrote the very book I'm here to replace. Chloe Petals is Mom's friend Chloe, whose real last name is definitely not Petals. I snap my eyes to the smiling woman stacking books by my aunt. I point at her. "You wrote *The Redcoat*."

She laughs. "I sure did. But you're not the demographic I was expecting. You've read it?"

My cheeks heat, which is really saying something because I'm always the guy who has no problem running to the pharmacy for condoms for my football teammates. "I read parts of it. I actually need to replace my friend's copy because I…spilled something on hers."

Chloe beams and turns around, reaching into one of the boxes. "Here you go, kiddo. On the house. Oh! Should I sign it?"

"I don't mind paying for the book."

Mom waves a hand and nudges Chloe with her shoulder. "Yes, sign it and tell the friend Odin's mother wants to meet her."

"You already did," I start to explain, the words out of my mouth before I realize the impact that will have. Mom and Aunt Emma clap their hands and Chloe wiggles around like she hit the lottery. They always act this way when one of my brothers or cousins brings home a date, which is why I don't do that.

"When did I meet her?" Mom taps her chin. "I would remember if my son introduced me to a special someone."

I sigh. "Don't call her a *special someone*, Mom. And you know Thora from the student law clinic, apparently. She's my research partner from class."

"Oooh, Thora," Chloe coos. "That's a great heroine name."

Mom squints at me. "Didn't you say you have a project together in a class? Sweetie, I thought you were doing a medical withdrawal? That paperwork is pretty important for NCAA eligibil—"

"Mom, I got it under control, thanks." I don't mean to snap at her, but everyone is always up in my shit about all of this. To Chloe, I explain, "My friend is Thora, T-H-O-R-A, and she's a huge fan."

Chloe scribbles something in the book and snaps it shut, handing it to me. "In that case, you should bring her to the event. It's sold out, but I happen to still have my two guest tickets to give away."

My brows fly up. Thora will bust an ovary if I bring her to see her favorite author in real life. I look at the date on the poster—this coming Thursday. We'll be done with our presentation by then. I realize that I've been sort of dreading the end of our time hanging out together, and this is definitely a way to extend that. Maybe she will wear that dress…

"I'd love that, thank you," I blurt as Mom and Aunt Emma exchange glances. It's no use trying to tell them there's nothing particular going on there. Thora is moving to another country in a few months.

She's also the only person in my life right now who didn't know me as Future Pro Football Player Odin Stag. It's refreshing, having her give me shit and fight with me, just for me. And it helps that she's cute as hell. I can already see her sitting ramrod straight in her seat, hanging on Chloe's every word during whatever conversation they're going to have.

I kiss Mom on the cheek, accept an arm squeeze from Aunt Emma, and salute Chloe with the book as I roll out of the store to find Thora, who is just now exiting her store with a huge plastic bag of clothes.

A smile splits my face, and I don't even care about the uneven sidewalk as I make my way toward her. "Listen," I start. "I never got to tell you my confession, but it's all good because I already made up for what I did."

She leans against the brick wall of the thrift shop, seemingly intrigued. "I forgot that you were telling me you did something bad."

"Oh, I'm bad, sugar." I wink at her and hand her the book. She glances down at it, confused. I lower my voice. "I ruined your book last night, but I got you a signed copy as a replacement."

She drops her bag of clothes on the ground and opens the book, chin dropping, eyes popping wide. "It's signed and personalized? Where did you get this??"

I hook a thumb behind me in the direction of the bookstore. "That's not all, though. There's an event here on Thursday."

She rolls her eyes at me like I'm the biggest idiot in Pittsburgh. "Duh.

It's been sold out for months. I wanted to go with Fern as a sort of farewell adventure."

My heart sinks, knowing I'm going to offer her both tickets and knowing I won't get to see her in the dress again or spend that time with her. I chalk it up to just one more thing I've lost this spring, but I tell her, "Well, I'm about to make your day, I guess." I pull the tickets from my pocket. "VIP seating and all."

Thora blinks at me, speechless. And then she tackles me into the wall with a hug that sends my scooter flying. Propped on one foot, I lean against the wall as Thora pumps her arms around me like she's giving me the Heimlich. "Thank you, thank you, thank you, you big, sexy hero. How do you have this? Are you made of magic?"

When she finally releases me and sees my scooter all tipped over, me perching like a flamingo to keep my boot off the ground, she starts laughing, and I join her because what else is there to do?

Odin keeps texting me to ask when we can finalize everything for our presentation, and I don't know why I'm avoiding his messages. The man got me tickets to meet my favorite author, and I'm leaving him on read.

It's kind of a lie. I'm avoiding him because I'm starting to think of him as more than just my research partner, and that's the sort of thinking that gets a girl in trouble. Nobody needs to explain to me that I'm balanced on a razor blade. Yes, I've been chosen as a Rhodes Scholar. However, the distance between acceptance and showing up in the United Kingdom is nearly insurmountable. I'm one missed bar shift away from not being able to afford all the details I need to get my ass abroad.

Speaking of, I need to see if someone will switch shifts with me so I can actually attend the event with Fern this week. Odin's face was interesting when he gave me the tickets. Like he didn't really want to hand them over or something. I figured out that his mom is on the panel of speakers, so I'm guessing he's anxious about me spending time with her. I will try to compose myself when I apologize to her about being a dick about this school project in his hospital room when he was coming to terms with his injury.

"Thora!" Fern snaps her fingers in my face across the table at lunch. "I've been talking to you for like five minutes."

"Oh. I'm sorry." I slide my phone under my notebook and fork a bite of soggy quinoa from the healthy station in the cafeteria. "I'm ready now."

She shakes her head and forks her own mushy grains. "I was saying,

Friday is my last recitation, and then I'm done. With college. Forever." She beams, actual rays of light shining out of her cheeks.

"It's definitely a weird feeling," I agree, tapping my fingers on my notes for my own math class, where I have definitely not been chosen as the TA like Fern. "It's going to take me a while to shake off the desperation."

"What do you mean?"

I shrug. "We're desperate to get out of here, you and me. Everyone knows it. And it's affected everything about us." She squints, considering, and I lean forward. "I don't own a robe, Fern. That's how little I know how to relax. Do you honestly think we're going to pop off on hikes or watch birds or whatever people do to chill in the U.K.?"

She laughs. "No, but I think we will probably meet up at some soccer matches, right? You'll sit with me to cheer on Wyatt?"

My chest shakes as I try to hold in a laugh. "I've never watched a sporting event in my life, except for what I can see from where I've been working for all of them at the bar or sports arenas." I tap my chin. "Maybe I'll get myself a job tending bar by Wyatt's soccer stadium just to feel normal."

Fern chokes down a final bite of her grain bowl. "I think they call it a football pitch over there. Or something." She pats my hand. "And you won't *need* a job as a bartender. You're going to be financially secure for once."

I nod. "Well, that's what I'm saying. It's going to take adjusting."

We're quiet for a bit until I remember that I haven't told her about the tickets. Her face lights up when I tell her about the bookstore event. "It doesn't go too late," I assure her. "You'll be able to get home in time to get your beauty rest before the final session as, Professor Fern."

"We can sleep when we're old," she says, gesturing for her ticket. "It will be so great to just go do something fun together. We never splurge on this kind of thing."

"Again," I say, tapping the table with my index finger for emphasis. "Adjustment. We are not normal, but we are working on it."

I never respond to Odin's texts before the presentation, but I do send him a detailed email and tell him to wear something nice for class on Tuesday. This makes me feel bad because I realize there's no way he can get dress pants on over his cast. At least, I don't think he can. I put on the dress and literally run out of the house Tuesday morning, so nobody can exhale a single puff of smoke on my new favorite material possession.

I arrive outside the class extra early and gasp when I see Odin in a shirt and tie. I had no idea he'd look like…*this* all dressed up, like a bulky GQ model with his broody blue eyes and perfectly styled hair. Even his earrings look classy, and I let my eyes trail down his body, halting when I get to the usual athletic shorts. A laugh explodes out of me, and he joins in.

He grins. "You said to dress nice."

"Oh my god, Odin, you're killing me." He spins in a circle on his scooter, wagging his butt and making me cry with laughter. "I can't believe you put a shirt and jacket on with mesh shorts."

He leans down and puts his mouth an inch from my ear, making me squirm and cling tightly to my bag when he says, "Make up your mind, Janssen. How do you want me?" And then he draws his head back and winks just as Professor Ferda arrives to open the classroom.

"Hey, you two," our instructor says. "Nice and early. Ready to rock?"

———

Odin has his notes typed on index cards. Not just written but typed and printed. I suddenly feel ill-prepared and sloppy next to him, and I never, ever feel that way about schoolwork. Like I told Fern, I worked my entire life toward this 4.0 undergraduate transcript, but I'm about to be shown up by a guy from the football team who, to my best estimate, only started showing up for class once he got hurt. I realize I'm being unfair because from what he's said and what I've seen, the athletes are pulled in a lot of directions, and they're helpless to go against what their coaches say if they want to keep their scholarships.

I zone out, focusing on his lips moving as I stand next to him, fidgeting in my cute shoes and designer dress. I realize the pattern on his tie matches the black and white houndstooth on my dress buttons and know he must have done that on purpose, based on what he remembered of the dress he only saw me in briefly. I know he is starting to think about me as more than a research partner, too, and that scares me even more. There's a reason I've avoided relationships. I can't afford one. Not yet. I still have too much to achieve.

Resigned to cut him off cold after class, I take a deep breath as he cues me up for my portion of the presentation. I adjust my posture, turn my glance toward the class, and perform the hell out of my piece of the argument.

"THAT WAS AWESOME." MY MOUTH BRUSHES AGAINST THORA'S HAIR AS I LEAN in to whisper in her ear. She flushes, my favorite shade of pink splashing across her cheeks in contrast to her dark hair. Why does she do that? I fucking love it, even if I don't understand that response from someone so obviously capable and kick-ass.

Professor Ferda smiles and gives us a thumbs up as the class titters in applause. I realize everyone is probably waiting for my hobbled ass to get back to my seat so the next group can go. I navigate the narrow space between chairs, bumping into shit with my knee roller.

Then I watch as Thora leans forward in her desk, totally paying attention to the next student presentation. I never, ever pay attention to those. I'm not going to start now, but I do watch as my research partner takes notes and focuses. She's probably deconstructing their arguments already and finding weaknesses.

I could walk out of here right now. I'm supposed to go immediately withdraw from school so I can get my medical delay or whatever it's called. I've stopped even bothering to check my email, so I have no idea how many of my other professors are still reaching out. Right on cue, my phone vibrates in my pocket with a message from Meech, demanding that I roll right up to his office as soon as my presentation ends.

I purse my lips and glance at Thora again. I want to do something with her after class rather than fade into her memory as some guy she knew once. She's about to go be a wizard or whatever at her fancy British school. And what will I be? A college drop-out with no career prospects and nothing to do but rehab an injury. It occurs to me that I'll lose my apartment, too, if I leave school. The Stag pad is in a building for student-athletes. Shit. I was going to stay one more semester until my eligibility ran out, and I left for the pros.

So, really, I'm an injured college drop-out who has to move back in with his parents. Yeah, I'm in no rush to deal with this paperwork.

A flutter of applause alerts me to the fact that the group has finished presenting. I watch Thora raise her hand and ask them if they could elaborate on the bias of one of the sources they used, and I laugh on the inside as she arches a brow in response to their inability to answer. She's not flushing now.

Class ends soon after, and I tug on the sleeve of Thora's sexy dress. "Hey." She turns. She's wearing makeup today, just a little. It makes her eyes look huge and her lips really, really good.

I drag a hand down my cheek. "You want to grab lunch? Celebrate being done?" I hope my voice doesn't give away how desperate I am for her to say yes. Because once she says no, that's it. We're not going to the author event together. We're just two people who did a research project for a class she needed to graduate.

Her face falls. "Oh, I can't today. I work."

I will my expression into a grin even though my insides are crumbling. "Well, then, I guess I'm following you for a drink." She smiles at that, and I'm surprised by the amount of relief I feel. "You going to wear that to tend bar?" I gesture at the dress I know she cherishes. I'm so glad she decided to wear it so I can memorize how it looks on her, highlighting every tiny dip in her figure.

Thora shakes her head. "Nah. I was going to change in the bathroom, and Fern was going to come grab the dress and take it to her place. Nobody smokes there..." Thora drops off like she's revealed too much about herself.

"I can take it to my place for you if that's easier. I know Fern takes the bus..."

Thora laughs, a delightful puff of sound. "Yeah, and you take forever on your scooter thing."

I waggle my brows. "Yes, but I have a basket."

———

I roll back to my place after Thora changes in the bathroom, where I tried desperately not to imagine her naked as she peeled off the dress and slipped into her jeans and tank. I ignore a bunch of texts from Meech and my coach. Instead calling one of my brothers to come run the dress up to my room. While I wait, I tear off my shirt, jacket, and tie, glad I wore a T-shirt underneath all that. I stuff everything in the bag Thora gave me, liking that our nice clothes are hanging out together.

Eventually, Gunny stumbles outside like he just woke up, which might be true since the hockey team is finished for the semester.

"Anything else, your majesty?" He eyes the plastic bag suspiciously and starts to open the snap to look inside.

"Mind your business. But can you run me to the Fuel Up? I'm meeting someone."

Gunnar squints and gives the bag a squeeze. "Someone, eh?"

"Can you take me or not?"

He scratches his nuts and yawns but eventually shrugs. "Yeah, let me go get my keys."

———

My brother drops me off without too much hassle, only cursing twice as he watches me struggle to get my knee scooter out of the back seat. "How much longer will you need that thing?"

I look upward, trying to do some quick math. "Two more weeks, I think. Then I get crutches. Or maybe I can walk in the cast? I have to ask."

He grunts. "That fucking sucks, bro."

"Yeah."

He looks at his phone. "I have class for a few hours. Want me to grab you after?"

I nod and slap the roof of his car. "Thanks for the ride."

When I get inside, Thora is pouring beers with both hands, smiling and wiggling her tiny butt to the music blasting. The place is pretty full. I guess a lot of people are celebrating the end of the semester. Next week are finals and then commencement. I tip my chin at a guy who vacates the end stool at the bar for me. I should care more that I'm this level of incapacitated, but I just don't.

While I wait for Thora to serve me, I realize my parents and uncles must be upset that zero Stag kids are getting their degrees this spring, as expected. Wes is playing pro soccer here in Pittsburgh, Wyatt is playing in London, Stellan is taking an extra year for some reason, and me? Well...

"Get you something?" Thora grins and leans her elbows on the bar in front of me. I don't even pretend not to stare at her tits.

"Shot of Glenfiddich?"

Thora rolls her eyes. "This isn't that kind of place, Odin. Best I can do is Johnnie Walker."

I arch a brow. "But does it have a Stag on the label?"

"I could draw one for you if that makes you feel more included."

I laugh and nod. "It would, thanks. I'll wait while you do that."

Thora flicks the tip of my nose and hops on a stool to grab a bottle of scotch from the top shelf. She pours me more than a shot's worth and slides the glass toward me.

"Wish you could do one of these with me." I look at her above the glass, smelling the warm spice of the liquor.

"I can do a shot of soda." She pours herself some from the nozzle into a plastic cup, which she taps against my shot glass. "Cheers, Odin."

"Skol," I say, making her laugh again. She takes an order from someone else, not even telling me what I owe her, which I guess is fine because I plan to sit here as long as she can stand me. I order a burger and another shot before switching to beer. I'm off the painkillers now, and I'm also off my nutrition plan.

My body doesn't know what to do with all the greasy food and alcohol. I can hear my stomach digesting against its will as Thora waits on a few more people, and then the lunch rush dies down, and I'm the only one left in the bar.

"You were great today," I tell her, spinning my empty glass in a puddle of condensation.

"You weren't half bad either, big guy." She gestures at her chest and points at me. "I wasn't expecting you to match your tie to my dress."

I tug on my imaginary cufflinks and glance down at my t-shirt, relieved to notice I have not spilled ketchup on myself. "I can clean up sometimes."

"Yeah, like I said, you only looked *half* bad."

"At least it was my good half." I give my leg a shake.

Thora sighs. "I really am sorry, Odin. I feel like I haven't said that enough. You must be floundering, trying to figure out what's next."

"Ha." I dab at my mouth with a napkin. "There is no next. I'm moving back in with my parents until I become one with their basement couch."

She frowns. "I used to not be able to see a future at all, you know. The first time my dad went to jail when I was in high school, I literally couldn't imagine what life would be like for me. I sort of thought I'd end up working retail or tending bar forever, but I couldn't even see that. I'd think about *after* high school, and it would just be…a black cloud."

"Relatable content." I stifle a burp. I must be well on my way to drunk. Thora doesn't offer me a refill, and I don't ask for one. I focus on my fries.

"But I had a really good mentor in high school. For some reason." She grabs the nozzle thing and a plastic cup and pours me a water without mentioning it. "They helped me apply for college, showed me scholarships, made suggestions. Don't you have someone telling you your options?"

"Oh, everyone's got opinions." I point at her with a French fry. "My uncles want me to go to law school. My dad has told me at least 700 times that I can coach college or pro ball with my playing experience. And let's see…my cousins have offered me free tickets to watch them play professional soccer, as if it wouldn't be fucking devastating to hear Stag this and Stag that while I'm stuck in a cast."

Thora's eyes crinkle around the corners, and her expression is hard to read. "I'm nervous, too, you know? About moving somewhere all alone, the unknown of it all, and the pressure."

I grip the bar with both hands and lean forward until my face is an inch from hers. "You have absolutely nothing to worry about. You're a fucking force, Thora, goddess of thunder." I'm close enough to smell her breath, and I know I'm going to kiss her. I want to grab the back of her head and pull her into me, yank her across the damn bar, and into my lap. She parts her lips, and I know she wants it, too.

But my brother Gunnar's voice slashes the moment. "Yo, Odin, if you want a ride home, I'm leaving now."

I sink back into the stool and turn to face him. He leans against the door to the bar, massive arms crossed over his chest, shit-eating grin on his face. That fucker absolutely timed his outburst to interrupt me kissing my new obsession. I turn back to Thora, who licks her lips and tucks her hair behind her ears. "I'll close out your tab," she whispers, and I nod.

I grab a bunch of cash from my wallet and slide it under my plate. "Have a great time at the book thing with Fern," I tell her.

If she responds, I don't hear her over the squeak of my scooter as my brother helps me out the door.

CHAPTER 19
THORA

I TAKE EXTRA TIME TO ADMIRE MY REFLECTION IN ONE OF THE OUTFITS I SCORED at the thrift store with Odin last weekend. While I'm looking at my butt in the mirror over one shoulder, my mom surprises me by tapping on the door and entering my room. "Oh, you look so nice, Thora."

I catch her eye, noting her weary face. "Thank you, Mom. I wasn't expecting to see you today."

She smiles thinly. "It was slow at the diner." She shrugs. "Thought I'd come home for a change." Mom has been working herself ragged. It's not lost on me that she's the sole contributor to the household once I graduate. I'm not exactly sure how my parents will manage once I move overseas. From the looks of my mother, she's not really sure, either.

I smooth my hands down my pants and smile at Mom. "Fern and I are going to a thing at the bookstore tonight. We scored free tickets." I don't tell her they were a gift from Odin or that he looked sad yesterday when he left the bar. Or that he almost kissed me first.

Mom would just tell me that I can't afford to get in trouble with a boy, and I would tell her that I know. I don't need to tell her I have an IUD courtesy of Planned Parenthood or that I'm pretty sure Odin won't be lured into petty drug crimes. Nor will he get sucked into the bottomless whirlpool of poverty if he gets a record and no access to any meaningful employment. I don't need to tell her any of that.

Instead, I kiss her cheek and grab my purse that's bulging at the seams just a little from the signed copy of the replacement *Redcoat* book. I head out to meet Fern at the bookstore.

Once there, Fern is waiting for me on the corner across the street, nervously eyeing the long line around the block of readers eager to get inside. "Wow," I tell her, pulling out my ticket. "I should have thought about getting here early to snag a good seat."

We cross the street, and an employee monitoring the line asks to see our tickets. I hold mine up, and they grin, waving an arm toward the front door. "Ooh, VIPs," they say. "Your seats are reserved right near the front! Enjoy."

Fern's mouth drops open, and I feel the weight of everyone's eyes on us as we bypass the entire line, shouldering our way into the bookstore, where there are as many folding chairs as possible have been squeezed into neat lines between the shelves. There's a small open space up front with a handful of chairs, each with a bright orange VIP sign taped to the back of the seat. Fern squeezes my arm, and we pick two chairs near the back of the special section. I'm really unused to this sort of treatment.

The closest I usually get to a performer is when I'm bringing them drinks before a show. Once, I was tending bar at the arena and I got to take a tray of shots backstage to the band opening for Radiohead.

Now I'm the lucky fangirl with the awesome seats. Soon, every chair in the shop is full, and Juniper Jones picks up the microphone, introducing herself as the host of the panel alongside Emma Stag and Chloe Petals. I wiggle in my seat, whispering to Fern that this is Odin's mom and aunt.

"I know," she hisses back. "They're all related to Wyatt, too, remember?" I swat her arm, secretly overjoyed that she has found such a great guy with a family that loves her as much as I do. I study Odin's mom's face as she talks about the history of rowing in the Allegheny region and her own experience rowing in the Olympics.

No wonder Odin's so obsessed with being a professional athlete if his father played pro hockey and his mother apparently dominated the entire world in rowing. Emma and Chloe start talking about their latest books and I've never been interested in reading nonfiction before now. Chloe Petals is delightful in real life, earnest and open, and I love how she and Emma talk about sharing their research into the sport. Chloe just made it all sexy while Emma—well, Emma made the real-life rowers sound pretty sexy, too, come to think of it.

I clutch Fern's arm as the authors each read aloud from their books, and before I know it, I'm in line to *meet* them. It's a good thing Fern is with me because, for the first time in my life, I'm struck speechless when it's my turn to greet Chloe Petals. Fern pinches my shoulder and greets Emma and Juniper, who peers around the shop and over our shoulders. "I thought Odin was coming tonight," his mother says, brow furrowed.

I shake myself out of my fangirl stupor and tell her, "He gave the tickets to me and Fern. It was so nice of him." I glance down at the book in my hand and then drag my eyes to Chloe's. "Thank you so much for signing my replacement book. Your writing is just—gah! You're my favorite."

She surprises me with a hug, pulling me in tight for a comforting squeeze. "You are so welcome! I always love meeting fans." She smiles at Fern. "Would you two like some photos?"

Emma laughs. "Fern is in plenty of photos with us. We're all going to be in the owner's suite next month when Wyatt starts in the London Derby."

Fern and the Stags start to talk about soccer, and my eyes are on the verge of glazing over when Chloe nudges me. "We have to move through the line, but we can do a selfie, just us if you want?"

I nod and snap a pic, sailing over the moon with the joy of being here, with my best friend, actually talking to authors. I'm suddenly sad to realize that Odin might have imagined being here with me. Was he thinking we'd go on a date?

Fern and I elbow our way out of the crowded shop with waves from the panel, and outside in the night air, Fern sinks against the brick wall of the shop, a smile spreading across her face. "I still can't believe I fell into this family," she coos. Fern never coos. We like each other because we are both practical and realistic.

But here I am, swooning right beside her. Maybe it's because graduation is looming, and things are finally falling into place. A few beats later, she pats my arm. "I teach my final class in the morning, so I better head home."

"Oh." I look at my watch. "Want me to wait for the bus with you?"

She shakes her head. "Wyatt pre-loaded my Uber account." A grin belies her frustrated tone. "I'll be home faster than you, probably."

She glances toward my house, and I nod. She taps around on her phone, and a few moments later, a hybrid vehicle swoops to a stop in front of us. "Catch up soon? We still need to deal with your passport, right?"

I nod and wave as she drives off, and I think again about Odin, sad at the bar. He's got my dress at his apartment. I need to go over there at some point to get it back from him, right? It's barely nine at night on the last week of classes. Surely, I won't be disturbing him if I pop over there now to thank him for the tickets?

The 54 bus chugs up Liberty Avenue before I can second-guess myself, and I hop aboard, heading toward Odin's place. I clutch the gifted book to my chest, realizing he never did tell me what he spilled on the original.

CHAPTER 20
ODIN

There's someone at the door. I can hear banging from my bedroom and then my brothers' voices as they greet the visitor. Probably someone from the hockey team come over to play video games with them since I'm holed up in my room moping.

I never withdrew from the semester, which means I will fail all my classes rather than have incomplete grades. Well, I guess I'm getting an A in my arguments class. I'm not sure if I've ever had an A before.

Not that I'm stupid. I've just always prioritized football because that was going to be my career for the next decade. Lotta good that did me.

The voices get rowdy, and I hear Gunny shouting my name. I'm already in bed with the ruined copy of Thora's book, planning to try to read the pages that aren't stuck together. I have no explanation for why I'm spending a beautiful spring evening in bed with a romance novel. I have no explanation for a lot of things these days.

The door opens, and I shove the book under my back. "What the fuck?" I snarl toward the entryway until I see who it is. "What are you doing here?"

Thora shuts the door behind her, a strange smile on her face. "Nice to see you, too, Odie."

"Do *not* call me that. Ever." I sigh and adjust my weight so the book is sort of off to the side. I'm not wearing a shirt and Thora notices. I let her, resisting the urge to flex my pecs as she stares at my chest. "Hi," I say, trying to start again. "I didn't realize it was you. I thought my roommates were just being assholes."

She smiles and drops a bag on my desk, shrugging out of her sweater. Hot damn, she's wearing one of those outfits she bought last week. A sleeveless top thing that nips in at her tiny waist and skinny black pants that leave nothing to the imagination but in a classy way. "Oh, they were being assholes. I'll spare you the details." She starts to tie back her hair. I want to scream at her to stop, to let me run my fingers through it while it's down and dark and all over her shoulders.

But then I think about what she just said. "What did those fuckers say to you?"

I move to sit up, and Thora laughs, shaking her head and sitting on the edge of my bed near my booted foot. "They're harmless. They were just giving you shit via proxy." She smiles at me and licks her lips. I sit up despite her earlier protests before I remember that she will see the book if I move. She points at it. "I came over to thank you for the tickets. And because you never told me what happened to my original copy of the book."

We both stare at the paperback. I'm not sure if she can see the wrinkled pages where the spooge dried, crusty and sticky. "I, uh…" Fuck it. What do I have to be ashamed of? She got herself off thinking about me reading her that book, and it was hot as hell. I look her straight in the eye, and my voice drops, husky and low. "After you left, I was polishing Gungnir and—"

"Gungnir?" Thora wrinkles her nose and raises one brow.

I flash her a full-watt grin. "Yeah. Gungnir. The Spear of Heaven."

"Oh, for fuck's sake, Odin." She swats me with the book, laughing until I yank it from her hand. "What happened to the book?"

"As I was saying! I was polishing Gungnir, and…I got jizz all over the pages."

Thora flushes from her throat to the tips of her ears. I watch the color bloom across her skin as she breathes, as her mouth drops open, and her pupils explode. "Odin." Her voice is an invitation, but the second I think about accepting, I realize there's no way I can perform.

I want to be rough with Thora, dirty. I want to dig my toes into the mattress and rut into her like…well, like a stag. I want to slam her up against the wall, bend her over my desk, and rail her from behind. And I can't do any of it. We stare at each other.

I'm not sure if she figures out what's going on in my head or what, but the next thing I know, she's standing next to me, slowly unzipping her pants and peeling them off her legs. She kicks off her shoes and then climbs back onto the bed, throwing a leg over my hips until she's sitting on top of me, staring as my chest moves up and down like a bellows. "What are you doing?"

She rubs her hands along my skin, and I hiss at the contact. I've been touching myself to thoughts of this for weeks now, telling myself it's okay to fantasize about her because she's leaving anyway. And she knows it because she presses a fingertip into my sternum and says, "This can't lead anywhere, but I really want you, Odin."

"Yeah?" I sound a lot more vulnerable than I want to come across. This is new for me. I don't love it.

Thora laughs. "Of course I want you. Look at you." She runs a palm along my chest, and the other one drops to her collar. "What do you say? Want to have at it 'til I leave town?"

This draws a laugh from deep inside me, shaking off the dreary cloud that's been hanging over my head all day. "Have at it? Did you just say that?"

"Oh, shut up, Odin." And then she's kissing me, leaning forward until her ponytail brushes along my chest. Her lips are soft and puffy, and she tastes sweet, like fruity gum. A moan escapes me as I deepen the kiss, bringing my hands up to her shoulders, to her neck, to her ass, where she sits on top of my growing erection.

"Thora." Her name is like some sort of faucet I open to drain away this darkness, this heavy dread that's followed me since the accident. I moan into her mouth and let my tongue tangle with hers. I wrap her hair around my wrist and tug, bending her head back so I can bite her throat. She likes this, rocking her hips against me when I nip at her skin.

I say her name again, thrusting up against her panties. And then I realize I haven't even really touched her yet, so I let go of her hair and squeeze at her ass. She's firm everywhere, tough like she's had to be, and I pull her down against me, rubbing her along my dick until I can feel her wet heat.

Thora is having her own adventure exploring my chest, digging her short nails into the space between my ribs. She grabs the book and throws it off the bed, and while I have her arms loose, I tug at her shirt up and over her head. "Shit, Thora, no bra?"

Her cheeks heat again, and she bites the corner of her mouth, shrugging. "I don't really need one…"

She starts to cover her breasts with her forearm, and I snarl, batting her hand out of the way and sitting up fully so I can tip her back in my lap and suck her nipples. Just as I hoped, I can fit almost her entire boob in my mouth, and I move between them, sucking and biting as she wriggles around and hangs onto my shoulders. We haven't even taken off each other's underwear, and this is already the hottest sexual encounter I've had…maybe ever.

This absolute beast of a woman shoves me backward with a shriek and starts crawling backward down my legs, tugging at the waist of my shorts and briefs in one handful. I raise my hips to help her out and close my eyes, so I don't have to see her struggle when she gets to my cast. If that happens, I don't notice because the next thing I know, Thora's mouth meets the head of my cock, and I practically black out.

Odin Stag is enormous. His entire body is proportional, and the dick I find inside his athletic shorts is hard and proud, pulsing and weeping precum from the uncut tip. I cannot help myself. I have to taste it.

And so, I do, lowering my head and sticking out my tongue to meet his hot skin as he hisses out a curse. I glance up to meet his eye as I slide him into my mouth as far as I can, and his expression might just ruin me forever. Odin is awed right now. There's no other way to describe the look he gives me as his hand gently drops to my hair, his fingers brushing along my cheek as I start to suck. I know my cheeks are hollowed out, and I almost feel my gag reflex kick in as he shudders involuntarily with what I assume is intense pleasure.

My name slips out of his lips, his deep voice practically purring. "Oh, fuck, Thora, that's incredible. Look how fucking sexy you look with me inside your mouth." He groans, his fingers in my hair tugging, a tingle along my scalp. I wrap one hand around the base of his cock and let the other explore his balls, warm and heavy in my hand.

As I bob my head up and down his length, I hear him slapping the mattress, and when I look at him again, he has the side of one hand crammed in his mouth, biting back a roar. Curious, I let my finger explore behind his sack, sneaking between his taut cheeks. I find the tight pucker of his ass and tap it, causing Odin to growl. I swear he flies into the air like a falcon.

I don't know how, but he turns and flips us both, so I'm on my back with my legs around his neck. "You want to make me cum before I fuck this pussy, Thora? Is that what you wanted?" Odin drags a finger along my panties, which are soaked to the point of ruin by now. He shoves them to the side, and my breath hitches as he slides one massive finger inside me. "Oh, this *is* a greedy pussy. You want the Spear of Heaven, Thora? Is that it?"

I laugh at his joke, but when I meet his eye again, I see he's dead serious. "We aren't joking about pussy. Not tonight." And then his face is between my legs, and his teeth are on my clit, and I forget to breathe as he wreaks havoc on my nerve endings.

"Odin. Holy shit. Wow." My hands scramble around the sheets, looking for something to grab as I feel the slow build of pleasure I almost never get from a partner. "It's so good," I whimper. He continues to lick, adding a finger inside me, pumping as he works my clit from the outside with his tongue.

"Do you always shave your pussy bare, Thora? Or is that just for me?"

I can't speak. I'm too worked up to answer him, but then he stops all his movement and begins lowering my legs. "What are you doing?" I try to sit up, and he gives me a side-eye.

"I'm taking off these fucking panties, so I have more room to work."

"Oh." My breath returns along with some semblance of thought. "You don't have to keep going. I can't really come that way. Remember how—"

"Thora." He puts one hand under my chin and looks right into my eyes, probably all the way into the back of my brain. "Do I look like I'm fucking bored?"

I glance down to where his other hand is stroking his massive erection, which…might be even harder than it was when I had my mouth around it. "Do you *like* doing that?"

He arches one brow. "Eating your pussy? Fuck yeah, I like it. I've been dreaming of doing that for weeks." He pulls open the drawer next to his bed. "Lie back."

I hear a familiar buzz and look over to see the blue cock ring I used when I got myself off alone here in the bed as he read to me from the chair. I now have a Pavlovian response to the sound and sight of it as Odin presses it against my upper thigh. "I said lie back, Thora." And Thor help me, I do as he commands.

I sink into the bed. My legs tipped open wide as he starts licking and stroking me again, now with the vibrating toy added into the mix. He teases me with it, holding it everywhere but my clit, but somehow the combination of his tongue, his fingers, the toy, and the knowledge that this is sexy to him…uncorks whatever usually holds back my pleasure during these sorts of encounters.

"Odin," I gasp, my hands flying involuntarily to my nipples, needing just that last bit of stimulation as the dam breaks and the pulsing, joyful white heat of pleasure bursts in my center, sparking through my limbs and back again. I must be screaming. I must be a mess. But I cannot find the energy to care, and then Odin's mouth is on mine again. I can taste myself on him, and I've never experienced that before, either.

When I open my eyes, he's smiling at me, an expression I know is dangerous for what this has to be: two people fucking around before graduation. A final, shuddering sigh slips out of my lips against his before he asks, "Can you keep going? Do you want me inside you?"

I should tell him no. I should get dressed and leave. I should delete his number from my phone before anything else happens that would potentially jeopardize me leaving this country. Instead, I reach for the drawer, where he has a strip of condoms, and I pull one from the row and tear it open. "Lie back," I echo, repeating his instructions earlier and figuring this will go easier on his injury if I'm on top.

He does as I say and watches as I roll the condom onto his dick. He feels so warm and stiff under my hand. I cannot wait to feel him stretching me open. I swing a leg over his hips and am about to impale myself on his delicious cock when he places a hand on my thigh. "Hang on." He flicks on the toy, grinning as he rolls that down his length. "Oh shit." His body trembles and shakes as he grows used to the sensation. "That's…wow. Fuck, Thora."

I grin, keeping his gaze as I slide onto him. We both moan as we press together, and I relish the feeling of fullness, the stretch as he opens me with his body. And then the toy is buzzing between us, pressing into him and into my clit at the same time. His mouth falls open, and there is that facial expression again, the one I cannot allow myself to return as I grip his shoulders and roll my hips. I ride Odin Stag as he chants my name, as his hands dig into my hips and pull me closer, offering me more and more friction. A second passes, or maybe it's an hour, but we're both coming. He swells impossibly large inside me, grunting and pulsing as my body jerks and spasms, the second orgasm hitting me much harder and longer like the first was just some warm-up act for the most explosive pleasure of my entire life.

When it ends, we stare at one another, terrified. Silently, Odin reaches for the toy to shut off the vibration, and as he slides out of my body, I nearly sob at the loss of him. I know he's right here beneath me, but I also know I cannot keep him and allow myself to want to.

"Odin," I whisper, shaking my head. "I can't."

He runs his fingers through the mess of my hair and nods. "I know." And he closes his eyes, rolling to the side to sit up and deal with the condom. He doesn't ask me to stay over, and I don't.

CHAPTER 22
THORA

I TRY TO RUSH OUT OF MY PARENTS' STINKY HOUSE AS SOON AS I WAKE UP. THE last thing I need is to catch whiffs of stale cigarette smoke while I'm trying to take a math exam. But as I dart through the kitchen, I spy my mother at the cluttered table, drinking coffee.

She offers me a watery smile, and I can tell she's been crying.

I purse my lips and open the back door, letting a gust of warm air into the kitchen as I sink into the seat opposite her and pat her hand. "Hey, Mom."

She blinks a few times and smiles. "Hey, baby." She doesn't add anything further, but I look down at the table. Between her hands, I see the red stamp of an overdue bill. My heart sinks, sensing bad news.

I tilt my head toward the paper. "Is that the electric?"

Mom shakes her head. "This one's from the piss tests."

"Oh." As part of my father's house arrest, he has to submit urine pretty regularly to verify he's not using, and each time it's at his expense, which is Mom's expense since he's not working, although he could be. I try to collect my thoughts and remember my research mission. He's not working because the jobs available to him are grueling, menial, and low-paying.

But also, he's just adding to my mother's burden, and that pisses me off. "How much is it?"

A tear rolls down Mom's face, and she reaches for my hand. "I'm not going to be able to take off next Sunday for Commencement." She waves a hand at the paper. "It's this or the rent, and we're behind on that, too."

———

Fern keeps staring at me from our seats on the bus as we head downtown in search of our student visa paperwork. She taught her final math recitation this morning, and I aced a final exam despite being up all night long. Now, we're hitting our checklists hard. Passports, visas, and bank accounts we can access from the United Kingdom without spending a zillion dollars on fees.

Fern pokes me in the nose at a red light, causing me to yelp. "What the hell is wrong with you?"

She squints and leans close to my face. "I was just checking to make sure you're alive." She snaps her fingers in front of my face.

"Will you knock that shit off? Fern. Stop it."

My best friend harrumphs but backs out of my physical space as much as she can on a crowded bus where I'm squashed against the window next to her. She hums. "What happened last night after the bookstore?"

I shrug. "Nothing," I lie. "I slept in my bed, in my parents' stinky house, and got up in time to make my mom breakfast for once." All truths there, the last part. It was good to see Mom for a bit, sipping coffee in the quiet before she dropped the bombshell on me

Fern shakes her head. "Something is going on. You know how it works, Thora. We tell each other our crap, and then we figure out a plan to solve or endure the problem."

I stare out the window, debating which news to break first: that I slept with Odin, and it was way more intense than it had any right to be...or that my mother revealed she can't come to my commencement. I turn to face my best friend and talk around the knot choking me from the inside. "I have to give my airfare money to my mom if I want her to be able to go to Commencement next weekend."

Fern's face falls. I know she's about to offer me money or tell me that her mom will take pictures and video or some workaround, but the truth is I really need to feel sad about this. "Don't tell me anything that will make it better, okay? Not yet."

She nods and drapes an arm around my shoulders. "That really, really sucks, Thora."

I rest my head on her, enjoying the familiar, soft weight of my person— of the friend who knows what it's like to sit on the edge of something better and feel the constant threat of it all being yanked away. I want *someone* to prioritize me, and it's not ever going to be my family, and the sooner I accept that the sooner I'll stop feeling this way when shit goes wrong.

My phone buzzes in my lap—a text from Odin. I wince before I read it, I'm not ready for any more emotional bombs to drop today. But it's pretty benign.

ODIN STAG

You get home okay?

I send him a thumbs up and turn to face Fern. "What would you do?"

She's quiet for a few blocks as the bus bounces over construction dips along Fifth Avenue. Hardly anyone gets on the bus on this stretch of road between the universities and the downtown office buildings. "I think I'd give my mom the money and get myself a slutty tank top to work some doubles at the bar."

I snort. "Two grand is a lot of double shifts."

She hums again and tugs on my arm, pulling me down the aisle and into the City-County Building and the passport office. We're waiting in line when she snaps her fingers. "You said two grand…was that for a round-trip ticket?"

I blink at her. "Well, yeah. I need to come back."

She shakes her head. "Not for an entire year. What if you just bought a one-way and figured out the rest once you're over there." She taps on the paperwork in her hand. "Maybe there will be a discount sale or something. I don't know."

I don't say anything as I consider her suggestion. She already has her phone out, searching for flights and I peer over her shoulder, feeling a lot less hopeless when I see the prices for one-way tickets. There is even a direct flight from Pittsburgh to London that I could work off the cost if I get picked to work at one of the country music concert venues this summer. I squeeze my friend and kiss her on the cheek. "That's a terrific idea, Fern Montgomery. Thank you."

I'm not sure if it's my improved outlook or our extreme preparedness, but the passport and visa applications are a breeze. That includes getting fingerprinted and having our retinas burned into the computer system—or whatever they did with our eyeball scans.

Fern suggests we take the train to her apartment for lunch, and soon, I'm nestled into her couch with peanut butter banana sandwiches and reruns of *Gilmore Girls* on the television. "I'm going to miss you," I tell her after a big swig of milk. "What if nobody over there understands me?"

She laughs. "They probably won't understand either of us. Between the Pittsburgh accent and our lack of refinement…" I stifle a burp and laugh. And then all my feelings settle in alongside the heavy peanut butter in my belly. "Seriously, though," she says, "You'll be an hour away. We won't have part-time jobs in grad school, you know. For one thing, we won't have work permits…"

That draws a laugh from me, but I suppose she's right. I will *only* be working on academic labor for the first time ever. Part of my brain immediately tells me I can always seek out under-the-table work in a pub. I entertain brief fantasies about sending money home to my mom so my parents can maybe cover their expenses without me.

I shake that away and quietly fantasize about walking over the Tower Bridge arm in arm with Fern, both of us in yellow raincoats. Because that's what I imagine people wear in London.

Fern takes my plate from me, sets it on the coffee table, and turns to face me, arms crossed. "Something else is up with you, though. What happened?"

I purse my lips. I guess it does no good to avoid telling her I slept with Odin since she's basically married to his cousin. I stare at the ceiling and blurt, "I went to the Stag apartment last night after you got on the bus."

When I look at her again, her eyes are wide and wild, and she's grinning like a weirdo. "How was it?"

I roll my eyes. "You know it was great."

"Seriously? It's never great for you with someone."

I grab a throw pillow and clutch it against my middle. "Yeah, well, I guess these guys know what they're doing in that department."

Fern flops back against the couch next to me again. "They really do. Or Wyatt does…"

"I told you he was the one to give your flower to."

She whacks my arm. "I told you to stop calling it my flower." We watch Rory and Lorelai Gilmore try and fail to prepare frozen pizza until Fern adds, "But if it was so good, why do you feel glum?"

"Because I like him. There. I said it." I sigh. "He's funny, and he gives me shit in a good way, and, well, he knows how to make me come, and now I'm leaving the freaking country."

"So?"

"What do you mean so? This is exactly the worst time to get involved with someone, Fern. I should be focused on my future. I need to work double shifts so my mom can watch me be the first person in my family to get a diploma. I don't have time for romance."

"Hmm." We're quiet again as the Gilmore gals have a similar discussion on the television. Fern points at the screen. "It's just that...so what if the timing sucks? Why not have a fling and enjoy yourself before you go?"

I consider this because I've been considering it since I left Odin's blue gaze late last night and felt the sting between my legs with each step I took today, reminding me of how he worked with me to find a way to make my body sing.

He wrote back at some point, reminding me he still has my dress and to let him know when I want to grab it from him. I should respond. I should say something about him wanting a booty call...keep things light. I should take Fern's advice and ignore my emotional connection to him while enjoying the pleasure sensations he knows how to strum up.

Fern continues, saying, "Enjoy it while it lasts. And maybe he'll visit Wyatt in London, and you can have a vacation booty call this fall."

Maybe she's right, and I can keep things light with Odin. Perhaps we can keep playing card games for sexual stakes, and if he gets a different cast, he can take me tubing in a river and make me come on a rock in the woods like a forest fairy. Or maybe all of that is a fantasy because nothing is easy like that. Not for people like me.

When the episode ends, I hug my friend. "I gotta go," I tell her, standing and stretching. "I'm working close tonight at the bar."

"Slutty tank top," she says, clicking off the television and walking our plates toward the sink. "Make lots of tips, friend."

She blows me a kiss as I back out the door to her apartment and make my way to work.

I leave Mom's text unread all day Friday while my cousin drives me to and from physical therapy. I also leave it unread while I shower for the first time without a boot on my leg. I mean…obviously, I don't take my phone in the shower. But the whole thing is a huge process I really shouldn't have tackled alone, and I'm not sure why I don't respond to my mom or call on any of my roommate-relatives to help me out.

Instead, I bite back moans of pain as I balance my ass on the tile and scrub my itchy-ass leg. I try not to look at the scar and bruising at the incision. I try not to think about what Thora might think if she saw me now, hobbled like an injured bird trying to scour lint from between my toes.

Thora.

Our night together was incredibly intense, and I know it scared her. She couldn't get out of here fast enough afterward. I don't know what the hell to do about her. She's leaving at the end of the summer. I know that. And yet, she's the best thing in my world right now.

I can't believe I went into that encounter thinking it would be terrible, I couldn't perform the way I usually do, do the things I typically do with women. Nothing about Thora is usual or typical.

I have no idea where she got the idea to play with my ass while she had my dick in her mouth, but I was a nanosecond away from exploding down her throat before I used some sort of ninja maneuver to flip us both over, cast be damned.

Post shower, once I have my cast back on, I'm about to face the music and read my mom's text, but the phone rings instead, and it's my dad. "Gah," I say by way of greeting.

"Never ignore your mother, Odin. It worries her, and then she pesters *me* about it." His tone is pretty neutral, so maybe this won't be as painful as I feared. No lectures. No litany of questions about my future.

"I was about to text her back," I tell him, grunting as I tug a pair of shorts up and over the cast. It's a new boot with some wedge in the heel, but I'm still only allowed to take it off to shower, and I've got two more weeks with the damn scooter.

"Yes, well, you waited too long. I'll be at the apartment in five minutes. I'll be double-parked, so start heading outside now." I don't have time to react to this news before he adds, "Are you good on the stairs yet? Should I park?"

I debate my response for too long because Dad hums, and I know he will park and offer to carry me. I am tall and coordinated enough to monkey-swing my way down the stairwell with my arms pressed to either wall, but I still need someone to carry my scooter down. I haven't yet gotten to the point where I want to throw it down the stairs and hope for the best.

By the time I get a shirt on and find my deodorant in Gunnar's bathroom—he's always stealing my shit, and I'm not going to miss that when I move out—Dad is in the doorway giving the apartment a condescending scowl. "Dad," I say, nodding my head in his direction. I roll over to him as he lets his face melt into a more familiar grin, and he opens his huge arms to wrap me in a hug. Honestly, I do feel better once I'm all wrapped up in a Tyrion Stag embrace. He's always been a good hugger.

"Lead the way, O-man. What should I do?" I demonstrate my hands-on-the-wall-and-swing-down-the-stairs technique, and he follows it with my knee roller. He blocked a hydrant with his ancient gold minivan, so I do my best to hurry into the passenger seat as if anyone would give hockey star Ty Stag a parking ticket. The man can, and has successfully, grinned his way out of everything.

Dad drives me to the house, pulling into the garage he recently redid and pointing at the ramp that has replaced the step into the kitchen. "You never know," he explains. "Seemed like a good idea. You know, in case your mother becomes infirm."

She hears this joke as we enter the house and whips him with a dish towel before pulling my face down so she can kiss my cheeks and ruffle my hair. "You had me so worried, Odin Theodore. Don't do that again." Holding me at arm's length, still awkwardly bent down, Mom studies my eyes like she's trying to look inside my head. "Go on and sit. I brought out the ottoman for you to rest your cast."

I don't bother to ask what inspired this private meal. I've been ignoring absolutely everyone but Thora, so I'm sure Mom has a notepad of prioritized to-do items to get my life back on track. The problem is, I don't think the tracks have been built yet. Or someone lost the blueprints. Or something.

Dad produces a huge takeout bag full of Mediterranean food, and my mouth waters at the smell of the hummus, feta, and fresh parsley. As predicted, Mom pulls out a yellow legal pad.

"I'm just going to dive in if that's okay," she says, not referencing the food but assuming full-on lawyer/judge mode. I nod because there's no stopping her once she starts questioning a witness. "I took the liberty of calling Brian. You remember your cousins' agent? He was Uncle Hawk's agent, too—"

"I know who Brian is, Mom."

She nods and takes a bite of cucumber. "Well, I told him you aren't pursuing representation any time soon." I silently swallow a mouth full of falafel and watch her cross AGENT off her list with a swift, precise pen stroke. "Now, you'll need to sign some paperwork from your coach, whom I've convinced to hold off pestering you for another week while you sort things out with academics. But anyway…"

I stop listening as Mom reiterates that my scholarship requires me to stay on the roster for the team during my rehab. She talks about minimum grade point average and academic eligibility and ten thousand things I already knew. I tune her out and bury my fingers in my hair, tugging it to feel the sensation on my scalp.

My life has exploded, and I can't even wallow. I have to do paperwork about it. When I open my eyes again, Dad has his hand pressed reassuringly over Mom's pen, and they're both staring at me.

"Hey," Dad says. "Tell me something good that happened this week." Mom nods and presses her lips together, setting the pen on the table.

I take a sip of my water and tell them about my presentation with Thora. "I think we aced it. Did I tell you she's a Rhodes Scholar?"

Dad's brows lift, and he nods, impressed. Mom grins. "This is the girl from the law clinic, right? She was so nice at the reading, although I thought you were coming along with her, sweetheart. I hope you didn't stay home because of your leg. I could have—" Dad squeezes her shoulder, and Mom stops rambling.

I take a deep breath. "Thora wanted to go with Fern." I hold my palms up. "I wanted them to have a nice night out."

Mom hums appreciatively. "Fern leaves soon. After Commencement, right? I think Wyatt is flying home to support her. Isn't that so sweet?"

Dad nods. "Very sweet, June-bug."

We all eat quietly until Dad grabs the notepad and scans the list Mom scrawled down an entire page. He looks at me and folds his hands together on top of the list. "What's one thing you can take care of this week, O?" He holds up a thick finger. "One thing."

I scratch my chin. I haven't shaved, but somehow, I suspect personal hygiene is not what Dad is talking about. I'm pretty sure I missed the window for the medical withdrawal, and I can't stomach being in the football building right now. Not with the team all high on success, working out next year's roster, and preparing for their own futures with the game. I'm sure the paperwork with Coach is important, but that feels as far off as going for a jog.

I think about Thora and what it means to her to finish a degree at all costs, let alone graduate school afterward. She mentioned how hard her mom has to work to support the three of them without a degree. My family is in a different place, financially, but it sort of feels like spitting in Thora's face to piss away the credits I've earned so far. I rap my knuckles on the table and look at Dad. "I'll call Meech and deal with my grades this semester. Maybe I'm not failing everything."

Both my parents smile. Mom reaches for her pen to cross something off the list, but Dad shakes his head and squeezes her hand. He looks me in the eye and says, "One step at a time, kid."

He's right, of course. My entire life has been derailed to the point where a shower takes me longer than it used to take me to run a 5k. Mom and Dad have ideas about what I should do—that much is obvious—but I have to figure out the next steps on my own. I'm not sure they understand that my even wanting to do that decision-making is a huge step up from last week. If it were up to Mom, I'd already have a new strategic plan for my life with goals, sub-goals, and a timeline.

Instead, I tell them I'm proud of getting my dirty dishes to the sink when I finish my pita. Everything is different now, and I know I can't stay in the apartment if I'm not an enrolled student. I know I can't stay on the football team if I can't play football anymore. I know all of that. But moving home isn't something I can handle right now, either.

Dad shoves an entire falafel ball in his mouth and swallows it, turning to me. "Come on, kiddo. I'll take you back to the Stag Lair."

I roll my eyes. He and my uncles have been trying to name our apartment ever since Wes and Wyatt first moved in. I hoist myself up onto my scooter just as Mom shouts that we can't forget more condoms for the safe and satisfied basket.

CHAPTER 24
ODIN

TURNS OUT, MEECH WAS MORE THAN HAPPY TO TALK TO ME ON A WEEKEND. I texted him about meeting up on Monday morning, but he called me the second my message went through and told me he was en route to my apartment—something about *his* boss getting in trouble if too many college athletes fail out of school.

I don't feel ready to make any decisions about the fall semester. It was going to be my final one, and I was probably going to graduate in December with a degree in psychology, even though I never really cared about psychology. It just had classes that fit the best around practice and weight training. Next winter, I was going to head to the pro football combine and enter the draft.

I explain to Meech that I'm fine with having a low C average for the semester. The A I'm looking at in my arguments class is holding everything together. He arranges for me to take an incomplete for a few classes until I can handle the final assignments sometime this summer. I can stay in the apartment—for now.

I don't have to leave the apartment except for physical therapy. For now.

It feels like a starting place.

———

I fall asleep Saturday night, wondering what Thora would think of my progress, which means I wake up Sunday confused about why I care what my class research partner thinks. It's not like she's reached out since we slept together. She's leaving the country. We were both just celebrating a job well done.

But I still have her dress.

Gunnar says he'll take me to the dry cleaner on the way to family dinner today, which feels like a fair trade. I hadn't planned on going, but my brother reminded me that Aunt Alice does amazing things with sweet potatoes and chicken. She's used to cooking for elite athletes, and it's not every day we get to indulge in a delicious feast that meets all of our restrictions.

Not that I have restrictions anymore.

Gunny squeezes his black BMW X5 onto Uncle Tim's street, lined with other black SUVs, signaling that we're the last to arrive. I aim my knee roller toward the front door, but Gunny shakes his head. "Aunt Alice said to come in around back this time."

I shrug and wait for my brother to open the fence, where I can see that the backyard is sliced in half by a new wooden ramp leading up onto the deck. I groan, realizing they must all be talking about me and my condition. I don't even want to know how this ramp got here, but I guess it's pretty cool that I can get into a place easily for once.

I roll into the kitchen through the sliding door and see Dad, Uncle Tim, Uncle Thatcher, and Uncle Hawk deep in conversation over a map of the neighborhood. They look like they've just gotten back from a run, all sweaty in matching Pittsburgh Forge shirts courtesy of Uncle Hawk.

Not going to lie; it's pretty cool that they are all still out there being active, even if they bitch and moan about their creaking joints. Dad has them all doing "yoga for mid-life," and there's talk of them hiring a private instructor for all the Stag men and their wives.

Gunnar scoops Aunt Alice up from behind and kisses her cheek as she swats at him. "Gunnar Stag, I've told you to stop lifting me in the air."

He steals a cube of chicken from the pan she's stirring on the stove. "But you're pocket-sized, Aunt Alice. I can't help it."

She swats him with her spoon. "And tell your brothers to stop picking at the potatoes. I set out nuts and pickles for appetizers."

My twin brothers, Alder and Tucker, holler from another room that they have finished the nuts. Then, some more of my cousins start cracking jokes about nuts and pickles until my mother whistles and tells them all to stop being buttheads.

I do love my family. This whole crew is loud, crass, and ridiculous, but everyone is on the same side, and that's the Stag side. I think back to when my cousin Wes's girlfriend ran into trouble with some creep from Soccer USA. The family all jumped in to make sure she and Wes had what they needed to sue that fucker and keep him away from athletes forever. It was the same when my cousin Wyatt had issues with his creepy bio dad.

Speaking of Wyatt, who is currently in London with his new pro soccer team, I'm a little surprised to see his girlfriend, Fern, here at Stag family dinner. I grab a cup of water and roll towards her, where she's deep in concentration with Aunt Lucy. "Hey," I say, scratching my chin. "Wasn't expecting you today."

Aunt Lucy shakes a finger at me. "Excuse me, sir, that is no way to talk to Fern. Of course, she's at family dinner. She's family now." Lucy squeezes Fern in a side hug, which Fern seems to find delightful.

Fern smiles up at me. "Hey, thank you again for the tickets to the book event the other day. It was awesome." And then she makes a face that tells me she knows exactly what happened afterward between Thora and me.

I clear my throat. "I'm glad you guys had fun."

Aunt Lucy furrows her brow. "Book event?" She locates my Aunt Emma across the room and hollers, "Emma Stag, have you been having literary festivities without us again?" The crowd goes silent while everyone tries to decide if they should be pissed off that my aunt would dare do any publicity without including twenty-plus members of the family.

Aunt Alice cuts the tension by announcing that dinner is served, and everyone forgets any potential slight in the rush for first dibs at the meal. I roll to my place between my brothers and shove my knee scooter out of the way once I'm seated.

Since Wyatt's abroad, Fern takes his usual chair across from me, and I ask her if she's ready for graduation next weekend.

Fern sighs dreamily. "Is it cheesy if I say I was born ready? Obviously, it's been a lot of work to get here, but I keep pinching myself because it's finally happening."

She forks a bite of food, and Aunt Lucy tips a ton of wine into Fern's glass, but Fern's smile fades a bit. I frown and ask, "What's with the face? Something wrong?"

She waves a hand. "Oh, no, Lucy pouring my drink reminded me that Thora's at work today."

The sound of her name sends my heart racing a little faster, and blood rushes to my groin. The other night was definitely not a "get it out of my system" situation. Or my system still has a lot more Thora Janssen in it. I clear my throat. "Isn't she always at work?"

Fern bites her lip and leans closer, voice low. "She's really doubling up, though. Ugh, she'd kill me for telling you this, but she had to give her airfare money to her mom for the rent so that Mrs. Janssen could be there for commencement next week."

I pause, letting that sentence sink in fully. "You're saying Thora is paying her family's rent?"

Fern nods. "They had some unexpected expenses. Thora's really upset. Ugh, don't tell her I told you." She sighs. "She's so close, Odin. It's hard to see the finish line getting bumped further away."

I nod, eating quietly while my mind races. I look around the table and glance out the back window at the row of six-figure cars that could finance Thora's life a million times over. Hell, last month's royalty check from the video game with my avatar could buy Thora upgraded airfare. Now she's working double shifts to pay her family's rent?

———

After lunch, I find my Uncle Tim in the kitchen rinsing dishes and loading the dishwasher, muttering to himself about noisy, nosy siblings. "Hey, Unc. Can I ask you something?"

He turns, looking delighted to be asked for advice rather than help scraping food from plates. "Sure thing, Odin. How's the leg feeling?"

"Meh. Pretty numb still." I tap on the cast. "It's not about that, though. I was wondering…how you'd go about giving money to someone who doesn't want to take money."

He smiles. "This is an excellent question. What sort of money are we talking?"

I throw one hand in the air. "Hardly any. Like a thousand bucks. Maybe two if I can finagle it."

He nods and squints over my shoulder toward his youngest brother. "Your Uncle Hawk has a foundation…would the…recipient perhaps be a woman in need of legal support?"

I purse my lips, considering. "She's trying to get to Oxford to study international family law policies. I want to pay for her airfare. I don't want to take money from Uncle Hawk's foundation."

Uncle Tim grins and rests a hand on my shoulder. "Ah, but we could funnel your gifted money *through* the foundation…we just need to convince her to accept it, right?" I nod. "Let's create a surprise micro grant program she can be selected for!"

I shake my head. "That sounds too easy."

He asks me what sorts of things the "recipient" is involved with at school, and I draw a blank until I stare at Fern and remember something Thora did a few months ago to help Wyatt. "She volunteers at the student law clinic on campus and helps people get free legal aid," I say. "She knows Mom from her guest lectures there."

Uncle Tim rubs his palms together. "Sounds like she's about to be chosen for a distinguished service award, doesn't it?"

He tells me to give him a few days to sort out the particulars and to create a way to hide my donation. I feel energized and excited for something, and I honestly never thought I'd feel this way again. It's like I won a game, and the game is getting Thora what she wants and needs. None of it makes any sense, but damn if it doesn't motivate me to be more of a human and less of a couch cushion.

CHAPTER 25
THORA

I stare at his text in between customers at the shitty hot dog stand in the baseball stadium. Why's he texting me? Okay, I know he's texting me about sex.

It has to be that, right?

It was good sex. He probably wants to have some more of it. He's such a dreamboat, and I can hardly believe this fling is real.

I'd definitely rather be doing Odin Stag than pulling hot dogs from boiling water at a food stand with no tips. When Mom said she could get us a last-minute gig during the day today, I thought she'd at least have us at a bar cart. Nobody tips the hot dog girl.

I pluck a dog from the water with a pair of tongs and snap a selfie, sending it back to Odin.

He sends me back a GIF of an old man squinting through a magnifying glass.

He's funny today. I like it.

ME

> Working the Black Sox game and then closing shift at the bar.

ODIN STAG

> Don't you have finals tomorrow?

ME

> Yes, Mom. What of it?

He doesn't need to explain to me that I'm burning the candle at both ends. It's nothing my mother hasn't done before. If she can pull doubles for weeks on end, I can handle it for a week until I finish my exams. Then I can probably almost get eight hours of sleep per day while I save up the rest of what I need to get my ass to England.

I ignore my phone for the rest of the ballgame, which ends at the top of the ninth because the Sox are losing like usual. Mom and I part ways, her taking a bus home and me heading into Oakland to work the closing shift at Fuel Up.

When I glance at my phone again, I see another text from Odin:

> You're acting like me, Janssen. Get some rest.

———

Tuesday and Wednesday bring more of the same, except I'm getting fewer messages from Odin during the day, and I need to remember to see my advisor one last time before the end of the week. I'm feeling pretty good about my performance on my last few exams, considering my legs and lower back throb constantly now, and I'm running entirely on coffee and anxiety.

I figure, these baseball players are knocking out games three days in a row. That has to be at least as much work as scooping up fries and nachos in the same amount of time. I'm basically a pro athlete, but my sport is food service.

I'm starting to feel the impact by the time it gets dark on Wednesday, though, and I'm messing up drink orders. I drop an entire pint of dark beer when I look up and see Odin sitting at the bar along with two of his roommates.

"Hey, now," Gunnar says, reaching around the tap for the glass I dropped. There's still an inch of beer left in the bottom, and he swallows it quickly with a wink in my direction. Odin looks at him with murder shooting from his eyelashes.

"Sorry, boys. I wasn't expecting to see you." I don't even have to force a smile; seeing them lifts my whole mood. "What are you having?" I tap my chin and squint at them, all lined up on bar stools. I know Gunnar and Odin are brothers, and Stellan is their cousin, but they really do all look very similar. The Stag genes must be potent.

That's an extremely delirious thought to be having right now, and if I needed further proof that I'm working too hard, I forget their drink orders the second they're done speaking. "Sorry." I pull out a notepad, something I never need unless it's swamped and we're serving food. "Tell me one more time?"

Odin frowns as his cousins order lite beers. "Just a lemonade, I think," he says, and they tease him. Truthfully, I don't know if I've ever served just a lemonade at the bar. Most people who aren't drinking alcohol get a soda or a mocktail. I first slide Odin's unusual drink and work on the foamy beers for his entourage.

Gunnar slides me a credit card and asks me to start a tab. I eavesdrop while he and Stellan ask Odin about his progress in rehab for his leg.

I immediately feel bad that I haven't asked him more questions or any questions since the first day I drove him there, when we changed the tire.

He talks about doing his regular upper body workout under supervision, as well as one-legged deadlifts and things on his good leg. "And then," he says sadly, "I'm almost up to spelling out the alphabet with the toes on my right foot. You know, real taxing shit athletes do."

Gunnar winces and wraps a thick arm around his brother while I wipe off the bar, trying not to look like I'm listening to every word. "I'm really sorry, brother. You know that, right? We all hate this for you."

Odin grunts and stares at the television, where pro hockey game replays dominate the four screens along the back wall. Soon, all three of them are watching in silence and I busy myself serving other customers. No wonder Odin was eager to work on our project in person and hang out afterward. He's really working through an identity shift from god among us to…a dude who has to work hard on ankle circles.

I can't dwell on this too long because a big table orders tater tots and vodka sodas. A wave of tiredness hits me as I'm waiting for the tots to come out of the fryer, and I almost cut myself slicing the limes for the drinks. I rally and arrange the drinks on the tray just as the bell rings for the appetizers. Happy I can bring it all out together. I turn around to grab the food from the service window and bring it to the kitchen. I guess I turn too quickly, though, because I'm lightheaded as I step behind the bar.

I'm not fully aware of tripping, but I do notice the wet slosh of the drinks hitting my shirt and the hot burn of the tot oil on my throat. The pain passes quickly as I am enveloped in strong arms, the smell of cottony laundry detergent and spicy deodorant.

T̲HE SECOND WE WALKED INTO THE BAR, I̲ KNEW SOMETHING WAS UP WITH Thora. Initially, I resisted going out with my brother and cousin, but now I am glad I have help as I watch Thora trip and fall with a tray full of glass.

I skid across the floor, not sure what happens with my cast, and scoop her into my arms as she hits the ground. She's all wet with spilled alcohol, and some people scream at the commotion, but I don't think she's cut anywhere.

When I glance up, my brother has hopped behind the bar like he works here or something, shouting how Gunnar Stag, hockey star, is here to treat everyone to a guest performance. I would laugh at his foolish behavior if I weren't so worried about the woman in my arms.

"Odin?" Thora struggles to get out of my lap, but I hold her tight. There's no way I'm letting her go back to the grind. Who knows how many hours she's already been working. Judging by the dark circles under her eyes, she hasn't slept since the last time I saw her, and that's been days.

I realize we are physically close for the first time since we slept together. Well. We didn't sleep, did we? We also didn't fuck. That was some next-level connection, and it rattled both of us. We can talk about it later, though. Right now, Thora needs a shower and a long sleep with nobody disturbing her.

Stellan sets my knee roller beside me. "I'll get the car," he says, turning immediately toward the door. Thora stops wriggling in my lap, and someone—maybe the manager? Comes around from the back and asks if she's all right.

"No," I shout at the same time she tries to insist she's fine. I growl. "She's exhausted. I'm taking her home to rest."

The woman puts her hands on her hips and glances around the crowded space. Midway through finals week and, the place is bumping. I know Thora will be pissed at losing the opportunity for tips tonight, but she can't be pushing herself until her body collapses and still plan to finish with the 4.0 grade point average she insists she needs.

Gunnar slaps the bar to get the manager's attention. "Hey, I'll be taking over for Thora there," he says, winking. I swear, every woman in the place swoons. What a clown. I'm grateful.

Thora has accepted that I'm holding her and rests her head against my chest. Her boss crouches down and asks, "Does he know what he's doing back there?"

I shake my head, and Thora shrugs. I glance up, and he appears to be pouring a beer to applause. The manager sighs. "Okay, well, get some rest. This is weird, but people seem to be into him."

I debate explaining hockey culture to Thora's bar manager, but if she doesn't understand by now, nothing I can say will help. Thora and I struggle to our feet. I grip my scooter with one hand, keep the other firmly around her shoulders, and guide her toward the door just as my cousin pulls up outside.

I don't know if Thora is just that exhausted or what, but she falls asleep against me in the back seat of Stellan's Jeep. It's only a few blocks to the apartment, just enough time for me to text my Uncle Tim that he needs to finalize the grant ASAP. I tell him it's an emergency, and he immediately responds that the plan is to give her the award at some ceremony Saturday night before commencement.

I glance at the woman in my arms and delete the message thread. I don't want her to catch a glimpse of anything and get suspicious.

Stelly turns around to look at me after he parks. "Want me to carry her?" I shoot him a death glare, and he holds up his palms. "Hey, man, I'm just an extension of you here. You know I have a boyfriend, right?"

I blow out a breath. He's right. I want to be the one to carry Thora upstairs, and six months from now, I could be. But the truth is I can still barely get myself to my bed. I nod, and my cousin comes around to the back seat to get my goddess of thunder.

"Since when do you have a boyfriend?" I follow along behind him, dragging my scooter and eventually leaving it at the bottom of the stairwell. Someone will bring it up to me and I can hop to my room once he gets Thora situated.

"It's new," he grunts, kicking open our door and striding into my room. He sets Thora gently on the bed, and she sighs and wakes up.

"Hey," I whisper. "You're at my place. I can sleep on the couch if you want, but you're staying over."

She opens an eye, and it glares at me, making me laugh. "Don't tell me what to do, Stag."

"Don't pass out from exhaustion at work, Janssen." I sit on the side of the bed, waiting to see what she says next.

She groans and rolls onto her back. "It's weird to just accept help."

"Get used to it, Toots. I'm helping."

She rolls her eyes. "Looked like it was your cousin helping, actually." And then she winces, recognizing that that was a low blow. I lie back next to her, and she rolls to her side. "I'm getting booze all over your sheets. I stink."

"There's been worse in my bed. At least it's not barf?"

She swats me, but there's no heart in her effort. She closes her eyes again. "I'm always the one cleaning up the mess. I don't know how to be the one someone cleans up."

I roll on my side to face her as I hear the unmistakable sound of my knee roller hitting my bedroom door. I owe Stelly big time for this. "Hey," I tell Thora. "Even with a jacked-up leg, I'm taking care of you tonight. Deal with it."

She bites her lip. "Why, though?"

I risk touching her face, letting a finger trace down her cheek. "I don't know. You got under my skin, I guess. I have nothing else to do."

That draws a laugh from her, and noticing that her shirt really is kind of gross from the spilled drinks, I hoist myself out of bed and hop over to my dresser. I pull out the smallest shirt I can find, make my way to the bathroom, and grab a wet washcloth.

When I get back next to her, she's half asleep again, and I start to peel off the soaked shirt. "I'm not getting frisky, honest," I whisper. She grunts. I get the shirt up and over her head and absolutely do not register that she, once again, is not wearing a bra…in public. I dab at her beautiful skin with the damp cloth, watching as goosebumps pebble her chest and arms. "Hold tight," I tell her, sliding the shirt over her head. It goes to her knees, which is good because I peel her jeans off next and get her tucked under the covers.

I open my bedroom door and toss her clothes in the hall, then text our apartment group chat, asking someone to run them through the wash before morning.

I flick off the light and am about to make my way out of there to the couch when her arm shoots from the bed and grips my wrist. "Stay," she says, a command and a plea all at once.

Even in the dark, I can see the need in her face, the hesitancy, and the fear about what it all means. She's leaving; that won't change anything, but we can be friends. I promised I'd take care of her broken body and all. I curl up against her in my bed, tuck her close against my side, and fall asleep with Thora Janssen in my arms.

I wake up in a panic, not sure where I am. And then I realize the hot coils wrapped around me are Odin's massive arms, and … I still sort of panic. But it feels different. I'm curled on my side, facing him, and I can make out the smooth features of his face in the dim morning light that sneaks around his curtains.

He's here because I asked him to stay last night. I remember tripping at the bar, him freaking out, and then I just succumbed to exhaustion once I realized Odin Stag wasn't taking no for an answer. Nobody has ever growled like that in defense of my health. God, his brother even took over my bartending shift. That could have gone really great or incredibly awful. I wonder if I'm fired.

Just as the financial panic about that sets in, Odin stirs, sees where he is, and pulls me even closer to him. "You're not sneaking away this time." His low voice vibrates through his chest. I love the rumble of it. His body is just so safe and strong and available to me right now. It's all very confusing and not something I'd like to allow myself to crave since it's all very temporary.

But maybe it's okay if I indulge for the day. Perhaps it's okay to let him hold me while I drift back to sleep, just for a minute.

———

I wake up again to a gentle shake and open my eyes to see Odin's blue ones in the bright light of full morning. At least I hope it's not later than morning. I sit up. "What time is it?"

He grins. "Not even eight yet. But I, uh, need your help with something."

I smooth my hair with my fingers, realizing I'm wearing a huge shirt Odin must have put on me last night. The cotton is soft and worn and smells like his detergent. I'd steal it if my parents' house didn't reek of smoke. "What do you need? I definitely owe you."

He shakes his head. "You don't owe me anything. But I'd love it if you could help me with this." He gestures at his cast. "I need to work on showering, and doing it at home is a benchmark for me." He drifts off, staring at the bathroom.

I watch his throat work as he swallows and then turns back toward me, brows lifted in a hopeful expression. I'm touched that he's making himself vulnerable for me after I was sort of forced to be vulnerable last night. Maybe we're a better match than I initially assumed. Okay, we definitely are. I rest a palm on his considerable thigh. "What can I do?"

He grins. "Mostly make sure I don't fall on my ass. I have a chair I'm supposed to use. I can take the cast off in the bathroom, but I still can't put any weight on my foot at all."

I nod and stand, facing the small bathroom. "It's going to be crowded in there."

"Think you can handle the press, Thora? I can get Gunny to help if you're overwhelmed."

I laugh. "I can handle a tight fit."

I expect him to make a joke about that, but he wheels his scooter into the bathroom and turns on the shower, setting out his towel on the counter. He starts to strip before I prepare myself, and there, in the bright overhead light, is the firm ass of Odin Stag. I can't help myself. I am powerless to resist laying a hand on it. It's right there in front of me.

"Don't push me," he says, then bends to remove the cast. I swallow, reminding myself that we are being vulnerable together. He didn't invite me in there to fuck in the steam. I'm not supposed to think about his skin all warm and soft from the hot water. He groans in pain, and my thoughts sharpen immediately.

I step closer as he places his palm on the tile wall, peeling off the boot cast with a creak of plastic hinges. I try not to look down at his heel, where I know his incision must still be pretty gross. He breathes out heavily through his nose, meeting my eyes as he pivots into the shower and sinks onto the chair.

Odin rests his head on the wall of the shower, letting the water fall over him. I can tell he's hurting but doesn't want to say anything about it. I strip off his shirt and step into the shower, putting shampoo in my palms and walking toward him.

His eyes fly open when my fingers dig into his hair, but then they drift closed again as his face eases. "That feels so good," he moans.

"Shh," I soothe, finishing his hair and reaching for his washcloth and the bar of soap. "Does it count against your therapy goals if someone else washes you off?"

He shakes his head. "My instructions were to safely enter and exit the shower independently."

"You did great. Where do I sign?" I urge him to lean forward, and he rests his cheek against my stomach as I scrub his back. His hands are still white knuckling the arms of the shower chair, and I'm not sure what hurts him specifically, but he seems to enjoy what I'm doing, so I continue.

"When do you have to be somewhere today? I can have my brother drop you off…" He sucks in a breath and twitches when I scrub his armpit.

"Ah, ticklish. Noted." I move the washcloth around to his chest. He leans back again, and his eyes are half closed, not staring at my tits, though one of his hands does find my butt cheek and gives it a squeeze. Tit for tat, I suppose. "I have one exam, and then I have my final meeting with my advisor to make sure everything is all set for graduation."

"Ung." He turns his torso, stretching or reaching for something, and I notice a pair of tattoos on his shoulder blades.

I touch them with a soaped-up hand, tracing the outline of a stag leaping over laurel branches. "Tell me about your ink."

He smiles. "All the Stags have that one." He points at his shoulder. "It's tradition."

"And the other one?" I move to scrub that side of his back, where a blackbird perches on a Viking helmet.

"It's dumb," he says and shrugs. "You know, Odin. Viking shit."

I smile. "Hi. My name is Thora. I don't think it's dumb."

Odin grunts and spreads his legs on the shower chair. I can't tell if he's half hard or if his penis is just like that all the time. When I was up close and personal with it, the thing was massive.

"I, um, think you should do your lower half," I tell him, and he opens his eyes, nodding. I back out of the shower and grab myself a towel from the cupboard where I saw him grab his earlier. "When does Wyatt get into town? I know he's accompanying Fern to London on Monday…"

"He's here," Odin says, leaning forward to wash one of his feet. I had never noticed his feet before, but they look strong. I like the tendons and calluses I can see. He moves to his injured leg and washes a bit more gingerly, blowing out another breath before explaining that Wyatt flew in late last night, but he's at his parents' house since they picked him up at the airport.

"He probably went to get Fern immediately," I say, patting my hair dry and looking around the room. "I, um, don't have any clothes but the fucked-up ones from last night."

Odin snaps off the water in the shower. "We washed those for you," he says. "Give me a minute, and I'll grab them."

And then he grips the chair handles, nostrils flaring as he concentrates on lifting himself using just one leg. I reach out to steady him, but he shakes his head. "I'm up." He hops a few times toward his bed, dripping water.

I laugh. "Let me at least wrap the towel around you before you soak everything in sight."

It's strange to be naked with him like this, blotting him dry before he eases himself back into the cast. There's nothing sexual about what we're doing, but it's intimate. Maybe more intimate than anything I've ever done. We're both aware of it as he tugs on a pair of mesh shorts and wheels himself from the room, returning soon after with my shirt and jeans from last night.

I step into the pants commando as Odin watches, shocked. I shrug. "I can do a test and a meeting with no undies. I'll change when I get home."

"Fuck, Thora." He drags a hand through his hair. "You're going to give me a stroke."

"That's what she said." We both laugh as I gather my things and leave, promising to touch base before I go to work in the evening.

———

My legal studies exam is a piece of cake, and I finish early enough that I can walk to my advisor's office at a leisurely pace. There's not a pre-law major here at the university, but between the political science classes and my work in the student law clinic, I feel good about my prospects after my fellowship year. Everything is so close I can taste it, and I shiver in anticipation as I gently knock on my advisor's door.

"Come on in, Thora," Mark says, his voice cheerful.

I wave and take a seat opposite his desk. "Just here for the final checklist for Sunday."

He chuckles. "Let's not get ahead of ourselves. There's still Saturday to deal with."

I furrow my brow. "Saturday?"

He looks at me over the folder he's studying. "Yes, the diploma ceremony. Surely you received the invitation?"

I nod. "I did, but I just thought it was optional. I didn't take off work Saturday." The night before commencement is one of the busiest nights of the year at Fuel Up. Not only will it be jammed with graduating students, but their alumni parents will also be in town, craving the nostalgia that comes with cheap, well-drinks. They always tip really well, those alumni parents.

Mark shifts uncomfortably in his seat, tugging at the collar of his shirt. "Thora, I, um, would really like you to consider attending. You're a Rhodes scholar. We'll be acknowledging that in the more intimate setting of just students from your major and—"

I shake my head. "I still don't have the funds I need to buy my plane ticket to BE a Rhodes scholar. I have to work on Saturday."

Mark gives his collar another yank and leans forward. "End-of-semester awards are granted at the ceremony, Thora. Let's say…you have a strong chance of receiving some funding." His eyes dart between his computer monitor and my face.

I frown. "I can't miss a guaranteed lucrative shift for a strong chance, sir. I'm really sorry."

Mark groans and pinches the bridge of his nose. "I'm pleading with you to attend," he says. "I'd like to offer my personal assurance that you will not regret it."

———

I leave his office deeply confused. I applied for every grant I could find, every bit of funding. Fern and I spent spring break last year making lists. If there was a scholarship, I'd be aware of it. Something feels off.

MY MOM INSISTS ON DRIVING ME TO PT ON FRIDAY, WHICH IS SORT OF WEIRD since she usually has court on Fridays. When I open the apartment door, she bounces on her toes a bit and looks excited. "It's all set, babe! We did it."

I arch a brow at her as I lock the door behind me. "What did we do?"

She swats my shoulder. "The scholarship! Your Uncle Tim worked it all out with the women's law foundation, and Thora will receive the award tomorrow night at her diploma ceremony." Mom wraps her arms around me and squeezes. "Want to be my date?"

"You're going?" This feels risky. If we show up at her event on Saturday, Thora will absolutely know my family is involved.

Mom nods. "I was always going. I was a guest lecturer at the student law group a few times this year. I'm giving a little talk. And now I'm giving a new award! I saw her resume, honey, and this award should have existed anyway. Dad and I are very proud of you for wanting to help, but keep the spotlight off yourself for doing so."

Mom talks about the importance of this kind of last-mile award as she carries my scooter down the stairs. I've perfected my monkey swing and we're in the car in minutes. Unfortunately, she invites herself to watch my entire session, but Mom takes an academic interest in this sort of thing since she has a background in elite rowing.

She even asks the therapist if rowing is a reasonable expectation for me for cardio. Mom knows about adaptive rowing machines that don't use the leg muscles at all, and I tune out while the two of them talk about my expanded workout potential. I can watch Thora receive this money. I can see her face when she realizes she doesn't have to worry about her plane ticket.

Mom drops me at home, promising to pick me up early tomorrow and take me to dinner before the ceremony. I wish we could bring Thora with us, but I realize there's absolutely no way to swing that without setting off her alarm bells. Instead, I text her a thank you for making sure my janky ass didn't slip in the shower like a senior citizen.

———

On Saturday afternoon, I cram myself into my business on top best with the most respectable shorts I can find to pull over my cast. I search for my cufflinks, remembering that they're in the top drawer of my desk where I hid the video game royalty check.

I look at the now-empty envelope, crumple it up, and toss it in the hall so someone can recycle it later. The whole scene makes me wish Wyatt were here, which is why I think I'm hallucinating when I hear his voice from the hall. "Littering now, O?"

I don't fight the grin that splits my face. I open my arms and my cousin steps in for a hug. Well, as close as he can get around my roller. He pats my shoulder. "I came to check in on you. Mom said you've been conniving."

His voice and expression are pleasant. That's unusual for him. "Um, yeah. Hey, man, you sound weird."

"It's called endorphins. I feel them now." He laughs. Then he stops laughing. "I feel bad bringing that up. Sorry."

"Nah. It's okay." I tug at my lapels and raise my brows at him. "Do I look okay for a smarty pants diploma thing?"

He laughs.

I return to my cufflinks and he reaches in to help. I watch his thick fingers struggle as much as mine, and ask, "Do you think Thora will hate this? The scholarship?"

Wyatt groans. "I think she will hate it if she knows you're involved. She and Fern...they have this whole thing about handouts. You got any food?"

He doesn't wait for my answer, but walks to the kitchen and returns a minute later crunching raw carrots. I say a quick prayer of thanks that I can at least eat proper snacks now that I'm not in training anymore.

I continue our analysis session, arguing, "It's not a handout, though. She should have this money."

"Mm-hmm." He swallows and gestures at me with a carrot. "I agree. I tossed some more money at Dad's foundation. They have a whole track now that funds the future lawyers, not just the legal funds for the women who need help. You did a good thing, dude."

"Thanks, man. That was cool of you to throw some of your millions back at the foundation. You look…happy. Beyond the endorphins, I mean."

"Speaking of," he swallows again. "I'm down to just one individual session a week with the team psych. Even got the green light to miss a session while I'm here fetching Fern." He grins.

"Is that a good thing?"

"Yeah. It means I'm dealing with my shit." Wyatt sits on my bed with the carrots. "The team there has a whole staff for mental health. There's a dedicated person who works with the injured guys."

That gives me pause. I look at him in the mirror over my shoulder as I smooth out my hair. "That's someone's whole job? Talking to injured athletes?"

"It's their whole ass job."

I want to ask him more about this, but I hear the door and the sound of Mom greeting Gunnar. Wyatt hops up to hug her and tells me he has to get going to Fern's award thing. I follow him into the living room, telling him to call me before he leaves town. Mom rolls her eyes when she sees me and pats my knee. "At least you wore a dress shoe."

I shake my foot. "And a dress sock. This is one of Dad's, I think." It's tall and yellow with tiny hockey sticks embroidered all over the material. She laughs, and we make our way to the car and onward to the ceremony.

We arrive at the law building, and Mom makes small talk with some of the professors, who acknowledge me the same way they did when I was ten. Like some kid who doesn't really belong in this room. Which is true. There's nothing for me here except Thora.

She walks in alone, wearing one of the outfits she got when we were at that store. Once again, it looks like it was custom-made for her. I slip away from Mom and roll toward my brilliant girl. Wait. Okay, fuck it. She's brilliant, and for the next month or so, she can be mine. We're at least friends. "Hey," I tell her, and her eyes shoot upward, widening in surprise.

"What are you doing here? Did you set this up?"

Thora's eyes dart around the room, and she fidgets with her purse.

"Did I set up a graduation ceremony for smart kids? No." I laugh to try and set her at ease. "I'm here with my mom. She apparently has been a guest lecturer for you guys."

Thora nods, and I watch her shoulders relax a bit. She bites her lip. "I called off work to be here. They were already mad at me about leaving halfway through Wednesday night…"

"Did Gunny not serve as a suitable replacement?"

That makes her laugh and I feel accomplished for a minute until someone in a suit bangs a spoon on a water glass and calls everyone to pay attention. "Good evening, scholars and families," the suit guy says. "If you could all please find a seat, we'll get started. I know we all have a busy day tomorrow!"

Some of the undergrads cheer and hug their families. Thora sits on the end of a row, alone. I try not to take it personally that she didn't sit with me. I did tell her I'm here as my mom's date. I zone out while they talk about how hard everyone worked for four years, how smart they all are, and how important political science is to society. I perk up when they start listing international fellowship awards and call Thora's name as a Rhodes scholar. I whoop loudly. Mom smacks me, but Thora turns and smiles at me, so I don't care.

Then, they call Mom to the mic. She gives one of her typical speeches about how she grew up in the foster care system and relied on scholarships and need-based aid to get through college and law school. She discusses the importance of family law to her judicial career and pivots to the women's law foundation and the work they do supporting their clients.

"And that's what really brings me here," Mom says. "I have one last surprise award for a student who has volunteered countless hours in the law clinic on campus and who has helped others achieve the small legal victories they needed in order to achieve big things in their personal lives. It's my pleasure to award a five-thousand-dollar grant to…" Mom points at Thora. "Thora Janssen!"

Thora turns white and stands with her hands over her mouth. I tug on my ear to make sure I heard correctly, but half the room is repeating the phrase "five thousand," and I have no idea what is going on. I promised like twelve hundred bucks to my uncle's foundation for the award, thinking I'd cover her plane ticket since that's what she was worried about.

Thora makes her way to the stage and takes the check, shaking hands as people take her photo. Mom wraps an arm around her and smiles, then slips away while other bigwigs from the college congratulate Thora.

"Mom," I hiss. "Five G?"

She waves a hand. "Oh, please. She needed way more than you

donated, and once some of the other law firms heard about her, they all chipped in. This seemed like a nice number to get her from here to there, don't you think?"

———

When I finally get Thora alone at the punch bowl, she's still rather white and shaky. "You gonna make it?"

I hand her a glass of the sweet liquid. Usually, I'm not able to drink something with this much sugar, but I'm still enjoying a no-restrictions diet, so I clink my plastic cup against hers as she stares at me. "Ooh, this is gross." I set my glass down on the catering tray in the corner.

Thora shakes her head. "Did you know about this?"

I sigh. "Thora. I had no idea you were getting five thousand dollars today," I tell her in all honesty. "But I loved watching your face when you did." I bump her shoulder. "You don't have to worry about shit now. You can just…fly off into the sunset."

She nods and continues sipping the punch she obviously finds acceptable. "I've never experienced not worrying. I don't know what to do with myself."

I grin. "I can think of a few ideas if you're stuck." I wink at her, and she shoves me, so I pretend to lose my balance and roll back in my scooter, causing her face to twist in alarm. "Just fucking with you."

"You are terrible," she digs a finger into my shoulder. "And those socks are atrocious."

"You love it. Come to my place and watch me take them off."

She sighs and shakes her head, setting her empty punch cup on the tray by my full one. "Nah. I gotta go get ready to graduate tomorrow. Isn't that wild?" She looks at the check sticking out of the pocket of her purse. "And I guess I need to stop by an ATM to deposit this."

I clutch my heart. "Thora. Do you mean to tell me you don't have mobile banking? There's an app for that, sweetheart."

She rolls her eyes. "Bye, Odin. See you around."

She turns to leave. "Call me," I beg, shooting my shot. "Let me take you out."

She looks down at the check and back up at me, and I watch as she spends an eternity deciding what to say next. "Yeah, okay," she says. "That would be fun."

I try not to jump or pump my fist in victory as she leaves the ceremony.

MOM SQUEEZES MY HAND ON THE BUS AS WE RIDE TOWARD THE ARENA ALONG with 10,000 other folks, all graduating today. "We're probably the only ones taking the bus to the ceremony," she says, smoothing her hair.

"First of all, definitely not. Second, we don't have to fight anyone for parking! We're way ahead of the game." Nothing is going to get me down today except maybe the thought of Fern leaving tomorrow. Neither of us has really taken the time to absorb the fact that we'll be separated for the first time in four years.

From the day I met her at first-year orientation, she's been my person—someone who understands my background and struggles and can really feel the magnitude of my successes when I have them. And today is definitely a success.

Mom dabs at her eyes with a crumpled tissue. "Nobody I know ever graduated from anything," she tells me.

"I know, Mom. But you set me up to do it." And it's true. My mother showed me the importance of hard work and perseverance every day of her life. Even if I don't understand what she gets from being with my dad, I still absorbed her ability to roll up her sleeves and get shit done. "And I'm going to work on changing things. You know, so other families have it easier."

She squeezes my leg and then stares at it. "Shouldn't you have one of those robes or something? For graduating? You did in high school…"

I laugh. "Fern has our gowns." I don't add that she kept them at her place so mine wouldn't stink. "We rented them." The bus stops at the bottom of the hill, and Mom and I join the herd of families huffing and puffing their way up DeSoto Street. The mood is joyful, like when we're working on game day and the home team is favored to win. Only I'm not working today. It's my show.

I'm still not over winning that award last night. I haven't told anyone. A small twinge of guilt pricks at my side, knowing I should tell my parents, but I won't because if they ask me for some of the money, I know I won't be able to tell them no. The second the money showed up as a pending deposit in my account, I bought a plane ticket and ordered a laptop. I don't want anyone to change their mind about the award.

I spy Fern at the bottom of the stairs, flanked by her mom and Wyatt. She starts jumping and waving, her blue gown billowing in the breeze. I hurry on ahead and clutch her hands, jumping with her in a circle as she tries to stuff the gown over my head. Wyatt clears his throat and hands us each a mortarboard and tassel.

I realize my mom hasn't met Fern's mom, Heather, or Wyatt, so I quickly introduce them. And then there's nothing left to do but line up while our families take their seats. Fern and I are oddly quiet as we listen to the band warming up before we march in.

"Hey," I whisper, squeezing her hand. We're supposed to organize by major, but with this many thousand people, nobody is taking roll or saying anything beyond the posters taped to the walls as an attempt to organize.

She turns to me, a dreamy smile on her face. I lick my lips, and she fishes a lip balm from a pocket somewhere. "Thanks. Also, I won a grant last night." Her eyes widen, and her mouth drops open. "Five thousand," I whisper.

She punches my shoulder. "Shut up. What for?" I explain how it was some legal aid reward for a student volunteer. "I don't remember anyone winning it last year, and it wasn't something I could apply for, so it really feels too good to be true, honestly."

"Hmm," she nods. "Any strings attached?"

I shake my head. "And it was a check to me, not the institution. I cashed it last night and bought my ticket *and* a functional computer. Oh, shit. I had it sent to your house, and you'll be gone." A tuba blares, and then the band starts "Pomp and Circumstance."

Fern leans her head on my shoulder. "You can still send stuff to my house. Mom will be happy to see you when you come pick it up."

We process into the arena and all the families pack the seats, cheering and waving. Fern somehow spots Wyatt and waves, face brightening. I'm shocked by a twinge of…something that Odin isn't there. Why would he be? I push down that unidentifiable feeling and focus on finding our seats and listening to the speaker tell us our lives are about to get awesome.

By the time the Chancellor tells us to stand and turn our tassels, I'm sort of numb and floating. Today is the day. I have reached the finish line. I'm a college graduate, and nobody can take that from me. Ever.

In a daze, Fern and I make our way back outside, eventually finding our moms and her man candy. They're very lovey, making out like fiends as Heather raises her eyebrows and tries to look at me and Mom.

"Well," Heather says. "Should we try to find lunch somewhere that's not mobbed?"

Mom presses her lips together. I didn't lay out any expectations beyond the ceremony. It hadn't occurred to me that, of course, regular families go out to eat or otherwise celebrate occasions like this. You'd think after years working in food service, that would be upfront in my thoughts. Mom stammers. "I, um…" She turns to me. "Sweetie, I have to get home to your dad, and then I have an afternoon shift. You know how it is with the fees."

I nod and hug her. "I know, Mom. I'm good."

Fern and Wyatt stop sucking face to wave goodbye to my mother, and the Montgomery crew invites me to Wyatt's favorite hole-in-the-wall deli for a sandwich, at least. "My treat," he says. And I accept only because he offered to run back inside and return my gown and Fern's to the rental collection.

"He's a keeper," Heather says, and Fern nods.

Lunch is all about England, how Fern leaves in the morning, and how she's going to make notes on everything I need to know and understand before I get there. At one point, Wyatt raises his water glass toward me and says, "Congrats on the award, by the way. Well earned, I'm sure."

And while I know Fern might have whispered it to him when I wasn't looking, I still don't quite understand how Wyatt knew I won an award. He must see my face contort, though, because he says, "Aunt Juniper leaked the news last night." He shrugs. "Stag family gossip. Sorry."

Fern squeezes his shoulder. "They all sent a video congratulating me, too." She kisses him until Heather clears her throat. They break apart and we talk more about the logistics of Fern's departure. And then the meal is over, I've hugged my friend goodbye for now, and I find myself with absolutely nothing to do.

I have no idea how to relax, let alone have fun. I was going to work tomorrow, but my manager gave away my shift after I fainted and then called off. I'm about to climb the Cathedral of Learning to stare out the windows at the city I'm leaving behind when my phone rings in my hand. Odin.

"Hello?" I know I told him I'd go out with him, but I wasn't expecting him to just call when I was on the verge of a meltdown.

"Congrats, grad. You are officially smarter than me."

I lean against the stone wall of the building, feeling the sunshine on my face. "I've always been smarter than you. Now I just have paperwork."

Odin's laugh is deep and slow. "What are you doing now? Wyatt just left with the rest of his shit, so I know you're not hanging with Fern."

I bite the inside of my cheek. I decide I don't have any reason to be coy or avoid the blatant truth. "I have no idea," I admit. "I have literally no plans."

He whoops. "I was hoping you'd say that," he says, voice urgent with excitement. "I have a really terrific idea if you're willing to drive my car for a bit."

I frown and push off the wall, walking toward a spot of shade. "What are you talking about?"

"Go pack an overnight bag and come to my place. I've got a top-notch celebration idea for us." I hesitate, confused by what he's asking. He continues, saying, "In fact, you don't even need to pack a bag if you don't want to. We'll just be naked. Come to my apartment."

"Odin Stag, you are insane. I am not going to be naked for an overnight trip."

"You better be naked for some of it, Janssen. Hurry your ass up and get here when you can." He hangs up before I can protest.

CHAPTER 30
ODIN

MY COUSIN WYATT TOOK HIS GIRL TO THE FAMILY SKI HOUSE FOR A ROMANTIC escape, and his fatal flaw was not checking the schedule to make sure nobody else would be there. I am committed to avoiding getting caught with my ass in the air by any member of the Stag family, so I cross out the next three days on the shared calendar.

I order a bunch of meal kits delivered to the house from a service local to the area, and I beg my brother to grab me a few bottles of wine from the store when he's out restocking on chips. By the time Thora hesitantly knocks on my door, I've packed the whole safe and satisfied basket along with a few outfits.

"Are you ready to be wined and dined?" I close the door behind me before she can engage Stellan or Gunnar in conversation.

Thora looks confused, so I hand her my knee roller and swing down the stairs. "The Stag family has a vacation house," I tell her. "It's like an hour from here. Super private. There's a hot tub."

She points to my cast. "Can you use a hot tub?"

I frown. "Good point. We'll just focus on other activities while we're there."

Thora squeezes around my backpack to open the front door of the apartment building, setting my scooter on the ground right outside the step. "What makes you think I want to be naked with you again?"

I wink at her. "I have so many more ideas for things we can do together, Thora Janssen. You are a college graduate. Don't you want to celebrate with the safe and satisfied basket?"

Her cheeks are pink, and I pull my car keys from my sweats pocket. I click to unlock my car and hoist myself inside as she tosses her bag in the back and climbs into the driver's seat. It takes her a long time to get it all the way up close enough that she can reach the pedals and see over the steering wheel. "Would it kill you to drive a car sized for regular people?"

I laugh. "You think you're regular-sized? You're fun-sized."

That has Thora roaring, and I'm glad I put her at ease. "Okay, you win. Tell me where to go." I direct her out of town and east on the turnpike for a few exits. We put the windows down and breathe in the mountain air when we get off the highway and wind our way along the curvy roads to the ski resort where our house is located at the top of the mountain.

"It's really quiet here in the summer," I promise. "There are people here for hiking and stuff, but there is absolutely nobody up on the slopes where the house is."

By the time Thora pulls into the driveway, she looks completely shell-shocked. I gotta admit, the house is pretty impressive. It's got a sloped roof and multi-story windows overlooking the woods. I hop out of the car and smile at the trio of meal boxes on the porch, which I shove inside the door with the front of my scooter. "Come on," I call to her. "Come see."

I grab her hand when she steps in the door, eyes wide at the sight of the great room. There's a remote-controlled fireplace along one wall and a massive sectional sofa. My favorite part is the huge wooden table that seats 20. She drops her bag on the floor and I tug her against my side, kissing her neck. "Welcome," I whisper. "Want a tour?"

She shakes her head, still staring.

I scratch at my chin, considering the open staircase leading up to most of the bedrooms. "Well, that's maybe okay because I don't think I can make it up to the second floor."

She chuckles. "I think we will be okay on this floor."

"There's a basement, too," I tell her. "That's where the foosball table is. And the theater room. And the hot tub, which we've already established I can't use..." My voice drifts off, and I stare out onto the deck, where the heated swimming pool is also off-limits while I'm still in the cast. Shit.

I let my hand trace along her arm as she looks around. "Are you okay? We can always play a game. Or watch a movie. I brought wine."

I stoop to pick up the bottle I shoved in the water bottle pocket of my backpack. I grin at Thora as I hold the alcohol, and she smiles, relaxing a bit. "Wine would be nice, I guess."

"You got it. Go sit." Thora folds herself onto the couch, looking smaller than ever, as I roll to the bar and grab us a few glasses. The wine is a screw top, which makes things really easy as I settle in next to her and pour us each a few inches. "To you," I tell her. "Congratulations."

She bites her lip. "I can't drink a toast to myself. That's weird."

I drape an arm around her, and she is receptive to that, so I scoot her closer to me. "What about…to relaxing?"

She clinks her glass to mine and nods. "To relaxing."

I reach for the remote and flick a button so the fireplace roars to life. She smiles and wiggles her toes as she sits cross-legged, leaning against me a little more. We sip in silence until she's put back about half her glass. "I still can't get over being done and having the grant. And not having to work. And—"

"Hey," I lean forward and set my wine on the table, turning to face Thora and putting a hand on each of her thighs. "You've had some big changes. Let me help you forget all that for a bit. Make you feel good." I let my fingers trace along her legs. She smells so nice, floral and leathery from my car, I guess. Or the couch cushions.

"What do you see in me? I'm mean to you." She leans back against the arm of the couch as I keep rubbing her legs. She sips the wine lazily and watches me touch her.

I grin. "You know I like it when you're mean to me." I stroke a finger behind each of her knees and she sucks in a breath. "And you like when I'm mean to you right back." I take the wine glass from her, set it on the table next to mine, and haul her onto my lap so she's pressed against my chest, face an inch from mine. "But how about if I'm nice to you for like a half hour?"

I swallow her laugh with a kiss and soon it's on like a remote-controlled fireplace. Thora wraps her arms around my neck as she presses her mouth into mine and I dig my fingers into her hips as I rock her on my length. "I'm so hard for you," I murmur into her mouth. And then I look at her face, eyes wild, so I bite her neck, and she gasps. "You like that? Do you get wet when I'm rough with you?"

I remember how I fantasized about fucking her against the wall, about bending her over and slamming into her from behind. I still can't do those things, but damn if I'm going to disappoint her while I have her on my lap. I pinch her nipples through her shirt because, of course she's not wearing a bra. Her hands scramble to pull off my t-shirt, and I reach an arm behind my head, pulling it off by the collar as she stares at me. I feel her nails drag along my abs, her tongue tracing the diamond in my earlobe. "I like all of it," she whispers, biting my ear as I pinch her nipples again.

She leans back to undo her jeans and yank them off while I work on my shorts. "Shit," I say. "The sex stuff is in my bag." I move to stand, thinking that I'll maybe hop over and get it, but she places a hand on my shoulder.

"I got it, Stag." And she saunters her tiny, naked ass over to my bag, strutting back over like some sort of sex goddess. She tosses it next to me on the couch. "Surprise me with your sack of goodies."

"Oh, honey, just you wait." I pull open the zipper. "Lie back." She arches a brow and does as I say. When one hand drops absentmindedly to her breast, I pop open a bottle of lube and squeeze a few drops between her fingers.

"What?" She gasps and then moans. "Oh, it's warm."

"Damn right," I tell her, smearing some more of it on my hands and massaging it into her nipples. And then I lap at one and then the other as she groans in disbelief. "And it's fucking cake flavored. Because this is a party."

CHAPTER 31
THORA

I'M LYING BACK ON ODIN STAG'S MAGICAL GUEST COUCH WHILE HE LICKS MY entire body, which he first spread with the warming lube.

I have never experienced this particular blend of sensations, and I don't know that I can go back to just regular feelings. This is twenty times better than the time I accidentally did coke at a party in high school and felt like a million bucks making out with a football player.

I guess I'm making out with a bigger, better football player now. And then I shut that thought down because, of course, Odin's badly injured. His cast bumps against my leg as a reminder as he works his way up from my pussy to my chest like he can't make up his mind where he'd rather linger.

And then he kisses me, and I can taste myself and the flavored lube, and I groan into his mouth. I'm falling to pieces right here underneath him, but his body is holding me together. "I want you so much," I pant, and he nods, grinning. He's so beautiful up close, even more so when he looks at me like I'm simultaneously made of glass and the most amazing thing he's ever seen.

"Look at you," he says, running a finger down my ribs, across my pelvis, inserting it inside my body, which welcomes the thick digit. "You're dying for it."

"Yes," I stutter. "I already said that. Come on, Stag." He laughs and reaches into the bag, pulling out a strip of condoms. "What all do you have in there?"

"Patience, Thora. You want my Spear of Heaven or not?" He starts to

557

roll on the condom as he laughs at his own joke. I admire him, naked and gorgeous, kneeling between my legs while he douses his sheathed cock in lube.

And then he slides inside me, warm and slippery, and I gasp because I feel so full and so damn hot. "Odin." My breath comes in pants as my hands grip his shoulders. He moans, nibbling at my shoulders with his perfect teeth, while he starts to thrust. I think the couch surface makes it easier for him to find traction with his cast, which he seems to have wedged against the back cushions.

He starts to rub at my clit, and I stop caring about his injury. I can't care about anything at all when he makes me feel this way, and it occurs to me that I just might be able to come without a vibrator if he can just keep doing that thing with his thumb while he thrusts. "Odin, don't stop. Please, I'm so close."

"Yeah?" He pulls his head back to look at me but continues to apply pressure with his thumb.

"Yes!" I squeeze with all my might, wrapping my legs around his waist. And I feel it starting. "Odin, I'm going to come. Just like that. Oh, Odin, it's happening." I think I start to cry as my body begins to pulse and shudder and gulp him in. I stare into his eyes, and it's just as intense as before, except it's warm and different, my eyes roll back in my head as the sparks of pleasure careen up and down my spine.

I think I'm screaming his name. I think I'm kicking his butt cheeks with my heels, like he's a horse I'm riding into battle.

"Fuck, Odin, shit." I'm panting. He's grinning and his thumb is still pressed against my clit as the waves subside.

"You came," he whispers, his hips still, cock twitching inside me.

"I did." I groan and poke his shoulder like I need to check if he's real. "You made me."

"I helped you." He plants a kiss on my nose. "You ready for more?"

I snap my eyes back to his and bite my lip. He's still hard, after all. He hasn't come. Could I do that a second time? "I want to try."

"That's my girl." He kisses me again and starts moving. Our eyes are locked together as he bites his lip in concentration. "Mmm, it's so wet."

I stare at the bottle of lube on the coffee table, noting its location in case we need more of it. And then I thrust my hips up to meet his, grinding myself against his pelvis while he lets out small sounds of pleasure...I don't even know he's aware of producing.

"Does this feel good? What do you like?" I want to make him explode just like he did to me. I want to pull him over that cliff with me.

He pauses his movement, props himself on one elbow, and traces my nipple with a finger. "Remember when you played with my ass?"

I laugh. "How could I forget? The sound you made was epic."

He flicks his gaze to the lube. "Would you want to do that again?"

I frown momentarily. "I'm not ready to lick back there if that's what you're thinking."

"No," he shakes his head. "I just meant…it felt really good. Your finger. And the lube is so nice…"

I reach for the bottle with one hand, tilting my chin to see above his shoulder as I squirt some into my hand.

He smiles as I set the bottle on the carpet and reach for his butt while he moves inside me. "Your ass is so firm." I pinch it with my dry hand.

"For now, I guess. Oh, shit, Thora." I slide a finger in between his cheeks and trace a hand down as low as I can reach. I curl up so my arm has more purchase, and I can just manage to tap the tight pucker that gives way as he buries himself deep into my body.

Our eyes connect as I gently slide my slippery finger inside his body, and his mouth drops open. Odin's entire frame begins to shudder, and he roars. I feel his cock swell and throb, and he just keeps on yelling, coming almost violently inside me until he drops his hand between my legs again, pressing my clit until another orgasm seizes me, too. My hand slips out from its exploration as I come in gasping waves. When it's over, I sink into the couch, and he collapses on top of me.

Heaving and panting, we hold each other until moving almost seems possible again.

CHAPTER 32
ODIN

"THAT WAS INTENSE." AFTER WE FUCKED, I DRAGGED THORA DOWN THE HALL to the bathroom and ordered her to get into the giant whirlpool tub, where I can dangle one leg out the side and pull her between my legs so she's lying back against my chest while the water swirls around us.

"Mmm. I liked it." Her eyes are closed, and she lets me play with her tits all I want, which is constantly. I could lie here like this for hours, a gorgeous woman in my lap, rock-hard nipples in my palms. "Where did you get cake-flavored lube?"

I shrug, adjusting my weight so I can shut off the water with my good foot. "It was in the basket. I don't ask questions. Maybe Stellan added that one."

She shifts so she can see me, resting her cheek on my chest, which also feels awesome. "Did you take the whole basket?"

"I dumped and ran, baby." She laughs. I kiss the top of her head like I'm allowed to do that. Like she's mine. Except I know she's not. We're here right now because she took a big step on a journey that's leading her far away from me. But I don't want to think about that right now.

She settles back in between my legs. I should be alarmed that I'm not getting wood again, but I came harder than I ever did in my life, so I'll chalk it up as a win if I can get there again after dinner. "So, I've seen the couch and the bathroom. You're telling me the other floors of this place are even nicer?"

"The nicest. You can go look around later. I'm going to cook dinner, and that'll take a while."

Thora sits up, and I hate it, so I pull her back, wanting her soft skin against me. "Odin," she says, "I'm not going to wander around your family's house without you."

I run my fingers through her hair, getting it wet so I can wash it like she did for me back at my place. "It's not like you're trespassing. But if you don't want to see the bunk room, that's your loss."

"I'm not sleeping in a bunk bed." She tips her head back, giving me more access to get her hair wet, and I reach for the shampoo, pouring some in my hand and starting to work it into her dark hair. It's straight and smooth between my fingers, and now she smells like soap instead of sex and lube.

"You better not sleep in the bunk bed. I was thinking we probably wouldn't sleep at all." She hums, and I wash her hair, then nudge her to scoot down further in the water so I can use my hands to cup water over it and rinse everything. Eventually, she turns, and we wash each other's bodies with the soap, her nipples impossibly hard, dragging along my chest when she leans forward to wash my back. Is she loving this as much as I am?

"Tell me about your travel plans," I tell her, to get my mind off the word "love" and the creeping feeling of attachment that is overtaking my brain.

Thora smiles. Her face is clean and bright and pink from the hot water. Or the sex. Or both. "I have everything set up," she tells me. "Passport. Visa. Ticket. I fly out on August 1, and Fern is meeting me at the airport. Which is good because my plane gets in super late at night, and I don't want to take the bus alone at one in the morning."

I frown at this. "You better not take a bus alone at one in the morning."

She swats at me. "I just said I wasn't. Wyatt has a car." Suddenly, I hate that my cousin will see my girl when she embarks on her life goal. My girl...that's not fair. I haven't earned the right to call her mine. We're just messing around while she waits for her next step, and I figure out what the hell my life looks like now.

I realize she has continued talking, and I lace my fingers together behind my head while she sits facing me in the giant tub. My leg is half asleep from dangling out of the tub, but I have my whole life to improve my circulation. This is my only chance to see Thora Janssen excited about international scholar orientation at Oxford.

"And then I'm pretty much on my own in the library," she says, clasping her hands together under her chin. She rests her elbows on my knees, and I press my legs together, pinning her in place. She giggles. I love it. "Nine entire months just learning about international family law and social services policy. I'm going to draw correlations and bring it all with me to law school. It would be great to do a Master's in Public Policy, too…what?"

She tucks her hair behind her ears. I shake my head. "Nothing. I just like hearing you talk about this stuff."

"You and Fern and nobody else." She sighs. "All right. I'm turning into a prune. You said you'd feed me."

Thora flicks the drain on the tub and the water starts gurgling out. "I guess you're in a hurry for my hot beef."

"Oooh, I do enjoy steamy meat." She cracks up as she steps out of the tub and, to my frustration, covers her body in a fluffy towel. "Do you need help getting out?"

I wish I could tell her I didn't. I wish I could do a lot of things, but I accept her hand and swing myself out of the tub, leaning against the side of it while I dry off.

Thora follows me to the kitchen, chatting about her packing plans while she pulls clothes from her bag and, unfortunately, covers up. I tug on a pair of shorts and start prepping one of the meal kits while we drink wine. It feels so natural, teasing her, talking about random shit like whether she needs compression socks for an international flight. "You're not middle-aged with circulation issues, Thora. I think you'll be fine."

She sips her drink. "I've never flown before at all…how should I know?"

"You never flew anywhere?" I offer her a spoon to taste the pan sauce while the meat simmers on the stove.

She closes her eyes and nods. "That's good. And no. I've never really left Pittsburgh much."

I think about my own childhood, traveling all over the world for my extended family's sports adventures. But none of that has prepared me for a future once my life got derailed. Thora has built herself a bulletproof plan, all within the confines of the Steel City.

I plate the food and realize I can't easily carry it all to the table, so I slide the plates onto the counter, and Thora hops up into one of the stools. We eat side by side, talking about nothing and everything until she slides her plate away, drops a hand to my crotch, and tells me to show her our bedroom.

I ABSOLUTELY CANNOT GET USED TO THIS. WHAT IS THIS LIFE WHERE I'M SWEPT off to a luxury cabin with a man who not only makes me come but cooks me dinner and plies me with delicious wine? I wake up cocooned in crisp, soft linens that smell so fresh and clean. And I've got a warm, hairy arm around my waist again, with Odin breathing softly into my hair as he holds me tight.

Maybe I can appreciate it for what it is: a perfect getaway. A gift for my graduation. Although, based on the sounds he was making last night again in bed, this is as much a reward for Odin as it is for me. We used that entire bottle of lube.

My body alerts me to the need to use the bathroom, and I struggle to free myself from his iron grasp. I eye the giant tub in the mirror as I fix my hair and brush my teeth. Did we really spend an hour in there just talking about my future? I realize I didn't ask him anything about his rehab or what comes next for him.

And then I gaze at his sleeping form and realize that was probably by design. Maybe this is an escape for him from thinking about all of that. I know his family is giving him a lot of pressure to make decisions and fill out paperwork. I heard Fern and Wyatt talking about that, and Odin has hinted at a few things.

I decide he deserves some more time to just mindlessly enjoy some pleasure, so I crawl my way back into the bed and reach in between his legs.

I find him hot and hard, and I smile, giving him a few pumps before I wrap my mouth around the tip of his cock. His eyes fly open, and he looks down at me, stunned, face-melting into utter joy as I plant kisses all along his shaft.

"Morning," I whisper, wrapping one hand around the base of his cock while I do my best to fit him into my mouth.

"Are you serious right now? Wow." Odin bites his lip, staring as I manage to get a few inches of his length inside my throat before I hollow out my cheeks and give a good, hard suck. "Oh, Thora. Gorgeous. Wow."

His hand drops to my hair, reverent, as he stares at me. I release him with a wet pop as I catch my breath and then hold his gaze while I suck with all my might, bobbing my head up and down, pumping him with one hand and cradling his balls with the other.

His body goes limp as Odin leans into the sensations, but soon enough, I feel him stiffen everywhere. "Thora, honey, I'm gonna—"

He tries to lift my head from his dick, but I send him a look. I know what I'm doing. I want to drink down the reward for this work. I want to make Odin Stag crumble to pieces because of me, and I want to be here to lick it all better at the end.

I wriggle my shoulders a bit so my nipples graze along his thighs, and that extra stimulation sends him right over the edge. Odin roars, one strong hand digging into the sheets while the other remains gentle in my hair. He spurts into my mouth, salty and hot, and I swallow down his release gladly. I want to get used to this. I cannot get used to this.

But there's today. And there's right now. And as I release Odin's softening cock, I stare into his blue eyes and see this massive man has fallen apart right here in bed beside me. It's a lot. But I chose this, and damn it, I'm going to soak it in.

"Morning," I tell him again.

He can't form words. He smiles lazily and pats the pillow beside him. I crawl back up and figure I'm going to rest my head next to him, maybe fall asleep some more, but he pulls me on top of him and kisses me, moaning into my mouth, pressing his lips into mine like he wants to fuse us together. "You're incredible," he says, tracing my chin with his finger, cupping the side of my face like I'm a treasured thing.

I can't speak, so I rest my cheek on his chest until his breathing slows, and he falls back asleep.

———

I don't remember falling back asleep, but I wake up to the smell of food cooking. I pad down the hall in Odin's t-shirt. He notices from behind the stove where he's folding an omelet onto a plate. "You better be naked beneath that," he says, tugging off his robe. He is, like before, just wearing athletic shorts. I like the opportunity to stare at this perfect specimen of the human body.

Well. Perfect, plus one small, injured part.

I sigh and hop up onto a stool. I sort of like eating at the counter with him this way. It's cozy despite the enormity of the house. "So, what's the deal with this place again? Who owns it?"

He hops up next to me and rests his cast on another stool. "My dad and his three brothers bought it together for Uncle Tim's 40th birthday. Now we all share it."

I look around the walls, covered in black and white photographs of a truly astounding number of boy children. "And you said there's a calendar for it?"

He nods. "And I double-checked." He squeezes my thigh and then lifts the hem of the shirt, peeking. I swat his hand away, and he laughs. "The whole family was all supposed to be at graduation this weekend." He takes a sip of juice. "Wes, Wyatt, and me. We were all going to graduate, and now…none of us did. Life is strange that way, I guess."

I hesitate, but since he brought it up, I decide to ask anyway. "What will you do about school?"

He nods, chewing and swallowing his eggs. He seems a little sad that his plate is empty, and I slide mine toward him. There's no way I can eat all this food anyway. He looks wide-eyed at my offering. "You sure?" When I nod, he continues talking. "Well, I finally did talk to my advisors. I got extensions for my classes. All except argument. Thank you very much for the motivation to get an A in that one."

I hold up my juice cup in a toast, and he clinks it against mine. "So anyway, in addition to a whole bunch more rehab, my big summer plans include geography homework and essays about sociology."

I finish my juice and dab at my mouth, hesitating again. "And then?"

"Then I have no fucking idea." He throws down his fork. "I can't play. I'm not even sure I'll be walking by fall. I'm just buying time until I figure out what the future looks like for a has-been athlete with no other marketable skills."

"Hey, don't say that." He scoffs. "I mean, you are an okay cook."

That draws a laugh out of him. I can't help but add, "it's nice that you can take some time, though. You know that you have support."

He nods. "Wyatt said something the other day that sort of stuck with me…but I don't know if it's possible."

My brows lift. "What? Tell me!" It's exciting to think he might have even a kernel of an idea for his next steps.

Odin blows a raspberry. "It's dumb. Maybe. But he said his team in London has a whole staff of mental health pros."

I clap my hands. "Sports psychology is a real thing for sure. You could go to grad school for that."

He shoulders me. "She says to the college dropout."

I shoulder him right back. "You just said you're fixing that, though. And don't get a big head or anything, but you're pretty decent at research and papers. That's most of grad school."

He grins at me. "Was that a compliment, Janssen?"

I throw my napkin at him, and he catches it mid-air. "This is my thanks? And I went to bat for you…" He stops mid-sentence and shakes his head.

"What do you mean?" I frown as Odin slides our plates toward the sink and pivots over there on his scooter, rinsing the dishes and setting them in the dishwasher. "Odin, what do you mean you went to bat? About what?"

"I didn't mean that. There was no bat." He starts hand washing the pan he used to cook the eggs in, and then he seems to change his mind. "Come outside on the deck with me," he says, starting to roll toward the sliding door. "Let's enjoy the view."

I can tell he's trying to change the subject, but in the spirit of enjoying myself, I follow him. The air is crisp here. I can hear birds and insects. I close my eyes and soak in the differences from the city. I wonder if this is what the scenery will be like at Oxford. If London is a similar city to Pittsburgh, what will life be like over there?

He wraps an arm around my shoulder and squeezes. "Pretty nice, right? I wish we could swim."

I frown at the pool. "Wouldn't it be freezing?"

He shakes his head. "Heated."

I roll my eyes. "I should have figured. Fancy-ass family." I sigh and stare over the deck railing at the trees beyond the currently grassy ski slopes. But then I think more about Odin's wealthy family and what he said at the sink. My stomach is uneasy. Something is off. I remember him showing up at the diploma ceremony, the way my advisor insisted I be there for a surprise award. A shiver rolls down my neck as I start to put it all together. "Hey, what did you mean? About going to bat."

He shakes his head and grips the deck rail. He is hiding something. "Did you have something to do with that scholarship? Is that why you and your mom were there at the ceremony?"

Odin grips the edge of the counter. "You're an amazing student, Thora. You deserve that money and more. You're doing good things in the world. I felt terrible that you paid your mom's rent so she'd come to graduation."

I fly back from the rail, horrified. "You felt bad?"

He throws a hand in the air. "Of course, I felt bad for you!"

I press my knuckles to my temples. All this has been way too good to be true. And now I see it for what it all was. "Am I your pity project? Is that what I am to you?"

"Thora. No. Wait. You're getting this wrong."

I cross my arms and stare up at him. "Then tell me what's right. Tell me you had nothing to do with that money."

He scratches the back of his neck. "Look," he starts, and I shriek and tug at my hair. I'm going to have to pay it back. I feel disgusting and cheap. I never wanted to be the object of anyone's pity, let alone a man I'm sleeping with. "Thora, I don't even know what the fuck I was going to do with that money otherwise. I can't live up to the expectations that were set when I got it from the fucking video game people."

I growl at him. I want to shove him in the chest but I'm adult enough not to knock him over while he's injured. "Odin, you can't just *sneak* and trick me. How am I supposed to react when I learn your entire family was talking about me? About how unfortunate I am?"

I groan and rush into the house, down the hall to the bedroom. I have to pack my stuff. I have to get out of here. Somehow. If I have to walk back to Pittsburgh, so be it. I hear him rolling down behind me. "I only gave some of the money. The rest was legitimately from lawyers all over the damn city who were impressed by you, Thora. It all went through the women's law clinic, I swear. It's a real award."

"Don't patronize me," I snap. "I've spent my entire life being patronized by people who think they know what's best for me. I thought you were different."

"Thora, please," Odin pleads. "I was just trying to help. My family has so much, and you work so hard—"

"Stop. Just stop." I hold up a hand. "I don't need you to remind me how hard my life is compared to yours. I don't need your family's pity money."

"It's not pity! God, you're so stubborn about accepting help—"

"And you're so used to throwing money at problems that you don't understand why this hurts me!" I ball my hands into fists and shake my head. "You know what the worst part is? I actually started to believe I maybe deserved good things. That I earned them on my merit. But this whole time, you were just another person who saw me as someone to fix." I tug at my hair. "I trusted you, Odin. What a mistake."

"Please sit so we can talk about this," he begs, hopping over to the bed and sitting next to my bag, where I'm stuffing in clothes and toiletries. "You're the only thing I have going for me right now, Thora."

I shake my head and yank off his shirt, stuffing my own over my head instead. "That's not fair, Odin. Everyone in my life depends on me utterly and fully. I thought you were someone I could maybe lean on."

"You can! That's why I wanted—"

I snarl. "Don't tell me that's why you gave me money. Just forget it. You'll never, ever understand where I'm coming from. I don't have a family who will pay my rent while I figure out my shit. I don't have anyone, Odin. I need to get out of here."

His face falls, and he breathes quietly for a few beats. "Take the car," he says. "My family can come get me."

I roll my eyes. "Of course they can." I groan and huff past him. "I'll leave your keys with your brother or whoever I can find."

I pause at the door, tears burning my eyes. "You know what kills me? I actually let myself believe you saw me as an equal. But I was just your charity case all along."

"Thora, that's not—"

"Save it for the next hard-luck case you want to rescue."

I slam the door to the palace in the mountains and cry the entire drive back to the city. When I get to Odin's apartment, I ring the bell, slap the keys into Gunnar's palm, and stalk off down the road as he shouts my name and asks what happened. Let him call Odin and ask.

A FEW HOURS LATER, ALL THREE OF MY BROTHERS SHOWED UP TO RETRIEVE ME. I didn't even call them, but since they arrived in my car, I guess Thora had already seen them and gone.

"Hey, man," Gunny says, sinking into the couch beside me. I don't even have the television on. I'm just staring into the fireplace, trying to figure out where I went so wrong. Thora thinks I pity her, but the opposite is true. I revere her. I find her to be extraordinary.

That feels like a bougie word, but it's the best I can think of. And I've spent hours just sitting here thinking about it.

I grunt at my brothers as the twins squeeze in on my other side.

Gunnar stretches and puts an arm around my shoulder. "Sooooo Thora stopped by…looked pretty pissed."

I nod and cross my arms. Alder and Tucker trade farts, probably trying to get a reaction from me, but I'm used to their antics.

Gunnar sighs. "We wanted to talk to you, actually. And since you weren't with Thora and you don't really leave the house, we tracked your phone."

Tucker nods. "Did you know I always know where you are, bro?"

I shrug, still not looking over at him and Alder. I'm sure Dad has our whole family tracked just in case, but I don't say so.

Gunny sighs. "We've been thinking about you and your bum leg, man. And our careers."

I frown and spare a glance at my brother. "What do you mean?"

He retracts his arm and pats my thigh. "You know hockey is different from football. I signed with the Fury two years ago."

"I know that." I still think it's weird that hockey drafts guys while they're still in college and waits around for them to finish before they start with the pros. And then it occurs to me that I think that's weird because guys can get injured. Seriously injured. Like me. "What are you saying?"

Gunny nods. "I'm leaving school." He points to the twins. "We all are. The twins got drafted in January. We don't want…" He drifts off without saying *we don't want to wind up like you.*

I pinch my lips together.

Alder winces. "We just…want at least a million bucks if we're going to get hurt anyway."

Tucker grunts. "Maybe you're only getting a million."

They start to argue about who is getting the better offer, and I hop up to my foot and extract myself from the couch.

"Odin, wait." Gunnar looks serious. "We wanted you to know that, like, this isn't all in vain. Or whatever."

I close my eyes and shake my head. "Gee. Thanks. Can you take me home now?"

Alder grunts, and I stare at him. "Mom said to drop you at the boathouse."

They start to walk toward the door of the ski house. Tucker asks, "Do you need to do anything? Burn the sheets? Scour the countertops?"

"I stripped the bed, jagoff." I pull the door shut behind me, and Alder types in the code to lock up.

"What the hell am I going to do at the boathouse?" I climb into the back seat of my own car. Tucker drives, and Alder sits up front with him. I don't want to interrupt their twin vibe. They're lucky they got drafted to the same team, so they can stay joined at the brain.

They're just all-around lucky… unlike me.

Gunny sings along to the radio for a few bars and then says, "I'm assuming you'll explain to Mom how you fucked up with Thora. Or maybe she'll make you work out with her. I don't know, man. I'm just following orders."

It's a weird, fast drive back into the city. I fall asleep for half of it and wake up with my face pressed against the window as my brother pulls off the highway onto the bridge toward Washington's Landing, where Mom keeps her fancy boats.

She used to take all of us out with her. Now, she mostly rows alone. But she's waiting in the parking lot as my brother rolls to a stop. I leave my bag in the car and grab my scooter from the back as the guys wave to Mom, who blows them kisses and then turns to me with a weird smile. "Come see what I have for you."

She heads down the ramp from the parking lot to the boat house, and I follow her, trying not to let the scooter roll away from me on the slope. Mom gestures at a boat propped on slings in the middle of the room. "Ta-da!"

I furrow my brow. "It's a boat."

She grins. "It's an adaptive rowing boat! I talked to your trainer and—"

"Mom, they're not supposed to just talk to you. What the hell? Don't I have privacy or something?"

She rolls her eyes. "I didn't discuss your particular situation. I asked what sort of rowing someone might try after an Achilles repair. This boat has a regular seat for me, and I set one up for you with just one foot pad. We'll each use two oars…"

I tune out as she babbles about how we will both hop in the river and splash our way around the island ten or twenty times. I don't bother to point out that I can't help her carry the boat to the dock, but she surprises me by unlocking little wheels on the boat slings. She's whistling her way down the ramp before I can respond, and she hoists the boat into the water on her own, reminding me that my mom is still jacked.

I scratch my chin and stare as she sets the oars up near the boat. "How will I get in? This is all awkward…"

Mom braces herself on the dock and tells me to squat low and take her hand. I do and step into the boat with my good leg, which is not the leg closest to the water. "You couldn't set up the boat in the other direction?" I grumble and clench my core as the boat rocks.

Mom steadies it with one foot. "Just sit down, kid."

I lower my butt into the seat, acknowledging that this is already a fantastic workout just climbing aboard. Mom is in her element in the seat behind me. "All right, O. Grab your oars. You remember. Yes, now strap your left foot to the boards. I set the footpad as big as it goes. I hope it works okay for your monster feet."

I grunt at her and get myself situated. I haven't rowed with her for a long time, but we sometimes do the rowing machine for workouts with football, and I'm sure my technique is still good. Mom pushes us off the dock, and when I glance over my shoulder, she's pretty much just holding the boat steady while I do all the work. She grins at me. "Doesn't the burn feel good, baby? Do you miss it?"

I glower at her because she's right. This feels amazing. My work at physical therapy has been very focused on small movements for my ankle. Then, I'm sometimes allowed to do seated upper body workouts, and if I'm very, very polite, Prachi lets me do one-legged squats.

But this is grabbing every part of my body except my right leg. I feel the movements in my hips. I feel my whole back working the oars in the river, and when I lean back, I feel the sun on my face as I dig in, which gets us going a little faster. "All right," I admit. "This is nice."

Mom chuckles and starts bossing me around like she's the coxswain. She must have already worked out today because otherwise, I don't think she'd be able to stand just sitting there holding her oars out of the way. We make a full lap around the island before she joins in, confident I'm not going to tip the boat with my uneven pressure.

We do two more laps before she calls it, and we approach the dock. There, we do the whole dance in reverse to get me out of the boat and the boat back up on the slings.

I lean heavily on my knee roller as I follow her. "That was pretty good, Mom. I'm sorry I was a jerk about it."

She smiles. "Just wait until you can walk on that cast. One of the guys from the masters team is an orthopedic surgeon. He thinks you could be rowing fully, regularly, by October."

I chew on the inside of my cheek. I haven't let myself think about October or anything beyond finishing my spring semester classes. Even that's new for me ever since my body broke.

"Mom, October is…I don't even know where I'll be living in August."

She beckons me to follow her to her car and helps me get my scooter in the back seat. Once we're both buckled inside, she turns on the air and says, "I was thinking about that, too. I know how much you love team sports. Did you know they have a crew team at Oxford?"

My eyes fly wide. "Mom, what did you do?" Thora's already furious with me for helping her fly to England. She will murder me if I show up there on the crew team. "I can't just enroll at Oxford. I didn't even finish college."

Mom waves a hand and puts the car in gear, heading back toward the bridge to the highway. "You'll finish your classes in a few weeks. Did you know the dean of admissions at Oxford was an Olympic rower, too?" I snort at my mother, who apparently has a PhD in meddling. Mom nods. "She's a little younger than me, but we're on the same online forums."

"Mom. You are insane. I can't just move to England and row boats now that I'm done playing football."

She scoffs like I'm the one being ridiculous. "Why not? You love team sports. You're an accomplished athlete. And you need a little time to figure out your next steps in the world. What's the harm in a little master's degree?"

"Okay," I pat her hand. "Let's pretend this idea isn't utterly ridiculous. Why Oxford? Why aren't you sending me to your old stomping grounds in Boston or something?"

She rolls her eyes, absolutely fed up with my apparent stupidity. "Two reasons, kid. First, you can compete for your university as a graduate student in the UK. Second, you can go win back your girl!"

Like it's so easy. Like she'd ever consider being mine. But Mom's idea does rekindle the curiosity Wyatt set off about a career in sports psychology. Who better to step into that role than someone who has walked that walk?

Mom drops me off at my apartment, where Wyatt's room is totally empty, Gunnar is half packed, and I realize that I'm powerless against the river of change flowing through my life.

Maybe my mom's idea isn't so ridiculous. It certainly beats living in my parents' basement while I figure out what comes next for me. Oxford is a big place. If Thora tells me to go pound sand, our paths don't need to cross. And I can get to some of Wyatt's games while I'm over there figuring out how to walk again.

I text Thora that I'm sorry, I'm here if she's willing to talk, and I lock myself in my room to scrape together a passing set of grades for the semester that just ended.

CHAPTER 35
THORA

Odin texts once a week to apologize and ask to talk. And I have zero time to deal with that nonsense. I'm too busy working double shifts all summer trying to pay him back for his pity portion of that scholarship. I can begrudgingly accept that most of the money came from actual charitable sources. Still, Fern confirmed that Odin donated his endorsement money from some video game to his uncle's foundation and told them to launder the money until it became a scholarship. For me.

It's embarrassing to think about the way I thought we were connecting, but he was actually just feeling sorry for the poor girl with formerly-incarcerated parents. God, what must he have been thinking about when I thought our eyes were locking, connecting despite our differences.

He and his savior complex can fuck right off. Which, I guess he did already. I don't know why I keep hoping he'll turn up at the bar. It's not like I've given him any hope of connecting. His family is probably vacationing in Ibiza or something glamorous. No, cancel that. They're probably all up in their mountain palace.

"Thora!" My manager snaps her fingers, and I shake out of my thought spiral. I've been on thin ice here at work despite years of dedicated work behind the bar. One little dizzy spell and one call-off...on arguably the busiest night of the year for a college bar...has put me in the doghouse for the whole summer.

I'm making bank right now, though, so I can't complain. I'm giving a lot of it to my parents and setting aside big chunks to pay Odin back as soon as I can figure out how to get him the money in a way he can't refuse or sneak back to me somehow. Fern says I'm being stubborn about this.

I'm counting down the days until I can see her again.

———

At the end of July, I work my last shift and untie my apron for the final time. I take the bus home, and since I'm leaving in the morning, I realize this might be my last time seeing this part of the city for a long time. I'll be different when I get back here. I press a palm to the window and stare at the streets below the Bloomfield Bridge. I look at the hospitals and university buildings that have defined my view my entire life. Everything that once felt so out of reach is finally within my grasp.

I pack the last of my things into my two new-to-me suitcases, and in the morning, I wake up earlier than I need to in search of my mother.

She's in the kitchen, wearing her work uniform, crying. "Oh," she says. "Hey, sweetheart."

"Mom." I wrap my arms around her slim, tired frame. I hear the familiar gurgle of the coffeemaker and try to imprint that aroma as my main memory of this house, of my childhood. "I wish you could come with me."

Mom snorts. "Yeah, right. Me travel abroad."

I pull back and stare at her. "You could visit me. I could help you get your passport. I'd help you."

She smiles and smooths my hair. "Thora, baby, I'm not cut out for that kind of stress. But it makes me proud knowing you'll be out there, showing them what Pittsburgh girls can be."

I lean against her shoulder, thinking how desperately I wish I could help her more, how her circumstances inspire my entire research focus, my fellowship application...everything. I consider that Odin maybe, could have felt similarly. But then I let that thought slip away so I can kiss my mother goodbye and splurge on a car service to the airport.

———

The flight is long and confusing for me. Am I supposed to tip the flight attendants who bring me free wine and food every few hours? Do people really pay extra for internet access when we have an entire library of free movies to choose from?

I keep my nose down, repeatedly clutch at my passport tucked into my bra, and finally make my way through customs and into the bustle of Heathrow's airport, which doesn't feel at all different from the crowded T station in downtown Pittsburgh after a hockey game.

My heart flutters in my chest as I search for Fern, and then I see her holding a giant sign with my name on it. She jumps up and down, hollering, and people stare. But who cares? We can be obnoxious Americans for a minute. "You're here," Fern squeals.

"You're here," I squeal back. And we dance in a circle around my bags, two scholarship girls from Pittsburgh here in London for graduate school. "This is surreal," I whisper.

She nods. "Come on." She grabs one of my bags. "Wyatt sent a car for us."

I chuckle. "Of course he did. It sucks that he's away. I would have given him a handshake or something to thank him."

She laughs and guides me toward a black car with a driver in a suit, eager to grab my bags and open our doors. It's a bit weird getting in a car with the steering wheel on the right, but I'm too tired to focus on it for long.

"You don't have to thank Wyatt," Fern says. "This is just something he likes to do to take care of me."

I run my arms along the leather interior. "Yeah, but you have to admit it's…maybe weird is the wrong word. But it's very different from what we're used to."

She smiles and closes her eyes, resting her head against the cushy seat-back. "I take care of him, too."

"Gross, Fern." I swat at her leg, and she laughs.

"Not like that. Seriously. Our relationship is very reciprocal. We have different love languages." I wish her comment didn't immediately make me think of Odin, causing my entire body to clench uncomfortably. I'm quiet for a bit, staring out the window as some of the city sights come into view. Fern says, "Hey, Geoffrey, can you make sure we pass The Eye? I want Thora to see it."

"You got it, guv," the driver says, winking at us in the rearview mirror. I keep my eyes focused out the window.

"Anyway," Fern says, "Wyatt is very generous with people he cares about. Which includes you because you're important to me."

I sigh. "Thank you. Thank him for me. You're important to me, too."

"Duh," she says. And then she drops a bomb: "And you're maybe important to other people in the Stag family, too…"

"Don't." I shake my head. "I can't." She's going to bring up Odin, and my heart can't handle all the conflicted feelings I have about him. He was supposed to be a spring fling, anyway.

"Why?" She pokes my shoulder. "He's kind of perfect for you. He gives you shit, and he's competitive like you. And he's smitten, Thora. Anyone could see…"

I turn to face her, spying the giant Ferris wheel Fern mentioned all lit up out her side of the car. "Okay, well, he's also super pushy and lives in a different country and has no life plan beyond living in his parents' basement." She bites her lip. I frown at her. "What? What do you know?"

She winces. "He doesn't live in his parents' basement."

"Oh. Okay, so he's still in a shitty athlete apartment playing video games."

"You like video games."

"Ugh!" I flop back in my seat and close my eyes. "That's not the point."

Her hand drops to mine and squeezes. I flip my palm over and squeeze back, wrapping our fingers together, enjoying being physically in my best friend's presence again, even if she's choosing right now to pester me about my spring fling.

"He's doing a master's in sports psychology," she whispers.

I open my eyes and stare at her in the dark, illuminated by the city lights, remembering what he said about that fledgling idea for his future before he revealed that he saw me as a charity project. "Well," I spit out. "That's fucking awesome." And it's true, but unexpected. "I love that for him." This last bit comes out with less vehemence.

The car eases to a stop outside a gorgeous apartment building, brightly lit by streetlights, with little awnings over the windows and flower boxes and a doorman in a red uniform. "You should text him," Fern says, unbuckling and accepting Geoffrey's hand as she exits the car.

"I'll think about it," I tell her, and I follow her upstairs to check out her incredible flat.

ALL THE MELATONIN IN THE WORLD COULDN'T PUT ME TO SLEEP THIS WEEK. MY body is wrecked with the time change. I eventually gave up trying to sleep at Fern's house and just stared out her flat windows at the London streets at night. The city isn't so very different from Pittsburgh…neighborhoods built and bisected by a river…cobblestones and old architecture sprinkled with new bike lanes and modern parks. It makes me feel at home in a way.

In the morning, Fern—well, with Geoffrey—drives me to Oxford and holds my hand while I sign in for the graduate student housing. I'm living in a glorious old building full of wee flats. My place is one room with a bathroom, tiny kitchen, and nook for the bed tucked in the wall where I can stare up at the beautiful wooden ceiling or stare out the window of the sandstone building.

I don't have much to unpack, and the kitchen comes equipped with *very* basic supplies…so Fern gives me a watery-eyed hug and heads back to her own school. The flat has built-in drawers and bookshelves, although I didn't bring any books to put on them. I fantasize about acquiring some while I'm here…old law texts and reference guides to policies from all the different nations that prioritize social services.

I fall back on the bed, clapping my hands, and pass out in the middle of the afternoon, which isn't going to do my jet lag any favors.

I wake up groggy in the middle of the night, and by four in the morning, I'm wide awake and ready to face my day. Too bad it doesn't begin for five more hours. I decide to teach myself about English tea and boil some water in the kettle on my tiny stove. I'm feeling very posh, pouring it into a pot with loose leaves Fern gifted me, but stirring and sipping in silence just leads to thoughts of Odin.

Honestly, I don't know what to make of the new information I've learned and processed. He figured out what he wants to do. He leveraged his family's wealth to do something nice for me. He told me I'm the only thing he has going right in his life. It's all too much, too soon, when I need to clear space in my head for this fellowship.

I will call him. Or text him. Eventually, I still intend to give him back his portion of that grant money. I even set it aside in a sub-account in my shiny new international checking account.

———

After two showers and a long session ironing my first-day outfit, I shoulder my laptop bag, toe on my red flats, and walk to orientation, knowing I look like what I am: a professional young woman starting graduate school.

The sun is shining, which I wasn't expecting, but I tuck my new raincoat in my bag regardless. I sign in for international student programming and mill around munching an actual crumpet.

"And where are you from?" A guy with a French accent holds a hand out toward me, a hopeful smile on his face.

"Pittsburgh. In the States," I tell him, shaking his hand and smiling. Look at me mingling. This isn't terribly different from bartending. Instead of hoping for tips, I'm looking to make professional connections, I remind myself.

"Ah, an American. What brings you to Oxford?" He leans against the mantle of a very ornate fireplace.

I swallow the last bite of crumpet and dab at my mouth with my napkin. "International Policy and Family Studies," I tell him. "You?"

He talks about microeconomics until my eyes start to glaze, but we're soon joined by a pair of students from India, here studying the impact of colonialism, and a German dude "reading" English literature.

I lose myself in conversations about relocation, learn that the Indian folks live in my same building, and enter our campus tour buzzing. As we walk across the impressive lawn, I snap a picture to send to my mom. Then I realize it's three in the morning back home. I sigh.

———

The rest of the day is a lot of the same. I repeatedly get to say, "I'm Thora Janssen, Rhodes Fellow." I like it when people are visibly impressed by my achievements. I could get used to this, I think. But it will take some time. I have to physically restrain myself from hopping up to get everyone a tray of water glasses at lunch and I thank the staff too profusely when someone serves tea in the afternoon.

I am grateful for a lull in conversation as people sip their tea, and I take the opportunity to step back from the cluster of other international students. I stand in the window, sipping, looking out at the people milling around campus. The professors here really do wear their academic regalia, or at least they're wearing it today, billowing around campus in bright red gowns and velvet caps.

Amidst the bustle, I think I see a familiar man limping, but I convince myself it's just the jet lag. There will be no massive football players here, with or without knee rollers.

But then I hear a scraping sound, and I turn to see a man walking with a cane, entering the room and sort of dragging a cast on his right leg. He's tall and fit, with bright blue eyes and a smile that has everyone in the space walking over to greet him.

Except me. I stand with a trembling hand; not sure I can trust my eyes until he approaches, and I catch a whiff of him. Cedar and lime and, well, swagger ooze from Odin Stag. I drop my cup to the ground when I see that it's really, truly him standing here in front of me. In England. He stoops to pick up the cup with his non-cane hand. "Pretty sturdy. I'm impressed it didn't break," he says, setting the cup on the windowsill.

"What are you doing here?" All I can do is hiss at him in disbelief.

"Well, I didn't come to mop up spilled tea, that's for sure, Janssen." He leans against the wall and smirks at me like we're just joking around on campus in Pittsburgh.

"What are you *doing* here?" I repeat, crossing my arms and looking around to see if people are staring. Some are, in fact.

"I joined the crew team," he says with a shrug, and I swat him in the shoulder. He grins. "I'm serious."

I scowl and take a deep breath. "Enough, Odin. That team is for students."

He grins even bigger, flashing dimples. I realize he's wearing pants for the first time since I got to know him. He's a whole mood, in dark jeans and a nice shirt beneath a blazer that hugs his shoulder muscles. He's got a leather belt on, and my traitorous brain creates an image of him whipping it off and dropping it on the floor with a clank as he opens his pants.

"Right," he says, reminding me that I'm in public. "I also enrolled in a sports psychology program here. Did you know they let masters students compete in sports in the UK? I'm a catch."

I blink at him, trying to understand what he's saying. That he, too, is a student. Here. Where I am a student. Close by. He leans in close and whispers. "Catch. That's a rowing joke. It slaps with the lads." And then he winks at me, and I can't take it anymore. I spin on my heel and walk out of the room.

"THORA, WAIT!" I TROT AFTER HER AS FAST AS I'M ABLE WITH THIS WALKING boot. I'm making a ton of noise with this thing, but she only gets as far as the stairs before I can reach her shoulder with my palm. "Can I talk to you?"

When she turns around, I see she's crying, and she crosses her arms over her body, shivering.

"Hey." I pull her close and wrap my arms around her, letting my cane drop to the ground and not caring what happens to it. "I swear I'm not trying to be creepy."

"You followed me to another continent?"

I shrug. "Lots of places have sports psychology master's...but I was kind of limited with my options for schools that *also* have crew teams where I can compete."

"What about your foot?" She burrows her face in my shoulder and inhales, and I tuck this knowledge away that Thora likes how I smell.

"I'll be out of this boot and mostly functional by October," I explain. "I might not ever run again, but rowing is a whole different thing." I grip her shoulders and hold her a forearm's length away so I can look into her eyes. "Thora, I can compete in something. Competition has been my whole life. My whole life. I thought that was over and gone. Rowing this summer has been huge for me."

She sniffs. "I'm really happy for you then."

She bites her lip and looks off to the side and I place a finger under her chin, turning her so she faces me. "But none of it has been anywhere near as great as I feel when I'm with you, Janssen." She blinks. "You light me up. And I wanted to be close to you." I watch her inhale a shaky breath. "If you don't want me here, I'll leave. I have some options in Cardiff, and if I really have to, I can go to Stirling up in Scotland, but it'll be cold as balls, and I'd much rather be close to you. If you'll have me."

Thora doesn't say anything for a long time. She just stares at me and opens and closes her mouth. But she doesn't wriggle out of my grasp or move her hands from where she anchored them near my elbows. I take a deep breath. "And I'm sorry I was sneaky about the grant. I just really think you're awesome, and I wanted to do something nice for you but not have you feel beholden to me or something." Again, silence. "So…is it okay? That I'm here?"

"You did all that to be near me?"

I nod. Tears are really starting to flow out of her eyes now and I want to dab them away but it's my turn to feel frozen in place.

"Odin…nobody has ever done anything like this for me before."

Her confession has me beaming, and I pull her close again, putting my mouth close to her ear. "Well, Thora, nobody has ever charged up my lightning rod like you before."

She groans at the bad Norse pun, but I know I'm in now. I tip up her face again and kiss her like I've been wanting to for weeks. Ever since she ran out on me at my family's ski house. I sweep my tongue into her mouth as I pull her close and she gasps when she feels me hard against her belly.

"Odin!"

I stoop to pick up my cane and run the tip of it along her leg. "Want to get out of here?"

She tucks her hair behind her ears and nods. "My place is very close by."

I nod. "Good."

———

She holds my hand and tugs me across the lawn to a fancy-ass building worthy of my smart woman. Her flat is on the first floor, and I sigh in relief when she pulls me through the door without having to go up a single stair.

So, I use that reserved energy to shove her against the wooden door in a rush of breath and wide eyes. "I can put weight on both feet now, you know," I tell her, biting her neck. "I've been dying to fuck you against a wall."

She starts ripping open the buttons on my blazer and then pauses. "Wait. I'm mad at you."

"I'll make it up to you." I start pulling her blouse from her skirt and easing it open as she glares.

"You railroad me when you get ideas, and you don't tell me things in advance. Like with the scholarship and just...showing up here at my new school."

I pause and press a palm on the door on either side of her head. "To be fair, gorgeous, you're always telling me to shut up or go away."

She sighs at this and returns to her work ripping off my clothes. She grunts in triumph as she pulls my belt loose and drops it on the floor with a thud. I yank down her skirt and everything underneath and then nudge her legs open with my thigh, hoisting her up so she's grinding her wet little pussy on my leg. "Do you want me to go away now?"

Her eyes flash. "You fucker," she grunts, rocking her hips. "You know I want your cock."

I grin and pull it out, fisting it as she stares and licks her lips. I kick my jeans off one leg and let them dangle above my casted foot. This will have to do. "My wallet is in my pants pocket," I admit after a few seconds pinching her nipples. "But, uh, I wanted to tell you that there hasn't been anyone but you in a long time. And I just got tested for my new team..."

She looks into my eyes, nostrils flaring as she considers. "I got a physical, too. Before I came here. And there hasn't been anyone but you."

I nod. "Nobody but each other, then." I kiss her neck. "I like being yours."

"Odin. I have an IUD."

"Yeah? So, you feel safe?"

I look into her eyes and hiss as she reaches for my cock, notching it at her pussy. "I feel safe with you, Odin. I want to feel all of you."

At that, I hoist her up, and she wraps her legs around my waist. I use one hand to line myself up until she slides onto me, and I brace her against the door, grunting like a caveman as I thrust into Thora. "I'm yours," I repeat. "There's only you. Only you, Thora."

She moans and her head starts rolling around so I reach in between her legs, right above where my bare cock slides in and out of her body, feeling like magic, and I press against her clit. "I want to make you come, gorgeous. I want to make you feel good."

"Odin," she breathes and stares into my eyes. "You feel amazing." Her body starts to pulse around me. It's been a long-ass time for me, and I'm not going to last, especially not with the slick, perfect glide of her body grasping at mine like the ivy on this building.

I press harder with my thumb, swirling and chanting her name, telling her how gorgeous she looks spread open on my dick against this door, and then she screams, one wrist clamped between her lips as her heels dig into my butt.

"Thora!" Her name is a strangled burst alongside the biggest orgasm I've had in months. I lean my forehead against hers, pressing her into the door as I spurt inside her until my release is dripping out from between her legs, coating both of us.

We stare down at the mess together, panting. I ease her legs to the floor and we both sink to the rug, where I trace the pool of my sticky, white mark on her thigh.

Sweaty, filthy, exhausted, we lie in each other's arms until we're both about to fall asleep. She hums contentedly, eyes closed, dark hair tangled around my arm. "Where do you live," she asks, not moving.

"It's not far from here. Grad student housing. Or whatever they call it." I try to get comfortable, but it's no use, so I accept the hard floor meeting my hip and pull Thora close. "But I'm happy to have it sit empty if you'll let me crash here. It's a first-floor setup! No stairs." I kiss the top of her head.

"How would that work?" She rolls to her side and drapes herself across my chest, chin digging into my sternum. I like it.

I shrug. "I don't know. Same as before, I guess. You'll kick ass at school. I'll do okay at school and kick ass on the water. And if I'm lucky, you'll cheer for me in between your projects."

Thora runs a finger along my jaw and across my lips, so I kiss the wandering digit. She smiles. "That all sounds kind of nice, I guess."

I shiver on the banks of the Isis, glad Odin's mom sent me a Snuggie-type garment, even if it does have a giant stag on the back. Let the people see who I'm rooting for, I say.

While I don't understand why the Cambridge and Oxford rowing teams compete against each other in December like maniacs, I'm really happy to be here cheering for Odin. Intercollegiate rowing is different here than how sports work back in the States. Oxford has crew teams for each college within the university, but then one fancy Blue Boat team that seems to line up with infamy over here the way varsity football does in the US.

Six months ago, I would have felt guilty about taking an entire Saturday to watch someone else do things for the whole day. I would have tried to work the bar in the boat house or squeezed in some work before and after the event.

But today, I woke up in my bed with my giant boyfriend wrapped around me, had morning good-luck sex, and wandered over to the river leisurely, with a thermos of tea, to sit with the other wives and girlfriends. And I'm going to hang out for the social after the races, too.

It's been a big term for me. I say term now, like a proper English schoolgirl, instead of semester. I've learned to relax, go sightseeing with Fern, and massage my boyfriend's shoulders after practice. He doesn't technically live with me because that would violate the rules, but we spend most of our time together.

I love it.

And I love him. I just haven't worked up the nerve to tell him yet.

I sit up straighter as I watch the judges line up the bow balls for the eight-seater boats. Odin is in the middle, a place he tells me is called the engine of the boat. He's out there in a unitard tank top, tiny socks, and little shoes that are actually built into the boat.

He's about ten weeks out of his cast now, rowing like a regular guy, he says. The official fires the starter pistol, and I hear the little shouty guys in the backs of the boats yelling at the rowers. "Power ten," they holler, and "move it."

I see them moving it, all right. I clutch my tea mug, watching Odin's shoulder muscles move in sync with the other athletes in his boat. But his body is the most beautiful. This is objective fact. Years of elite training have done him a million favors in honing his muscles.

The woman next to me elbows me. "Look at your man go!"

I nod. "He's worked really hard to be here."

The Oxford boat creeps ahead of the Cambridge boat, oars flying, and hardly any water splashes as these guys move with perfect form. I feel my cell phone buzzing in my pocket and realize Odin's mom is waiting for an update. I know they're streaming the race live online, but I'm sure there's a lag. I told Juniper I'd try to respond, but now I don't want to look away as the rival boat starts gaining on Oxford.

Yesterday afternoon, I was presenting data on the correlation between family support policies and reduced recidivism across multiple European countries' correctional systems. Odin stood in the back, pumping his fist silently while I talked to a crowd of intellectuals from around the world. He wore a bespoke suit and then took me out to dinner at the nicest pub in town, telling me he could listen to me talk about justice and equity forever.

Old Thora would have protested and insisted on paying. When we arrived four months ago, I kept trying to give him his scholarship money back. But I've learned to appreciate the gifts he gives me as just that: no strings attached. They are offerings from his heart, things he wants me to have because it makes him happy to see me succeed.

I'm sure I would have felt proud of myself without him here. I probably would have felt confident in my role here, my power as a researcher, and knowing that my work matters. But having Odin at my side for all of it? Cheering for me and doting on me? It's like a dream I never dared to imagine.

When the coxswain notices the Cambridge boat creeping ahead and starts bellowing at Odin's team to use "Pick it up, lads!" I fly to my feet, the stag Snuggie dropping to the grass.

"Stronger strokes, Odin Stag," I scream through my cupped hands.

"Eat their water!" He doesn't turn his head to face me, but I catch a glimpse of his lips turning up in a smile. The Oxford guys kick it into a new gear, and the boat catches Cambridge. I run along the course, closer to the finish rope. "Come on, Blue." My throat is hoarse as I watch the eight rowers' knees and arms moving in unison. I can see the muscles of their thighs, the ripples in their shoulders and backs as they dig and dig until it's over. As the boat glides to a stop, Odin pumps a fist in the air.

He's so happy when he's competing like his body was made to do this. Sure, he's doing great in his coursework. And he's really looking forward to working with a professional sports team someday, helping the athletes balance the mental aspects of competition … and coping with injuries that prevent them from doing what they love.

But for now, he gets another chance to be a beast. To tax his body to the limit and feel that glory from working in unison with his team.

Back on land, I see him looking for me, and I run to him, Snuggie flapping in the wind as he wraps his long, sweaty arms around me. "Thora! Did you see that shit?"

I kiss his neck, tasting salt. "I did, babe. You were amazing." He turns to wave at a passing fan, and I glance down at the thick vertical scar on his right ankle, which is a reminder that all of this is fleeting.

His muscles bulge around the spandex uniform, and his bare feet look strong, gripping the dock. He's in his element here, and he wants me to be part of it, holding me close and kissing me again and again. "Ugh," he moans. "I have to help put shit away. But you'll meet me inside?" He points at the boat house, where fans are heading, some joyful, some frustrated.

"Of course I will." My smile widens as he grips my arm. "Hey." He looks down, eyebrows raised, body poised to go and help his team with the boat. I pull his palm to my chest and press it above my ribs. "I love you, Odin. I love you so much."

The smile that splits his face is bright enough to catch a glare from the river. "Thora, I've loved you since the day you showed up in my hospital room," he says, lifting me off the ground so my face is level with his. "I've been waiting and waiting for you to feel ready to say it."

I kiss the tip of his nose. "I'm ready now," I tell him. "I never want to stop."

He kisses me, lips cold despite his internal furnace. He spins me around, and I laugh at the beauty of all of it. "I love you," I repeat.

"I love the hell out of you," he says. He sets me down. "Okay, that one was a little weird." He pulls my hand up and presses a kiss to my palm. "I love you, and I need to go put this boat away."

"Go," I tell him, and he steps backward, waving.

I snap a picture with my phone as he walks toward the boat, his torso turned toward me, arm waving, smile shooting sparks my way.

I missed a hundred messages from his family asking about the race. Apparently, the online stream didn't work. I send the photo to his family group chat, telling them, "My man, the victor. They crushed those light blue Cambridge Smurfs."

I also sent the picture to my mom, telling her I wish she could have seen Odin row, and promising her that she'll get to meet him at Christmas. Dad got a job washing dishes at the diner where Mom works, and things have been a little better back home. I might not ever be able to help lift enough stigma and baggage to help my parents directly, but I know my work will make a difference for other families like mine.

I know Odin Stag will be at my side wherever I go, rooting for me and making life work together. I used to think commitments to other people would be a burden, that opening myself up to anyone, but Fern would hold me back. I see now how these connections Odin has forced upon me have opened my world.

I grab a beer for each of us and sit on a bench at one of the long tables to wait for him.

———

My body relaxes when he arrives, gray sweats over his uniform, sandals on his still-bare feet. He slides onto the bench and pulls me into his arms, kissing me before reaching for his beer. "I love you," he says. "I'm going to say it twenty times an hour now."

"I love you too." I clink my cup against his, lean my head on his shoulder, and sip my drink happily. "Hey," I say, turning again to face him. "Did I ever thank you for following me here?"

He grins. "No, but that's okay. I can tell you need me."

"Oh, I need you, do I?"

He nods and finishes his beer in one more gulp. "You need it bad, Thora Janssen." He squints, studying me, and then leans in close. "In fact, I think we should get out of here."

"You don't want to stay and celebrate with your team?"

He shakes his head, hops to his feet, and reaches for my hand. "What I want is you, Thora. Always."

"Mrs. Janssen, I couldn't eat another bite." I toss my napkin to the side and pat my stomach appreciatively. Thora was nervous as hell about coming to her parents' house for Christmas. I promised her I was absolutely fine with whatever was inside there, but her dad surprised her by revealing that he quit smoking months earlier.

Thora cried and walked through the rooms of the house, sniffing pillows and touching curtains. I mean, sure, the guy switched to nicotine gum, but it's way less stinky, and apparently, it's covered by his insurance. They have that now—insurance. Thora also cried when her parents let her help them with the paperwork for that a few months ago.

"You guys just seem so healthy," Thora sniffles. She hugs her mother tightly. They're about the same size, which is tiny. Mr. Janssen grunts and pops another piece of gum in his mouth, flicking the television over to a hockey game. I join him on the couch, looking to see my brothers on the screen. "Hey, the twins are starting," I say, and Thora pats my shoulder. She's not really a sports fan unless I'm competing, but she will agree to watch Wyatt, Wes, and Cara play soccer if I bribe her with sex. I guess I have to get her into hockey now that the Stags are back in the game.

Thora's dad stares at me like he's just putting it together that Odin Stag is related to Alder, Tucker, and Gunner Stag. "Your people play for the Fury?"

I bark out a laugh. "Well, yeah, man. Not sure about Gunny right now, actually. You know he got in a bit of trouble back in Vegas."

Thora's dad nods and crosses his arms. "Absolutely ridiculous to go there for pre-season."

I hold up my hands because what am I going to do about my brother's antics. Twenty minutes later, after a bunch of clangs from the kitchen, Thora comes up behind me again and leans her chin on my head. "You ready to go?"

I know that tone, and as much as I'd like to watch my brothers play hockey, I'd rather destroy the rental Thora and I got in my parents' neighborhood. "Thanks for everything, Mr. and Mrs. Janssen," I say, snatching Thora's coat from the banister and draping it over her shoulders. "We'll see you New Year's Eve at my uncle's house? For shrimp?"

Her parents nod and kiss her and hug her and pat my arms and then I'm back behind the driver's seat of my G Wagon, massaging the steering wheel like it's one of my girl's thighs. "Hey, lady," I whisper to the black leather glory. "You miss me?"

"Are you talking to your car? That's it, I'm not letting you anywhere near my boobs." Thora laughs and buckles her seatbelt, and I head east up Liberty Ave.

"Who said I want your crusty old boobs? Maybe I'm sick of them." It's a lie, and we both know it. I'm obsessed with Thora's bra-free rack, and I reach across to give it a pat.

I screech the car to a halt in the driveway of the rental house, and she giggles and runs up the stairs to the front door. I run right after her, still appreciating how easily I can move around in the world after six months of intense rehab. The reward for all that is right here in front of me, stripping off her fancy pants lacy tank top, and holiday sweater.

"I love you," I tell her, tackling her to the floor inside the front door.

She pounds her fist on my chest and laughs, tugging at my own sweater. I take mercy on her and kneel above her so I can undress more easily, but I keep a knee on her leg so she can't wriggle away. I do love a game of chase with her, but she has me all worked up and I want her. Right now.

Naked, panting, I grab my length and give it a good tug while she watches, licking her lips. "You hoping for a candy cane, Thora? Something hard and sticky in your stocking?"

"You are absolutely insane." She shoots her feet around my waist and pulls me toward her body. I happily tip over and reach for her, parting her folds and finding her wet and hot and slippery.

"Oh, hello." I grin and pump a finger in and out of her body while she wriggles on the rug.

"Yes, yes, I want you, too. I'm sorry I threatened to take away my boobs. Oh, god, yes, please keep doing that." I am stroking her with two fingers now, stretching her out. I usually like to make her come at least once before I slide my cock inside her, but things are getting desperate up here for me.

With a grunt, I thrust inside my lady. "Yes, Odin, god, yes," she says, nails poking into the tattoos on my shoulder blades. She sinks her teeth into the side of my neck, and I growl, pulling back onto my knees and hauling her ass off the ground so her hips are on my lap.

I'm very deep inside her this way, and I can watch her chest shaking as we slam together. "This is all yours, Thora." I punctuate each word with another thrust. "Every. Thing. I. Have."

"Love you," she wails, bringing her hand between her legs.

"Yes, beautiful, touch yourself for me." I wrap an arm under each of her thighs, spreading her even wider and giving me more leverage to pull her into my body.

Thora releases strangled sounds of ecstasy as her fingers fly over her clit, her other hand scrambling to grab my arm, my leg, the rug. I feel it when she starts to come, and I soar over the cliff alongside her, grunting with the effort and then flopping forward to join her on the rug.

"Merry Christmas," she whispers, eyes fluttering open like she can't decide if she can remain awake.

"Hm," is all I can manage in return.

"We hardly ever do it in a bed," she says, rolling onto her back and blowing hair out of her mouth. "Why is that?"

"Because we have imagination. Because I can't control myself when I'm near you. Because the whole world is a canvas for our art."

I roll onto my back and lace my fingers together behind my head.

Thora roars with laughter and sits up. "Odin Stag, the things that fall out of your mouth."

"You love it," I say, winking at her in the glow of the twinkle lights on our rented mantle.

She sighs and lies back down, arms around my middle, head on my chest. "Yeah," she says. "I really do."

Thank you for reading Forging Chaos! If you want to know what trouble Gunnar
Stag gets into, read his book
Playing for Keeps.

*Can't get enough of Odin and Thora? My newsletter subscribers get a bonus
scene.*
Sign up at LaineyDavis.com